Five Stories of Untam
in a Wild State

The

LONE STAR

Romance

COLLECTION

Cathy Marie Hake
& Kimberley Comeaux

BARBOUR
PUBLISHING

Member of the
Evangelical Christian
Publishers Association

Printed in Canada.

CONTENTS

ONE MORE CHANCE

by Kimberley Comeaux

Dedication

*For my husband, Brian, who always encourages me
and then helps make dreams come true.
And to my son, Tyler, my precious gift from God.
You're the best!*

Prologue

East Texas, 1883

It was Sunday morning and silence had fallen among the congregation of the First Church of Springton. Coupled with the stony silence was a morbid curiosity, the kind of curiosity that compels folks to gather at hangings and peep out their windows during gunfights.

Of course, most of them knew what it was all about. When the good Reverend Parker had proclaimed his uncompromising revelation, right after his closing prayer, they'd all been expecting it.

"There's a sinner among us," he'd said in a booming voice. He was bent over his large wooden pulpit when he'd said this, his hands gripping the sides until his knuckles shone white. His bushy gray eyebrows arched dramatically over cool blue eyes as he slowly scanned the audience. Though he was seventy-two, Reverend Parker could easily intimidate when he chose to. He had a severe appearance: He was tall and skinny with a shock of iron gray hair and skin that resembled untreated leather. But it was his way of looking at a person that could scare the sin right out of a man, whether he was in need of it or not.

Adelaide Hayes sat in the next-to-the-last row beside Mattie Mae Higgins and Mattie's husband, Charlie. Adelaide's eyes narrowed at the preacher. Everyone knew that Reverend Parker and Mrs. Hayes had never seen eye to eye. It appeared to Adelaide that what the preacher was about to do would not build any bridges between them!

Eighteen-year-old Rachel Branigan nervously twisted a plain white handkerchief in her trembling hands. The reverend's accusing glare was trained on her, and she had to force herself not to lower her eyes. He wanted her to break down in tears, to throw herself on his mercy and beg for forgiveness.

But she had nothing to be sorry for. She knew she must remember that.

"'The wages of sin is death,'" Reverend Parker quoted, bringing his fist down with a bang. "And fornication, my brothers and sisters, is sin!"

An automatic response of amens echoed about the church.

Reverend Parker shifted his piercing eyes to the man who sat next to Rachel. "Brother Jebediah, bring your niece to stand before God and this congregation," he ordered.

7

Rachel felt five sweaty fingers close around her wrist. For a moment she fought his hold. Embarrassment and panic enveloped her like a tight glove. A part of her wanted to believe that none of this was real, that it was only a nightmare and soon she would wake up.

But she was only kidding herself. It was worse than any nightmare she'd ever dreamed. Much worse.

Abruptly she ceased her struggle, realizing that she was fighting a losing battle. Jebediah Pierce stood and jerked Rachel to her feet, then pushed her out into the aisle.

The short walk to the front of the church seemed to take an eternity. Whispers and murmurs came from all directions. Eyes that held condemnation and scorn seemed to prick her skin like tiny needles as they focused on her.

She wanted to run away and hide. She wanted to find a place where their eyes couldn't see her and their words couldn't hurt her. It wasn't her fault this had happened. Why couldn't they understand?

Reverend Parker looked down at her from the high position behind his pulpit. Rachel lifted her chin and stared back at him.

"Do you, Rachel Branigan, admit your sin, and do you seek forgiveness for your wicked ways?" he asked, his voice harsh and accusing.

Rachel swallowed back the rage that rose within her at his words. "I've committed no sin," she announced clearly. She was relieved there had been no quaver in her voice.

A rumble sounded from the congregation at her statement. Reverend Parker pounded his hand on the pulpit. "Silence!" he ordered and was immediately obeyed. His gaze narrowed at Rachel's stiff posture and defiant stare. He seemed taken aback by her denial of guilt.

"Dare you stand there and *lie*? Are your sins not enormous already?" he charged.

"No!" She shook her head helplessly. "I'm not lying!"

"Then you deny, woman, that you are with child?"

She lowered her gaze. Pain ripped through her chest. Tears pricked the back of her eyelids. "No," she answered softly, "I don't deny it."

The crowd erupted again. Addie Hayes gripped the pew in front of her as if she were trying to prevent herself from leaping up and rushing to Rachel's defense.

Rachel forced herself to speak. "Do you think, Reverend, that I got into this condition all on my own?"

"Of course not. Tell me the name of your partner in this sinful act!" he commanded.

Rachel opened her mouth to speak but cried out in pain when Jebediah's hold on her arm tightened.

"Mind what you say, girl," he hissed in her ear.

Determined not to acquiesce to the man's threats any longer, she jerked her arm from his grasp and shouted out before her uncle could stop her. *"Milton Pierce!"*

The crowd seemed to gasp in unison. Three rows back, a tall lanky, young man leaped to his feet. He had blond, greased-back hair; and his normally pale, ruddy cheeks were now flaming red. He pointed his finger in the direction of his accuser and yelled, "That's a lie straight from the pit of. . ."

"Brother Milton!" the reverend interjected.

Milton had the sense to lower his eyes, as if he were sorry for his outburst, though Rachel knew that he wasn't. Milton didn't care what people thought of him.

"Come stand beside your father, Milton," he was ordered.

Rachel felt herself begin to tremble as Milton came near. It had been this way ever since she'd moved in with her uncle and his family three years ago, after her parents were killed. But she'd never dreamed Milton was capable of doing what he'd done to her. . .that he would rape her.

"Brother Milton, are you the father of this unborn child?" Reverend Parker asked, his tone far less judgmental than when he had accused Rachel.

Milton's features held a pasted-on expression of innocence as he lied. "No, Reverend Parker, I'm not."

"That's a lie!" Rachel cried out, despite her resolve to remain calm. "Please believe me!"

"Quiet, *woman!*" Parker growled, then turned back to Milton.

"Are you telling us that you did not lay with this woman?"

"No sirree, I did not!" Milton exclaimed with a look of indignation.

The nightmare was getting worse. Rachel closed her eyes and fought to hold back an ocean of tears. "No. . . ," she whispered hoarsely. She was ignored.

"And I'll tell you something else, too, Reverend. She tried to throw herself at me, but I refused!" Milton continued.

"That's not true!" she screamed, finally getting their attention. Blinded by desperation, she lunged past Jebediah for Milton. Her movement was thwarted when her uncle grabbed her arm and yanked her to her knees.

She didn't know if it was because her arm and knees hurt so badly or because her heart ached like nothing she'd ever felt before, maybe it was a combination of both, but her eyes filled with tears and she could no longer keep them from falling.

With as much dignity as she could muster, she pulled herself up, wincing at the pain, and directed her gaze toward the reverend. "Reverend Parker, if. . .if you c–could please. . .*please* let me have my say," she asked, her voice shaking.

Reverend Parker appeared to be put off by this request; but to everyone's surprise, he waved an impatient hand in her direction and told her to speak quickly.

Sniffing back tears, she took a deep breath and began to recount what had happened on that horrible day.

"Three months ago, Milton trapped me in the stables. He. . .he said that if I screamed, he'd hurt me. . .bad. I—I tried to run away from him, but he threw me to the ground. He kept hitting me. Not. . .not on my face w—where you could see, but on my stomach. . .and my chest. And then. . ."—a sob caught in her throat and she shut her eyes tightly, trying to block the horrific image that played in her head—"he. . .attacked me. He made me. . ." She took a deep breath and looked pleadingly at the reverend. "Reverend Parker, Milton *raped* me."

Sounds of shock ran rampant through the congregation.

For the first time since the church service had ended, Reverend Parker appeared doubtful. He looked at Milton, who was shaking his head as if he were shocked. "Is there any truth in this, Milton?"

"Of course not, Reverend," he vehemently denied. "I would never do that!"

Jebediah interrupted at that moment. "Uh, Reverend, I have four ranch hands that will testify that each of them has been with this girl," he lied. Rachel closed her eyes wearily. She knew he would pay the men to say this if he had to.

Parker looked at Pierce with surprise. "Is that right?"

Jebediah nodded. "That's right, Reverend."

The whispers that passed among the people slowly quieted. Rachel found the reverend's narrow gaze on her once again. She silently begged him to believe her.

But either God wasn't telling or the reverend wasn't listening.

"I ask you again, Rachel Branigan. Will you repent of your sins and right your wrongs with God?"

Helplessness poured through her like cold rain. The lie Jebediah had just told the whole congregation had ruined her anyway. She could tell a lie or the truth—it no longer mattered. To this town, she was an outcast. Unworthy. A sinner.

She looked back up to the reverend and took a deep, shaky breath. "No, I will not confess. I have nothing to confess."

Chaos erupted among the congregation. Shouts of hurting, judgmental words were hurled at Rachel. Her uncle merely gave her a look of disgust and walked to stand by his son. Milton had a pleased, smug look on his face. The reverend was a picture of righteous indignation.

Rachel stood there, her shoulders slumped in defeat, her face white, and her eyes lowered in humiliation. Her heart was filled with hopelessness.

Reverend Parker raised his hand and immediately the crowd quieted—waiting, anticipating.

"Since you refuse to acknowledge the error of your sinful act, you are, therefore, cutting yourself off from God. And as long as you continue thus, you will not be welcome in this house of God!" he declared with finality.

Tears continued to flow down Rachel's cheeks in silence. Her whole world seemed to be closing in on her, suffocating her. She looked up and focused on the wooden cross positioned behind the preacher.

One more chance, Lord, she prayed, *just give me. . .one. . .more. . .chance.*

Then, without looking at anyone, Rachel turned and walked out of the building.

—⁓—

Santa Fe, New Mexico Territory

The streets cleared immediately. Only two men were standing on the dusty street now. It was so quiet in the desert town, the men could hear each other's breathing—one calm and even, the other fast and shallow. Even the piano from the saloon across the street had quieted.

But there were eyes watching. Some curious. Some dangerous. Some downright deadly.

But then again, they were playing a deadly game. A game that would produce only one winner.

Snake Barnes stood across from the gunslinger as a bead of sweat followed a slow, wet path from his forehead to the tip of his nose. Fear was plainly written on the smaller man's face, his hand twitching nervously as it hung beside his holster.

The gunslinger, C. J. Stone, knew something was up. He just didn't know what. Stone was one of the most notorious gunslingers and bounty hunters in the West. Snake Barnes was just as famous—for his cowardliness.

So why had Snake called him out? C. J. didn't really want to shoot him. He had a bounty on the run, and he knew he was close to capturing him. He didn't have time to play "quick draw" with the likes of Barnes.

But that nagging at his memory didn't let up. What had he heard about Barnes recently? There was something important he should remember. . . .

Snake drew his pistol. C. J. was faster. But neither gun ever fired a shot. The shots came from behind C. J. Three bullets hit him—one in the leg, one in his back, and the other grazed his head.

He fell face down in the dirt.

As the last shred of light and awareness played through his mind, C. J. recalled what he'd been trying to remember before. Barnes had joined the Jenkins gang. Jenkins had been trying to kill him for years, ever since C. J. killed his brother in a gunfight.

Jenkins's coarse laugh overhead proved it. "There's more than one way to bring a man down," he told C. J. in a sly, smooth voice.

C. J. could no longer feel his pain. He was dying and he knew it. He wondered if there was a hell, because he had a pretty good idea he wouldn't make it to heaven.

One more chance, God, he prayed, for the first time in his life. *Please give me. . .one more chance. . . .*

Then everything went dark.

Chapter 1

Three Years Later
Springington, Texas

The lone church bell rang out, temporarily disrupting the quiet mourning of the townsfolk who had gathered at the cemetery. The midday sky was dark with angry clouds, but no rain fell. The gloom perfectly fit the mood of the moment.

Reverend Parker was dead.

Rachel stood at the large picture window of the general store that sat just off Main Street. Peering off into the distance, she watched as people started making their way back to their horses and carriages.

She felt strangely numb; not sad, not elated, just numb. In the three years since that fated day, the good reverend had not spoken one word to her, as if to do so would somehow soil him. Nor had she ever returned to the white clapboard church at the end of the street.

She wasn't welcome.

Rachel really didn't know what she would have done during that hard time if it hadn't been for Adelaide Hayes. The fifty-three-year-old widow had marched right out of the church behind Rachel and didn't ask but demanded that Rachel go home with her. She had said she needed help at her store and that Rachel was just the right young woman for the job. She'd even provided her with a room next to Adelaide's above the shop.

In the three years that Rachel had lived and worked with her, they had never spoken of it, but both knew—without Addie Hayes, Rachel Branigan would have been without hope.

At first, Rachel had been afraid that hiring her on would affect the store's business, but it hadn't. It was the only general store for miles, and folks simply had no choice in the matter. It either was that or travel sixty miles north to Tyler.

Most folks either ignored her completely or acknowledged her with tolerance. They'd never forgiven nor forgotten what had taken place three years earlier. Reverend Parker had never let them.

Rachel sighed as she backed away from the window and glanced about the store. Life had been unkind to her, but God had given her the grace to endure it. God had also blessed her with the most precious gift she'd ever received.

Her daughter, Caitlin.

Rachel was quickly shaken from her musings when, from the back of the store, her old tomcat let out a loud screech. A high-pitched giggle immediately followed.

Rachel smiled and called out, "Caitlin Branigan! Leave that poor cat alone, young lady!"

She tried to look stern when her two-and-a-half-year-old daughter came running into the room, but failed miserably. Caitlin was just too cute and too charming to frown at for long.

She looked up at her mother with beautiful, innocent eyes and said, "Pway wit' cat, Mommy."

Rachel lifted Caitlin up into her arms so that they could see eye to eye. "Yes, darlin', but the cat doesn't like his tail pulled. That's not playing nice, now is it?"

Caitlin's face took on a guilty look. "Not nice."

Rachel planted a kiss on her daughter's cheek and put her back on the floor. "Don't do it anymore, Caity, or you'll not get any of your aunt Addie's chocolate cake for supper!"

Caitlin's eyes widened at her mother's words. "I be good, Mommy," she promised and ran back out of the room.

Rachel watched her daughter's silky black curls bouncing over her back and shoulders as she left her. A wave of melancholy washed over her as she thought about Caitlin and all she'd had to do without.

Rachel knew she'd done the best she could with her, but the fact remained, every child needed a father as well as a mother. And to be truthful, every mother needed a husband to share the trials and burdens of parenthood. After three years, she was afraid that her dream would never be a reality. Not in this town. Not with her reputation.

For a year she had been bitter toward men in general. The rape had left mental scars. And for that whole year, she'd let the wounds fester and eat her up inside. But with Addie's help, she'd managed to let go of the bitterness. She no longer held every man she came across accountable for what happened to her. Little by little she came to realize that she *did* want a man in her life. A man who loved her and wanted to marry her. A man who would take Caitlin as his own. But did such a man exist? Rachel prayed that he did.

Chiding herself for daydreaming, Rachel walked back to the storeroom to check on Caitlin. All was well. She was returning to the store when the front door swung open and Adelaide Hayes came breezing in. With a flick of her wrist, her hat was off and swinging from a peg of the hat rack in the corner, where it had been tossed with practiced skill.

"Well!" she began in her usual crisp, no-nonsense tone. "It's a new day dawning for Springton! Today begins a new chapter!"

Rachel frowned after her. "What do you mean?"

"The reverend, of course!" She grabbed an apron from behind the counter and pulled it over her head. "His brand of religion has poisoned these gullible folks' minds long enough. As I see it, it's time for new blood around here!"

"Addie!" Rachel gasped. "I thought you liked the reverend."

Addie snorted. "Where did you get that fool idea? I tolerated the man, that's what I did! Ain't no hard-nosed man going to keep Adelaide Hayes from going to church, no sir! And after what he did to you?" She shook her head in disgust. "Like I said, it's time for new blood. That's why I put myself on the nominating committee! 'Course, old Harold Ray Norton didn't like the idea of a woman being on their committee one bit! But I told him he couldn't stop me!" She grinned at that. Rachel knew that Addie liked nothing better than getting Harold Ray's goat.

"I don't understand why you and Harold Ray don't go and get yourselves married. You two fight like you've been married twenty years already!" she teased.

Addie gave Rachel a wide-eyed look. "Goodness no, child! If we got hitched, we just might start getting along! Then I would have nothing left to look forward to! I'm an old woman, Rachel Branigan. I have to take my entertainment anywhere I can get it!"

They both laughed at that, then Addie went to the back storeroom to get some canned goods to restock the shelves. Rachel watched her go, and her smile slowly faded into a worried frown.

She dearly hoped that the reason Addie didn't openly court Harold Ray had nothing to do with Caitlin and herself. Sometimes Rachel wished that she could support herself in some way other than working in Addie's store; that way, maybe Addie wouldn't feel so responsible for her and Caitlin.

Addie came back into the store with an armload of canned beans, and Rachel went over to help her place them on the shelves.

Please, God, Rachel prayed, *help me not to be a burden to Addie. Make a way where there is no way. . . .*

—⚬—

One Month Later
Santa Fe

Caleb Joseph Stone neatly folded the last one of his shirts and placed it into the leather trunk. He glanced about the room that he'd occupied for the last three years and, after deciding that he had packed everything, closed the trunk and snapped it shut.

An ironic smile curved his lips and he shook his head. C. J. Stone wouldn't have been caught dead traveling around with a gentleman's trunk. What he couldn't pack in his saddlebags, he didn't take with him. He ran his hands over his new clothes and fingered the tie at his neck. Nor would C. J. be wearing a Sunday-go-to-meetin' suit, either!

But Caleb Stone, the preacher, would.

It all still seemed unbelievable to him. If a man had asked him three years ago, before the Jenkins incident, if he would ever consider becoming a man of the cloth, C. J. probably would have shot him!

That day had forever changed his life.

After the Jenkins gang had cleared out of town, the townsfolk had slowly emerged from their hiding places and curiously gathered around his bloody, prone body lying face-down in the dust.

They had thought he was dead. The undertaker had already started making his way out to collect the remains and prepare the body for burial.

That's when his salvation came.

Reverend George and Mary Ellis had broken through the crowd, declared him still living, and then carried him home with them.

They never gave up hope. Even after the doctor extracted the bullets from his body and told them that he didn't think the gunslinger would live, they had kept on believing and praying. As the injured man lay unconscious, he heard their prayers.

And he had lived. Everyone declared it a miracle. They couldn't believe the clean-cut gentleman walking through the church doors one Sunday morning was the same man who had been gunned down months before.

Every day, after his recovery, C. J. had told himself that this was the day he would pack up and ride out of there. But the day would pass and he would find himself still residing with the Ellises. At first he didn't know what drew him to them. All he knew was that, before, he had no one to care for him or to worry after him; but here, he was loved. The Ellises didn't seem to care about what kind of man he was, how dangerous it was to house someone like him. The Jenkins gang could have found out from any-one in town that he still lived, and that would have been the end of things; Jenkins probably would have ridden in and killed them all.

The longer he was around George and Mary Ellis, the more C. J. wanted what they had. He wanted the peace and contentment they possessed. He wanted to know this God that they kept talking about. The only time he had heard the name of God mentioned in his lifetime was when someone had used it as a curse.

Caleb knew he didn't want to return to his former way of living. It was a lonely, worthless existence. He wanted to do something with the life God gave him, to help someone like the Ellises had helped him.

When he finally made the decision to become a minister, it hadn't been all that difficult. It had seemed like the most natural decision in the world. He couldn't wait to have his own church, to teach people like the reverend had taught him. He had so much love stored up in his heart that he had only begun to give it out. The time to begin was *now*! He was ready.

"Are you nearly packed?" Mary Ellis asked from the doorway.

Caleb turned and gave the woman, who had been like a mother to him for the past three years, a smile. "Near 'bout," he replied.

Mary drifted on into the room and picked up a couple of his shirts and placed them in his traveling bag. "It sure is going to be lonesome here without you," she mentioned casually. "I remember when you came here. You had some of the coldest, meanest eyes I've ever seen and you near 'bout gave me a fright every time you spoke."

She looked him over from head to toe. "Now look at you. So tall and distinguished, those green eyes of yours just a-gleaming with warmth and goodness." She shook her head wryly. "I still think that hair of yours could use a good barber, but at least you shaved off that horrible mustache."

Caleb chuckled. "How did you say I looked? Like an outlaw?"

"Well, with all those stories you've told me about your gunslinger days, I wasn't too far off the mark!"

"Well, thanks to you and George, all that's changed now." He paused and thought before he asked a question. "Do you think that I'll do all right in Springton?"

Mary gave Caleb a maternal pat on the back. "Caleb, the way God has blessed you with your gift for talkin', those folks in Springton are going to love you. Just look at how the people here in Santa Fe responded to your preaching! You even had old Buzzard Grisham's attention. He hasn't managed to stay awake for a whole sermon in ten years!"

Caleb smiled and proceeded to buckle his travel bag. "Well, it's not my doing. I can feel God moving through me when I'm up there in the pulpit. It's not my words I'm speaking but Him speaking through me," he said modestly.

"You're a good man, Caleb Stone. And just remember that God can work anything out when you come up against tribulations. Because you will have them. Especially in a town like Springton."

Caleb studied Mary's worried face. "You're thinking about your brother again."

Mary nodded. "Being the sister of the Reverend Cecil Parker is not something I'm proud of. And I've heard that his religious snobbery has rubbed off on a lot of his former congregation. I just want you to be careful and not let them discourage you."

Caleb reached out and gave her a hug. "I'll be all right, Miss Mary. Don't you worry about me, okay?" he said in his husky drawl. "I reckon it's those poor ol' Texas folk that you need to be worrying about, getting an old gunslinger for a preacher."

She pushed away from him and planted her fists on her ample hips. "Now don't you go talking like that, son. Those folks don't know what you used to be; and if you're smart, you won't tell them. That old part doesn't matter anymore. You're like Saul in the Bible. Once God changed him and gave him the new name of Paul, it didn't matter what he had been. It only mattered what he did with himself after that."

He chuckled and held up his hands in mock surrender. "All right, all right! I give up!" She joined in his laughter and then gasped in surprise when he reached over to plant a kiss on her cheek. "I love you, Miz Mary. I don't reckon I've ever told anybody that, but you've been like a mama to me. I won't ever forget it," he told her solemnly, his green eyes reflecting his feelings.

She flustered about a bit, a little embarrassed but profoundly honored to receive such a compliment. "I love you, too, son. Now, go on and get your bag and your trunk out to that wagon. George is out there waitin'."

He grinned and gave her a wink before reaching for his trunk.

Chapter 2

What do you mean you won't buy my eggs?" the small but feisty little woman demanded, pointing to the basket whose contents were in question.

Rachel, standing across from her, took a deep breath and mentally counted to ten. This woman definitely knew how to make Rachel's Irish temper flare. "Mrs. Hawthorn, I cannot buy any more of your bantam eggs because I can't sell them. People want the larger eggs. These are too small," she explained slowly and carefully.

"Humpft!" the woman snorted. "And who, Miss High-and-Mighty, put you in charge of these things? I want to talk to Adelaide about this! I reckon she'll set this matter straight!"

Rachel's chin rose a half an inch, and she glared down at the Hawthorn woman. "Mrs. Hayes isn't here. I was left in charge."

"Where is she?" the woman demanded.

"She's getting the parsonage ready for the new minister. And I doubt she has time to be disturbed!"

Mrs. Hawthorn narrowed her beady eyes and shook her finger in Rachel's face. "This ain't the end of this, missy. You just see if it ain't!" she declared, then proceeded to march toward the door.

Her path was blocked, however, by the tall, nicely dressed gentleman who stood in the doorway; neither woman had seen or heard him enter.

Caleb Stone swiftly stepped aside, seeing that the elderly lady had no intention of stopping.

For a moment Caleb stared after the older woman, then he looked back to the girl standing at the counter. He couldn't help but smile with amusement at the scene he'd just witnessed.

His smile froze, however, as his vision became adjusted to the dimmer light inside the store, giving him a clear view of the woman with the long black hair. She was absolutely beautiful.

If this isn't the prettiest woman I've ever laid eyes on, I'll eat my hat! He stopped just short of saying it out loud.

He realized he was staring at her when he noticed the blush that suddenly tinged her cheeks.

He blinked and cleared his throat, embarrassed that he'd been standing there like an idiot. Caleb walked over to her and extended his hand. "My name is Caleb Stone, ma'am. I'm new to Springton."

"Hello, Mr. Stone," the woman answered, her voice floating over him like summer rain. She reached out and placed her hand in his.

The feel of her warm palm touching his sent a tingle up his arm that seemed to reach his heart. He couldn't help lowering his head and brushing a kiss along the back of her hand.

But when he heard her gasp, his head snapped up. Her face had grown even redder, and she seemed shocked at what he'd done. It suddenly occurred to Caleb that kissing a lady's hand might not be the sort of thing a minister practiced. Then another thought formed. In his whole life, Caleb never once had courted a decent woman. His experience usually had consisted of those ladies of somewhat shady reputation. They were the only ones who would have anything to do with a gunslinger anyway.

This was a dilemma.

Slowly he let go of her hand and fixed a polite smile on his face. Never before had he been nervous around a woman. Well, there was a first time for everything, because he was practically shaking in his boots!

The second that the gentleman entered the store, Rachel had felt something stir in her heart. Everything about him appealed to her. The neatly combed but overlong hair, his warm green eyes, the lopsided grin, the way he stood so straight and tall, even the way he loosely held his hat in his hands. He was a very handsome man.

And when he'd bent his head to kiss her hand, her heart had nearly pounced right out of her chest. She couldn't control the gasp that escaped her lips.

She quickly dropped her gaze and tried to compose herself. For a moment she had almost let herself believe that a gentleman like this Caleb Stone could be interested in her.

It was no use fooling herself. Once he found out about Caitlin and the fact that she was an unwed mother, he wouldn't come around kissing her hand anymore.

Rachel cleared her throat. "Was there something. . .um. . .something I could help you find, Mr. Stone? In the store, that is?" Her voice didn't shake, but she couldn't bring herself to look at him.

Now he knew he'd overstepped his boundaries. He could instantly feel the barrier she had erected around herself. He wondered if an apology would do any good.

He decided, instead, to act like it hadn't happened. "You know, you never did tell me your name."

Rachel finally did raise her blue gaze to his. Bashfully she returned his smile. "Rachel. My name is Rachel Branigan."

"Rachel Branigan," he repeated slowly, savoring each word and committing it to memory. "Well, Miss Rachel Branigan, the pleasure is all mine."

She nodded her head and once again lowered her gaze to the counter in front of her. An awkward silence followed, both of them searching for something to say.

Caleb wondered if that bullet that had hit his head had done some real damage after all. He was as nervous and awkward as a schoolboy. He could only thank God that he wasn't packing a gun anymore. The way he was feeling, he would probably shoot himself in the foot!

"Well," Rachel began, "was there a particular item that you were looking for?"

Caleb took a deep breath and tried to clear his muddled thoughts. "Uh. . .yes! I wanted to see about opening up an account here. I'm just moving in, and there will be a few things I'll be needing." He grinned sheepishly. "And maybe you could help me with that, Miss Branigan. You see, I'm an old bachelor and don't know the first thing about setting up housekeepin'!"

She laughed, and he joined in her laughter. "Not a pretty picture, I'm afraid," he said. "Think you could lend me a hand?"

"Stop by tomorrow. Mrs. Hayes, the owner of the store, and I will give you all the help that you need, Mr. Stone." She reached over for the small file that held the accounts. "I'll just need for you to give me your address and your employment information."

For the first time in his whole life, Caleb could proudly state what he did for a living (if he didn't count the two years that he worked as a carpenter in Sante Fe). He was a preacher. A respected position in anyone's opinion. So when he gave her the information that she asked for, he was a little anxious to see what kind of reaction that he would get from Miss Rachel Branigan.

"I'll be living in that little white house by the church. I think they call it the parsonage. You see, I'm the new minister."

The reaction he got was not what he'd expected. In all his life, Caleb couldn't remember ever seeing a person turn white so fast.

It gave him pause for a few moments. It occurred to him that maybe he'd slipped and said "bounty hunter" instead! No. He was positive he'd said "minister."

"Miss Branigan? Are you all right?"

She made herself stop gaping at what he had just said. Hadn't she known that it would be foolish to hope that he was different? She had just never thought—not in a million years—that this handsome man would turn out to be a preacher!

She forced herself to take a calming breath and then plastered a pleasant smile on her face. "Of course! I'm fine. It's just that you don't look like a. . .preacher." She hoped that the last word had not sounded as bitter as it tasted on her tongue.

Caleb gave her a searching look. "Is there a certain way a preacher is supposed to look?" he teased, obviously trying to lighten the mood that had grown leaden.

Rachel looked at him sheepishly. "I guess that was a silly thing for me to say."

He smiled gently at her and said in a quiet way, "Miss Branigan, I would never think that you were silly. I'd even bet that you were rather a smart lady."

She looked away, embarrassed. "You don't even know me, Mr. Stone."

"It's just a hunch. I've found that I'm rarely wrong about these hunches." He suddenly pulled back from the counter and placed his hat back on his head. "I'll look forward to seeing you tomorrow, Miss Branigan." He tipped his hat smartly and left the store.

Rachel stared at the closed door long after the little bell attached to the top had stopped jingling.

—⁂—

Addie Hayes and her best friend, Mattie Mae Higgins, stood on the small porch of the parsonage. Addie, eyes squinting and hand shading her brow, anxiously scanned the street for anyone who might resemble a minister.

"See him yet?" Mattie Mae asked in her scratchy voice. In an automatic motion, her hand flew to her salt-and-pepper hair to smooth any stray wisps.

"Nope. Not hide nor hair of 'im," Addie answered with a sigh. "Maybe he wasn't on the train. Roscoe said he didn't see anyone get off that train that looked like a preacher."

Mattie Mae snorted at that statement. "Roscoe Smith can't see anything clearly unless it's within spittin' distance. He's blinder than that old mule Harold Ray keeps tied behind his house!"

Addie appeared to ponder something for a few moments, then asked, "Wonder why he keeps a blind mule tied to his house? That never made a lick of sense to me."

"Why, for company, of course! I once caught him kissing the old varmint on the nose."

Addie looked shocked. "You didn't!"

Mattie Mae nodded in a superior way. "Saw it with my own eyes. I'm surprised that you didn't know how he felt about that mule, seeing as how you're sweet on him and all."

Addie's blush showed from her graying hairline to her rose-tinted toes. (No one in Springton knew that Adelaide Hayes painted her toenails!) "Why, Mattie Mae Higgins, I'm sure that I have no idea what you're talking about!" she huffed indignantly.

Mattie Mae laughed at that, then looked back out to the street. "Addie, who's that young fellow walking this way?"

Addie squinted again and shook her head. "I don't rightly know. You don't suppose he's the new reverend, do ya? It sure would explain why Roscoe didn't see him."

"I don't know. He's a right nice-looking fellow, isn't he?"

"Humpft! I wouldn't know, Addie Hayes! I'm a married woman. I don't notice such things as that!" she said indignantly, though she couldn't bring herself to stop staring at the man.

Addie planted her hands on her hips and looked over at her friend. "Well, for someone who ain't noticin', you're sure looking hard enough."

This time it was Mattie Mae who colored. "Oh, hush up, Adelaide! Look! He's opening the gate!"

Caleb was walking through the gate when he saw two elderly women staring at him. With a charming smile, he approached them. He reached the bottom step of the stairs and lifted his hat off his dark head in a gallant gesture. "Good afternoon, ladies. I suppose you've been waiting for me to arrive. I'm Reverend Caleb Stone." This time, he had no intention of doing anything but shaking their hands. He'd learned his lesson on that score. "It's a pleasure to meet such lovely ladies as yourselves."

Slowly, they each extended a hand to the new minister. Neither of them had so much as nodded.

"Oh. . . ," Addie managed to say.

". . .my," Mattie Mae helpfully finished for her.

Addie was the first to speak. "You don't look like a preacher!"

"Oh, for goodness sakes, Addie! What a thing to say!"

"You just said the very same thing not three minutes ago, Mattie Mae Higgins!"

"But I wasn't addlebrained enough to say it right to his face!"

"Well, let me tell you something. . ."

"Uh. . .ladies?" a deep voice spoke up, interrupting their arguing.

Caleb watched as their irate gazes turned on him; then, realizing what they were doing, each woman slowly looked away with embarrassment. They both became suddenly interested in smoothing their calico skirts.

"Hello there!" a loud voice called from the gate.

Both women looked up with relief at Harold Ray Norton as he unknowingly came to their rescue. "Harold Ray Norton, this here's the new reverend, Caleb Stone," Mattie Mae quickly stated.

A look of surprise crossed Harold Ray's weathered face when the tall man turned around to face him.

Finding their shock rather humorous, Caleb grinned and extended his hand to Harold Ray. "These ladies here were just telling me that I didn't much look like a preacher to them."

Harold Ray looked scandalized. "Why, Adelaide Hayes, you knew that the letter stated that the new minister would be thirty-two years old."

"But Addie told me she just didn't realize that he'd be such a handsome man!" Mattie Mae said slyly.

Addie nearly choked. "I said no such a thing!" Her face steamed bright red, and Harold Ray broke out into a hearty laugh.

Caleb had to bite his lip to keep from laughing. Quickly he turned to address Harold Ray. "I have a trunk back at the station. I was wondering if you might know where I can get a wagon to haul it up here to the house?"

"Got one right here, Reverend. Be happy to fetch it for ya! You just let these ladies take ya on in and show ya around the place."

"Thanks, Mr. Norton. I'd appreciate it!" He shook the older man's hand and turned his attention back to the ladies.

Wanting to avoid any more embarrassing moments, the ladies hopped into action. "Come on in, Reverend. Mattie Mae and I cooked you up a delicious peach cobbler!"

Caleb's grin was a mile wide. "Just lead the way, ladies," he said as he motioned for them to enter the house ahead of him.

Being a preacher did have its rewards!

Chapter 3

Night had descended upon the small Texas town, though the brightness of the full moon above prevented total darkness. It was a beautiful night. A night for taking long walks with a sweetheart or for sitting with family on the front porch after a full, satisfying supper. It was a night to share.

Maybe that was why Caleb was feeling such an intense loneliness. He propped his big shoulder up against the pillar of his front porch and sighed. Sure, he had felt this way before. This pretty much was the story of his life. But never before had another feeling accompanied the loneliness—a feeling that was just as intense, just as disturbing.

It was an urgency, he realized. An urgency to do something about his solitary state. Before, it hadn't mattered that there was no one waiting at home for him. Women to him had been a convenience when you needed them and a nuisance when you didn't. He never cared whether he impressed a woman or not. It just didn't matter. But then again, *nothing* much mattered to the old C. J. Stone.

Now it mattered, and Caleb knew why. The reason was wrapped up in one beguiling, beautiful, and mysterious package named Rachel Branigan.

The memory of her had forced its way into his mind all afternoon. At first he had tried to convince himself that the only reason he kept thinking about her was that, as a minister, he would be needing a wife. Mary Ellis had placed that little jewel of wisdom in his ear every chance she got. Not only had she mentioned it, she paraded every available female in the Santa Fe area through their parlor and would casually drop an introduction as if it had all been a coincidence!

But Caleb's mind usually ran on one track. And at the time of all those tempting introductions, his mind had simply been on something other than getting himself hitched. Every minute of the day, when he wasn't working at his job, he was studying. Finding a wife simply was not a top priority. After all, he had done just fine without one for thirty-one years. Waiting another few years wouldn't kill him.

Then why, all of a sudden, did it feel like it would?

He chuckled softly at himself. He had spent less than ten minutes in her presence and already he could hear the clanging of wedding bells.

Pushing away from the pillar, he walked down the porch steps and sauntered over to stand under the gaslit streetlamp. He gazed down the main street of town. Not much was happening. A few men lingered, smoking their cigars outside of the saloon. A couple men staggered out the swinging doors, their drunken laughter drifting slowly over to him.

The saloon crowd was one of the first things that he planned to work on in this town. Like almost any other minister would, he wanted the saloon to be closed down. But he didn't plan to accomplish that by posting ladies outside to sing hymns or by preaching hellfire and brimstone from the pulpit every Sunday.

No, Caleb had another plan. He would simply get to know the men who frequented the establishment and let them get to know him. He understood their way of thinking and what they were going through because he'd been there himself. Those men were on his heart, and he hoped he could make them listen and understand that God loved them.

Excitement shot through him as he thought about everything he wanted to accomplish. The saloon was only one of the many areas that he felt he needed to attend to.

His biggest project would be to set up a decent orphanage in town. The orphanage where he had been left at the age of ten was a nightmare. He had been starved and beaten for no reason; and he, along with the rest of the older children, was put to work in the factory that the orphanage owners operated. Not once had he been looked at by families who were seeking to adopt. He knew he had to get out of that situation or he would die, so he fled.

He wanted to create a healthy, happy environment for orphaned and abandoned children—one where they would feel loved and wanted even if no one ever came to adopt them.

There were so many things that he wanted to accomplish. But he was realistic enough to know that it would all take time.

His eyes drifted to the general store just down the street. A smile curled his lips as he considered that maybe his mind wasn't so one-tracked after all. For even though his pastoral duties weighed heavily on his thoughts, his mind also was filled with the sweet face of Rachel Branigan.

Tomorrow couldn't come soon enough!

—⁂—

"Mama! No go bed! No!" Caitlin complained to Rachel in her high-pitched little voice as her mother tucked her into bed. "Pway! Pway!"

"Caitlin, my sweet, you'll have plenty of time to play tomorrow. Now, give me a kiss and close your eyes," Rachel directed gently.

A big wet kiss was delivered to Rachel, accompanied by a fierce hug. "Night, Mama," she said with a yawn, her blue eyes already closing.

Rachel smoothed her hand over her daughter's black curls. "Good night, lass. Sweet dreams," she whispered and reached over to dim the lamp's flame.

The room was feeling a little stuffy, so Rachel walked over to the window and lifted it halfway up.

It was a lovely evening. The stars were shining. There was even a cool breeze. But instead of being refreshed by the beauty of the night, Rachel just felt lonely. She hated feeling this way.

And she felt guilty, too. God had given her so much to be thankful for that she knew she shouldn't waste time feeling sorry for what she didn't have. But talking to the new preacher today had stirred up those old feelings and brought to mind all those old dreams. She wanted a husband to take care of her and Caitlin. She wanted someone to love her and cherish her.

The preacher, she believed, was just the kind of man who could make a woman feel like she was queen of the world. Rachel couldn't put her finger on exactly what it was that made her think that of him; but looking into the man's eyes today, she was sure she'd seen a generous and kind heart.

And he'd looked at her like she could be a queen. *His* queen!

But by tomorrow evening, he would probably know. It wouldn't take long before Caleb Stone was fully informed of who in town was a heathen and who was not. And since she had been banished from the church, she was definitely listed in the heathen column.

Sometimes she wondered if God felt that way about her, too. Addie always assured her that God knew Rachel's heart and saw the goodness in her. But sometimes that was hard to accept due to the way everyone treated her.

A flash of white at the end of the lamplit street caught her eye, and she tilted her head to investigate.

Her heart skipped a beat. It was him. Caleb Stone. He was standing just inside the white picket fence that surrounded his house. With his arms folded, he rested them on the flat top of the gate. The wind was ruffling his dark hair, and he appeared to be in deep thought.

If only it could be, she thought. *If only it could be.*

Suddenly his gaze lifted, and she knew that he'd seen her. She knew she should look away, but she couldn't do it. He couldn't seem to break away, either, because his eyes never wavered.

—⁓—

At first Caleb had thought it was only his imagination—he had been thinking about her so hard that he had somehow conjured up her image. But then he realized she was real. And she was looking at. . .him! Caleb could feel his heart pounding inside his chest. He kept his eyes glued to her image, afraid that if he blinked, she would go away. But she didn't.

Did she feel the same attraction for him that he did for her? A surge of hope swept through him.

He took a deep breath, then allowed himself to smile the smile that was just bursting to come forth. He raised a hand and gave her a brief wave.

—⁂—

The preacher had waved at her! That meant he still didn't know. So tonight she would pretend. Tonight she would let herself dream.

Slowly, almost hesitantly, she lifted her hand and returned his wave. A smile lit her own face as they continued to look toward each other.

She stayed there at the window only a moment more, just so she could remember. And she *would* remember this night and this feeling. She would remember that for one moment in her life, she had felt pretty and adored. She would remember it because it probably would not happen ever again.

Then she lowered her eyes and walked away from the window.

—⁂—

Caleb's smile softened but did not leave his face as he watched Rachel disappear behind a filmy curtain. He vaguely noted that his heart was still pounding and his hands were sweating. One little wave from the woman, and he was a mess.

"Hey, preacher man!" a loud, drunken voice called from the street, breaking into Caleb's thoughts. Caleb lifted his head and peered thoughtfully at the figure that stood swaying before him, waving a half-empty whiskey bottle. "Why don'tcha (*hick*) come on o'er an' join us?"

That statement brought on snorts of laughter from the three men lounging in front of the saloon.

Caleb swallowed a grin and opened the gate. "Don't mind if I do!" he called out. "I've been wanting to get to know all of you!"

They all stopped laughing.

Chapter 4

The next morning, Caleb sat in the town's only restaurant and hotel, eating breakfast. The church council had set up an account for him there since he was a bachelor. He watched as townsfolk, mostly men, dined in the relaxed atmosphere. He wondered if any among them attended the church.

A tall, brawny young man walked in and, upon searching the room, headed toward Caleb. The star on his chest marked him as the town's sheriff.

"Reverend Stone?" the man asked in a friendly tone.

Caleb nodded and stood up. "Name's Caleb. You the sheriff?"

"Yes. Lee Cutler." They shook hands. "I heard you would be eating here and thought I'd come and introduce myself."

"Well, it's nice to meet you, Lee. Have a seat!" He motioned to the empty chair across from him.

When both men were seated, Caleb asked the sheriff, "Are you from Springton originally?"

Lee shook his head. "No. I moved here five or six years ago. I'm from Houston—near there, anyway. My father has a ranch down there. I was in the Rangers when I came through on the trail of a suspect. I liked it here; and when the sheriff position opened up soon after that, I checked into it, got the job, and moved here." He shrugged. "Anyway, I've felt for a long time that Springton's church needed someone new and fresh to come in and challenge us. I guess we've all become sort of comfortable. I'm looking forward to hearing you Sunday!"

Caleb reached up and rubbed a finger across his chin. "Now, Lee, don't be afraid of putting me under any pressure or anything." They both laughed, although Caleb's laughter was a little shaky. "This is my first church, and I've gotta confess that I'm nervous. There's a lot I want to accomplish, but I want to do things right."

Lee nodded. "I have no doubt that you'll do just fine."

During breakfast, Caleb felt that he'd made a friend. And as a man who'd always been a loner, that was a new—but welcome—experience.

They parted company, and Caleb made his way to the general store. He'd gone to bed thinking about Rachel Branigan; and upon waking this morning, he began counting down the minutes until he would be able to see her again.

He had almost reached the store when Rachel walked out and began sweeping the boardwalk.

"Good morning, Miss Branigan!" he called. His heart was pounding so hard, he feared it could be seen visibly pulsing beneath his shirt.

She wasn't dressed any special way. She wore a simple blue skirt and white blouse. But her beautiful, shiny black hair was swept back on the side and tied with a blue ribbon, from which it cascaded down her back. He wondered if it was as soft as it looked.

She turned her vivid blue eyes in his direction and smiled when she saw that it was him.

———

Rachel looked over to find the new preacher coming up the boardwalk. Just the sight of him nearly took her breath away. He was smiling at her, and she guessed he probably hadn't yet heard about her past. He wouldn't be smiling if he had, she was certain of that.

Hadn't it been that way with the other young men in town?

"Hello, Reverend Stone. Come on in and I'll help you pick out your things," she said, turning to open the door.

He rushed up and reached for the door before she could. "I'll get that, and please, just call me Brother Caleb. I start looking around for someone else when people call me Reverend!"

She laughed and agreed that she would do as he asked.

Addie looked up as Rachel and Caleb walked through the door. Rachel smiled at her, but Addie just stared thoughtfully at the two of them. Addie always seemed to have the ability to look at Rachel and know what was going on inside her mind. Could she read Rachel's attraction for the preacher? If she did, she obviously didn't approve.

Rachel knew that if that were true, it was only because Addie worried that Rachel might be hurt.

"Howdy, Miz Hayes!" Caleb spoke up, diverting Addie's attention from Rachel. "I sure did enjoy the fine meal you ladies prepared for me last night. Hadn't eaten like that since I left Santa Fe!"

Addie smiled at him; but before she started helping him with his shopping, she gave Rachel a warning look.

———

An hour had passed, and Caleb had just about everything he needed for his house. He purchased supplies ranging from soap to lamp oil, and from linens to a garden rake. He should have been thrilled about getting all of his shopping out of the way, but the fact is, he wasn't.

For one thing, he was frustrated, though he was careful not to show it. He had talked to Rachel for an hour and still was no closer to knowing her than when he had walked into the store. She was polite and nice to him, but distant; it was almost like she was a little bit afraid of him. Now, he would understand her being afraid of what he used to be, but a preacher? It made no sense.

Impatience was another thing eating at him. He wanted to court her, but she wasn't acting like she wanted to be courted!

He sighed quietly. He wasn't sure he was going about this courting business right. Maybe he should ask Lee Cutler's advice. There must be some kind of special technique that he didn't know about.

—⟋⟍—

"It looks like we're going to need one more box," Addie said as she packed all of Caleb's purchases.

"I'll get a box," Rachel said and headed off to the storeroom.

When she was well out of sight, she leaned against the wall, pressed her hand over her beating heart, and let out a long breath.

How could she continue to pretend she wasn't interested in him? He was so charming, and she could tell he was very interested in her.

She wished. . .well, it would do no good to dwell on what could never be. Her life was what it was; and unless she moved away from Springton, it would always be this way.

Being with Caleb Stone made her heart ache for things that every girl dreams of: a husband and family. She had Caitlin and was very thankful for her sweet little girl, but she wished there was a man with whom she could share her precious daughter's life.

She looked over at Caitlin where she slept on a pallet on the floor. It wasn't fair that Caitlin was growing up without a man in her life. There was no way that Rachel would ever want Caitlin to be involved with her real father, but she wished there was someone.

Someone just like. . .Caleb Stone.

Rachel had only been gone a minute or two when Prudence Primrose came breezing through the mercantile door. Her dull gray dress was buttoned up so far that it went beyond being modest, bordering on prudish. Her brown hair was tucked tightly in a bun at her nape, not a stray hair in evidence anywhere. And as always, her nondescript features were pinched into a disapproving frown. (Mrs. Primrose made it her business to disapprove of nearly everything other people did.)

"Mrs. Hayes," she acknowledged in her haughty, condescending way.

"Mrs. Primrose."

In the storeroom, Rachel froze. Prudence Primrose was here? Rachel slumped against the door frame. Would Prudence tell Caleb about her?

Carefully she peeked around the corner and looked at the threesome.

Rachel thought that Prudence Primrose couldn't have picked a worse time to shop in the store. She prayed that Addie could take care of the woman's needs and usher her out the door before anything was said about Rachel.

She saw Prudence's speculative gaze fall on the preacher. She obviously hadn't been introduced. "Mrs. Primrose," Addie began, "I don't reckon you've met our new minister, Reverend Caleb Stone. Reverend, this is Prudence Primrose."

"Mrs. Primrose," Caleb greeted politely.

She nodded coolly as she looked over his appearance. "Well, your hair is mighty long. How does your wife put up with it?" she asked in her usual direct manner.

Addie lifted a brow as if knowing what Prudence was fishing for. "Reverend Stone is a single man. I believe you were out of town when we learned about him in church."

Rachel cringed at the smile that spread across Prudence's face. Prudence had a daughter who was seeing the other side of twenty and still had had no offers for her hand. Prudence no doubt thought that Patience could do far worse than to be a minister's wife.

"Can I help you, Prudence?" Addie asked, obviously breaking into the other woman's thoughts.

Prudence dragged her eyes from the preacher and answered, "I need a bag of sugar and two bags of flour, Adelaide."

That meant Addie would be coming back to the storeroom. It also meant that Prudence would be alone with Caleb.

Addie had just walked a couple of steps when Prudence spoke. "I don't suppose you've met that woman Adelaide lets work here at the store, have you?"

The question came out of nowhere, and at first Caleb didn't respond—he merely stared at the woman. "I'm sorry, ma'am, but are you talking about Miss Branigan?"

Prudence looked very smug at being the one to enlighten the preacher. "Yes, of course. Have you seen her daughter, too, Reverend Stone?" she asked pointedly.

———

Caleb's whole body froze. Daughter? Was Rachel married? He felt like someone had just pulled the rug out from under his feet. "Uh, no, ma'am," he answered lamely. He didn't know *what* to say.

Prudence nodded sternly. "She's not married, of course. Never has been. In fact, she created a huge scandal by claiming. . ."

"STOP IT! Why can't you mind your own business, Mrs. Primrose? You have no right to do this to me. No right!" With tears clouding her eyes, Rachel turned and ran from the store. She never once looked at Caleb.

Caleb's head was spinning with everything that just happened. Confusion warred within his heart and his head. He didn't know what to make of what Prudence had told him and Rachel's reaction to it.

The only thing that stood out clearly was Rachel's tears.

"Please excuse me," he said, walking off in the direction Rachel had fled.

He ignored Prudence Primrose's gaping mouth and Addie's concerned frown and went to find Rachel.

He found her sitting on the ground by the small stream that flowed near the store. Her face was buried in her knees, which were pulled up to her chest.

He sat down beside her.

Rachel knew it was Caleb Stone next to her, but she didn't care. He was a preacher; and now that he knew the gossip about her, he'd start spouting Bible verses at her about the wages of sin and then he'd never come around her again. It was so stupid of her to hope for something that could never be.

"Rachel?" he asked hesitantly, bringing his hand up and patting her on the back. "Please don't cry. I'm sure Mrs. Primrose didn't mean. . ."

Her head flew up and raging wet eyes glared at him so fiercely that he was startled. He immediately removed his hand from her back.

"Go on, Preacher. Tell me what a big sinner I am. Tell me that I should have told you all about it before I allowed you to associate with the likes of me!"

He shook his head with a frown. "Miss Branigan, I don't know what you're talking about! I don't even understand what Mrs. Primrose was saying. And please don't put words in my mouth!" he answered. "I make up my own mind about things, and I have never called anyone a big sinner, nor will I ever do so. That's for God to judge, not me."

She studied him a moment more, then looked away, a cynical look on her face. "Everyone judges, Reverend Stone. Why should you be any different? Three years ago, I became pregnant after my stepcousin raped me. This town practically tarred and feathered me because they thought I'd gotten into this predicament because I was an 'unprincipled woman.' So don't tell me you don't judge, Preacher. I saw the look on your face when you heard I had a daughter."

Caleb felt every bitter word that rolled off her tongue. Rachel had been raped? It made him angry to think of it—angry that someone had so badly hurt this precious woman. And he could only be truthful with her about his reason for his look of shock at hearing about her daughter.

"I thought she meant that you were married, Rachel. That's why I was shocked. I had been trying all morning to get around to telling you that I'd like to come calling on you."

Chapter 5

You *what?*" she asked, disbelief clearly evident in her face.

He smiled gently. "I said I want to court you, and I couldn't do that if you were already married, now could I?"

She looked at him and absently wiped her tears with the back of her hand. "Oh. Well, I guess you know it would be impossible for that to happen now." She was aware that she sounded disappointed, but she couldn't even attempt to hide it. Just the thought of him having *wanted* to court her was so unbelievable.

If only she were just a normal girl with an ordinary life. . .

He didn't answer for a moment. He ran his gaze over her face and hair. And then, with a curious gleam in his eyes, he reached out and took a strand of her hair between his thumb and forefinger.

"No, Rachel, I don't know that," he finally answered. "I still want to come calling on you. I just realize now that it will be a little more difficult to court you than I'd anticipated." He gently laid her hair back on her shoulder.

"Oh, Brother Caleb, you just don't understand. *No one* in this town, except for Addie, believed me when I told them about the rape. I was brought in front of the church and told never to come back because I would not admit to the sin of fornication!"

He shook his head in disbelief. "They *expelled* you? From the church? But Rachel, why didn't you explain what happened?"

Rachel laughed bitterly. "I tried to explain, but no one would believe me. Especially Reverend Parker! I haven't been back since!"

"Well, then you must come back now," he declared, as if it were a simple matter. "We'll show them that I believe you should be in church. Some of them may even change their opinions of you."

"They won't change their minds, Caleb. You don't know these people, what they're capable of. All the sermons in the world won't change their minds." She waved her hand above her head in a gesture of futility.

He reached out and took her hand in his. "I know that, Rachel. But *God* can!" He held her hand tightly. "I want to do this for you, Rachel. God changed my life around, and I believe He may have sent me here to help change yours, too."

Rachel marveled at the fervor and belief in his voice and eyes. She wanted to believe as he did. For so long, she'd prayed that God would give her another chance at life. Sometimes she felt as though He'd forgotten her; but maybe, just maybe, He'd been waiting for the right moment to act in her behalf.

It was foolish to hope. Foolish to want to believe.

But somehow, she did.

She nodded her head. "Maybe you *have* been sent from God. I hope so, Brother Caleb; but I don't want you to lose favor in this town because of your association with me."

He jumped up, pulling her up with him. "We'll cross that bridge when we come to it, all right?" He brought her hand up to his chest. "Will you come this Sunday?"

She looked down. "I don't know. Please. . .please give me time to think about it. . . ."

"Of course," he said in a low voice. She brought her eyes back to his. "I can wait, Rachel. However long it takes, I'll wait. Do you understand?"

She smiled at him shyly and nodded.

"Good!" he declared and let go of her hand. "Now, let me walk you back to the store, and you can tell me about this daughter of yours." They started walking, and he said before she could speak, "And by the way, I liked it when you called me just Caleb."

She looked at him in dismay. "I didn't!"

He winked at her. "You did."

They both laughed, and she started talking about Caitlin as they made their way to the store.

—⚭—

Sunday morning, the sun shone brightly upon the congregation of the First Church of Springton as people made their way into the building. Caleb stood at the door and greeted them as they entered.

He finished shaking a hand and then smoothed his lapels for the fourth time since he'd arrived that morning. He hoped he looked all right. The truth was, he was so nervous, he could hardly stand still. What if he wasn't what they'd expected? What if he said or did the wrong thing?

But, no. God chose him for this job. He would help Caleb get through the morning.

One question plagued him, though. Would Rachel come to church?

—⚭—

As Rachel sat at her window and watched folks enter the little church building at the end of the lane, she knew she wasn't ready to attend church herself. Maybe she'd never be ready.

Caleb's words kept playing in her mind. She wanted to believe that he could help change things for her. She wanted to let herself hope that he'd be able to call on her as he'd said he would.

But this was *his* day. To go into the church today would take all the attention away from him and his carefully prepared sermon and put it all on her.

She promised herself that she would go. . .someday.

Just not today.

—⁊⁊—

Harold Ray stood behind the huge wooden pulpit and nervously cleared his throat. It was well known that there was nothing he hated more than standing in front of a crowd and making a speech. He cleared his throat again and ran a hand over his already-slicked-back hair.

The congregation had quieted down and sat looking at him, willing him to get on with things.

Addie gave a quiet snort and leaned over to Mattie Mae. "Look at how his Adam's apple keeps jiggling up and down. Maybe he should have brought his old blind mule up there with him for comfort!"

"Oh hush up, Addie. Quit being so mean and listen!" she scolded, while trying not to laugh.

"I would, uh, like to, uh, introduce everyone, uh, to our new. . .preacher. We're, uh, proud to, uh, have him here with us!" He let out a relieved breath, glad to have that over. "Reverend Stone," he added, waving his hand toward where Caleb stood on the tiny dais.

Two little girls who sat in front of Addie and Mattie Mae put their heads together and giggled. One of them rolled her eyes and said, "Uh, uh, uh. . . ," and was immediately scolded by their mother.

By now, tears of laughter were gathering in Addie's eyes. Caleb shook Harold Ray's sweat-drenched hand and stepped behind the pulpit. A feeling that this was right swept over him as he placed his hands on the smooth wooden surface. If he hadn't been sure before, he was now.

This was God's plan for his life.

"Thank you, Harold Ray," he said with a nod and a smile, then looked over the congregation with a broad sweep that took in every face. A warm light shone in his green eyes, and there was an open friendliness to his face that immediately put everyone at ease.

"The Bible speaks of the followers of Christ being brothers and sisters in Him. In a sense we are to be a family, to look after one another like a family is supposed to do. To love one another like a family loves its members." He paused and watched as the congregation gave nods of approval and uttered hearty amens.

"That's what I want everyone in this church building today to think of when they think of the First Church of Springton—that we're family.

"I also want to thank you for allowing me to fill your pulpit. I have to admit that I may be different from the kind of preacher you are used to. I'm not a fancy person. On the weekdays you'll probably catch me dressed in overalls and riding a horse. And I don't mind being addressed as Brother Caleb."

He smiled then, a smile that instantly drew people in with him. Many smiled back. "I'm always here to help you. In the daytime or the middle of the night. If you need anything, I'm here for you. Like I said, we're family." He opened his Bible then. "Now, if you'd all open your Bibles to. . ."

—⁂—

Caleb wearily sat down on the front pew and stretched his legs out in front of him. Closing his eyes, he allowed himself to go over in his mind everything that had taken place that morning. He thanked God that he'd had a sermon that seemed to touch people. It just felt good to know that God trusted him enough to lead this congregation. It was daunting, but he felt he could handle the challenge.

He stayed in the pew for a few minutes more and simply basked in the presence of God that seemed to fill the building.

"Hello?"

The hesitant female voice startled him from his relaxed state. He jumped up and turned toward the back of the building, where a woman and a little girl stood.

Rachel. He watched as she fidgeted with her little girl's bow, then wiped her palms on her own skirt. He smiled as he reached them. He noticed that she began to relax.

"Your daughter?" he asked as he bent down to her level.

"Yes, this is Caitlin. Caitlin, this is Brother Caleb. He's the new preacher," she said.

Caleb's heart melted at the sight as eyes so much like Rachel's looked at him curiously. "Hello, Caitlin. My, you're a pretty little girl!" he said as he tugged on a strand of her ink-black hair.

"Hi, Bruddah Caley!" she returned as she reached out and pulled on a strand of *his* hair!

The two adults laughed. "I'm sorry," Rachel said. "I should have warned you that shyness is not one of her problems."

He looked up at Rachel and grinned. "I think she's beautiful. Just like her mother."

Rachel blushed and looked away momentarily.

Caleb just smiled at her. "May I?" he asked, indicating with his hands that he wanted to pick up Caitlin.

Rachel nodded, and he hoisted the little girl up and onto his shoulders. She squealed with delight, and he motioned for them to go up front and sit down.

—⁂—

Longing washed over Rachel as she watched her daughter and Caleb getting to know one another. This was the way it was supposed to have been. But the man playing with her daughter should be her father. Caleb Stone would make a wonderful father.

She had to blink several times to keep the tears at bay. Maybe it was being in this building again or something, but Rachel felt like the walls were closing in on her. She couldn't let Caleb see her fall apart again. She had to be strong.

A hand came around her shoulder, and she realized that Caleb, Caitlin on his shoulders, now was at her side. She guessed he'd been watching her.

"I know it bothers you to be here, Rachel. I'm here with you, and we'll get through this together, all right?"

"I'm sorry, I. . ."

"Shhh. . . It's okay, Rachel. No apologies. I'm just glad that you're here." He took Caitlin off his shoulders and waited for Rachel to sit down; then he joined her, putting Caitlin on his lap.

"How did the service go?" Rachel asked.

Caleb chuckled and ran a finger across his chin. "Well, they didn't fall asleep or walk out in the middle of my sermon, so I guess it went all right." He thought a moment and absently brushed a hand lightly down Caitlin's head. "It felt right. Just like it feels right to me that you are in this church."

She looked away. Uncertainty marred her features. "I don't know about that. That was one of the reasons I didn't come to the service today—I didn't want to ruin this special time for you. Not your first day, in your first church."

He put his hand along the back of the pew and leaned closer to her. "I appreciate your thoughtfulness, Rachel. But it was unnecessary. I was more concerned about you this morning than I was about how my service would go."

He hesitated, looking deep into her eyes; it was almost as if he could see what she was thinking. "I've thought a lot about you since Friday, Rachel. I want you to know that I've not changed my mind about wanting to court you. I want to get to know you *and* Caitlin better and for you to get to know me."

Her eyes started to tear up again. "Caleb, you shouldn't say things like that to me. If anyone suspects your intentions, there will be nothing but trouble."

He put his hand on her shoulder. "Rachel," he said, his voice intense. "Do you care anything for me? Are you trying to let me down easily because you don't feel the same way I feel for you?"

She gasped. "Oh, no! Please don't think that, Caleb. You don't know *how* much

I care for you. I'm just so frightened that we both might get hurt."

Caleb became still at hearing her declaration. "You care for me," he repeated in a voice full of wonder.

Caitlin chose that moment to start wiggling, wanting down.

Impulsively, Rachel reached over and kissed Caleb on the cheek. "We'd better go. And don't stop trying to convince me that this can be real. I want it to be so badly, Caleb."

With that, Rachel took Caitlin by the hand. "Good-bye," she said, and Caitlin parroted the word and waved to him.

"Good-bye," he said faintly as they walked down the aisle and out of the church.

He fell back against the pew in a daze, his hand over his cheek. Two things kept running through his fogged mind. She cared for him, and she had kissed him.

He was a very happy man.

Chapter 6

L eander Cutler lifted his hat off his head as he entered the hotel dining area. A wide grin spread across his face as he spotted the person he'd been looking for.

His long, lean legs carried him quickly to the table in the corner, where Reverend Stone was wolfing down a very tall stack of flapjacks.

Caleb looked up and saw Lee coming toward him. He'd enjoyed getting to know the lawman in the three weeks Caleb had been in town. They had a lot in common, and it was nice having a friend with whom to share meals.

Lee stopped at the empty chair facing Caleb and announced himself. "Well, you were right. I ain't never heard a sermon preached quite the way you did it yesterday!"

Caleb leaned back in his chair and narrowed his eyes in mock seriousness. "Is that some sort of backhanded compliment, or are you insulting my life's work?"

Lee barked out a loud laugh but put a quick damper on it when he noticed everyone staring his way. He shrugged and plopped down into the chair. "Let's just say I had never thought about the story of Jesus walking on the water in a humorous way. The way you described poor old Peter losing his faith out in those waves, well, I got pains in my stomach from laughing so hard. But when you brought the point around about folks like me being just like Peter at times, well, I saw myself going down in all those waves. It made me really think about my own life, Preacher. I've gone to church on and off my whole life, but it's never really meant anything to me. But yesterday, although I didn't walk down the aisle, I made a commitment to God in my heart, to serve Him." He paused and thought a minute, a little embarrassed about his admission. "Do you think that's enough?"

Caleb smiled proudly. "It's a decision of the heart, Lee. All you have to do is really mean it. Walking down an aisle just gives some folks a little extra faith is all." He reached over and gave him a friendly slap on the shoulder. "I'm happy for you, Lee. Being a Christian isn't an easy life, but it's a fulfilling one."

The serious mood was broken when the hotel owner's daughter came over and took Lee's order. Her hazel gaze kept going from one man to the other.

Lee snickered when she finally walked away. "Reckon Miss Suzy, there, can't make up her mind who she's sweet on—me or you."

"She's a fine woman, but I'll let you have her," Caleb offered gallantly.

Lee narrowed his eyes. "That wouldn't have anything to do with all those trips to the mercantile, would it?" he asked shrewdly.

Caleb hadn't told anyone how he felt about Rachel, but he'd managed ways to see her nearly every day. It didn't matter if it was only for a few minutes; he was just content to know that she cared for him, just as he did for her. Even though he couldn't publicly court her and call on her, he knew they would have a future together one day. No one else would do for him.

"That's what a store is for, isn't it? To stop by and purchase what you need?" he asked evasively.

Lee studied his new friend for a moment. "She's real pretty. Probably the prettiest girl in town. I was interested in her myself when I first came to Springington," he said, causing Caleb to look up at him sharply. Lee just ignored the look.

"I'd been here three days when I was duly warned about her, Caleb. That Primrose woman saw me greet Miss Rachel on the street one day, and she didn't hesitate to fill me in on what happened three years ago. I guess you know 'bout that?"

A grim expression stole over Caleb's face. "I know about it. I also know that Mrs. Primrose's version and Rachel's version of the story aren't one and the same."

Lee nodded. "To tell you the truth, I've always felt that a person's past was their own business; and, Lord knows, I wouldn't want anyone poking around in mine. I could tell she was a nice girl and wasn't the scarlet woman Mrs. Primrose painted her to be. But after she got me well informed, she issued a warning. What it all boiled down to was, if I wanted to continue to be the sheriff of Springington, I'd do well to stay away from Rachel Branigan."

Caleb's jaw clenched and an angry flush rose on his face.

Lee sighed. "I didn't feel anything toward her. I hardly knew her. She never paid much attention to me anyhow. I didn't figure it was worth losing my livelihood over. I ain't met a girl yet who was worth that."

Caleb fiddled with the silverware by his plate as he thought about what Lee had told him. It sounded, more and more, like he wasn't just fighting against a few people for Rachel. He was going to have to fight the whole town!

Because he and Lee had become friends and Caleb really needed someone to talk to, he confided, "Lee, Rachel was attacked and molested by her stepcousin, Milton Pierce. Rachel told everyone that and was never believed. But, Lee, I believe her."

Lee studied his friend for a moment and then nodded his head. "Then that's good enough for me, Preacher. You sound like you want to try to do something about it."

"As a matter of fact, I do. I just don't know how I'm going to do it!"

"Why, Reverend Stone! Just the man I wanted to see!" A boisterous voice intruded upon their conversation.

Lee watched as Caleb raised his head curiously. Caleb turned his head and looked back over his shoulder at the man walking in their direction.

Jebediah Pierce.

"Morning, Mr. Pierce," Caleb greeted, praying at the same time that the smile on his face didn't look as forced as it felt.

Jebediah puffed out his flabby chest and strutted over to the preacher's table. He was a man who prided himself on his attire whenever he rode into town. As usual, he sported his brown suit with the matching vest, and around his neck he wore a thin ribbon tie like he'd seen the big ranchers wear back in Houston.

Today, he'd apparently decided it was about time he had a visit with the new preacher and make his presence known.

"Good morning to you, Brother Stone. No, no. Don't get up. I'll just pull me up a chair and join you, if you don't mind." He didn't wait for an answer. He sat down, and that's when he realized the sheriff was seated there as well.

"And how are you, Sheriff Cutler?" Jebediah greeted.

"Oh, fair to middlin', Pierce," Lee drawled unexpressively.

Caleb narrowed his eyes on the rancher as the man turned his attention back to him. He wondered what Jebediah was up to. Nothing good, he guessed. He'd probably like to know where that boy of his was. There were rumors about that he'd joined up with a gang of outlaws that had been stirring up trouble around this part of Texas. Lee had said that he was just waiting for Milton to mess up and that he had a cell with Milton's name on it.

After a bit of small talk about weather and ranching, Jebediah finally got to the point. "Reverend, I'm not sure that you're aware of this, but I was considered by the late Reverend Parker to be sort of his assistant on certain occasions," he announced.

Caleb's face remained unreadable. "Is that right?"

"Why, yes! He valued my opinion on many matters, and I hope that you'll feel free to come to me when you need help of any kind."

Caleb nodded pleasantly. Or so it appeared. On the inside he was fighting to remain impartial and not let his feelings for the man get in the way. He knew that Jebediah Pierce could have stood up for Rachel, but instead he'd turned his back. How could he forget that?

"I'll keep that in mind, Mr. Pierce. And by the way, I met your niece the other day at the mercantile. Rachel Branigan?"

The veins of Jebediah's forehead bulged at the mention of her name and his face became red. "That woman is no kin of mine. Any connection she had with our family became severed when she. . ."

Caleb interrupted, "I heard the story, Mr. Pierce. I just don't happen to believe that it was like everyone is saying. Didn't you, even just once, wonder if she was telling the truth? What if that little girl, who everyone ignores like she has some horrible disease, *is* your granddaughter?"

Jebediah began mopping his brow with a handkerchief. "No, Brother Stone, I did not. I believed my son." He put the hankie away and looked at the preacher with a show of outward calm. "But that's just water under the bridge, isn't it? Reverend Parker dealt with that."

Caleb's temper was about to reach the boiling point. He knew anger was something a minister, especially a new one, should always control, but. . . He was leaning forward to give the man a good piece of his mind when he felt a hard, swift kick under the table. He saw Lee frown and shake his head.

Suddenly Caleb reined himself and his anger back in. How had he let himself get so out of control? He was about to make a scene in a very public place over a matter that was important because it was personal. He would find a way to resolve the issue, but not today. He would be wasting his breath with this man.

"Well," he said, letting go a deep, cleansing breath. "I believe the truth always has a way of letting itself be known."

He got up from the table and tossed a couple of coins by his plate. "I'd better be going. I have visitations this morning. Give your wife my regards, Mr. Pierce. I'll be stopping by to see her soon about the Sunday school class she volunteered to teach."

Jebediah looked bewildered at the sudden impending departure of the preacher. "But I. . ."

Caleb ignored him and continued. "You have a nice day now." He looked at Lee. "I'll be seeing you, Sheriff."

Lee jumped up himself. "I'll walk out with you, Preacher. I need to be going, too."

"Well," Jebediah stammered, "good morning. . .I. . ."

They both tipped their hats and kept on walking till they were out the door.

Outside, Caleb stopped and leaned against the railing where folks kept their horses tied up. He was frowning and looked troubled. "I don't know how to thank you, Lee. I nearly made a fool of myself in there."

Lee shrugged. "I probably would have done the same thing if I'd been you."

"Yeah, but I've got to get a handle on this thing," he replied, shaking his head.

"Oh, by the way," Lee said, "Harold Ray is expectin' about four horses to come in today. He told me that he wired a Dallas ranch about what you wanted. One of those should suit you fine."

"Okay, I'll drop by and let him know that I'm interested," he said, excited about finally getting a horse. "I was beginning to think I'd be stuck forever riding that rickety old buggy you lent me, Cutler! 'Bout broke my neck when the wheel went flying off yesterday evening!"

"That's 'cause you don't know nothin' about how to drive one of those things!" Lee tossed back with a grin.

Caleb laughed and readily agreed. "You're right. I guess you'll have to teach me sometime."

"Not before I make out my will. I might not survive the experience!"

Caleb shook his head and put his hat back on his head. "See ya later, Sheriff."

"See ya, Preacher."

Caleb stopped at Harold Ray's stables to find out what time he needed to come by later that afternoon.

Harold Ray lifted his hat, scratched his head a little bit, then put it back on. "Wahl. . .I suppose they're comin' 'round five o'clock today. You can stop back by then."

Caleb nodded and thought a minute before he asked the next question. "Uh. . .Harold Ray? I wanted to ask Rachel Branigan if she could stop in here and look at the horses with me. I know how a lot of folks here in town feel about her, but we've become friends and all—"

Harold Ray waved him to a stop. "Never did cotton to the way this town handled that situation. If you ask me, I think it's high time that Miss Rachel had a gentleman friend! Addie and me talk about it all the time!" he said gruffly.

Caleb had seen the old man and Addie together. He should have known that Addie would have an influence on how Harold Ray felt about Rachel.

Caleb smiled at the man. "I'm much obliged, Mr. Norton! See you at five." He tipped his hat and walked out.

Chapter 7

Caleb was headed to the mercantile to see Rachel, just as he did every day. She was still shy with him, and he hated having to make excuses to see her. But he wasn't about to give up hope.

Caleb had nearly reached the mercantile when one of the "ladies of the evening" from the saloon walked by him. She pulled her shawl around her bare shoulders and shabby dress and looked at him warily.

He felt sorry for her. Like so many people in the world, she, too, needed Christ. Ignoring the woman or feeling superior to her would not help her situation. So he tipped his hat and said to her, "Morning, ma'am."

At first she looked startled, and Caleb saw her eyes fill with tears. She cleared her throat and quickly said, "Morning, Preacher." Then she scurried around him.

Caleb turned and looked after her with a worried frown; and when he turned around again, he nearly ran into Prudence Primrose and her daughter, Patience, who were standing right in front of him.

"Brother Caleb," she said smartly, her face pinched tight with disapproval, "maybe you are not aware of this, but that woman you just spoke to is not someone the decent folks of this town associate with. A minister has to remember things such as that."

Caleb, who usually just nodded and let her words go in one ear and out the other, became irritated. He was not in the mood to listen to anything Prudence Primrose had to say! "Mrs. Primrose, I only said hello. Jesus didn't ignore people just because they weren't acceptable to the 'decent folks.' We should follow His example."

She quickly backed off. "Of course you are right, Brother Caleb. I wasn't sure you knew whom you were talking to. I—"

"I knew, Mrs. Primrose. I hope you ladies have a fine day," he said as he tried to move around them.

"Oh, there was something else I wanted to mention, if you don't mind," she said, stopping his escape.

He stifled a sigh. "And what is that, Mrs. Primrose?"

She thrust her chin up in the air, the way she always did when she had something that she thought was of great importance to tell. "It's been brought to my attention that you've been seen at the mercantile quite a bit. I hope you are not becoming friendly with that Rachel Branigan. It didn't set well with me that day you went running out after her. I just want to warn you—"

"Uh, Miss Patience? I heard that you can sing. Would you want to sing a special song this Sunday at church?" he interrupted, not wanting to get into the subject of Rachel again.

That shut Prudence right up. She actually smiled and clasped her hands together. "Of course she will! Tell him, dear, that you'd love to!"

Patience began batting her eyelashes at him (he'd noticed that, while she was being ignored, she hadn't batted them even one time). "Why, of course I will, Brother Caleb! Sure is awful nice of you to think of me."

Oh no, he thought as he watched her give him a flirtatious smile. *Out of the pot and into the frying pan!* He certainly didn't want Patience to think he was giving her special attention.

"I'm just relying on what someone told me, Miss Patience. Let me know your selection so I can make an announcement." He tipped his hat once more. "I'll see you both Sunday." He was quicker about going around them this time, and he succeeded.

All this was being observed (in a subtle way, of course) by Addie and Mattie Mae from the window of the mercantile, while Rachel listened to their chatter. She was sorting through the candy and taking the empty boxes to the storeroom.

"Wonder what that was all about?" Mattie Mae pondered aloud.

"Hmm. I don't know, but Prudence's mouth is hangin' open like she wasn't done talking," Addie mused.

Mattie Mae sighed and backed away from the window. "Oh well. Show's over. Let's get these books dusted off."

They headed off toward the back of the store to the bookshelves. They got together every week to dust the books and to share any news they'd heard that week. (They would never, of course, call it gossip!)

They each grabbed a dust rag and a book and sat down on a pair of stools.

"That Brother Caleb is something else, I'll tell ya!" Addie commented. "Why, he don't care a hoot or holler what folks think of his methods of doing things. The man's been sittin' outside the saloon every night, talkin' to men as they go in and out. Says to me that most of those men wouldn't set foot near his church doors, so he just goes to them instead! Why, it seems to be working, too. Saw old Dusty Ramsey sittin' in the back pew Sunday morning. The old coot had shaved his whiskers and even combed his hair." She looked thoughtful for a moment. "You know, I believe that's the first time I've ever seen old Dusty sober!"

Mattie Mae nodded. "Yeah, he's doing a right fine job!" she agreed.

Rachel grinned as she listened in on their conversation. She loved hearing about

Caleb and everything he was doing in the town. She looked over at the last of the boxes and sighed. Work wasn't going to get done by daydreaming and eavesdropping.

She picked up the empty boxes and carried them to where the older women were. "Addie, I'll be in the storeroom," Rachel told the storekeeper.

The little bell above the door tinkled as soon as she had spoken, signaling the arrival of a customer. Addie didn't move. She just looked over at Mattie Mae and said, "See about the customer first, will ya, Rachel?"

"I wonder who it is?" Mattie Mae asked.

Addie lifted a brow and looked down at the watch pinned to her dress. "That'll be the reverend," she said.

Mattie Mae looked at her oddly and strained to see over the shelf they were sitting behind. "How in the world did you know he was coming here?"

"It's eleven o'clock. Comes in here every day about this time."

"What for?"

Addie shrugged, her eyes on her dusting. "Paper."

"Paper?"

Addie looked at her with patience. "Preachers make notes for their sermons, don't they? I reckon that's what he needs paper for."

"He buys paper every day?"

Addie nodded. "A tablet each day."

Mattie Mae whistled softly. "That's an awful lot of note taking!"

"I reckon."

—⁊⁊—

Rachel came from the back of the store, an excitement dancing around in her chest. It was the same every time Caleb came into the mercantile. She knew he came to see her, though they both pretended that wasn't why he was there.

She found him looking through the tools in the store's third aisle. He apparently was very interested in what he was examining, because he didn't hear her as she came up behind him.

"Hello, Brother Caleb."

Caleb whirled around when he heard her voice, not knowing she was so close to him. He reached out to steady her as she took a step back, but she bumped into a stack of cans and lost her balance. Before he knew it, she was falling; and because he was holding on to her, he fell right with her.

"Oomph!" they both grunted as they hit the floor. Caleb had made an attempt to help break her fall but instead ended up falling across her body.

Immediately he lifted his head and looked at her startled face. "Rachel! Are you hurt?"

She looked like she was having a hard time breathing, and she mumbled something that he couldn't understand.

"What? I can't understand you, Rachel? What's wrong?"

"YOU'RE SQUASHING THE LIVING DAYLIGHTS OUT OF ME! GET OFF!" she forced out in one breath.

"Oh!" Caleb mumbled, chagrined. He clumsily pushed away the cans and scrambled to his feet.

"I'm sorry, Rachel. Let me help you up," he said, offering his hand.

She let him lift her up, and, after a quick check, realized that she was unhurt. She looked up to find Caleb watching her with concern. "I'm okay," she assured him. "Really, I am."

He reached for her hand and held it between both of his. "I hope so, Rachel, because I would never forgive myself if I'd harmed you in any way."

He looked so upset. She was touched by his concern. "You didn't. Now help me pick up these cans before Addie skins us both," she said with a teasing smile.

He let go of her hand. "Oh no! We don't want to make the old girl mad!" he said, laughing, and quickly went to work.

They restacked the cans in no time. "Okay!" Rachel exclaimed, dusting off her hands. She turned to Caleb. "Did you need more paper today?" she asked innocently.

He passed her a dry look. "No ma'am. I think I have enough paper to last quite awhile now."

She laughed. "Well, what can I get you today? Do you need any tools?"

"No. I came by to ask you if you would meet me at Harold Ray's stables. I'm meeting him around five to get a horse from him. Thought you might want to be there when I pick one out."

Her smile fell. "I don't think so, Caleb. Somebody might see me."

He let out a frustrated breath. "Please, Rachel. I know you worry about that, but I really want you to come today. Nobody will notice if you come at, say, five-thirty, will they?"

She knew she should say no, but looking at him and knowing how much he wanted to be with her. . .

"Okay, Caleb. I'll meet you at the stables," she relented. "But please make sure nobody sees us, all right? I'm worried about you, not me."

His smile was back. "Great. And I promise everything will be fine." He picked up her hand and gave it a quick kiss. "I'll see you this afternoon!" And with that he left the store.

Rachel was still staring at the closed door when she overheard the ladies talking.

Mattie Mae spoke up. "Okay, Addie Hayes. What's this all about? What is going on between those two?"

"They are friends and that's all. Now stop trying to make mountains out of molehills, and let's get back to work!"

"Humph!" Mattie Mae snorted. "Friends or not, no one is going to like them being seen together. It'll cause nothing but trouble, Addie. Trouble!"

"I know, Mattie Mae. I know."

Rachel closed her eyes tightly for a second, then went back to get the boxes.

Chapter 8

Harold Ray had a small corral behind his stables. As Caleb approached the three horses grazing there, he knew which one was his. The horse had a shiny black coat and stood tall—it obviously was the product of excellent bloodlines.

Caleb leaned on the fence beside Harold Ray. "See one you like?" Harold Ray asked. "They're all three good riding horses, but they are also buggy trained, if you need them for that."

Caleb nodded his head and studied the horses once more. "Let me have a look at the black one there."

Harold Ray opened the gate and grinned at the preacher. "Figured that would be the one you liked! Go on in and look him over." He motioned Caleb forward.

The horse eyed Caleb warily as he approached the animal. He reached out his hand, and the horse jerked his head away but didn't back up.

"Whoa there, boy," he called softly to the horse. "That's right. Easy now. . ." This time the horse stood still and let Caleb's hand stroke his nose and then his neck.

"He's a beauty, ain't he?" Harold Ray commented behind Caleb. "He was a little skittish when he first got here, but it seems like he has calmed down some. He'll do good for you!"

Harold Ray brought the horse into the stable and they saddled him. They were still standing talking when Rachel and Caitlin walked in.

"Come on in, Rachel!" Caleb called out when she seemed hesitant about entering.

Rachel shut the door behind her and looked at both of them.

Caleb motioned for her to join them, aware of her nervousness. He felt so proud when she walked up and stood by him. He knelt down and picked up Caitlin so that she could get a better look at the horse.

"What do you think?" he asked them both, though his eyes were on Rachel.

Rachel looked at the horse and said the first thing that came to her mind. "He's so big!"

The two men laughed. "Yes, he is that." He directed his attention to Caitlin. "What do you think, darlin'? Do you want to touch him?"

Caitlin seemed to ponder this for a moment. "Horse spooky!" she said, but the next minute she had her chubby little hand on the horse's mane, lightly touching the coarse hairs with her fingertips.

"Spooky, huh?" echoed Caleb. He threw both Harold Ray and Rachel a wry look. "Not spooky enough that she's afraid of him, apparently."

Rachel laughed and shook her head. "There's not much that scares her, I'm afraid. She's too curious to stay afraid for long."

Harold Ray spoke, then excused himself, saying he had to go check on the two horses still in the corral.

Rachel's nervousness returned the moment Harold Ray walked out the door. And Caleb knew it.

"Hey," he called softly to her so that she'd look at him. "It's okay. Harold Ray is not going to say anything about you being here."

She shrugged. "I know. He's really sweet. I'm just not used to any of this, Caleb."

He put Caitlin down and then reached out to tuck a loose hair behind her ear. "I know. But I'm so glad that you came."

She smiled. "Me, too." She took Caitlin's hand and looked toward the door. "But I guess we'd better go. It's going to be dark soon."

He nodded. "I'll watch to make sure you get back all right."

"Just make sure—"

He waved away her concern. "I won't be seen, Rachel. I promise."

When they got to the door, he stopped her before she could open it. "Rachel, I have an idea. Why don't I meet you tomorrow for lunch, out by the stream. Nobody ever comes by there at that time of day, and I'll even bring the food."

She paused, and he had a sinking feeling that she was going to refuse. It was like there was a war going on in her head. Then she looked at him and blurted out, "Okay. We'll be there."

He couldn't believe she'd agreed so quickly. He felt like throwing his head back and giving a victory yell, yet he did his best to appear calm. "Great!" He opened the stable door and lovingly ran his eyes down her pretty face. "I'll see you tomorrow, then."

She shyly nodded. "Good night."

He stood at the door and watched as she made her way to the mercantile. "Good night," he whispered, his voice floating out after her in the night.

When she arrived at the store and went inside, he closed the door and yelled, "Yee-haw!"

He felt a little foolish when he turned around and found Harold Ray staring at him like he'd lost his mind.

Rachel and Caitlin were the first to arrive at the pretty spot beneath the willow tree. Her hands shook as she tucked back a stray hair that had blown across her face. Not for the first time, she glanced down at her clothes to recheck her appearance. She wore a pink calico skirt with a white shirtwaist. Nothing fancy. Should she have dressed up more? Maybe she shouldn't have come at all.

Caitlin found the water and ran toward the edge.

"No, Caity!" Rachel called out as she caught up with the enthusiastic two-year-old. "You mustn't get so close to the water without me, lass. I wouldn't want you to fall in!"

She pointed out a couple of minnows that were swimming by. Caitlin wanted to try to catch them, but Rachel talked her out of it.

They were still talking about the fish when they heard Caleb's horse galloping up behind them.

Caitlin immediately forgot about the fish and fixed her attention on Caleb and his horse. "Spooky horsey! Spooky horsey!" she chanted, jumping up and down as Caleb dismounted.

Rachel's heart was pounding in her chest as he walked toward them. *He surely must be the most handsome man in all of Texas,* she thought. His longish black hair was wind-tossed, his sun-bronzed skin was flushed from the ride, and his green eyes sparkled in the sunlight.

All of a sudden, she realized that she had fallen in love with him. It was like he'd been made just for her. Surely God would work something out, she prayed.

"Hello," he said in a low voice. He was looking at her peculiarly; and after a moment, Rachel realized that he was looking at her just like *she* was looking at *him*!

"Hi," she returned softly.

They stood there looking into each other's eyes; and for a moment, nothing in the world mattered except for them and that moment.

"I missed you, you know," he said.

She blushed and replied, "I missed you, too."

But Caitlin was being left out and was not happy about it.

"Caley! Caley! Pick up! Pick up!" she cried and held up her arms for him.

They both laughed. He scooped the little girl into his arms and hugged her. "Caley, huh? Never been called that before."

"Caley," she said with a nod, as if saying "and that settles the matter!"

Rachel smiled and shook her head. Then she pointed to the willow tree. "I have a blanket spread out over there; and if you'll get the food, I'll lay it all out."

"All right. Come on, Caitlin! Let's go get the food." He hoisted her up onto his shoulders, and she squealed with delight.

Rachel watched them and felt a small ache in her heart. Caitlin had missed so much, not having a father. She realized that her little girl was becoming fond of Caleb. What if she got attached to him and he gave in to the dictates of the town and stopped coming around to see them?

Rachel was afraid that it would devastate them both.

But she wasn't going to think about dismal and depressing thoughts today! She ran toward the blanket where Caleb and Caitlin were already heading and went to work putting out the food.

They had a wonderful picnic. Caleb had gotten plenty of food from the restaurant, and they listened to him tell stories about his life in Santa Fe and his surrogate parents, the Ellises. He also got Rachel to talk about herself. Mainly, about her life before her parents were killed.

After they finished their meal, Caleb took Caitlin riding around the meadow on the big black horse (which Caleb still hadn't named). And he promised to bring Rachel back to this place, when Caitlin wasn't with her, and give her a ride also.

They were packing up the food and the blanket when Caitlin went skipping off to pick flowers that were growing by an old stump.

Caleb fastened the basket to the saddle. "I can't say when I've had a more pleasant day." He turned and smiled at her. "Thanks for coming today, Rachel. You two are special to me, and I'm thankful for every moment that I have with you."

Rachel's heart melted at the precious words. "Caleb, you shouldn't say things like that to me, *but*," she quickly added when he opened his mouth to argue, "I'm so glad you did. I enjoy being with you, too; you've brought so much to our lives, Caleb. I can't tell you how much."

Caleb's throat developed a knot, and it became hard to swallow. No one had ever meant so much to him. No one had ever affected him like Rachel Branigan did.

But one word, spoken by Caitlin, destroyed the moment.

"Snake."

That word sent both Caleb and Rachel into a frozen panic. Caleb's head snapped up to look where Caitlin stood. Coiled in front of her, its head arched back in a curve and its tail rattling a warning, was a rattler.

And it was ready to strike.

Rachel turned and with a cry started to run toward her daughter. Caleb grabbed her and held her still.

"Don't! If you frighten Caitlin and make her move, that snake will strike."

Rachel whimpered but nodded her head. She was shaking, and Caleb knew it took everything within her not to run to her little girl.

Luckily, Caitlin didn't seem to be upset at seeing the snake. She apparently had no idea it was dangerous and could bite. She watched the rattling tail in fascination.

Sweat started to bead on Caleb's forehead as he slowly reached into his saddlebag and brought out his six-shooter.

Rachel gasped when she saw the gun flash in the preacher's hand. He sent her a brief look of warning, then turned his attention back to the rattler.

Slowly and carefully, he inched forward. His heartbeat pounded in his ears, and he had to force his arm to be steady. One shot was all he'd have. And it had been three long years since he'd touched a trigger.

He was close enough, he knew. He cocked the gun and took aim.

But Caitlin moved and the snake struck.

Later, Caleb wouldn't remember the moment he knew to pull the trigger. It had been all instinct and reflex.

Just like it had always been.

The snake's head exploded in midair. Caitlin screamed and fell backward.

"CAITLIN!" Rachel screamed and rushed to her daughter, who lay prone on the ground. For one horrifying moment, she thought Caleb had shot her.

But Caitlin was already trying to sit up by the time Rachel reached her. Her face was pale and teary. "Snake was gonna get me!" she cried as she threw her trembling arms around her mother's neck.

"Shhh. It's okay, sweetheart. Caleb got the snake. It's all right now," she said softly into her daughter's satiny hair.

It wasn't until she spoke his name that she realized Caleb had not walked over to them. She looked over her shoulder at him.

He was still standing where he had fired the pistol. His eyes were dazed as he looked down into his hand where the six-shooter lay. His face was white as a sheet, and he was shaking.

"Caleb?"

He looked up, but she could tell he wasn't really seeing her. It was as if his mind was occupied, like he was somewhere far off and very frightened.

She felt afraid for him but had no idea why.

Slowly he lowered his eyes to the pistol and held it tightly in his fist. He blinked one time, then again, and looked as if he were just becoming aware of his surroundings. His grip loosened on the pistol. Without looking in Rachel's direction, he walked over to his horse and put the gun back into the saddlebag.

Caleb closed his eyes for a moment and leaned his head forward to rest on his saddle. He breathed in deeply. He sent up a silent prayer of thanks and a small plea for strength. For one terrifying moment, it had all come back to him. The power of holding the pistol in his hand. The adrenaline that surged through his system. But this time he hadn't been in complete control. This time he was gripped by fear.

Fear and guns were a deadly combination.

He could have missed.

"Caleb?" Rachel called out. He felt her warm hand on his back. "Are you okay?"

He pushed back from the saddle and turned toward her. Rachel looked at him with concern as she cradled Caitlin in her arms. "Is she all right?" he demanded.

Rachel nodded. "She's just fine, Caleb. Thanks to you."

"Caley!" Caitlin cried and then flew into Caleb's arms. He caught her easily and held her against his chest. He held out his other arm, and Rachel joined them.

Rachel and Caleb really couldn't have said how long they stood that way— Caleb with an arm around each of them, holding them to him as if they were his dearest possessions. And they both had to laugh when Caitlin started wiggling, wanting down.

It lightened both of their moods.

But it was getting late, and Caleb knew Rachel had to get back to her job.

"Thank you, Caleb. I could never repay you for what you did. I just hope that *you* are all right," she said with concern.

He smiled, though there was a weariness in his eyes. "I'm fine." He patted her arm. "Now you two get on back. I'll watch to make sure you get there all right."

She nodded and gave him one last searching look, then she and Caitlin began making their way back to the mercantile.

Caleb was mounting his horse when he felt it, a prickly sensation that started at the back of his neck and ran down the length of his back. It was another one of those things that he'd not experienced in three years.

In the past it had never failed him.

Quick as lightning, he whirled around and searched the trees that lined the far side of the creek. Nothing. He relaxed and chuckled to himself. He chalked it up to leftover nerves from handling the gun today. He let out a breath and took one last look at the thick woods, then mounted his horse.

—⁊⁊—

From his resting place beside a tree, a slightly drunk Snake Barnes watched the rider fade from his view. He rubbed his eyes and shook his head.

"Nah! It couldn' be," he mumbled to himself. "Tha' looked like Stone!"

He sighed, scratched his whiskers, and pulled himself up. He swayed but caught himself.

"Gotta tell Jenkins 'bout this," he said aloud.

He then made his way back to the gang's camp, chuckling all the way.

Chapter 9

The tapping at his door brought Caleb awake immediately. He'd always been a light sleeper. In his former line of work, that had been a necessity.

He was grumbling to himself about it being the middle of the night when he opened the door. At first he didn't see anyone. Then he looked down.

Whatever he'd expected, it certainly hadn't been two blond-headed children wearing ragged clothing and looking at him like he was their only hope.

Ten-year-old Jessie Holt stood bravely in front of the frightening man, gripping his five-year-old sister's hand. Their mama and daddy had died a few weeks back of influenza, and they had been left in their aunt's care. She wasn't a particularly good person, though; and when she'd heard that the preacher in this town had talked about starting an orphanage, she wasted no time in finding his house and dumping them off. All they owned in the world were the clothes on their backs and a crudely written letter their aunt had sent the preacher.

Caleb stared at the children for a moment, wondering what they were doing at his door, particularly at this time of night. He opened his mouth to ask that question, but the boy held a piece of paper out to him.

Puzzled, he reached out, took the paper, and smoothed it out so that he could read it. The writing was messy and almost illegible, like a child had written it. But the message was all too clear: These kids had been abandoned.

And they expected *him* to take care of them.

He did what most men would do in this kind of situation—he panicked. Then he went in search of help.

—⁂—

Addie and Rachel nearly fell over each other as they came rushing out of their bedrooms at the same time.

Rachel pushed her tangled hair out of her eyes. "Who do you think it is?" she asked a startled Addie.

"I don't know, but I guess we better go down and see!" she answered. "Oh, wait!" Addie added as she disappeared back inside her room. When she returned, she was holding a shotgun.

Rachel gasped. "Addie! What in the world are you going to do with that?"

55

"It's for protection!" she declared.

"Addie Hayes, I don't think I trust you with that gun! Do you even know how to use it?"

"I've seen it done."

Rachel's eyes narrowed in the darkness. "Addie, just because you went all three nights to see that Wild West traveling show, it doesn't make you Annie Oakley!"

"Shhh!" Addie hushed her as they walked into the store. The shades were pulled and the room was dark. She walked quickly to the side of the door. "Get back, Rachel," she hissed. "They could start shootin'."

Rachel rolled her eyes but did as ordered.

Addie cocked the rifle with a flair that would have done Wild Bill proud and shouted out, "Okay!" She pushed the lock on the door and threw it open. "Hold it right there. . . ."

Her voice trailed off into a whisper when she looked into the amused eyes of Reverend Stone.

"Saw the Wild West show, did you, Miz Hayes?" he asked with a straight face.

"Is she goin' to shoot us?" a voice asked below them.

Addie and Rachel's gaze zeroed in on the two children standing next to Caleb. But the children didn't seem to notice the attention. Their eyes were trained on the barrel of the shotgun pointed in their direction.

"Oh!" Addie cried with a red face. She quickly propped up the gun inside the door. "Come on in, Brother Caleb."

"Brother Caleb, whose children are these?" Rachel asked as the threesome stepped inside.

Caleb wearily removed the hat from his head and laid it on the counter. "Ladies, meet Jessie and Emmy Holt. They're from Louisiana. Their ma and pa died about six weeks ago, and their aunt dropped them off at my front door just a little while ago."

"You mean she just left them with you and rode off?" Rachel asked in disbelief. "What was her reason?"

"I didn't talk to her. She wrote a note for Jessie to give to me, and it didn't say much."

"She said she wouldn't be able to find her a husband if she was saddled with two kids," Jessie explained calmly, drawing the adults' attention. He looked so much older than his ten years as he stood calmly before them, still holding his sister's hand.

Ever the crusader, Addie became indignant. "I say we hitch up a few wagons and see to finding this woman. We'll bring her back here to face her responsibilities!"

"Now, Miz Hayes," Caleb interjected. "She'll just go dump them off some other place. Next time it could be a worse place than my house."

Addie grew quiet as the truth set in. Everyone knew that a lot of bad things could happen to innocent children in this day and age.

Rachel smiled down at the little girl as she asked Caleb, "Brother Caleb, what do you need us to do?"

Caleb seemed to hedge on his answer. "I was hoping that. . .maybe. . .you two could watch them for me tonight. I don't have extra bedding for the other beds in the house. I'm just not prepared."

Addie nodded. "Of course we will. Come on, kids. Let's get you into some bed-clothes, and I'll show you where you can sleep!"

Caleb and Rachel watched with amazement as Addie hustled the children up the stairs before either of them could answer.

Caleb shook his head. "Is she always like that?"

Rachel giggled. "Yep. She's probably thirty-five years older than me, but I can't keep up with her!"

It grew quiet in the room, and for the first time, they realized that they were all alone.

Caleb looked around as if searching for something to say, then gave up and just looked back at her.

"I'll be here as early as I can get here in the morning," he finally said.

She blinked and realized that she'd been staring at him. "Oh. Uh, okay," she stammered. She started to turn away, but he took her chin between his thumb and finger.

He leaned forward and softly kissed her lips, then backed away.

"Good night, Rachel." His voice sounded as if it had been raked over sandpaper.

He was out of the building, and Rachel realized that she hadn't uttered a word since the kiss. She didn't even tell him good-bye.

Rachel would always wonder if she'd walked back up those stairs that night or if she actually had floated.

—◊—

The next morning, before Rachel had even come downstairs, Caleb and Addie talked about what he must do.

He'd discussed his plans with the church board about starting an orphanage. They were in favor of doing so, although they'd planned for it to be further in the future. For now, he'd have to keep the kids at the parsonage until he could find them a good home. He would also need to build an extra room onto his house. For that, he'd need the church members' help.

But the biggest problem he faced was finding household help during the day. Who would cook their meals? He couldn't take them to the restaurant for each of their meals. Who could fill this role?

They both voted for Rachel. Rachel, however, was horrified by the plan.

"You want me to do *what*?" Rachel blurted out to Caleb. "You two can't be serious!"

Caleb took her hand in his. "Rachel, just listen, all right? What better way to get folks used to seeing us together? And just think of the time that we *will* be able to spend together every day, Rachel!"

Addie glared at Caleb. "Now, hold on there, boy! Just what are your intentions concerning Rachel?"

Caleb let her hands go and threw his arms up in surrender. "Perfectly honorable, Addie. I've been telling Rachel that I'd like to court her. Well, if we can't be together as a couple in public just yet, at least we can get to know each other better with her helping with the kids at my house."

Addie crossed her arms under her bosom. She looked stern. "I hope you realize what you're up against, 'cause it won't be easy." She turned to Rachel. "And you, young lady. How do you feel about all this?"

Rachel glanced at Caleb, then back at Addie. "Oh Addie, I don't know. Ever since I met Caleb, I've wished I was a normal girl with no past to drag around with me. I don't want this to make things worse for us. I hope and pray things *will* work out," she said truthfully.

Addie sighed and dropped her arms. "Oh, all right. Just watch everything that you do, you hear? I 'spect God will work this out, if it's His will. You just got to be careful!" She pinned Rachel with another look. "Now tell me straight. Are you going to help out this poor man or not?"

Rachel looked at Addie, then Caleb. He looked back at her with pleading eyes.

"Yes. I'll do it," she said. "I just hope we're all not sorry later on!"

—❦—

By that afternoon, word had spread throughout Springton about the children. Folks came to the parsonage with clothes for the children and enough food to last several weeks. Bobby Joe Aaron, one of the owners of Aaron Brothers Sawmill, came by and offered the lumber and labor needed to build an addition onto the parsonage.

Bobby Joe was one man Caleb had yet to figure out. He came to church Sunday mornings with his little girl and his three brothers, but he rarely socialized. Addie had told him that Bobby Joe's wife had left him when his daughter was only a baby. His wife later died, but Bobby Joe didn't show any interest in finding a replacement for her. He seemed like a sad man. Caleb prayed that he might be able to reach out to him someday.

His final guests were Prudence and Patience Primrose. He let them in and they met the children. Prudence barely acknowledged them, but Patience cooed and made over them like she'd never seen children before. Then she'd turned her attentions Caleb's way.

She was sweet on him, that much was obvious. And somewhere along the line, someone must have told her that batting her eyelashes was attractive to a man, because she could bat those lashes faster than anything he'd ever seen. And she giggled. There wasn't anything that wore on his nerves faster than a giggling female.

Unless, of course, the giggle was sweet and sounded like bells. Like. . .Rachel's!

"I just wanted to tell you, Brother Caleb, that I would be happy to come around some night and cook for you. I know you must have a lot of volunteers, but I can come anytime you want!" Patience offered with a lot of the batting and giggling thrown in.

"Oh, well, I—"

"Now, we won't take *no* for an answer, Reverend," Prudence interjected. "Patience is an excellent cook, and a man with children in the house needs a woman around who can cook!"

There was more than one way to take that little speech, and Caleb wasn't going to think about the other! "Well, you see, Miz Primrose," he began, "I have hired someone to come and take care of the house and fix our meals."

Twin pairs of eyebrows rose at that. "Who? I can't think of a soul who has the time, unless it's the Widow Miles; but she's seventy years old if she's a day. She won't have the energy."

"Miz Primrose, it's not the Widow Miles." He paused, then just blurted it out. "Rachel Branigan will be helping us."

They both froze upon hearing Rachel's name.

"It was really thoughtful of her," Caleb continued. "I mean, she has a daughter and a lot of work to do at the store. But she cares about children and doesn't want to see them suffer. I'm sure they'll appreciate having a woman around, too."

He stood up. "Well, I notice it's getting dark outside. I'm sure you two will want to be on your way," he said, ignoring the suspicious look from Prudence.

"Reverend Stone. I really think you should rethink this! I—"

"Now, now, Miz Primrose. What we do for others, we do for God! You wouldn't want to take away her blessing, would you?" He opened the door. "It's been a pleasure, ladies. And I'll look forward to your song this Sunday, Patience," he added, hoping to distract them.

It worked. Patience, batting and giggling, replied, "Why, thank you, Reverend! And we insist that you come eat Sunday dinner with us. The children, too, of course!"

"That's right, Reverend. We'll see you Sunday!" Prudence confirmed.

Caleb opened his mouth to decline the invitation, but he couldn't come up with a single excuse.

Patience waved and Prudence nodded, and before he could even think, they were walking through the front gate.

What would Rachel have to say about this?

Chapter 10

A grim-faced Lee greeted Caleb the next day when he entered the sheriff's office. Lee was one fellow who always seemed to be in a pleasant mood. It was unusual to barely get a greeting out of him, as was true just now.

"Hey, Lee. What's got you so down in the mouth?" Caleb asked, trying to shake Lee's mood.

Lee shuffled the papers on his desk and sighed. "I just got a report of a stage robbery, and this time a man was shot. It's the second time this month this has happened, and frankly, it's got me worried."

Caleb frowned and sat in the chair facing Lee's desk. "Who are they?"

Lee shrugged and reached up to rub his neck. "That's just it, Preacher. Nobody knows who they are. We don't think they're from around here. Other than that, we have nothing; we don't even know what they look like. They all wear hats and cover their faces."

Caleb pondered what Lee had just told him, and already he could feel his own instincts kicking in. "What about horses? Do any of them have distinguishing marks? And have any strangers been seen hanging around together?"

Lee did smile then. "Are you sure you didn't miss your calling, Preacher? Maybe a career in detective work?" he teased.

Caleb cringed on the inside and hoped it didn't show on his face. The last thing he wanted people to know was that he used to hunt down outlaws for a living. He wasn't ready for folks to know. Not yet. He wanted to live a normal life for a while.

"No, that kind of life isn't for me," he commented casually. "Just hate to see good folks get hurt."

Lee nodded. "You an' me both." He looked at the report in his hand. "It's just so strange, you know? Whoever has been setting up these robberies has to know something of the area and the routes the stages run. This particular one was a gold shipment headed to Dallas. It took a route different from what it normally would travel." He let out a frustrated breath. "I wonder if this gang really *is* local boys? I mean, they would almost have to know the area to find the spot where they ambushed the coach."

Caleb ran a finger across his chin. "Either that or they recruited a local to help them. Has anyone, maybe someone who's been in trouble before, been missing or maybe disappeared for long periods of time?"

"I don't know, but that's a good place to start looking. I'll send a message out to Billy Aaron and see if he can help me with this." Lee stood and gave his friend a shrewd look. "Are you sure you aren't after my job?"

Caleb looked at him with a horrified expression and held his hands out in front of him. "Not me! I'm just a country preacher," he declared. "I think I'll stick to that occupation for a while."

Lee laughed. "Well, that's good. Maybe if you can get everyone saved around these parts, I won't have so much work to do."

Caleb got up from his chair and grinned at the sheriff. "Ah. . .but work is good for you!"

"I don't know about that," he replied as he stood and walked Caleb to the door. "Work is one thing, dealing with this gang of outlaws is another. Just be praying that we find out who they are soon. Otherwise, folks are going to be running scared around here."

"Will do," he answered and gave Lee a friendly slap on the arm.

As Caleb walked down the street in the opposite direction from that which Lee had taken, he couldn't help being bothered by what Lee had said.

Stagecoach robbers. He'd been acquainted with quite a few of them years ago. He'd even shot a few. But he couldn't help thinking of one gang of outlaws in particular who stood out from all the rest, one he was never likely to forget.

The Jenkins gang.

—๑๑—

Early the next morning, Rachel stood at the parsonage door trying to draw up the courage to knock. Her knees were shaking, her hands were sweating, and her lip was bruised from chewing on it. She was a wreck!

But she was so excited about being with Caleb, and all day long!

She knocked once and the door flew open. There stood Caleb, looking about as frazzled as a man could get.

"I didn't think you'd ever get here!" he told her in exasperation.

She glanced at the watch pinned to her blouse. "I'm five minutes early!"

"They woke up an *hour* ago!"

She laughed and pushed him back into the house, closing the door behind them. "You poor thing. And kids are such *fearsome* creatures, too." She laughed again.

Caleb frowned as she found humor at his expense. "But Jessie refuses to get ready for school, saying he won't leave his sister. And Emmy won't talk to me at all. She just sticks her thumb in her mouth and refuses to get out of bed." He plopped down on the sofa and laid his head back to stare at the ceiling. "I'm not sure I can do this, Rachel. I haven't been around kids since I *was* one!"

Rachel propped her hands on her hips and stared down at the helpless man. "Caleb, honestly! They are children who need a lot of love and attention. They're scared and worried about where they'll wind up next. It will just take a little time for you all to get to know one another."

He raised his head and looked at her skeptically. "Easy for you to say—you're used to kids." He looked around him. "Hey! Where is the little darlin', anyway?"

"Addie's watching her this morning. I'll go get her later," she explained. "Now, I'm going to start breakfast, and you need to pull yourself together and get the kids to wash up and come to the table!" With that, she whirled around and headed for the kitchen.

Caleb stared after her in amazement. He realized that his shy little Rachel had transformed before his eyes into a confident woman and mother who knew what she was about. *She's in her element,* he thought with wonder. *She would make a man a perfect wife.*

As he went after the children, Caleb decided that *he* was going to be that man.

—◊—

Jessie was still adamant about staying in his bedclothes so that he wouldn't have to go to school, and Emmy finally had to be picked up and carried to the table. But at least they were there.

As Rachel put the food on the table, she thought she'd never seen a more disgruntled group!

"Why, good morning, Emmy and Jessie. I'll bet you two are hungry! We all have a busy day ahead of us, so you better eat up," she chattered, despite the fact that they weren't responding to her. "There's chores to be done and duties that we all need to work out. First we'll go through all the clothes we've been given and see what fits and what won't."

"I ain't goin' to school," Jessie announced suddenly, his chin tipped up defiantly.

"No, not today. But tomorrow you'll have to go before you get too far behind in your schooling," she said without so much as blinking an eye. She just kept spooning up eggs and putting them on their plates.

"I ain't going tomorrow, either. I ain't leavin' Emmy!"

She did look at him then. "Jessie, you are not going to do Emmy any good if you stay here with her and neglect your learning. I imagine you'd love to get a job one day and take care of her, wouldn't you?" she asked nonchalantly.

He nodded. "It's my duty to care for her!"

She smiled at him. "All right, then! You go and learn how to read and write and work arithmetic so you can make yourself a living, and I'll teach Emmy all she needs to know about how to be the perfect lady," she said as if the matter had been settled.

Jessie wore a questioning expression on his face, but he didn't say anything. Emmy had taken her thumb out of her mouth and was actually smiling at Rachel.

Caleb was amazed. Everyone seemed happy and content at the moment, and all were eating their breakfast with gusto. He shook his head as if trying to clear it and took a bite of a biscuit.

And the woman could cook, too. Was there anything she *couldn't* do?

The rest of the morning, they made quick work of getting clothes sorted and their room set up. Since the parsonage only had one bedroom, all three of them would have to share it until the other room was built.

As the day wore on, Rachel went after Caitlin, and she watched Emmy open up when the little girl came into the room. Caitlin had brought her dolls, and for the rest of the afternoon the two girls played contentedly in the parlor.

Jessie, anxious to prove how grown-up he was, pitched in and helped Caleb move furniture around and do some minor yard work.

They'd all worked so hard that they were exhausted by the time supper was on the table.

Rachel blotted her mouth on her napkin and finally began to tell Caleb about a decision that she'd made.

"Caleb?" she started out softly. He looked at her, and she nearly lost her nerve.

"What is it, Rachel?"

She took a deep breath and plunged ahead. "I've decided to attend church this Sunday."

Pure joy broke out on Caleb's face. "Rachel! Why, that's wonderful! When did you decide this?"

She shrugged. "Oh, I've been thinking about it awhile, and I believe I'm ready."

Caleb, happier than he had been in a long time, tossed back his head and gave a triumphant shout. He then jumped up and pulled Rachel up with him.

The kids cheered as he twirled her around. They finally stopped, and Rachel giggled. "You're still spinning!"

He hugged her to him. "That's how you make me feel all the time, Rachel." They stared at each other for a wonder-filled moment. Suddenly they were kissing and putting into that kiss all the things that they couldn't put into words.

"Oh, yuk! They're *kissing!*" Jessie exclaimed in disgust.

The sound of his voice had the effect of a bucket of cold water thrown on them. They sprang apart and stared at each other as if seeing one another for the first time.

Rachel put her hand over her tender lips. "Oh my goodness," was all she could say.

Caleb took a deep breath and grimaced. "I'm sorry, Rachel. I. . ." He stopped when he noticed that all three pairs of eyes were staring at them with great interest.

Even little Caitlin was holding her hand over her mouth and giggling like she'd observed something naughty.

He took Rachel's arm and pulled her toward the door. "Sit still," he ordered the kids. "We'll be right back."

On the way to the parlor, he racked his brain about what he would say to her. He'd worked so hard to get her to trust him. All he needed was for her to pull away from him now.

He directed her to sit and sat beside her. "Rachel, I—"

"Oh Caleb. Will you just be quiet? If you say you're sorry one more time, I'm going to be insulted."

He opened his mouth, shut it, then opened it again. "You're not. . .mad at me?" he asked hesitantly.

She smiled at him. "I'm not angry with you. If anything, I'm more convinced of my feelings for you. You make me happy, Caleb. Before you came along, I was resigned to living life without a man. I had accepted my fate. But when you came to town, I began to hope and dream." She scooted closer to him and put her hand against his rough cheek. "I don't ever want to go back to my old life. I want you in my life, Caleb."

He nearly stopped breathing. "Rachel," he whispered hoarsely as he reached up to grip the hand touching his face. "Are you saying that you love me?"

Rachel's eyes filled with tears and she nodded her head.

Tears sprang to his own eyes, but he didn't care. He folded her in his arms and pressed his mouth against her ear. "I love you, Rachel," he told her fervently, his voice breaking. They stayed in each other's arms for a minute more, soaking up the warmth of the feelings that flowed between them.

Slowly, he pulled back and wiped his eyes. She smiled at him and touched his face. "You missed one," she teased as he blushed.

Together they walked back into the kitchen and acted like nothing had happened between them. But in their hearts, they knew something had happened and that nothing would ever be the same again.

Chapter 11

The next couple of days were blissful. Rachel's being with Caleb each day enabled the two of them to get to know each other much better.

Rachel still worried about what people were saying, of course. The townspeople were far from being willing to accept her. She knew there was widespread talk about her being Caleb's housekeeper. She wondered if there would ever come a day when people would stop looking down their noses at her and start treating her like one of them. She tried to have faith, but it didn't come easily to her.

Now it was Sunday, and her faith would be put to the test. She looked at the door of the white clapboard church and remembered a time when scornful eyes had judged her and found her guilty.

She knew that if it were not for Caleb, she would never be able to go through with this. But she'd promised, so here she was.

Rachel had purposely arrived late. She figured that she and Caitlin would just slip in after the singing started and find a quiet, inconspicuous seat in the back row. That way she could make a quick departure afterward.

She knew it was cowardly. And it wouldn't make any headway into what she and Caleb had wanted to accomplish, either. Next Sunday, she promised herself, she would work her way up to the next to the last row.

Maybe.

When she pushed the door open and stepped inside, her heart promptly sank. It was apparent that more folks attended Sunday morning services now than they had three years ago; there wasn't a seat to be had anywhere.

With the exception of the front row.

Her first thought was to jerk the door open and slip back outside—nobody had noticed her yet. The piano was cranking out "What a Friend We Have in Jesus," and all in the congregation were singing like they meant it.

But no sooner had her hand reached for the handle than Addie (who just happened to be sitting on the front row next to that empty seat) looked back and saw her. In her usual forthright way, she motioned wildly with her hand for Rachel and Caitlin to join her.

Frantically she shook her head and tried again to escape. But folks had already started glancing back toward her with curious eyes, thanks to Addie; and Rachel realized that she hadn't been as ready for this as she'd thought. Not really.

That's when the song came to an end and Caleb stood up in the pulpit he'd been sitting behind. That's also when he saw her.

She was trapped, her escape thwarted. Her heart seemed to sink right through the floorboards of the building.

Caleb smiled like a man who'd just seen daylight after thirty years of darkness. "Miss Branigan," he stated, to her eternal mortification. "Come on in. We're glad to have you!"

Maybe he was, but the rest of the congregation clearly didn't share his opinion. They stared at her as if she were a pesky insect that should be swatted or at least shooed away. She wasn't encouraged by their response.

Caleb Stone was going to get an earful after the service!

Like a prisoner walking to the gallows, Rachel started the trek down the narrow aisle. It required tremendous effort not to compare this church experience with her last time, years earlier. Caleb's kind face and understanding eyes made it all easier, of course. But she was determined that he was still going to be in trouble!

After what seemed like a thousand years, she made it to her destination and quickly sat down, hauling Caitlin up in her lap.

She would get through this. She would!

Caleb preached his sermon, and the service was about to come to a close. One of the deacons was saying a closing prayer when Rachel realized with surprise that, sometime during the service, she had relaxed.

It had been the sermon. Caleb had preached about the crucifixion of Christ, about how the Lord's own people had turned against Him. Then Caleb explained how Christ's disciples and close friends betrayed Him and denied knowing Him. How, despite knowing the truth deep in their hearts, they rejected Him and went along with the crowd.

Then he'd told this story:

"There once lived a man and his wife in a little village near Tucson. The man was respected in the town, a blacksmith. His wife was expecting their first child, and life seemed to be treating the man just fine. People liked him. He was fair and honest in his dealings; and because of that, his business thrived.

"One day a stranger came to town so that the blacksmith could shoe his horse. The blacksmith did that, but his customer wasn't satisfied with the work and refused to pay the man for the job.

"The blacksmith was outraged, of course. He knew that the work he'd done for the stranger was excellent and that the man was trying to cheat him out of his payment.

"There were a lot of people on the street that day, and they heard the loud, angry voices of the two men. As the customer mounted his horse, still refusing to pay, the blacksmith shouted out that if he ever came back to his shop again, he'd be sorry.

"The next morning, a loud knock sounded on the blacksmith's door. The sheriff was waiting when he pulled it open and asked him where he had been the previous evening. The blacksmith explained that he'd gone fishing, alone. The sheriff told him that a man was found in the back of his shop, dead from a gunshot wound to his chest. It was the man that the blacksmith had argued with the day before.

"The evidence against him was convincing. He was arrested and a trial was held. In the end, he was found guilty. All the people turned their backs on him, even his wife. No one believed that he was innocent.

"They hung him. The town thought justice had been done.

"About a week later, a young man who was known in the town for being a little rowdy and reckless walked into the sheriff's office. He looked bad. His eyes were bloodshot, and he didn't look like he'd eaten anything in a while. He confessed to the sheriff that he was the one who had killed the man.

"Every person who'd known the blacksmith was ashamed. His wife was so sick about what she'd done that she stopped caring about herself or anyone around her. She seemed to give up on living. She bore a son shortly after the hanging; and in the five years that the little boy lived with her, the only words she ever spoke to him where laments about the trial and how wrong she'd been. After five years she took him to an orphanage, left him there, and he never saw his mother again.

"That man," Caleb told them quietly, "was Joseph Stone. My father."

A collective gasp had gone through the congregation when he said that.

He'd closed the service by saying, "This week I want each of us to search our own heart. I think there are things in all our lives that need fixin' before we can take the time to try to fix somebody else. God told us in His Word to leave the judging to Him. If one of us is in sin, then believe me, God will deal with that person. But in the meantime, we need to love and support each other instead of finding fault with one another."

He then smiled and stepped down from the platform to stand on the same level as the congregation. His concluding words had been, "I think your lives will be richer once you replace the hate and condemnation in your hearts with love."

The prayer was now over, and everyone was leaving the church. Rachel sat and tried to swallow the lump that had formed in her throat.

He'd done it for her. All of it. The friendly greeting, the sermon, the story. . .everything.

She looked over her shoulder to where he stood at the door, shaking hands with people as they exited the church. For one brief moment, he seemed to sense her stare and looked her way. It was a quick glance, but she'd seen what he wanted her to see.

It was love—deep as the ocean and endless as the midnight sky. He loved her and she loved him.

"Are we gonna stand here all day or are we going to get on home?" Addie complained beside her.

"I'm hungwee!" Caitlin sang out.

"All right, all right!" Rachel grumbled good-naturedly, and they started down the aisle.

They were the last ones to leave, and Caleb watched as they made their way toward him. "Well? What'd you think?" he asked. She could see that her answer was important to him.

She smiled and tried to share with him what was in her heart. "Thank you, Caleb," she whispered as he took her gloved hand in his own. "I don't know what to say, I. . ."

He squeezed her hand. "You deserve no less, Rachel." To anyone who happened to see their exchange, it looked like he was merely wishing her good day.

"Well, Brother Caleb, why don't you come over to our place today and have dinner with us," Addie suggested.

Caitlin jumped up and down. "Pwease, Caley! You come! You come!" she chanted, latching onto his leg.

Jessie came up then, holding Emmy's hand. "We're going to the Primrose house today. I heard Mrs. Primrose say on the way out of the house the other day that Brother Caleb would make Patience a mighty good husband," Jessie chose to inform them all.

Caleb had been shaking his head at Jessie, but it did no good. "Rachel, it's not what you think!" he quickly tried to explain.

But Rachel wasn't mad. She was laughing! "Oh Brother Caleb," she managed to get out, "you should see your face!" She laughed some more.

"Yooo-hooo!" a voice trilled from the steps outside the church. "Are you ready to go, Brother Caleb?"

Caleb looked down at Patience as she batted her lashes and smiled at him. "Yes," he said. He could feel the blood rushing to his face. "I–I'll be right there."

He looked at Rachel and frowned at the mirth on her face that she made no attempt to hide. "It's not funny!" he insisted in a sour whisper.

"I didn't say a word," she insisted, then waved at him as she and Caitlin, with Addie trailing behind, walked down the steps.

He looked down at Jessie, and the boy shrugged his shoulders as if saying, *What did I do?* Emmy just smiled at him. Caleb closed his eyes and sighed.

"Well, come on, you two. Let's go," he said as he ushered them out of the church.

When they arrived at the Primrose farm, Caleb noted that it looked about like he'd expected it to look. Nothing fancy. Everything was in it's place, clean and practical. The inside of the house was pretty much the same.

He watched as Prudence ordered Patience to set the table and do several other menial chores. For the first time, he really took a look at Patience. She was so nervous about getting everything right for her mother that she dropped her usual facade. She wasn't *that* unattractive, she just didn't do anything to fix herself up. She wore the same plain brown dresses that her mother wore and none of the lace and frills that most young women her age were so fond of. He wondered if it was because Prudence wouldn't allow her to wear such things. Probably.

Caleb felt a little guilty at being so irritated by her and began to feel sorry for her.

The rest of the afternoon turned out just as he'd expected it to. Prudence lectured him about the qualities a preacher must have in a wife. Then she expounded on the many talents and qualities that Patience possessed. She was the perfect candidate for a preacher's wife, according to Prudence.

The children were quiet throughout the meal. Of course, they couldn't have gotten a word in edgewise even if they'd wanted to.

Caleb wondered what Rachel was doing and thought about what Prudence Primrose would say to him if she knew he considered Rachel to be perfect preacher's wife material.

He lived for the day when he could tell her.

Chapter 12

A week had passed, and Rachel couldn't remember ever being this happy and content. Because of Caleb's sermon and his hiring her to keep his house, folks around town had started to loosen up around her. Some had even smiled at her the day before in church. She was beginning to wonder if Caleb had been right. Maybe he *could* help change the attitudes of people around her.

Feeling lighthearted, she scooped Caitlin up in her arms and ran the few steps to Caleb's gate. They were laughing and were not aware of the three ladies who stood on the front porch, blocking her way.

Rachel had walked all the way up the steps before she noticed them.

Prudence Primrose, Isabelle Duncan, and Effie Lawrence stood in front of the door like soldiers creating a barricade. Their heads were held high, their shoulders were thrust back, and all had expressions of grim determination pasted on their faces. They took a menacing step toward Rachel and Caitlin that caused Rachel to step back against the porch railing.

Rachel could feel little Caitlin gripping her hand fearfully, and that made her angry. How dare these women scare a helpless child! She opened her mouth to tell them so but was cut off.

"We've decided," Prudence motioned her head to include the other two ladies, "that you are not fit to take care of the reverend and his children! You've already led one man astray with your sinful ways, and you'll not bring about the downfall of this good minister!"

Rachel gasped, so hurt and shocked that she was unable to reply. Caitlin began to whimper.

Isabelle Duncan walked up. "We've seen how you look at him in church. You've got him bamboozled into believing that you're good and innocent, when we all know better!"

"How dare you say these things to me and scare my little girl!" Rachel cried out at last. "You don't see anything but what you want to see! I'm sick and tired of all of you judging me like you have the right. You don't! Now, move out of the way. I have a job to do!" she demanded, as angry as she'd ever been.

She pushed them aside; and as she reached for the door handle, the door swung

70

open. Caleb stood there; and after seeing Rachel's face, he glared at the three stern women standing behind her.

"What is going on here?" he demanded.

Caitlin cried out his name and flew into his arms. He caught her easily and naturally and held her little body close. "Can I help you ladies with something?"

Prudence eyed with distaste the frightened child in his arms. "We came to warn you, Reverend! We've noticed how this woman is worming her way into your good graces, and we felt it our duty to make you aware so that you can be on your guard against her!" Having said this, she crossed her arms across her chest and thrust out her chin.

Caleb was nearly shaking with anger. "Miz Primrose," he began, his voice hard, "Miss Rachel is a friend of mine, and I'll not have you call her names or make false accusations about her character! She's here to help me keep house and care for the orphan children who live here and *not* because of any of the things that you've accused her of today!

"I'm sick and tired of folks making hasty judgments against others when it's not their place to do so. Reverend Parker was wrong to do what he did to Rachel. Instead of trying to comfort a young woman who was attacked and violated, you people shunned her."

Effie and Isabelle were the first to speak up. They apologized profusely to the preacher and then to Rachel.

Rachel watched as a variety of emotions crossed Prudence's features, ranging from shock to anger.

But suddenly, as if she had decided not to make a scene, Prudence lowered her eyes with false humility. "Accept my apology, Reverend," she mumbled. "We were merely concerned for your well-being."

Caleb looked displeased with the halfhearted apology, but he answered, "I understand, as long as you think about what I've said."

Prudence nodded weakly and said, "Come along, ladies." Together they left the preacher and Rachel on the porch.

Rachel and Caleb had just stepped into the house when Caitlin began crying that she'd left her doll out on the porch.

"I'll get it," Caleb volunteered.

When he reached the porch, he saw the women standing at the gate. They didn't notice him as they spoke.

"She's brainwashed him! That's just what she's done!" Prudence hissed to her companions, thinking they were out of earshot.

Isabelle gaped at her friend, "Oh Prudence, I don't think—"

"The reverend had a point, Prudence. . . ," Effie argued.

"Don't tell me her Little Miss Innocent act got to ya'll, too! She's a liar and a fornicator! Believe me, I know one when I see one!" Prudence declared.

Her friends looked at each other and then back to Prudence, their expressions doubtful. They'd always followed Prudence and believed every word she said. On this matter, however, it seemed they were not sure.

But neither said another word, and all three left, headed back toward town.

Troubled, Caleb stooped down and picked up the doll. Then he went into the house.

His troubles fled, however, the moment he saw Rachel's worried face. Caleb went to her and took her into his arms.

"It's going to be all right, Rachel," he comforted.

She shook her head against his chest. "It's not, Caleb. They're talking about us. I knew this would happen."

He pulled her back so that he could look her in the eye. "Don't give up now, Rachel. This will work out. I'll find a way, all right?" Gently he reached up and wiped away a tear that was slipping down her cheek.

"But I don't want this to ruin your ministry. If one person starts spreading things about us, then they'll start believing it."

He shook his head with confidence. "Rachel, I don't believe God is going to let that happen. I can't explain how I know this, I just feel it. . .in here," he said, placing his hand over his heart. "And if I wasn't sure, I'd simply take you and Caitlin and move someplace else!" He grinned. "That may not be such a bad idea anyway. Then we could be married right away!"

Rachel stared at him. "Married?"

He nodded and suddenly sank to one knee. "Rachel Branigan, please say that you will marry me and become my wife." She opened up her mouth, but he waved away her concern. "I know we can't make it public right now, but I need to know one thing for sure. After we find a way around all this gossip and these judgmental attitudes, will you marry me?"

Her tears started again. "Oh Caleb." She sighed and ran her fingers through his soft black hair. "Yes," she answered. "I'll marry you!"

"Yeeee hiiiii!" he whooped. He jumped up, grabbed her around the waist, and planted a big kiss on her surprised lips.

Little feet came running into the room. "Oh, yuk!" Jessie complained. "It's nothing. They're just kissin' again."

Emmy laughed and started dancing around them. Caleb let Rachel go, picked the little girl up, and planted tiny kisses on her cheeks while she giggled in delight. It was the most emotion either of them had ever seen Emmy show, and it delighted them.

Caleb turned to Jessie, and the boy quickly backed up. "I gotta go to school," he said with more enthusiasm than he'd shown in a while. "Good-bye!"

Caleb smiled and raised his eyebrows. "Maybe that's the way to get him to go to school without complaining. Threaten to kiss him!"

Rachel rolled her eyes. "Yes, but he left without eating breakfast, and he's at least forty minutes early!"

"Well, if you'll make something up, I'll run it down to the school for him," Caleb said, embarrassed that he hadn't thought of the problem first.

Caleb was coming back from the school when Addie ran out onto the boardwalk and motioned for him to join her. Curious, he trotted across the street and into the store.

"What do you need, Addie?" he asked, noticing the worried frown on her face.

Addie shrugged. "It's probably nothing, but I thought you needed to know that someone was in here yesterday asking questions."

Caleb froze. "Who was he? What kind of questions?"

Addie thought a minute. "Well, he was asking about you. He said he knew someone with your last name once and wondered if it was you or a relative. He was sort of medium height with wiry blond hair but had black eyebrows and lashes. Looked really strange. I didn't get his name, though."

Caleb racked his brain trying to remember who that description fit. And then it clicked.

Jenkins had a boy named Yancy who rode with him. He had wiry blond hair and black eyebrows. People often commented on his odd looks, although Jenkins always did his best to make sure the boy covered up well so that no one could identify him.

Dread was building in Caleb's heart. Jenkins must have found out about him. And if that was true, no one around him was safe.

He excused himself, asking Addie to let him know if the man came back, and left for the sheriff's office.

It was time that Lee Cutler knew what was going on.

—◦—

Lee was sitting at his desk when the preacher came in. He threw down his pen and stood up. "Well! To what do I owe this pleasure?" he greeted.

Caleb shook his hand. "I have something I need to tell you, Lee. I may need your help," he stated grimly.

Lee became serious and motioned for Caleb to take the seat across from him.

"Three years ago, I worked as a bounty hunter in the New Mexico and Arizona area. If the outlaws didn't come peacefully, I didn't hesitate to put them out of *my* misery, I guess you could say." Caleb's mirthless laugh was tinged with sadness. "I was after a man named Bill Jenkins. He was a leader of a gang of outlaws that mainly robbed banks and held up stages. They would as soon kill you as look at you, and they left a lot of innocent deaths along their trail. I found Bill in a saloon one day; and when I tried to take him in, he drew his gun on me. I was a fast shot and I killed him.

"Well, old Bill had a brother who set me up in a bogus gunfight. I was shot from behind several times and left for dead." He shook his head. "They *thought* I was dead.

"A preacher and his wife took me in and that's how I met the Lord and felt the call to preach. I haven't even thought about seeing that gang again. I would never have imagined that they could be here in Texas!"

Lee propped his elbows on the desk and leaned forward, clearly shocked at what he was hearing. But he waited for Caleb to finish.

"They know I'm here, Lee," he finally said. "It's like a nightmare come true. They will come for me; and when they do, they won't care who gets in their way. I'm not so much scared for myself as I am for the rest of the people in this town. What if he finds out about Rachel and Caitlin? He'd use them to get to me."

Lee put out a hand. "Now hold on, Preacher. That's what I'm here for. I know who you're talking about, and believe me when I tell you that I'm close to capturing and arresting them." He hesitated for a moment, then continued. "But that's not all. Milton Pierce is with them."

That name brought forth such anger that its ferocity surprised even Caleb. He knew he had to let God help him deal with the animosity he felt for Rachel's attacker. But to think that he was riding with his enemy. . .

"How did you find out?" Caleb asked.

"We've been gathering information about each of the gang members from witnesses and victims. Milton's bandanna got yanked off by an angry man who refused to give up his gold watch. The man never lived to tell about it, but someone else happened to see Pierce." He added, "Milton Pierce wasn't the one who did the shooting. At least he doesn't have murder on his list of offenses. Not yet, anyway."

Caleb leaned forward. "Do you think you have a prayer of arresting any of them? I want to see Jenkins brought in, but I want Pierce more. If we can get him to confess. . ."

Lee nodded. "Then Rachel will no longer have to live under the stigma of being a wanton woman," he finished for him. "I'll tell you what, I'll contact the other towns in this area and see if I can get some help with this. If we all work together, we may be able to solve *all* of your problems."

Caleb stood and put his hand out to Lee. "I sure hope so, Lee. Also, there is a man asking around town about me. He's one of Jenkins's men. If you can get hold of him, you may get him to lead you to Jenkins."

He placed his hat back on his head. The men exchanged good-byes, and Caleb headed back to the parsonage.

He wondered how he would be able to tell Rachel about his past. But he knew it was time.

Chapter 13

Rachel and Caleb had made plans to meet at their special place by the stream the next evening. He'd asked her to come alone and made plans for Addie to watch the children. He'd said he had something important to tell her.

As she waited, anxiety ran rampant through her. What did he want to say to her? Was it about them? Was he having second thoughts?

Her dismal musings evaporated the minute he rode up. He jumped off his horse and took her in his arms.

"Caleb?" she said with concern.

"Are you okay?" he asked, running his eyes over her to be sure. "I should have told you to wait for me and not come out here alone." He shook his head and let out a deep breath.

Rachel placed her hands on his chest and made him look at her. "What in the world are you talking about? Why wouldn't I be okay?"

He knew he wasn't making any sense. "I'm sorry, Rachel. I'm just worried about you being out here alone. I don't want anything to happen to you." He stepped back a step but grasped her hands in his.

"I brought you out here so I can tell you about my past," he told her.

Rachel studied the strain on his face and remembered another time when she had seen that look on his features. "I've been wondering when you would tell me about that," she said gently.

"Wait right here." He walked over and took a rolled blanket from his saddle and spread it out on the ground. They sat on the blanket, and he began to share with her what was on his mind.

"I haven't always been a preacher," he began.

She just smiled. "I didn't figure you had been. I know the Springton church is your first."

He tried to smile but failed. That's when she realized that what he wanted to say was important to him.

Caleb spared himself no mercy as he described his past. He painted a picture of a hardhearted, selfish man who had done nothing unless it profited him. He told her of the outlaws that he'd killed. He wanted her to see the hard, cold facts of what he'd been and where he'd come from. It was the way he saw himself whenever he remembered.

But Rachel saw something different. She saw a young man who'd been abandoned, abused, and hurt. A man who hadn't believed in the potential goodness of life, so he immersed himself in the bad.

She didn't realize she was crying until Caleb turned to her and touched one of her tears with a gentle finger. The hardness that had etched his features changed to despair. "Ah, Rachel. . .I'm so sorry I had to tell you this. I know it's hard to hear. I had to tell you, though, before we married. I will understand if you—"

She put two fingers on his lips to stop him. "You don't understand, Caleb. I'm not crying because I'm disgusted at what you were. I'm just so sad that you had to go through your whole young life thinking that you weren't worth anything."

It took a moment before her words made sense to him. A lump lodged in his throat and tears filled his eyes. How had she known how he'd felt all those years? How could she see past all the horrible things that he'd told her and understand the emptiness that had eaten at him day after day? But she did.

She knew it was because she loved him.

He blinked a couple of times and managed to hold back tears. "I love you, Rachel."

"I love you, too, Caleb. And it doesn't matter what you've done or where you've been. What you have become makes you special to me. Your kindness and caring has extended to everyone in Springton, and there's not a soul here who hasn't been affected by it."

He was a little uncomfortable with her praise. "I've only done what I feel God has called me to do."

She nodded and decided not to argue the point. "I know."

"Still want to marry me?" he asked, feeling a strand of her hair.

She smiled. "I haven't changed my mind yet!"

An eyebrow arched. "Yet?"

"You just better be on your best behavior!" she said saucily.

He laughed and leaned over to her, pressing his lips against hers in a warm, soft kiss.

They stayed by the stream awhile longer, then she left him to walk back to the store. All the way there, she relived over and over in her mind that tender kiss.

Maybe that's why she failed to see the woman standing just outside the corner of the store. The woman had seen the innocent kiss and the dreamy look Rachel wore on her face as she drifted back to the store. The woman's arms were crossed tightly against her chest and her mouth was pinched in a disapproving line.

Prudence Primrose narrowed her eyes, then disappeared behind the building, unseen.

—◊—

A wagon was parked out in front of his house when Caleb returned home. In it sat a man and a woman. He noticed that Harold Ray was standing beside the wagon.

Caleb pulled back on the reins and climbed down off his horse. "Can I help you?"

"Reverend?" Harold Ray greeted with a tip of his hat. "This here's Ken and Wilma Whitten. They just moved into town. Ken's gonna be working out at the sawmill."

Caleb nodded to them both, his eyes curious. "Pleased to meet you both. I'm Caleb Stone."

The Whittens returned the greeting politely. They seemed like decent folks to Caleb. He waited for Harold Ray to explain why they were there.

Harold Ray went on. "The Whittens were wanting to see about taking in a child, and I told them about the kids that you have here."

Clearing his throat, Caleb managed a smile. "Well, their names are Jessie and Emmy Holt. Their parents passed away a few months back, and they need a good family to love and take care of them. They're both wonderful kids." Caleb stopped, unable to continue. He'd never stopped to think about how he'd feel when Jessie and Emmy left him.

He knew now—horrible.

Mrs. Whitten threw a panicked look at her husband, and Mr. Whitten patted her hand, apparently trying to reassure her. He looked at the preacher and told him, "Uh, Reverend, we would love to take both children, but we can only afford one child. We'd had our hearts set on a boy."

Caleb blanched. "But you're talking about separating a brother and sister who have looked after one another all their lives. You can't take one and leave the other, Mr. Whitten."

Harold Ray spoke up then. "Brother Caleb, things like this happen when you're running an orphanage. You know that firsthand. Most probably, someone around these parts will take the little girl. They'd still get to see one another at school and such."

Caleb knew the practical truth behind Harold Ray's words, but he also knew that separating the children would be wrong.

"Mr. and Mrs. Whitten, I have to give this some thought. Separating the children is a big decision to have to make. I'll need time to think and pray about it," he told them.

Mr. Whitten nodded. "I'll check back with you in a couple of days, Reverend." He tipped his hat and they rode away.

Caleb got back on his horse and rode straight to the mercantile.

—⚬⚬—

The minute Caleb walked into the store, Rachel knew something was wrong. Caleb had tried to smile as he entered but failed miserably.

"What's wrong?" she asked.

Caleb didn't answer immediately. He first looked at the two children who were playing on the floor with Caitlin. He hoped they were far enough away that they wouldn't hear him.

"Someone wants to adopt Jessie."

The only word that registered in Rachel's mind initially was "adopt."

"That's wonderful, Caleb! How—"

"They don't want Emmy."

Rachel's excitement disappeared as quickly as it had developed. "Oh no. Caleb, what are you going to do?"

He rubbed a hand over his face. "I don't know. They can't afford to take in both of them, they said. I know I have an obligation to see that the children find homes, but I just can't do it. I can't separate them." He felt so helpless.

Rachel was quickly on his side. "Of course you can't! They would be scarred for the rest of their lives if you tore them apart!"

Addie nodded. "I agree, but you have to wonder if this may be their only chance at a family. You aren't going to get an orphanage going for some time. What are you going to do then?"

He shook his head. "I don't know, Addie. But I'll think of something. I'd better get the kids back to the parsonage and put them to bed."

As they were gathering the children's belongings, Caleb asked Rachel if she would come with him and help tuck them in. She agreed.

They had gotten Emmy all tucked in and she was nearly asleep, when Jessie asked in a low voice, "Are you going to separate us, Brother Caleb?"

A stunned Caleb and Rachel glanced at each other, then looked back at the boy. He was trying to be brave, but his eyes were moist and red.

Caleb knelt by his bedside and laid a hand on the boy's chest. "No, I'm not. I'm sorry you heard that; I was hoping to keep you from knowing." He paused and looked at Jessie. "You do know this could be your only chance to find a family, don't you?"

Jessie shook his head. "But aren't *we* a family? Can't you be my pa and Miss Rachel be my ma?" he asked earnestly.

"But we're not married, Jessie."

"But you're goin' to be," he countered with certainty.

Caleb's eyebrow rose. "You have big ears, don't you, son?" He chuckled and looked up at Rachel, who just shrugged.

"Well, I guess that's just something we will have to see about. It may be awhile before Rachel and I will marry. . . ." He was hedging, but he had no idea what Rachel would think about keeping Jessie and Emmy for their own.

"I can wait," Jessie said.

"Well, good night then," Caleb said and turned down the lamp.

In the parlor, Caleb pulled her down beside him on the sofa. He took her hand into his own and looked into her eyes. "Rachel," he began. He paused, then started again. "Rachel, what would you think about, well. . .about. . ."

"About keeping Jessie and Emmy?" she supplied for him.

Chagrined, he chuckled. "Yeah, that's what I was trying to ask."

"Caleb," she scolded and tugged at his hand playfully. "You know I love those kids just as much as you do. If you want to keep them, then we will." She sighed. "I just don't know how long it will be before we can be together."

"It will happen," he insisted. "But before you leave, I have something to say that I forgot to tell you about earlier. Do you remember me telling you about the gang that set me up?" She nodded, and he continued. "Well, they are in this area and I think they know I'm alive."

Rachel's eyes filled with horror. "Oh no! Caleb, what will they do?"

He tried to calm her. "Now, don't worry about me. Lee Cutler is alerting all the surrounding towns and thinks the gang will be arrested before they can do anything."

He reached up and cupped his hand around her jaw, rubbing his thumb across her cheek. "I'm telling you this because I want you to be careful, too, Rachel. If Jenkins finds out that you're special to me, he'll try to get to me by using you. So make sure you have someone with you at all times."

"I will, but you promise me that you'll be careful, too."

He smiled at her and agreed. He gave her a brief hug and helped her up from the sofa.

The walk home wasn't far; and though she protested, he walked her halfway and made sure she got home all right.

On the way back to the parsonage, he again had the feeling that he was being watched. Cautiously he glanced around him; and when his eyes fell on the saloon, a shadowy figure walked out from behind a post, then turned and sauntered back into the saloon.

Caleb's dread increased twofold. He'd been spotted and they knew where he lived.

And now they knew he was seeing a woman.

He just hoped they wouldn't find out that the woman was Rachel.

Chapter 14

Rachel continued to cook and keep house for Caleb and the children, and she'd been faithfully attending church services for four weeks. It was true that the folks of Springton were a lot friendlier toward her, though they didn't accept her fully. The reason for the improvement, she knew, was her association with Caleb.

When two people were as much in love as they were, it was bound to show. It didn't help any, either, that Caleb was always looking at her and smiling. If someone had the nerve to ask him straight out how he felt about her, he'd have told the person. Rachel was sure of it. She knew that he felt no shame in loving her and saw no reason to hide his love.

But Rachel saw plenty of reason to be careful. And the truth was, she was sure that the people of Springton would never accept her as the wife of their minister. Not with the slightest bit of doubt lingering in their minds about how Caitlin was conceived.

Her fear of the future grew day by day. The last thing she wanted to do was hurt Caleb's ministry. And it would hurt him if they made their love public. She had no doubt of that.

But Rachel said nothing to Caleb as another week went by. And on Monday afternoon, when Prudence Primrose walked into the store just before closing time, she had a feeling that things were about to become worse.

"I'd like a word with you, Miss Branigan," Prudence demanded as her hawkish gaze landed squarely on Rachel.

A trickle of dread ran down Rachel's spine. Prudence seemed intent on a purpose, and it didn't take three guesses to figure out what that purpose was.

"What is it that you'd like to talk to me about, Mrs. Primrose?" she asked.

Her eyes narrowed shrewdly, and she wasted no time in getting to the point. "We both know why I'm here, girl. It's about your chasing after the preacher!"

Rachel swallowed and stared down at the counter. "I don't know what you mean."

"Don't add lyin' to the list of all your other sins! I've seen the way you two look at each other. The whole town has seen it! It's disgraceful, the way you've been throwing yourself at him."

Rachel's head snapped up. "I have not thrown myself at him and we've done nothing wrong or sinful. We are friends!"

Prudence scoffed at that. "Friends?" she sneered. "You're trying to lead him down the path of sin!"

Rachel gasped at her crudeness. "I am not!"

"That's what the town thinks," she informed, with relish. "People are starting to talk. They're thinking that they might not want a preacher who has associations with a woman of ill repute!"

Rachel paled. "That's not true. . . ." But she knew very well that it could be the truth.

Prudence watched Rachel's reaction with a look of satisfaction. "Oh yes, it is true! Folks expect their minister to marry a good, decent woman. Not a woman who gets herself with child, then blames it on someone else. The preacher may believe your lies and he may have gotten some of the town to think a little better of you, but it don't mean that they accept you. It just means that they don't want to appear judgmental!"

Rachel's heart was pounding in her chest. A heavy feeling of dread spread over her body, and tears swelled behind her eyelids. She'd somehow known it would come to this. She'd let Caleb convince her that it wouldn't, but he'd been wrong. As right as it felt, they were not meant to be.

Not at the expense of his ministry.

Prudence was right. The longer Caleb and she continued their relationship, the worse things were going to get.

She lifted her eyes to the merciless woman and saw fanatical determination in her gaze. Despite the fact that the woman was right in what she was saying, Rachel had to wonder why this mission to sever the relationship between she and Caleb was so important to her. To what lengths would she go to keep her away from the town's minister? It was almost frightening to think about.

"Well, Mrs. Primrose, you seem to have all the answers. How am I supposed to do this? The children still have to eat and need someone to care for them."

Prudence's mouth formed into a grim smile. "I have arranged for the Widow Miles to come in and cook their meals."

She had it all planned, Rachel realized. "But she's so old! The children need someone to play with them and look after them. I—"

"*And,*" she continued, cutting Rachel off, "I suggest that you make it clear to the reverend that you no longer desire his company."

Rachel shook her head in disbelief. Caleb would never believe that.

"I just have one more thing to say." She leaned closer to Rachel. "If you don't stay away from him, I will tell everyone that I saw you two by the creek all alone, and you were kissing!"

Rachel knew what people would think of that. "But we weren't! He just kissed me once. . . ."

"*Do we understand each other?*" she demanded.

Rachel felt ill, but she had no choice. "Yes," she said.

She stood and watched the door close behind the meddlesome woman. The impact of what she'd just agreed to do hit her. A sob rose from her chest and to her lips. Both hands gripped at the fabric covering her chest as if it were an attempt to prevent her heart from breaking.

"No, no, no. . . ," she sobbed mournfully. Her knees gave way and she sank to the floor. Her hands came up and covered her wet cheeks as sob after sob wracked her body.

All her hopes, her dreams, were dead.

She must let him go.

—⁂—

At six o'clock, a knock sounded at the parsonage door.

"Miss Rachel's here!" Emmy called out as she started toward the door.

Caleb, who was just as delighted as Emmy, got to the door ahead of her. "I got it, Em," he called unnecessarily as he turned the knob and threw open the door.

"Good even. . .ing." His excited welcome drifted to a whisper when he realized it wasn't Rachel at the door but Mrs. Miles. "Uh. . .Mrs. Miles. Is there something I can help you with?"

Eloise Miles smiled kindly at the preacher. She was getting up there in terms of age, but she was still as spry as a bird. Her cheeks were wrinkled in a permanent smile, and her faded blue eyes always twinkled.

"I'm here to cook for you. Prudence came to see me this morning and told me Rachel had decided this was too much for her, what with working at the store and all, so they asked me if I could take over. Told 'em I'd be right happy to oblige."

A feeling of dread ran through Caleb as he stepped back to let the lady inside. He numbly showed her to the kitchen, then left her to her work.

"Miss Rachel's not coming, Papa Caleb?" Emmy asked, looking around for her.

He glanced down at the child, then over to the window. "I don't know, Em. It doesn't look like it." What had happened? It didn't make sense. He'd seen Rachel just this morning, and she'd said nothing about the work being too hard for her to handle or that she was thinking about quitting.

He had a bad feeling about this, a feeling that frightened him.

"Mrs. Miles, I'll be right back," he called to her, then ran out of the house.

When Rachel wasn't at the store, he looked for and found her right where he thought she'd be—behind the store by the stream.

"I thought I'd find you here."

Startled, Rachel whirled around, placing a hand over her chest. "Oh! Caleb. How. . .how did you find me here?" she asked lamely.

"The question is, darlin', what are you doing here?"

Rachel stared into his confused, hurting face for a moment, then looked away. She couldn't look at him and tell him straight to his face what she needed to say. "I. . .I don't think I'd better cook for you and the children anymore."

"Was this before or after you had a little chat with Prudence Primrose?"

Rachel closed her eyes and took a deep breath. Caleb wasn't going to make this easy. "She has nothing to do with this."

With what sounded like a growl, Caleb grabbed her by the shoulders and turned her to face him. "Don't lie to me, Rachel. Mrs. Primrose talked to you today, didn't she?"

"Caleb. . ."

"Didn't she?" he demanded.

Rachel hated the anger and the hurt she saw in his eyes. "Yes, but everything she told me was true."

He let out an exasperated breath. "What do you mean?"

She pushed away from him and wrapped her arms around her middle. "This town is never going to accept me as your wife, Caleb. They are starting to talk. Already they think that I'm trying to lead you into sin!"

He reached for her, but she backed away. The rejection cut him like a knife. "Then we will go someplace else," he told her. "A place where no one will know what happened to you three years ago." He knew he sounded desperate, but he didn't care.

"We can't run away, Caleb!" she cried. "And you can't walk away from a work that you haven't finished yet, a work that you said yourself God brought you here to do."

He was the one who turned away this time. He stared blindly at the trees across the creek. The ache in his chest was becoming hard to bear. Rachel was right on one point—he couldn't leave his job unfinished. But that didn't mean she was right on everything. "No," he finally answered in a strained voice. He turned back to her and caught her face between his rough palms. "But I can't lose you either, Rachel. I can't."

Tears filled Rachel's eyes and rolled down her cheeks, wetting his fingers. "Don't you understand, Caleb?" she whispered sadly. "If you marry me, you'll lose their respect. Then your work here will be over. I can't let that happen."

"You're wrong, sweetheart. They've already begun to soften their attitude toward you. Given time, they'll know that you're a godly woman. They won't care one way or the other if we marry," he argued.

She reached up and pulled his hands from her face, trying to break free of him. But he grasped her hand tightly. She sighed and went on. "The only way they'd ever accept me in this town would be if they had proof. And that could only happen if Milton confessed to what he did to me. That isn't going to happen, Caleb."

"But it could, Rachel!" he insisted. "If Lee can prove that Milton is running with the Jenkins gang, maybe he can be bribed into telling the truth."

"No," she stated, successfully pulling her hands free and backing away. "We can't wait for that or believe that the sheriff will catch him. It's over."

He felt his body turn to stone. "What do you mean by that?"

A sob rose in her throat, and she swallowed hard to keep it down. "I can't. . .see you. . .anymore," she stammered between sob-filled breaths.

Disbelief radiated through his every pore as Caleb stared at her. "You don't mean that. You can't mean that."

"I do," she whispered. "I'm sorry. . . ."

"You're sorry?" he asked incredulously. "I love you, Rachel. You love me. You're going to just throw that away?" He shook his head fiercely. "I won't let you do this!"

"You don't have a choice, Caleb," she insisted. "It's the only way."

Caleb could only stare at her while his eyes filled with tears. He turned his head and wiped them away in an angry motion.

He felt as though a piece of himself was being ripped away. After a long moment, he spoke in a whisper, "I can't believe this is happening."

She blinked back a fresh load of tears. "Caleb. Please. . ."

"Don't stop coming to church because of this, Rachel," he said, and she had to think about what he meant. She hadn't expected him to think about that.

"No. . .I will. . .come."

She saw him wipe his eyes again. "And. . .I won't be coming by the mercantile anymore. Sundays will be difficult enough."

She sniffed and wiped her face on her sleeve. "All right," she answered. For what seemed like an eternity, they just stood there. An oppressive silence hung thick between them. She was the one who broke it.

"Good-bye, Caleb," she sobbed as she started to flee past him.

But as she passed by him, he grabbed her arm, and she finally got a good look at his face. His eyes were red, his face ravaged with grief. "I'm not going to tell you good-bye, Rachel. I love you now and I'll love you when I'm eighty. I'll go along with what you want. For now. But know this—I'm not giving up. I'll never give up." With that, he let her go.

And before she threw herself in his arms and begged him to forget everything she'd just said, she stepped away from him, gathered up her skirts, and with a heart-wrenching sob, ran back to the store.

Caleb watched with eyes that were now dry as the woman he loved more than anything walked out of his life. What he felt now went beyond tears. It went beyond any hurt he'd ever known.

But he'd told her the truth. If it took until his dying breath, he'd find a way to make Rachel Branigan his wife.

He'd never give up.

Never.

Chapter 15

The next morning, Lee eyed his friend across the dining table with concern mixed with curiosity. This was the first time they'd eaten together since the children had come to live with Caleb, and Caleb knew he was putting a real damper on the meal.

"Well, aren't you just a joy to behold this morning!" Lee finally commented.

Caleb pushed his half-eaten food back and threw down his fork. "It's Rachel," he admitted.

Lee just nodded. "What's the matter? Thought things were going good for ya'll," he drawled.

Caleb ran his hand through his hair, making a mess of it. "I did, too. I mean, I knew there were obstacles that we still needed to work through, but I never dreamed that she'd just give up!"

Lee's brows shot up in surprise. "She jilted you?"

He nodded grimly. "That's what it amounts to. She apparently had a conversation with Prudence Primrose. I don't know what was said, but it was enough to convince Rachel that I'd be better off without her."

Caleb took a sip of his coffee and leaned his elbows on the table. "I have to tell you, Lee. I don't know what I'm going to do if I can't figure out a way to get her back. If I could find a way to get to Milton, I'd get a confession out of him, you can be sure of that!"

The waitress came by at that moment and gave them a refill on their coffees. Lee waited for her to leave and then he told Caleb, "Well, I may just have some good news for you."

"I could sure use some."

Lee pulled out a piece of paper. On the paper was a crude drawing of a young man. "This came by courier today. The deputy in Red Town managed to shoot him in the arm when they interrupted a stage robbery. He got away, but I think this is the man you're most interested in."

Caleb looked down at the drawing and knew that he was looking at the face of Milton Pierce, although he'd never met him. His hand shook as he picked up the paper. "Do you have a plan?"

Lee nodded. "Already working on it. I'm betting that he'll head home to the Pierce ranch. If that's true, Jebediah ain't goin' to let us waltz in there and arrest his son. I think we've both seen that he's blind where Milton is concerned. If he's there, I'm going to take a group of temporary deputies and *make* Jebediah hand him over. I'm hoping Milton's ready to bargain for his life, both for Rachel's sake and for Jenkins's downfall."

Excitement shot through Caleb. If they could get Milton to talk. . .a future with Rachel might not be so far off after all.

He leaned forward and looked Lee in the eye. "I want to ride with you when you go out there to bring him in."

Lee sat quietly in contemplation, then nodded. "Consider it done."

Caleb relaxed then and leaned back in his chair. "In the meantime, I'm going to do a lot of praying."

"We both will," Lee agreed.

With hope looming on the horizon, Caleb suddenly regained his appetite. He pulled his plate back to him and dug in. The food was cold, but he hardly noticed.

—⁂—

One minute Rachel was dusting with a small soft cloth, the next minute she was crying in it. It happened every time she glanced at the stack of writing tablets from which Caleb had made numerous purchases when he'd first come to Springton.

It was the same with anything else that she associated in her mind with the preacher. Sitting through a church service without so much as shedding a tear was a huge accomplishment for her. But it hurt to look at his face and see the sadness lurking in his eyes. And she felt his pain when his gaze would collide with hers and then he'd quickly look away.

He was hurting and it was all her fault.

She started crying again.

Addie found her in this state when she came back into the store. With a sad shake of her head and a cluck of her tongue, she walked over to Rachel and handed her a clean hankie from her pocket (she now kept an ample supply on hand, since Rachel was in this condition so frequently).

"Honey child, you can't keep going on this way," she scolded gently as she patted the weeping woman on the back. "You're going to make yourself sick."

"I know," she conceded in a shaky voice. Rachel made an effort to wipe away her tears but more fell to replace them.

"Land sakes, you both are a pitiful pair. The preacher walks around here thinking he's foolin' everybody with his false cheerfulness. But anybody can see that his eyes are red from sleepless nights and that he's lost more than a pound or two in the last three weeks. You cry at the drop of a hat and walk around here like you don't care if you live or die. Ya'll can't even look at each other! You're miserable! And for what?" Rachel sniffled and opened up her mouth to answer, but Addie did it for her. "I'll tell you what for! It's because of your stubbornness, Rachel Branigan!"

Rachel gasped. Addie had never talked to her this way.

"I figure you think you're being some sort of martyr by giving him up. But I think you're just too scared to take the risk of admitting you love each other!"

"That's not true!"

Addie ignored her comment. "You let one person convince you that you'd never be accepted as his wife! Did you ask anybody else their opinion? Oh no. You just took Prudence's word for it! Don't you know that the people of this town love Caleb? They can see that he lives what he preaches. Don't you suppose that even though they may have some worries about you being a preacher's wife, they'd accept you because they trust him?"

Rachel's tears were fully dried on her face now. She didn't like what Addie was insinuating. "I want them to accept me because they believe the truth about what happened—that I was raped and not a 'woman of ill repute' as I've been called."

"You're breaking his heart because you're too proud to accept a compromise?" Addie asked in disbelief.

Rachel wanted to cover her ears. She didn't want to hear the truth in Addie's words. "You don't understand. . . ."

Addie shook her head sadly. "You're right. I don't understand."

Rachel watched as Addie turned away but not before she saw the disappointment in the woman's eyes. "I'm doing this for Caleb!" she tried to explain, but Addie said nothing.

Rachel felt panic rise in her chest. Was Addie right? Was it just her pride that she was trying to protect?

Prudence's threat rose in her mind. No. She couldn't allow Prudence to tell about them being at the stream. Folks would get the wrong idea.

She was doing the right thing. She had to believe that.

—៣—

Caleb walked out of Lee's office, closing the door behind him. He'd just gotten word that Milton had gone back to the ranch. And because there were now wanted posters bearing Milton's likeness posted all over the area, Jebediah had given most of the ranch hands time off, keeping around only the few that he trusted most. So it just made their plan easier.

Lee believed that Milton, if captured, would turn in his own grandmother for a deal enabling him to skip the hangman's noose. So not only did he think that he could get him to testify against the Jenkins gang and get him to divulge information about the gang's whereabouts, he also believed they could get a confession out of him about the attack on Rachel.

Caleb dearly prayed that would happen as he walked away from the sheriff's office and headed for the parsonage.

He was aware that someone was about to pass him on the boardwalk and reached up to tip his hat. He stopped dead in his tracks when he saw that it was Rachel.

"Rachel, wait," he said, taking her by the arm.

"Hello, Caleb," she said, not looking at him.

He thought about how he'd missed this woman, about how lonely he'd been this past week. He thought about how much he loved her and that he wanted to bend down and kiss her until he'd driven all her doubts and fears about them from her mind.

She glanced around at the people nearby, noticing that some were beginning to stare. She pulled at her arm. "Caleb, please. . .people will see us!"

That was it! He'd had enough. He'd listened to all her paltry reasons and gallantly stepped away when she'd insisted. And how did that leave him? Feeling ten kinds of miserable. Well, it was about time Miss Branigan listened to what *he* had to say!

With little strain, he bent down and scooped her up in his arms. She tried not to squeal when he whisked her away into the alley between the sheriff's office and the doctor's office and out of public view. He then carefully set her down on a dusty crate and pulled up another for himself.

Shocked by his actions, Rachel struggled to regain her voice. "What. . .do y–you. . .think—"

He laid a hand over her lips and knelt down in front of her. "I *think* it's high time that you stop being so noble and listen to what I have to say for once! And I mean it, Rachel. Really listen."

Taken aback by his authoritative, even aggressive tone, she gave him a small nod and said nothing. To be honest, she was a bit afraid to speak. He looked so angry! And it was directed at her.

He took a deep breath. "I can't live like this anymore, Rachel. I don't care what Mrs. Primrose threatened you with. I don't care anymore about what anyone thinks about you or me or *us*. I just want you to think about what you are throwing away." He shifted and took her hand. "Not many people find what we have. It's a gift. And I think we would be just throwing our love back in God's face if we let this town tear us apart."

He brought her hand to his lips. "I've missed you, sweetheart," he said sadly.

"Oh Caleb," she whispered tearfully. "I've missed you, too. So much."

Before he could register the meaning of her words, Rachel launched herself at him, winding her arms around his neck so tight that he had a hard time breathing.

What did a little breathing matter, though? He was holding his woman in his arms! That was the important thing. His own arms came around her and held her close. How many nights had he stared out into the night, remembering what it felt like to hold her? How many times had he caught the smell of honeysuckle and remembered the sweet smell of her hair? How many times had he looked anxiously toward his front door before remembering that she wouldn't be coming anymore? He loved her and he missed her. She was his heartbeat. How was he supposed to live without that?

They finally broke apart, and she wiped her cheeks dry.

"I'm sorry, Caleb. Addie told me that I was being selfish and proud, but I didn't want to believe her. I'm just so scared, though. Things are so uncertain. And then Prudence says that she'll tell everyone that she saw us at the stream kissing. You know what people will think about that!" she gushed.

Caleb sighed grimly. "So that's what she did. She blackmailed you."

Rachel nodded.

He smoothed his hands down her arms in a loving gesture. "Rachel honey, you might be scared about what the town will think or say about us, but they'll just have to work that out for themselves. I'm not worried about any of that. All I know is that I want you for my wife and I'm not going to hide it anymore! I love you now and I'll love you forever. The question is, is it worth it to you? Is our love worth risking the town's judgment and possibly their rejection?"

He knew he should tell her about the plan to capture Milton and make him confess, but he had to know if she was willing to take a risk for him and their love.

"Yes," she said simply. "Our love is definitely worth it."

They were just about to kiss when they heard a voice behind them.

"Well, hooray! And now that you two have kissed and made up, do you mind stepping out of my alley, please? All that sweet talkin' and sparkin' is upsetting my prisoners," Lee said with his usual dry wit.

Caleb and Rachel looked in the direction Lee had pointed. Sure enough, there were three barred windows; and in two of them there were scruffy-looking faces pressed against the bars, giving them their rapt attention.

Lee thought it was hilarious. Caleb didn't really care. But Rachel thought she'd simply *expire* of embarrassment.

Caleb shook his head, took Rachel by the arm, and escorted her back to the mercantile.

Lee's laughter followed them all the way.

Chapter 16

When Rachel and Caleb arrived back at the mercantile, Caleb greeted Addie and Caitlin. Addie inquired about the children, and he told her that the Widow Miles was watching them for him.

She took off her apron and tossed it on the counter. In her usual direct style, Addie bluntly said, "Well, I guess you two will want to kiss and make up, so I'll just go upstairs. Holler when you're done."

With that, she and Caitlin left the room.

Caleb rubbed his chin and chuckled. "The woman never ceases to amaze me!" He looked down at Rachel with laughing eyes. "Now about the kissing and making up, it sounds like a good idea to me!" he teased, his eyebrows moving up and down.

Rachel put her hand up as if to stop him. "No kissing until you tell me what you were doing in the sheriff's office!"

Caleb shrugged cautiously. "Lee and I are friends."

She studied him a moment and decided that he was acting too casual, as if he were trying to hide something.

"Caleb, I want to know what is going on. Are you having trouble with those outlaws that you once knew? Because if you are, I would like to know!"

Caleb could see that she was becoming upset, so he took her hand and set about calming her. "This is about Milton Pierce," he told her truthfully.

She was confused. "What about him? I thought he was off in Houston somewhere."

Caleb shook his head. "He's been running with the Jenkins gang. Apparently he got himself shot while running from a stage robbery. They didn't catch him, but they knew he was hurt pretty bad. Lee just found out that he's gone to his father's ranch."

Rachel's eyes grew large. "Is he going to be arrested?"

"Just as soon as Lee can get to him. But the sheriff thinks he may have a tough time. Jebediah's hiding him, not admitting to anyone that he's there." He paused and looked at her seriously. "We're going to go in and get him."

"We? Tell me you're not going with the sheriff, Caleb. You could get yourself killed. Jebediah's probably got his men guarding the place! What if—"

He let go of her hand and placed his hand across her mouth. "I know what I'm doing, Rachel. I feel like I need to do this. For you. . .and for me, too. He deserves to be behind bars, not only for his recent crimes, but for what he did to you. I aim to help make sure that he gets his due."

Taking his hand away from her face, she put both her arms around him. "Caleb, I understand, but I'm scared for you. I wouldn't want you to get killed for me. He's just not worth it."

He wrapped her in his arms and held her close. "I love you, Rachel, and I'm not going to do anything foolish. All right?"

She nodded against his chest, but he could feel her shaking. He could tell her that they were going to try to get Milton to sign a confession about the rape, but he didn't want to get her hopes up. Instead, he comforted her the best way he knew how. And that was to make her laugh.

He leaned back from her embrace and arched a brow. "We could try that kiss now. You know we've been accused of kissing or wanting to kiss twice now. I don't think we should disappoint our accusers, do you?"

It worked. She laughed. "You are a crazy man, Caleb Stone!"

He grinned. "Do you like to kiss crazy men?"

"I like to kiss *this* crazy man," she said saucily. She surprised him by standing on her tiptoes and kissing him sweetly.

He returned her kiss and stored it in his memory so that he would be able to recall it later that night if things got tough.

Okay. So maybe that wasn't his *only* reason for kissing her.

—⁓—

It was nighttime when they rode up to the ranch. They had the place completely surrounded with eight men. Lee and Caleb would do the confronting. The others would back them up.

Thus far, they'd only seen one of Jebediah's men. They had him covered; but Lee thought there would be at least three men, according to one of Jebediah's former ranch hands.

A bird whistle sounded, alerting Caleb and Lee that another man had been spotted.

One to go.

Quietly, they crept behind a wagon, then darted behind a bush along the side of the house.

"Now what?" Caleb asked.

"I don't know," Lee answered. "I'm worried about there being another one of his men about. Chances are he's not even out here, but I hate to take that chance." He studied the windows and roof line of the house.

They sat there for another ten minutes; and when it appeared that all was clear, Lee gave the signal and he and Caleb ran for the door. They were almost there when they heard a warning whistle. Without thinking, they dove to the ground just as a gun fired.

"Aargh!" Lee cried and grabbed his shoulder.

Caleb looked his way, then turned to see if another shot was coming. One of Lee's men had taken care of the gunman, though, by clubbing him over the head with the butt of a pistol. Caleb hoped that was the last one because, danger or no danger, he had to see about Lee.

He crawled over to where the lawman lay on his back, writhing in pain. Caleb quickly tore open his shirt and checked the wound. Thankfully, Caleb found that the slug had gone all the way through and the wound wasn't bleeding too badly. He ripped the rest of Lee's sleeve off and tied it tightly around the wound.

Lee had managed to bring himself under control, although his shoulder hurt like the dickens! "I'm all right. Just let me up."

"You need to stay put or you'll bleed to death!" Caleb argued.

Lee winced as he sat up. "Just who's in charge here? Me, the sheriff, or you, the preacher?"

Caleb snorted and gave him a hand. "All right, you lead, and I'll catch you when you pass out."

Lee didn't find that funny. He shrugged off Caleb's hand.

With his good arm, Lee banged on the door. "Open up, Pierce. I know that you can't be so deaf as to not have heard that gunshot, so come on out here!"

Sure enough, Jebediah's voice came from behind the door. "I ain't got nothing you want, Sheriff. You got no right to be on my land."

"Pierce, I'm standing here with a bullet hole in my shoulder and I'm not in the mood for games. Now, either you just open up this door or my men are going to just start shootin' until you do!" Lee ordered.

Slowly the door opened, and Jebediah came around it, holding his shotgun at the ready. He looked at the pale, wounded sheriff and then at his partner.

His eyes grew wide as saucers. "Brother Caleb?" he sputtered with disbelief.

Caleb shook his head in disgust and came forward. "Put that gun away before you hurt somebody else, Pierce." He took Lee by the arm and pushed Jebediah's gun aside. Caleb helped Lee inside the house to a chair, then lowered him down into it.

He checked the wound and saw that the bleeding had slowed. Absently he asked Jebediah, "You got any whiskey on hand? We need to make sure that wound doesn't get infected."

Pierce took offense at the question. "I don't keep spirits of any kind in this house, Brother Caleb!"

"No, you just harbor criminals here, eh, Jebediah?" Caleb shot back.

Lee pushed Caleb's hand away. "Stop fussing around me like an old woman, Preacher. I told you I was all right; I just need to sit down a moment. Now, let's get what we came here for." He turned his irritated gaze to Jebediah. "Where is he, Pierce? And don't tell me you don't know what we're talkin' about."

Jebediah looked from the preacher to the sheriff and let out a defeated breath. He motioned toward the hallway.

"He's in the last bedroom on the right."

Lee got up, and he and Caleb walked back to where Pierce had directed them. They let themselves in and saw Milton lying in bed, his arm in a heavy bandage. He was still asleep, and it gave Caleb great pleasure to wake him.

He yanked the covers off the bed and pulled Milton's skinny legs to the floor.

"Hey, what's this all about? What are you doin'?" he muttered as he rubbed his eyes and pushed his hair out of his face.

Caleb was the first person he was able to focus on. Milton sneered, "What are you doing here, preacher man? Heard that Jenkins was out for your hide? I'd be running scared if I was you."

Caleb just looked at him, stone-faced. "Jenkins is a sad, pathetic man who uses men like you to do things that he's too chicken to do himself. And you, Milton. You're a selfish man who thinks that he can take what he wants and do what he wants without paying a price for it. You believe Daddy will always get you out of a fix. Well, this time it ain't gonna happen. This time, you *will* pay."

The click of a gun switched Milton's attention to the second person in the room. He'd not even noticed him there.

Lee, his gun cocked and aimed, said dryly, "I still think you missed your calling, Preacher. I couldn't have said it better myself." He bent down and picked up a pair of wrinkled pants from the floor and threw them at Milton. "Now, stand up real slow and nice, Pierce. We're gonna take a little ride and lock you up in a nice cozy cell. How does that sound?"

Milton threw Lee a look of hatred but didn't say a word. He stood, yanked on his pants, and let Lee escort him out of the room.

When Caleb came back into the parlor where Jebediah still stood, he stopped. "You have never done him any good by taking up for him when he didn't deserve it. You've let him get away with rape, and you almost let him get away with thieving and robbing."

Jebediah looked older than his fifty years. "He's my boy, Brother Caleb. It was my obligation to look after him."

Caleb shook his head sadly. "To look after him, yes. To lie and cover for his bad behavior, no. Milton has a lot he's going to have to answer to the law for. You,

Jebediah, have to answer to God for what you've done." He gripped the man's arms. "It's not too late, Jebediah. It's never too late with God."

Jebediah looked up at Caleb, then looked away and gave him a vague nod. It would take time, but Caleb was not about to give up on the man. God could work a miracle in Jebediah's life just like he had in Caleb's own.

That night, he let himself into his empty house. The kids had spent the night with Mrs. Miles; and for the first time in a while, he was all alone.

He readied himself for bed; but before he lay down, he fell to his knees and prayed.

He prayed that God would take away the bitterness he felt for Milton and Jebediah. He prayed that God would allow Milton to sign a confession about the rape so that Rachel could be free of the stigma she'd lived under.

And last, he gave thanks to God for the wonderful woman He had given him and prayed that he could be the man she desired and deserved. Someone who could help erase all the hurt and pain she'd felt over the past three years. Someone who would give her all the love and devotion that she'd always dreamed of.

He was such a different man than he used to be—he'd learned that tonight. He didn't feel the need to use his gun to settle a score or to use physical force to get his point across to Milton. Instead, he felt like he was in control of his anger and his emotions.

He was growing. Maturing. And hopefully he was becoming the man God wanted him to be.

—⁂—

Rachel was still awake, though the hour was late. She'd been worried about Caleb and had been praying that he would be all right.

What a man he was. Sometimes it was hard to believe that he was real. He was a man who would always be her champion, who would always cherish and protect her, and who would always show her how much he loved her. He *already* did those things. He was her love. He was her very best friend.

She thought back to the prayer she'd prayed just three years before. *Please give me one more chance, God. . . .*

And He had given her His best.

Chapter 17

As Caleb entered the jail cell occupied by Milton Pierce, he noticed that Milton's eyes were bloodshot and that his hand shook as he ran it through his greasy blond hair.

Lee, who'd insisted on being there despite his pain, motioned for Caleb to sit on the chair across from Milton.

Caleb thought about what he was feeling as he sat down across from the man who had all but destroyed Rachel's life three years ago. He had thought he'd feel rage, but at the moment he felt nothing but pity.

Lee looked at the man and started the meeting. "Pierce, I know you're aware that the penalty for your crimes could put you in a hangman's noose if you're convicted. And since we have two reliable witnesses who have placed you at two of the stage robberies, your chances of being found innocent are practically nil," he told the man bluntly. "You do understand this?"

Milton, his face pale with fright, nodded.

"I want you to testify against Jenkins and any of his men that we manage to arrest. But that's not all we want from you." He looked at the preacher and then back at Milton.

"From your response to him last night, I know that you're aware that this man is Reverend Caleb Stone. You also know that he's acquainted with Jenkins and he's been helping me with this case. But he also has an interest in one of your crimes that has apparently gone unpunished."

Milton turned his suspicious gaze to the intimidating man sitting beside the lawman. "I know what you want. Yancy told us how you've been sneaking around and seeing her. You ain't the first one that's seen her," he said crudely, with a nasty smile on his face.

All pity he'd felt for the man fled. He leaned forward in his chair, and Milton was no longer facing Caleb Stone the preacher. Milton was facing the man that Jenkins and the boys had said was colder than ice and harder than nails. He knew he was looking into the face of C. J. Stone.

"Let me tell you what's going to happen, Pierce. Lee's going to hold a town meeting in about an hour. At that time, I either read a signed statement saying that you're guilty not only of robbing those stages but also of the assault and rape of Rachel Branigan, or that judge is going to find himself with absolutely no mercy. If that happens, before you can so much as sneeze, you'll find your scrawny neck inside a hangman's noose!"

Milton swallowed hard and began to sweat. "What do I get out of this. . .this deal?" he asked nervously, his eyes shifting back and forth between the two men.

Lee took over the conversation. "If you agree to testify and sign a confession to the rape, I can guarantee you a minimum of seven years in a state prison; and then you'll have to sign a statement that you'll never come within two hundred miles of Springton before you can be released. If you do, the original charges will apply, and you'll be prosecuted and returned to prison."

Without hesitation, he agreed.

———⟨W⟩———

Rachel stood in front of Prudence Primrose's door and lifted her hand to knock. She couldn't think of why Prudence had sent her the note asking to see her. She hoped it was because she was now sorry for threatening Rachel. It would be wonderful if she and Prudence could talk this out and come to an understanding.

But it wasn't Prudence who greeted her at the door. It was a man. A man with a gun pointed right at her chest.

"Get on in here, woman, but walk in nice and slow," the man growled at her from under his bandanna.

Terrified, Rachel did as she was told. She was then shoved roughly to the floor. Painfully she sat up and looked around the room.

Prudence was standing on the other side of the room, staring at her. Confused, Rachel looked back at the gunman. "What's going on?" she cried.

They ignored her, and Prudence walked over to where the gunman was. "I'll just be leaving now. You've got what you wanted."

Yancy Jenkins laughed an ugly laugh. "You ain't going nowhere." He grabbed her by the arm, ignoring her protests, and shoved her on the floor behind Rachel. With swift movements, he tied their hands together behind their backs.

He checked them carefully; and after deciding that the ropes were secure, he left the house.

As soon as the door closed, Rachel asked, "What is this all about?"

"Don't get all huffy with me, missy. I don't know what they want. All I know is that they made me write you that note and promised that I could go free once you got here."

Rachel wondered how much of a hardship it had been for her to write that letter. "Why you? Why are they here?"

She felt Prudence shrug. "I suppose they stopped at the first place they came upon that was away from town. I'm just glad that Patience is off at a friend's house this morning."

Rachel realized that these men must be the gang of outlaws that Caleb told her about. And if that were true, Caleb was in trouble. *Please, God,* she prayed, *protect Caleb.*

"I heard one of the men mention that Pierce had been riding with them for a while," Prudence said suddenly.

Rachel shook her head as if to focus on what Prudence was talking about. "What are you saying?"

Prudence laughed bitterly. "It must be why you're here. He must have gotten tired of your accusations against him," she said snidely.

Rachel had had all she could take of this woman; and realizing that she might not make it out of this alive, she decided to tell Prudence Primrose what was on her mind. "You know what, Prudence? I think that you're a self-absorbed, bitter old woman who takes great pleasure in finding fault in everyone but yourself! You've kept what happened to me alive and fresh in everyone's mind, and for what? That's what I can't understand. Why do you even care?"

Prudence was quiet. Rachel wished that she could see her face to get some idea of what was going through her mind.

Rachel went on. "You know that we may not make it out of here alive. I know what those men want, and we are just a means to get it. It would be a shame to die with all this bitterness and the lies between us, wouldn't it? Well, I'm going to tell you the truth once and for all. I was raped by Milton Pierce over three years ago. I was not, nor am I now, an adulteress or a fornicator.

"And while I'm giving it to you straight, I might as well tell you this. If I get out alive, I'm going to marry Caleb Stone whether you or anyone else in this town likes that or not!"

Silence filled the room.

"Well, aren't you going to say anything?"

That's when Rachel heard the sniffle, then a voice said softly, "I was jealous."

Rachel heard the pain laced through that simple admission. She couldn't believe what she was hearing. "But, why?" she asked, more confused than ever. "You have everything, Prudence. A lovely daughter, the respect of the townspeople, and a fine farm. I don't understand!"

"But you see," Prudence began, "I thought you might be getting a second chance, the second chance that I'd always wanted but never received. Not the way I wanted it, anyway."

"Why did you need a second chance?" Rachel asked carefully.

Prudence was quiet for a moment. "Before I came to Springton, I became pregnant with Patience."

When she said nothing more, Rachel commented, "Yes, I've heard about your husband dying, leaving you with child."

"That's just it. I was pregnant, but I wasn't married."

Rachel's mouth gaped at the news, and she was glad that Prudence couldn't see her face. "You mean you were raped, too?"

"No, I wasn't." And while Rachel was trying to digest all this, Prudence told her the rest. "I was nineteen and foolish. I let myself be talked into an illicit relationship; and when I became pregnant, my parents kicked me out of the house and the boy wouldn't have anything to do with me. I came here to stay with my mother's aunt. It was her idea to create for myself a dead husband." She sighed and her shoulders slumped forward. "I thought that I would eventually get married. But I was never a pretty woman; and I soon found out that, while men might respect me, they weren't interested in marrying me.

"My aunt eventually died and left the farm to me." She cleared her throat and sniffed again. "I guess I wanted to punish you for *my* sins. Can you ever forgive me?"

Rachel's heart broke for the woman. "Of course I forgive you, Prudence. We all have things in our lives that we have to deal with. Sometimes we just aren't sure *how* to deal with them."

"Thank you, I—"

Prudence was interrupted when the outlaw came back into the house. "What's all the yakking about in here?" he growled. He waved his gun in their general direction. "Now, sit there and shaddup, or else!"

They didn't question what the "else" was, and neither said another word. But they both had a lot to think about.

—※—

By the time Caleb left the sheriff's office, he held in his hand the evidence of Rachel's innocence and the key to their future. He ran down to the mercantile to tell Rachel, but Addie told him that she'd gotten a note from Prudence and had gone out to meet her at the Primrose farm.

That didn't make sense to Caleb. "What did Miz Primrose want?" he asked.

Addie shrugged. "Don't know. Rachel said she was tired of being intimidated by her and hoped that Prudence wanted to make amends. But if she didn't, Rachel was planning to tell her to leave her alone. It's about time that girl stood up for herself!"

"Well...," Caleb said with a shrug. He didn't know what to do now. He really wanted Rachel to be at that meeting. "Can you leave Rachel a note and tell her to meet me down at the church for the meeting? I really want her to be there."

"What's going on?" she asked curiously.

Caleb smiled. "I have some news that's going to change this town forever!" he told her cryptically.

Addie raised her eyebrows. "Must be some news. You can bet *I'll* be there!"

Caleb laughed, aware that Addie wouldn't want Mattie Mae to be there and know something that she didn't.

As Caleb left the mercantile and made his way to the church, an uneasiness gripped him. He stopped in his tracks and looked around. There stood a short, nondescript man with a worn cowboy hat pulled low over his eyes. It was Snake Barnes.

"Well, looky here! You cleaned up real nice, Preacher Stone," Snake taunted with heavy sarcasm.

Caleb quickly scanned the area. He thought Snake was alone, but he wasn't sure. "What do you want, Barnes?"

"Wellll," he drawled, "I believe we got something *you* want, preacher man. She's real purdy, too."

Terror engulfed Caleb. "You've got Rachel."

Snake gave a nasty laugh. "Yeah, we do. And if you want her back, you're going to have to meet Jenkins."

Caleb was tired of playing games. He grabbed the front of Snake's shirt. "Spit it out, Barnes. What's it going to take to get Rachel back?" He was more scared than he'd ever been in his life.

Snake wished he hadn't taunted the man. How could he forget how frightening Stone could be? "A gunfight. Jenkins wants to meet you on Main Street at sundown. Wants to fight one-on-one, fair and square."

Caleb sneered. "Just like last time, huh? When your buddies shot me in the back?" He let go of Snake with a shove. "I don't fight anymore. Your boss has wasted his time."

Snake swallowed nervously. "That's the deal, Stone. Take it or leave it. Jenkins wants you dead, and he is bound and determined to be the one to see the deed done. He said that he'd bring the girl with him. She'll be released when we're safely out of town. Until then she's our insurance. No fight, no girl."

Caleb suddenly felt helpless. How could he fight when he'd set all that aside years ago and given his heart to Jesus? How could he face someone in a gunfight knowing that he would have to kill or be killed?

But he knew that he really had no choice. They had Rachel.

"I'll be there," he said, his face devoid of emotion.

Snake nodded and hightailed it out of there.

Caleb began to pray.

Chapter 18

Winter was beginning to set in, and the temperature had dropped signifi-cantly since morning. Because of that, everyone had crowded inside the church; and they all were waiting uncomfortably as Lee Cutler walked up to the pulpit. He put his good hand up to bring them to attention.

"I'm glad you could make it here this afternoon," Lee began. "I called you here because of the recent stage robberies we've had in these parts. I've got one of the gang members in my custody, and we have reason to believe that the others might be coming into town."

Panic spread through the room. Nothing like this had ever happened in the little town. Folks didn't know what to do.

"Now just hold on," Lee shouted, waving his hands. "I've got several towns back-ing us up with their lawmen, and I've contacted the Rangers. The best thing you can do for you and your family is to stay in your houses or your places of business and don't be out alone."

He seemed satisfied that they'd calmed down, so he continued. "Now, this may come as a shock to some of you, although many of you have seen the wanted posters, but the outlaw we caught is Milton Pierce."

Whispers went around the room, but apparently word had already gotten around.

"I've got a sworn confession from Milton. He not only confessed his crimes, but he agreed to testify against the other gang members," Lee continued. "He also con-fessed to a crime he committed three years ago, and the pastor will tell you about that," Lee told the crowd when he saw Caleb slip in while he was talking.

The crowd turned to watch the preacher walk forward from the back of the church.

Caleb approached Lee and whispered something in his ear. Immediately alarmed, Lee nodded and ran out of the church. Slowly Caleb turned and faced the confused crowd.

"Three years ago, this church was responsible for being the judge and jury for a young woman. She had told everyone she'd been attacked and molested, but almost no one believed her. And for three years, Rachel Branigan and her daughter have lived with the shame and have been outcasts within this community." He held up a piece of paper in his hand. "This is a signed confession from Milton Pierce admitting that he did indeed do moral and physical harm against Miss Branigan."

The crowd looked at one another but was strangely quiet. Guilt and shame were evident on their faces. There was nothing they could say.

"I came here today to let you know that I've asked Rachel to be my wife and to find out if we will have to move to another town or be welcomed by you to continue in ministry here. But that's all changed."

Concerned faces looked up at their pastor expectantly. "Today," he continued, "I was confronted with my past. Only a couple of you know that I'd been a gunfighter and bounty hunter before I became a Christian."

Shocked murmurs went through the crowd.

"The gang that you were warned about in this meeting is the very same gang that shot me down three years ago. They thought they'd killed me, and they very nearly did. Unfortunately, they have found out about me, and they are determined to finish what they started.

"I've just learned that they've kidnapped Rachel," he said, his voice wavering.

Gasps sounded throughout the building.

He waved them down. "Please let me finish. I don't have much time." He cleared his throat, but it felt like it was closing on him. "The only way that I can get her back safely is to meet their leader in a gunfight. Because of this, I am asking you to pray. Pray that God will give me guidance, because if he wins, I will die. If I win, I must step down because I cannot take another man's life and still be your spiritual leader. Thank you." He stepped away from the pulpit.

The crowd immediately surrounded him, many insisting that they wanted him to remain as their pastor while others offered their help in getting Rachel back. But Caleb heard none of it.

All he heard was the prayer he silently prayed again and again. *Please help me, God. Please help me, God.*

—⁘—

Caleb stood on the street and waited for Jenkins, his guns strapped to his belt. There had only been enough time to inspect and clean them to make sure they were in working order and no time to practice his draw.

It didn't matter anyway. It'd been three years since he'd drawn a pistol. An hour's practice wouldn't make much difference.

It was all up to God.

Five minutes later, he saw them. But what surprised him was that they not only had Rachel but Prudence Primrose as well. He wondered how she figured into this.

The boardwalks were scattered with curious and concerned folks. A lot of them were looking out from the windows of the various buildings along the street. He knew that Addie had the three children tucked safely away from danger inside the mercantile.

Jenkins's men hung back but watched the crowd carefully as Jenkins dismounted and walked to the center of the street.

Caleb's eyes strayed to where Rachel sat in front of one of the outlaws, a knife at her throat. He hoped that Lee knew what he was doing, because if that man harmed Rachel in any way, he would take care of the outlaw himself.

If he was still alive by then.

With great difficulty, he made himself focus solely on Jenkins. The man smiled tauntingly and looked him up and down.

"Wooowee! Look at you, Stone. You done gone and got all respectable," Jenkins drawled, trying to anger the emotionless man.

But Caleb didn't respond to his taunts. "I'm ready when you are, Jenkins."

Jenkins snorted but backed up and readied himself.

Mere seconds seemed like hours as the two men eyeballed each other, waiting for some sign to draw.

Jenkins must have gotten tired of waiting. But his hand had no more than touched the butt of his pistol when Caleb beat him to it. Staring him right in the face was the barrel of a gun.

Slowly, without taking his eyes away from his foe, Caleb walked forward until the gun was inches away from Jenkins's face. He reached and took Jenkins's pistols and tossed them on the ground.

"Tell your men to let the women go, Jenkins," he ordered softly.

Jenkins just sneered and yelled, "Kill 'em!"

But Stone only smiled. "I don't think so," he said and looked over Jenkins's shoulder.

Confused by the silence, Jenkins looked around and found that lawmen had surrounded his men.

The men holding the women immediately raised their hands in surrender. Caleb knew they weren't *that* stupid. There were too many lawmen. Yancy let them take Rachel and nodded for the other man to do the same with the older woman.

Lee personally came over and cuffed Jenkins and led him away.

They'd finished untying Rachel's hands when Caleb reached her and swept her up in his arms.

"Rachel!" he cried and held her tighter. "I nearly went out of my mind when I heard that they had you. Are you okay?"

Tears were seeping out of her eyes as she laughed for joy. "I'm okay now," she told him. "I was so afraid that I would never see you again."

He set her down and cradled her face between his palms. "Me, too, sweetheart. Me, too." Then he placed a soft kiss on her waiting lips.

A cheer went up, startling Rachel. She looked around them and saw almost the entire town's population surrounding them, all clapping and whistling. Confused, she looked at Caleb; but he just smiled and said, "They're just celebrating our engagement!"

"But...," she began but was bombarded by well-wishers as well as many people bearing apologies for mistreating her for three years.

God was bringing understanding and forgiveness to a people who had been without for too long.

—⁓—

Three months later, Rachel was standing outside of the church dressed in a beautiful wedding gown, waiting to meet her future husband. She couldn't believe that the day had finally arrived.

Caleb had wanted to get married right away, but Rachel insisted on waiting for his friends, George and Mary Ellis, to arrive and for George to perform the ceremony. But time flew by so quickly, she'd had barely enough time to get things ready as it was.

Rachel looked at Addie, who was fussing over the ribbons tied in Rachel's loose hair. It looked like there might be another wedding soon. She and Harold Ray had been inseparable for the last two months, and Addie had confided that he'd asked her to marry him. Addie was taking her time, though, on giving poor Harold Ray an answer.

A couple of late-arriving guests slipped past her and into the church. Lee Cutler was one and Patience Primrose was the other. Lee looked sort of hassled, and Patience looked very determined.

Caleb had told Rachel that Patience had turned her attentions toward Lee as soon as Caleb announced his intent to marry. Lee had said that Harold Ray's mule would start talking before he'd ever court Patience. Caleb had taken great pleasure in telling Lee the Bible story featuring a talking mule.

Lee was not amused!

The door opened again, and it was Mattie Mae waving at her, letting her know that it was time to go in.

Taking a deep breath, Rachel entered the church. She lifted her eyes and caught the look on Caleb's face.

Caleb stared at his wife-to-be in awe. She was the most beautiful vision he'd ever seen.

His heart was beating madly as she walked up to join him, staring into his eyes all the way. He saw the love that was clearly written in her eyes, and he knew that she saw the exact same thing in his own. He nervously reached his hand out to her and felt the sweetness of her touch as her fingers found his own.

The ceremony was a simple one; and when Reverend Ellis pronounced them man and wife and asked Caleb to kiss his bride, a collective sigh resounded in the church.

Reverently, Caleb cupped his bride's face in his hands and lowered his mouth to hers. He sealed their union with a kiss that was filled with such love, passion, and sweetness that a few giggles and chuckles could be heard throughout the room.

Smiling (and just a little embarrassed), the new husband and wife turned toward the crowd and started for the door. But suddenly Caleb stopped. He went back to the front row where the children sat, picked up Caitlin, grabbed Jessie's hand, and motioned for Rachel to get Emmy. Together, with the crowd cheering happily, they walked out, a family.

COURTIN'
PATIENCE

by Kimberley Comeaux

Dedication

To James and Dianne Kennedy.
My best friends, who just happen to be my parents.
I love you.

And to my friend and critique partner
Debi Luna.
Thanks for all your help!

Chapter 1

Patience Primrose was on her way to becoming an old maid. At least, most folks in the small Texas town of Springton thought so. It was true that she didn't have many prospects as far as potential husbands went. And now there were even less since the Reverend Caleb Stone had just married.

Patience sighed as she watched from her side of the room as Brother Caleb and Rachel Stone greeted the well-wishers attending their wedding reception. Patience had once entertained thoughts about the preacher. Every female in Springton had entertained the same thoughts. But Patience had been so sure that she could catch him. According to Emma Hadley's *A Young Lady's Guide to Courtship and Marriage*, she should have been the one walking down the aisle in a white dress.

She'd followed everything the book had suggested on getting a young man's attentions: batting her lashes at him, giggling when he said something funny, and always looking at him with adoration. Well, the batting-the-lashes thing was getting tiresome and making her eyes ache, the giggle was getting on *her* nerves, and she didn't always feel like looking at the guy as if he were the next best thing since chocolate cake. But the book had boasted that one hundred women had procured husbands by following Emma Hadley's advice. There had to be something to it!

Her mother said that she ought not read such nonsense, that the Bible would have all the information that she'd ever need.

Well, while it was true that she loved to read the Bible and prayed diligently to God, all she could think of was how the biblical Esther went to all the trouble to get her husband, entering a contest of beauty! She told her mother this. Prudence Primrose was not amused, but then, nothing really amused her anyway.

So, here she was. Twenty-one and still unwed. If only she looked like the bride, Rachel. She had beautiful black hair and a lovely peaches-and-cream complexion. Patience knew that she, herself, was no beauty. Her skin was rather pale, and her hair was a dull dark blond that she kept pulled back in a tight bun. She longed to wear her hair down like many of the other young women, but her mother told her that dwelling on hair and looks was nothing but vanity, and that was a sin. But even Emma Hadley's book encouraged "making the most of your God-given attributes and features."

Patience let her gaze slide past the groom and latch onto the handsome man standing by the preacher. Sheriff Leander Cutler was a fine-looking man. Tall and broad-shouldered, he stood a good two inches taller than the preacher. He kept his sandy blond hair cropped short, and his eyes were a strange golden color. Around town, the girls called him the golden man because he had a tan from all the time he spent outdoors.

Yes, he would make some woman an excellent husband. Could Patience be the one who could snare him? It didn't seem likely. She'd been trying to get his attention for a month now, and either he was dense or he was ignoring her. Emma Hadley's book said not to get discouraged, that patience and perseverance would bring rewards.

Well, so far it had only brought irritation from the sheriff. What was she doing wrong?

—ᨳ—

Lee Cutler shifted from one foot to the other as he stood and tried to concentrate on what Caleb and Rachel were saying to him. He'd started feeling sick just this morning; and his stomach was now cramping so bad, he wasn't sure how much more he could stand. He wondered if he'd picked up a stomach virus.

Except no stomach virus had ever hurt like this.

The pain suddenly intensified, when Caleb nudged him with his elbow. "Lee!" Caleb whispered, getting his attention. "You didn't forget those train tickets, did you? The train leaves in a little over an hour."

Lee blinked and realized that Rachel and Caleb were looking at him curiously. *Tickets? Tickets!* Chagrined, he reddened, reached inside his coat, and withdrew them from his pocket. "Sorry, Preacher."

Caleb frowned and opened his mouth to say something; but Jessie, the little boy that Caleb and his new wife were going to adopt, pulled on his jacket. As always, his attention shifted immediately to them.

The room was looking sort of fuzzy, Lee thought. If he could only focus.

Why couldn't he focus?

—ᨳ—

Patience looked at Lee with concern. She watched as the preacher and his new wife left his side and walked over to the door, apparently getting ready to leave.

She looked back at Lee and noticed that he was still standing there. Why wasn't he walking them out? Come to think of it, he didn't look like his usual vibrant self. Patience saw him start to sway. Frantically, she looked around, but no one seemed to notice him. They were all looking at Rachel and Caleb.

Patience did the first thing that she could think of—she scrambled over a row of chairs in front of her, then ran to where Lee stood, or rather, swayed. She reached him just as he began to fall. She threw her arms around him, all his weight leaning on her slim frame. She didn't know how long she could hold him.

"Help!" she whimpered, barely above a whisper. For a second, she couldn't breathe. She couldn't see, either. Her face was buried in his black vest, a button grinding into her cheek.

Abruptly, his body was lifted off of hers and blessed air filled her thirsty lungs.

"Patience Primrose! What are you doing with your arms around that man?" her mother screeched from overhead.

Patience opened her eyes and saw that her mother, Brother Caleb, Rachel, and mercantile proprietress Adelaide Hayes were standing around her.

"He was falling and I...," Patience tried to explain.

"Land sakes, Patience. You ought to have more sense than to launch yourself over a pew like a hooligan and grab ahold of a man like that! Everybody in the church saw you," Prudence Primrose nagged as she helped Patience straighten her clothes.

But Patience wasn't paying attention to her mother. Her eyes were on Lee, who was conscious now but halfway lying in a chair. Doc Benson was bent over him, and Lee was shaking his head.

Patience shook off her mother's hold and knelt beside the handsome sheriff. He didn't look good. His eyes were clenched and he was gritting his teeth in pain. "How is he, Doc?" she asked fearfully.

"Foolish boy!" Doc said gruffly. He opened up his shirt and pointed to the tiny puncture marks all along his side and wrapping around his back. He ran his hand over the festered skin. "Looks like he got into a fight with a few porcupines. If they get infected, they can make you powerfully sick. It looks like he got into a whole nest of them."

Caleb nodded. "He told me about getting into them a couple of days ago. Said he'd been camping and accidentally rolled over on them. But why would they be making him sick now?"

"It takes days sometimes for an infection to settle in," Doc Benson explained.

Lee moaned and Doc snapped into action. Quickly he called a couple of men over to carry Lee to his office. Patience followed them and tugged on the doctor's shirt. "Doc, can I do anything to help?"

Doc looked beside him and measured her up quickly. "You sure can. Mary is gone to her sister's today, and I don't have anyone to assist me. I'm going to have to clean and disinfect these oozing wounds. As far as his apparent stomach cramps are concerned, I'll just have to give him a dose of laudanum."

Patience hesitated for a second. *Oozing?* A wave of nausea bubbled up within her, but she quickly squelched it. She could do this. For Lee, she could do anything.

"Okay, Doc. Just show me what to do," she told him. Her voice didn't shake, did it?

Doc gave her a knowing look as though he could read her mind. But he accepted her help anyway. "Let's get this man to the clinic, then."

—⁓—

It wasn't as bad as Patience thought it'd be, once she got past her horror of seeing all the "ooze," as Doc called it. Lee wasn't in any mortal danger, but he was very sick. The doctor said that he would probably run a high fever for a few days because of the infection.

After what seemed hours, Doc finally stepped back. "That's it, or at least all I can do for him right now. Let's just hope that we can get this under control. At least we got all the quills out of him." He walked to his basin and began washing his hands. Weariness was evident in the droop of his shoulders and the slowness of his movements. Patience had no idea how old the man was. With his dark brown hair that was peppered with gray and the crow's feet that fanned the corners of his eyes, she guessed that he was in his fifties. She'd known him all her life. He'd been the one to bring her into the world.

Patience finally got the nerve to ask the most important question. "Doc. . .is he going to be all right?"

Doc sighed and continued to dry his hands as he walked back over to her. "Yes, but he's going to feel a might poorly for a few days. And he's not going to be able to take care of himself. Unfortunately, I don't have the space to keep him here. And since that boy hasn't seen fit to find himself a wife, I'm going to have to find someone to care for him."

"I'll do it!" Patience blurted.

Surprised at her outburst, Doc just looked at her with raised eyebrows.

"I. . .I mean, he can stay at our house and my mother and I can take care of him," she stammered. Her mind was racing. What an opportunity! He'd be in her house, with her all day for several days! She'd show him what a good wife she'd make. By the end of his stay, he'd be begging her to marry him!

Doc nodded, his relief apparent. "That would be a great help. Of course, it will need to be okay with Prudence."

Ordinarily, she knew Prudence wouldn't agree to this idea at all. But lately, her mother'd been acting so strange since her abduction. Patience had a feeling that her mother wouldn't mind.

"Hey, Doc?" Brother Caleb called softly as he stuck his head through the office door. "How's he doing?"

Patience could tell that Caleb was very worried about his friend. *Poor man, he should be on his way to his honeymoon, not standing around outside of a doctor's office.*

The tall and broad-chested minister sauntered into the room. His black, long-ish hair had been tossed by the wind; the coldness of it had put color in his high cheekbones. Caleb Stone was unlike any preacher that Patience had ever known. Which was one of the reasons that she'd been drawn to him in the first place.

"He should be fine, Brother Caleb." Doc motioned for him to stand by the examination table. "He's going to be weak for several days; but, if God's willing, he should recover."

Caleb nodded but didn't look convinced. He reached over and put his hand on Lee's still fingers. He said a prayer over him, while Doc and Patience lowered their heads in agreement.

"Maybe Rachel and I should put our trip on hold. We can set him up in Jessie's room so he'd have someone to look after him," Caleb began, referring to his adopted son.

"You don't have to worry about that. The Primroses will be taking him in. Now, you just need to concentrate on taking that pretty little bride of yours and catching that train. We'll watch over him while you're gone. You just keep on praying for him, and he'll be fine."

Patience could tell Caleb was clearly torn. On one hand, he wanted to stay and be the one that looked after his friend. On the other, he had a wife now with whom he needed to spend some time alone.

"All right, Doc," he relented. He looked at Patience, and she couldn't help but cringe at what she knew he must be thinking—she was desperate for a husband, any husband. She'd been a pest around the preacher, always trying to get his attention, flirting. And now she was going to be taking care of his best friend.

Oh, he knew what she was about, all right. She'd made no secret of the fact that she liked the sheriff. But she prayed that he would also see that she was sincere about looking after him and seeing that he got well.

Couldn't they see that she was a good woman, that looks weren't everything? Couldn't they see that she would make a good wife, that she would love and cherish the man who would marry her?

Would she ever get the chance to prove it?

"Miss Patience, I'm much obliged that you're looking after him," he said finally.

Too tired to be coy, Patience merely nodded tiredly. "You're welcome, Brother Caleb. I'll do my best to see that he pulls through."

Caleb nodded, and after one last look at Lee, he left the room.

Patience looked at Doc. "I'd better go tell my mother and then get the house ready. Do you think you can have him brought out before sunset?"

Doc agreed that he would, and Patience went out of the office. There was so much to do. The room needed to be dusted and the linens changed.

Everything had to be perfect!

Chapter 2

For three days, Lee slept fitfully most of the time, burning with fever. Patience and her mother were exhausted in their care for him. They took turns dribbling broth and water down his throat and mopping him down with cool water to keep the fever down.

Patience had really been surprised that her mother had agreed to Lee staying in their home. Prudence wasn't normally a kind person. She was usually the first one to pass out judgments and to tell someone what she thought their problem was, but she was not the one to help them. But three months ago, something had happened to Prudence; and she hadn't been the same since.

She'd been kidnapped by a band of outlaws.

Patience was not quite sure how it had all happened, because her mother refused to talk about it.

It all had to do with the fact that Caleb Stone, the minister who'd just married a few days ago, had a past as a gunslinger. The Jenkins gang had tried to kill him once; and when they found out that he was in Springton, they'd tried to get to him again. Only they'd decided to use the woman that he was in love with, Rachel Branigan, to do it.

They'd ridden up to the Primrose ranch and apparently forced Prudence into sending for Rachel. Rachel came, and both Prudence and Rachel were tied up for hours while the gang made their plans of revenge on Caleb. Soon after, they were taken into town and were released when the sheriff and his deputies had taken over the gang. Whatever happened to make her mother so different must have happened while she was tied up with Rachel.

Her mother had never approved of Rachel before that. She especially didn't approve of her as a pastor's wife, because Rachel had a child and was unmarried. It had been the result of a rape, but her mother and the rest of the town had called her an adulterer and had ostracized her.

But when the truth had been made known to everyone about Rachel's circumstances, Patience's mother had been one of the first ones to admit that she'd been wrong. Definitely out of character for her mother!

Although her mother was acting differently, it was a welcome difference.

"Patience," Prudence called, coming out of Lee's temporary bedroom. "He looks like he's coming around. I'm going to go make up some more broth. Why don't you go in there and check on him?"

Patience hopped up from the dining table, where she'd been resting, and ran to the bedroom. For the past three days, she'd been living for this moment, the moment when he'd wake up and thank her profusely for taking care of him and nursing him back to health. Maybe he'd see her in a different light. Maybe he'd realize that she was the woman that he needed in his life. Maybe. . .

"Where am I and what are *you* doing here?" he growled the moment she entered the room.

Patience's shoulders drooped. Maybe she'd just forget about the man.

Taking a deep breath, she straightened her shoulders and walked over to the bed. "Hello, Lee. You are at my house, and I am here because I live here," she recited calmly, folding her arms about her middle.

Sheepishly, Lee looked at the room, at himself, then back at Patience. He felt more than just a little petty for sounding so mean. It was just that he'd been dreaming about Patience. That was the whole problem. He didn't *want* to dream about the woman. But now that he understood that he'd been in her house and probably hearing her voice, well, it was a little more understandable. That had to be the reason!

The woman aggravated him. She'd been following him around for weeks, and he was getting tired of it. His friends were even starting to tease him about it. Especially the preacher!

He and all the men in town thought that Patience, while a nice girl, was rather plain where looks were concerned. And she had an irritating way of giggling and batting her eyelashes that could get downright annoying!

And besides, he'd sort of decided to court the new schoolteacher in town, Susannah Butler.

"I'm sorry, Miss Patience. Waking up in a strange place made me jumpy." He tried to sit up and then winced.

Quickly Patience went to him and helped him to sit up by putting her arms around him. "Sheriff, please be careful! Your sores are still healing," she scolded like a mother hen.

Lee was so surprised at the pleasant way that she smelled that he didn't protest her fussing over him. She smelled like flowers. . .vanilla! That was it. She smelled like vanilla. He was about to take another sniff when he stopped himself.

Maybe that was what she wanted him to notice. First he'd be smelling her perfume, next she'd expect to go acourtin'! Well, it would take a little more than vanilla to get him to do *that*!

Carefully, he leaned back away from her. "That's fine, Miss Patience," he said politely, then breathed a sigh of relief when she let him go.

She straightened then and blushed, realizing that she'd just had her arms around him. Awkwardly, she smoothed her sweaty hands down her apron and looked about the room. "Uh. . .Mother is bringing you some broth. I'm sure you're hungry," she said lamely, trying to fill the uneasy silence of the room.

He fumbled with his covers as if he felt awkward and nodded. "What's wrong with me?" he finally asked, confused.

"Doc said that those porcupine needles made you sick; they got infected," she explained.

He was quiet for a minute, a puzzled expression on his face. "But I didn't feel sick after I got punctured with them. But they sure did hurt when I had to pull them out!"

"I don't know," Patience answered. "I think Doc said something about the infection not coming until days later, something about not being cleaned out after you removed the quills." She shrugged.

His stomach chose that moment to growl. "I feel like I've not eaten in days!" Lee said with a laugh.

"You *haven't* eaten in days!" Patience informed him. "Three days to be exact!"

Lee's brows shot up in disbelief. "Three days? Aw, man! I've got to get out of here and down to the office! I've got a hearing I've got to get ready for. And I promised Miss Susannah that I'd escort her to the church social. . . ." He struggled to get out of the bed but wasn't having much luck.

"You missed it."

Lee's head snapped up and his brows lowered in a frown. "Huh?"

Patience looked at the man and wondered why she was even trying to get his attention. The man was so dense. And it hurt more than she thought it would to know that he was interested in the schoolteacher. "I said that you missed it. The church social was last night," she explained, with just a little hint of satisfaction.

He groaned but kept up the effort until he was sitting up in bed with his feet on the floor. "Oh well. I still need to get to the office."

Patience walked around the bed and stood in front of him. She put her hands on her slim hips and glared at him. "You are not going to go anywhere! Billy Aaron has been running things and doing just fine. Nothing much ever happens, anyway. So you just get back in that bed and rest!" she ordered firmly.

For a moment, Lee could do nothing but stare at her. Mercy, she was a fussy package of goods! Never would he have believed that mousy, little Patience Primrose could be so bossy. And she hadn't batted her lashes once since she'd been talking to him. He didn't know whether to be irritated at her boldness or applaud her for being so gutsy.

Instead, he just gave in and fell back into the bed. Lord knew he was tired. And having to deal with this woman just made him more tired.

She smiled with obvious satisfaction. "Mama will bring your broth shortly." She walked to the bed table and took the worn Bible from the drawer. "Why don't I read something to you while we wait?"

Lee eyed her warily and thought that there was something fishy about the gleam in her eyes. But it *was* the Bible—how deceptive could she be?

Without waiting for his answer, Patience pulled up a chair and opened up the Bible. "Okay, let's see. I'll just begin where I left off reading this morning." She glanced at Lee, then back to the page, and began, "Song of Solomon 4:3: 'Thy lips are like a thread of scarlet, and thy speech is comely: thy temples are like a piece of a pomegranate within thy locks. Thy neck is like the tower of David builded for an armoury, whereon...'"

"Stop!" Lee quickly interjected, seeing where the Scripture was heading. Patience looked at him, a question in her expression. "Uh...I think I'd just rather rest, if ya don't mind."

Patience smiled an innocent smile that Lee didn't believe for a minute! "Well okay, Sheriff. If you're sure."

"I'm sure," he said quickly. Was it him, or was it getting warm in the room?

She shrugged as if fighting to keep back a grin. "I just find the Song of Solomon so romantic, don't you?" she asked sweetly.

"Uh...I guess so," he muttered uneasily, very uncomfortable with the subject.

He may be irritated with her, but at least she'd gotten his notice. It was quite an experience to have Leander Cutler's full attention. In chapter four of Miss Hadley's book, it stated, "To procure the young man's notice, you must first make certain that he knows who you are! Engaging him in witty and clever conversations is vital in this delicate process."

Well, the sheriff may not be bowled over by her attempt at witty conversation, but he definitely knew she was alive!

At that moment, Prudence came into the room, carrying a wooden tray laden with a bowl of delicious-smelling broth.

Lee wasted no time in spooning the warm liquid into his mouth. He was so hungry, but he had a feeling that the broth wasn't going to fill the void. By the time he was through, his strength was drained; and he was grateful when Prudence took the tray and both she and Patience left the room.

Carefully, he scooted down to lie flat. He thoughtfully fingered the bandage at his waist. He really should have taken care of this when it'd happened. He knew that porcupine needles could make him sick if the wounds became infected; he just didn't realize how sick.

He was sorry, too, that it had made him miss that church social. He'd been interested in the new schoolteacher, Susannah Butler, ever since she'd arrived just two months ago. They'd spoken a few times at church, and he'd finally gotten enough nerve to ask her to the social. He'd felt lucky that she'd agreed to go with him. He knew that, because she was so pretty, there'd been many eligible men who had shown her interest. Her hair was a glorious auburn that she kept knotted at her nape, while little curls fell all about her face. Her skin was pale and dusted with a coating of very light freckles that danced across her nose and cheekbones. When she looked at him with those blue-green eyes of hers, it could knock the breath right out of him! He'd figured that she would already have a date, but amazingly she said yes to him. Now he wondered if she'd gone with someone else.

He hoped not. He figured that it was getting time for him to marry and have a family. Miss Butler would make the perfect wife.

—⁂—

Patience sat at the sturdy wooden table, absently running a finger along the wood grains.

She looked up when her mother sat down beside her. Prudence wore a worried expression, and Patience had a feeling that she wanted to talk to her. She felt suddenly confused—her mother dictated, but never communicated openly and certainly never worried.

"What's wrong, Mama?" Patience asked warily.

Prudence looked at her daughter strangely for a moment, as if she wanted to say something. Patience wished that she would. She wished that she could pour out her heart to her mother and then be given a comforting hug as she'd seen other mothers do with their daughters.

But, as usual, Prudence did none of those things. The moment passed and Prudence shook her head. "Nothing," she murmured, then turned toward the sink and began washing a pot.

Patience sighed. If she didn't talk about the feelings swirling around her, she'd just break down and never stop crying. Why was it so difficult for people to love her? Her mother didn't show that she loved her, she didn't have any friends who expressed such emotions, and the sheriff definitely didn't love her and didn't show any signs of starting!

Sometimes she even wondered if God loved her. It seemed a selfish and silly thing to contemplate, but she found herself thinking it anyway. There were so many people who were smarter, more upstanding, and better looking than she was. Why would God bother with a plain, average country girl like herself?

Then again, she thought, *why would anyone?*

Chapter 3

The next day, Lee felt a little more like himself and not nearly as tired as he had been the day before. His stomach still ached, but he was able to sit up on his own—thank God!—and needed no more help from Patience.

It wasn't that he was bothered yesterday when she'd helped him up. Why would that bother him? She was just an acquaintance. A distant acquaintance. One that just happened to help him out in his time of need. That was all.

And he would have really believed that, except for the dreams. . . .

For goodness' sake, he didn't even want to think about them! They were ridiculous! In his dreams, Patience was so different. Pretty, even. And he'd been holding her hand and kissing her tenderly. She stood in his house as if she belonged there. Ridiculous!

He really needed to concentrate on getting out of here and going home. That was the answer. And besides, he knew that she liked him; and he didn't want her getting any wrong ideas!

—⁂—

The only "idea" that Patience was getting was that if she wanted to get the sheriff to start thinking of her as serious courting material, she was going to have to work harder!

Eagerly, she opened Emma Hadley's book and turned to chapter five.

Upon occasion one might encounter certain problems pertaining to the young man, himself. One problem might be if he has shown significant interest in another young woman. Miss Emma wants to assure you that, unless there has been an engagement announced, all hope is not lost!

Study the young woman who has captured his regard. Perhaps she wears her hair a certain way or carries herself in a manner that is attractive to him. One can garner much insight on studying one's rival. . . .

Thoughtfully, Patience bookmarked her page and closed the volume. "*Studying one's rival. . .*" Hmm. Maybe if she learned what he liked about Susannah Butler, she could become more of what he wanted.

Taking a fortified breath, she put the book down and started toward the sheriff's room. She had work to do.

When she entered the bedroom, she was surprised to see Lee sitting up. He looked up, scowled at her, then stood carefully.

Patience merely folded her arms around her middle and sighed. Then she waited. Sure enough, he stumbled, rocked unsteadily on his feet, then plopped back down on the bed.

She'd already watched him do this three times today!

He glanced her way again and growled, "Don't say it."

She put on an innocent face and raised her arms in a "surrender" position. "I didn't say a word."

He let out a long, weary breath and sank back down onto his pillows. "I've got things to do. I don't have time to be laid up like some invalid!"

Patience made a show of smoothing her brown cotton skirt, then took the seat next to the bed. "Well, I have something that I think might cheer you up," she said pleasantly. "I've asked Billy Aaron to stop by and fill you in on what's been happening at work. He'll be here in a few minutes."

Patience was rewarded with an unexpected smile. She found herself smiling back.

Lee watched the smile transform her ordinary face into something quite...pretty, actually. Her eyes sparkled and her cheeks bloomed with color.

Not that he noticed such things, of course. He was just touched that she would think of inviting Billy over so that he could catch up on what he'd missed. There were several cases that had been worrying him since he'd awakened the day before. And talking to Billy would certainly ease his mind.

He wondered if it would be impolite to ask about Miss Susannah. Taking another look at her face and how she was looking at him, he decided it would be. And it would probably hurt her feelings.

"Well," he said, breaking the moment, "I appreciate you asking Billy over."

She blushed at his acknowledgment and looked down at her hands. "I knew you were worried and. . ." She drifted off with a shrug.

He looked around the room and racked his brain trying to think of something to say. "Uh. . .would you like to stay and visit with us when he arrives?"

She looked at him quickly, and Lee saw a strange look pass over her features. "No!" she practically shouted, then took a deep breath. "I mean. . .no. I'm sure that you have outlaw and crime things to talk about, and it would only be a hindrance having a female in the room. And besides, I have somewhere I need to be."

He raised his eyebrows, wondering at her reaction. "Oh? Where are you going?"

"Nowhere."

He scratched his head. "But you just said. . ."

"I meant," she interrupted, "that I have nowhere special to go. I've just got some things to do, is all. Is there anything else you want to ask me?" she demanded with exasperation.

Women! Who could figure them out? She was making his head hurt. "All right, all right! I was just making conversation!" he said defensively.

"Oh. Well. . ." She glanced at the clock on the wall, just beyond the tall bedpost. A knock sounded from the other room, and they could both hear Patience's mother opening the front door.

Patience hopped out of her chair. "Well, that will be Billy. Have a good visit." She hurried toward the bedroom door.

"Thanks. I will!" he called after her, but he wasn't sure she'd heard him. What was wrong with the woman? And where was she going that made her not want to tell him? Not that it was any of his business. It just seemed strange that she was so reluctant to tell him.

Then a thought hit him. What if she was meeting a man? Did Patience have a beau? He laughed under his breath at that thought. Of course not. It was clear as spring water that she was still interested in him. Meeting a man? Not likely!

But then again—

"Hey, buddy! Did you decide to join the livin'?" Billy Aaron asked cheerfully as he let himself into the bedroom.

Lee greeted his friend and deputy, but his mind was only on half of the conversation.

One question kept buzzing around his mind.

What was Patience up to?

—⟨⟩—

Her mother would have said that she was up to no good! But that didn't stop Patience from knocking on the door of her rival for Lee's affection, Miss Susannah Butler.

The door opened, and a very pretty, tall redhead appeared on the other side. Her dress was something out of those fashion magazines that Mrs. Hayes kept in her store. Made of light blue-green linen and trimmed in delicate lace, it fit her figure perfectly. The color even matched her eyes. Like most redheads, she had pale skin; and even her freckles added rather than took away from her beauty.

She was everything that Patience wished that she could be—elegant, graceful, and beautiful.

Holding back a sigh, Patience held out the pecan pie that she had brought with her. "Hello, Miss Butler. I'm Patience Primrose. I've not made your acquaintance since you've arrived in town, so I thought I'd come by and welcome you to Springton," Patience recited with more enthusiasm than she felt.

Susannah's face lit up in a delighted smile. "Well, aren't you the sweetest little ol' thang!" she exclaimed in a soft Southern drawl that took Patience by surprise. "Is that delicious-smelling pie for me?"

Bemused, Patience simply nodded her head. Susannah Butler was a Southern belle? *Maybe that is the attraction. . . .*

"Well, won't you come in? I've been so busy with the school that I haven't had time to meet many folks around here. Here let me take that," she said as she took the pie from Patience's hands and ushered her into the little house.

Visiting with Susannah was an eye-opening experience for Patience. Never had she met a woman who could talk as much as she! In fact, Patience couldn't remember saying more than fifteen words the whole thirty minutes that she visited.

And she learned more about her than she ever thought she would in just one visit. She learned that Susannah was from Charleston and that she was Bobby Joe Aaron's late wife's sister. But most importantly, she learned that although Susannah was acquainted with Lee, she didn't seem all *that* interested in him. Who she did seem more interested in and talked about in length was her brother-in-law, Bobby Joe.

Interesting.

Patience did come to some theories about what attracted Lee to Susannah, though. It was quite simple, actually.

He liked her Southern accent.

So she'd just have to. . .get one.

———

After Billy left, finding himself all alone, Lee took the time to really talk to God and thank Him for sparing his life. According to Doc, he was lucky that he didn't get bit by one of those animals. If the creature had been infected with rabies, Lee might have even died from it.

That really shook him up. Up until now, he'd thought of himself as pretty invincible. As a Texas Ranger and a lawman, he'd faced danger and life-threatening situations many times; but he'd never been affected as he was now. Suddenly he was looking over his life and was unsatisfied at what he saw. He knew since making a new commitment to Christ, he'd taken a step in the right direction; but he still had some growing to do.

He realized what he wanted was a family. A home, wife, and kids, and maybe a dog or two. Maybe it was because his best friend, Preacher Caleb Stone, had just gotten himself hitched. Whatever it was, he knew that he wanted it more than ever.

The pretty face of Susannah Butler came to mind, and he wondered if she was the one for him. She certainly seemed perfect. He could look at her and listen to her talk for hours. But was that enough on which to base a relationship? He knew also that she was a Christian, and that was the most important thing.

Quietly he bowed his head as he sat up in his bed and prayed. "Dear Lord, I pray that You show me the direction that You want me to go. If it's Your will that I marry,

I pray that You bring the right woman into my life, like You did for the preacher. I also want to thank You for sparing my life and making me realize just how precious life is. I pray that I may be a man after Your own heart, Lord. Thank You. In Your name I pray. Amen."

What did God have in store for his life? He couldn't help but feel that whatever it was, it was going to happen soon. He didn't know why he thought this, but he just knew.

—⁂—

Patience, standing just outside of Lee's bedroom door, leaned silently against the door frame and closed her eyes. *He was praying for God to send him a wife!*

What would it be like to be loved by a man like Lee? A man who took time to talk to God and thank Him for his life. Such a man would never ignore the ones that he loved and never would he allow them to feel neglected or unloved. His wife would feel cherished and secure.

She would just have to work harder. She must become someone that he would love. Someone like Susannah Butler.

Someone. . .other than plain old Patience.

Chapter 4

G ood mornin', Sheriff," a singsong voice sounded through his sleep-fogged brain. For some reason, a vision of Susannah Butler arose in his mind. It was the voice that made him think of her. It sounded strangely. . .Southern.

He peeped out of one eye to see who was in his room, and all he saw was Patience standing there. He knew it was just too good to be true to think that Susannah had come to pay him a visit. He sighed and opened the other eye. Patience was carrying a tray piled with a lot more food than they'd been feeding him before. His stomach growled with anticipation.

"Is that eggs and bacon I smell?" he asked, his voice heavy with sleep.

Patience smiled, batting her lashes. "Why, it sho' enough is!" she exclaimed in her newly practiced accent.

Lee looked at her as if she'd just spoken in a foreign language. "What's wrong with your voice?"

She placed the tray across his lap. "Whatever do you mean, Sheriff?" she drawled, giving him another smile and another round of extremely fast eye batting.

"You sound funny, and you're starting to do that thing again with your eyes," he told her bluntly as he picked up his fork and scooped up a good-sized helping of eggs.

Patience frowned and her shoulders drooped. If Susannah were here, he wouldn't say that she sounded funny! She made a quick mental note to never bat her eyes again. Emma Hadley couldn't be correct about everything!

She cleared her throat. "Uh. . .it must be the spring air. . .or. . .something," she explained lamely.

He didn't seem to hear her, though. He was much too busy eating.

Ignored again, she thought. She looked about the room, then down at her wringing hands. "Well, I'll just leave you to your breakfast," she muttered and started out of the room.

"Wait a minute."

Patience stopped, not quite believing that she had heard him correctly. Slowly, she turned toward him. Against her better judgment, hope started to bloom within her chest.

Lee motioned toward the chair by the bed. "Why don't you keep me company? Unless. . .you have something to do?" he asked sincerely.

The cows had to be milked, the eggs needed to be gathered, and the chickens needed to be fed. "No," she heard herself answer. "I can stay for a few minutes."

Lee saw the hopeful expression on Patience's face and had a moment of doubt. He didn't want her to think that he was attracted to her, but he found himself enjoying her company. For the last two days, he'd found Patience to be surprisingly easy to talk to. She was intelligent and funny, at least when she wasn't trying to spin her feminine wiles on him.

He hoped that she would realize that they could be friends and get over her apparent infatuation!

He took another bite of his food and swallowed. "I was just wondering if you can fill me in on what's been happening around here in the last few days? Billy let me know about what's been going on as far as the law goes; but I feel like the world kept spinning and living, and I slept right through it."

Patience put on a saucy grin and sat in the chair beside him. "You're not telling me that you want to know all the gossip in town, are you?"

He took on a look of mock indignation. "Hasn't anyone ever told you that men don't gossip?" he admonished.

Patience scoffed at that statement. "Someone forgot to tell Mr. Harold Ray Norton about that. If it's worth knowing, he probably knows about it. Of course, he probably hears it from Miz Hayes," she told him, speaking of the storekeeper and her beau.

"You have a point," he agreed, smiling.

For a moment they sat in silence as he finished the rest of his breakfast. He wiped his mouth with his napkin, and Patience took the tray and placed it on the bedside table.

"Now," Lee said as he settled back against his pillows. "What's been happening around here?"

Patience filled him in on the little things that happened during the week, and then she casually brought up the ice cream social that he'd missed.

"Everyone was there," she told him. "Susannah was there, too," she added, testing his reaction.

It irritated her when he immediately perked up. "So. . .how is she doing? Was she there with anyone?" he asked, trying, but failing in his act of nonchalance.

Patience stifled a sigh. "Oh, she's fine. Just fine." She fiddled with the pleats in her skirt. "She didn't come with anyone to the social, but I did see her talking a lot to Bobby Joe Aaron."

His eyes narrowed. "Oh, really."

She nodded, looking out toward the small window, just beyond his bed. "Yes. They're related, you know."

He immediately looked relieved. "Related? I didn't know that. I didn't even know that they knew each other."

She shrugged. "Well, I guess that they're not really related. I mean, she was his late wife's sister."

"Oh." His shoulders slumped, and Patience realized how much he liked Susannah.

Was it worth it? Was it worth trying to get the attention of a man who clearly preferred someone else? At first she'd only been attracted to him because there weren't many bachelors around Springton. No good Christian men, anyway. He just seemed like good husband material.

But now, after spending so much time with him, Patience's reasons for liking him had changed.

He had a fine quality about him. But more than that, there was something about him that seemed to reach out to her and speak to her woman's heart. She loved to hear him laugh. She loved to sit and talk with him. Everything about him was interesting and attractive to her.

Patience knew that he liked talking to her, but she was also smart enough to realize that he felt no attraction to her as a woman. He treated her as if she was his little sister or his pal. Would that ever change? Or would she have to be content with being only his friend and watch him as he courted Susannah Butler or some other woman?

Looking at him now, seeing the concern that he had for Susannah, Patience couldn't bring herself to give up. This was too important. He was becoming too important to her.

She couldn't give up. Not yet.

"You know, I never heard Billy Aaron speak of even knowing Susannah," Lee told her, breaking into her thoughts.

Patience puzzled over that little bit of information. "Hmm. That's strange. When I talked to her she acted like. . ."

"You talked to her?" he interrupted.

"Yesterday, I went. . .I mean. . .uh. . . ," Patience stammered, realizing what she just said and mentally kicking herself for the slip.

"Wait a minute. You saw her yesterday? Where?" he demanded.

Patience looked at his suspicious face and sighed. "I went to her house."

"You *what?*"

Patience jumped up from her seat and started pacing about the room. "I went to her house. Is that a crime?" she asked, throwing up her arms dramatically.

He opened his mouth, then shut it. "Well, no. It just seems strange that you would go there. I didn't know you were acquainted," he finished lamely.

"Why should you know? I don't remember us being acquainted until you fainted at my feet!"

"I did not faint! I passed out!"

Patience rolled her eyes. "Thank you for clarifying that!"

But Lee was not to be deterred. "Why did you go to Susannah's house, Patience?" he asked once again.

Patience's mind raced. She couldn't tell him the real reason. But she couldn't lie, either. So she compromised. "I just went to get to know her. She is new in town, you know."

Lee stared at her for a moment. "You just suddenly got the urge to befriend her yesterday?" he asked, unconvinced.

Patience pulled up an innocent face. At least, she hoped it looked innocent. "Yes. Do you have a problem with that?"

Lee sighed. It just took too much effort and energy to understand this woman. He knew there had to be more to this visit with Susannah, and he just hoped that she wasn't trying to sabotage his chance for a relationship with the pretty teacher.

Then he felt bad for thinking ill of Patience. She didn't seem like a spiteful person, and he knew that he shouldn't judge her.

"Well," he said finally, "I guess I'll try getting up and getting dressed today. I feel much better." He slowly got out of bed; and for the first time, he didn't feel light-headed.

Patience rushed over to him. "Be careful, Sheriff!" she admonished. "Maybe you're rushing it."

Lee put his hand out, stopping her words. "Miss Patience, I'm doing fine. I'm feelin' plenty good enough to take care of myself." He smiled at her, flexing his arms out. "You and your mother have done a good job taking care of me, and I know you must be anxious to get me out of your hair."

Patience felt her heart drop to her toes. He was leaving? So soon? Logically she knew that he'd have to leave sooner or later, but she was hoping that it would be much later. She needed more time to figure out what he wanted in a woman. She needed more time for him to get to know her and she, him.

What would Emma Hadley do? What would she say at a time like this?

Patience thought for a minute and suddenly got a wonderful idea.

"You have been no trouble at all, Sheriff. But I'm sure you know what's best for you," she said happily. She went to the tall pine armoire and opened it up. Carefully she took out the clothes that he'd arrived in, all freshly laundered. "Here you go." She handed the clothes over to him.

Patience noticed that Lee looked relieved that she wasn't making a fuss about it.

Obviously, he was expecting her to do that very thing.

He took the bundle and nodded to her. "Thank you," he said, his voice holding a question, as if he was unsure of what she was about.

"I'm sure you're anxious to get back to keeping all of Springton safe and sound!" she said briskly as she picked up the tray of dishes. "I'll just let you get ready."

She walked toward the door, and he called after her, "Uh. . .yeah. Well, thanks."

When she got to the door, she paused and turned to Lee. He was standing there, poor man, like he was waiting for the next shoe to fall.

And it did.

"Oh, by the way," she began. "I wouldn't think of letting you fend for yourself while you are getting your strength back. I'll be bringing meals to your work and your house so that you won't have to worry about all that." She waved her hand airily about and with a pert smile, she left, closing the door behind her.

As usual, he felt emotionally drained when Patience left the room. Talking to her was like being on a boat during a storm—tossed up and down and left feeling dizzy in the end!

He was sure that she was up to something, but what? Surely she wasn't using the meals just to get close to him! He did have to eat, and heaven knew he'd rather eat someone else's cooking than his own.

He shrugged and proceeded to dress himself. It would be good getting back to his house. He lived on a moderate-sized piece of land outside of Springton in a small house he'd built himself. It wasn't much, consisting of just two bedrooms, a living room, and a kitchen; but he had plans to build on to it. His father and brother had come up to help him, and they'd made it sturdy.

But as small as it was, it still felt too big to live there all by himself.

Suddenly a picture of Patience filled his mind. She was standing out on his little white porch. He shook his head and wiped his eyes. He really was going to have to stop doing that! Why was he constantly thinking about her?

It must have been because he was in her house and constantly seeing her. At least it made him feel better to think that!

It was definitely time to go home!

—⁘—

When Patience took the tray to the kitchen, her mother was standing there waiting for her. She didn't look happy.

"Patience Primrose, it's already nine o'clock and not one of your chores is done. This farm doesn't run itself, you know. If you would spend less time mooning over the sheriff and reading that worthless book that you've always got your nose stuck in, maybe we could get things done." She folded her arms under her bosom and narrowed her eyes at her daughter. "And I hate to say it, but you're making a fool of yourself over that man. Practically throwing yourself at him! He's not unconscious anymore, and it's unseemly for you to be in his room for the length of time that you've been spending in there!"

Patience lowered her head, shamefaced. "But, Mama, I didn't mean anything by talking to him, and I'm not *throwing* myself at him," she defended, though it came out weak. She always had a hard time standing up to her mother.

Prudence just shook her head and started rinsing out Lee's dishes. Patience stared pensively at her mother. She needed desperately to talk to another woman about what she was feeling, but she didn't know how her mother would respond.

"Uh. . .Mama?" she began. "Could I talk to you about something?"

Prudence sighed impatiently, but didn't stop what she was doing. "Mercy, girl. All you do is yap! What is it now?"

Patience bit her lip and looked down at her clinched hands. "How does a woman go about getting a young man's attention? I mean, how did you and Papa meet? Did you like him before he liked—"

The dishes crashing in the sink stopped Patience from continuing. Prudence whirled around, her face white. "I don't want to talk about that, you hear? Ever! You just leave it to the Lord to find you a man. Chasing after one don't bring nothing but trouble, you hear? Trouble!"

With that, Prudence stomped out of the house.

Shocked, Patience stood staring at the door. What had she said that was so wrong? All she'd mentioned was her papa.

Slowly Patience sat down at the kitchen table, her mind racing. For as long as Patience could remember, they'd never really talked about her father. When she was little, she remembered her mother saying that he'd died and that had been it!

What was it about her papa that got her mother so upset? Had he been a mean man? Did they not get along?

Patience pushed a stray hair from her face and looked longingly at Lee's bedroom door. Was her mother right? Should she just wait on God to send her the right person? But what if God wanted Lee for her, but he was just being too stubborn to realize it?

No. She must persevere! And she must keep trying to become the woman that Lee wanted!

Chapter 5

A winter chill was in the air as Patience drove Lee back to his house. Patience guided the wagon with the ease of one who'd been handling a team of horses for a long time.

It was late October; and though summer had lasted way into September, it was now staying cool throughout the day. They passed several homesteads and farms on their way to his house. A lot of the trees had been cut down and cleared for farming or grazing. But between the clearings, the oak trees stood tall, their leaves painting the skyline in several shades of gold and orange. And, of course, there were the pines. The smell of them tickled her senses like a gentle perfume.

It was the smell of home, and she would never tire of it.

But her attention was not on the trees or the way they smelled. It was on Lee and the fact that she would miss him being with her every minute.

Thank goodness, their ride was not a short one!

Lee's homestead was located not more than four miles from her mother's; but because of how the roadways were laid out between properties, they ended up having to drive twice that far. So far their conversation had consisted of the weather and the scenery.

It wasn't what Patience had in mind at all when she suggested that she be the one to drive him instead of getting Billy Aaron to do it. Somehow she'd pictured a romantic ride where he'd suggest that, because of the chill, she move closer to him. She could almost see them all cuddled up and talking intimately.

So far, when she'd told him that she was chilly, he'd taken off his jacket and handed it to her. When she protested that he might catch a chill, he told her that the cold didn't affect him that much.

Patience sighed. This was not going the way she'd imagined it. Nothing ever did when dealing with the sheriff of Springton!

She discreetly peered at him from the corner of her eye. He was looking out over the land and smiling. She watched as he took a deep breath, breathing the clean, crisp air, and then let out a contented sigh.

Her heart started beating a little faster as she looked at him. It wasn't only because he was a handsome man, but that he had a confidence about him. A demeanor that implied that he was happy with his life and his world. He just had to be the most perfect man she'd ever encountered. She wondered if Emma Hadley had ever encountered such a man; and if she had, would she even have been able to capture his affection?

She looked ahead and saw his little white house far in the distance. "Oh! Isn't that where you live?" Of course, she knew that it was his house, but she didn't want him to think that she knew *everything* about him.

He nodded and, for the first time, looked her way. He opened his mouth to say something, but nothing came out. He had the strangest look on his face.

What *was* he thinking?

Lee knew exactly what he was thinking; he just couldn't believe he was thinking it.

He'd turned to tell Patience about his land, when he'd looked at her and noticed that the wind has loosened several curly strands of her hair and her cheeks were rosy from the chill. But it was her eyes that caught his attention. They were a brilliant light blue that seemed to light up her whole face.

She was lovely.

Confused, he hastily looked away.

"Were you going to say something?" Patience asked him.

He took a breath and decided that he was cold and must have been hallucinating. "I was just going to say that I hope Billy Ray did a good job of feeding my livestock while I was gone."

She looked at him a second and then nodded. "I'm sure that he did. You know Billy is always proud to do something for you."

Glad to have his mind on something else besides her, he chuckled. "He's a good man. I know that he'd like nothing better than to be a full-time lawman himself. But Bobby Joe would never let him go without making him feel guilty about not sticking with the family business." He took a deep breath while looking over the horizon. "I just wish that Bobby Joe would loosen up, you know? Daniel and Tommy give him plenty of help."

Patience was silent for a moment. "Have you tried to talk to him?"

This time Lee's laughter contained no humor. "I've talked and talked till I'm blue in the face. It's almost as if Bobby Joe's life is so miserable, he wants to make everyone else feel that way, too."

"That is such a sad story about his wife. I mean, first she runs away, leaving a daughter behind; then only a few weeks later, we hear that she died—from what, no one seems to know. I can't imagine what that poor man is going through. Bobby Joe was so different back then, when he first got married. They'd both seemed so happy. How can a marriage just break up like that? What would make her leave?" Patience asked.

That question disturbed Lee a great deal. He had just arrived in town when the scandal of Bobby Joe's wife leaving hit Springton. And since he'd decided that he would like to get married and have a family, he worried that the same thing could happen to him. He knew that it was important that, whomever he married, God be the center of the relationship. Since he'd made a new commitment to Christ several months ago, he was striving to get his life in order and be the kind of man God would like him to be. It wasn't easy, but the rewards of living for Christ were so great.

He finally answered her. "I don't know, Miss Patience. I do know that Bobby Joe has pulled away from the Lord. If a couple doesn't pray together and trust God together, I believe that they won't have a firm foundation for their marriage. I know that when I turned away from the Lord, my life didn't have the meaning that it does now that I'm walking with Him."

"I agree. Sometimes, God has been all I've had. If I didn't have Him to turn to, I don't know what I would do."

That sentence struck Lee as odd. He turned and looked at her and was puzzled by the wistful expression on her face. "What do you mean, Miss Patience?" he had to ask.

Immediately, she stiffened as if realizing that she'd spoken aloud. "Nothing. I was just talking," she quickly said with a shrug, dismissing it as nothing.

But Lee had a feeling that there *was* something more to her words. He assumed that since Patience had grown up in Springton, she had plenty of friends whom she could turn to. And then there was her mother. But as soon as Lee thought it, he mentally took two steps back. No, her mother wasn't the kind of woman a daughter could confide in. In fact, Lee had never met such a harsh, judgmental person. *What must it be like to live with her?*

They finally reached the road that led to his house. Lee focused his attention on his surroundings.

It really felt good to be home.

—⁂—

When they had stopped in front of his house, Lee climbed down from the wagon and started to tell Patience good-bye. But when she looked at him and smiled sadly, he stopped.

"I hope that you will take care of yourself, Sheriff. It's been nice getting to know you," she told him sincerely.

He opened his mouth again to answer her, but what came out wasn't what he'd intended. "Why don't you come in while I fix us a cup of coffee? Maybe it'll warm you up for your trip back."

Her face lost its sad expression and brightened as she smiled. "That would be mighty nice, Sheriff," she gushed enthusiastically.

He mentally gave himself a kick for the hopeful look that he'd just put on her face. He'd promised himself that he wouldn't encourage her, and here he was inviting her into his house! What was wrong with him?

He smiled halfheartedly and then reached up to help her from the wagon. He put his hands at her waist, and he couldn't help but marvel at how small she was. Deciding to concentrate on the task at hand, he lifted her to the ground. She braced her hands on his chest to get her balance.

The moment her hands touched him, he felt a stream of warmth run through his body. Shocked, he looked at her and into her bright eyes and unconsciously tightened his grip on her waist.

He felt strange, almost mesmerized, as they stared at each other. She seemed as taken aback as he.

—⁂—

Patience felt as though she couldn't catch her breath. The moment Lee put his hands on her waist, she became more aware of him than she'd ever been before.

She flexed her fingers on his chest and could feel the warmth of his skin beneath his cotton shirt. His face was so close to her own, she could almost imagine him leaning closer and kissing her.

What would it feel like to be kissed by this wonderful man?

She saw that his eyes were growing wider; and much to her embarrassment, she realized that she was beginning to lean closer to him.

Quickly, he let her go and stepped several steps away from her.

"Uh. . .we'd better get on in before we freeze!" he muttered and clumsily turned and ran up the steps to his door.

Patience didn't move at first. She took a deep breath and willed her cheeks to return to their natural color instead of the blaring red she knew they must be. What he must think of her! She'd practically leaned over and kissed him. Patience had never been more embarrassed in her life.

Taking a fortified breath, she straightened her shoulders, walked up the steps and through the door that he was holding open for her. She looked at him as she passed him, but Lee didn't look up.

When she entered the house, she was surprised at how neat the house was. There weren't any signs of frills or ruffles, but it was neatly decorated in a clean style a man would choose. The curtains on the windows were a pretty blue color that matched the pillows on the beige couch. Above the fireplace was a pretty landscape painting with several small pictures placed on the mantel. She guessed that they were of his family.

"You have a nice home," she commented, hoping to break their awkward silence.

He came up behind her, but not too close. "Thanks. My brother and father came up to help me build it a couple of years ago."

She turned and gave him what she hoped was a bright smile. "Where do your brother and father live?"

"Right outside of Houston on the Lazy C Ranch with my mama. My brother helps him run it, but I never was interested in the ranching business. From the time I knew what a sheriff was, I wanted to be one. I'm just glad that my parents understood," he explained.

"Which is why you understand Billy's situation," she surmised.

His grin was sheepish. "Yeah, I guess you're right." He ran a hand through his hair and glanced about the room. "Well, let me go and get that coffee made."

"No," she said, stopping him. "I'll go make it. You just sit down and relax. I can find everything."

By the weary look on his face and the slump of his shoulders, she knew that she'd guessed correctly. He merely nodded and sat down on the couch.

She went into the kitchen and tried not to dream that this could be *her* kitchen.

Lee was clearly tired, so she didn't stay long. He walked her to the door and on the way grabbed up his jacket that she'd draped over a chair.

"Here. Put this on. You can return it to me later," he offered, holding the coat open for her.

She nervously turned her back to him so that he could drape it around her shoulders. Was it her imagination or did his hands linger on her shoulders longer than they should have?

But she dismissed that thought. Of course not. He only regarded her as a friend or. . .a sister! He practically ran off when he thought that she might kiss him, didn't he?

She turned back to him and smiled. "I put the hamper of food I brought in your pantry. If you need anything, just let us know."

He nodded. "I will. Thanks. You be careful riding home."

She stared at him a minute more, then turned and walked out to her wagon. She noticed that he watched at the door while she climbed into the buggy and rode out of sight.

What was he thinking?

Lee was thinking about the fact that he'd almost kissed her! He couldn't get over the feeling that had swept over him when they'd been standing close. For that moment, it had felt good to have his hands on her waist and her hands on his chest. He'd wanted nothing more than to reach down and brush her lips with his own. It had seemed right somehow.

Lee shook his head as if trying to clear it. It was the close proximity to her that was making him confused. It had to be. Now that he was home, things could get back to normal. He could start concentrating his efforts on courting the woman that he really wanted—Susannah Butler.

She was the woman for him. Beautiful, gentle, and graceful. Just the kind of woman a man needed to come home to after a hard day at work. He would never get tired of looking at her. That was for sure.

And while it was true that he hadn't had much time to talk to her, he was sure that they would have a lot in common.

Patience wasn't the only woman that he could talk to!

Tomorrow. Tomorrow he would go and pay her a visit. That surely would get his mind off of Patience Primrose and back on the right track of rational thinking!

Chapter 6

Getting motivated to get out of bed and go to work wasn't an easy chore, as Lee found out the next morning. His mind was raring to go and get things done, but his body was moaning and groaning for him to stay put.

When his hungry animals started protesting, he finally got up. "All right, all right," he grumbled as he slowly got dressed.

His livestock consisted of three horses and five head of cattle. Just enough to meet his needs and not be a bother to care for. There wasn't a whole lot of crime to deal with in a small town like Springton, but what little there was kept him busy. He didn't want to have to spend his extra time and money trying to run a large spread, too.

With the feeding done, he made his way into town and to the jailhouse, which also contained his office and two jail cells. It was empty when he arrived, so he got to sit and catch his breath for a few minutes.

He didn't get to rest for long, although the man who walked through his door was a welcome interruption.

"Preacher!" Lee greeted the town's minister with a grin. "How's married life?"

The two men shook hands, and Caleb Stone sat in the chair in front of the desk.

"Married life is wonderful. You should try it some time," Caleb answered, a satisfied gleam in his eye.

Lee laughed. "I don't know. I might think about it one of these days. When did you get back?"

Caleb lifted his hat off his head and ran his fingers through his messy black tresses. "Last night. We were going to come in today, but Rachel was anxious about the kids. I was sorta missing the little boogers myself! I'm just glad that we got someone to run the orphanage for us so we didn't have that worry." He stopped and stared at Lee, his gaze, as always, keen. "You doing all right, Lee? You still don't look that good."

Lee gave his friend a wry grin. "Thanks, Preacher."

Caleb didn't smile. "Are you sure that you should be back at work so soon?"

Lee waved off his concern. "Doc says I'm fine. I just don't have all my strength back, is all."

Caleb studied him a minute more and seemed satisfied. He nodded and then a teasing smile lit his face. "So...did Patience Primrose get you all taken care of?"

Lee eyed him warily. "Yeah, she and her mother did all right," he said.

Caleb nodded and pretended to have great interest in his hat. "Hmmm... And how was Patience? Did you two get along?"

"What do you mean?"

"I was just wondering if your feelings had changed any where Patience is concerned. I mean, living with someone for nearly a week can bring a whole new perspective to things. And she is sweet on ya...."

"No!" Lee immediately denied. Upon seeing Caleb's eyebrows raised in question at his vehement denial, he cleared his throat and spoke more calmly. "Patience is a nice girl, but we're just friends. I made that clear to her."

"Ya did, did ya? So no more batting her eyelashes and giggling?" Caleb asked. "She got the point that you're not interested?"

Lee glowered at the preacher. "You know good and well she ain't easy to convince. You had to get engaged to someone else before she got the point!"

"So what are you going to do? Get yourself engaged?"

Lee smiled. "I'm working on it."

That got his attention. Caleb popped forward in his chair. "You're what?"

Lee leaned back. "I said I'm working on it. Been thinking 'bout courtin' that new schoolteacher, Susannah Butler."

Caleb thought for a moment. "Isn't she Bobby Joe Aaron's sister-in-law?"

"That's what I heard," Lee said with a shrug. "Anyway, I was supposed to go to the ice cream social with her before I got sick. Thought I'd ask her to a picnic this Saturday."

"Sounds like you got this thing all figured out."

Lee smiled smugly. "I've got a plan, if that's what you're asking." He looked at Caleb more seriously and then told him what had been on his heart recently. "Lately, I've really been praying that God would send me the perfect mate, like He did for you. I really want to do God's will."

"Then I'll be in prayer for you also," Caleb told him, but then paused. "You know, Lee, what you may think is God's will for you may not be right at all. And then, sometimes what we would never consider in our own minds may be what God wants for us."

"What are you saying?" Lee asked, confused.

Caleb took a breath and shook his head. "I don't know. I just felt God wanted me to tell you that."

Lee groaned and ran his hand over his face. "Don't do that to me, Preacher. You can't just throw something out there and not explain it!"

"A little mystery in your life is good, Sheriff. I don't make up these little insights; I just deliver them," he said with a shrug. Then he laughed. "Maybe if you didn't have all these women troubles, you'd be able to hear Him for yourself."

At that moment, Patience breezed into the office. "Why hello, you all!" she said in a strange accent.

Caleb glanced at Lee and then turned in his chair to face Patience. "Been down South lately, Miss Patience?" he asked, as if quite amused.

"Why no, Brother Caleb," she answered and quickly changed the subject. "You all are back from your honeymoon?"

Caleb nodded. "Yes, I was just telling Lee here that the married life was something he should experience for himself."

Lee stopped himself from rolling his eyes. He was getting paid back for all the times that he teased the preacher when Patience had shown interest in him! He could practically see the marriage-minded wheels in Patience's head spinning.

"You're thinking of getting married, Sheriff?" Patience asked with great interest.

"No!" Lee practically shouted.

Patience's eyebrows lifted, and Lee admonished himself for letting all this marriage talk get to him. "I mean, I hope to one day; but I'm not in a big hurry."

Patience smiled at him. "That's the way I feel, Sheriff!"

Lee could tell that Caleb was biting his lip in an attempt not to laugh. Lee gave him a withering glare.

"Seems like you two have something in common," he casually mentioned.

Lee hopped up from his desk. "Didn't you mention that you had something to do, Preacher?" he asked, looking pointedly at Caleb.

This time Caleb chuckled aloud. "Well, if I don't, I'm sure I can find something to do." He got up and donned his hat, tipping it in Patience's direction. "Miss Patience, you have a good morning."

Patience beamed at him. "You, too, Brother Caleb."

They both watched the preacher close the door behind him, and then Patience turned to Lee with a smile. "He seems happy, doesn't he? Marriage must agree with him."

Lee had about all the marriage talk he could take this morning. He *especially* did not want to discuss it with Patience! "Yeah, uh. . .well. Did you need me for something this morning?" he asked briskly.

Patience looked down at the basket and the jacket she'd been holding. "Oh yes! I brought you some muffins. I thought you might not feel like fixing yourself anything, so I made extra for you. And I also wanted to return your jacket and thank you for letting me borrow it last night."

It was the first time he noticed that she had her hands full. It made him feel a little guilty for being so short with her. "I appreciate it, Miss Patience. I was getting a little hungry."

"Well, we surely don't want you to starve!" she exclaimed as she put the basket on his desk, then laid his jacket beside it. She was speaking with an accent once again.

He just had to ask.

"Uh. . .Patience, why do you keep doing that?"

She frowned, but kept laying out the contents of the basket. "Doing what?"

He put his hands on his hips, then let them fall at his side again. "That thing with your voice. You sound. . .funny!"

That got her attention. She looked at him with a strange expression on her face. "I don't know what you mean."

The accent was gone. He narrowed his eyes. "There you go again. Now it's gone."

She giggled nervously. "Really, Sheriff. . .," she muttered, picking up the basket and hurrying toward the door. "Well, I'll just leave you to your breakfast!"

"You're not going to join me?" he called after her.

She opened the door and plastered a smile on her face as she looked back at him. "No, no. That's okay. Good-bye!" With that she stepped out and shut the door behind her.

Lee chuckled, then laughed out loud. He had to admit, Patience was fun to tease. He never knew what that girl was up to or what she was going to do next!

He sighed happily and sat down, savoring the muffins and the sweet rolls that Patience left behind.

And there was one more thing he liked about Patience.

The woman could cook.

Patience walked over to the bench that sat outside the sheriff's office and slumped down onto it.

What a disaster! She'd practiced all morning on that Southern accent, and all she'd managed to do was to make Lee think she was even more strange.

She bent over, cupped her face in her hands, and groaned. This wasn't going to work. She was an utter failure at this sort of thing. She was going to die an old maid. That was all there was to it!

"Patience?" a sweet Southern voice asked overhead.

Slowly Patience raised her head; and after taking a look at the woman in front of her, she wished that she'd never looked up. What she didn't need was to see her competition looking more beautiful than ever.

Patience pulled her eyes away from the radiant pink-striped gown—redheads weren't supposed to look good in pink, were they?—and then looked down at her own plain, beige dress.

Forget the accent, Patience thought, *I need new clothes!*

She made a mental note to think on that later and looked back up at Susannah. "Hi, Miss Butler. How are you?" she greeted.

Susannah smiled and sat down beside her. A wave of honeysuckle drifted over to Patience, as the pretty woman straightened the frills and ruffles on her skirt.

"I'm so glad I ran into you!" she began. "I surely did want to thank you for that dee-licious pie you brought to my house."

Susannah was so nice, it was hard not to respond to her enthusiasm. "You're welcome, Susannah. I'm glad you liked it."

"I also wanted to ask you if you would come to dinner at my house tomorrow night. I'm just having a few people over that I've met in the short time I've been here. You know, so that I can get to know everybody a little better. It'll just be the pastor and his new wife and Bobby Joe, if he'll come, and his brother, Billy. Oh, and I plan on asking Sheriff Cutler. That's where I was just headed."

Patience's heart dropped. "The sheriff, huh?"

"Oh yes," Susannah gushed. "Isn't he a handsome man? Those golden eyes of his can just make a girl's heart go all aflutter! And I heard that you took care of him! Wasn't that just sweet of you! I do hope that he's recovering nicely."

Patience didn't know when she'd felt so depressed. Susannah thought Lee was handsome. It was clear that she was attracted to him. And with Lee reciprocating those feelings, where did that leave Patience?

Home alone with Mama for the rest of her life. That's where. It was a depressing thought.

"He's doing fine. He's in his office. I just came from there," Patience answered faintly.

Susannah beamed. "Oh good! Well, I'll just run in there and ask him if he'll come." She hopped up and tugged at her little pink gloves. "Can I count on your being there?"

Patience knew that she shouldn't go. It would be humiliating to be in the presence of this woman and the pretty preacher's wife, Rachel. She would look so plain in comparison. But she didn't want to leave Lee alone with this Southern beauty, either. "I'll be there," she answered.

"All righty. I'll see you around six tomorrow?"

Patience nodded and with a friendly wave good-bye, Susannah let herself into the sheriff's office.

Staring after her, Patience felt envious. Susannah had everything that Patience wished that she had. What chance did she have if Susannah truly did want Lee for herself?

Patience turned away and looked down the street. She couldn't let herself think like that. The feelings that Patience had for the sheriff had become something strong and powerful in the days that she'd gotten to know him. To think that he'd never be hers was more than she could handle at that moment.

There had to be a way.

She got up and took another look down at her dress. *Clothes.* She needed to do something about her clothes. But what?

She looked down the street and saw the sign of the mercantile swinging in the wind. She wrapped her woolen shawl tightly around her and made her way in that direction.

Chapter 7

When his office door opened once again, Lee didn't even look up. He just assumed that he knew who it was—Patience. "I really do need to get some work done here," he said firmly and kept on writing.

"Oh! Well, I promise I won't take up much of your time, Sheriff," a musical Southern voice answered.

Lee's head popped up, and he was greeted with the lovely presence of Miss Susannah Butler. "I'm sorry I was so rude," he said quickly. "I thought you were. . . uh. . .someone else," he finished lamely.

She seemed to float across the room to where he sat. At the last minute, Lee remembered his manners and jumped up from his seat and motioned toward the empty chair. "Won't you have a seat?" he offered politely.

"Why, thank you." She sat in a puffy cloud of striped pink and white and proceeded to pull off her dainty gloves. "I just wanted to stop by and invite you to a dinner party at my house tomorrow night. I'm only inviting a handful of people, just those I've become acquainted with recently. I would be most honored if you'd be counted among my guests," she implored with a sweet smile.

He looked at her for a moment and blinked, amazed that she hadn't even taken a breath during her whole speech. "Well, sure! I can be there. What time?"

She clasped her hands together in an apparent show of joy. "Oh, that's wonderful! Everyone is arriving at six. And don't worry about bringing anything—I'm cooking plenty of everything. I also invited Billy and Bobby Joe, too; though I don't think that Bobby Joe will come. He's such a stubborn old thing. And Daniel and Tommy can't come because they are out of town, but I did invite the preacher and his wife and they said that they would be happy to come. Oh, and I almost forgot, I also invited. . ."

The door opened and Lee couldn't help but take a breath of relief that someone had interrupted her. Had she talked so much before? He couldn't remember that. Maybe he'd found it irritating because he was feeling so poorly and weak. That had to be it.

Texas Ranger Gene Brown stepped into the office, dragging a cuffed, scruffy-looking man behind him. "Lee! Glad to see that you're out and about. Unfortunately I've got a present for you," he greeted as he yanked the outlaw to his side.

Susannah, upon seeing the man, jumped up from her seat, clasped her hands to her chest, and gasped aloud. "Mercy!"

Lee was instantly next to her. "Gene, why don't you lock up our guest, there, while I escort Miss Susannah outside," he said as he tossed Gene the keys.

Gene nodded and halfway dragged the man toward the cell.

Lee took Susannah's arm and ushered her outside.

"I'm sorry about that, Miss Susannah. But you never know what's going to come through my office. I mean, it is a jail, too," he explained.

"Oh, don't be a silly-willy, Sheriff. I'm perfectly fine. That poor man just startled me, is all," she said, waving off his concern. She pulled her gloves back on in a smart fashion and gave him a breezy smile. "But that was awfully gallant of you to come to my rescue like that!"

She laid her hand on his arm and smiled at him.

—⁂—

Patience let herself into the mercantile and went directly to the section of the store that she was most interested in. The material.

"Hello, Patience!" Addie Hayes, the store's owner, called out from behind the counter. "What can I do for you today?"

Patience walked up to where she stood and motioned to the shelves behind Mrs. Hayes. "I just wanted to look at your material, Mrs. Hayes. I was thinking about making a new dress."

Addie smiled and then turned and looked at her inventory. "Hmmm, let's see. I have some of that gray cotton that your mother likes so much and, of course, the brown wool if you're looking for warmth. It's October and getting colder every day!"

But Patience shook her head. "No, I was looking for something. . .prettier?" she explained, her voice uncertain. She scanned the shelves, and her eyes lit on the green silk material on the third shelf. "Something like that."

Addie followed to where Patience was pointing and asked, "The green?"

"Yes."

"Now, this is a pretty color!" She pulled it loose and held it against Patience's face. "Oh, and look at that. It just brightens your whole face!"

Patience wasn't expecting the compliment. She blushed. "Do you really think so?"

"It certainly does! You could sew a fancy dress using this material!"

Patience's face fell. "Oh. I'm sorry, Mrs. Hayes. I can't get this. I never have gotten the hang of using a sewing needle. Mama makes all my clothes and she would surely pitch a fit if I brought this material to her to sew. And besides, I don't have enough money for silk," she finished sadly. She let herself touch the pretty silk one last time before she let it go.

Addie studied her for a moment, then nodded her head as if coming to a decision. "You know, Patience, I've had to run things by myself ever since Rachel got married; and it sure is rough on an old woman like me. I don't suppose you would want to help me a few days a week, would you? You could buy all the material you want, then Rachel could sew them for you."

Hope welled within Patience's heart. Did she dare? "But Mrs. Hayes, my mother would have an absolute fit!" she lamented, voicing her worst fear.

Mrs. Hayes rolled her eyes at that. "Oh fiddlesticks! I've dealt with Prudence before. You just leave her to me." She tapped her cheek in contemplation. "In fact, why don't I drop by and ask her myself? It'll sound better coming from me, anyhow."

Patience bit her lower lip and looked down at the beautiful green silk again. She could see herself entering a room wearing the green silk fashioned in a flowing, stylish gown. Lee wouldn't be able to miss her in this color!

She looked back up at Mrs. Hayes. "All right, let's do it!"

Addie laughed, as if she and Prudence had butted heads before and was looking forward to the chance to do it again! "I'll be by around seven this evening."

Patience giggled with excitement. "Okay! See you tonight!" She turned and practically skipped out of the store.

When she ran down the steps, she had visions of beautiful dresses dancing around in her head. She turned to walk to her wagon, which was parked by the sheriff's office, and froze.

Lee and Susannah were standing closely together, right by her wagon. She had her hand on his arm, and they were gazing into each other's eyes.

"Oh no!" she whispered. She tried to swallow; but to her horror, tears began to gather in her eyes.

She blinked furiously, determined that she was not going to let this upset her. She was not going to cry!

"Aren't they just the cutest couple?" a high-pitched voice commented.

Patience turned slightly and saw Amy McLain and Jessica Buford standing with their heads together, their attentions fixed on the couple across the street from them. Amy and Jessica were the same age as Patience and had been schoolmates of hers. Both were married to the sons of the town's only banker.

But they had never been Patience's friends.

Jessica giggled. "I'll bet he's thrilled to be out of the Primrose house! Can you imagine having to endure five days with Prudence? And poor, plain Patience couldn't have been much company to him! She's such a mousy thing, isn't she?"

"I'll say," Amy agreed while patting her chestnut curls that were all still perfectly in place, despite the wind. "I can't imagine the poor thing ever finding herself a husband. She'll probably end up an old maid."

Jessica nodded. "Well, we really do need to make Susannah's acquaintance. She seems like someone that we would want to befriend."

Patience's tears were abandoned in favor of anger. How many times in her life had she had to endure the pettiness of girls like those two? Never had they asked her to join in with them or invited her to their parties. When she'd been younger, she'd tried so hard to get them to like her, but they'd just ridiculed her more. Poor plain Patience. So pathetic in her attempts to be in their circle. Never belonging.

She never really belonged anywhere.

And as usual, she let them walk away without saying anything in her own defense. They never even seemed to notice her standing there.

Taking a deep breath, she prayed that God would help her with her anger, then started across the street to her wagon.

—◆—

Lee returned Susannah's smile and glanced down to where her hand rested on his arm.

But something was wrong. Her smile, while it had dazzled him in the past, didn't do a thing to him today. He'd dreamed of her touch, but there was no spark or warmth now that she actually was touching him. He felt disappointed.

He suddenly thought of last night, when he'd helped Patience from the wagon. Her touch had made him feel more than he cared to admit.

Susannah was the woman he was interested in. Shouldn't her touch have more effect on him?

A movement in his side vision made him look up. Patience, wrapped tightly in her woolen shawl, was coming toward them. She didn't even look up as she walked to her wagon and climbed into it.

He didn't know what made him do it, but he stepped away from Susannah's touch.

"Oh! Hello, Patience!" Susannah called out.

Patience looked at them as if she didn't know they'd been standing there. "Oh, hello, Susannah. . .and you, too, Sheriff."

Lee cocked an eyebrow at her cool voice. "Going home, Miss Patience?"

She noticed, just then, that he'd stepped away from Susannah. That melted her coolness considerably. Maybe she had more of a chance with the sheriff than she'd realized. He'd actually moved away from the fair Susannah to acknowledge her! With a genuine smile, she answered, "Yes, but I'll be back to bring you some lunch, Sheriff."

"I'd be most obliged."

She waved good-bye to them both and rode away.

Susannah watched as the wagon disappeared down the street. "I really like Patience. She's a real sweet girl, don't you think?" she commented.

Lee agreed. "Yes, she is," he murmured thoughtfully.

"Well, I surely hope that we can become fast friends! I could really use one, being that I'm a stranger to this state!"

Lee looked at her curiously. "Aren't you friends with Bobby Joe Aaron and his family?"

Her bright face suddenly darkened. "Not really, although I've tried to be. . ." She tugged her shawl closer around her and changed the subject. "I guess I should say to-di-loo, and I'll see you tomorrow night. Now, don't you forget about the dinner. I just think. . ."

"I won't!" he quickly interjected. "I better get back in and see about that prisoner."

She smiled. "Okay, Sheriff. Good-bye, now."

"Good-bye," he said, and they both turned to go their separate ways.

Lee went back into the office, where Gene was waiting for him.

"What's his story?" Lee asked, motioning toward the outlaw, who had already made himself comfortable on the cot inside the cell.

"He and his brother have hit a couple stagecoaches in this area. I brought him to you in hopes that his brother will show up and try to bail him out. I know you are shorthanded around here, but I wanted to ask if you could keep a round-the-clock watch while he's here. If we can get his brother, we'll have a much better case. He's wanted in Louisiana, Arkansas, and Texas."

Lee nodded. "I'll see if my deputies can help out."

Gene slapped him on the shoulder. "Good. I'll be checking in." He picked up a paper from Lee's desk. "Here is a picture of his brother. You might want to get them copied and post them around town."

"I'll run them by the newspaper office."

Gene picked up his hat. "Okay! You take care, you hear?"

"Will do," Lee answered.

—⚏—

After Gene had left, Lee sank back down into his chair.

"You can have as many deputies as you want guarding this place. It ain't gonna make no difference. If Otis wants me out, then he'll get me out," the outlaw spoke from his cell.

Lee, not in the mood to deal with the man, wearily rubbed his eyes. "Look. . ." He glanced down at the papers Gene had given him. ". . .Powell. I'm not in the mood to play my-brother-is-tougher-than-yours, all right? Just sit there real quiet-like and we'll get along just fine. I might even let you eat lunch." Then he silently groaned. Lunch! He'd need to make provisions for meals for this wise guy. Then he remembered Patience. Maybe she could run down to the inn and pick something up for him.

"You'll be sorry," the outlaw spoke again.

Lee rolled his head back and looked beseechingly heavenward. "I'm already sorry."

Chapter 8

Sheriff Cutler was becoming more and more dear to Patience, and Patience was afraid that she was becoming more and more. . .like a sister to him. Worse than that, she felt she was being a pest!

She'd taken his lunch and had even run down to the inn to get food for his prisoner. He'd seemed glad to get the food; but when she'd suggested she sit with him, he told her that it wasn't necessary. That he was going to work while he ate. In fact, he barely even *looked* at her the whole time she'd been in his office.

She was obviously getting on his nerves. That had to be the problem. But she didn't know how else to get his attention. The only thing that she could come up with was to alter her appearance.

But she needed the mercantile job to accomplish that. And for that, she needed her mama's blessing.

It wasn't soon in coming. Prudence threw an absolute fit!

Patience knew that she would. How could her mother ever understand how Patience felt? Though she'd lived alone all these years, Prudence had once been married and had borne a child. Patience would never have a chance to do any of that unless her mother gave in. She needed the job Addie Hayes offered. It would not only give her extra money for new clothes, it would give her a sense of self-worth.

"My daughter does not have to work like a common laborer! I'll not have it, I tell you. She doesn't get her work done around here as it is."

Addie Hayes folded her arms about her middle and gave Prudence a direct look. "Patience would only be helping me out in the afternoons. There'd be plenty of time to get her chores done around here."

Prudence turned her shrewd gaze toward her daughter. "And why do you want this job? What are you up to, girl?"

Patience forced herself not to cringe from her mother's tone. She bravely stood her ground. "I would like to have my own money, Mama. I'm twenty-one years old, and it doesn't look like I'll be getting married. Not yet, anyway. So I want to do this for myself." She braced herself for her mother's harsh words, which she knew would probably come.

"All you're going to do is cause folks around here to talk and to speculate about why you have a job! They will think we're hurtin' for money. Is that what you want to do, girl? Bring shame to this house?"

"No. You know that I don't want that, Mama. I just want to make a little money on my own."

"Selfishness! That's all it is!" Then Prudence sharpened her gaze on Addie. "And you! You're sticking your nose where it don't belong! Well, I wash my hands of it!" With that, she got up from her chair and walked out of the room.

Embarrassed at her mother's rudeness, Patience hastened to explain. "I'm sorry, Mrs. Hayes. I don't know what's wrong with Mama lately. She's acting awfully strange. I. . ."

Addie waved her words aside. "Oh, you don't have to explain your mama to me. Rachel told me she's going through a lot of things on the inside. You just keep praying for her; she'll be all right."

Patience reached up and smoothed a stray strand of hair from her face and tucked it behind her ear. "I just wish I knew what's wrong with her. I mentioned my father the other day, and she acted like I'd just asked about the devil himself!"

Addie shook her head, confusion marring her brow. "I don't know about that. Never knew your father. Prudence was already widowed when she came to Springton."

"I know. But other than telling me that he'd died before I was born, she's never mentioned him. I guess I'm just curious about who he was." She shrugged. "But I don't reckon that I'll ever know."

Addie reached out and patted Patience on the hand. "Well, don't worry yourself sick over it. Maybe working at the store will get your mind off it. You are old enough to make this decision for yourself, Patience, whether your mama likes it or not."

Patience was thoughtful for a moment. She'd never openly defied her mother before, but she could see the truth in Mrs. Hayes's words. She was a grown-up. It was something her mama would have to learn to accept. She looked up into Addie's eyes and brightened. "I'm really excited about working for you, Mrs. Hayes. I do so want to be able to purchase pretty cloth for new dresses. I've got to do something to attract the sheriff, or I'm afraid that I'm going to end up an old maid!" she wailed.

Addie practically crowed. "Oh ho! So that's how the wind blows, does it? Well, you just leave it to Rachel and me. We'll get you all prettied up! You just wait and see."

"Oh Mrs. Hayes. Do you really think you can?"

Addie smiled and arose from her chair. "Yes, I do. Now, let me go so you can go on in and get your beauty rest."

Patience giggled excitedly as she got up and walked her to the door. "I'll see you tomorrow."

Addie waved. "Just be there around nine. That will be fine."

"Okay," Patience answered. "Oh, and Mrs. Hayes?" she called out.

Addie turned and looked back at Patience.

"Thank you."

Addie just smiled and climbed into her buggy.

—◊◊◊—

The boards creaked softly as Lee stepped out onto his little porch and eased his lanky body into the swing. The crickets were out and singing in full chorus; their song had a peaceful effect on Lee as he nudged the swing into a gentle sway.

He'd gotten Billy Aaron to bunk at the jail for the night to keep watch over their prisoner. He really hoped they caught Otis Powell soon. It was hard finding men to volunteer for things like taking the night watch. Lee knew that he'd probably end of up doing most of it himself. He just wished he'd get all his strength back so he'd be up to it when his time came.

But even the singing of the crickets could not wipe away the nagging guilt he was feeling for snubbing Patience today at the office.

He had come to a decision about her, and he was trying his best to carry it through. He'd decided to act cool so that she would stop getting her hopes up about them having any kind of relationship. He saw the expression on her face, the attraction for him that was written in her every look. She was much too sweet a girl to be hurt by his rejection. He had to do it now, before it was too late.

He laid his head back on the swing and stared up at the blue ceiling of his porch. He'd just finished painting it that color because one of the women from church had said that it would stop dirt-daubers from building nests in his eaves. They would see the blue and mistake it for the sky. That's what he was told anyway. He supposed he wouldn't find out till spring.

Spring. . . Would he be married at that time? He figured that he'd go to this party, and afterward, he'd invite Susannah on a picnic the next day. From there they would start dating frequently. Everybody would see them together and start acknowledging them as a couple. At Christmas he could present her with a ring, and by March they could be married.

Lee smiled. It sounded like a good plan to him.

Except. . . Oh, he shouldn't be thinking it. He shouldn't let doubts creep in! Yet he couldn't help but be, well, bored when she started talking on and on, as she tended to do. That was just her vivacious personality, he supposed. But could he live with that for the rest of his life? Why couldn't she just have a normal conversation with him like. . .Patience.

He closed his eyes and grimaced. He wasn't going to think about her anymore! He especially wasn't going to compare her with Susannah.

Patience was his friend. So he guessed it would be okay to think of her that way.

It didn't mean anything. It didn't mean that *she* meant anything to him!

He blew out a breath. Why was everything so confusing? He'd been so clear about everything before he ended up in Patience's care. So sure of what he wanted.

Now. . .he wasn't sure about anything.

—m—

Patience drove up to Susannah's house at a quarter past six. By the wagons and buggies lined up in Susannah's small yard, Patience could see that most everybody was there. From inside the house came a hum of chatter, peppered with a dash of laughter here and there.

Lee's horse was tied to the only tree in the yard.

He's here.

Patience closed her eyes for a moment, gathering needed strength. She opened them and, with a fortified breath, stepped down from the wagon. Carefully she smoothed the pleats of her best dress and tucked the curly stray strands of her hair back into place.

Her dress was made of a dark blue material that would have been quite attractive. . .on a brunette. On her, it merely made her look paler than usual. And the neck of it was so tall, she felt like she was choking at times. But it was better than anything else she owned. It would simply have to do until she could purchase the green silk.

She walked the few steps to the house and knocked on the door.

Susannah opened it after a few moments and smiled broadly upon seeing her new friend. "Patience! I was just beside myself when six o'clock came and went and you weren't here yet. Please, come on in! I was just about to set supper on the table."

She took Patience's hand and pulled her into the parlor, where the rest of the guests were gathered.

"Looky, you all! Patience did make it, after all!" she announced to the whole room. Then she turned to Patience. "You know Reverend Stone and his wife, of course, and Billy Aaron—his brother didn't come—and over there is Lee."

Patience looked over to where the sheriff stood, conversing with Brother Caleb. But when Susannah said his first name, he lifted his head and his gaze clashed with Patience's.

Lee had been merely curious at hearing his name spoken, but he froze when he saw Patience standing there. He'd heard someone else come in, but he'd been interested in something the preacher was saying and hadn't looked up.

He didn't know that she would be here.

Was there anywhere he could go that Patience Primrose wasn't?

Very politely he nodded to her and turned his gaze back to the preacher, only the preacher was no longer paying attention to him. He was looking at Patience, too.

And before Lee could open his mouth to stop him, Caleb was already talking. "Miss Patience! We're glad you're here. Now everything is even. Billy can sit beside Miss Susannah and Lee, here, can escort you to the table."

Lee glared at him and whispered under his breath, "I'll get you for this, Preacher."

Caleb continued to smile as Patience made her way over to where they were.

"Hi, Brother Caleb," she greeted first. She then looked at Lee with a wary expression that made him feel like a complete heel. "And how are you, Sheriff?" she asked, sounding tentative.

Lee made himself relax and squelched his irritations. "Hi, Patience. That lunch you fixed today was mighty tasty." Actually he hadn't really tasted it. He'd felt so horrible for treating her coolly that he hadn't felt like eating.

Patience's face lit up prettily. "Oh thank you, Sheriff! It was my pleasure!" she gushed. The wary look was gone, replaced by a dreamy sort of look.

He'd done it, again. He'd gotten her hopes up.

"Okay, you all! The food's ready, if you all would follow Billy and me into the dining room!" Susannah announced, taking Billy's arm.

Lee watched Susannah precede him into the dining room. The preacher and Rachel were next. That left him and Patience.

Cautiously, he looked sideways at her and saw that she was watching everyone leave the room. She seemed to be waiting for something.

With a sigh, he held out his arm to her. She blushed and carefully reached up and put her arm through his.

Lee felt that touch all the way to his toes.

Shocked, he looked down at her hand, then up to her eyes. She was a tall girl, so it wasn't hard to look directly into her eyes.

She was wearing the same expression he was. She quickly looked away, and her blush blossomed to a deep red hue.

Taking a breath, Lee tried to rationalize why her touch would, once again, make him feel this way, why Susannah, his dream girl, could touch him and he felt no different. But one tiny little touch from Patience sent his senses reeling.

There had to be an explanation. A logical reason for this.

Chapter 9

He ignored her all the way through dinner. Oh, he'd answer her when she asked him a question; but other than one-syllable answers with a less than halfhearted effort, he ignored her.

It was what happened after dinner that Patience would forever remember as the "dessert disaster."

It all started when Susannah announced that she was serving dessert. Patience remembered a passage from Miss Emma Hadley's book about the eloquence of serving: "A young man's head is easily turned when presented with a young woman who shows elegance and refinement in the way she serves a table."

So Patience hopped up immediately and offered her assistance. It was going so well. She first served Billy, carefully pouring his coffee and then gracefully setting his plate of chocolate cake in front of him.

Then she got to Lee. Once she'd served his coffee and cake, she felt so proud of herself that she'd looked at him and smiled.

Her eyes met his. She smiled brighter. He, staring at her as if mesmerized, smiled back. And then. . .*it* happened.

She fell flat on her back!

She'd liked to think that there had been a reason for her to trip. But, in fact, it had been nothing but clumsiness. She'd been so overwhelmed that he'd smiled at her, that she'd stepped back. The heel of her shoe had gotten caught in the hem of her dress. And the next thing she knew, she was on the floor, staring at the ceiling.

She sat up, and that was when she noticed everybody's reaction. Susannah gasped and came right over to her. Billy looked shock. The preacher stood up, looking concerned. Rachel put her hand over her own heart and asked if Patience was all right.

But it was the sheriff's reaction that really upset her.

He laughed.

And he laughed. In fact, the nitwit couldn't stop laughing!

Susannah helped her up and began fussing over her dress. "Oh, you *poor* thang! I am *so* sorry that something like this has happened. I should have insisted on getting the dessert myself. I just feel plumb awful, is what I feel! I. . ."

Patience put her hand out. "It's all right, Susannah," she interrupted. "Really, I'm fine."

At once, everybody started gathering around her, helping her to her chair and picking up the few utensils she'd dropped. But the laughter coming from the chair beside her could not be ignored.

Rachel, ever mindful of others' feelings, spoke up. "Really, Sheriff. It's not very nice to laugh at her. Patience could have been really hurt."

Lee made a show of trying to stop, but failed. "I'm sorry, Patience, I really am. It's...," he laughed again, "that I...," another outburst of the rude sound, "can't seem to stop!"

Tears filled Patience's eyes, though she tried very hard to keep them at bay. "Um...I think that I will go now. It is getting late," she said, quickly standing up. She deliberately turned her back to Lee, not wanting him to see her tears.

Susannah looked crestfallen. "Oh Patience. Please don't cry. Did you hurt yourself, after all?" she asked innocently; but Patience wished she could have just been quiet.

"I really need to go," she answered and walked briskly to the parlor to get her shawl. That was when she made her decision. She'd taken enough teasing in her life to know when something was pointless. And a relationship with Leander Cutler was just that. She was going to leave the man alone.

—⁂—

Patience's leaving and Susannah's mentioning the girl's tears put an abrupt stop to Lee's laughter. He honestly didn't know what had happened to him to make him laugh. He supposed that it was that he and Patience had become such good friends that he treated her as he would have if it had been any of his friends who'd ended up all sprawled on the floor. He laughed.

But now he knew that he'd been wrong. Terribly wrong. He'd made her cry. He felt like such a heel.

He got up to go to her, but Rachel stopped him.

"I know that you didn't mean to, Lee, but you've hurt her feelings. I think you are the last person she needs to see right now," Rachel told him.

Lee felt the sting of her words all the way to his gut. Now more than ever he wanted to make things right with her. But he nodded reluctantly. "All right, Rachel. But please tell her I'm as sorry as I can be."

Rachel told him she would and hurried from the room.

She caught up with Patience just as she was climbing onto her wagon.

"Patience, wait!"

Patience gripped the hard wood rail on the wagon and closed her eyes. Why couldn't she have been faster? She didn't want to talk to Rachel, or anyone, for that matter. She just wanted to be left alone to find a quiet spot to have a good cry.

But Rachel could not be ignored. For one, she was the pastor's wife. Two, she was too nice; and Patience knew that she was just trying to help.

So, she quickly dried her tears and slowly turned and stepped back off of the wagon. "I'm okay, Rachel," she told her, trying, but failing, to sound brave.

Rachel walked up to her, her eyes shining with compassion. "No. You're not okay, Patience. I know that Lee hurt your feelings in there." Patience started to disagree, but Rachel went on. "And I know how much you like him."

Patience looked at her with dismay. "You do? Oh *great!*" She threw up her hands. "I suppose the whole town knows that I am making a fool of myself over him."

Rachel reached out and took her hand. "I know because Caleb told me. He saw how you looked at Lee at his office the other day. He's seen that same look on my face, Patience. That's all."

Patience looked down at her hands and thought fleetingly that she had never had a friend to talk to, a friend who would offer her comfort. But here Rachel was, offering just that. Patience slowly raised her eyes to the pretty woman. "I don't know what I'm going to do, Rachel. When it started, I just figured he'd make a good husband. But now. . .now it's different. I can't explain it," she said with a frustrated shake of her head.

Rachel squeezed her hand. "You don't have to. I know what it's like to love a man you think you could never have. Even to want a life that seems impossible."

A tear rolled down Patience's pale cheek. "But look at you, Rachel. You are so beautiful, and Brother Caleb loved you from the beginning. And now look at me." She let go of Rachel's hand and held her arms out on either side of her. "Sheriff Cutler won't even *consider* that I'm courtin' material! He looks right past my plain face and latches on to Susannah's pretty one. Why couldn't I just be someone else? Someone who he could love," she wailed and slumped against her wagon, burying her head in her hands.

"That's the biggest bunch of self-pity I've heard in a long time!"

"What?" Patience's head snapped up at Rachel's scornful tone.

Rachel put her hands on her hips and made a *tsking* noise. "I'll admit, I said the same thing plenty of times after I was molested and after the church rejected me. But to wish that you were someone other than what God created you to be is just like telling God that He made a mistake when He made you!"

Patience blinked. "But. . .well I. . . ," she started and stopped. Then she sighed. "You're right."

Rachel nodded. "Of course I'm right! Now, Addie told me that you were going to start working for her tomorrow." After Patience nodded her head, she continued, "Well, I'm going to get sewing on that new dress you wanted, and we're also going to get to working on *you*!"

Patience felt a little dizzy. "Me?"

"Yes, you. I didn't say that God didn't give us the good sense to work with what we have. Sometimes we just need to do a little polishing!"

"Okay," she answered, though she hadn't a clue as to what Rachel was talking about.

"Be at my house right after you get off of work, and I'll tell you what we're going to do!" Rachel all but ordered.

"Okay," Patience answered again.

Rachel smiled broadly. "Well, then! I'll let you get on back home! You be careful!" And with that, Mrs. Rachel Stone sashayed back into the house, leaving Patience bewildered and excited all at the same time.

—⁂—

"You look worried, Lee," Susannah said from behind him. He was standing at her window and watching as Patience rode away.

Lee turned and schooled his features to a pleasant expression. He didn't want her getting the idea that he had feelings for Patience. Not when he needed to get onto the business of courting her!

"I just feel bad for hurting her feelings. I didn't mean to laugh at her. Patience and I have become friends, and I didn't think she would mind," he said with a shrug.

Susannah wrung her hands. "I do hope she is all right."

Lee looked back to the window. "Patience is a good sport. She'll be okay." He had to believe that. He could not dwell on her anymore. He had to get down to the business at hand.

Courting business.

"Uh. . .Susannah, I wanted to ask you something." He turned once again to face her.

Susannah smiled and linked her arm through his, leading him back to the dining room. "Ask away, Sheriff!"

He took a deep breath. "Would you like to take a stroll with me down by the stream tomorrow?"

Susannah twirled around, facing him, and laid a hand on his arm. "Oh, that would be delightful, Sheriff! What time shall we go?"

"Around noon? I'll drop by and pick you up."

—⁂—

Patience was halfway home when her wagon wheel broke. Stunned, she looked over the flickering ears of her horses, then bent to peer over the side.

Broken.

Patience blew out a frustrated breath as she straightened and looked around in the moonlight, trying to get her bearings.

She was by the Aaron brothers' sawmill. Good. The brothers lived in a big house beside the mill. Surely they could help her.

She was climbing out of the wagon when she remembered something she'd heard at the party. Daniel and Tommy were out of town and Billy was still at Susannah's. She couldn't remember what had been said about Bobby Joe. She hoped that he was home.

The wind was getting colder, and Patience's thin wrap wasn't enough protection from the biting weather. Carefully, she stepped onto the dirt road and searched through the darkness for the cutoff that led to their house.

She found it and also found something else—the row of shacks that housed a lot of the workers from the mill.

Instantly, Patience became frightened. Most were decent, but she'd heard tell that they liked to drink at night. Mama had always warned her that men did bad things when they were drunk.

She'd just have to be quiet as she passed them. And hurry. She must hurry.

As she made her way down the narrow road, she could hear the laughter coming from some of the shacks. One man was singing at the top of his lungs, but they were all inside. Thank God.

But when she'd just passed the last house, her luck ran out. Suddenly the door flew open and out came three huge, burly men.

And they were all staring at Patience.

"Would you loo' at this, men!" one of them drunkenly exclaimed.

The one in the middle, whose hair was redder than any hair Patience had ever seen, walked toward her. "Are you looking for me, darlin'?" he growled.

Patience screamed and turned to run. But her feet failed her for the second time that night. She tripped over the hem of her dress and went sprawling in the dirt.

Suddenly they were all kneeling around her, pulling at her. "No, no. . . Please. . . Leave me alone! Please. . . ," she cried, as she tried to fight them off. *Oh God, please, God. Don't let them hurt me. Please, help me, oh God!* she prayed fervently.

Then God sent a miracle.

The click of the gun cocking was what stopped them, but the voice was what sent them running. "Let her go and get back to your houses."

Patience looked at the owner of that hard, commanding voice and saw the uncompromising face of Bobby Joe Aaron.

"Oh Bobby Joe. . . ," she wept. "Thank you. Thank you so much."

He knelt down beside her and gently helped her up. "What in the world are you doing out here, Patience? Don't you have more sense than this?"

She stood with his help and looked down at her soiled dress. Her hands were skinned and her hair was cascading all about her shoulders, having completely fallen from its knot. "My wagon broke down and I was trying to find you. I've been at Susannah Butler's house," she explained and looked up at him.

He opened his mouth to say something, but then stopped and stared at her.

She stared back warily. "What's the matter?"

Bobby Joe shook his head, bemused. "You. You look. . .different." He reached out as if to touch her hair but, at the last minute, caught himself and drew his hand back. His face, once again, became unreadable.

Patience just stared at him, not quite knowing how to take that comment. She'd known Bobby Joe all her life, though their families rarely socialized. And since he was almost ten years older than she was, Patience could count on one hand the number of times that she'd actually spoken to him.

His words seemed to hang awkwardly between them. "Well, let's get you back to the house. I'll send some men down to see about your wagon."

Patience nodded and wondered if the rest of the time in his company was going to be as strange as this had been.

Chapter 10

The Aaron house was massive. All three stories of it stood tall among the beautiful pines that surrounded the home. It was the only house in Springton that was made of brick. Jeremiah Aaron, Bobby Joe's great-grandfather, had hauled them in all the way from Chicago. There were three tiers of porches and balconies that were supported by six huge, white pillars.

It was the first time that Patience had ever been in the house. She was more than a little intimidated as she stepped over the threshold and onto the shiny marble floor.

Bobby Joe closed the door behind him and offered to take her shawl. She turned her back to him, and he took the garment and threw it and his own jacket over the hat tree standing by the door.

"Why don't we go into the library?" Bobby Joe suggested as he gestured toward an open door off the hallway. "There should be a fire in there so you can warm yourself."

She nodded, but her mind raced. A library? People actually had libraries in their houses? Goodness!

Patience had never seen so many books in her life. Being a book lover, she yearned to pore over the titles to see what she could discover.

Instead, she followed Bobby Joe to the hearth, and together they held their hands out to the warmth of the crackling fire. She turned to thank him for his hospitality; but when she looked at him, she noticed that he was already looking at her. And probably had been looking at her the whole time.

Was there something on her face? Self-consciously she put a hand up to her cheek but felt nothing but her clean, chilled skin.

Why had he been staring? Her face must have reflected her confusion, because he suddenly blushed and quickly looked away.

Patience looked away also, more confused than ever.

"Well," Bobby Joe said after they stood there in an awkward silence. "I'll go tell my men to see about your wagon." And with a polite nod, he walked out of the room.

She opened her mouth to say something, but he was already gone. *Bobby Joe is a strange man,* she thought for the umpteenth time that night. With a shrug, Patience turned back to the shelves of worded treasures and smiled. She really hoped that he wouldn't rush. And without another thought for her rescuer, she grabbed a couple of books and began to read.

—⁂—

Fortunately, they were able to fix the wagon wheel. Patience, her arms loaded with books that Bobby Joe had gallantly lent her, readied herself for her ride home.

She laid the books carefully in the back of the wagon, then turned to Bobby Joe, who was standing quietly by.

"Thank you, Mr. Aaron, for all your help." She paused and glanced toward the back of her wagon with a smile. "And for the books."

He actually smiled. Patience couldn't help but marvel at what a handsome man he was when he allowed himself to relax. "It was nothing."

He looked down at his feet as he shuffled the toe of his boot in the dirt. "Look," he began, "I know it's none of my business, but a pretty girl like you don't need to be riding around unescorted. Next time, someone may not be there to rescue you."

Patience's mouth fell open in shock, and she stared at his nonchalant expression as he looked everywhere but at her. It was almost as if he was embarrassed saying it.

Then she realized something. Gruff old Bobby Joe Aaron was really a nice guy—he just didn't want anyone to know it!

And he thought she was *pretty*?

Blinking a couple of times in amazement, she looked away from him. "I'll be careful, Mr. Aaron. I don't ever want to be caught alone again. I thought they were going to. . ." Her voice faltered.

"But they didn't," he interjected firmly.

She nodded her head and looked at him. "Thanks to you."

He waved off her praise. "Here. Let me help you up."

He took her hand as she stepped into the wagon. Patience straightened her skirts, then picked up the reins.

Looking at him, she asked, "You'll be right behind me?"

He nodded and put his hat on. "I'll be behind you all the way. Don't worry."

She watched as he mounted his horse and realized that with him watching, she wouldn't need to worry.

—⁂—

Patience's mother met her at the door and she didn't look happy.

"Where—have—you—been!" Prudence demanded, emphasizing each and every word. She was dressed in her plain, white nightgown that buttoned high on her throat. Her hair was still in its severe knot at the base of her neck. Patience thought fleetingly that she'd never once seen her mother with her hair down.

Patience looked away and brushed past her mother to step into the room. "The wagon wheel broke," she said shortly. She was so emotionally drained, she didn't want to be having this discussion now.

Prudence closed the door behind her and stood, back stiff, with her arms folded tightly at her middle. "It didn't seem to be broken when you rode up!"

Patience took a deep breath and sank down into a chair. There was no way her mother would let her go easily; she would have to explain the whole thing. "I was coming home from Susannah's house, when my wheel broke. I was right by the Aaron brothers' sawmill when it happened. Mr. Aaron invited me in and then got some of his men to fix it for me, then he followed me home on his horse," she explained, deliberately leaving out the part of the attack.

Patience watched as a red, angry flush spread across her mother's face. "What if someone had seen you with that man? Don't you realize what would have happened to your reputation?"

Patience shoved her hair out of her face. "Mama, I didn't know what else to do, I—"

"I'll tell you what you don't do, Patience Anne—you don't go into a young man's home at this time of night! You should have waited outside!" Prudence raged.

"Mama, you don't understand the situation."

"Oh, I think I do understand! You just don't think, girl! Are you hoping that Bobby Joe Aaron will want to marry you, now? If you are, you are—"

"I was nearly raped!" Patience all but screamed at her mother. Tears of frustration pooled in her eyes. "I was trying to find the Aaron house when some of his men attacked me. If it wasn't for Mr. Aaron, I can only imagine what would have happened to me."

Prudence's face paled. "Patience, I . . ."

"He took me into the house to get me away from them and to make me feel safe. Which was the same reason he followed me home tonight. Because he was worried about me." Silent tears were flowing down her cheeks. Her eyes pled for her mother to understand, to offer her comfort.

Prudence stood up and walked to where her daughter sat. Her hand reached forward, and for a moment, Patience thought she was going to hug her. But then she pulled it back and stepped away. "Well, it seems you've had a rough night. You'd best get on to bed."

Patience watched her mother leave the room. A familiar sadness swept over her, urging more tears to fall. But she had cried enough. Determinedly, she wiped her face with the back of her hand and stood to walk to her room.

She passed her small mirror that was perched on her dresser, then on impulse she stopped and looked into it.

Hesitantly, she reached up and touched the curls that surrounded her face. She'd always hated her curls; her mother had told her that they were unbecoming and she must wear her hair tightly knotted to hide them.

But Bobby Joe Aaron had remarked that she looked different, even...pretty! No one had ever called her pretty before.

She sighed, pushing her hair away from her face in a frustrated gesture. "If only Lee thought I was pretty," she said aloud to her reflection.

But maybe with Rachel's help, he would.

—∞—

The next morning, before Patience left the house for her new job, a message was sent to them. "A message from the sheriff," Billy said as he handed the note to Patience.

For a day so full of promises, it was amazing how one little note could darken it so fast. Lee didn't want her to bring food around to him anymore. Said he was feeling well enough to eat at the inn once again.

The truth was, he did not want to see her anymore. He didn't want her bothering him. Especially after she made such a fool of herself last night. It was just as well, she thought, remembering her resolve to stay away from him. This would just make it easier to keep her promise to herself.

—∞—

The real truth was that Lee was having conflicting feelings about Patience, and it was getting in the way of his courtship of Susannah. He could not allow himself to see Patience anymore. He'd felt so terrible about laughing at her. She pulled at his emotions like no other woman ever had, and he didn't want her to. She wasn't right for him. Susannah was the woman he needed.

He'd decided not to have her bring his lunches in an effort to push her away. He hoped she wouldn't be too hurt by his rejection.

He shook his head, trying to shake off his guilty feelings. Today was a new day, he told himself. Besides, he had a date with Susannah to eat a picnic lunch and nothing was going to stand in his way.

Especially not Patience Primrose.

—∞—

By lunchtime, Patience knew she'd never worked so hard, but had so much fun. Adelaide Hayes was a tiny woman who had more energy than anyone Patience had ever encountered. Together they stacked canned goods, folded material, and restocked the dry-goods shelves.

Mrs. Hayes and her friend Mattie Mae Higgins were now dusting the books at the back of the store. Patience had offered her help, but the ladies insisted that they could do it by themselves. With a shrug, Patience donned her shawl and grabbed the basket of food that she'd packed for herself. Since it was such an unusually warm day, Addie had suggested that she take her lunch by the stream situated just behind the mercantile.

Humming softly to herself, Patience enjoyed the cool breeze blowing gently on her face as she walked. The water was surrounded by shade trees, but Patience decided to walk a little farther to find a nice place in the sun. It was still too cool for shade.

A small strand of hair came loose from her knot and blew across her face. Patience started to tuck it back, but stopped. Discreetly, she took a quick peek at her surroundings, then reached up and took the pins from her hair. Her scalp tingled as she shook her curly strands loose. She was prudent enough to pin the sides up. She didn't want to look like a ragamuffin!

She'd just walked around a clump of willow trees; and when she saw what was on the other side, she froze.

To her dismay, there sitting on a beautiful blanket of blue and white lace was Susannah and sitting with her was. . .

Lee.

Chapter 11

*T*urn around and pretend that you didn't see them! was the first thing that ran through Patience's mind. She didn't want to see this. She didn't want to see the man she loved cozying up to someone else.

But that idea blew away like feathers in the wind. For at that very moment, Susannah looked up and saw her.

"Patience! Why isn't this just a pleasant surprise! Look yonder, Lee! It's Patience!" She tugged at Lee's arm. But he was already looking at her, though he didn't say anything.

Susannah apparently didn't notice his reaction because she hopped up and went to Patience. "And just look at your hair!" Susannah exclaimed, clasping her hands together in delight.

Patience reached up to her wind-tossed hair with a sinking feeling. She'd forgotten about her hair. Hurriedly, she tried to explain. "I was just. . ."

"It's absolutely de–lightful! Patience Primrose, you stinker! You have the most beautiful hair I believe I've ever seen! Don't you agree, Lee?" she asked without looking at him for an answer.

That was a good thing; because when Patience glanced at Lee, he was still staring at her strangely. As a matter of fact, he was looking at her just like. . .Bobby Joe Aaron had the night before.

Susannah noticed Patience's picnic basket. "Were you going to eat by yourself?" she cried.

Patience nodded and opened her mouth to reply, but she wasn't given the chance.

"Why, we can't allow that, can we, Lee?" No response. "You must join us! Come, come! Sit! There's plenty of room for all three of us!"

Patience was horrified. "Oh no, I couldn't. I. . ."

Susannah sat down and started taking food out of her basket. "Oh, sure you can," she replied. "Tell her she can stay, Sheriff." This time the question demanded a response; and when she didn't get one, Susannah looked up at him. "Sheriff? Lee!"

Lee heard his name, but not all that clearly. Frankly, he'd been in somewhat of a stupor ever since he looked up and saw Patience standing there surrounded by all that. . .*hair*! Where had all those lovely curls come from? Suddenly a face that usually looked pale and plain and slightly pinched looked totally different when framed by her dark blond hair. She was. . .pretty!

She wasn't supposed to be pretty.

For some reason he didn't want to examine, he got really irritated. And he showed it.

"Why are you wearing your hair like that?" he snapped at her.

Patience looked away, her face losing its smile and becoming withdrawn. Beside him, Susannah gasped.

"Sheriff Cutler, sir! You're going to hurt her feelings! *Again!*" she added with emphasis. She cleared her throat and put a hand at her neck as if to collect herself. "Now, I think you owe Patience an apology so that she will feel comfortable joining us."

Lee grimaced at her tone. He could tell Susannah was a schoolteacher when she talked like that. It made him want to ask that she not send a note home to his mother!

And when had they invited Patience to join them? Wasn't this supposed to be a date? He specifically did not want to think about Patience, much less have her join them!

One look at Susannah's face changed his mind. She looked stern and disapproving. He wasn't sure he liked this side of her.

Reluctantly, he looked at Patience, trying to squelch his feelings of concern over having hurt her again.

"I'm sorry, Patience," he told her, and he meant it. "You might as well join us. There's plenty of room."

—⟋⟍—

Well, when he puts it like that, how could I possibly refuse? she thought sarcastically. How could she not feel insulted at his treatment of her?

More and more, Patience was determined to set the man out of her mind. How could she ever think that this man was looking at her in an admiring way? He was probably thinking about something else when he'd worn that strange look earlier.

He was probably thinking of Susannah.

Maybe he didn't think she was pretty, but someone else did—Bobby Joe Aaron. Maybe she'd start casting her amorous aspirations *his* direction!

Who needed a man like Leander Cutler, who treated her so shabbily? Who needed a man who, for all accounts and purposes, was in love with someone else?

You do, her heart seemed to whisper to her. *You do. . . .*

—⟋⟍—

The picnic was a disaster. Try as she might, Susannah could not generate a pleasant conversation or salvage whatever pleasant mood they might have started off with.

Lee seemed uptight and uncommunicative the whole time, and Patience acted as if she might burst into tears if she talked too much.

Poor Susannah. Even she gave up after awhile and joined them in their stilted silence.

—∞—

The picnic had turned a perfectly wonderful day into a dreadful one.

Patience was so upset about it, that she completely forgot that she was supposed to meet with Rachel after work.

She had just climbed up into her wagon when Rachel ran up to her. "Patience! Wait! Did you forget that you were supposed to come to my house?"

"Oh no!" Patience cried out in dismay. "I did, but let me tie the horses back up and I'll come right over."

Rachel smiled. "I'll wait for you and walk you over."

Patience smiled back, marveling at how she felt a kinship with this woman. One that, strangely enough, she was even feeling for Susannah. After a lifetime of having no real friends, two friends was a little overwhelming, but very welcome.

"All right," she called out and climbed from the wagon. At Rachel's house, Patience sat in a chair as Rachel slowly circled her, eyeing her closely. Her hand was on her chin with one finger tapping thoughtfully, while her eyes squinted with concentration. Patience heard a lot of "mmmm's" and "hmmm's."

"Okay, stand up," Rachel finally said.

She said it with such command that Patience immediately obeyed. Rachel might be little and petite, but she sure was bossy!

Rachel took Patience's measurements and worked with her hair for at least twenty minutes. She took her hair down and put it back up three different times in three different styles.

Finally, Rachel was satisfied with the way Patience's hair looked. She took a step back and smiled. "Perfect!"

Patience's eyebrows lifted with excitement. "Do you have a mirror? I want to see!"
"No."

Patience frowned. "What do you mean 'no'?"

Rachel held her arms out on either side of herself. "We're not finished. Now, follow me."

Patience sighed, but obeyed. She followed Rachel into her and Caleb's bedroom. She watched as Rachel went to her wardrobe and took out a garment made of peach-and-white cotton. The sleeves were puffed and edged with ruffles. The neck was rounded with a pretty white collar. The skirt was slim and slightly gathered with pleats at the back. It was so pretty and feminine.

"It's beautiful, Rachel!" she said wistfully.

"It's yours."

Patience looked at Rachel with disbelief. "It's mine?"

Rachel nodded. "I had made it for a lady in Tyler, but she decided on a different color. I held on to it, hoping I'd be able to use it for something else. After I talked to you last night, I came home and took some tucks and made a few adjustments. According to my measurements, it should fit perfectly." She held the dress out to Patience.

Reverently, Patience reached out and took the dress. Carefully, she held it with one hand, while touching the exquisite workmanship with the other. "I don't know how I can pay you right now. I. . ."

Rachel laid a hand on Patience's arm. "It's a gift, Patience. You've been on my heart ever since Caleb and I returned from our honeymoon. I wanted to give you this so that when you wore it, you would know that someone was thinking about you and praying for you."

Rachel dropped her hand and smiled gently at Patience. "I've felt that you needed a friend, and I'll be honest with you—I've needed one, too."

Tears welled up in Patience's eyes. "I would love to have you for a friend, Rachel."

"Then, it's settled," Rachel declared, with tears in her own eyes. "Now, let's get that dress on so that you can see how pretty you look!"

Patience laughed. "I don't know about that, but I do want to get into that dress!"

After a lot of unbuttoning, buttoning, and straightening, the dress was finally on. Rachel stepped back, once again inspecting her work.

A look of pure wonder spread across her face. "Oh Patience. . . ," she whispered in a voice filled with awe.

"What? Oh Rachel, I want to see!" Patience cried impatiently.

Rachel took Patience by the hand and led her to a full-length oval mirror.

This can't be me was the first thing she thought upon seeing her reflection. The woman staring back at her was elegant and graceful. Patience Primrose was frumpy and plain.

Her hair was pulled up, but Rachel had cut strands of hair so that they curled and framed her face. And then there was the dress. In it, she didn't look like her too-skinny self, but rather slim and elegant. It fit her perfectly.

"I can't believe this is me." Her voice was full of wonder.

Rachel crossed her hand over her chest and looked quite pleased with herself. "Well, believe it!"

The sound of a door opening drew their attention from the reflection. Childish chatter and the clomp of little footsteps resounded throughout the house. Rachel's face lit up. "Caleb and the children are home! Come on. Let's show Caleb."

Suddenly, Patience was unsure of herself. "I don't think. . ."

Rachel rolled her eyes. "Come on, Patience. Courage, girl, courage!" Then she pulled her from the room and into the parlor, where Caleb and the children were.

Caleb grabbed at his hat and took it off his head. "I didn't know you had company, Rachel." He held his hand out to Patience. "I'm Reverend Stone, ma'am. And you are?"

Patience looked at him in disbelief. "It's Patience Primrose, Brother Caleb. Don't you recognize me?"

Rachel playfully swatted his arm. "Caleb Stone, you are such a tease!"

She turned to Patience with a shake of her head. "Of course he knows who you are, Patience. That's just his way of saying that you look nice."

She looked at Brother Caleb and saw the teasing glint in his eyes as he smiled at her. She wasn't sure what to say.

"I didn't mean to tease, Patience. I think you look very nice." He rubbed a finger across his chin as if contemplating something. "I cannot wait till Lee sees ya!"

Patience's mouth thinned. "Thank you, Brother Caleb, but I don't care if I ever see the sheriff again!"

The preacher winced. "Did I say the wrong thing?"

Rachel intervened. "Children, did you all have a good time looking at Harold Ray's new horses?" she said, addressing the children.

Jessie, the eldest of the children that they were in the process of adopting, answered, "Yes ma'am. My favorite was the palomino!" he exclaimed, excited.

Emmy and Caitlin both asserted that they both liked the black mare with the white spot on its forehead.

Patience watched the family converse, grateful that the subject of Lee Cutler was dropped.

The reverend hit too close to the truth when he commented about Lee seeing her with her new look. She so wanted to know what he would think. She wanted to know if he thought that she looked pretty, that she could be someone he could love now that she looked different.

But her mind was made up. More and more she realized that if Lee didn't like her as plain Patience, she didn't want him. She wanted him to like her for her—not for what she looked like.

She once again looked at the reverend and his wife as they laughed with their children. Brother Caleb had loved Rachel despite what the town had thought of her. He wanted her for his wife, and nothing was going to get in his way.

That's the way Patience wanted to be loved. And more and more, she believed that God would help her find it.

Somewhere out there was a man who would love her and cherish her like the reverend loved Rachel.

She no longer believed it was the sheriff.

Chapter 12

The next morning was Sunday, and everyone was sitting in their pews and listening to Brother Caleb introduce the soloist for that morning when Lee finally arrived. He couldn't believe he'd overslept. He had an old rooster that woke him up at five-thirty on the dot, every single morning. And Lee was sure that the ornery critter had probably crowed his heart out this morning, too, but he hadn't heard it. He'd slept right through it.

And it was all Patience's fault.

He couldn't believe it when she'd shown up yesterday at his picnic with Susannah. She must have planned it. Somehow she heard that he was taking Susannah on a picnic, and she'd deliberately set out to sabotage it!

She wasn't going to get away with it. He was going to. . .

Just then, Susannah caught his eye. She gave him a little wave to let him know that she'd saved him a seat. Hurriedly, he made his way to the second row from the back and sat beside her.

He looked across the aisle and nodded to Billy and Daniel, then looked back to Susannah.

She smiled at him. As usual, she looked pretty as a summer's day in her yellow dress made of silk. "I thought you weren't coming," she whispered close to his ear.

"I slept a little late this morning," he whispered back in response.

"You're just in time to hear her!"

He looked up to see who "*her*" was.

He should have known it'd be Patience. He dreamt about her, he saw her at dinner parties and on outings with other women, and she popped up in his mind at the most unusual times. Why should today be any different?

Only. . .wait a minute! This wasn't the Patience who sat by his bedside when he was sick, the one who laughed with him when he felt blue after being away from work so long. This wasn't the quiet, mousy girl who brought his meals and who ran away from a party after he'd cruelly laughed at her. No. This was someone different. Someone he didn't know! This Patience had her hair curled and styled, and she was all gussied up in a shade of peach that made her skin glow like gold. A dress that fit her figure perfectly.

He hadn't known that Patience even *had* a figure.

What had she done to herself? First, it was the hair thing at the picnic and now this.

Lee didn't like this one bit. He had firmly convinced himself that he wasn't attracted to her, and here she was making it harder for him.

Then she began to sing. It was not the first time he'd heard her, for she sang often. But it was the first time her voice affected him.

Her sweet, clear tones floated over him like a warm balm. He couldn't say what the song was, because all he could hear was the sincerity and passion behind those words.

He was captivated.

—⁂—

Patience saw him come in and sit by Susannah. Not that she cared, of course. It was merely an observation.

No, today was a new day. She was going to sing her song and step down. She wasn't going to look at the sheriff. Not once!

Okay. . .maybe one little peek. As she sang, she cast a quick glance his direction and then looked quickly away.

He was looking at her, and knowing that almost made her forget the words. Not wanting to take away from the meaning of the song by messing up, she firmly put Lee to the back of her mind, closed her eyes, and began to put her heart into it.

Patience loved to sing. She always thought it was the only thing that she did do well. It was the only thing her mother ever complimented her on, so she practiced often. And it was a way for her to forget her problems and dreary life. But best of all, she could express her feelings to God in a way she couldn't with a prayer.

When it was over, Brother Caleb came up and thanked her, and she stepped down to take her seat. Most of those who caught her eye were smiling at her with looks of appreciation, with a little wonder mixed in. They were obviously surprised at her new look.

And they weren't the only ones.

She hadn't meant to look at Lee, but her empty seat was situated right in front of him and Susannah. Her eyes just naturally went to him. For a moment, it seemed all time had stopped.

Their eyes met and held. Patience felt as though she couldn't look away. Something strange was happening to her, and it was wonderful and terrible all at the same time. Wonderful, because his warm gaze made her feel beautiful and wanted. Terrible, because she knew he was feeling something, too; yet he would continue to deny it till his dying breath.

And deny it he would. . .later. But not now. Not at this moment. Why couldn't he look away? Why did he feel as if he were drowning in her gaze? Emotions that he couldn't even begin to fathom were building up so heavily within his chest, he felt as though he couldn't breathe.

"Sit down, Patience! What's wrong with you?" Patience's mother hissed at her, yanking on Patience's skirt.

It made both of them jump, each becoming aware of their surroundings. Lee glanced around and to his chagrin everyone was staring at them! Even the preacher. In fact, Caleb was smiling at him as if he knew something Lee didn't.

As Patience whirled around and sat down, Lee felt his face burn; and he knew that he must be the color of the Red River. He glanced over to Susannah, and she was giving him a searching look. He looked away, not wanting her to read what must have been clearly written on his face.

He was attracted to Patience Primrose.

He could deny it to his dying day, but there it was. It didn't mean anything, of course. He'd been attracted to a lot of women. This time was no different.

Just for reassurance, he reached over and took Susannah's hand. He heard her breath catch in a small gasp; and when he glanced at her, she was looking at him as though he were crazy.

Maybe he was crazy. Like a little boy that had just gotten his hand slapped for stealing from the cookie jar, he let go of her hand and placed it back on his own leg.

Things weren't going according to his plans. He was supposed to be growing closer to her, building a relationship with her, not letting his foolish feelings for another woman get in the way!

Susannah was the woman he was going to marry. Now if he could just get her to believe that.

No. If he could just get himself to believe. . .

—⁂—

Two weeks passed; and no matter how hard Patience tried not to, she kept running into Lee. She knew that he thought that she was following him around, but she really wasn't. It was just that they were both working in town, and he always seemed to be going the same direction that she was going!

And worse, she always seemed to interrupt his attempts at courting Susannah.

If Lee wasn't irritated before, he was now.

Patience had done her best to keep him out of her mind. She worked three days a week at the mercantile and had earned the money to buy material, and Rachel was making her dresses out of it. She was wearing her hair in the style that Rachel had taught her, though her mother griped about it at every chance. But Patience was an adult now, and her mother just had to realize that!

Something else had happened to Patience that had never happened before. She began getting gentlemen callers! Men she'd never known existed were coming up to her and asking to escort her to church or were bringing her flowers.

She didn't know what to think. It was all very flattering, but she couldn't help wishing that they were the sheriff.

It was Saturday morning, near lunchtime. Patience had started to go up to Addie's room above the store to eat with her, when a knock sounded on their door.

Addie sighed. "I'd best go see who it is. It may be important."

Patience patted her on the arm. "You go on up, Miss Addie. I'll go check."

Addie nodded and went up the stairs.

Patience went to the door and was surprised to see Bobby Joe Aaron standing there.

"Oh! Hi, Mr. Aaron. Can I help you with something?" she asked, marveling at the way he looked. He'd really gone out of his way to fix himself up! His hair was all slicked back, and he was nicely dressed in a black vest and pants with a crisply ironed shirt.

Then she noticed the little girl standing beside him. It was his daughter, Beth.

"Hi, Miss Primrose. Beth and I wanted to stop by to see if you'd join us for lunch," Bobby Joe asked her shyly. Shy was not a word one would usually apply to Bobby Joe, but he was sure acting timid!

Or was he just unsure of himself?

Patience looked at him, then looked down at his smiling daughter. "Oh. . .well. . . sure! Let me go and tell Addie, and I'll meet you back down here. All right?"

Bobby Joe nodded, and his daughter said, "Oh goody. I told you she wouldn't say no, Daddy!"

His face turned red. "Beth, don't. . ."

"I'll be right back," Patience interrupted, not wanting him to take his embarrassment out on his daughter.

She did think it was funny, though. But she waited until she was out of earshot before she laughed aloud!

—∞—

Lee was sitting with Susannah in the dining room at the Springton Inn. He'd asked her to lunch and felt pleased that she'd eagerly accepted. They were moving right along, now that he'd gotten his mind off of Patience. It was true that she kept popping up everywhere he went, but he was doing pretty well at staying focused on his courtship of Susannah. In fact, he was just about to invite her to attend church with him when *she* walked in.

"Not again," he groaned aloud without realizing it.

Susannah looked at him quizzically. "What's wrong?"

"Huh? Oh. . .nothing. I was just thinking about. . .something," he answered lamely.

She was something all right. Today, she was wearing blue. Not just regular blue, but rich, royal blue. The neckline was scooped and showed off a little of her chest and her neck. He noticed that her skin wasn't merely just pale, it was luminous.

"What is Bobby Joe doing with her?" Susannah whispered beside him.

What did Susannah mean? At that moment, he realized that Patience wasn't alone. She was with Bobby Joe Aaron and his daughter, Beth! What was *he* doing with her?

But then again, why was Susannah worried about it? He glanced at her and saw a look of hurt cross her face, but it was quickly masked by a friendly, sunny smile.

He looked back and saw that the trio was headed their direction.

"Aunt Susannah!" Beth cried out and ran to throw her arms around her aunt. Susannah hugged her and greeted her with the same enthusiasm.

Slowly she looked up to her brother-in-law. "Hello, Bobby Joe."

Bobby Joe visibly stiffened beside her. "Hello, Susannah," he said coolly.

Lee frowned and wondered at the hostility that radiated between them. Then he wondered how Susannah could ignore Patience like that!

He had been ignoring Patience for two weeks now. He guessed it wouldn't hurt to be nice to spare her feelings today. He stood and greeted her. "Hello, Miss Patience."

Patience's face was an unreadable mask as she looked back at him. "Hello, Sheriff Cutler."

Lee's frown deepened. When had she stopped looking at him with adoration? Then it struck him that she didn't look like a woman who was pining away for him! Wasn't she affected at all after the way he'd ignored her?

And why was she with Bobby Joe Aaron? The thought kept menacing him.

"Can we eat with, y'all?" Beth asked. "Look! There's enough room!" She motioned to the three empty chairs at their large round table.

"Uh. . .I don't think. . . ," Bobby Joe began.

"Well, we were just. . . ," Lee chimed in.

"We really couldn't. . . ," Patience said graciously, causing the frown to return to Lee's face.

"Isn't that a wonderful idea!"

All eyes went to Susannah. She looked at everyone with innocent eyes. "Well, for goodness' sake! Are you all going to stare at me all day, or are you going to sit down and have some lunch?"

—⁂—

It was a disaster. Maybe not as bad as the dinner party had been, but it was close.

Bobby Joe, who earlier had been friendly and a little talkative—as much as Bobby Joe could be—suddenly clammed up and became a stone-faced grouch.

Susannah was talking more than was even normal for her and trying to make everyone believe she was so happy, though it was obvious by the looks she kept sending Bobby Joe she wasn't.

And then there was Lee. He was acting just plain strange. He would look at Bobby Joe, then look at Patience, and a grim look would spread across his face. He did this about every five minutes; and after awhile, Patience got tired of it.

Leaving her plate barely touched, Patience pushed back from the table and stood. Immediately, the two men stood up with her. "I'd better get back to work." She turned to Bobby Joe. "Thank you for asking me to lunch, Bobby Joe and Beth. We must do it again sometime." *Alone.* She didn't say it, but it was clearly implied.

Bobby Joe nodded to her with an apology in his eyes. "Yes. We will," he agreed. "Can I walk you out?" He reached for his jacket.

She held out a hand. "No. That's okay. You sit and finish your meal." She smiled at Beth. "It was nice talking with you, Beth."

The seven-year-old waved at her.

Hurriedly, she said her good-byes to Susannah and Lee and quickly made her way from the inn.

—⚊⚊—

Lee didn't even think twice about it. He jumped up, threw down his napkin, and excused himself. "I'll be right back," he mumbled and ran out of the restaurant.

In three quick steps, he had caught up with Patience.

Steering her into a nearby alley, he then turned her toward him. "What's going on between you and Bobby Joe Aaron?" he demanded.

Patience blinked a couple of times. "Pardon me? I don't see that it's any of your concern, Sheriff Cutler!" she announced huffily.

His lips thinned. "See? You know me better than you know him, and you don't call *me* by my first name!"

"For your information, *Sheriff Cutler*, I've known Bobby Joe since I was a child. And besides, he asked me to call him by his first name!"

"And I see that you gave him the same privilege," he charged, pointing a wild finger in the direction of the inn.

"That's right, I did!"

"Well. . . ," he blustered, searching for words, aware that he was behaving like a lunatic. "I don't like it!"

She actually laughed at him. "Well, la-de-da! I don't care if you like it or not!"

"Well, maybe you won't care about *this*, either!" He grabbed her by the shoulders and kissed her.

Chapter 13

Touching her lips was like getting zapped by lightning! Stunned, he let her go and stumbled back a step. He watched as she brought a hand up to her face, her eyes full of amazement.

For a moment, they did nothing but stare at each other and try to catch their breath.

Why had he done that? He'd been courting Susannah for over two weeks now, and he'd done nothing but hold her hand! Now, here he was kissing the one woman he did not want to become involved with!

At that point, he lost all reason.

"I do hope that you don't think that kissing me means anything!"

Her mouth fell open with a gasp. "I didn't kiss you! You kissed me!"

He pointed his finger at her. "Well, you made me do it! And besides. . .*you* kissed me back!"

She grabbed his finger and shoved it out of the way. "I didn't make you do anything, Sheriff Cutler!" she taunted. "I think you have been *wanting* to kiss me! That's why you did it!"

He narrowed his eyes at her mean little smile. "That's just wishin' on your part, Miss Primrose! It will be a cold day in El Paso before that will happen! And I want you to stop following me around, too!"

"I haven't been *following* you around! How dare you. . ."

"Every time I'm on an outing with Susannah, you show up! Don't tell me it's a coincidence!"

"Okay! I won't tell you! I'll just let you wallow in your conceit!"

"Conceit, is it? Don't tell me you weren't hoping that I'd court you when you told Doc to bring me to your house. Well, it didn't work then, and it's not going to work now! I'm not going to court you, Patience. Not ever!"

Lee thought he saw her wince, but he wasn't sure. Even as the words were coming out of his mouth, he regretted what he said. But she rallied back quickly.

"Don't worry! I don't want you," she sneered. "Just make sure that you don't 'accidentally' kiss me anymore. I'd rather kiss. . .*Bobby Joe*! In fact, I just might do that. *Today!*"

His face darkened. "Now, don't you do anything stupid, Patience, I..."

"I didn't say you could use my first name, and I'll do whatever I please!" She started past him. "Now, if you'll excuse me..."

He grabbed her arm, but his grip was gentle. His face lost its anger, and a look of concern replaced it. "I mean it, Patience. Don't do anything stupid just to get back at me." He looked away for a moment, trying to collect his thoughts. "He's not a churchgoing man. You should keep that in mind."

She smiled at him sadly. "I'm not planning to marry him, Sheriff. And what do you care, anyway, huh? You've ignored me and...and laughed at me...and insulted me. You don't have the right to tell me anything." With that, she pulled her arm from his grip and walked away from him.

She waited until she was well away from him before she broke. She leaned against the back side of the store building and covered her face with trembling hands.

She was through with that man. She didn't want to see him and especially didn't want to talk to him. She wouldn't marry him if he was the absolute last man on earth!

Not that she ever would be given the chance.

—⟶—

Patience showed up at church the next morning, sporting her new green dress. Rachel had told her it was the latest design from New York, and she had fashioned a small hat to match it.

While the dress caught everyone's eye, it was the little girl holding her hand that made everybody do a double take.

Patience could just imagine what they were all thinking of her coming in with Beth Aaron, but she didn't really care. The little girl was so eager to go, Patience couldn't have said no, even if she wanted to.

It was really the sheriff's words that made her bring up the idea with Bobby Joe in the first place. When he said that the sawmill owner wasn't a churchgoer, *Well,* Patience thought, *it wouldn't hurt to invite him to go with me.*

Unfortunately, he turned her down, but Beth had chimed in that she would like to go. Bobby Joe didn't have any concerns about the matter, so they agreed that Patience and her mother would pick Beth up the next morning.

As usual, her mother balked, saying that she could just imagine what people would think! Instead of riding in the wagon with her daughter, Prudence went with a neighbor.

That was fine with Patience. She didn't feel like dealing with her mother anyway.

She guided the little girl into the nearest pew, not really looking at whom she was sitting by. She got Beth all seated and patted her on the head. Then she looked up at the person just on the other side of the child.

She really should start paying more attention....

Lee watched as Patience came in and sat by Susannah and himself. He noticed that she looked well rested and refreshed.

At least somebody *got some sleep last night.* He hadn't gotten any! He kept playing Patience's parting words over and over in his head, and he knew that he'd been behaving in a manner that was unbecoming and unchristianlike. Who was he to judge Bobby Joe, when he could treat another person the way he'd treated Patience?

He admitted to himself, finally, that he was very attracted to Patience Primrose. He didn't want to court Susannah, nice and pretty as she was. He wanted to court Patience.

He couldn't understand why it took him so long to figure that out. Probably it was because he'd been swayed by others' opinions.

Poor Patience was talked about and laughed about and called a plain old maid by every bachelor in town. He'd thought he was too good for her.

What a fool he was.

The truth was, Patience was too good for him. She was honest and kind, and someone with whom he could sit down and have a real conversation. She was a true friend and could be more than that to him.

But it could be too late.

He glanced down at the child beside her and wondered what was happening between her and Bobby Joe. Were they courting? He dearly hoped not.

Not when he wanted his chance at courting Patience.

"I can't believe it!"

Susannah's outraged whisper pulled his attention away from his thoughts of Patience. He looked sideways at her and saw that she was near to crying. "What's wrong?" he asked, his voice full of concern.

He watched as she looked over at Beth with a longing expression, then looked back to the preacher. "Nothing."

Huh? He sighed silently and then glanced Patience's way. As if she felt his gaze, Patience turned her eyes to him. Then she lifted her head, looked down her nose at him, sniffed, then looked away.

Lee had just been royally snubbed!

Great! he thought morosely. He was sitting by two women who either hated him or wanted to cry all over him for no reason.

He felt a pull at his sleeve, and he looked down to see Beth staring at him. She grinned, showing him two big spaces in her mouth where teeth should be, then she winked at him!

He bit his lip to keep from laughing, then he moved his eyes back to the preacher. At least somebody liked him!

She couldn't *believe* she had sat by Lee Cutler! Of course, he would think she did it on purpose, the conceited man!

Well, let him! She no longer cared what he thought.

Susannah could have him!

Lee was taking Susannah back to her house, when he decided to ask her again what was wrong. She'd been strangely quiet ever since they'd left the church.

Susannah sniffed and blinked, obviously trying hard not to cry. "I've been asking Bobby Joe for months now to let me spend time with Beth. He always says no. Do you know that he won't even let her come to the town school? He hired a tutor to come to his house three times a week to teach her. It just hurt my feelings, I guess, to see that he allowed Patience to bring her to church." She looked off in the distance for a moment, then looked down at her clenched hands. "I guess they're getting close, huh?"

Her words struck fear into his heart. He wasn't the only one thinking it, then. "I don't know, Susannah. What's between you two anyway?"

She shook her head. "I don't know. I guess he blames me for my sister running off. Then to find out she died without him ever being able to understand why she did it. . ." She let out a breath. "She left for reasons that I don't understand; and by the time she reached our parents' house, she was dying. There was nothing I could do. Nothing anyone could do."

"Well, he's a lot different since his wife died. He's really bitter."

"I know," Susannah answered sadly. "I just wish I could help him." She shrugged her shoulders. "Maybe Patience can."

Lee felt like shouting *No!* He didn't want Patience helping anybody but him!

They were silent for a moment. Lee knew what he had to do, he just didn't know how or the right words to say. He took a deep breath and just told her.

"Susannah, there's something I need to tell you. . . ."

"You're in love with Patience," she interrupted him calmly.

"Now, I've never said anything about. . .about. . .*love!*" he sputtered. "I just. . ." He stopped suddenly and looked at her with amazement. "How did you know what I was going to talk about?"

Susannah smiled at him and patted him on the cheek with a gloved hand. "Oh Lee. It's been obvious to me for weeks. I was just wondering when you were going to notice."

Lee scratched his head. "But I thought you'd be mad at me for courting you all these weeks. . . ."

"I'm not in love with you, either, Lee, so you can quit worrying."

Lee opened his mouth and then shut it. "You're not?" he finally asked.

She laughed. "No, but I have really enjoyed your friendship. Now, what you need to do is forget about me and start working on winning over Patience!"

Lee blew out a frustrated breath. "I don't think she'll let me. And you said it yourself, she may be leaning Bobby Joe's direction."

Susannah sat back in her seat and crossed her arms around her middle. "I hope not," she murmured.

Lee studied her face and began to realize things he'd totally missed before—that Susannah had her own feelings for Bobby Joe. Why hadn't he seen it before? But he kept his thoughts to himself.

With a flick of his wrist, he snapped the reins to urge the team to a faster pace.

Chapter 14

It was two weeks later, and Patience was busy writing up Mrs. Perkins's purchases when Lee walked in the door.

She determinedly ignored him as he milled around the store. "Here you go, Mrs. Perkins. You have a nice day," she told the newly married woman while handing her the bundle of goods.

Mrs. Perkins left, and Patience got out a dust rag and began to wipe down the counter.

Lee sauntered over to her and leaned against the edge of the counter. "Hello, Miss Patience," he greeted.

She made a show of cleaning a spot on the counter that was well away from him. "Sheriff Cutler," she greeted coolly.

He walked to where she was. "When are you going to stop ignoring me, Patience?" he said with simmering impatience.

She avoided looking at him and walked to the opposite end of the counter. "The last I heard it was still pretty warm in El Paso, Sheriff Cutler. And I *didn't* give you permission to use my Christian name!"

Lee shoved a hand into his hair and smoothed it back in a show of frustration. "Come on, Patience. It's been two weeks since I said that. When are you going to forgive me?"

She turned to him finally, looking down her nose at him. "You're forgiven. Now, if you'll excuse me, I've got work to do." With a regal lift of her chin, she went to an aisle where she had started stocking paper and pencils.

"Well, if you forgive me, will you go with me to the fall social the ladies club is throwing this Saturday?" he asked while following her.

She kneeled on the floor and took a stack of tablets out of a box. "No. I already have a date." She carefully placed them on the shelves and prayed her hands wouldn't shake.

She still had deep feelings for Lee, no matter how she tried to convince herself otherwise. But she knew he was only coming around and inviting her out because he felt guilty for saying all those mean things to her. He didn't really want to be with her.

"Who is it this time?" he stressed. "This is the second man who's called on you this week, and it's only Tuesday." She'd been called upon at her home by Jake Norton, Harold Ray's widowed son.

She smiled with satisfaction, knowing that her loose hair hid her face. "Not that it's any of your business, but I'm going with Bernard Touchet."

"The Frenchman?" he exclaimed with derisiveness.

"He's not from France, but from Lafayette, Louisiana. I suppose you could call him Cajun French."

"He's only lived here for a month! You don't know what kind of man he is." Lee was pacing back and forth at this point.

Patience started counting the pencils in the box. "And I suppose you do?"

Lee stopped and looked down at her blankly. "Well. . .no! And that's the reason you don't need to go to the social with him!"

Patience looked up at Lee curiously. He sure was acting funny. "I didn't realize your role of sheriff extended to who courted whom!"

Lee's mouth thinned. "Okay, here's another for you. The man is in his mid-forties! He could be your father!"

Patience sighed and threw the remaining pencils back in the box. She kept losing count. Unless she got rid of him, she was never going to get any work done. Slowly, she stood and dusted off her dark blue skirt.

"I am tired of having this conversation. Aren't you supposed to be guarding that outlaw or something?"

Lee shook his head absently. "I'm on night duty. Billy is with him now."

Patience planted her hands on her hips. "And I suppose you haven't been home to rest either, have you?"

Lee shook his head. "No, but. . ."

She took the sheriff by the arm to pull him toward the door, but she had forgotten what touching him did to her. It made her go all soft inside. It made her dream of him taking her into his arms and kissing her again.

She was so moved by the warmth of his arm that she just stood there.

Lee felt it, too. Carefully, so as not to scare her away, he covered her hand with his own. The touch of her soft skin brought back memories of their kiss. How wonderful it felt having her in his arms.

He wanted more. He wanted Patience to be his wife.

But he couldn't just blurt something like that out. No. He had to woo her and court her.

That was, if she'd let him!

Patience had been more than stubborn for two weeks now. He knew that she still felt something for him. He also knew that he'd hurt her badly. It was going to take time to win back her trust.

And now that she'd been going out with other men, he knew that she wasn't getting serious about Bobby Joe Aaron, so he had more time to win her.

But what was with this Frenchman? He'd come into town last month and bought a large spread just outside of town. Already he was building a house that rivaled the Aaron mansion. That meant he was rich. How could Lee compete? Lee was a man of comfortable, but meager means. He couldn't give Patience a big fancy house or fancy clothes.

What he could give her was his love.

Love! He'd never thought about it much, but it was true. He was in love with Patience Primrose.

She was still holding onto his arm and looking at him. He was so overwhelmed by his feelings for her that he did what came natural.

He bent to kiss her.

Dingaling-aling-aling! The sound of the bell made her jerk away from him.

Lee tried to pull her back, but it was too late.

Startled, Patience looked at him with accusing eyes, then ran to the front of the store.

Though frustration gnawed at him, he took deep breaths and forced himself to be calm.

And he stayed that way until he saw who had come in the door.

It was the Frenchman.

Patience smiled at Mr. Touchet as he walked up to her. Lee had completely gotten the wrong idea about them, and she'd allowed him to believe it. In truth, she enjoyed Mr. Touchet's conversations since he'd been coming into the mercantile, and she had felt a kinship with him, much like a niece with her favorite uncle.

He would tell her stories of his life in Louisiana and about their unique culture. And best of all, he'd seemed to enjoy talking to her, too. In fact, it seemed that he sometimes came to the store just to talk to her. He constantly wanted her to tell him about her life and the things that she'd done growing up. But most of all he made her feel good about herself. Something she hadn't felt in a long time, despite the wonders that Rachel had wrought in her appearance. While it was true, she was getting a lot of attention from the young bachelors in town, she couldn't forget Lee's words. She couldn't forget that he'd said that he'd never court her.

So she welcomed any chance she got to talk to the gentleman. Mr. Touchet was just a very nice, older man who probably thought she reminded him of his own daughter. Lee shouldn't have been so suspicious, anyway.

But he was. Lee didn't like the fact that this stranger was so chummy with the girl he was in love with. Who was he? What did he want?

Billy had reported to him that this Mr. Touchet came over to the mercantile quite a bit and only on the days that Patience worked.

Maybe he was one of those dirty old men who stalked helpless women! Well, he would just have to get through Leander Cutler first.

Bernard Touchet gave Lee a friendly smile. "Good evening, Sheriff!" he greeted in his accented voice. "How are you today?"

Lee nodded to the man without returning his smile. "Howdy, Mr. Too-chet," he said in an exaggerated drawl, deliberately mispronouncing his name. "What brings you to town?"

"Oh, dis and dat," he answered vaguely. "I always drop in to say hello to de belle of all Texas!" he commented with exaggerated hand movements.

It was all Lee could do not to roll his eyes. The man was slick, he'd grant him that. One look at Patience and he could tell she was eating up all that malarkey he was shoveling out. It made Lee sick. . . .

That he didn't think of it first.

Maybe that was why she was dating all those different guys. She liked all the attention. They probably flattered her and told her how pretty she looked.

He'd never once told her how much he liked her new look. Probably because he wished sometimes that she would go back to her old self so he wouldn't have so much competition.

And he wouldn't be so jealous.

"Well, you're right about that, Mr. Touchet," Lee finally answered, only he was looking at Patience. "She is the prettiest little lady around."

After making that comment, he nodded to them both and left the store, pleased that he'd left Patience with her mouth hanging open in disbelief.

"De young sheriff, he's in love with you, yes?"

Patience managed to close her mouth and look at Mr. Touchet. "What did you say?"

Mr. Touchet waved in the direction of the front door. "Sheriff Cutler. He is in love with you," he confidently stated.

Patience just shook her head and laughed as if he'd told a great joke. "Sheriff Cutler does not love me, Mr. Touchet. He feels bad because he hurt my feelings and he wants to make up for it. He's feeling guilty, not amorous!"

Mr. Touchet frowned. "Why do you not believe in yourself? You are a lovely and kind woman." He stared at her for a moment, then raised his eyebrows as if realizing something for the first time. "You do not think you're lovely or special, do you? You do not think dat a man such as de sheriff could love you!"

Patience looked away. "Mr. Touchet, I really have a lot of work to do and. . ."

He reached out and placed a hand on her shoulder. "You are, Patience. You are a special person. Do you not know dat all of God's creations are beautiful in deir own way? You must believe dat He made you beautiful, too. Not just on de outside, but on de inside!"

Bernard Touchet spoke with such conviction, she felt tears rising in her throat and eyes. If only she could feel that way. If only. . .

All she could do was shake her head.

Mr. Touchet nodded his head. "I see dat it will be up to me to see dat you believe! So just be prepared!"

That made her smile. "I will," she whispered through her tears. She wanted him to succeed.

But she wondered if he could.

Chapter 15

Patience sat in her kitchen, reading one of the books that Bobby Joe had sent her, trying to ignore the agitated movements of her mother as she furiously cleaned a room that was already spotless.

This particular behavior had been going on for a month now. Patience couldn't begin to understand what had upset Prudence, but she knew that something must have. When she'd asked, she'd been given some vague answer about there being nothing wrong.

But this was strange behavior for even *her* mother.

She thought about how Mr. Touchet had tried to help lift her spirits that very morning and wondered why she didn't try it with her mother. Prudence had never reached out to her, so Patience had never tried to reach out to her mother for fear of being rejected.

Well, Patience was tired of being fearful of doing things that might hurt her feelings. So she took a deep breath and began to talk.

"So, Mama, what did you do today?"

Prudence didn't miss a beat with her dusting. "This and that, Patience," she answered briskly.

Patience smiled in remembrance. "You know, I heard those very same words today at the mercantile. Only they were pronounced funny. But I guess they talk like that in South Louisiana. That's where Mr. Touchet is from, you know."

Patience didn't notice her mother had stopped dusting. "He's such a nice man. Have you met him yet, Mama? Mama?" she queried again when she got no answer the first time.

She stared at her mother's stiff back and frozen position. "Mama? Are you all right?"

Slowly Prudence turned, and Patience was shocked to see her mother's face was white. "You met. . .Mr. Touchet?" she asked faintly.

Patience nodded, not sure what was wrong.

Her mother was breathing fast and heavy. Prudence grabbed the back of the chair to steady herself. "Did he. . .say anything to you?"

Patience was getting scared. Her mother didn't look good at all. "What was he supposed to say, Mama?"

Her mother stared at her for a good long minute, then relaxed a little. "Nothing, I...nothing," she muttered, shaking her head.

"Mama, do you know something about Mr. Touchet that I should know? He seems nice, but if he's a bad person, I need to know. I mean, he's escorting me to the fall social and..."

"He's what?" Prudence cried. "Oh dear Lord. Oh God. Help me. Please..." She grabbed at her chest and started the heavy breathing again. Then she stumbled backwards, almost falling.

Patience jumped up from her seat and ran to her mother. "Mama, what's wrong? Please...talk to me!" She placed her arms around her mother's trim waist. She was shaking all over.

"This is terrible, so terrible...," Prudence muttered over and over.

Patience was really scared now. Her mother was still clutching at her chest, and Patience worried that she could be having some kind of attack.

Slowly, she led her mother to her bed and helped her lie down. Prudence seemed out of her head—she kept muttering things and now she was crying.

"What's wrong with you, Mama? Are you sick? Please tell me what I need to do," she begged her mother, but it was no use. It was as if she couldn't hear her.

There was only one thing to do. She had to go and get the doctor.

After closing her mother's door, Patience ran and grabbed her coat and put it over her nightgown, hurrying from the house.

There was no time to harness the horses, so Patience threw a saddle over one of them and prayed that she wouldn't kill herself riding into town. She'd never been any good at riding, but tonight she'd just have to take a chance.

For once, her mother needed her.

Clumsily, she climbed onto the horse that she called Cactus, because she was always so prickly, and squirmed around until she got her seating. Cactus must have sensed her anxiety, because for once she didn't try to throw her.

Wind whipped through her loose hair and tore at her gown as she urged Cactus into a faster run than she was used to. It was so cold, and her legs were partially exposed from straddling the horse. She forced herself to think about what she had to do to help her mother so that she wouldn't think about how badly her teeth were chattering.

Finally the dim glowing lamplights came into view. Doc's office was located in the middle of the town, just down the street from the sheriff's office. It was really a narrow two-story house that contained his office on the bottom floor and his residence on the top.

When she got there, she slid off her horse. Her leg muscles screamed in protest, and she almost stumbled. Determinedly, she made it to the door and pounded hard on the wooden surface.

"Doc! Doc, please wake up! It's Patience!" she yelled at the door. "Mother is ill! Doc! Doc?" It was no use. She could see that the lights were still out and the house was very quiet. With a sickening feeling, she realized that the Doc and his wife weren't home.

Frantically, she ran into the street and started searching for anyone who could help. Her eyes fell on the saloon. Raucous laughter filtered out into the night and made Patience shiver. It reminded her of the night she was attacked.

There was no way she was going *there* for help.

She looked down the other way and saw the sheriff's office. She let out a relieved sob when she saw a light burning in his window. Lee had night duty with the prisoner! He would know what to do.

She left her horse tied to Doc's post and ran to the sheriff's office.

—m—

If he hadn't been so exhausted, it wouldn't have happened. He'd tried so hard to stay awake, but the prisoner wasn't in the mood for chitchat, and he'd been unable to keep his eyes open. Somehow, he'd drifted off into a dreamless, exhausted sleep.

"*Click!*" was the only sound he heard, but it was enough. He went from very sleepy to wide-awake in a matter of seconds, which wasn't hard to do with a pistol pointed at his head.

Standing behind the gun was a face that only a mother could have loved. Black stringy hair fell from the man's pointed skinny head and around his stark face. He had sunken, beady eyes and a crooked nose. And when he smiled evilly at Lee, he displayed a mouthful of yellow, rotten teeth. It was a face he was familiar with. The outlaw's brother had returned for his own.

"Welllll, looky here!" he drawled snidely in his reedy voice. "Looks like the law ain't too fierce around these here parts!"

The outlaw looked over to his brother. "Bubba, you all right?" he yelled out, looking quickly back to Lee.

"Yeah, but it sure took you long enough to get here," he whined.

Otis smiled. "Ain't that gratitude for ya?" he spoke to Lee. "He always was the spoilt one in the family." He laughed, and Lee nearly doubled over from the smell of his breath.

Lee didn't say a word. He kept trying to think of a way to reach for his gun.

Otis finally stopped laughing at his own humor and got down to the business at hand. "Okay, Sheriff. Where do you keep those keys?"

Lee didn't say anything for a moment; but when he saw the deadness in the man's eyes, he realized that the man would as soon shoot him as look at him. And

Lee wanted to live. He wanted a life with Patience. He wasn't ready to die now.

"In the desk drawer," he replied coldly.

Otis moved in closer. "Well, why don't you get it?" he demanded, his voice sarcastic. "And don't try anything, because I'll plug you full of holes if you do!"

Sweat began to bead on Lee's forehead and fall down into his eyes. Slowly, he reached down and grasped the drawer handle, pulling it open.

Lee looked at the keys and then up at Otis. There was a gun inside the drawer. Did he dare?

His chance came when he saw Otis turn to his brother and say something. He got a good grip on the handle and trigger and started to lift the gun out of the drawer when the door opened.

Lightning fast, Otis whirled around and fired.

Everything happened in slow motion after that. The force of the bullet knocked Patience against the door frame. Lee, shocked and horrified, reacted by aiming and shooting Otis. Almost in harmony, they fell to the floor.

Thinking his aim had been true, Lee dropped his hand and ran to where Patience lay. "Patience!" he cried as he stepped over Otis to get to her.

Suddenly Lee was falling. Someone had grabbed his ankle. He managed to turn, as to not fall on top of Patience. He was just about to regroup and point his gun at the source of who made him fall, but he was too late.

Otis was already standing up, his pistol aimed steadily at Lee. Otis glanced at his bloody arm and laughed nastily. "You just nicked me, lawman. I guess good help is hard to find in backwater towns like this, huh?"

Lee dropped his gun, his concern for Patience only. "Otis, listen. You have to let me check the girl. She's just an innocent bystander in all this," Lee pleaded.

Otis sneered as he picked up Lee's gun. "You can check her after I get Bubba out of here."

Slowly, he made his way to the desk and felt around for the key, his eyes and gun remaining on Lee.

Lee looked over to Patience. He could see the hole in her leather coat and the red stain on her gown where the coat gaped. But hope arose in his heart when he saw the faint movement of gown. She was alive!

He briefly closed his eyes and gave a prayer of thanks to God, then he opened them and watched as Otis let his brother out of the cell.

Then Otis waved his pistol in a gesture telling Lee to move into the cell. "Now it's your turn to spend a little time behind bars," Otis said with a terrible smile. "Pick the woman up and get in."

Lee cast a worried glance toward Patience and then looked pleadingly back at Otis. "Otis, please. She needs a doctor. If you'll just let me..."

"My heart's bleedin', Sheriff. Now quit wasting my time and get in here!" he ordered menacingly.

With a sinking heart, Lee lovingly gathered Patience in his arms and carried her into the cell. While he laid her on the cot, he heard the clang of metal hitting metal as the cell door shut. He didn't relax until he heard them leave the office.

Quickly, Lee stripped the coat off of her and ripped the gown open at the shoulder.

Tears of relief and joy gathered in his eyes when he saw the wound. It seemed that he hadn't been the only bad shot that night. The bullet had merely grazed her shoulder; and although it had bled a lot at first, it had already started slowing.

Patience hadn't fallen unconscious because of her wound. She had only fainted!

Chapter 16

P atience. *Patience!*" She heard someone call from a long way off. What was touching her face? It felt like someone was tapping her cheeks. It certainly was annoying!

"Come on, Patience! Wake up!" *Tap, tap, tap.* . .

Well, the voice sounded like Lee, but Lee couldn't be trying to wake her up! Maybe her mother had a cold.

Tap, tap, tap. . .

Irritated, Patience slapped the object that was tapping her face. "Mmmm. . . Quit it," she mumbled.

She barely opened her eyes and saw Lee's face looming before her. "Oh. . .it *is* you," she said and then closed her eyes.

Two seconds later, her eyes sprang wide open as she stared at Lee in disbelief. "Lee! What are you doing in my bedroom?"

Lee looked at her as though she'd lost her mind. "Patience, we aren't in your bedroom. We're at my office," he explained patiently. His face looked haggard and weary.

She frowned. "What are we doing in your office?"

He looked at her, biting his lip as if contemplating what to tell her. "Uh. . . You don't remember coming in here?" She shook her head, and he sighed. "Well, you did, and. . .you were shot." He pointed to her bandaged shoulder.

Patience looked over and saw the blood all over her nightgown. Then she noticed the bulk of the bandage that he'd made from a pillowcase underneath.

"You shot me?" she asked with disbelief. "Am I all right? I'm not dying, am I?"

Lee let out an aggravated breath of air. "No, I didn't shoot you, Patience! How could you think that? And you're not dying. Believe me, you wouldn't be this chatty if you were. You were just nicked; you're fine."

She shook her head and winced at the pain—her shoulder was really aching. "Who shot me, then?"

"Take it easy," he soothed, laying a gentle hand on the bandage, making sure it was still tight. "Remember the outlaw I was guarding?" She nodded. "Well, his brother caught me off guard, and you got caught in the middle. Then they locked us up in here," he said, motioning about the cell.

She looked over at the bars. "We're in the jail cell!"

"Yeah. And I don't think we're going to get out of here until daybreak, when Billy comes in to relieve me."

For some reason the meaning of that comment didn't register because suddenly her memory was triggered.

"Oh no!" she cried, sitting up. She tried to ignore the pain in her shoulder. "My mother!"

"For goodness' sake, Patience! You're going to make it start bleeding again!" He checked her bandage again. "Now, what's this about your mother?"

She grabbed Lee's arm. "Lee, I think my mother is ill. I tried to find the doctor, but he wasn't home! That's why, when I saw your lights, I came over here!"

"I was wondering what you were doing out this late. . .especially after what happened to you the last time."

Her eyes widened. "You know about that?"

He nodded grimly.

She looked at him for a moment, then shook her head. "Lee, we have to get out of here!" She jumped up, walking to the door and shaking it.

Lee followed her and took her by her good arm. "Patience, just calm down. We ain't goin' nowhere! Now tell me exactly what happened with your mother."

Patience reluctantly allowed Lee to lead her to the cot. "We were talking about me meeting with Mr. Touchet, and she suddenly turned pale and began shaking like she couldn't stop. She grabbed at her chest and ran to her room." She looked pleadingly at Lee. "Sheriff, we've got to help her!"

Lee held his hands up, trying to calm her down. "Whoa, there. Now it seems to me that your mother wasn't ill, she was just upset over this. . .this Touchet feller." He snorted. "She ain't the only one!"

Patience frowned. "But why would his name upset her? She's never met him."

Lee was thoughtful for a minute. "But what if she had? What if he did something to scare her, and she is afraid? Has she been acting differently since he came into town?"

Patience thought back over the last month and how her mother rarely left the house. "Now that you mention it. . .she has been acting strange," she admitted.

"Okay, now think about this. She knows something bad about him and is scared of meeting up with him, then you come along and say that you are acquainted with him, and she gets upset!" Lee surmised.

She didn't look convinced. "I don't know, Sheriff. What if you're wrong? What if she's really sick?"

Lee sighed and leaned against the wall. "Then worrying about it ain't going to help matters none. We just have to pray and hope for the best."

But at least they were quiet.

"I want everyone to be quiet and listen for a moment, okay?" She looked around the room and glared at them all until they nodded in agreement. Quickly, she told them everything that had happened, from her trying to find the doctor, to how they ended up in the jail.

There was nothing but silence that followed her incredible story.

Prudence cleared her throat. "Well, be that as it may, it doesn't matter. You did spend the night together, all alone, therefore, you must get married."

"No!"

"Okay."

The words were spoken at the same time.

"I cannot believe you agree to this!" Patience looked at Lee.

Lee just shrugged. "It doesn't look like we have much choice!"

Patience knew that was the way he felt—that he was only agreeing to the marriage because her mother was forcing him. Because of appearance. It just stung to hear it from his lips. She lowered her eyes and looked away.

As soon as the words were out of his mouth, he wanted to take them back. That wasn't what he wanted to say at all! He wanted to tell her that he wanted to marry her because he loved her! But thanks to his big mouth, she'd never believe it now.

"Patience...I..."

"What do you mean, *no*, young lady?" her mother demanded.

A defiant, determined look came over Patience's expression as she faced her mother. "It means that I will not marry Leander Cutler! It's humiliating to marry a man who feels forced into it!"

"Patience, that's not..."

"Miss Patience, I realize that it's not the most ideal way to get married, but I was under the impression that you and Lee were friends. Surely a marriage based on friendship can grow into love," the preacher tried to counsel.

Lee tried again. "But I already..."

"That wasn't the way you felt about Rachel, was it, Brother Caleb? You both already loved each other. That's what I want!" Patience told him with quiet conviction.

"But I can..."

Once again Lee was interrupted; and he felt so frustrated, he didn't know what to do!

"Oh, for goodness' sake, get on with it, Reverend!" Prudence ordered, her impatience evident. "And you, Patience! Not another word!"

"I won't do it!"

"You must do it!"

"Patience, I..." Lee tried to butt in.

"Patience, please be reasonable—"

"I am being reasonable—"

"I'm trying to tell you—" Lee tried again.

"You have to marry him."

"I don't."

"I am trying to say something here!" Lee yelled out over their voices. Once they were silent, he continued, "Now that I have your attention, I would like to tell Patience something."

He turned to her and looked into her eyes. "Patience, what I've been trying to tell you is that I. . ."

"What's going on in here?" a new voice interrupted Lee.

Everyone turned to see that Bernard Touchet had walked into the office, and he didn't look happy.

Lee's shoulders drooped. Why was this so difficult? He just wanted to tell her he loved her!

"It's none of your business! Now, please leave!" Patience's mother told the Frenchman coldly.

Lee, Patience, and Caleb were all shocked at her frosty tone. She sounded almost hostile!

Mr. Touchet's face turned an angry red. "It is so my business! Why is Patience locked behind bars? And why is she covered with blood?"

The preacher tried to soothe the strange situation. "Uh, Mr. Touchet, sir, we are having a private conversation here. I'm sure that we can talk to you later."

Mr. Touchet ignored the preacher, his eyes staying steadily on Prudence. "You know that I have a right to know."

If steam could come out of Prudence's ears, Lee was sure that it would be doing it at that very moment. "You gave up that right a long time ago. Now, leave!"

Patience jumped up from the cot and walked to the cell door. "What does that mean, Mama? How do you know Mr. Touchet?" Patience asked in a strangely frightened voice.

Lee's protective instincts rose up within him, and he quickly went to stand behind Patience. "Could you please let us out and then we can continue this conversation after Patience has been checked out with the doctor?"

Caleb shook his head. "But we don't have the key!"

Lee sighed and wondered what else could possibly go wrong.

"Should you tell her or shall I?" Bernard Touchet asked Prudence. Apparently they were in their own little world over there. They hadn't stopped glaring at each other once!

"Tell me what?"

"No one is telling her anything!" Prudence told him.

"That I'm your. . ."

"Goodness! What's all the hoola-ba-hoo? Did someone have a party and forget to invite me?"

Lee groaned inwardly and decided that it *could* get worse.

Susannah sashayed into the room and came up to the jail cell. "Oh my stars! What are you two doing in there? And, Patience! You're bleeding! What happened to you? Is everyone going to just stand there, or are you going to let them out?" she demanded to the room at large.

"We don't have the key," the preacher started to explain.

"I was shot, Susannah!" Patience told her friend.

"Lee shot you?"

"No, I did not. . . ." He stopped and threw up his hands and stalked away from the cell door. "Forget it, just forget it!"

He turned back to them. "Can somebody go and find Billy? He's got an extra key."

"Reverend, can you please just marry them before the rest of the town finds out?" Prudence cried out desperately.

"Marry? Are you and Lee getting married?" Susannah asked.

"No!" Patience answered emphatically. "But they are trying to make him marry me!"

"They are not making me do anything. I. . ."

"But this is wonderful!" Susannah cooed.

Patience just shook her head in confusion. "Why is it wonderful?"

"Could somebody please go and get Billy?"

"I'm right here!" Billy announced from the doorway.

Lee let out a breath of relief. "Please tell me you brought the key to the cell door."

"Don't let them out before you pronounce them man and wife!" Prudence demanded.

The preacher shook his head. "But, Mrs. Primrose, I can't do that until they say their vows and. . ."

"And I'm not going to say them!" Patience announced.

"Billy, open this door now!"

Billy fumbled in his pocket for the keys; and when he brought them out, they were immediately snatched out of his hands.

"They are not coming out until they are married!" Prudence declared, holding the keys in the air, where they were promptly snatched from her own hands.

"If she doesn't want to marry, she doesn't have to!" Bernard Touchet declared, now holding the keys in his hand. He stepped closer to the lock.

Prudence threw herself in front of it. "I will not let you do this! You don't belong here!"

"I do belong here, Prudence. Now, move!"

"Excuse me!" Susannah's Southern voice broke into the chaos. "I know it's none of my business, but I'm awfully curious. Why do you think you belong here, Mr. Touchet? Are you wanting Patience for yourself?"

Mr. Touchet sputtered, "Of course not! Do not be so ridiculous!"

Lee knew that this was not the time to go into this, but he'd been wondering the same thing about the Frenchman. He walked back to the cell door and looked right into the eyes of Touchet. "Then why don't you tell us why you're here."

Bernard Touchet looked at Prudence. "Tell them," he ordered her.

"No," was her answer.

His mouth tightened grimly, and he looked at Lee, then past him to Patience.

For some reason, Lee reached out and put his arm around Patience, sensing she would need his comfort.

And he was right.

"I'm your father, *mon cher*."

Chapter 18

Lee was the one who took Patience to the doctor's office after Mr. Touchet finally let them out. Patience hadn't said a word since her father had shared his secret with everyone, and Lee was worried about her.

She had gone so still and pale, only looking at her mother in question. But Prudence wouldn't make eye contact with her. Silently, Lee had taken her arm and led her out of the jail and out of the building.

Now Lee was pacing around in Doc's outer room because Doc insisted that he couldn't come in while he examined her.

Lee looked despairingly at the closed door and wondered what was happening. Was Patience all right? What would this revelation mean to their future? Would it make a difference?

Not that it mattered to him. He loved Patience no matter whether she was born legitimately or not. But he could not predict what Patience would do. She'd been so adamant about not getting married before, he feared this would just give her another excuse to refuse.

What would he do without her?

Lord, please help us find a way through all this mess! And please let Patience realize I'm telling her the truth when I tell her that I love her. . . .

"You can come in now," Doc said as he peered around the door, interrupting Lee's prayer.

Quickly, Lee followed Doc into the room and found Patience sitting on the examination table, robed in a large brown dress. It obviously belonged to Doc's wife, but Lee was happy to see her out of the bloody nightgown.

He walked up to her and reached for her hands, which lay folded in her lap. "Patience, darlin'? Are you all right?"

He was relieved when she looked at him tiredly and gave him a half smile. "I'm okay." She looked down at their entwined hands; and when she raised her gaze back to his, she had tears in her eyes. "Lee, what am I going to do?"

Lee threw Doc a glance, and the doctor mumbled something about having to check on his wife and then left the room.

Then Lee did what he'd been wanting to do ever since Patience had walked into his office last night. He put his arms around her and held her.

She began to cry. The sound of it tore his heart right in two.

———~~~———

She didn't mean to cry. But the moment that Lee put his arms around her, she couldn't help herself. Never in her whole life had anyone offered to hold her when she was hurting. And now this man, the man whom she loved with all her heart, was offering her the very thing she'd needed so many times in her life.

Tenderness and compassion.

When her tears began to subside, he handed her his hanky to wipe her eyes.

"How can I ever forgive my mama?" she said in a ravaged voice.

He gently took the hanky from her trembling hands and began to wipe the places that she had missed. "Why don't you hear her side of things before you start worryin' about that?"

"But she lied to me, Lee. All these years she's let me believe that my father was dead! And now I find out that not only was my father alive—Mama was never married to him!"

"Patience. . ."

"No!" she said firmly, pushing away from him. Her tears were gone, and anger had taken its place. "Do you know how judgmental she has been toward me all my life? She's never been considerate or kind to me. She's never taken me in her arms like you just did and offered me comfort. All she's ever done is rule my life!"

"Patience, I want you to calm down and listen to me," he ordered as he took her shoulders in his hands. She obeyed mainly because she was stunned that he'd used such a harsh tone with her. "I didn't mean to yell at you, but I need you to listen to me."

Just hearing his voice calmed her down. With him, she felt safe, as if she could lean on him and he'd take her problems on his capable shoulders. She nodded her head to him.

He took a breath and began to speak. "I think it's important to talk to your mother, and I'll tell you why. Just think how she felt when she found out she was with child and unmarried. And why didn't Touchet do the honorable thing and marry her? It seems like the blame should not fall only on your mother's shoulders."

She opened her mouth to speak, but he stopped her. "No, wait. You said your mother was always strict with you and judgmental. Don't you think that she was just trying, in her own way, to make sure that you didn't make her mistakes? Yes, she went about it the wrong way. But in her mind, I'd imagine she did the best that she knew how."

Patience bit her lip and thought about what Lee was saying. "I know there is some truth in what you are saying, but. . .I just don't know. . . ."

"I know that it won't be easy. Forgiving and forgetting will take time. But I know that God will help you if you'll just trust in Him." He took her hands into his once again. "I'll be here, too."

Patience looked into his eyes, afraid to read anything into that statement. "You will?" she asked faintly.

"Yes, I will, if you'll let me. Patience, I want you to marry me."

She felt as if she couldn't breathe. "You do?"

He smiled tenderly. "Yes, I do."

Patience wanted to believe that he wanted to marry her, but she told herself that it couldn't be true. Someone like Lee Cutler wouldn't want to marry someone like her. "You're just afraid of a scandal, Lee. You don't really want to marry me."

He actually laughed! "Oh Patience, how can you even think that I would marry you for that reason? I'm not afraid of a scandal." He stepped back and tugged at her arms until she had scooted off the table and was standing in front of him. He let go of one of her hands and gently cupped her face in his palm.

"I love you, Patience. That's the reason I want to marry you."

Patience searched his eyes and face, looking for some sign that he wasn't telling the truth. But for the first time, she saw the love shining through his eyes and smile. "Oh my goodness! You're telling the truth," she said faintly.

He nodded. "I'm telling the truth. Now, you tell me the truth. Do you love me?"

Patience wondered if the man was blind or just crazy! "Of course I love you!" she cried. And with a jubilant laugh, she launched herself into his arms.

He caught her and hugged her tightly to him. "Ah darlin', you've made me a happy man," he told her, then bent his head to kiss her.

After a moment, he looked up and asked her, "Does this mean you'll marry me?"

She nodded. "Yes! Oh yes, I'll marry you!" This time it was she who kissed him!

—∞—

Lee felt like a thirsty man who had finally reached the river. He returned her kiss, telling her without words the feelings that were swirling around in his heart.

His lips left hers, and he planted little kisses on her cheeks, moving up to her eyes and then back down to her nose. That made her giggle.

He leaned back and smiled at her. "Liked that, did you?"

She sighed happily. "I can't believe this is happening. I keep wondering if it's all a dream and I'll wake up."

Lee stopped smiling. "Patience Primrose, I don't ever want you to talk like that again. You are such a beautiful and special person, it is I who feels lucky to have you!"

Her eyes teared up again. "Thank you for that, Lee."

He shook his head. "I'm going to make you a promise right here and now. I promise that I will do everything in my power to make sure that you never feel unworthy or unloved again. When you're feeling down, I'll be there. When you need someone to talk to, I'll be there.

"But you need to remember this, too. God will be there for both of us. If we pray together and always keep Him first in our lives, Patience, our lives will be so good together."

"I know," she told him in a shaky voice. "He's already done so much for me. He's given me two good friends and let me have that job when I really needed something for myself. But most of all, He's answered my prayer. I prayed that you'd be the one He chose for me, and He granted it!"

To Lee, it seemed like a good time for another kiss; and he was just about to touch her lips with his own, when the door to the doctor's office opened.

"Whoa there, boy! You haven't said your 'I do's' yet!" Caleb told them with a teasing glint in his eye as he came into the room.

Caleb wasn't the only one who entered. In walked Prudence and Mr. Touchet, also.

Protectively, Lee put his arm around Patience. He could feel her shaking, and he tightened his hold to reassure her.

"Patience, I'd like to talk to you. . . ," Mr. Touchet began.

"No!" Prudence interrupted. She stepped past him to get closer to Patience. "I want to tell her what I should have told her a long time ago."

She closed her eyes for a moment, then opened them. Her face was set with determination. "Twenty-two years ago, I got involved with Bernard. We courted for a short time, and I thought I loved him. He started pressuring me into having. . .relations. . .with him without the benefit of marriage. It was wrong and very much a sin; but I went along with it, thinking he would marry me."

Tears started filling her eyes, but she blinked them back and continued, "I be-came pregnant and I told him about it, hoping that we could hurry up and marry and nobody would find out. Well. . .he said he couldn't marry me because his family would never accept me. Instead he married someone else.

"My parents were horrified, and they did the first thing they thought of, and that was to send me off to Aunt Ida's house here in Springton. When I got here, it was Ida who thought up the idea of me being a widow. I went along with it and tried so hard to mold myself into a better person."

"You became a strict, religious-minded woman who wouldn't bend even for her own daughter," Patience spoke out, her voice scratchy from crying.

Prudence threw up her hands. "Don't you understand I didn't want you to end up like me? I did what I thought was best."

Patience stepped out from Lee's embrace and walked closer to her mother. "Couldn't you have just shown me a little attention? Couldn't you have loved me?" she cried out, pointing to her chest.

Prudence put a hand over her mouth as a sob rose out of her throat. "Oh Patience. I do. . .love you. Please. . .please forgive me. Please. . ." She broke down completely and covered her face with both of her hands.

Huge tears rolled down Patience's cheeks. "Oh Mama. . ." She wept and threw her arms around her mother. "I do. I do forgive you. I just never. . .knew. I never knew. . .you loved me."

Lee looked at the preacher, and they shared an understanding glance. Caleb had apparently known about all this, because he didn't look surprised. Lee sure wished he'd known so he could have been prepared to say something to Patience to comfort her.

When they'd cried all their tears, the women separated, wiping their tear-stained faces.

Lee stepped forward and placed a hand on Patience's back. "Are you all right, darlin'?" he asked.

She nodded. "I'm okay."

He wasn't convinced, but they could talk about it later. He looked around the room and noticed that, although the preacher was still with them, Mr. Touchet had slipped out of the room.

"He said that Patience needed to deal with one parent at a time. She can go and talk to him when she's ready," Brother Caleb told him.

Lee turned to Patience. "I think that is a good idea, don't you?"

She nodded wearily. "Yes, I'm a little overwhelmed; and I need time to think about it all."

He grimaced. "Well, this is probably not the best of circumstances to announce this, but Patience has agreed to marry me."

Prudence opened her mouth to say something, but Lee stopped her. "But not today!" he told her emphatically. "Patience should have a big wedding with a pretty dress and the whole works. She deserves it. But she also needs time to deal with her father being alive and the issues between you and she."

Prudence simply closed her mouth and nodded.

"In the meantime," the preacher spoke up, "why don't all of you come over to the house? Rachel always cooks so much for the children, there's always plenty left. She'll want to hear the news of your engagement."

Lee threw Patience a questioning glance, and she nodded her head. He smoothed his hand up and down her back in a comforting gesture as they followed the preacher out of the office.

Chapter 19

On Christmas Eve morning, Patience was still in bed, though it was well past nine, dreaming of Lee. It was such a beautiful dream. Lee was in his best suit, standing in a mist of clouds, reaching his hand out to her. He was smiling and telling her to. . . Hmmm. Patience couldn't quite make out what he was trying to tell her.

Patience tried to run closer; but as dreams sometimes went, her legs felt heavy and she was unable to get to him as fast as she wanted. Finally, she could hear him better. He was saying. . .

"Wake up, Patience!"

Wake up? That was a strange thing for him to say!

"Patience Anne, are you going to sleep all day?"

Patience was jolted awake by her mother's voice; Lee's voice drifted off into dreamland. Sleepily, she blinked and saw not only her mother but Susannah and Rachel standing by her bed.

"What are y'all doing here?"

Susannah giggled in her delightful way, and Rachel put her hands on her hips and shook her head. "Patience, as much as you longed for this day to come, I can't believe you have to ask that! We're here to help you get ready!" Rachel explained.

Patience sat up then. Suddenly, her heart filled with gladness, and her stomach fluttered with excitement. Of course! How could she have forgotten?

It was her wedding day!

Susannah ran to the window and pulled back the gingham curtain. "And look, Patience! It snowed last night! Just enough to make everything pretty and white!"

Patience crawled out of bed and looked at the snow-covered landscape. The sun was glistening through the iced-over trees, making them sparkle like jewels. It was all just perfect.

"It never snows at this time of the year," she commented.

"Well, Caleb would say that God likes to give wedding presents, too," Rachel said as she joined the women at the window.

Patience stared out and tried to blink back the tears that came to her eyes. "God has already done so much for me. I feel like I don't deserve any more!"

"Now, I won't hear talk like that, young lady!" her mother said from behind her in a brisk voice. Prudence's hands came to rest on Patience's shoulders, and she felt a warm feeling of contentment run through her that she was sure she'd never get used to. "You deserve all God has for you!"

Patience and her mother had come a long way since that confrontation in the jail two months earlier. With the pastor's help, they were able to work through their feelings and past fears and come to a closer relationship. They still had a ways to go, but God was surely working a miracle.

"Okay, enough dillydallying! We've got work to do!" Susannah said, stepping away from the window.

"We sure do," Rachel chimed in. "Your mother has fixed you a good breakfast, so you can get in there and eat. But you need to hurry because we've got to do your hair. . . ."

"And get that dress and veil on! With all those buttons, it's going to take awhile!" Susannah finished for her.

Patience laughed with delight. "Okay, okay! Boy, you two are bossy!" she exclaimed as she grabbed her robe and followed them into the dining room.

—⁂—

After breakfast, they all went to Rachel's house so that they would be near the church. The three women worked for over an hour brushing, teasing, pinning, buttoning, and tugging. Patience stood or sat patiently as they did their jobs, wishing they would hand her a mirror so she could see the progress.

But as usual, Rachel liked to wait until everything was finished so she could make a grand production of it.

And *finally* she was ready. Patience stood in front of Rachel's oval floor mirror and stared at herself with awe and disbelief.

Her dress was made of the finest silk that Adelaide Hayes was able to buy. It was her gift to Patience. Rachel and Susannah had worked together on her dress, and they'd done a superb job.

The gown was high at the neck and the bodice fashioned of the most delicate lace. The bell-like sleeves were puffy and fell inches above the elbow with an undersleeve fitted all the way to her wrist. The skirt was full, but smooth, gathered at the back and fastened by a large pearl-edged bow. The dress fit her figure perfectly.

Her hair was loosely knotted at her nape and parted down the middle, tendrils of blond curls framing her face. She wore a circlet of roses with a long lace veil attached to the back like a crown around her head.

Patience felt like a fairy princess.

Prudence walked up to stand beside her. There were tears in her eyes as she looked at her only daughter through the mirror. "I'm so proud of you, Patience.

You really make a beautiful bride."

Patience smiled radiantly at her mother and hugged her. "Thank you, Mama," she whispered, squeezing her tightly.

After a moment, Susannah announced that it was time for them to go. She was in a pretty gown of green and was to be Patience's maid of honor.

A flutter of nervousness ran through Patience's stomach as she followed the women to the church. She felt a little like she was still walking around in her dream from this morning. It seemed to take forever to reach the church, although it was only a few steps away.

Bernard Touchet was waiting for her at the door. The dapper man that she had, just yesterday, agreed to call "Daddy" was to walk her down the aisle to her future husband.

Theirs was a relationship far from resolved, but they had made a few small steps on understanding what had happened years ago.

He'd explained to Patience and Prudence that he'd been pressured by his parents to marry someone else. And when Prudence had told him she was pregnant, he'd gotten scared and married the other girl. Because his wife was from South Louisiana, where his parents were originally from, he'd gone down there to live. He knew that he was running away from Prudence and their child, and he had never forgiven himself nor forgotten what he'd done.

He'd started his own rice farm, and he and his wife had planned to raise their children in the large plantation house that he built for them. But when his wife and his child died in childbirth, Bernard began to look for Prudence and Patience.

Unfortunately, her parents would not tell him where she was, and no one else in the town of Shreveport knew.

Off and on, he'd taken time off from his work to look for Prudence. His break came when he read in the paper about the Jenkins gang being arrested in Springton, Texas. It had told the details, commenting that Prudence Primrose had been kidnapped and then released by them.

Bernard had sold his farm and come to Springton in hopes of apologizing to Prudence. He knew it would not be easy for her to forgive him, but he hoped for some sort of place in both her and his daughter's life.

Prudence was still standoffish with him, but Patience knew that deep inside her mother still loved him and would soon be able to forgive him. Despite all that had happened, Patience couldn't help but want him in her life.

She'd so yearned for a father and now she had one. Life was too short to stay mad at one man and one woman's mistake.

That was the reason she asked her father to walk her down the aisle.

From inside the building, Patience could hear the strains of the wedding march beginning. Her mother kissed her on the cheek and allowed Jessie Stone, the pastor's son, to walk her into the church and show her to her seat.

Next, after throwing Patience a reassuring wink, Susannah walked in.

Rachel took the bride's hand and squeezed it. "Now it's your turn, Patience. Don't be nervous. You look beautiful," she told her with confidence.

Patience nodded her head and took a deep breath. "I'm ready," she told her father as she took his arm.

Slowly, they entered the church and began to walk down the aisle. She was so glad that the town had never found out about the incident at the jail. And where her father was concerned, they all assumed that he'd been thought dead from the war and they had been unable to find him. Patience and her mother did nothing to deny nor confirm the rumor. They all felt safer letting the townspeople think that than to allow her mother to feel more shame. And if anyone was a little confused about their last names being different, they were much too afraid of Prudence to ask.

Patience looked forward, to the front of the church. The preacher was standing there in the center, and then her eyes fell to the handsome man standing beside him.

Lee was dressed just like in her dream. So tall and handsome robed in his dark suit. He was staring at her with such a look of love that it nearly took her breath clean away.

She wanted to laugh when Billy, his best man, nudged him with his elbow and, when Lee glanced at him, wiggled his eyebrows and nodded in Patience's direction.

Lee just looked back at Patience and smiled proudly.

She was the luckiest woman in the world!

—⁂—

Lee felt as though he was the luckiest man in the world. What a woman she was! And she was *his*!

His heart was pounding hard in his chest as his eyes swept over his bride. She looked so beautiful in her white gown. The only color was the red Christmas flower in her hands.

It seemed fitting that they marry on such a holy day of celebration. Every year, from this day on, they would not only celebrate Christ's birth, but they would rejoice in their marriage as well.

Finally, she was beside him. Bernard guided her hand to Lee's arm, and Lee felt her sweetness and warmth as she held onto him.

He didn't think. He just bent down and placed a gentle kiss on her smooth cheek.

A tinkle of laughter drifted over the congregation, and Caleb gave them a mock frown. "You're supposed to wait until the end of the service for that!"

Lee felt his face burn, and he smiled sheepishly at Caleb. "Sorry," he whispered.

He glanced at Patience and relaxed when he saw her trying to hold back a laugh.

The ceremony was beautiful. There wasn't a dry eye in the whole place by the time it was through. And when Lee finally got another chance to kiss his bride, every female heart went to fluttering as they dreamed of their own weddings, past and future.

Epilogue

After a two-week trip to New Orleans, a wedding present from Bernard Touchet, Patience and Lee returned to Springton. So many things had happened, they soon realized, while they were honeymooning.

First, the Powell brothers—the outlaws that had shot Patience—had been arrested in Oklahoma, and it looked like there weren't going to be any jailbreaks this time.

Second, they found out that Patience's mama and daddy had gotten married in a quiet ceremony at the pastor's house. According to Prudence, it was so that they could live in the same house together to stifle any gossip. But Patience saw the emotions that passed between her parents and knew that it was a happy union.

Third, Lee had a friend in the Rangers who was part of the crowd that welcomed him and Patience home. And he'd told them that he'd been down in South Texas for the last few weeks and reported that El Paso was "so cold that icicles were hanging from the cactus." Somehow, that *didn't* surprise the happy couple.

But once everybody left them at the train station, they headed out to her mother's old farm and began to move her things into his house.

She was busy hanging her dresses in his wardrobe, and he was unpacking a box of books. "Remind me to give Bobby Joe his books back. He let me borrow a few of his, and I've forgotten all about returning them," she said as she shook the wrinkles out of one of her best dresses.

"Well, darlin', I would hope that Bobby Joe wasn't in your thoughts while we were honeymooning!"

She rolled her eyes at his mock jealousy.

They worked quietly for a few moments until Lee began to chuckle. "I don't think this one belongs to Bobby Joe!"

She looked over her shoulder to see what he was talking about and froze.

In his hand was Emma Hadley's book, *A Young Lady's Guide to Courtship and Marriage*!

She dropped the dress and ran over to take the book. "Give me that!"

He held it high and shook his head. "Wait! I want to see what this says!" He opened up the book, still holding it over his head and out of her reach. "'Batting your eyelashes and giving a gentle giggle lets a gentleman know that you have his complete interest. A gentleman always likes to feel as though he is the most important man in the room,'" Lee read aloud.

He looked at her with disbelief. "That's why you were batting your lashes? Because you read it in a book?"

She had never been so embarrassed in her life! She could have sworn she threw that book away a long time ago! "Oh, give me that! And quit laughing!"

"I thought you had something wrong with your eyes!" Lee exclaimed and began to chuckle.

She finally was able to grab the book out of his hand. She whirled around, intent on leaving the room, when he grabbed her arm.

"Ah, don't leave, sweetheart! I was just joking!" He lifted her chin so she would look at him. He shrugged his shoulders. "Hey, it worked, didn't it?" he said arrogantly.

She rolled her eyes and hit him playfully with the book. "Oh, please! Is that your head I see swelling?"

He laughed and with a flick of his wrist tugged the book away from her and tossed it across the room so that he could take her into his arms. Holding her close, he put his face near to hers so that their foreheads touched.

"Why didn't I realize that you were the one for me right away? Then you wouldn't have had to read that book and follow that awful advice!"

She sighed. "Because you thought Susannah was the perfect one for you."

"Nah. . .I think that I was just fighting my feelings for you and using her as a shield. But know this, darlin', I thank God that He opened my eyes, and I'll never let you go!"

"That's good, because I wasn't planning on letting you go!" she said saucily, then gave him a kiss that made his head spin.

TO LOVE MERCY

by Cathy Marie Hake

Prologue

April 3, 1892
Aboard the Anchoria in the Atlantic

Y ou'll stay together?"

Robert Gregor curled his hand around his father's. "Aye, Da. You've my word on it."

"Dinna be grieving, boy-o. 'Twas my wish to see you to the New World. As for me, my destination's heaven. God and your mama will welcome me with open arms."

The ship rolled gently, and sorrow as deep as the Atlantic washed over Robert. It didn't come as a sudden shock but as a swell, carrying him from the security he'd known and leaving him adrift. *Not yet. Please not yet.* "We'll see land in another day."

"That you will." His father had a way of putting together words to intensify their meanings. He'd done it now, and Robert felt the tide of life shift in those moments.

"Rob?" Duncan looked down from the upper bunk. His black hair stood up boyishly, making him look only half his age.

"Go fetch Christopher." Robert knew his eldest brother would be pacing the deck. A restless man, Chris avoided situations where he'd bare his emotions or soul to others. Had it just been the four of them, he'd have stayed, but the ship teemed with hundreds of folks with nothing better to do than mind everyone else's business. Christopher left the crowded steerage compartment round about midnight, grief ravaging his features.

Lord Almighty, must You take Da yet? Robert knew the answer. As a doctor, he'd witnessed births and deaths aplenty. Powerless to do anything but give comfort, he smoothed back Da's thinning gray hair. "Save your breath, Da. The others'll be here soon, and they deserve to hear your love."

Minutes later, Christopher shouldered past the neighboring berths and knelt by the bunk. Duncan came to a halt behind him and rested a warm, calloused hand on his shoulder. Robert saw the tension in their jaws, the sheen of tears in their eyes. The Gregors were stoic with others, but amongst themselves, they always loved, laughed, and wept unabashedly—except for now. Time grew short, and Robert knew his brothers' hearts were breaking, as was his, yet they both stayed strong for Da's

213

sake. A man ought to slip from this world and into God's arms with the peace of knowing those he left behind would fare well.

"I've been blessed to have ye, lads." Dad drew in another breath. "Stay close to the Almighty so we'll meet again at heaven's gate."

Each of them gave that promise without reservation.

Da squeezed Rob's hand. "My da's watch—to Chris." He stared at his eldest and whispered, "Time is a gift, dinna waste it."

Christopher nodded solemnly.

"Bible—I'm wanting Duncan to hae it. He's a man of deep thoughts and quiet truths fit to soothe the soul."

"I'll treasure it, Da." Duncan bent closer. "I'll have a son and read to him as you read to us. He'll know the Word of God, and Da—I'll name him after you."

A smile chased across Da's features. *Aye, Da'd been right,* Robert observed. *Duncan just spoke words that gave comfort.*

Da then turned his head. "Robert—"

Rob leaned down and looked steadily into his father's eyes. "You already gave me my gift, Da. I know what you sacrificed for me." The compensation Da received for the arm he lost while working in the zinc mine had paid for Robert's medical schooling.

Da smiled. "Mama's ring. I kept it for ye, Son. Caring for bodies makes a doctor close off his heart so he doesn't have to feel the pain. Dinna do that. Take a chance at love."

Within the hour, it was all over. Rob wrapped Da; Christopher pushed everyone away and cradled his lifeless form up to the deck; Duncan carried the Bible. During the voyage, they'd assisted with other burials, but this was different. All three of them stood in a sorrowful knot as Chris prayed.

The *Anchoria*'s captain made a motion as he somberly said, "Lord, we commend the body of Micah Gregor to You and commit his mortal body to the deep until the day of Your return."

It was over. Those who had come up to pay their respects murmured their condolences, then wandered off to leave the brothers some privacy.

Duncan opened the Bible. The ribbon marker was set in the book of Micah. He cleared his throat and read in an unsteady voice made thick with tears, " 'He hath shewed thee, O man, what is good; and what doth the Lord require of thee, but to do justly, and to love mercy, and to walk humbly with thy God?' "

Christopher nodded solemnly. "Da did those things."

Rob wrapped his arms about his brothers' shoulders. "Aye, and we will, too, in his honor."

Chapter 1

Ellis Island

The Gregor brothers stood shoulder to shoulder along the ship's rail as the *Anchoria* cut through the choppy waters. The copper Statue of Liberty towered over their vessel, but her long-awaited welcome felt empty since Da wasn't beside them to see the grand sight.

Duncan nudged Rob. "I'm thinking she has the biggest feet I've ever seen."

His joke lightened the tension. All three brothers chuckled. It made sense that Duncan would notice such a detail, him being a cobbler.

All about them, folks craned to see the sight. Mamas clutched their children close, and men stood a bit taller. Freedom. Opportunity. They'd scrimped, saved, sacrificed, and some nearly starved to come to America. Seeing Liberty did something—they'd gotten here... Didn't that mean other dreams and hopes could come true, too?

"Ellis Island," a sailor announced through a megaphone. "First-class passengers, please remain aboard. We will assist you with all your needs. Second class and steerage, gather your belongings and prepare to disembark."

"Remember what I told you," Robert murmured to his brothers. He shot a meaningful look at a woman coughing into her handkerchief. Americans didn't want diseased immigrants flooding their land. Processing newcomers through this facility allowed officials to turn back those they determined might be sickly. Robert had known that fact full well, but Da refused to listen. He'd insisted on making the voyage.

"We're hale as horses," Chris said as he withstood a hefty bump from someone on his other side. "I'm heartily sick of being crowded. I'm going below to get our gear."

"I'll come along." Duncan shifted sideways.

Robert didn't say a word. He'd given Da his promise that they'd stick together, and he'd meant it. From here on out, he'd be sure to keep what was left of his family intact. After an overcrowded, noisy voyage, the steerage compartment was eerily empty and silent. They walked down the companionway and wended past bunks to reach the berth they'd shared with so many others.

215

Chris and Duncan knelt and yanked Duncan's trunk from beneath the bunk. Filled with a cobbler's tools, the thing weighed a ton, but Duncan hefted it with relative ease.

Robert turned his hand over and felt under the bunk for a package he'd secured there when they'd first boarded.

"Is it there still?" Chris asked in an undertone.

"Aye." Rob untied the corners and carefully reclaimed his precious supply of medications and medical instruments. Theft below decks had proven to be a persistent problem, and he'd taken care to protect these things from sticky fingers and shifty souls. "I'll put this in my bag with the rest of the things now."

Two battered suitcases, a physician's bag, and a cobbler's trunk. The Gregor brothers carried all their worldly possessions off the ship and onto American soil. In short order, workers herded them through lines and into a large wooden building. Workers chalked numbers on the immigrants' baggage and gave them pasteboard tickets for each piece.

"I'll have that." A man tugged at Robert's valise.

"No." Robert held fast. "I'm a physician. 'Tis my bag."

"Why didn't you just say so?" The man shot him a disgruntled look and went on down the line to the next men.

Duncan folded his arms and looked about. "Aboard the ship, the noise all rolled back on us. Here, I can make out all of the different tongues. How are they ever going to be able to ask us all questions and understand our answers? 'Tis like the Tower of Babel in here."

"Chris," Robert elbowed him. Christopher had an uncanny ability to learn languages. "How many do you hear?"

"German. Dutch. French. Russian. Some of it sounds like Latin, so I'd venture that it's Spanish or Portuguese." He shrugged. "Probably both. Judging from clothing, there are Slavs aplenty, too."

Their group spent time in what looked remarkably like a livestock pen. Older folk slumped on wooden benches and toddlers fussed.

Women went one way; the men went the other. Robert watched in silence as each man underwent a cursory examination. Those with light sensitivity or red, runny eyes received marks on their coats. So did the ones whose coughs revealed consumption.

A father and son ahead of them were drawn off to the side; the son's eyes were diseased—would the father stay in America while his son was shipped back home?

Lord Almighty, what a horrendous situation. Da wouldn't have made it through this. You took him from us, and that was hard enough—but to have a stranger rip us apart would have been unbearable. I didn't realize at the time just how merciful You were being.

"Destination?" The tall man at the desk looked at Duncan for an answer.

"Texas," Christopher answered. He pulled Connant's letter from his vest pocket and carefully laid it on the desk. Connant had enclosed a note with that letter, warning them that New York teemed with immigrants. Officials would be glad to hear the brothers would leave the area.

"I can see you're all brothers." The man gave them a friendly smile. "Black Irish?"

"Scots," they said in unison.

"Brawny ones at that." The man scribbled something on a document. Robert wondered how someone in the midst of this madhouse managed to stay cheerful all day. Perhaps the news that they were headed clear off to Texas pleased him. *God, thank Ye for Connant's friendship and sound advice.*

"What trades do you boast?"

"Doctor, cobbler, and miner." Christopher jabbed his thumb at each of them in turn.

"Make yourselves useful, men. America needs men of peace and productivity." He stamped something and waved them onward.

"Now what?" Duncan frowned. "I'm not liking this business of them keeping our belongings somewhere."

A lanky man with a fringe of bright orange hair beckoned them. He'd gathered several others around him who all looked to be from the Isles. "Immigrant Society!" he called loudly.

"Connant wrote about them." Robert headed that way.

"There we are, then." The man smiled broadly. The lilt in his voice sounded wonderfully familiar. "America's a wondrous land, and I won't be sayin' otherwise, but I need to warn you that many an unscrupulous man waits across the harbor. They'll make promises and take what little ye've left, but 'tis little to no help you'll get back. The Immigrant Society will help, and 'tis honest. If you ken where ye be headed, we'll help transport you there at minimal cost and less fuss."

—⁂—

"Minimal cost and less fuss turned out to be an honest assessment," Robert said later as he tucked his black leather bag beneath the train bench and took a seat.

Duncan chuckled. "It bewilders me, it does, how you recall every last word a body says. How long's the trip to Texas?"

"Three days." Christopher folded his arms across his chest and scanned the others filling the train car.

Robert watched the other passengers, too. Long ago, he'd learned he watched people just as avidly as Chris, but they saw entirely different things. Where from his clinical perspective he saw undertones in complexions, strained breathing, guarded moves, and grimaces from pain, Chris focused on eyes and hands because he'd learned to measure a man's ability to help or do harm. Together, they would evaluate their fellow travelers and exchange terse comments if something struck them as important.

Duncan, on the other hand, slouched in the seat so he'd be at eye level with a small boy. They'd struck up a conversation, and once the train set in motion, Duncan wrapped his arm about the lad's shoulder and nudged him to rest his head against Duncan's ribs. It wasn't but a few minutes ere the lad fell fast asleep, and the mama gave Duncan a look of sheer gratitude.

"Well?" Robert didn't even look at Chris when he asked.

"Left of the bald man in the green jacket—man's armed to the teeth. Behind us three rows are two Poles with more fight in their eyes than brains in their heads."

"That's all?" He slanted a glance at Chris and gave him a slow, easy grin.

"Aye." Chris pulled the brim of his hat down over his eyes, folded his arms, and stretched his long legs out before him. "I could whip all three of 'em without breaking a sweat, and you could wash the scratches on my knuckles afterward if you were of a mind to be helpful." His chin dipped to rest on his chest, he let out a throaty chuckle, and before long he slumbered.

Robert couldn't sleep. Then again, he'd learned to do with less sleep than most men needed. Relentlessly, the train chugged across the nation, belching clouds of black smoke and covering mile after mile of this huge, strange country. The rhythmic *clack, clack, clack* as they advanced didn't make him sleepy—it energized him.

Three days. Three days of stopping here and there. Of changing trains. Of going through big, stately cities that looked newer than anything Scotland boasted, past grand stretches where nothing but forests commanded the land, and past patchwork plots covered by verdant crops. The streets weren't exactly paved with gold, but from where he sat and what he saw, Robert knew America offered what every man craved most: an opportunity to make something of himself.

Back home, the zinc mine was played out. Christopher would have faced the humiliation of having no way to earn a living. Folks couldn't spend money on shoes when their bellies were empty, so Duncan had experienced a severe drop in demand for his skills. Even Robert found he'd been paid far less reliably by his patients. This would be a fresh start. They'd have a meager beginning, but that thought didn't trouble him, or his brothers, one bit. Strong, motivated men could forge a new life. Besides, they had one another, and they had God. In the end, those were what mattered most.

—◊—

Mercy Ellen Stein clipped the floss, turned over the dish towel, and smiled at the pattern. Violet-blue morning glories trumpeted across the corner, and she closed her eyes for a moment to imagine just how well they'd match the pale blue cabinets in Otto's house. Otto would be here for supper in less than an hour. Tonight they'd choose which Bible verses and hymns they wanted for the wedding. In preparation for that, Mercy had marked her favorite selections in the hymnal on the piano.

The family Bible always rested in the place of honor—a small oak table. Depending on the season, *Grossmuter* used to change the little tablecloths. Since her death last year, Mercy had followed the tradition. Fall's maple and sycamore leaves embroidered on ecru cotton gave way to holly and ivy linen at Christmas. During spring and summer, partly for fun and mostly because dust was so prevalent, a whole variety of scarves decorated with flowers and birds took turns each week. In honor of their wedding plans, Mercy had used the satin one with delicate orange blossoms and airy tatted lace edges.

The hope chest in her room held a plethora of such linens. She didn't need this dish towel at all, but she enjoyed needlework. The bodice of her wedding gown bore testament to that. She'd spent hour upon hour doing French cut lacework on the white cotton. They couldn't afford satin, but that didn't trouble her. Grossmuter had taught her to draw contentment from making ordinary things beautiful—and though it would be brazenly proud to speak the words aloud, Mercy believed her wedding gown to be the most beautiful thing she'd ever created.

Otto's mother came over yesterday to help her pin up the hem. She'd pronounced the dress exquisite. After Grossmuter died, Otto's mother had become Mercy's confidant and mentor. Helpful and kindhearted, Mrs. Kuntsler would be a fine mother-in-law.

The back door banged and feet pattered on the new linoleum floor. Jarred out of her musings, Mercy called out, "Walk in the house, Peter."

Her little brother swung around the corner and half shouted, "*Grossvater* said I can keep one of Freckle's puppies!"

Setting aside the almost-finished dish towel, Mercy laughed. "I suppose you've already decided which one."

"Come see!"

"Why don't we set the table first?"

"Mercy, I can't wait. Please come now."

She couldn't resist her eight-year-old brother's pleading brown eyes. "Okay. Let me check the roast first. The puppies aren't going anywhere."

Mercy glanced at the pan of green beans she'd cook in a little while, set potatoes on to boil, and peeked under the flour-dusted towel to be sure the dough was rising. The yeasty smell promised tasty rolls.

"You said you'd check the roast." Peter wriggled with impatience. "You're looking at everything else."

"You'll be glad later when you sit down to a good meal." She opened the door to the Sunshine stove and pulled out the gray roasting pan. Fragrant steam billowed as she lifted the lid. "Mmm." Quickly, she clanged the lid back down and pushed the pan back into the oven. No use letting out any moisture. Grossvater and Otto both loved gravy, so she'd want every last ounce of drippings she could get.

"Otto eats a lot," Peter said as she took his hand and started toward the barn. "That roast better be really big."

"Men who labor hard work up hearty appetites. Otto works hard, so he eats a lot. So does Grossvater. Someday, you'll do the same thing when you're doing a man's work around here."

Peter's lower lip poked out. "I work hard around here."

"Yes, you do." She resisted the urge to ruffle his wind-tousled brown curls. She hadn't meant to hurt his feelings. "Fast as you're growing, you'll soon be a man."

His face brightened. With that issue resolved, he seemed to concentrate on their destination. Peter tugged on her hand, silently urging her to walk faster.

Mercy wished she'd taken time to put on her shoes. Grossvater scolded her whenever she came out to the barn barefooted. It was just that with the oven's heat and spring sunshine, she'd peeled off her shoes and stockings in the house.

"If I guess which puppy you want," she teased Peter, "you have to gather eggs this week."

"Nuh-unh!" Peter yanked away and streaked ahead.

Caught up in his joy, Mercy laughed and ran after him. Early evening sun slanted into the barn, lending a golden glow to everything in sight. A horse whinnied, feet shuffled the straw-covered ground, and Freckle growled.

Mercy's eyes hadn't yet adjusted to the dim place, but she guessed what was happening. "Peter, be careful. Mamas don't take kindly to someone handling their babies."

A muffled sound made her stop and tilt her head. Something wasn't right. It was then that she saw Grossvater's legs and boots sticking out from a stall. She cried out in alarm.

"Shut up."

Mercy spun to the side. Cold horror washed over her. A stranger stood three feet away. Light glinted off the wicked-looking knife he held to Peter's throat.

Chapter 2

What do you think?" Connant Gilchrist swung his arm in a grandiose gesture.

Robert took in the room with nothing short of delight. "It's perfect. And so modern!"

"Old Doc Neely's widow didn't know what to do with it. She sold the house and moved back to Boston to be with her daughter. The office—well, she told the mayor she reckoned the town folks bought most of this when they paid Doc for his services. The city council voted to pass it on to the next qualified physician."

"It sure pays to have friends in the right place at the right time," Chris said as he tested the examination table by pressing his palms downward on it.

Sturdy. Robert assessed the table with glee. He'd worked on many a patient who lay on a wobbly dining trestle. *Good height, too. I won't have to hunch over when I perform surgery.*

"You came in through the waiting room." Connant jerked a thumb toward a wide flight of stairs. "Two rooms up there—Doc Neely kept one as a sick room and used the other for himself on nights he needed to stay and keep watch on a patient."

"Stove there is big enough to cook on when you're not boiling instruments," Duncan said. "After being crammed in that ship, even a small bedchamber will feel roomy."

Connant nodded. "You can ask the bank for a loan or wait till you save up a bit, but the lot here's plenty big enough. You might want to be building a wee house and a shop for Duncan in the back."

"So the land is ours?" Robert gave his childhood friend a startled look.

"Aye, and why not? I put a stipulation in the contract, though." His grin looked smug as could be. "Says you have to stay here five years, else the land and all of the supplies go to the next doctor."

"That's more than fair."

Christopher's face darkened. "Is there a problem so no one wants to stay here?"

"Flash floods, scorching summers, and occasional tornadoes. Worst of all, the cook at the diner serves charcoal instead of food." Connant recited those flaws in a gratingly cheerful tone. "As my memory serves me, none of the lot of you ever did more in a kitchen than burn perfectly good food to cinders."

"True," Robert groaned. The best he could say about the food in the steerage compartment of the *Anchoria* was that it filled a stomach. Then again, the same could be said of anything the Gregor men cooked.

He walked over to the cabinet containing pharmaceuticals and noted a generous bottle of bicarbonate of soda. Good thing, that. More often than not, if they cooked for themselves, the Gregor men ended up needing bicarb to settle their bellies. He continued to scan the bottles and vials. All bore neatly printed labels and sat in alphabetical order. "Atropine. Belladonna. Calomel. Cascara sagrada. Chloroform," he read aloud. "I take it there's not a local apothecary since the supply here is so complete?"

"That's right. I have a key for the file cabinet. Doc kept his patient books locked in there."

"Good. Good." Privacy was important, and Robert planned to maintain it. Nonetheless, it would be wise for him to read the records so he'd be familiar with the cases he'd be taking on.

He turned toward the filing cabinet and made note of the fact that both drawers locked. *I'll move some of those bottles and vials into the second drawer.* In the years he attended school, he'd seen more than a few patients grow dependent on certain elixirs and compounds. At the earliest opportunity, he'd lock away most of the laudanum, cocaine muriate, and morphine sulfate.

Duncan looked down at his hands and made a face. "Half the soot from that train fell on me. We'd best wash up, even if the food at that diner turns out to be as black as the mess on our shirts."

Duncan and Christopher stripped off their shirts over at the washstand. "You're a filthy mess, boy-o," Duncan teased Chris.

"No more than you." Chris nudged him to the side. "But the admission galls me. Fill the pitcher again. I'm planning to scrub my head, and you can rinse it. I'll return the favor."

"I should go first. You've such a big head you'll use up all of the water!"

Robert let their good-natured horseplay fade as he continued to walk about the office, opening drawers and taking stock of what was on hand. *In my wildest dreams I never thought this is what I'd find. Everything I read said how backward the American West is, but this is the best medical setup I've ever seen. Holy Father, help me to use these things to Your glory.*

"Quit daydreaming and wash up. We're hungry," Chris called over to him.

Rob looked at his brothers. "I'm not daydreaming. I was standing here thinkin' on how proud Da would be to see such a grand arrangement."

"Aye, he would." Duncan nodded.

"True." Chris nodded curtly then tacked on in a raspy tone, "But he'd not want us to starve half to death whilst you gawked around. Let's go eat."

Duncan walked back to the waiting room where their trunks sat. "I'll get your clean shirt."

The cool water refreshed Robert. He scrubbed, enjoying the astringent scent of the soap. He moaned aloud at the simple pleasure of Connant pouring a pitcher of water over his head to wash out the dust, soot, and soap.

Dripping wet, shirtless, and with his suspenders hanging down, he wheeled around when someone burst through the door to the building.

"Sheriff!" A strapping man swayed in the doorway. "I killed him."

"Killed who?" Connant pushed the man into the nearest chair. "Who did you kill, Otto?"

"Don't know."

Robert assessed the man quickly. His eyes were wide with shock, his whole frame shook, and he'd been violently sick all over the front of himself. "Are you hurt?"

"No."

"Tell me what happened," Connant rapped out.

"They're hurt."

"Who?" Connant demanded.

"Mercy." Otto groaned, then leaned forward and retched.

Robert automatically held out the towel even though nothing came up. He turned toward the luggage to grab his bag.

Duncan had opened the trunk and gotten out shirts. He tossed one to Robert. Christopher's shirt hung open, but he'd moved on toward the next item of business. He was strapping on his gun.

"The Steins live about three miles out," Connant said as they all barreled through the door. He grabbed the reins to his own sorrel mare and yanked Robert up behind him. "That's Otto's horse," he told Christopher.

Christopher said nothing. He was swinging up into the saddle as Connant set off.

Robert leaned forward. "How many in the family?"

"Three. Old man and his two grandkids. Girl's engaged to Otto; the boy's a mere lad."

They dismounted and entered the house first. Something was burning in the stove, but the place lay empty. Chris and Duncan had gone toward the barn. "Here!" Chris bellowed.

Duncan exited the barn carrying a schoolboy. Blood dripped from a lump on the boy's head. Robert determined he was breathing well as Duncan rasped, "Old man's alive."

Once inside the barn, Robert paused by the body of a man. Connant had his pistol drawn and shoved Robert ahead. "It's not Stein."

"Back here," Christopher called. He squatted beside an old man and was slicing through his britches with a knife.

The lanky older man lay unconscious. Robert shouldered past Chris and knelt by the man's chest to quickly assess his condition. *Pale. Clammy. Shock. Breathing slow. Pulse thready.* An ugly bruise on his jaw proved he'd fought, but the real injury was impossible to miss. The pitchfork in his thigh hadn't hit an artery, but the extent of the damage couldn't be determined yet.

A young blond cradled the old man's head in her lap. She was tenderly smoothing his brow with her shaky hand, but the sight of her made Robert's stomach lurch. Her dress was torn, and hay clung to the back of her shoulders and hair. Her left eye was starting to swell shut, and other marks at her throat and wrists let him know she, too, had been hurt.

Robert knew he could patch the old man back together. The girl bore wounds no man could heal.

—⁓—

She knew the sheriff. The black-haired men were strangers. The first one—the one with the gun—scared her; the one who knelt closer touched Grossvater with a mixture of confidence and care. He looked her in the eye and spoke in a low tone, "I'll be able to fix him up. He'll be fine."

He sounded reassuring, but Mercy couldn't respond.

"My brother's going to take that out of his leg, and I'll hold a compress on it to keep it from bleeding. We'll be moving him into the house. Do ye ken what I'm telling you, lass?"

She swallowed and nodded.

Grossvater moaned a little when they did the deed, and she bit back a cry.

" 'Tis a good sign that he's feeling his leg, lass. I'm thinking the wound will make a mess of his bed. Is your dining table sturdy?"

She nodded and led them inside.

Another stranger in her kitchen looked much like the other two. He had Peter sitting in a chair and was dabbing at a knot on her brother's head. Peter jabbered about the puppies.

"This is Dr. Gregor, Mercy," the sheriff said as he gave the kind-voiced man's shoulder a quick pat. "He'll help your granddad."

She wrapped her arms about her ribs and stepped back.

"I could use some bandages. Do you have any?"

Mercy went to the cabinet where they kept the liniment, Epsom salt, and bandages. She set all of the bandages at the head of the table.

"There's a fine help." He pulled out a chair and patted the seat. "You sit here. If your grandda wakes, you'll be nearby. I'm wanting you to drink this for me, too." He set down a glass of water.

She slipped around the edge of the room and did as he directed, then watched in silence as he used the things from his black leather bag. Nothing he said seemed real. Most of it was muffled, but the tone and cadence lulled her.

Finally, he finished tending Grossvater. After he knotted the bandage in place, he took Grossvater's pulse again.

"Well?" one of the other men asked.

"I'm cautiously optimistic. Let's put him to bed."

The sheriff and the other man carried Grossvater to his bedroom, and the doctor took a look at the bump on Peter's head. "Nothing wrong there this won't cure." He drew a glass tube from his medical bag and pulled out a sourball.

"Thanks!" Peter popped the candy into his mouth and regained his usual, cocky grin.

The doctor turned and held out his hand to Mercy. "Let's go see to things."

When she stood, her legs felt rubbery. Even so, she didn't take his hand. They walked across the kitchen, but to her surprise, he murmured, "They'll put your grandda in a nightshirt for you."

"Oh. Yes. Thank you."

He didn't touch her, yet his nearness made her sidestep. He pushed open the door to her room.

Mercy stared inside. *The tub. What is the tub doing in my room? And who put out my nightgown? It's not bedtime yet.*

"Miss Stein."

She jumped at the sound of her name.

"I'll stay out here and make sure no one bothers you. I thought you might want to bathe. Afterward, I'll see to your bruises and such."

Once in her room, Mercy locked the door. She didn't want to undress with those men here, but she caught sight of herself in her mirror and choked back a sob. Her dress was in tatters and her hair hung in snarls. Those were just the outward things.

I can't stay like this. Grossvater and Peter need me. Her hands shook so badly, she could scarcely undress. Everything took great effort. It hurt to move. She stepped into the big galvanized tub, then knelt. All of the scrubbing in the world couldn't make her feel clean.

Chapter 3

The thin walls of the house didn't block out the sound of her weeping. Robert and Duncan exchanged a glance.

"Mercy's crying." The lad stopped eating the inside bits of the roast Duncan salvaged for him. "Does she need a hug?"

"She's upset that the bad man hurt you and your grandda." Duncan tapped the edge of the plate to divert the boy.

Peter wrinkled his nose. "You said Grossvater is going to be fine. I'll go tell Sis my head doesn't hurt too much."

Duncan put a restraining hand on the boy's arm. "Doctor will tell her. Hearing it from him will be more reassuring."

"Is she scared that bad man will come back?"

Connant and Chris were out in the barn at this very moment, loading the body onto a buckboard. Duncan shook his head. "I give you my word, lad—he'll never bother you again. Now you finish eating, then we'll chop up the crisp bits of that roast and go feed them to your dog. After whelping, a mama dog needs lots of food."

After they'd left with the body and while Duncan took Peter out to feed the dog, Mercy's door opened. Instead of putting on her nightwear, she'd donned a rust-colored calico dress. Avoiding looking at Robert or speaking, she sidled into the other bedroom.

Robert stood by the door and watched as she smoothed the quilt over the old man's chest, then combed back an errant lock of his white hair. Her hand shook.

Though she'd washed her hair, it was too thick to towel dry well. Wisps that didn't make it into the simple bun started to coil around her wan face and nape, reinforcing a vulnerability that tore at him.

She didn't seem in a hurry to leave her grandda's side, and Robert struggled with that fact. If she drew comfort from seeing the old man was all right, that was good. She deserved solace whatever the source. Then again, he needed to examine her and hoped to have it finished before Peter came back into the house.

Hooking his thumbs into his suspenders so he'd appear friendly and casual, Rob said quietly, "He's resting well. With time and attention, he'll be up and about."

"Thank you."

226

She whispered the words so quietly, he almost didn't hear her. The hoarse quality to her whisper worried him. *Is she having trouble breathing? She has marks around her throat. If she screamed...* Robert shut down that line of thought immediately. It caused his ire to flare brighter, and she needed him to stay composed. He made the next overture. "Come out to the kitchen. I'll examine your eye."

She ducked her head and turned to the side, as if to hide the bruising, swollen eye.

"If we put a cool compress to it, you'll not look so bruised tomorrow." He paused. "Your little brother's out feeding the beasts in the barn."

She shuddered. "Peter—"

"We'll talk about him." Robert tilted his head toward the kitchen table. "Come."

'Twasn't an easy span of time, those next minutes. Mercy Stein left her grandfather's side only to hear about her brother's condition. Wary as could be, she tried to keep as much distance from Robert as possible.

Robert turned his back on her and took a dishcloth from the rod by the pump. He dampened it, then methodically folded it into a compress. Each move he made was deliberate in an effort to keep from spooking the lass. As he drew close to her, she flinched.

"There, now. This will make a difference." He extended his hand and offered her the compress.

"I don't need it. Tell me about Peter."

The lass has grit. Robert laid the compress on the table easily within her reach and turned back to his bag. "Other than the bump on his noggin, he's right as rain."

The corner of her mouth twitched in acknowledgment.

After taking a few items from his bag and closing it, Robert approached her again. This time, he pulled out a chair and sat at an angle from her—close enough to touch, far enough that she wouldn't feel crowded. "This is witch hazel."

He opened his other hand. Cotton wadding tumbled free. "I'll dab this on your temple, throat, and wrists. It'll lessen the soreness."

She cringed back into her chair. "Don't need it."

"Miss Stein, did you hear Sheriff Gilchrist? You know I'm a doctor."

"I have witch hazel if I decide to use it."

"I'm here to help you," he said gently. He waited a beat, then stated, "Something happened in the stable."

Her breath caught.

"Women are delicate, easily hurt. It would be wise for me to—"

"Leave me alone!"

He stood and picked up the cotton wadding piece by piece, then took up the Thayer's witch hazel. "I'm going to take these into your chamber and bring out the tub. You want your privacy, and I'll honor that. Witch hazel is very safe and mild.

A woman can use it anywhere she hurts. Do you understand me?"

He got no response and didn't wait beyond a heartbeat. His shoes made the only sound in the small wooden home as he went to her chamber. A tidy little place it was. An airy green-and-white quilt covered the iron bedstead, and matching cushions covered both a small chair and a dowry trunk.

A dowry trunk—no doubt filled with all sorts of useful linens she'd prettified as she dreamed of a happy future. Robert winced. The dreams could still come true, but she'd not go to her wedding with the joy of an innocent bride. Otto knew already. At least she'd be spared having to tell him.

Lily of the valley. He inhaled again. The scent from her soap lingered in her room. Robert lifted the tub and carried it through the kitchen to the back door. As he emptied the water into a flower bed, Duncan and little Peter came strolling back. Peter went on inside while Duncan stopped.

"I'll spend the night here. I want to be sure the old man's all right when he awakens. The lass isn't in any condition to do much, and if they needed help, the boy's too young to fetch it."

Duncan nodded. "Should I stay?"

"Nae. 'Tis already hard enough on the lass. The last thing she needs is folks hovering."

—⚶—

Hours later, Robert moved from the old man's bedside and peered over the trundle to be sure Peter was sleeping well. Mr. Stein had awakened an hour ago. He answered questions appropriately and worried about Mercy and Peter before slipping back to sleep. In a day or two, he'd learn the truth. For now, he slept with the same innocence as his grandson, deaf to the sound of his granddaughter's sobs.

Where's Otto? Connant said she and Otto were engaged to be married. If ever a woman needed comfort, now was the time. She deserved all of the solace and reassurance Otto could give.

Robert carried the kerosene lantern with him to the parlor. A photograph of a woman and the old man in his younger days standing in front of a different house was propped beside another photograph of a family of four. The third photograph was of the children with their grandparents. It didn't take much to deduce that Mercy and her little brother were orphaned and reared by their grandfather. *Puir lass hasna had an easy life.*

Even if Peter hadn't knelt and said a bedtime prayer, Robert would have known this was a believer's home. A well-thumbed hymnal, a much-loved Bible, and little colored picture cards from Sunday school bespoke that these people lived their faith. *And their faith was just put to an awful test.*

He didn't want to snoop. Casual observations were fine, but this parlor held too many personal touches. Robert went to the kitchen stove where he stirred up the coals. Spending the night here was a prudent choice, but it wasn't a comfortable one.

He wanted to be sure Mr. Stein didn't brew a fever and hadn't lost his mental abilities. Between the punctures in the old man's leg and the bump on the back of his head, either of those complications could occur. So far, neither had materialized. Robert had confidence in his own professional skills, but medical science could only do so much. His faith in the Great Physician's healing knew no bounds, and he sought wisdom and assistance from the Lord for each case. In regard to Mr. Stein's welfare, his prayer was being answered.

Robert also stayed for Mercy's sake. He knew she didn't want him there, but folks often resented a physician's presence because it underscored problems they wanted to deny. She might seek care from him still; he'd discovered that in the dark of night, folks sometimes could ask a doctor things they couldn't speak of in daylight.

He'd set a pot of coffee on to boil after he tucked the boy in for the night. Sickened by the violence these people had suffered, Rob hadn't bothered to eat. Grumbling in his stomach now made him lift the towel draped over a pan. The yeasty smell drifted up to him as he gazed at the dough that had risen and finally fallen flat. Fried in a dab of bacon grease, such dough still gave an empty belly satisfaction.

The scents of fried bread and coffee filled the house. Robert sat down at the table and ate by the light of that single lantern until a faint creak made him look up.

Still wearing her calico dress and clutching a shawl about her, Mercy slipped out of her own room and directly into the other bedchamber.

Robert walked to the doorway and whispered, "Peter's been sleeping like a bear. Your grandfather woke about an hour and a half ago. He knew where he was. He's able to move his leg and wiggle his toes—both excellent signs. I expect him to make a full recovery."

"I'll watch over them. You should go."

"I've no doubt you'd hover like a guardian angel if you had the chance, but 'tisn't necessary. I'm stuck here. I've no horse, and even if I did, I couldn't find my way back to town since I just arrived today. After I change the dressing on his leg in the morning, I'll leave."

She pulled the shawl more closely about her shoulders.

"You've yet to slumber, and you need your rest. I've powders in my bag that will help you fall asleep."

"No, thank you."

Robert grudgingly admitted to himself that Mercy shared a trait of his own—she knew her mind and stuck to her plans. Often, that perseverance paid off, but in this case, her stubbornness resulted in needless suffering. He decided it wasn't worth arguing with her. If anything, she needed to feel she'd regained control—however simple or slight it might be.

"Forgive me, Miss Stein. You're barefoot and likely catching a chill whilst I natter away the night. I'll go back to my coffee. If you'd like, I can pour you a cup."

"I'll retire." Though she stated her plan, she made no move to carry it out.

Robert turned and went back to the table. So that was the way of it. She'd refused to brush past him to leave the room. He couldn't fault her for being skittish; she had just cause to be wary—extremely wary. He'd have to earn her trust, and from this encounter, he reckoned it would take a good long while.

—⁓—

Mercy woke and promised herself it was just a bad dream, but that false hope disappeared the minute she rolled out of bed and hurt all over. Deep purple-black ringed her left eye, and she turned away from the mirror as she pinned her braid into a bun.

The door to Grossvater's room stood open. A quick peek reassured her that he and Peter still slept soundly. Usually, Grossvater would be stirring, if not up by now. Knowing how he'd chafe at being kept in bed, Mercy hoped he'd sleep late.

She tiptoed past the doctor, too. He'd fallen asleep with his head resting on his folded arms at the dining table. The settee in the parlor was far too short for a man of his height to stretch out on. Just seeing him made her balk. She'd need to speak to him before Grossvater woke up. Would he honor her request to keep what happened from Grossvater?

Otto. Surely Otto wouldn't tell anyone. He'd shelter her from the humiliation of others knowing the full truth of what had happened. He'd responded to her screams and come—too late to stop the worst—but Otto knew what happened and killed that awful man. *I'm glad he's dead. Glad. He can't come back to hurt me again.*

Steeling herself, she stepped into the barn. Bile rose, and she swallowed it. Just off to her right was where *that man* died at Otto's hand. Another few steps and she was near the place where he'd held the knife to her sweet little brother's neck, then struck him in the head. Her legs shook so badly, she could hardly walk deeper into the barn. Over there, in that straw, he'd. . .

She stumbled and pressed the back of her hand to her mouth to keep from crying out. Evalina's lowing jarred her back to what she needed to do. *I can go on. I can. I'll do my chores and make it through the morning. Then I'll make it through the afternoon.*

Mercy rested her cheek against Evalina's warm side and listened to the *shhh-shhh-shhh* as the bucket filled with the rhythmic motions of her hands. The smell of milk, hay, and cow were so common. After promising herself that staying busy with tasks would keep her from remembering, Mercy discovered she'd been lying to herself.

How could life ever be ordinary again? Swollen as her left eye had become, she could see only a narrow strip out of it. The cuffs on her sleeves rubbed against the tender bruises on her wrists.

Shame and embarrassment kept her from accepting care from the new doctor. He'd tried to be helpful, but Mercy wanted to forget what happened. The aches in her body, heart, and soul wouldn't let her forget, though. The doctor said he'd leave this morning. She hoped he'd keep his word—in fact, that he'd sneak in, check on Grossvater's leg, and be gone by the time she got back to the house. She didn't want to face him—or anyone—today.

Pouring the milk into the separator strained her wrists. Everything she'd done this morning—combing her hair, washing her face, milking the cow—all of the simple pleasures of life had been tainted by painful reminders. Mercy felt a bolt of hatred. She'd never hated before, but she knew exactly what the emotion was. *I'm glad Otto killed him.* The thought went through her mind again. *Even hell is too good for a wicked man like that.*

A roar of pain echoed from the house.

Chapter 4

Mercy tossed aside the milk pail and ran for the house. She tore through the door and ran full tilt into Grossvater's bedroom, only to bump smack into a broad back. She shoved the doctor aside and stopped cold. The sheriff stood by the bedside, and anguish contorted Grossvater's dear face. She'd seen that look only once before—when Grossmuter died.

Grossvater turned his head and looked at her. Tears filled his eyes.

"What have you done?" she cried to the sheriff.

Hands curled around her shoulders from behind. She immediately struggled to free herself.

"Shh, lass."

"You told! You didn't have to tell him." Tears she couldn't hold back broke forth as her knees gave out. Strong hands gently tightened about her—not in binding restraint, but in comfort. The doctor kept her from collapsing.

"There'll be time to talk later," the deep baritone said from over her shoulder.

Mercy buried her face in her hands as the doctor turned her and led her from the room. He took her to the kitchen, leaned against the cupboard, and held her as she fell apart. "Why?" She finally looked up at him. "Why didn't you protect him? You could have spared him."

"Connant told him, Mercy." Slowly, he wiped tears from her cheeks.

"He had no business, no right—"

His blue eyes were somber and his face grim. "Peter was already awake. I sent him over to the neighboring farm with a request to borrow some honey. Your grandfather woke, and his first words were about the two of you."

"You didn't have to—"

"One look at your face, and he would have known, Mercy. No man could mistake the truth."

She closed her eyes and bowed her head. *So everyone who ever looks at me again will know? Lord, how will I ever endure such shame?*

He clasped her to his chest and held her there. His heart beat steadily beneath her ear. Quietly he said, "I'm sure Connant wanted to spare you from having to tell him, Mercy. You're worried about protecting your grandfather; Connant was trying to make this easier on you."

She pushed away. "Easier? Easier! Nothing about this is easy. It is awful. It is evil."

"You're right. What happened was evil."

Sheriff Gilchrist's boots shuffled on the plank floor. He cleared his throat. "Mercy? Your grandfather wants you."

Mercy started to cross the floor, then paused. She didn't look at the sheriff or the doctor. Clutching her hands together, she murmured, "You men should go now. There is nothing for you to do here." Her voice caught, then she added, "Too much has already been said and done."

As she entered Grossvater's bedroom, she heard the screen door shut. *If only I could run over, slam the door, and lock out the world.*

"Mercy," Grossvater said from the bed. He'd wiggled his way up until he sat propped against the headboard. His face was ashen, his eyes haunted. It broke her heart when he silently stretched his arms wide to take her to his breast.

She wanted to fly across the room as she had when she was a small girl and lost her parents. He'd held her tight and provided a secure, loving life. Grossvater and Grossmuter did everything they could to fix her broken world. Grossvater couldn't fix this, though. She was a woman now, and she'd have to live with this tragedy. Mercy tried hard to control her tumultuous feelings as she walked toward him with measured steps. "How are you feeling? How is your head? Your leg?"

"I'll heal. But you, sweetheart—"

She sat on the edge of the bed and carefully leaned against him. His arms enfolded her. "Don't say anything, Grossvater. Please, don't."

He bowed his head and kissed her hair.

—⚬⚬—

Mercy stopped abruptly at the sight of the full egg basket by the chicken coop. *Who's been here?* Chills raced up her arms. Evalina lowed over in the pasture. *I left her in the barn!*

Mouth dry and heart pounding, Mercy started to back toward the house. *It can't be that man again. Otto killed him. Otto—he probably came over to help. That's it.* She let out a shaky breath. *Sturdy, reliable, devoted Otto. He still loves me!*

The grating sound of a shovel indicated someone was in the barn, mucking out the stable. Yes, Otto would have thought of the animals' welfare. The knot between her shoulders lessened, and she called out, "Otto?"

Footsteps sounded in the barn.

She tried to smile, but doing so pulled the skin. That tightness, teamed with the way she could only see a slice of anything from her left eye, registered. *He'll see my face. I shouldn't have called to him.* Mercy spun toward the side.

"Whoa!"

A scream ripped from her chest.

"I wasn't meaning to alarm you, lass." The doctor's hands hovered beside her arms, but he didn't make any contact.

Shuffling backward, Mercy called out, "Otto!"

"Rob?" A man stood in the barn's doorway.

It's not Otto. He hasn't come ever since—

"I startled Miss Stein, Chris. 'Tis all." The doctor looked at her. "I came by to check on your grandda."

Mercy made no reply. She led him to the house and stood by while he changed her grandfather's dressing. As he tied it into place, he said, "Mr. Stein, whilst you're recovering, you'll need a strong back and an extra pair of hands about the place. I've brothers—either Christopher or Duncan will ride out each morning to help."

"I could use the help, but I need to be up."

The doctor nodded. "That you do. Your muscles will weaken if left unused. My brother Duncan made you a walking stick. I'll allow you to use it 'round the house, but 'tis all. No taking the steps off the porch for another few days, else you'll suffer a terrible setback."

After Grossvater was up in a chair in the parlor, the doctor left. Mercy fussed around in the house all day. Though her hands stayed busy, her mind spiraled into a near panic. Four endless days had passed, but Otto hadn't yet come over. She took bread from the oven and searched for something—anything else to do.

Heavy footsteps sounded on the veranda, then someone knocked. "I'll get it," Grossvater said.

Though she didn't know that he ought to be moving around much, Mercy allowed Grossvater to answer the door. She didn't want anyone to see her.

"Come, Mercy." For the first time since *it* happened, Grossvater sounded like his old self.

Mercy wiped her hands on the hem of her apron and went to him. As long as she kept her face turned, no one would have to see—

"Otto's here." Grossvater's words stunned her. Otto never knocked. Fully assured of his welcome, he always barged in.

"I killed a man." Anguish permeated Otto's stark words. Emotion contorted his features. "With my own hands, I killed him."

"You did." Mercy didn't move an inch. *Look at me. No, don't. But at least draw me into the shelter of your arms.*

"It was a bad thing." Otto's voice was nothing more than a ragged whisper.

Mercy couldn't hold back a strangled sound. The man she loved was trying to reassure her and chose his words so as not to shame her. The doubts and worries the past days fostered gave way to relief. She stepped forward, finally free to lean into Otto's consolation. Her arms barely started to close around him; her bruised cheek scarcely grazed the fabric of his shirt when he jerked away from her.

Mercy's head snapped back. "Ot—"

"I killed a man!" He stared at her. This wasn't the Otto she knew. His eyes weren't sparkling with laughter or lit with gentle love.

Her arms dropped woodenly to her sides.

Grossvater hobbled closer and managed to keep his balance while still wrapping an arm around her shoulders. "You did your best, Otto. You tried to protect those you love."

Leather creaked loudly in the awkward silence as Otto shifted from one boot to the other.

"With God's help, we will get beyond this," Grossvater said.

I don't know that I'll ever get beyond it.

Otto cleared his throat. "The wedding."

Not our *wedding?* The *wedding?* Mercy started to tremble anew.

"It's thoughtful of you, Otto, to give my granddaughter a little time."

In that moment, Mercy knew the truth. Otto's expression told her more than words could. The brutal truth hit her. "There will be no wedding."

"Mercy—" Grossvater began.

The dainty ring burned as she twisted it off her finger. "I no longer hold you to your promise."

Although Otto didn't reach for it, he didn't make an attempt to try to reassure her that their love could weather this catastrophe.

Tightening his hold on her, Grossvater growled, "There's no reason to be hasty—"

"I do not blame her," Otto said thickly. "I cannot live with myself, knowing I have killed a man."

"There's nothing wrong," Grossvater said, "with a man protecting those he loves."

Mercy trembled—unsure of what to do. *Can it be that Otto needs my love and acceptance now, more than ever, just as I need his?*

Otto looked at her. Never once had she seen him cry, but tears traced down his sunburned cheeks. "It was not about protection. He'd already done his worst. I sought vengeance." His hands came up and formed an ever-tightening circle. "I took a man's life. How am I to know God would not have redeemed him someday? All that was right and pure between us—what he did couldn't ruin that. What I did— that defiled everything."

Grossvater took the ring from her nerveless fingers and passed it to Otto.

—⁂—

"Excuse me." Robert pushed through a gaggle of women at the mercantile and frowned. "Stand back. 'Tis too close in here." If it weren't for the cracker barrel behind Mercy and Carmen Rodriguez propping her up, the lass would be flat out on the plank floor.

His inclination was to scoop her up, but Robert quelled that at once. Mercy spooked too easily. If she roused much, she'd likely fall apart as he carried her to his office. He knelt beside her and hoped she couldn't hear the suppositions the busybodies behind him whispered. When the community heard of Otto killing a man, Otto's mother sought to defend her son—but at Mercy's expense. As if the poor lass hadn't suffered enough, she'd been denied the ability to keep what had happened private.

Miss Rodriguez used her hankie to blot Mercy's brow. "If you help her over to my house, I can see to her. It's probably just. . .constriction."

Robert slid one hand behind Mercy's neck and unfastened the uppermost button on her high-collared shirtwaist. Taking her pulse necessitated unfastening the mother-of-pearl buttons on her cuff. Mercy's lids began to flutter, and he announced, "With that stove roaring, 'tis hotter than Lucifer's laundry pot in here. Miss Stein? Ah, there we are." He tilted her wan face toward his. "The heat's claimed you. Miss Rodriguez here is going to accompany us back to my office."

"I—I just need a moment." Mercy's words sounded every bit as faint as she looked.

"I agree." He nodded. "A short rest and a nice dipper of water will go a long way toward helping you."

Miss Rodriguez patted her. "I'll stay right beside you. The nice doctor is going to help you up now." She drew closer and whispered, "Mercy, he's strong. He can carry you."

The very last vestige of color bled from Mercy's face.

"She'll lean on me. We all understand the necessity." Robert pulled Mercy to her feet and wound his arm around her slender waist.

Back in his office, Robert managed to get Mercy alone in the examination room. She promptly declared, "Truly, I've recovered. It was just the heat."

"I'm not so sure of that."

Primly buttoning her cuff, she said, "If it's not the heat, then it must be something I ate."

Robert pressed a glass of water into her hands in order to keep her seated on his examination table. He asked several questions, purposefully posing them in a rambling fashion so she wouldn't have a sense of what he needed to ascertain.

"This is unnecessary. It was simply the heat. Just as you said at the mercantile, all I needed was water and a short rest. I'm better." She looked ready to make a dash for freedom.

Sick to the depths of his soul, Robert rested his hand on her forearm. "No, you're not. Miss Stein, you're with child."

Chapter 5

Cold dread washed over her. For weeks now, she'd lived in terror of this possibility. Night and day, she'd begged God to spare her this. The last two weeks, her anxiety had mushroomed. Still, she didn't want to believe it could be so. "I truly must go." Mercy twisted to the side and slid off the table.

"Miss Stein—"

She shook off the doctor's hand. "Grossvater needs me." Desperate to get away, she opened the door out into his waiting room.

Carmen Rodriguez hopped to her feet. "Are you feeling better now? You've never swooned before."

"Then I suppose it was my turn. I really must get home."

"I'm due to pay a call on your grandda." Dr. Gregor picked up his black leather satchel. "I'll accompany you."

"Oh, that's so kind of you. I'd have worried myself sick if Mercy went home alone."

"Mercy!" Peter burst into the doctor's office.

"What are you doing out of school?"

"Teacher sent David to get more chalk from the mercantile. He told me—"

"Tales," Mercy said flatly. "We do not listen to tales, Peter. Now you march right on back to school."

The doctor waited until her little brother left, then he chuckled. "And to think I always thought growing up with *older* brothers was difficult!" As Carmen laughed, he smoothly took hold of Mercy's elbow. "Now that everything is settled, let's go see your grandda."

"He's fine. You saw him, yourself, at church just yesterday—and the two Sundays before that, as well."

"Aye, that I did. After six weeks of healing, the time's come to regain the strength in his limb."

"Can you do that?" Carmen pressed a hand to her bosom. "It's nothing short of miraculous how you didn't have to amputate. No one expected him to ever walk again."

"God gets credit for all miracles," the doctor said. "I take responsibility for the more ordinary—like teaching Mr. Stein some movements so his strength returns."

"And that Mercy rests," Carmen added. "Good-bye, then. Oh! Mercy, Leonard brought over a pound of coffee. He said that's what you came to town for."

Using that as an excuse to break away from the doctor's hold, Mercy reached out and accepted the bag. "I'll be sure to thank him when I go get my horse." She knew the doctor didn't own a horse, so Mercy figured she'd neatly managed to get rid of him entirely.

She wasn't that fortunate. Five minutes later, as they rode out of town, he'd finished telling her about how his brother Chris had bought the dappled mare for a pittance because it had been in such sorry shape. Clearly his medical skills extended toward beasts, too.

He cleared his throat. "My apologies for speaking so much, but I assumed you didn't want anyone asking questions, so I dominated the conversation."

Surprised by his insight, Mercy still grasped at the opening he'd provided. "Dr. Neely said he'd taken an oath to give patients privacy. Did you take that same vow?"

"Aye. The Hippocratic Oath."

"Good. Then you are not going to tell anyone. . ." She couldn't bring herself to even say the words.

Dr. Gregor said nothing.

Terrified that a prompt agreement didn't spring from his lips, Mercy halted. So did he. Ever since *that day*, she'd hardly looked directly at anyone. Deeply shamed, she couldn't. But this was too important. "You took the oath. You must uphold it."

" 'Tisn't a secret that can be long kept."

"It can be kept until Grossvater is strong. Then I can go away." She tore her gaze away from him and stared off in the distance.

"Lass, your grandda willna be fully recovered for almost four more months. You'll not be able to hide the truth until autumn."

"Of course I can." *I have to.*

"I canna begin to imagine how difficult this is for you, but I'll be speaking plainly. Your brother will say something about you fainting. Even if you admonish Peter to remain silent, any one of a half dozen of the people who were in the mercantile will mention the episode to your grandda."

The reins slithered through her fingers. Everything was slipping through her fingers—her love, her reputation, and now even this.

The doctor leaned forward and collected a rein. Pressing it back into her hand, he murmured, "For your own sake as well as his, don't you think it would be best if we told him now?"

She gave no answer. They reached the farm shortly thereafter, and the doctor's brother sauntered in from the nearest field. Either or both of the doctor's brothers came each day. At first, they'd come into the house to ask Grossvater what needed to be done. As he'd improved, Grossvater made it a point to be out on the porch to meet them.

The doctor dismounted and helped her down. His brother strode over, and the two of them greeted each other as if they'd been separated for a year. The second Duncan turned her way, Mercy dipped her head.

"Your grandda is in the barn, Miss Stein. I brought over some of my tools, and he's repairing harnesses and the like."

"That was good of you. I'll go get lunch."

Duncan chuckled. "Only for yourself. We found the sandwiches you left and polished them off. Rob, while you're here, take a look at Freckle's runt."

"He's in the barn?"

"Aye." Duncan headed back out to the field.

The doctor looked at her. "Would you like to eat first?"

Rage swept through her. "First? The decision is mine to make."

"Yes, 'tis." He didn't pause for a second to frame his reply. "But Freckle isna about to let me near her wee little pup unless you're there."

He'd spoken the truth. Freckle didn't mind anyone playing with the other puppies, but she'd become unaccountably protective of the runt. Heaving a sigh, Mercy walked toward the barn. *It's only Monday. I'll have a few days as long as I make sure Peter says nothing.*

"*Schatze!* Did you have a nice trip to town?"

Mercy evaded the question. "Grossvater, look at you! I didn't know we had so many leather things."

A proud smile lit his face. "These are just the things that needed care. Most were still in working condition, but with a little attention, they'll last much longer."

The doctor set down his satchel. "That saddle is a thing of beauty."

"It was my son's." Grossvater gently buffed an edge. "Mercy's mama gave it to him the year they were married. Peter is about the age where he will treasure it."

"So you will give it to him for his birthday?" Mercy nodded. "He will be very pleased."

"If you're done riding for the day, I'll unsaddle your horse," the doctor offered.

"Ja, that is kind of you." Grossvater smiled. "And then I will ask you to help me hide this saddle."

Mercy added, "Peter's birthday is next month—on the fourth of July."

"There's a fine date." The doctor sauntered out to get her horse.

Independence Day... But I'll never be free again. In the doctor's absence, Mercy slipped away from Grossvater and leaned over Freckle's box. She scratched between the mutt's ears. The whole time the doctor unsaddled her horse, she lavished attention on Freckle and admired each pup. Finally, she lifted the runt. "I'll bring her right back."

"Duncan tells me the wee one isna feelin' so chipper."

Grossvater let out a deep sigh. "She crept out of the box today and followed Peter. While he was doing the milking, Evalina stepped on the runt's tail."

"Let's see." The doctor stepped closer. Mercy tried to hand him Dot, but he made a dismissive gesture. "I'll be better able to assess her tail if both hands are free."

His breath washed over her wrists, and Mercy longed to pull away. Deft and gentle, he examined the runt. The very last place he touched was its tail, and the pup whimpered.

"Ooch, now, there's a shame." The doctor crooked his forefinger and rubbed the runt between her ears, just as Mercy had done to Freckle. "Puir wee pup. Tail's broken."

"I feared that." Grossvater sounded grim. "Freckle's been licking it, but the skin's broken, and the runt'll get gangrene. We'll put it down before Peter gets home."

"He's blaming himself already," Mercy murmured.

"Now, that's premature." The doctor finally took Dot from her and cuddled the pup to the center of his broad chest.

Half an hour later, Mercy put Dot back with Freckle. "She doesn't have the part of her tail with the spot that we named her for."

"Stubby." The doctor's voice sounded vaguely humored.

Grossvater chortled. "Stubby! *Ja,* it is a good name."

Mercy straightened up.

"Mercy." Grossvater's voice suddenly sobered. "You do not laugh? *Was ist den loss?*"

What is the matter? Grossvater sometimes lapsed into German when he was emotional. He looked from her stricken expression to the doctor and back. Then he groaned and rubbed his hand down his face.

Everything in her wanted to scream a denial, to run. But no sound would come out of her mouth, and her feet wouldn't move.

The doctor pressed something into her hand. Mercy stared down at the handkerchief for a moment before she realized she was crying. Finally, she rasped, "I will go away."

"*Nein!*" Grossvater got to his feet and limped with the cane as fast as he could toward her.

"Are you wanting to be alone?" the doctor asked her softly as Grossvater approached.

Mercy nodded. A moment later, she and Grossvater wrapped their arms about one another. He stroked her back. "I won't let you go. You are not to blame, and neither is the child."

"But, Grossvater—" She couldn't put into words all she felt.

"No sneaking off to hide." He held her tighter. "I have worried there might be a child. I have prayed. This child—we will love it, for it is yours."

The ball in her throat made it hard to speak at all, but she managed a strangled whisper. "I don't know if I can."

"We can." Grossvater's voice held great determination. "Ja, with God's help, we can do this."

Mercy clung to him. *With God's help? Why did He not help me so all of this didn't happen? Even if just the baby didn't happen? How am I to trust Him to help me now, when He's ignored my cries for so long?*

———❦———

"Dr. Gregor?"

Rob halted and looked across the street. "Aye?"

Carmen Rodriguez motioned toward him. He crossed the road and joined her on her veranda. "I've been wondering. . ." she half whispered. Color filled her cheeks. "Mr. Stein is doing whatever you showed him to do, and his recovery is remarkable. I was wondering. . ."

When her voice trailed off, Rob accepted the glass of sweet tea she extended toward him and sat in a wicker chair. He'd intentionally waited until he knew what she wanted. Ever since Mercy swooned in the mercantile almost a month before, folks tried to get him to speak about her. Some meant well; others were gossipmongers. Either way, he refused to discuss any private matters. Since Miss Rodriguez wished to broach a different topic, he'd listen. "You were wondering?"

"Could I do the movements? Would they help me?"

He made no pretense at ignorance. The lass had a noticeable limp. "You were quite young when you broke your limb, weren't you?"

She nodded. "Doc Neely wanted to amputate, but Papa wouldn't consent to it."

"When you showed interest upon hearing about the therapy, I made the assumption that you were hopeful something might benefit you, as well." Rob looked her in the eyes. He'd learned early in his career that patients inevitably coped better with bad news when given the dignity of a direct response. "I took the liberty of examining the medical journal Dr. Neely kept. The problem is that your bones knit together in puir alignment. Motion exercises address muscular problems, not skeletal. I'm sorry I canna make a difference for you."

"I suppose," she said in a tight voice, "I should be grateful for what I have."

"I'm sure the Almighty never tires of hearing our gratitude." He looked out at the garden she tended every afternoon. "What happened? Just yesterday your garden was brimming with blossoms, and most of them are gone now."

"Ada Meister's wedding is tomorrow." She clenched her hands in her lap. "You know what they say—the woman who marries in June is a bride all her life."

Rob hitched a shoulder. "To my way of thinking, 'tisn't when you marry—'tis whom. Even so, it was kind of you to share your flowers with Miss Meister."

"Thank you."

They exchanged a few more pleasantries, then Rob excused himself. As he started down the steps, Otto Kunstler passed him. They exchanged nothing more than a polite nod, but Rob overheard him.

"Hello, Miss Rodriguez. Is your sister home?"

The rest of the afternoon passed with an assortment of cases that demanded the doctor's attention. His last patients were from two towns over. Suspecting that they, like Carmen Rodriguez, were hoping for a miracle, Rob took additional time with the Heims. In the end, all he could do was tell them the sad truth.

"I'm sorry, Mr. and Mrs. Heim, but you'll not be having any children."

Mrs. Heim sobbed quietly, and her husband held her close. He looked just as shattered. "Are you sure?"

"Aye." Rob explained the details as gently as he could.

Chester Heim heaved a sigh. "We were told the same by the doctor in Austin. We hoped he was wrong. Lena and I—we talked about it. If there is no hope for us to have a child of our own, we would consider adopting."

"If anything comes up, I'll keep you in mind."

Wearily washing his hands, Rob let out a long sigh. *Mercy is carrying a babe that was forced upon her; the Heims desperately want a child and cannot have one. It's not for me to question Your ways, Father, but I have to admit I dinna understand them. Common sense says the solution to everyone's problem is clear, yet that's man's planning and not Your wisdom. Unless, or until, You give me a clear sense that You want me to approach Mercy about relinquishing her babe, I'll wait in silence.*

"Kunstler!" Grossvater's voice sounded loudly through the open barn door.

Mercy swiftly set Stubby down next to Freckle and headed toward the other exit. Ever since Otto broke their engagement, the only time she'd seen him was at church. Never once had he offered to come help with the chores or crops when Grossvater was unable to work. Not once had his mother thought to bring by food. When gossips whispered about the babe Mercy carried, it hurt. But buried in that hurt was the hope that Mrs. Kunstler would come and speak privately with her, to let her know what to expect, to console her and promise to help with the birth. Those hopes were in vain. Mercy tugged on the barn's back door.

It was stuck.

Chapter 6

Otto would come inside and walk the length of the barn so he could inspect the reaper. For a moment, Mercy considered scrambling up into the hay loft. *No. This is my home.*

She sat back down beside Freckle's box and filled her skirts with puppies. A minute later, Grossvater and Otto came inside.

Otto caught sight of her and averted his gaze. Still, he kept coming. He stood above her and cleared his throat. "Miss Stein, those are fine hounds there."

Miss Stein? This man who was supposed to have been her husband now greeted her as if she were practically a stranger. Mercy looked down at the wiggly little bundles of fur and nodded. "Ja, they are fine, indeed."

To her relief, Grossvater leaned against the wall of the stall. "Even the runt is growing to good size."

"Everyone knows Freckle's pups all become good hunting dogs." Otto hunkered down and reached for a solid brown male. "Since the day you promised me a puppy, I've looked forward to claiming one."

Mercy sucked in a pained gasp as memories washed over her. *He used seeking a puppy as an excuse to come over, and he asked me to marry him that afternoon.* Unable to quell the emotions, she blurted out, "More than one promise was made that day."

Otto's head shot up. Finally, he looked at her. "So is that what you want? For the sake of a promise you would marry a man who cannot bear to look at you? Who, every time he sees you, remembers how he slew a man? You would want me to rear the child of the man I killed?"

"What I want?" Her voice shook. "Do you think I want any of what has happened? To bear the pain, the shame, and to carry a child? No! I don't want any of that. I wanted a man who would love me regardless of what life brought and who would stand beside me in the bad times. You were right to break your promise to wed me, because you are not that kind of man."

"Mercy," Grossvater said softly.

Her eyes swam with tears. "I do not know whether my grandfather is calling my name or reminding me to treat you with mercy."

"This has been very. . .difficult for both of us," Otto said.

One by one, she placed the puppies back in the box. "In three weeks, the pups will be weaned. We will reserve that one for you." She went into the house, opened the bottom drawer of her wardrobe, and pulled out a white bundle. Until now, she'd dared to hope that Otto would overcome his upset and realize his love for her was stronger than what had happened. He wouldn't.

Slowly, she unfolded the beautiful gown she was to have worn. All of it wouldn't fit in the stove at once, so she cut it. Piece by piece, she burned it. As the last threads burned, Mercy retied her apron strings. Her waist hadn't changed a bit. In time, it would expand, but she didn't know when—and she couldn't ask anyone. Never had she felt so alone.

—⁂—

"I thought to ask your opinion of this drawing." Rob laid the floor plan out on her dining table. "It's a house plan."

Drying her hands on a dish towel, Mercy said, "I've seen many plans in *American Woman's Home* and in *Ladies' Home Journal*."

"On the train from New York, everyone shared their books and magazines. *Scientific American* captured my attention. It featured some of George Barber's homes."

Mercy merely nodded.

"My brothers both think I'm daft for mailing away for this, but it seemed to me that since Barber is already well known for his plans, it only makes sense to lean on his experience."

"Then why do you ask me what I think?"

"Because you're a woman. Three bachelors are liable to overlook something important when it comes to the practicalities of running a household. When Chris or Duncan marries, it would be a shame to find out we'd forgotten or been ignorant about an essential."

"What makes you think Mr. Barber has not given thought to such matters?"

"He," Rob paused and gave her a rascal's smile, "is a man, too."

Mercy approached the table hesitantly. Robert didn't move an inch. Ever since the first time he'd seen her, she'd been jumpy—and understandably so. But over the last few months, he'd made a subtle attempt to show her understanding and make her feel safe.

Manufacturing excuses to be around her was fairly easy. He was passing by the Stein spread while making house calls, he needed to confer with whichever brother happened to be out in the field that day, the Stein mailbox at the mercantile was full. . . In the churchyard, he'd make sure to compliment her on a dessert she'd sent home with one of his brothers or praise her for having accompanied the choir on the piano. Delivering the babe would be difficult enough—hopefully, he could get her accustomed to his presence so she wouldn't be overwhelmed when the time came.

"You have two plans," she said.

"I can see why you'd think so since they both have doors and a veranda. The one to the left is the downstairs. The one to the right is the upstairs. The upstairs veranda can be enclosed later to form another bedchamber."

"I see." She leaned a little close. "This is the kitchen?"

"Aye." He glanced at how her kitchen was arranged. "I imagine it would be set up similar to yours."

"No." She shook her head. "Grossmuter and I often regretted not having a mudroom. Everything gets tracked in." She pointed toward a room. "What is this here?"

"Duncan's shop. We don't need a separate dining room—the kitchen will suffice. He can do his—" Rob watched as she shook her head. "What's wrong?"

"Do not mistake me. Being a cobbler is an honorable profession, but the leather—much of it together in the same place smells bad. Between the smell and the hammer pounding on it, it would not be pleasant in the house."

"Good point." He tapped a pencil on the edge of the blueprint.

"A workshop just a stone's throw from the house would work. That would free up space for your house to have a mudroom. You could divide that space and make it useful. The pantry you show here, beneath the stairs—it will not work well because you and your brothers are all tall. What if you have a mudroom, washroom, and pantry here?"

"An indoor washroom?" Robert chortled. "That's very progressive. I like it! Is this a good spot to place the stove?"

She made a few more suggestions, then went over to the stove and stirred a pot. "When will you build the house?"

"Within the next month or so. I'll telegraph a company in Knoxville, Tennessee. They'll mill and cut the lumber, then send it by the railroad."

She dropped the spoon. "You are mail-ordering a house?"

"Aye, that I am. It will save considerable time and labor here, and the cost of the kit is actually quite thrifty by comparison."

"A kit."

Amused at how she echoed the word, Rob chuckled. "Indeed. The notion takes a little getting used to." He slipped a different page to the top of the stack. "This is the exterior view. When I order it, I'll tell them not to send all the spindles and such."

"Gingerbread." She returned to the table and said, "Grossmuter called all of the lacy scrollwork and wooden fancies gingerbread."

"Now there's a grand description." He shrugged. "But I couldn't care less about how it looks on the outside. 'Tis the inside that counts."

"This is too much, but a little would give charm to the house." Mercy tapped the fanlike piece spanning from the peak of the roof to the eaves on either side. "Can you keep some of it?"

"What do you recommend?" Rob felt a spark of hope. For the first time since the tragedy, Mercy seemed to be coming out of her shell. He'd hoped the sketches might be a good tool for drawing her into a conversation. With a few leading questions, he enticed her into discussing the plan in infinite detail.

After a while, she went back to the stove. "In a month, the wheat harvest should be done, and the corn harvest won't quite be ready. That was good planning. The farmers will be able to help you."

"Speaking of help. . ." Rob scribbled a note to himself in the corner of the page before rolling it up. "I'd like to hire you to cook for the men who come work."

She shook her head. "Not one penny have you or your brothers accepted for the care or the help you have given."

"And you've not accepted a single penny for all the delicious meals you've sent to us." He crooked a brow. "Have you ever eaten at the diner?"

"Once."

"And only once." He nodded. "That says it all. Indeed, my brothers and I all agree—our cooking is no better than the diner's. We've come out far ahead on the bargain. And since we're on the subject of food, I'm trying to find a way to invite myself to lunch. Whatever you're cooking smells delicious."

"Ham and beans. And you are always welcome at our table."

"That's so wonderful to hear!" As Mrs. Kunstler scurried in from the wide open door where she had obviously been eavesdropping, Robert noted that Mercy startled at her interruption. Mrs. Kuntsler looked from Mercy to Rob and back again before continuing, "Things work out, don't they? And now my Otto won't be worried about hurting your feelings as he courts Ismelda."

Color rushed to Mercy's face, then bled away just as rapidly. She shook her head.

Rob took the spoon from her, set it down, and pushed her into a chair. Keeping a hand on Mercy's shoulder, he looked at Otto's mother. "Mrs. Kunstler, you misconstrued matters."

"What was I supposed to think?" Her gaze kept darting from Mercy to him. "You're alone, together, in the house. Decency—"

"I'm sure you didn't mean to question Miss Stein's reputation or impugn my integrity." He stared at her.

"I—um—it, well, of course I didn't." A nervous smile twitched across the woman's face.

Rob directed his attention toward Mercy. "I'll get you some water."

"Oh, I'll do that." Mrs. Kunstler pumped water and hastily shoved the glass into his hand. "I didn't mean to upset her."

"Drink." He pressed the glass to Mercy's mouth. Beneath the hand he kept on her shoulder, he could feel how she shook. Mercy reached up and took the glass from him. For a fleeting second, Rob considered asking if Mercy wished for him to leave. Just as quickly, he dismissed the notion. Distraught as she was, she might still swoon.

He curled his hand around hers and lifted the glass to her mouth again. At the same time, something odd occurred to him. In the three months he'd been in America, he'd been astonished by the Texans' hospitality. Not only did women always offer refreshments and extend an offer for a meal, but they went so far as to take a gift or food whenever they went calling on someone else.

But Otto's mother came empty-handed.

"Mrs. Kunstler, since Miss Stein isn't feeling her best, I'm sure you'll understand—"

"I—we are still neighbors." The woman started wringing her hands. Rob took in how fine beads of perspiration dotted her face and she couldn't maintain eye contact. For her, the situation had to be uncomfortable, but he didn't consider that even a fraction as important as Mercy's heartbreak.

"We are still neighbors," Mercy said in a bleak tone. "Your son was here yesterday. He still plans to borrow Grossvater's reaper and claims one of Freckle's pups. But me?" Her voice caught. "He said he cannot bear to look at me."

"He scarcely sleeps, remembering how he killed that man."

Mercy took another sip of the water. " 'It is not good that the man should be alone; I will make him an help meet for him.' That is the verse from Genesis you recited to me the day Otto asked me to marry him." Mercy set the glass on the table with exacting care. "God does not change, but man does. Otto still needs a helpmate, yet he no longer wants me." Her head came up and she squared her shoulders. "Was there any other reason you came today?"

Mrs. Kunstler slumped against the table. "We thought it best for you to know before you saw them together. Please, Mercy, be kind to them."

"You speak to me about kindness?" Mercy shook her head. "You are the one who went about town telling everyone how that awful man shamed me."

"I didn't want anyone to think badly of my Otto if you were with child! I did it for you, too."

Ruthlessly wiping away her tears, Mercy whispered in a raw tone, "Do not tell me this. You did not do it on my behalf. This is the first time since it happened that you have come here. You did not seek to help or comfort me. Today you have not come to ease my burden. What you ask is for me to make things easier on your son. It wasn't necessary." Mercy rose. "He is the man I was to have married, and the love I held for him would keep me from wounding him in any way."

Aching silence filled the house. Robert cupped Mercy's elbow. "Go lie down, lass. You need to rest."

"I need to churn butter." She sidled toward the stove, moved the pot off the heat, and then wiped her hands on her apron. "You will both go now."

He and Mrs. Kunstler went outside. Stopping by her mare, Robert glowered at Otto's mother. "Am I to understand that you've not sought her out to give her a woman's advice?"

"The situation is strained. I'm not the right woman to—"

"No," he agreed abruptly. "No, you're not."

"You don't see—"

"I see all too clearly. I'll help you onto your horse. You don't belong here." Once Mrs. Kunstler left, Rob stared back at the house. *Three months. It's been three months. All this time, I thought she was being comforted and counseled by a woman who could show sensitivity. What kind of doctor am I? I've failed a seventeen-year-old lass who's been facing this all on her own. No more.*

Chapter 7

Her palms were moist. Mercy traded the house plans from one hand to the other so she could slip her hands on the edge of her apron to dry them. Duncan arrived this morning, declaring the doctor needed the plans. Of course, he did that immediately after promising Peter that they'd go fishing once the weeding was done.

Though early in the day, the June heat had begun to build. The door to the doctor's office was open. Mercy stood at the threshold and decided she ought to knock—after all, the doctor didn't just work here, he and his brothers lived here, as well.

"Hey, Rob!" Christopher Gregor appeared in the hall and shouted up the staircase as he yanked Mercy inside. "The plans are here!"

Of all the brothers, Christopher was the one who never ceased to startle her. His actions were invariably swift and often unexpected. Mercy barely kept from screaming.

Chris grinned at her, completely unaware of how he'd practically sent her into a panic. "Rob said you think we ought to keep some of the embellishments on the house. You'd better be ready for a fight, because I'm holding out to eliminate every last one."

"It's your house." She managed to scoot away from him.

"That's what I'm telling them. I'll do most of the construction. I used to do a lot of the mine construction back home."

"Oh."

"Good morning, Miss Stein." The doctor descended the stairs.

"I gave your brother the plans." She started to turn toward the door to make a quick escape.

"Actually, while you're here, I'd appreciate some help."

"No fair askin' the lass. It's your own fault." Chris folded his arms across his chest and growled at Mercy, "He slept through breakfast."

"I didn't mean anything about food," the doctor snapped.

Chris leaned toward her. "Pay no heed to his surly attitude. He gets that way often enough. One night with a few paltry interruptions, and he gets cranky."

"So you need some breakfast?"

"No, I dinna need you minding my belly." The doctor scowled at his brother. "Go make yourself useful."

"Nae. 'Tis too much fun staying here for the moment."

"This is a touchy subject," the doctor began.

The whole matter seemed far too dubious. Mercy murmured, "Then perhaps you ought to have someone else assist you."

"I seriously doubt anyone else could help." The doctor heaved a sigh. "Come out to the back."

"You go on ahead. I'm not fool enough to chance it," Christopher announced.

"Coward," the doc muttered.

Mercy tagged along and tried to ignore the smell of scorched oatmeal as she passed by the stove. She had no idea what she was getting roped into, but the brotherly banter struck her as amusing. Once she reached the back steps, she gave the doctor a confused look.

Features strained, he whispered, "So you dinna know what to do, then, either?"

She blinked. "About what?"

The doctor cringed at the normal volume she'd spoken in and whispered even more softly, "That." He pointed to a huge pasteboard box.

Mercy leaned forward, looked inside, and started to giggle.

"Now then"—the doctor's brows puckered—"'tisna all that funny."

"Just yesterday, you told me you were going to get a house kit. I didn't think you meant this kind." She went down on her knees by the box where a cat was nursing a litter of kittens—but in contrast to all the other marmalade-colored babies, one was black and white.

Doc leaned down and clamped his hands on her upper arms as she reached for the baby skunk. He murmured, "I wasna askin' you to get rid of the beast—just for some advice. I read about them, and I dinna think it's wise for you to be so close."

"He's a spotted skunk. If he's ready to do mischief, he'll stand on his hands." She didn't pick up the kit. Instead, she rubbed each of the tiny kittens in the litter. "They're all about the same age and size—about six weeks."

"So how do we reunite him with his mother? And how do we get rid of them all?"

Mercy sat back on her heels. "Spotted skunks don't stay any one place for long. They roam. The mother could be anywhere—in a rotten log or an abandoned burrow. She probably came to the house because you've set food out for the cat."

"So she could return tonight and reclaim her kit?"

"It is possible but not probable. When mothers and their babies are set apart, they don't come back together again." She turned to look at the doctor. "What you read told you how stinky a skunk is, but they are shy creatures. They only protect themselves if they feel threatened."

"Why do you think three grown men are whispering and tiptoeing around?"

Mercy smothered a smile. "He isn't old enough to be completely weaned." She paused a moment and decided to tease him. "Spotty. You should name him Spotty."

"There's no need to name something when it's not staying."

"Hey, Rob," Christopher's subtle-as-an-ox whisper drifted out to them. "I've never been happier that you're the doctor."

"Why?"

"I just read something." Chris stuck his head out the door. "You can operate and take out the stink glands. Yep. You're the doc." Just as quickly, Chris disappeared again.

"There's no need to be hasty," the doctor said.

Mercy grimaced. "Actually, after four weeks, they start to practice spraying. By six or eight weeks—"

"We're not keeping it around that long!"

"If the mother took him out at night, he's about six weeks."

Looking thoroughly disgruntled, the doctor announced, "His mother will come get him tonight."

Suddenly the humor of the situation evaporated. Mercy averted her gaze. "Just because you want something does not make it happen."

Dr. Gregor sat on the wooden plank veranda beside her. " 'Tis a harsh truth you just spoke."

Mercy tried to rise, but he stopped her. "Dinna run, lass. You needn't speak a word a-tall. I plan to do a bit of talking." For good measure, he scooped a kitten from the box and tucked it into her hands.

"I have chores to do at home."

"A woman's work is ne'er done. Or so my ma always said, God rest her soul." The corners of his bright blue eyes crinkled. "I canna be certain whether she's finally resting in heaven, or if she's still bustling about with a broom, trying to make the streets of gold gleam brighter."

The image coaxed a twitch of a smile from her.

"I oughtn't cast stones. My brothers taunt me about my tidy ways."

"Your patients would develop infections if you were slovenly."

He inclined his head as an acknowledgment. "Aye. But I also remind them cleanliness is next to godliness." He glanced over his shoulder, then whispered, "Betwixt thee and me, 'tisna always the case. Times when my soul's been the most troubled, I've tried to busy my hands so as to keep from thinking or praying."

Her breath caught.

"My da—he passed on to Jesus just a day before we reached America."

"I–I'm sorry."

"I still grieve for him, but 'tis only my selfishness that causes me to. He was ailing for a long while, and now he's whole once again and in heaven. A mining accident took his arm several years back—'twas the guilt money they settled on him that paid for my medical training. He claimed God took a bad situation and used it for good."

Anger flashed through her. *He'd better not tell me it's all for the good that I'm with child and Otto has abandoned me.*

Unaware of her reaction, the doctor kept talking. "But 'twasna until his last hour that Da pointed out something that was right before me for years. I cared for Da—leastways, for the needs of his ailing body. But Duncan—he's a man with a knack for wrapping quiet comfort like a blanket about others whose hearts and souls are aching. Chris—well, he manages to scowl others into behaving so peace is maintained."

Mercy concentrated on tracing the soft stripes in the kitten's fur. The doctor was right: the Gregor men were vastly different in their strengths and personalities.

"None of us is good at everything. We have strengths and weaknesses. God created us that way so we'd rely on Him and on our brothers and sisters." He reached over, gently stroked the kitten, and said in a somber tone, "You're a fine woman, Mercy Stein. Aye, you are—but you're going to have to lean on God and others to help you through all that lies ahead."

She started to tremble. "I must leave now."

He took the kitten and gently put it with its littermates. "I'll walk you out."

It would be rude to refuse his assistance rising from the veranda. Once she was up, Mercy snatched back her hand. Her plan was to dash down the steps and go around to the front, but the doctor stopped her.

"We obviously have a mama skunk close by. Go back through to the front." As she started through the doorway, he added, "Is there anything I should put out to entice that mother to come get the kit?"

Relief flooded her. She could salvage her pride by leaving on a better note. "What did you have out last night?"

Chris must have overheard her, because he started to chortle.

Mercy gave the doctor a questioning look.

His neck and ears went red. "Leftovers."

"Dinna believe him." Chris served his brother a wallop on the back that would have felled a smaller man. "Rob tried to bake beans. I've chewed on softer bullets."

It's my fault. I was rattled yesterday and didn't send food home with them. She stared at the far wall and said, "Eggs. Skunks like eggs."

"How many?"

"I'd suppose you have only one female and her litter of kits."

Doc chuckled. "One's more than enough. I meant, how many eggs should I put out? Half a dozen?"

"One or two."

He looked uncertain. "Fried?"

"Raw." She hastily added, "Still in the shell."

Christopher seemed to find the whole exchange vastly amusing. Until today, he'd always been so stern. Discovering it was nothing more than bluster made her bold. Mercy walked toward freedom and called back over her shoulder, "Christopher Gregor, you owe me for helping you out. It's going to cost you."

"Is that so?"

"Ja." She turned to the doctor. "I count on you to make sure he pays this debt."

"You just name it," Doc said.

"I can hardly wait." Christopher looked too smug.

She gave the doctor's brother the same look she used on Peter when he misbehaved. "Gingerbread."

"Uh. . .I'm not any better at cooking than my brothers."

The doctor tried to smother his laughter with a cough.

Mercy cast him a quick glance, then mused, "But you are good at building things?"

"That's a fact." All of a sudden, Christopher's face contorted. "Not my house!"

"Our house," the doctor corrected. "Miss Stein, what will satisfy the debt?"

"I'm a fair woman." She ignored Chris's rude snort and continued. "The fan-styled inset at the apex of the eaves. And if the mother returns and takes away the kit, whichever is cheaper: a spindled veranda or scalloped clapboards for part of the building."

"If the skunk is gone, you'll have both, and we'll be coming out better on the bargain."

"You're demented." Chris shook his head. "Any sane person would want a skunk as far away as possible, and you're trying to get it to come up on the porch!"

"You suggested I bring a skunk into my office and perform surgery on it!"

Mercy left, surprised she was still smiling at the Gregor brothers' antics. But she'd ridden no more than five feet before it happened again. Women gave her pitying glances and turned away. The tiny bit of happiness she'd had withered, and misery swamped her.

Chapter 8

"No gingerbread. Not a stick." Chris stomped into the surgery and half bellowed, "Did you hear me?"

"Half of Texas heard you." Rob calmly placed a bottle of arnica on the shelf and shut the door to his pharmaceutical cabinet. "I take it we still have the skunk?"

"No, we dinna. *You* now have two!" Chris glowered at him. "I'm working at the farm today. You and Duncan can find a way to rid us of those beasts."

Rob stood chest-to-chest with his brother and glared at him. "You're not going."

"And why not?"

"You'll bellow at the lass. She canna take it. I'll send off the telegram to order the house, and you can start the foundation."

"I can't yet. Connant insists we have a cellar to hide in when there's a storm. He hounded me until I relented and said I'd dig it." Chris looked exasperated. "I'm too busy to worry about cowering from a gust of wind."

"Last day of last month, Bell and Falls counties lost ten men to tornadoes. Connant has yet to steer us wrong about America."

"Exaggeration. It has to be. These Texans pride themselves in telling tall tales. Connant's always had a talent for stretching the thinnest thread of truth into a yarn. He's warmed up to the Texan tradition. Every time he mentions a tornado, it gets more powerful. He started with telling me about the hail that's the size of a fist. Then he had flying cows. At last telling, brick houses were torn to bits."

"You gave your word; you'll dig the shelter."

Rolling up his sleeves, Chris muttered, "Hot as it's getting, I'll probably be striking Lucifer with the shovel—and most likely within the first few inches."

"Now look who's spouting Texas-sized tales!" Rob folded a paper up and tucked it into the pocket of his vest. Miserably hot as the summer had proven to be, he felt a spurt of thanks that the men didn't feel it necessary to wear a coat and hat.

"It's a crying shame Connant wasn't stretching the truth when he told us it gets hotter than the hinges to Hades in the summer."

"Speaking of the devil's domain. . ." Rob stared at his eldest brother. "I've waited for you to tell the truth about those trips to Thurber."

Chris shrugged. "I haven't lied."

"You've not been forthcoming with the real reason you went, either." Rob knew Chris had spent time in the mines. "Did you think I wouldn't recognize the cough?"

Chris didn't look in the least bit unsettled or repentant. "Don't fault me for doing my trade."

"We're relying on your talents with construction. It's time to build the house. You're getting irritated about me getting called out in the wee small hours, and Duncan's snoring is driving me to distraction."

"Duncan's busy with all manner of leatherwork, and your practice is booming."

Rob knew he had to tread lightly. Chris was a proud man. "Aye. I canna deny either of those statements. But we'd have to pay dearly for anyone else to do the construction. We're relying on your skill."

"I haven't done a scrap of work on it yet."

Rob nodded. "And glad I am that you haven't. You were where you were most needed. The Steins would be in sorry shape had you not worked their land."

The tension in Chris's jaw eased only slightly.

"It's not just the farming you do that's vital. You've seen how skittish Mercy is." He saw Chris's eyes flare. "Having a strong man there lends her a sense of safety."

Chris grunted.

Rob knew he'd succeeded in making his point. With Chris, it was better to back off so he felt he'd made the decision. "You're so big and ugly, there isna man nor dog that'd tangle with you."

"I'd tell you to look in the mirror, but you'd break it." Chris stared out the window. "I'm not done in Thurber. I'm going back for two more days."

Rob glowered.

"It's lignite. They're opening shafts four and five, and some idiot set up shoring in them that's got exposed nails. You use your knowledge to save lives. This time, I'm using mine. One spark and the whole thing would burn for months."

"Which is why I don't want you down there at all." The railroad desperately needed the soft coal, but Rob didn't want his brother to continue mining. Mining ruined a man's lungs, if it didn't claim life or limb first. "You're done with that trade."

"In case you didn't notice, I didn't ask what you thought."

"We pledged Da we'd stay together."

"I'm still in Texas!"

"Not good enough," Rob shot back.

Chris banged his fist against the back of a chair. "I'm not about to concede to your whims. Not after you decided our house needs to have more frills than an Easter bonnet."

"Sore over that, are you?"

"No." The corner of Chris's mouth kicked up. "Any gingerbread's going to go on Duncan's workshop, and I'll pound you into the ground if you warn him."

"You haven't succeeded in distracting me. I still expect you to put mining behind you after these last two days of consulting."

"You haven't distracted me, either. Duncan gets any of the silly frills."

Rob nodded. "We have a deal."

"You've wasted half the morning. I have a stupid basement to dig in the heat of the day now that you're done clucking like a hen."

Rob grabbed his medical satchel and a slip of paper. He'd already composed the order for the house—including all of the "standard" features, which included a plethora of the frills Chris was grousing about. In addition to the house, Rob had estimated enough boards to construct the partitions in the downstairs to create the washroom and Duncan's workshop. He grinned to himself. Chris agreed to the bargain that Duncan got all of the gingerbread—but Chris didn't consider one important fact: Duncan could put the gingerbread wherever he wanted to.

—⁂—

"Grossvater is in the cornfield." Mercy pinned Peter's shirt to the clothesline.

Doc didn't stride off. Instead, he announced, "I sent for the house and extra lumber to construct Duncan's workshop."

"The men will all want to help, but this kit—will it come with instructions?"

"Aye, and each piece is numbered. 'Twill require two cars on the train to hold all of the material."

Mercy kept hanging up clothes. "Two! That much to make a house?"

"It surprised me, too." Rob reached over and held the hem of the dress she'd taken from the basket.

"You'll get wet." She tried to tug it away.

"I'm sweltering, lass. That's not a threat, 'tis a promise." After she pinned the calico dress to the line, he pinched the cloth on either side of the waist. "You'll be needing new frocks soon."

Mercy pretended she hadn't seen nor heard him.

"You've not asked, and I'm—"

"I'm not asking anything." She snapped a dishcloth in the air, then savagely pinned it up.

"Between Christmas and New Year's." His words came out in a patient tone. "I just thought you might want to know."

Heat soared from her bodice to her forehead. Rattled, she tried to jam the wrong end of a clothespin onto the line.

"If it's too hard for you to discuss, I could write down a few things for you."

"Let me be!" Once she cried out the words, Mercy felt guilty. "I don't want to be rude. Just please leave me alone."

"I respect you immensely, Miss Stein, and I'll respect your wishes." He didn't even pause but changed the topic. "Your grandda is healing better than I anticipated, but I'd best not find him working too hard. If he is, I'll scold him like he's six instead of sixty."

"Duncan's with him."

"Good, good." He nodded. "Duncan's grown quite fond of your grandda and Peter. They didn't get a single nibble whilst fishing yester noon because the three of them kept trading jokes and made too much noise."

"Fish don't have ears."

"Ah, but they do." The doctor pulled a pair of britches from the basket and held it to the line so she could hang it. "They have an ear stone and little hairs inside at the back of the head. They sense vibration—much like you feel the vibration of a tuning fork or a bell."

"Hmm."

"Just because we canna see something doesna mean 'tisn't there."

Everyone knows that. Why would he say such an odd thing?

"Though I canna see the Almighty, I still know He's with me because of how He resonates in my heart."

I used to feel that way. Now I don't. God hasn't listened to me or talked to my heart for months now. She glanced at the doctor, and he gave her a quizzical look. Embarrassed at her thoughts, she stammered, "It is odd, you speaking of fish and God in the same discussion."

His eyes twinkled. "Ooch! Now, lass, many a man will tell you 'tis no place like sittin' by a stream with a pole in your hand to let your heart go still. 'Be still, and know that I am God.' Aye, I'm thinkin' that verse applies to the hours when I fish."

Eager to veer away from discussing spiritual matters, she pretended to play with a clothespin. "So then, go talk to Grossvater in the cornfield. Maybe he could take you fishing sometime."

"That I will."

As the doctor walked off, Mercy hung the last of the laundry and went to the garden. She picked some vegetables and took them inside. The doctor had said he stayed busy when his heart ached. Mercy envied him. *No matter how hard I work, nothing fills up the emptiness inside me—nothing but that evil man's child.*

Chapter 9

No being surly," Rob warned Chris as they rode to the Stein farm.

"Of course he willna be surly." Duncan thumbed back his hat. "'Tis Peter's birthday, and Chris wouldna think to spoil it with a dark mood."

"I'm not surly." Chris shifted the box on his lap. "I'm impatient."

Duncan looked at Rob. "Peter's growin' a year older today, and I'm thinking Chris is going backward in age."

"You chose more fireworks than I did." Chris gave Duncan a mock scowl. "But if you think they're just a schoolboy's toy, I'm sure Mercy would let you stay in the kitchen and wash dishes while the rest of us enjoy the lights—don't you think, Rob?"

"We'll not light a single one till everyone can enjoy them."

Chris smirked. "Duncan, you're my witness. Rob just volunteered to do dishes."

"Aye, that he did!"

Rob chuckled. "Since when did I mind getting my hands wet? Washing dishes is a far sight easier than sterilizing my instruments."

Duncan moaned.

"Keep talking about that." Chris grinned at Rob. "Duncan goes green whene'er he even hears about blood and gore. It means there'll be more food for us."

As they approached the farmhouse, Peter ran out to greet them. "We get to have a picnic! Grossvater said we could!"

As they hitched their horses, Peter hopped from one foot to the other. "You got three horses now?"

"Aye, we do." Chris gave his gelding an affectionate pat.

"Was yours sick, too?"

"Nae. Just bad tempered. His owner didn't know how to treat him."

"There's not a beast alive Chris couldn't charm," Duncan boasted.

Mercy came out onto the veranda. "Except a skunk."

Rob chortled. "Aye, and that's the truth. Chris, will you be telling the lass, or do I?"

Mercy's eyes widened. "The skunk didn't—"

"No," Chris snapped. He heaved a sigh. "You were right. The skunk was in that log. While she went to our porch for the eggs, I chopped up the log so she'd move on."

"And she took every last one of her kits with her," Duncan added.

Rob gave Mercy a slow smile. "So mayhap you ought to be reminding Chris what gingerbread is to go on the new house."

"I'll remind him later." Mercy pushed a golden strand of hair behind her ear. "I wouldn't want to spoil his appetite."

"Mercy made a cake for me. Wanna come see?"

"Later, Peter." Mercy made a shooing motion. "Go take the blanket and spread it out. Don't lay it by the redbud tree. There's an anthill there."

"And after I do, I getta choose a watermelon."

"Now I think I'm going to have to set this box down and help you with that chore. We'll find the biggest watermelon in the garden."

Peter went up on tiptoe. "What's in the box?"

"A surprise." Chris set the box down on the veranda. "It'll be the last thing we do today."

Peter shuffled backward. "It's not a switch is it?"

"What," Rob asked, "would make you think of a thing like that?"

"Johann's father says that when he's been naughty."

"I see." Rob heard the gritty undertone in Chris's voice.

"Mr. Honig is a firm man, but fair." In spite of the heat, Mercy wrapped her arms around herself. "It's a case of his bark being worse than his bite."

"That's good to know." Chris straightened up.

"I think you'd better worry about my bite." Rob grinned. "I'm smelling fried chicken. While the others go spread out the picnic blanket and choose a melon, I'll come help with the food."

"That kind of help will leave the rest of us hungry," Duncan predicted.

"He wouldn't do that to us." Peter looked up at him. "Would you, Doctor?"

"Never. I'd be sure to save out three pieces—one for you, another for your sister, and the last one for your grandda."

"Does the gizzard count as a piece? It's awful small."

"Seeing as it's your birthday, I'd save that one for you as a treat."

"Okay, but I like the leg."

"Hey!" Chris looked at Duncan and half bellowed in outrage, "They're plotting to leave us out."

Duncan crooked his finger at Peter. A moment later, he whispered something in the boy's ear that sent him into a fit of giggles.

"The both of you are up to no good."

"And what else would you expect of us?" Duncan settled his arm around Peter.

Five minutes later, Rob held a tray with dishes on it. A substantial thump sounded from one of the bedrooms, and an immediate *shhh!* followed.

"What—" Mercy wheeled around toward that room.

"Else do we need to take out?" Rob cut in as he stepped in front of her. He tilted his head toward the direction of more rustling and winked. "That chicken platter is heavy. Do you want to take it out now"—he shook his head from side to side—"or get it on the next trip?" He nodded.

Mercy took the cue. "Perhaps the next trip. Right now, I could take the potato salad out."

"Aye. That's a fair plan. So off we go. How many watermelons are in your garden?"

"I haven't counted." Mercy stepped out of the house.

Rob followed and immediately set down the tray and held a finger up to his lips. He shut the door and stomped twice in place, then lightened his footfall to imitate the sound of them walking away. He winked at Mercy.

She carefully set down the bowl she carried and gave him a baffled look.

He held up one hand and crooked one finger at a time to count down five seconds. "Ah ha!" Rob shouted as he threw open the door.

Peter screamed, and Duncan caught the platter of chicken before it fell. They traded a guilty look.

"What's wrong?" Chris demanded as he hastened up the steps.

"What's wrong?" Duncan groused. "I'll tell you what's wrong. You didn't cause sufficient diversion!"

Mercy's eyes popped wide open. "Christopher, you were a part of this, too?"

"It's your fault," Chris retorted.

Pressing her hand to her bosom and sounding completely bewildered, Mercy said, "I am to blame?"

"Aye, 'tis a fact." Chris nodded.

Rob smiled at her. "You're a grand cook, and we're desperately hungry men."

Mercy laughed. "You are all little boys having your fun. Now everyone, carry something and we will have supper."

Duncan held fast to the chicken platter and headed out the door. The look on his face dared anyone to reach for a bite. Mercy slipped to the side and picked up the bowl she'd set down while Chris rumbled to Rob, "She thinks 'twas all a game."

Duncan let out a bark of laughter.

Rob couldn't. He was too focused on Mercy to pay much attention to his brothers. For the first time since he'd met her, Mercy had laughed.

Throughout supper, Rob hoped to hear her laugh again. Chris and Duncan were in rare form, teasing one another and pulling Peter or Mr. Stein into the middle of nonsensical debates. Mercy smiled a time or two, but that was it.

After they'd demolished the supper and decimated the cake, Chris surveyed the scattered collection of plates. "Well, Rob, I'm thinking you willna hae to work too hard, washing the dishes. We practically licked them clean for you already."

"Speak for yourself," Duncan said in an affronted tone. "You might hae eaten like a ravening beast, but I didna stoop to that level. Neither did Rob. We sopped up the last morsels wi' Mercy's fine bread."

"That, we did." Rob grinned. "It was efficient and mannerly. Mercy, you'll have to excuse Chris. He's never been one to act civilized."

The banter continued as they carried everything back to the house. Even as Rob washed the dishes, Duncan dried them, and Mercy put them away, lighthearted teasing kept on.

"Now?" Peter pled. "Now can I see what's in the box?"

"Sure." Duncan swung Peter upside down and carried him in that position out onto the porch. " 'Twill be dark enough to play with these in just a little while."

"I can't open the box when I'm hanging like this."

"Rob," Chris asked, "did you hear that? Peter's nine now, and he's still a weakling. Do you have a tonic to help?"

"Eww!" Peter squirmed. "Tonics taste awful. I don't want any!"

Duncan flipped him right side up and set him down. "I dinna blame you. Rob's potions taste e'en worse than his cooking—and that's saying a lot."

Peter knelt by the box and pried off the lid. "Grossvater! Look! A giant paper candle!"

"It's called a Roman candle." Duncan sat beside Peter. "It's a firework. They're beautiful but dangerous."

Peter accidentally bumped the box. "Mercy! There are two of those Roman paper candle fireworks."

"Gently lift those off and look deeper in the box," Rob instructed.

Peter eagerly complied. Three more layers yielded an assortment of fireworks. "Can we set them all on fire now?"

"It would be safest to have a few buckets of water on hand first," Rob said. "Don't you think so, Mercy?"

"Ja, that would be wise."

After Peter fetched the water, Rob insisted that three buckets of sand were also smart. "If something accidentally goes up in flame, we need to be ready."

Mercy gave Rob a puzzled look as Peter dashed off after one last bucket. "Do you not want him to set off the fireworks?"

"Oh, we will. I was delaying a bit because when it's darkest, the lights shine more brightly."

They all enjoyed the showers of light. As the last one burst into a wondrous display, Rob looked at Mercy. He'd hoped to see joy shining in her eyes. Instead, the sadness he saw there made his breath freeze in his lungs. Just as quickly, he tamped down his emotions. Pity would cripple her. The prudent thing to do was to treat her just as if she weren't tormented by the violence that begat the bairn she carried. *If I'm to be able to treat her medically, I must not allow compassion to weaken me. She has friends and family—there are a strong handful of those, but she'll have but one doctor—me. They can fret o'er her emotions. Me—'tis her health and that of the babe with which I must concern myself. I'll guard my professional demeanor and keep enough distance that I not lose my objectivity.*

———※———

Mercy filled a bucket with cool water and grabbed a pair of dish towels. She walked out into the field.

"Danke." Grossvater dipped the first towel into the water and handed it to Duncan, then wet the other. The men continued to discuss plans for threshing as they cooled down—first with the damp cloths, then by taking huge gulps straight from the edge of the pail.

"Lunch will be ready in an hour." She headed back toward the house. Duncan and Christopher Gregor had participated in the reaping of the fields, and the wheat had dried. Men in the county pulled together to do the next step—moving from one farm to the next with the big steam threshing machine. Women helped one another feed all those hungry men—at least they always had. This year was different.

Grossvater owned the only reaper in the county, and everyone had borrowed it. Years ago, all of the farmers went together and bought a thresher. Each farm used it in turn, in the same pattern as the reaping went. The Stein farm would be the first to have all the men come for threshing.

But Mercy knew the women wouldn't all come with big vats of food and fill the day with happy chatter. They barely spoke to her at all, and only when it was unavoidable. Carmen and her sister felt the same way the doctor and his brothers did—that she bore no blame for the child. Asking Carmen and Ismelda to come help cook had been embarrassing, but Mercy had done so to avoid the shame of not being able to feed the men.

She dreaded threshing day. Three days later, as soon as the men began to arrive, Mercy knew her fears had been well founded.

Chapter 10

My mother—she is not feeling so good today. She sent this." Otto pushed a large bowl into Ismelda's hands.

"She's sick?" Ismelda made a sympathetic sound. "Is there anything I can do to help?"

Mercy tore herself away from the scene just outside her kitchen door. It all hurt so much—for Otto to be courting another girl so soon, for his mother to have suddenly turned cold and silent, and for the women to all shun her as they did.

Over the next half hour, man after man arrived. A few ventured toward the kitchen with a dish or loaf of bread. Weak excuses accompanied those offerings.

Working feverishly, the three women did all they could. Carmen had come over for the past two days to help make things in advance. Even then, as the men all washed up at the huge tubs of water and Mercy scrambled to put the last dishes on the tables, she worried there wouldn't be enough to satisfy them.

Texas held many different cultures, but until recently the German community had stayed pretty much to itself. Foods the men expected were on the table—ham, roast beef, fried chicken, mashed potatoes and gravy, cucumber salad, coleslaw, pickles, pickled beets, watermelon pickles, green tomato relish—but also now, there were dishes they'd not known. The exotic dishes Carmen and Ismelda made seemed so out of place—yet Mercy pretended the spread was the same as it had traditionally been.

Grossvater raised his hand in the air, and the men went quiet. "I want to thank all my friends and neighbors for their help. Let's say grace and eat!"

Well-worn straw hats came off.

The food flew off the tables just as quickly. Between filling cups and putting out more food, Mercy had an excuse to dash around and not speak.

In times past, the men spoke little as they ate—mostly just, "Pass me the gravy," and, "Good chicken, Miss Stein." This meal, as if to make up for the lack of women calling things to one another, the men tried to fill the silence with hearty jokes or conversation. The awkwardness didn't keep them from decimating apple pie, raisin pie, blue plum kuchen and cakes. The custard with caramel on it that Carmen called "flan" seemed to please the men.

When the men went back to work, Carmen surveyed the tables. "I've never seen men pounce on food like that!"

"They liked your ta-mals."

Carmen laughed. "Tamales. I didn't make them very spicy. If I want, I can season them so your tongue begs for deliverance."

"I like sweet foods and tangy things—not so much the hot ones." Mercy stacked the empty pie tins. "I hope a little of your flan is left. The men praised it lavishly."

"A few grunts are lavish praise?" Ismelda shook her head. "Such a strange custom."

"Be sure I am very thankful for all your hard work." After the dishes were all washed, dried, and put away, Mercy pressed a small cloth bag into Carmen's hand. "Molasses cookies."

"Oh, you know how I love them!"

Ismelda gave her a hug. "Thank you, Mercy, for letting everyone know that we're still friends. I know you truly wish Otto and me every happiness."

"I do." Mercy stared down at the grimy hem of her apron. "You saw today—the other women didn't come. I will not blame you if—"

"Nonsense!" Carmen gave her a stormy look. "You're my friend. Nothing will change that."

"Exactly." Ismelda grinned. "Now will you write down the recipe for that cucumber salad?"

Mercy obligingly did so. By late afternoon, the chugging of the M. Rumley steam thresher stopped. Not long after, all the men left. Those whose wives sent food came to the back veranda to fetch the dishes, and Mercy had all of the dishes lined up there for them—each with a small bag of molasses cookies to show her thanks.

There were enough leftovers for her to feed Grossvater and Peter supper. Mercy didn't have much of an appetite. She went to bed and curled up, feeling horribly alone. Always in the past, threshing was a day of joy—thankfulness to God for a good harvest mingled with the merry visiting of neighbors. *But God let that man hurt me, and the women who are my sisters in Christ have turned their backs on me.*

Sleep wouldn't come.

The sky was still violet. Soon, the rooster would be crowing the sun up. Mercy lay in bed and stared at her bedside table. A thin layer of dust covered her Bible. She hadn't read the Word for weeks now. Setting aside quiet time for devotions was too hard. The minute she ceased doing chores, she started drowning in a sea of feelings.

Deciding what to make for breakfast, she shoved off the sheet. It was far too hot to use blankets. Suddenly, she froze. Lying still, she closed her eyes and tried to steady her breathing. A few minutes later, it happened again—an infinitesimal fluttering low in her tummy. Light as butterfly wings, the sensation came and left again.

The baby?

Mercy slid her hand down the soft-from-a-hundred-washings cotton night-gown. Resting her palm where she'd experienced the sensation, she waited. And waited. And waited.

Is that you?

—⁂—

"Hello, Dr. Gregor! Welcome! You're just in time—the men are coming in for lunch."

Rob didn't dismount immediately. "I was concerned about you, Mrs. Kuntsler. My brothers said Otto mentioned you were feeling puirly."

"I'm hale as a horse. I don't know where—" She halted abruptly as color rushed to her cheeks.

Crossing his hands on the saddle's pommel, he looked across the table. "Mrs. Grun, I'm glad to see the terrible sprain you had yesterday has healed so swiftly. You're walking without any difficulty. Mrs. Voran, Mrs. Stuky—I'm gratified to see your children are bounding around so easily. I was made to understand they were ailing yesterday, as well."

Mrs. Kunstler bustled past him and waved the men over. "Come. Yes, come now. Dinner is ready. There is plenty!"

Chris yelled, "Rob, what are you doing here?"

Rob shrugged. "A whole lot of nothing, much to my surprise. Just yesterday, you said many of the women or children were sick. I'm delighted to report everyone's in the very pink of health."

Rob joined the men at the washstands, then ate with them. As he rose, he said, "What a grand meal this was. I've never seen men eat half as much. You women—all of you women—worked hard to keep sufficient food on the table."

"We all help one another," Jakob Lintz said.

"Ahh. So that's it." Rob nodded his head sagely. "None of the ladies went to help at the Stein's threshing yesterday. I'm supposing 'twas because none of us Gregors thought to pledge that one or two of us would work the threshing on the Stein's behalf." He let out a big sigh. "I'm relieved. Aye, I surely am. I should have known better than to worry as I did."

"Worry?" someone asked.

"Aye. I'm ashamed to confess I worried mayhap something else was behind puir wee Mercy working her fingers to the bone. Now I see 'twasna a case of anyone reviling the lass. Glad I am of it, too. She's but an innocent lamb, hurt in the verra worst way by a godless beast of a man. She and the babe—I'm glad to know you'll all be thinkin' kindly of them and extending Christian charity toward them through the coming months and years."

"I'm sure you're right, Rob." Duncan stood and scanned the young women who stood around the edge of the yard, their hands full of empty pie plates. "I'm betting not a man here hasna given thought to the fact that it could have been his daughter or granddaughter who fell victim to such a tragedy. Connant told us this community was strong in the Lord. 'Twas our fault—the Gregors should have pledged to you all that we'd represent the Steins. From now on, you can count on us."

"Aye, that you can." Chris slapped a straw hat on his head. "Now I'm getting back to work ere I yield to the temptation to take a nap after all that food."

Rob rode over to the Steins'. Mercy was in the garden wielding a hoe. Rob dismounted and chuckled. "I canna help wonderin' whether you're merely killin' that weed or if you're trying to send it clear down to the devil himself this verra minute!"

"I'd gladly send him and all his brothers."

"This is a lovely garden patch. You must have quite a fondness for sweet corn."

"We all do." Mercy surveyed the long rows of corn. Suddenly her eyes went wide and her hand went to her middle.

"The babe's bootin' you, eh?" Rob made a casual gesture. "The timing is right. The next three months, you'll not be feeling so sleepy. The last three, you'll be worn out and have your back achin' fiercely, but that's all to be expected."

"Oh."

She's not cutting me off. I dinna dare push too far, but the lass needs help. Lord, give me the wisdom and words she needs.

" 'The barest of flutters,' " he smiled. "That's how the first mother-to-be I doctored many years back described it. Later, she declared that same babe was stompin' in hobnailed boots inside her." Hitching his shoulder, Rob admitted, " 'Twas her eleventh babe. My hands caught him—a fat, squalling boy—but that woman took a mind to tell me half of what I needed to know wasna in my medical texts."

"She told you this? Your patient?"

"Aye, and right she was." Rob casually patted his chest pocket. "Now there's a pity. After each visit I paid her, I wrote notes to myself. Ever see that small red book I carry? I could quote page upon page, but still I carry it with me on the days I'm to see a woman who's in a motherly way."

"Why?"

"That book serves as a reminder that 'tisna always the mind that teaches us the important things—ofttimes, 'tis the heart."

Mercy started hoeing again with a vengeance. "You're supposing everyone has a heart. You're wrong, Doctor. Write that down in your book, too."

Chapter 11

As soon as the bitter words left her mouth, Mercy regretted them. They were honest—but too stark. Concentrating on a small dirt clod, she beat it into oblivion as she muttered, "I should not have said that."

"And why not? There's nothing wrong with speaking the truth as you see it."

"I'm not a child. You do not need to humor me."

"I'm not humoring you. As a matter of fact, I think you have plenty of call to question if anyone has a heart. You've suffered greatly because of what others have done."

She stared at the soil. "It was not others about whom I spoke. It is myself."

"Without a doubt, Miss Stein, you have a heart of gold. You love your brother and grandda. You even pet baby skunks."

"It does not say much for my character that I care for the young, the old, and the helpless. These days, those are all I do care for."

"Your heart has been wounded as surely as any other injury you have suffered. To my way of thinking, there's nothing wrong with you guarding yourself. You need time."

"Time will not help." Mercy stared at the earth. If anything, time would only make matters worse. People already shunned her. How much worse would it become when her belly grew huge? And how would they treat her after she had the babe?

How will they treat the baby? The thought made her breath catch. Until this morning, she'd resented the life she carried. All she'd been able to link it to was the horrific act. Only now things seemed different. That life was so very small, so helpless. *The gentle-as-raindrop patter I felt inside—how could I have thought I would hate such a thing?*

"Time doesn't cure everything." The doctor let out a rueful chuckle. "If it did, I'd be out of business. What I've found is, as weeks and months go by, we gain wisdom and are better able to make decisions."

"I have no decisions to make." Mercy's head shot up, and she stared at him. "These days, all I do is live with the way things are because of what others have done or thought or believed."

"I'd be a fool of a man if I said what others think and believe doesna matter.

Instead, though, why not give some consideration to what it is that you think and believe?"

Embarrassed that she'd been blurting out thoughts she ought to have kept private, Mercy decided to sidestep his probing question. "What I think is that I have chores to do. All the talk in the world won't get them done."

"These cabbages here look ripe and ready. How many are you wantin' me to pick?"

"I didn't mean for you to set your hand to my work!"

The doctor squatted down and absently brushed a little dirt from the side of the nearest head of cabbage. "I wasna born with a scalpel in my hand. Some of my most cherished memories are of helpin' Ma in our garden." He smiled at Mercy. "I confess, I often took a can along, just in case a worm turned up. Fish and vegetables make a fine meal."

"Why did you come here today?"

"I had a couple of reasons." He reached toward her. "Knife."

"How do you know I have a knife with me?" Ever since *that day*, she'd carried a knife in her apron pocket.

"Any practical woman would when her garden brimmed like this." He accepted the knife, cut a cabbage, and hefted the head a few times. "Round and heavy and the color's good." He tilted his head to the side. "I've said the selfsame thing about a few of the babes I've delivered."

I knew not to trust him. She turned away as she said in a flat tone, "You came to talk to me of the child of my shame."

"Stop right there." He straightened up and stepped in front of her. "Whatever else you think, Mercy Stein, know this: I have not, and I never will think of you as being shamed. Shame implies you did something that makes you guilty. You did nothing wrong."

"If I did nothing wrong, then why is God punishing me?" She slapped her hand over her mouth and stepped backward, away from him. Something hit her ankle, and she started to fall.

"Careful." The doctor's fingers clamped around her wrist and drew her upright. His strength amazed her. Until now, he'd always been restrained and gentle. His brothers came and did physical labor, so the fact that he was every bit as tall and broad as they hadn't registered. "The hoe was behind you, lass."

"You're strong." It came out as an accusation.

"That fact needn't trouble you. I've taken an oath to heal, not to harm."

Mercy stared at him. *How did he know I'm afraid?* Just as quickly, she resented the fact that he knew of her vulnerability. "You talk too boldly."

"I'm a plainspoken man. Hiding behind fancy words never suited me. Cutting to the heart of a matter is best. I admire how you've been doing that today. The things you've said thus far—you've shown rare courage for admitting what others would gloss o'er."

Courage? Mercy shook her head. "How can you tell me not to be troubled by your strength in one minute, only to suggest I'm brave in the next?"

"Because until you're honest enough to confess your doubts and fears, you canna get beyond them. God created us with physical bodies, but just as surely He filled us with feelings and placed a soul within us. 'Tisna just your body that is changing. Your feelings and faith are, too. You've come to the point where you recognize that fact."

Mercy watched him nod his head as if he'd just solved the problems instead of starkly laying them out. Loneliness swamped her. No one could possibly understand—

"I'll not insult you by spouting platitudes and saying I know how deep your sorrows flow." The doctor gave her wrist a tiny squeeze, then loosened his hold and slid his hand down until his fingers laced with hers. "I came today to promise to help you through the weeks and months—aye, and e'en the years ahead. As your doctor, I'll inform you what to expect.

"If you'd like, I'll loan you my little red book. I took care not to write the woman's name in it, and she gave me leave to put down whate'er I wished. You needn't worry that we'd be prying into her privacy. Think on it and let me know if you'd like that. Since you dinna hae a mother or grandma here to instruct you from a woman's perspective, it might be nice."

Mercy couldn't unknot all of the feelings coiling inside her. His offer was everything she needed but not what she wanted. Why couldn't one of the ladies from church pay a visit and privately teach her such intimate things? But the women all kept their distance and withheld their counsel—yet the doctor didn't because he felt she and this babe were blameless.

"You asked why God is punishing you. Terrible things happen, but they are not always His doing."

"But He lets them happen."

"There's no denying that." He paused. "Hae you e'er noticed that for all the trials that beset Job, God ne'er took His hand off the man? Just as surely as I stand here and hold your hand in mine, He is with you and has not loosened His grip."

One by one, Mercy uncurled her fingers. She dragged her hand free from the doctor's hold. "Job's friends still stayed by his side."

The doctor snorted. "Some friends. Even Job's wife told him to 'Curse God, and die.' That kind of help is worse than none a-tall. Job held fast to his faith, and that's why the story has such a grand ending."

"There's not a good ending for my story. There can't be."

"I disagree. To say that, you give up your faith in God's love and goodness."

Mercy closed her eyes. Pain washed over her. The loneliness she felt wasn't just for friends. In the maelstrom life had become, she'd lost her faith, too.

"Earlier, you asked why God's punishing you. In the midst of all this, dinna be shy of asking those hard questions."

"It makes no difference," she said in a tone that sounded as heavy as her heart felt. "There are no answers."

"I've noticed something. Christians who grow up as believers most often come to a crisis at some point in life. 'Tis then all they were told is stripped away. All they have left is a skeleton of faith. Just as your grandda has had to work to build up his wounded muscles, you have to build up your strength of faith so you can continue on your walk with the Lord. 'Tis by asking the questions, praying, and reading the Word that you will succeed."

I can't get past asking the questions. Praying and reading the Bible—I can't. As soon as she told herself that, something inside shot back, *Can't, or won't?*

—⚬—

"Here is your book." Mercy's voice was barely audible as she palmed the tiny leather book to Robert.

He casually tucked it into his pocket and surveyed the huge assortment of crates and dishes in the back of her buckboard. "You brought enough food to feed an army for a year."

"Everyone is talking about your house kit. I expect a whole army of men to come help. They would come anyway, but their curiosity will have them arrive early and leave late."

"Hot as it's been, it makes sense that we start early." Rob hefted the closest crate. "Do you have any particular order to this?"

"That one can be stored back—it is for late in the day. This one," she said as she started to lift another, "I will need—"

"Put that down." Rob's throat ached with restraint. It took every shred of self-control not to roar the order at her.

"It is not heavy. I—"

He shifted the crate he held to one side and jerked the other from her. "Go open the screen door."

She scampered ahead. Once inside, Rob set down the crates and turned on her. "You canna be lifting things like this."

"I'm not weak. I put them all in the wagon myself."

"Miss Stein, it has nothing to do with strength. Your delicate condition—" The color flooding her cheeks left him feeling crass and mean. He'd made his point, so he changed tactics. "Three men live here. We're strong of muscle but feeble in the kitchen. Stay here and direct us as to where you want each crate to go."

"Cabbage and carrots in this one," Duncan announced as he carried in a bushel basket.

"Go ahead and put those wherever you want," Chris said as he entered on Duncan's heels. "I've got strudel here. I'm taking it upstairs. If either of you says a word about it, you won't get a bite."

Mercy shook her finger. "Christopher Gregor, you behave yourself."

"I am. I offered to share this with my brothers."

"You will share it with all of your brothers in Christ tomorrow morning."

"If any is left, I will." Chris sounded downright reasonable.

Mercy smiled. "You cannot always have whatever you grab for."

Chris scowled at Rob. "She's teasing, right?"

Mercy's head dipped. "I am not that kind of woman."

"Hey—I didn't mean—"

Rob swiped the strudel and set it on the cramped "kitchen" table. "Chris, you're thinkin' with your belly instead of your brain. Mercy, you'd think the man's never eaten a single morsel."

"Your logic is flawed," Chris snapped back. "It's because I've eaten Mercy's strudel that I'm claiming it. She should be flattered by that fine praise."

"Mercy, Chris is too dense to apologize properly." Rob tapped the toe of his boot a few times. "But now that Chris has given it consideration, he's wanting to let you choose another piece of gingerbread for the house."

"I am not!"

Duncan slapped Chris on the back. "We should have known you'd be in a generous mood, Chris. Mercy, he wants you to choose two."

Mercy's head was still bowed. Rob glared at Chris to make him watch his words, then pasted on a smile. Tilting Mercy's face upward, Rob asked, "So what do you think?"

"I think you Scotsmen are crazy."

"Not as crazy as my house is going to look," Chris muttered.

"*Our* house." Duncan shoved Chris toward the door.

"I'm going to have the last word," Chris growled. "Just you wait and see."

Rob stepped closer to Mercy. Her eyes widened and the pulse at her throat pounded far too fast. *I've got to teach her she's safe with me.* "I have to tell you something secret."

Chapter 12

Y ou do?"

He nodded and crooked his finger. She hesitated for a moment, then leaned the tiniest bit closer. Rob cupped his hand and leaned toward her ear. "Chris and I have an agreement."

Her brows puckered.

"He decided to give all of the gingerbread to Duncan, and I agreed—other than all of the pieces he owes you."

"Duncan does not know this?" Mercy started to pull away.

Rob closed the space and whispered, "Duncan doesna know yet. . .but the jest is on Chris. He wasna mindful of his words when we came to the pact. Duncan gets all the gingerbread—but Chris didna think to say where Duncan had to put it."

Mercy's lips parted in surprise.

"Whatever this is," Chris declared as he returned with two large pans, "it smells good."

"It is not for you." Mercy scooted past Rob and swiped a pan from Chris.

Chris let go, but he got a fierce look on his face and held fast to the second one. "Why not?"

A smile lifted Mercy's lips. "Because you do not like gingerbread."

—⁂—

"I've never seen such a mess," Mercy said that noon.

"Ooch, 'tis true." Rob wiped his brow. "But 'tis an organized mess. Since Chris has gotten everyone working on a specific portion of the kit, the chaos has ceased."

Mercy heaved a sigh. "You are a man of science, Robert. An intelligent man. How can you stand in the midst of this madness and hold out any hope that such confusion will build your house?"

"I have faith."

Mercy gave him a dubious look.

Rob motioned toward the lot. "The frame is almost done, and the external walls are coming along. Suddenly, everything will fit together. Wait and see."

"Two days. It has been two days, and still, it has so far to go. Do you know that these same men who are helping you all get together and put up an entire barn in just one day?"

"By tomorrow, the bulk of the work will be done. The rest, Chris wants to do on his own. He's gotten excited by the challenge."

"Excited? Is that what you call it when he complained about the bay window? Or is excited when he stubbed the toe of his boots against the scalloped shingles for the bottom half of the front wall?"

"Nae, lass. Those moments were just mild irritations. Excited was when he bellowed because you'd bested in that bargain you struck." Rob chortled softly. "I dinna think Chris will e'er eat strudel again without thinking on how he agreed to put that onion top on the turret instead of the plain cone design he planned on."

Mercy grimaced. "In truth, Rob, I thought that was all a joke. I did not think your brother took me seriously."

"It served him right. His greed got the better of him."

"Are you saying that because he ate that whole strudel all by himself?"

The doctor's mouth kicked up into a rakish smile. "I'm not going to answer. Just you wait, though—after tomorrow, the house will be well on the way. And better still, after that, Chris will be so busy with constructing the rest, he'll not be restless and underfoot all the time."

"Perhaps I should make more bargains with him. Was there any special piece of the gingerbread you liked?"

"Let's see. You have the fan at the apex of the eaves, the onion top on the turret, and the bay window. . .and there's the fish scale clapboards in the middle third of the front. . .and the spindled veranda."

"Don't forget the pretty scrolled gingerbread in the upper corners of the windows."

"I couldn't forget that." The doctor's grin grew wider still. "That was when Chris started moaning that the place was going to wind up looking more like a wedding cake than a house."

"I think you are enjoying this," Mercy accused.

"And I think, Mercy Ellen Stein, that you are a very smart young woman." The doctor walked off, calling, "Chris, Mercy and I were just talking. . ."

Chris let out a groan that sounded over all the hammering.

—⁕—

"What a pretty new apron!" Carmen greeted from her veranda.

"Thank you." Good manners demanded Mercy acknowledge the compliment, even though she'd hoped no one would notice her apron. Instead of the bibbed, tie-in-the-back aprons she'd always worn, this one reminded her of a pretzel. The front hung from neck to hem, but the back pieces swooped up to the opposite shoulders.

Instead of accentuating a slender waist, this one was meant to hide a tummy that now bulged outward.

"Everything's ready." Carmen hobbled down the walkway. "Duncan Gregor brought over canning jars last night."

"Good." Relief flooded Mercy. She didn't want to have to walk down the street and into the mercantile. Ever since the week of threshing, people had changed. The women didn't avoid or shun her anymore—but they took pains to avoid the topic of childbearing, babies, and child rearing. That left awkward silences and tense moments whenever Mercy was around.

Her hand slid into her apron pocket. The doctor's little red book was there. Every couple of weeks, he'd slip it to her. She'd pore over the pages at night in her room. Each time she returned the book, Mercy felt as if she'd lost a friend. Every time the doctor left it in her keeping, solace blanketed her.

"What are you daydreaming about?"

"Oh!" Mercy jumped. A thought flashed through her mind. "I cannot remember if I took the iron off the stove."

"In this heat, you shouldn't be ironing anything other than Sunday-best clothes." Carmen linked arms with her and started dragging her across the street.

"This is the wrong way," Mercy said in a wry tone.

"I suppose I'd better warn you, we have more to do than we'd planned on."

"Why is that?"

"The doctor's been paid for several accounts in the past week."

"I see."

Carmen giggled. "Mercy, you're too nice. Ismelda's been moaning all morning about it."

"She decided she liked the pickles we made last time with the cucumbers."

"But this time, it's—well, you just have to see this for yourself." Carmen led her around the side of the doctor's office to the yard between it and the fancy new house as she whispered, "I didn't want to miss this."

Mercy took a look and started to shake.

—⁂—

It would be rude to laugh. Truly, it would. Mercy covered her mouth and pretended to muffle a cough while she marshaled her self-control.

Duncan stopped poking at the armadillo and rapped on it with his knuckles. " 'Tis like a knight's armor."

"There's got to be a chink in it. Every defense has a weakness," Chris declared as he rolled the creature over.

The doctor came out of the house with every cutting tool ever invented. "Good morning, Mercy! Have you seen them?"

Mercy bit her lip and nodded.

The doctor laid out an ax, a cleaver, four knives, a saw, a scalpel, and a pair of pruning shears. " 'Tis a most curious beast. The exoskeleton is osseous—reminiscent of a turtle or a crab, but—"

"Rob," Chris half growled, "hot as 'tis, the beasts are going to cook in their shells if you muse all the morning long about their scientific merits."

"I doubt the hide's usable." Duncan drummed his fingers on the odd-looking beast.

"My grandmother had a purse made from one," Carmen said. "She used it to carry all of her healing herbs."

"Very interesting." Duncan stared at the armadillo more critically. "So how was the shell cut?"

While Carmen and he spoke, Mercy sidled closer to the doctor. She slid her hand into her pocket and fingered the little book, took a deep breath, and passed it to him. Subtle as could be, he tucked it in his pocket.

"I saw Cletus." The sheriff sauntered up. "He said he paid you four armadillos. Any of them a hairy screamer?"

"Hairy screamer?" Mercy echoed.

The doctor turned his attention on the sheriff. "Are there different varieties?"

"Don't be so gullible, Rob." Chris elbowed him. "Connant's grinning like a fool. This creature is so odd, God wouldn't have created more than one type. Even Mercy thought 'hairy screamer' was absurd."

"Chris, you're such a skeptic," the sheriff said. His grin didn't fade in the least. He nodded toward the armadillo on the battered wooden table. "Those are good eating. Taste a lot like—"

"Chicken?" Chris inserted in a disbelieving tone. "Have you noticed how everything is supposed to taste like chicken? Snake, for example."

The sheriff ignored him. "Pork. Armadillo tastes like a nice, juicy pork roast. Funny things, though. They can swim."

"Texas tall tale," Chris muttered.

"Texas tales are an important tradition," Mercy said. "You are supposed to admire them."

"That's right," the sheriff nodded. "But armadillos' talents don't stop at swimming. They can jump hip high when they need to."

The doctor chortled softly. "Aye, Connant. I'm supposing though they've wee, stubby legs and claws made perfect for burrowing, they'd far rather jump o'er fences than skitter below."

"This one's got the best-looking hide. Let's butcher one of the others first." Duncan dropped it down beside the other three.

With a shriek, one of the others jumped astonishingly high and plopped loudly onto the table.

Instantly, the doctor whisked Mercy behind his back. Duncan shouted, and Carmen screamed. Mercy couldn't see around the doctor's broad shoulders, and he kept her against his spine in an unyielding hold. "Check the others," he ordered someone.

The sheriff's whooping laugh stopped just long enough to declare, "You wouldn't have believed me if I said they sometimes play dead."

"Cletus said they were dead," Duncan said.

"Well that one is surely dead now," Chris asserted.

The doctor's hold eased. In a lithe move, he turned around and held Mercy by her shoulders. "Are you all right, lass?"

She nodded.

" 'Twas a shock. Let's sit you down."

"I'm okay."

Carmen let out a nervous giggle. "I told you we had to be here, Mercy."

The sight on the table made Mercy's brows rise.

Dr. Gregor pivoted to block her view and tugged on her arm. "Come, now. 'Tisna good for you to see such things."

Mercy looked into his steady eyes. "I think Christopher has been taking lessons from me—from when I kill chickens. But I just use the axe and behead a chicken. Your brother—he used the ax and a knife and—"

"If," the doctor interrupted as he tried to divert her from what his brother had done, "your fried armadillo tastes half as good as your fried chicken, 'twill be fine eating, indeed."

"Oh no." Carmen shook her head. "Roasted, barbecued, or in a casserole. That's how they're cooked."

"I told you they don't taste like chicken," the sheriff groused.

"When you have them butchered, we'll cook them." Carmen looked at the creature. "After all, we don't want to open the oven and have one hop out of the roasting pan."

"Are you sure?" The doctor searched Mercy's face.

She nodded solemnly. "Yes. He'd track the drippings across the floor so we couldn't make gravy."

Chapter 13

When other helpers fail and comforts flee,
Help of the helpless, O abide with me.

obert followed the soft alto notes of the plaintive hymn and found Mercy
in the field. She wore a cloth bag over her left shoulder and was stoop-
ing to pick beans. The fullness of that gathering sack couldn't hide the distinctly maternal shape of her form.

"Hello." Rob plucked several beans and slid them into the gathering sack. For
the first time, Mercy didn't reflexively flinch or scoot away to avoid any proximity.
He hummed a few bars of the hymn, then picked a few more beans. Without looking at her he said, "The hymn you're singing—'twas a scant week or so after my ma's
death that I heard it for the first time."

"I'm sorry. Did I make you sad?"

"Does the hymn make you sad?" he countered.

Her brows puckered. "It is not our way to speak of our feelings."

"Yet you asked me about my feelings." He held up a hand to keep her from
apologizing. "It didn't offend me, Mercy. It touched me, knowing my reaction mattered to you. You've a tender heart. Knowing that as I do, canna you see how I'd care
for your feelings just as you'd care for mine?"

"Sunday, the pastor—he said we must live by faith, not by feelings."

"Dinna ye think the God who gave us those feelings knows us well enough to
understand them? And that He walks beside us e'en in the valleys when the shadows
are the darkest?"

She shrugged and continued to pick beans.

"The passage in Ecclesiastes comes to my mind. Recall how it speaks of the different seasons in life? On how there's a time to weep and a time to laugh, a time to
mourn and a time to dance? 'Tisna that we're not to have the feelings. We're to hold
fast to God regardless of the moods of our hearts."

Her hands slowed. In a barely audible voice, she whispered, "I'm reading my
Bible again."

Again. The lass stopped for a time. The revelation didn't surprise him, but Rob ached for her. "God will honor your diligence. Aye, that He will. Are ye havin' a rough time talking to Him?"

Mercy's eyes grew huge, and tears filled them.

Not waiting so she'd feel pressed to give him an answer, Rob took the gathering bag from her shoulder and slid it onto his own. "Mercy, we're meant to bear one another's burdens. Just as surely as I can hold this bag, I can hold you up to the Lord. Indeed, I have been all along. I was remiss in not telling you that afore now."

Her tears spilled over.

Why didna I think to say anything long ago?

"It's so hard—praying. I don't have the words to say."

"You were talking to the Lord when I arrived. Your soul was reaching toward Him in song because your heart was too muddled to put everything into words."

"Do you think so?" Anguish tainted her thready voice.

"Aye, that I do. He hears our thoughts. He knows the desires of our hearts. Even when we're so burdened all we can manage is to groan or cry, He understands. God is faithful. He abides with you, Mercy Stein."

On the ride out to the farm, Rob had thought about presenting the possibility of Mercy relinquishing the babe and having the Heims adopt it. Each evening, he'd prayed over that issue, but God hadn't directed him to say anything yet. Rob looked at her and knew the truth: The lass couldn't make a wise decision until her heart was spiritually settled. Until then, it would be cruel to say a word.

A thought occurred to him. "Do you remember Peter's birthday?"

"The fireworks." She cleared her throat. "You Gregors brought fireworks. They were beautiful."

"Do you recall us discussing how there was only a half-moon and few stars?"

She nodded.

"A good thing, that—the darker the sky, the brighter the fireworks glow. 'Tisna that the fireworks wouldn't go off just as well on a full moon's eve, but the contrast wouldna be the same. So, too, in our journey with God—on fair days, the sunlight is all we need to get by, but in the dark of night, if we seek His light, 'tis a thing of rare beauty. You might want to think on that."

Mercy nodded slowly. They worked in silence for a short time, then she cleared her throat. "Did your brothers tell you? Something is getting into the last of the melons and our pumpkins."

He chuckled. "Aye, and you ought to hear my brothers discussing how best to trap an armadillo. They took an immediate liking to that meat."

"They are hoping in vain, because Grossvater showed the tracks to Peter. He said the pest is either a raccoon or a 'possum. They have front prints that are much alike, but a 'possum's rear print is funny—it is because they have something like a thumb back there to help climb trees."

"So is it a raccoon or a 'possum?"

Mercy paused a moment. "I don't recall!"

"Is either of them edible?"

She wrinkled her nose. "I have heard they are, but I have never prepared them, either."

"I dinna dare ask Connant. He'd take advantage of my ignorance and weave a tale for the ages. After that crazy armadillo jumped and screamed, I'm liable to believe just about anything he'd concoct about these wild animals in America."

"You didn't have any of these animals in Scotland?"

"Skunks, armadillos, and opossums are all American creatures."

"Was it hard to give up all you'd known and come so far from home?"

"'Twas equal parts anticipation and fear. Losing Da on the way near broke my heart—but my brothers. . ." He tucked more beans in the sack. "We're here together. That's what counts."

"And so now you make a new home."

Rob winked at her. "And we built one, too. Chris is proud of that house. Dinna e'er take exception to his grumbling. He takes a secret pride in finding ways to complain just so we can admire it aloud all over again. Remember those scalloped shingles for part of the clapboarding? Just last night, he stood in the yard and complained that our house has more scales than a fish."

Finally, a smile chased across her face and brightened her eyes. "You must tell him something. He isn't a Scotsman any longer. By telling such a tall tale, he proved he is now a Texan. That means it is not just a house; now it is a home, for this is where you will all stay. Texans never want to leave."

"So you're stuck with us forever." As soon as he spoke the thought, Rob practically dropped the harvesting bag. *I almost said "me" instead of "us." How can it be?* Just as quickly, the answer struck him with blinding clarity. *Da was right. He warned me I'd close off my feelings so I wouldna feel my patients' pain. All along, I've struggled with keeping my distance from Mercy. More and more, what she needed and wanted mattered to me. The reason—'tis plain as can be. Over these months I've lost my heart to the lass, and I didna even know it.*

—◊—

Reluctantly, Mercy shut the hymnal and got up from the piano stool. Ever since the doctor pointed out how she'd been using music to talk to God, she'd found great solace in singing, playing, or even humming. Then, too, the Psalms of David suddenly took on a whole new meaning. He'd been sorely troubled often in his life, yet he'd used his psalms and played his harp to tell God how he felt.

The spicy scent of pumpkin permeated the house. Pumpkins with stems would store well for a long while, but those without stems tended to spoil. She'd baked three pies and six loaves of pumpkin bread and had roasted pumpkin seeds. Tomorrow she and Carmen would make pumpkin marmalade and can puree.

Puree. Mercy stared out the window. *When do babies start eating food like that?*

Peter burst through the door.

Mercy automatically called out, "Wipe your feet!" Stubby scampered past her. She heaved a sigh and swept up the pup. "Peter, you know the rule. You must train—" Her voice died out as Grossvater shouldered past Peter to ease something through the door. He took a few steps into the house, then set the oak piece on the floor. A light push set the cradle into a gentle rock.

"There!" Grossvater nodded approvingly. "It is still as good as it was when I made it to hold your own papa."

Mercy started to shake as the runners rocked a rhythm of impending doom.

Grossvater wound his arm around her. "The day I finished this and gave it to your grandmother, we put it by our bed. Each morning, we stood beside it and prayed for a healthy child and that we would be good parents. I will stand beside you, Mercy. We will pray those same things."

I don't know if I can be a good mother. And Grossvater—he is old. He will not be here all of the years it will take to rear this babe. Panic started to envelop her. Her heart hammered loud in her ears. Gott in Himmel, *how will I ever—*

"We can do this together," Grossvater crooned.

Mercy bowed her head. She didn't want to admit her doubts or confess her worries. Regardless of his assurance, the fears exploded.

"Mr. Stein," a voice came from the doorway. "Have you—"

The beat got louder and drowned out the man's words. Boots stepped between her and the cradle—the doctor's boots. Instinctively, Mercy reached for him as everything started to swirl around her.

Chapter 14

There now, lass." Rob blotted Mercy's colorless face. He wasn't sure whether he was trying to comfort her or reassure himself. On a medical level, she was fine—but that didn't take into account her feelings. *In the midst of her panic, she reached out to me. That counts for something.*

Another mewling sound came from her as her eyes fluttered again. This time they stayed open. Rob fought the urge to scoop her into his arms and murmur all was well. Instead, he leaned over her bed and said in a stern tone, "You canna be wearin' that whalebone cage any longer."

As she gasped, Mercy's hand fumbled beneath the bedsheet.

"I cut it off. An absolute wonder 'tis that you've not been swooning thrice a day whilst being constricted so severely." The whole time he chided her, he tenderly petted back tiny wisps of hair that coiled around her face.

"You cut it?" Her whisper held a squeak of outrage.

"The laces, I did." He scowled. "Though if you dinna give me your word that you'll leave it off, I'll consider cutting some other part to render it unusable."

Color filled her cheeks as she turned her face away.

Determined to be matter-of-fact so she'd get over her embarrassment, he stated, "You needn't fret o'er this discussion. 'Tis common sense, a woman not trussing herself up whilst she's with child—especially in her last months."

Mercy refused to look back at him. Rob placed his hand on her tummy, and she went as rigid as her stays had been. "The babe—'tis growing fast now and needs to be free to tumble." As if on cue, the mound beneath his palm squirmed. "In this next month, the freedom you give the babe is vital—'twill allow him to settle his head downward. Trussed in the corset, your body canna yield sufficient room. I'm tryin' to spare you a breech birthing."

Still, she said nothing. Until now, Mercy hadn't ever allowed him to examine her. Other than peppering their private conversations with medical information and providing her with the little red book, Rob hadn't been in a position of asserting himself. *May as well seize this opportunity.* He slid one hand over hers and dragged it downward. "Feel this? 'Tis round and hard—the babe's head. Down here, 'tis round, too—but soft. 'Tis his backside."

At least she wasn't jerking away.

"When he's kicking and pushing, which side do ye feel it on most?"

A few seconds passed, then she feathered her fingers to the left.

"Ah, so that's the way he's facin'." Rob chuckled. "And kickin'! He's got some strength."

Mercy pushed away his hands. "I have work to see to."

"As do I. I'm on my way out to pay a call on the Stukys."

"Someone is sick?" Finally, Mercy looked at him.

"Not exactly." Rob hitched his shoulder. "Their stallion's got more spirit than sense. He kicked out of his stall. I put stitches in him late last week, and the time's come to remove them."

"They don't have a goat or a mule." Mercy held the sheet clear up to her nose. "One would help."

"How would a goat help me remove sutures?"

"A goat or a mule in a stable makes the horses calm down. You could borrow Sadie."

"Sadie has a knack for chewing my clothes. I'll have you come along."

Mercy's eyes grew huge. "Are you calling me a goat?"

Rob stared at her. "Of course not. How did you—oh." He gave her an apologetic grin. "I can see how that must have sounded. I meant that if I had you along, you'd make Sadie behave while Sadie made the stallion mind his manners. Somewhere in the midst of that, I lost both my mind and my manners."

"It was a simple mistake is all."

He turned toward her wardrobe. "I presume your blue-and-white frock is in here." Ignoring her splutters, he opened the door and carried on in a conversational tone, "I'm not one to pay much mind to what a woman wears, but this one you've stitched for yourself caught my attention."

"Because it's the size of a revival tent," she muttered.

"Nae, not a-tall. My ma—she had a plate she dearly prized. Delft, she called it. This frock, it puts me in mind of that plate. Just seein' you in it makes my day improve."

She blinked in surprise.

"I'll drape it here and wait for you out in the parlor."

"I need to stay and see to supper. Peter can go with you."

Rob didn't argue with her. He left her room, pulled the door shut, and walked over toward the kitchen where Mr. Stein and Peter stood.

"My granddaughter—"

"Is fine." He grinned at Peter. "When your sister grew faint, I'm sure she accidentally put Stubby in the cradle. Best you take him back out to the barn ere she sees him in there."

Peter snickered and dashed to freedom with the puppy.

Rob cast a glance at the bedroom door. "Mercy's needing some fresh air. I aim to have her accompany me to the Stu—" Rob halted when Mr. Stein shook his head.

"This is not done." Mr. Stein's voice came out in the barest of whispers. "You do not know our ways. For a young man and woman to spend time together, alone—"

"I've been in Texas a little over half a year." Rob stared into the old man's eyes. In that moment, everything felt so right. "I'm fully aware of the implications. I came here today to declare my intent."

Mr. Stein shook his head. "I made a mistake once before. Without praying about it, I told Otto he could have my granddaughter as his wife."

"I've not spoken rashly." Robert tapped his chest. "In my heart and soul, I ken Mercy's the one for me."

"Robert Gregor, you're as fine a man as God's made, but that doesn't change my stance. I'll not lean on my own understanding and let her suffer heartbreak as the result again. Until I'm certain that it is God's will for her to be yours, you are not to court her. This isn't about what men think or want. It's about waiting on the Lord and seeking His wisdom."

"Fair enough," Rob said. "Until I spoke with the Almighty o'er this, I kept silent. God doesna change. He'll be givin' you the same assurance He gave me."

Sadness radiated from Mr. Stein's craggy features. "Only a great work of God will give my Mercy any peace."

Hearing Mercy's soft footfall, Rob pointed at the pie and raised his voice ever so slightly. "Give her two pieces. I'm supposing she was so busy baking, she forgot to eat at midday."

Her door opened and she emerged.

"Mercy, when you brought lunch out to the field, you did not eat." Her grandfather shook his finger at her. "You must eat for two."

"If I eat any more, I'll grow bigger than Evalina!"

"You're hardly in danger of being even half the size of your milk cow." Rob rubbed his jaw thoughtfully. "If you give me your word that you'll not skip meals and will have either a glass of Evalina's fine milk or a slice of cheese between those meals, we'll not fuss at you about what you eat."

"You need not fuss. When I'm working in the kitchen, I take tastes."

"Mercy Stein!" Rob managed to sound scandalized. "You baked today. Are you telling us you licked the bowls?"

A fetching blush tinted her cheeks. "And what do you know about licking bowls, Dr. Gregor?"

"Not nearly enough. 'Tis the drawback of having big brothers." He gave her a woebegone look. "From now on, I'm going to have to plan a house call on the days you bake. Aye, I am."

———

"Is he gone?" Carmen peeked around the door.

"Who?" Mercy pretended not to know what she meant.

"The doctor." Carmen came in and clomped toward the table. "Duncan mentioned his little brother was coming by here today."

"It is hard to think of the doctor as being anyone's little brother." Mercy finished icing the cake. She fought the urge to look at the bowl over on the counter. The doctor had swiped his finger all along the inside of the bowl and licked the batter off his finger as the cake baked in the oven. Once or twice a week he came by. Though he never stayed long, his visits invariably left Mercy feeling. . .better.

Carmen leaned against the counter, but she didn't take off her shawl. "All three of those Gregor men could masquerade as giants."

"Ja, this is true." Mercy looked at her friend. "But something is bothering you. Why don't we have some coffee and cake and talk about it?"

Carmen's features twisted. "You might not want me to stay."

"Nonsense." Mercy put down the butter knife and poured two cups of coffee.

"I don't know what to say or do." Carmen flopped onto a chair. Her dark eyes filled with tears. "I love my sister. You know I do."

"Of course." Mercy sat beside her.

Carmen snatched her hand and held it tight. "Her good news is our bad news. Mercy, Otto asked her to marry him."

The news left Mercy feeling strangely old and empty. "You must tell Ismelda I wish her to be happy."

"But doesn't it break your heart for Otto—" Carmen pressed her fingers to her mouth. "I'm sorry. That was rude of me."

"You didn't mean to hurt my feelings, and you have not." Mercy stared through the open doorway to her room and spied the cradle. "Things have changed. Otto is a different man, and I am a different woman. The dreams of my girlhood are long gone."

Carmen's hold on her hand tightened. "It's a good match, but I'm jealous. Isn't that awful of me? Mercy, no man has ever expressed any interest in me. I'm the older sister. By custom, I'm supposed to marry first—but I'm going to be a crippled old spinster, and Ismelda will have a husband and children."

Mercy twisted and pulled Carmen's head down onto her shoulder. Holding her, she whispered, "It is hard when dreams die."

"What do I do now?"

Mercy finally straightened up and rubbed her back. "All around us, we see girls marry and have babies. We both assumed that would be God's plan for us, too. Now, instead of telling God what we think, we have to ask Him what He wants."

"I'm in trouble then." Carmen sniffled and tried to smile. "I'm far better at talking than at listening."

"Me, too. I've started to sing hymns and recite Bible verses. I read one a few days ago. It was where David is talking to Solomon. 'For the Lord searcheth all hearts, and understandeth all the imaginations of the thoughts: if thou seek him, he will be found of thee.' So see? God knew our dreams. But it is our job to seek Him instead of what we imagined for ourselves."

Carmen looked at her for a long while. "You're right, Mercy. You have changed. Months ago you were a girl with stars in your eyes. Now you are a woman."

"Life changes us all. I'm trying to change in the ways God wants me to. I have to—not just for myself, but for my baby."

Carmen didn't end up staying long. After she left, Mercy added seasonings to the split peas and a ham bone in the simmering soup pot. Finished with other chores, she sat in the rocking chair in the parlor and darned Peter's socks. Once those were repaired, she stared into her sewing bag. A small ball of yarn and several crochet hooks rested there. Slowly, she took out the yarn and selected a hook.

The first thing her mother taught her to crochet had been a cap for her doll. As Mercy started the hook into motion, she began to sing the hymn her mother had sung that day. *"Weißt du, wie viel Sternlein stehen... Do you know how many stars..."*

—◊—

"Dr. Gregor!"

Rob kneed his mount toward the fence. "Mr. Stein."

"I have something to ask."

Rob kicked out of the stirrups and dismounted. "Aye?"

"This baby my granddaughter carries—what do you think?"

"I think he's going to be healthy enough to bellow down your house." Rob grinned. "Which is why he should grow up in mine."

The old man's weathered face broke into a smile. "So you would allow Mercy to keep this child?"

" 'Tis borne of the woman I love. That alone will cause me to love him." Rob tipped back his hat. "If Mercy wishes to keep the babe, 'twill be ours."

"*If* she wishes to keep it?" The old man looked scandalized.

"Aye." Robert didn't back down. "You and I love Mercy and will love her child. But Mercy—she was forced. In the end, she must decide whether she can love the babe entirely or if it would be best to give him to a childless couple. It is a choice only she can make."

"Have you said something to her?"

"Not yet." Rob squinted toward the house. "I know of a couple, but that doesn't mean they are meant to have this baby. I've held my silence and waited for Mercy and God to show me what's right."

"But a woman who could give away her own flesh and blood—"

"Is a woman who is honest with herself and willing to give that baby a better life than she herself could give the child, holding the feelings she may have. I love Mercy. That love willna change regardless of whate'er decision she might make."

Mr. Stein let out a long sigh. "I was so busy praying about whether you were right for her, I never thought to pray about if I was giving her the right guidance myself."

"Grossvater!" Peter shouted from the porch. "Supper!"

Mr. Stein slapped Rob on the back. "Come. Stay for supper."

They stopped at the pump and washed up before entering the house. "I hope you don't mind—" Rob began.

Mercy turned from the stove. "I've said you are always welcome. Peter saw you, so we have a place waiting—see?"

"What have you done?" Mr. Stein's voice was rich with emotion.

Rob had been so intent on Mercy, he'd not noticed anything else. He looked over his shoulder at Mr. Stein.

Mercy breezed past them and into the parlor. "I've been busy." A shy smile flirted at the corners of her mouth as she started to tuck little bits into her sewing box. "It's probably well past time that I started making my baby some clothes."

Never before had he heard her say, "*My* baby." It was always, "The baby." It wasn't just what she said, but how she said it, too. Rob knew then and there that God was going to bless him with a wife and child at the same time.

Chapter 15

So I learned an important lesson," Ismelda said as she clipped a thread. She gave Mercy a wry look. "It doesn't matter how long he's lived in Texas, a German farmer still doesn't know what he's asking for when he says spicy food is okay."

"I've tasted your chili. I know better." Mercy finished hemming the baby gown.

"We made mild tamales for lunch. You don't need to worry." Carmen patted her hand.

"I do love your tamales." Mercy smiled. "That, and your sweet corn casserole. For Thanksgiving, you might want to make that."

"Otto won't need to wash away the taste with a whole pitcher of milk," Carmen teased. "Ismelda, stop snitching my scissors!"

They continued to chatter and sew. As lunchtime neared, Mrs. Kunstler arrived, and she brought along a gentleman. "Isn't it lucky you are in town today, Mercy? I've been wanting to introduce you to Chester Heim. He's my cousin's cousin."

Mercy stammered what she hoped would pass for a polite greeting as she tried to subtly cover her large tummy with a length of cloth. A woman with a mere month to go before having a child only associated with family and very close friends. It was embarrassing enough for Otto's mother to have introduced her to this stranger—surely she wasn't trying to play matchmaker!

Carmen gave Mercy a confused look.

"Ismelda, why don't I help you set the table?" Mrs. Kunstler bustled away.

Mr. Heim mopped his brow. "Miss Stein, I've been eager to meet you. Please understand how much this means to me."

"I'm sorry. I don't—"

He sat beside her on the settee and grabbed her hand. "Time is short."

Mercy snatched her hand away. "Mr. Heim, excuse me."

"The baby, I want it," he blurted out.

Carmen bolted out of her chair. "Mr. Heim, you need to leave."

"My wife and I—we'll take it!" Mr. Heim clamped his hand around Mercy's arm. "It's for the best. I know you'll agree."

Mercy stared at him in horror. In a matter of seconds, Mrs. Kunstler was standing beside him, testifying to his character. At the same time, he was pleading on behalf of his wife. Carmen had fled, and Ismelda stood in mute horror.

"You can rid yourself of your shame this way," Mrs. Kunstler declared.

"You won't be encumbered," Mr. Heim asserted. "Someday, maybe another man will come along. You wouldn't have to confess—"

"That's enough!" The doctor's bellow silenced the room. He strode right up to Mercy. "Mr. Heim, you are to leave now."

"No." Mr. Heim puffed out his chest. "You knew about this, but you didn't help us. I'm taking matters into my own hands." He turned back to Mercy. "Don't you see? This way you won't be completely ruined."

"Mercy was never ruined." The doctor's voice came out in a rumble that would make thunder sound like a mere whimper. He knelt beside her. "I'll let no man slur her."

"I didn't mean it to sound badly," Heim stammered. "You're alone, Miss Stein. My wife and I—we want children."

"Miss Stein is not alone. She has family who love her." The doctor slid his hand over hers. "Aye, and there's a man who loves her, too."

Mercy tore her gaze from Mr. Heim and gawked at the doctor.

" 'Tisna like I'd planned, but I dinna regret making my declaration." He squeezed her hand.

"He's the one, Doctor." Carmen limped back through the front door, her features strained. "He needs to leave."

"Everyone needs to calm down," Mrs. Kunstler said.

Mr. Heim tugged on Mercy's sleeve. "Listen to me. My wife and I would give your baby a good home. If the doctor will take you, the two of you could have your own children."

"If I'll take her?" Rob's voice resonated with outrage. "I'd be blessed if she'd take me!" He stared into Mercy's eyes. "Your value is far above rubies, Mercy. Whate'er decisions you make, they need to be based on what you know and feel deep down in your soul. Dinna allow anyone to discount how special you are, for you are a daughter of the King of Kings." He rose and helped her to her feet.

The minute she stood, self-consciousness flooded her. Mercy knew just how huge she looked.

The doctor tilted her face up to his. "You're every bit as beautiful as you are innocent."

He had her halfway across the street before Mercy could speak. "Are you taking me home?"

"In a manner of speaking." He took her into the beautiful home that they'd built and seated her on the veranda. "Wait here for a moment." He left and reappeared in a matter of seconds. Kneeling beside her once again, he pulled a thin gold band from his pocket. "My Da's last gift to me was Ma's ring and a piece of advice. He knew caring for bodies makes a doctor close off his heart so he doesn't have to feel the pain. He warned me not to do so but instead to take a chance at love."

Mercy stared at the ring. *So he's willing to take a chance and marry me out of pity.*

"Clear down to my soul, I love ye, lass. 'Tis been hard, waiting to tell you. I pledged to your grandda I'd not court you without his leave. It's felt like an eternity, but I finally gained his permission yester noon. I'm askin' you to be my wife—and for no other reason than the love God gave me for you cannot be denied."

Slowly, he tucked the ring in her palm and curled her fingers around it. "You hold my heart in your hand. 'Tis a matter all on its own. I canna expect that you dinna have questions or concerns, so I'll not mince words.

"The child you carry—I'll honor your decision whate'er you choose to do. Just as I love you, I'll cherish this wee one and rear him as my verra own. But if you sense you canna love him without reservation, I'll understand if you wish to allow others to take him into their hearts and home."

She swallowed. "So you're not trying to salvage my honor so the baby is not a—" She couldn't bring herself to say the vile word.

"Blessing. *Each* child is a blessing." He looked at her steadily. "You've two separate decisions to make, Mercy. On one, I've told you I'll support whate'er you decide. On the other, though. . ." He lifted her closed hand and kissed it. "I'm going to do everything in my power to sway you into consenting to be my bride. I'll love you with every breath I ever take, Mercy. Marry me."

Her hand stayed in his, but she turned it over. "A woman in my condition does not think of finding a man who can love her. I once said I wanted a man who would love me regardless of what life brought and who would stand beside me in the bad times."

"I'm that man." The truth sparkled in his eyes.

"But there is another part. That man—I should love him with all that is within me." She opened her fingers, and the ring fell into his palm. "I care for you—and today, I find I care for you in a way I did not realize. It does not seem possible."

"With God, all things are possible. This love is from Him, Mercy."

The last reservation she held crumbled. "I do love you, Robert."

"Duncan! Go fetch Mr. Stein. Chris, grab the parson. We're getting married!"

Mercy yanked on his sleeve. "Robert! I cannot get married. Not like this."

He cupped her face in his hands. "The day I showed you the plans for the house, I told you I couldn't care less about how it looked on the outside. 'Twas the inside that counted. Well, I meant that then, and at the same time, I'm taking those words back this verra minute. You're beautiful, and you're wearing the delft frock I fancy. You couldna be more perfect than you are at this moment. I'm not goin' to give you a chance to change your mind. Nae, I'm not."

"There's no need to rush."

"Ooch, lass, I've been longing to profess my love for you. Now that I have, I dinna want to cross that threshold unless I'm carrying you across it. I'm a reasonable man. I'll give ye a whole hour."

"An hour!"

He nodded. "Carmen can help ye wi' some of her posies. She and her sister can fuss wi' your glorious hair and make themselves pretty so they'll stand alongside you. Aye, since I'll be havin' Duncan and Chris stand wi' me, it's fitting your two friends are there. Your grandda and brother—they're the only others who really matter, aren't they?"

Mercy thought for a moment, then admitted slowly, "Yes."

"Good! Then 'tis set." He gave her an enthusiastic kiss.

One slim hour later, Carmen finished brushing Mercy's hair and topped it with a flower wreath she'd hastily made. "You're beautiful!"

"Here. We made this for you." Ismelda pressed a bouquet into her hands.

Mercy's lips moved, but no sound came out.

"Ready?" Grossvater asked.

"Yes," Carmen answered. She and Ismelda rushed to the front pew.

Autumn sunlight poured through the church windows. Mercy wondered how that could be because she felt so cold. Robert wasn't waiting at the altar for her, and fear welled up. Unaware of her feelings, Grossvater walked her down the aisle. He got her to the front of the church then patted her hand.

It wasn't until then that Robert's brothers entered. Chris came first, and then Duncan. By then, Mercy wasn't cold at all. She couldn't be—not after the shocking sight of the men wearing red, green, and white tartans that bared their knees!

"They're wearing *skirts!*" Peter blurted out.

"Kilts," Chris corrected him.

"Highlanders wear their kilts for important occasions," Mercy declared. She was marrying into Robert's family, and a wife owed her husband loyalty and allegiance. Not only was Robert marrying her, but his brothers were showing their acceptance of the union by wearing their odd garb. Her chin lifted. "I'm honored."

Chris and Duncan had already been standing straight and tall, but at her words, their backs nearly snapped from pride.

Robert approached her. He, too, wore his tartan. Having gotten over the original shock of seeing the men in their kilts, Mercy decided then and there that no man had ever looked half so handsome as her groom did in his kilt. His voice was as warm and steady as his hands when he held her close and proclaimed his vows.

Mercy repeated her vows, and each of the promises she made came straight from her heart.

"What God hath joined together, let no one put asunder," the pastor said at the end. "You may kiss your bride."

"We Gregors have a special tradition." Robert smiled as he pulled a length of cloth from the leather tie at his waist. The cloth matched his kilt.

Draping the cloth over her shoulder, he quoted:

> *"As fair art thou, my bonnie lass,*
> *So deep in luve am I,*
> *And I will luve thee still, my dear,*
> *Till a' the seas gang dry.*

> *"Till a' the seas gang dry, my dear,*
> *And the rocks melt wi' the sun!*
> *And I will luve thee still, my dear*
> *While the sands o' life shall run."*

He drew her close, and his kiss promised all the love she could ever dream of.

TO WALK HUMBLY

by Cathy Marie Hake

Chapter 1

Y"ou've got to come now!" Duncan Gregor shouted hoarsely as he burst through the door.

Carmen Rodriguez's gasp of surprise turned into a groan as the flan she'd been tipping out of the pan slithered and slopped into an unsightly mess on the plate. "You're early. I thought we were having supper at six."

"Nae, lass. 'Tisna that a-tall!" Duncan slumped against the door frame, his chest heaving and his blue eyes huge. "Mercy—the babe!"

"Why didn't you just say so?" Carmen ripped off her apron and put on a fresh one as she hobbled toward the door. "What does Robert say?"

"Rob's not at home! He's out somewhere."

Well, that accounts for why he's flustered. Carmen gave Duncan a reassuring smile. She fought the urge to smooth the wayward lock of inky hair back from his forehead. "I'll stay with Mercy while you go fetch him."

"We canna recall where he went." The man sounded as though he'd been forced to gargle vinegar before making that confession. His gaze swept the house. "Where's your sister? We need all the help we can get."

"Ismelda is at Otto's, helping his mother. She'll be back by six for supper."

"Why can't everyone stay put? Especially Rob. A man who's about to become a father has no business gallivanting off."

"He's a doctor," Carmen pointed out.

"Exactly." Duncan glowered at her. "And just who else is supposed to be helping Mercy through her travail?"

He'd left the door wide open when he barged in, so Carmen stepped out onto the veranda. Cool days like this always made her left leg ache. She'd broken it as a child, and the bones hadn't healed correctly. *It's nothing—especially in comparison to Mercy's travail.*

Duncan cupped Carmen's elbow. "I'm worried about her."

"I'm sure she'll be fine." She reached to shut the door.

Duncan muttered, "This is takin' too long." He shut the door, swept her into his brawny arms, and carried her across the street to the clinic. Once inside, he roared, "Where'd you put her, Chris?"

Silence met them.

Carmen tried to wiggle so he'd put her down. Bad enough her crippled leg kept her from being able to dash around in an emergency—but for him to cart her any farther rated as complete humiliation. "They're probably still at home."

Duncan's face went colorless. "Oh no." He kept possession of her, plowing out the back door and across the yard to the house he shared with his brothers and new sister-in-law. "I'm counting on you."

"I'd do my best, but I've never helped at a birth."

"And you shouldn't have to." Under other circumstances, his scandalized reaction would have amused her, but Carmen couldn't make fun of Duncan. The poor man looked downright sick. "I'm countin' on you to talk sense into Mercy. Tell her she has to wait awhile to have the babe. And be sure to make her promise to go to the clinic. 'Tis safer there."

"Safer?"

"Aye." Dark head bobbing emphatically, Duncan declared, "Rob's got enough medical equipment and drugs there to cure every man, woman, child, and beast in three counties. Whate'er Mercy needs, he'll have it on hand." He kicked open the front door and strode in. "Chris! What's takin' you so long? You were to have Mercy at the—"

"She's refusing to budge." Christopher Gregor looked thoroughly disgruntled.

"Hi, Carmen." Mercy sat in the rocking chair and patted her tummy. "It looks as if we're going to have a New Year's Eve baby."

"Not if I can help it." Chris glowered at her. "You could cooperate and wait a day or so."

"At least go to the clinic," Duncan tacked on as he let go of Carmen's legs and slipped her to the floor. The man looked terrified, yet he instinctively handled her with consideration and didn't turn loose until he was certain she'd become stable on her feet. "Don't you think that's a grand notion, Carmen?"

"I—"

Mercy curled her hands around the chair's arms and rocked faster. Carmen wasn't sure who moaned—but it wasn't Mercy. About a minute later, Mercy relaxed. "I'm having this baby here, Duncan, and you're not going to change my mind."

"We'll see to things." Upon making that declaration, Duncan nodded to Chris.

The brothers bracketed the rocking chair and hefted it.

Mercy let out a surprised yelp.

"What are you men doing?" Carmen stared at the odd scene.

"She wants to be in the rocking chair. We're humoring the lass." Chris spoke as if she'd turned into a half-wit.

Duncan jerked his jaw in the direction of the door. "Run on ahead to the clinic, Carmen. Aren't you supposed to be boiling water or something?"

"The reservoir on the stove is full." Mercy tapped Duncan and Chris on their shoulders. "And unless you put me down, the roast in the oven is going to burn."

"Don't care about the roast. I'm more worried about the wee little bun in your oven." Duncan ignored her insistent tapping and started to walk. Ostensibly not to be dissuaded from his convictions, Chris followed suit.

"If you men carry me to the clinic, I'm just going to walk right back here."

"The pangs are addling her mind," Duncan muttered.

"No, they're not." Mercy wheedled, "It's still early. Robert's books say labor is likely to last twelve hours, if not twice that long. You can't expect me to spend my first New Year's Eve as a married woman anywhere other than in my husband's wonderful home."

Carmen secretly admired Mercy's wiles. She'd obviously come to understand she couldn't fight both of her brothers-in-law, so she'd divided them by appealing to Christopher's pride at having built the house. Chris stopped walking, and Carmen suspected as anxious as Duncan had grown, he'd carry Mercy in circles all night if someone didn't intervene.

"I'm relieved to see you men are trying to protect Mercy from any eventuality." Carmen smiled at Duncan. "It's going to grow nippy tonight. Just in case Mercy relents and decides to have the baby in the clinic, you'd better go light a fire in the stove there so she won't catch a chill."

"Put water on to boil, too," Chris demanded.

"I'll stay right here with her." Carmen motioned to set down the rocker.

—※—

Two hours later, Duncan stared at Carmen and ground out, "Cookie cutters?"

"Of course." Mercy concentrated on cracking eggs into an earthenware bowl. "When everyone comes to visit the baby, we need to show them hospitality. You don't want to shame me by making me face them without cookies."

"Plenty of cookies don't require cookie cutters." Chris scowled as he motioned behind his back to make Duncan put away the ironing board. Until Mercy took a mind to bake cookies, she'd ironed every shirt in the house twice.

"But those are everyday cookies." Mercy dumped two cups of sugar into the mixture. "Guests should receive special cookies."

"Anyone paying a visit to a house with a new baby ought to be bringing the cookies." Duncan paced from one end of the kitchen to the other. During his third transit, he tucked away the ironing board. "Aye, no doubt about it; they should be bringing the cookies. I distinctly recall Ma taking food when she went to a home where there'd been sickness or death."

"I'm neither sick nor dying." Mercy looked suitably appalled at his comment.

Chris mopped his brow. "But you're going to be the death of us, trying to have this babe with no help at hand."

"Don't you insult my dear friend that way." Mercy waved a wooden spoon in Carmen's direction. "She'll help me. Won't you, Carmen?"

Though her apprehension far outweighed her confidence, Carmen nodded. After all, her friend needed her, and loyalty demanded she be a staunch ally.

Duncan pulled Carmen from the kitchen. "Some kind of help you are! You were supposed to get her to the clinic, not to the oven!"

"I had a choice to make—either I make you happy or I comfort my friend who happens to be in labor." Carmen stabbed her finger into the center of his broad chest. "I didn't think I'd have to listen to a grown man whine—especially when a woman under his roof is in labor and has yet to let out a single cry."

"I dinna whine!" He looked thoroughly affronted. "I'm reminding you of what's important. Cookies willna matter a whit if she or the babe dinna get through the ordeal."

"You need to have more faith," she whispered. "Now go on over to my house. Ismelda just used the cookie cutters yesterday. They're in the orange box to the left of the sink."

"This is it, woman. I'll not be humoring any more of these ridiculous requests."

Carmen pretended she didn't hear him. Truthfully, for the last couple of hours, Carmen had concocted a variety of tasks for Chris and Duncan to accomplish. It kept them from hovering, at least part of the time.

Duncan shook his finger at her. "Dinna feign innocence. You ken full well what I mean."

"You could cooperate. Staying busy has kept Mercy from panicking about the fact that Robert's not here."

"He'd best better hie on home." Duncan's brows knit. "Chris sent Connant after him over an hour ago."

"We have to stay calm. You go get the cookie cutters. I'll set the table." Carmen returned to the kitchen. Mercy urgently motioned to her, and Carmen headed her way. With every step, she promised God she'd do any number of good deeds as long as she didn't have to deliver this baby on her own.

Mercy pulled Carmen close. "I've done it now."

Chapter 2

Carmen clamped her lips together to hold back a moan.

"I wasn't paying attention. I didn't just add sugar to the cookies. I added a whole cupful to the mashed potatoes!"

Disbelief forced Carmen to laugh. She tightened her apron strings. "I'll add a few eggs to make them hold together, then fry slabs."

"Like potato pan–caaa—" Mercy curled forward and lost the last part of the word. When the pain ended, she fretted, "I wanted this supper to be perfect."

"You've talked the men into wearing their kilts, Chris brought in a log that could burn for a month, and the pewter candlesticks are at least a half inch shorter after you set Duncan to polishing them. It'll be a supper they remember for a long time."

Mercy let out a doleful sigh. "I was talking about the food."

"The roast is big enough to feed everyone for three days." Carmen cast a quick look at the door. "Duncan and Chris are so worried that I don't think they'll taste a single bite they wolf down tonight, anyway."

"It's taking Robert a long time."

"You, yourself, said it'll be hours yet." Carmen hoped with every fiber of her being that her words were true.

"Ja. You work on the potatoes. I'll start rolling out the cookie dough—oh, and put the apple cider on the back burner. I want to mull some spices in it and serve it with dessert."

"I think," Carmen glanced about furtively before continuing, "we ought to have Chris and Duncan take the cookies over to the clinic to bake."

"They'll burn half of them." Mercy grinned.

"Fine. We'll have to mix up another batch. That'll keep them occupied a little longer. I'll hurry and start boiling rice. It'll go with the roast and gravy."

Chris and Duncan fought over who got to go bake the cookies. It was then Carmen fully appreciated just how terrified they were that they might have to help with the delivery. She sent both. They'd return to the house only long enough for Mercy to plop the next round of cookies on the sheets, then run off to the clinic oven again.

"That's the last of them," Mercy announced as she handed her brothers-in-law the cookie-laden sheets. "Chris, you and Duncan, when you've baked them, change into your kilts, and we'll have supper on the table when you come back." She waited until they were gone, then pled, "Can you haul me out of this chair? I'm not moving so good."

"Sure." Carmen helped her up.

Mercy stood, curled forward, and moaned with the next pang. When it was over, she straightened and said, "The table looks beautiful. I wish my husband were here to see it."

"I'm sure he'll get here soon, Mercy." *He'd better. I'm starting to get as nervous as Duncan. Well, I'm not going to let Mercy see that. If she can stay calm, so will I.* "The only thing left is for me to make the gravy."

"I can do that. Will you get some honey from the pantry?"

"Sure."

The door opened, and Ismelda came in. Holding the plate with the destroyed flan, she gave Carmen an uncertain look.

"Oh, flan!" Mercy sounded truly thrilled over the mess. "I love your flan."

Ismelda asked, "*¿Olvidó de traer este?*"

"Yes," Carmen answered her sister in English, "I forgot to bring that. I was excited because Mercy's in labor."

"How wonderful!"

"Tell that to Duncan and Chris." Mercy's wry smile slid into a grimace.

By the time they sat down to supper, Carmen tried not to fault Chris and Duncan for seating Mercy, then hastening to the chairs farthest from her for themselves. After all, they were gentlemanly enough to pause long enough to seat Ismelda and her on either side of Mercy. Folding his hands, Duncan said, "I'll ask the blessing."

Carmen bowed her head. Duncan's prayers never ceased to touch her. He spoke to the Lord in a way she'd never heard a man pray—with a rich blend of reverence, respect, humility, and love. Tonight's prayer ought to be particularly special.

"Lord, the food looks good, but the only blessing I'm asking tonight is for You to help our Mercy through and for the babe to be all right. Amen."

" 'Men," Chris chimed in.

While Carmen blinked in astonishment over the prayer, Chris picked up the carving knife and proceeded to hack a picture-perfect roast into an assortment of chunks spanning every possible shape and size. Carmen consoled herself that the irregular hunks would hide how lumpy the gravy was. And the gravy would add moisture to the rice, because it turned out a tad dry. Those paltry facts were lost on the men, who inhaled the food with blinding speed.

Mercy barely picked at her plate.

"What's wrong?" Chris squinted at her.

"Nothing." Her lips thinned, and she went silent.

"Nothing?" Chris threw back his head and groaned. "If Rob doesna walk through the door in the next five minutes, I'm goin' to skin him alive."

"You will not." Mercy let out a small sigh and pushed away her plate. "I'm just being choosy tonight. I wanted to save room for dessert."

"Me, too!" Carmen hopped up. As she and Ismelda cleared the table, Carmen seriously questioned her own sanity. Mercy had accidentally thickened the apple cider instead of the beef broth and drippings to make "gravy." In order to salvage the situation, Ismelda turned the broth to gravy and Carmen "fixed" the cider.

"What's for dessert, Mercy?" Chris sounded hopeful. "You said you had something special planned."

"I'll bet you've never had this before," Ismelda murmured.

"That's right. It's a new recipe." Carmen slapped the fried, sweetened mashed potato slabs onto plates, added diced apples, spooned blobs of flan atop them, and then topped the whole affair off with a mulled, spicy apple "glaze."

Mercy attacked hers with gusto.

Chris gave his serving a dubious look. "What is it?"

"Happenstance," Carmen blurted out as she picked up her fork.

"Probably another Texas dish," Duncan said. "There's not been one yet I haven't liked."

Duncan's fork practically created sparks on the plate, he ate so fast. Chris matched him bite for bite.

Carmen exchanged a look with her sister. "Ismelda, why don't we share mine? I made a plate for Robert, but if Connant comes back with him, we wouldn't want him to go without."

"Connant could have Rob's, and Rob could go hungry," Chris growled. " 'Twould serve him right for leaving his kin in a time of great need."

Duncan nodded as he pushed to his feet. "Food was good. Filling. You ladies worked hard cooking it, so Chris and I'll do the cleanup."

"Yeah." Chris rose. "And since nothing's keeping you here, Mercy, Carmen and Ismelda can take you over and settle you in the clinic now."

"I can't go to the clinic!"

Chris scowled at Mercy. "And suppose you give me a good reason why not?"

"She's not in her nightdress," Ismelda replied.

"You can jolly well change once you're there." By now, Duncan and Chris bracketed Mercy like a pair of menacing gargoyles.

Suspecting they were about to pick up Mercy's chair once again, Carmen tapped her fork on the edge of her dessert plate. "Once Ismelda and I finish our. . .uhh. . . happenstance, we'll be happy to help Mercy change. Won't we, Sister?"

Ismelda looked at the dish, and Carmen had the sinking feeling her sister was going to either use this as an excuse to get out of eating the mess or offer to help Mercy and allow Carmen to eat it all by herself. Alarmed at either possibility, Carmen gave her little sister a behave-yourself look.

"You take a bite, then I'll take one."

Relief flooded her. Carmen assessed the dessert and decided the safest thing to do would be to isolate and eat each item independently. She speared an apple and popped the slice into her mouth.

It seemed Ismelda came to the same conclusion. She took a miniscule dab of flan.

"You'll be here until the Second Coming, eating that slowly." Chris drummed his fingers on the back of Mercy's chair.

"My friends are ladies, not field hands." Mercy's voice went up in volume, then petered out on the last word.

"Another one? She's having another one." Distress tainted Duncan's voice. "I'm not liking this one bit."

"What aren't you liking?" a voice asked from the door. "And why are the lamps on over in my clinic?"

—⁂—

Duncan bellowed at his brother, " 'Tis far past time you showed up!"

Robert set down his medical satchel. "I'm sorry I'm late for supper. It couldna be helped."

"You should have had your sorry hide home hours ago," Chris grated.

Maddeningly casual, Rob crossed the room, pressed a kiss on Mercy's temple, and said, "Aida and Stuart had a wee little boy tonight. Mother and child are right as rain."

"What were you doing there?" Chris bristled. "You were supposed to be at the Stukys'. I sent Connant there to fetch you."

"I said I was going to Stu Key's." Rob hadn't straightened up. He stayed down close to Mercy and said softly, "I take it you're planning to make me a father tonight?"

She bit her lip and nodded.

"Now then, that's a fine piece of news. And 'tis plain to see you're faring well. Since the day we knew you to be with child, I've prayed 'twould go easy on you. God is faithful."

Duncan stared at his brother. Clearly, he didn't understand just how serious this was—either that or he was demented. "Mercy's been having pangs for hours now," Duncan intoned, trying to get Rob to comprehend the gravity of the situation.

Rob crooked a brow. "Have you, now?"

"Only since noon." Mercy's smile faltered, then disappeared entirely.

"Noon!" Chris roared. "And you didn't tell us then?"

Rob wheeled around and stood nose to nose with his oldest brother. "Dinna raise your voice at my wife!"

" 'Tis you I'll yell at. She needed you, and you were off with another woman!"

"Stop this!" Mercy's eyes filled with tears.

"Now look what the both of you did." Duncan swiped the napkin from Mercy's lap and blotted her face. "Upsettin' a wee mother-to-be. Shame on ye."

Carmen rose. "I'm sure you gentlemen will excuse us."

Now that Rob was home, Duncan's nerves settled. Asking Carmen to come had been a move of desperation. It wasn't right to ask an unmarried woman to play midwife. Carmen hadn't confessed to being worried, but Duncan knew she'd calmed tremendously since Rob arrived. He could tell because her accent grew thicker when she was upset. Suddenly, her tongue's rich-sounding roll when she pronounced *R*'s and the softening of the *T* sounds weren't as strong.

"You can't go!" Chris went right back to yelling.

Clearly not intimidated, Carmen glared at Chris. "I wouldn't dream of leaving her tonight. The only place I'm going is upstairs to help Mercy change into her nightdress."

"That's a fine plan." Rob's voice took on his everything's-under-control flavor. He wound Mercy's arm about his neck and scooped her out of her seat.

She turned her face into his neck and started to cry.

"There, now. There you are. Aye, lass. You needn't worry a bit now." Rob kept a steady stream of reassurances as he carried her up to their bedchamber. Even after they were out of sight, Mercy's weeping drifted down the stairs.

"I'm thinkin' you're right. Mercy might want a woman's help," Duncan said quietly to Carmen.

Carmen nodded. Compassion shimmered in her deep brown eyes. He admired the woman. Others in the community hadn't known how to react to Mercy since her child was conceived by an act of violence. They'd kept their distance; Carmen hadn't wavered in the least. She'd been a stalwart friend.

He decided to repay her kindness. "Whilst you're up there with her, I'll dump out your happenstance. No use in all of us sufferin' indigestion."

Carmen's eyes grew huge.

"Did you think we didna see Mercy put sugar in the mashed potatoes?"

Ismelda squeaked, "Why didn't you stop her?"

"I couldna bear to rattle the lass." He pulled out Carmen's chair. Duncan fought the urge to carry her up the stairs. He'd already dented her pride by carrying her across the street earlier in the day. She did her best to get around and ignore the pitying glances folks gave her. Indeed, she managed life quite nicely. But if he offered her assistance, she'd likely take it the wrong way.

Carmen mounted the stairs methodically. Soon after she disappeared from sight, Rob appeared. Rubbing his hands together, he announced, "I'm hungry as a draft horse."

"Eat dessert first," Chris advised as he shoved some of the disastrous dish at Rob.

Duncan swiped the plate right out of Rob's hand. "We canna have him gettin' sick. He's got to deliver the babe."

"Mercy's never made anything that didn't taste grand." Rob reached for the happenstance again.

Ismelda giggled. "But Mercy's never been in labor before."

"How far along is she?" Chris dumped chunks of meat onto a plate. "How much longer?"

"I can't say for certain."

"You're usually able to give a fair estimate," Duncan said.

"Aye." Rob shot a look at Ismelda, who'd taken the dessert plates to the back door to rid them of the monstrous concoction. Rob's voice dropped to a confidential whisper, "But those women have been long married." He paused a moment to choose his words carefully. "And they dinna suffer crippling modesty."

Duncan grimaced. He rested his hand on Rob's shoulder and gave him a powerful squeeze as a sign of his support. *Rob told Mercy he'd been praying for her to have an easy delivery. I never gave much thought to how hard this will be for her—and for him, too. Lord, You hae the power to calm them and ease things. Please grant them that.*

"You're in your kilts." Rob accepted the plate of roast and rice from Chris.

"At your wife's request." Chris grinned. "We may well be in Texas, but she's showing promise. With time, she'll understand the honor of marrying a Highlander."

Rob ate quickly and cast a look at the stairs.

"You need to get her o'er to the clinic," Duncan urged.

"She's wanting to hae the bairn in our own bed."

"Make her see reason." Chris started pacing. He practically mowed over Ismelda. "It's 1892. Modern women should avail themselves of the best medicine has to offer. Your clinic is the finest there is."

"I promised my old-fashioned bride a solid half hour of privacy so she could wash up, change, and have Carmen help her with her hair. After that, we'll see how she is."

"Half an hour?" Duncan shook his head in disbelief.

"She's rattled. Carmen has a knack for making Mercy feel better. Just you wait. I'd estimate that right about now, my wee wife's calming down."

"I will not!" Mercy shouted from upstairs.

Rob winced.

"No, no, no, no." Mercy's voice went from a shout to a strangled moan.

"That doesna sound like a woman who's finding her serenity. Go help her, man!" Chris shoved at him, and he raced upstairs.

Less than a minute later, Mercy's voice held a shrill edge. "You promised thirty minutes!"

Rob came back downstairs, grinning like a fool. "Things are progressing well."

"If that's 'well,' you'd best stuff cotton in your ears once you hae her at the clinic. The lass is liable to scream you deaf once she's in the thick of it."

"Bein' a mite temperamental is a fine sign. It indicates a woman's toward the end."

"Toward the end of her rope, I'd say," Chris muttered.

Someone knocked once while opening the front door. Connant stuck his head into the house. "I'm relieved to see Rob's horse. I've ridden all over and couldn't find him. How's Mercy?"

They all looked toward the ceiling. As if she'd heard Connant's question, her stricken voice echoed down the stairs. "No one needs to know!"

Connant's eyes widened. "I'll go now."

"She didna hear you. She's talking with Carmen." Rob motioned him in. "Come. Eat."

The sheriff looked appalled at the notion. "I've got things to do."

"Is that so?" Rob asked. His tone sounded entirely too entertained.

"I'll help." Chris rushed toward the door, to freedom.

"No. No. Everything's under control. Happy New Year." The sheriff shut the door with obvious alacrity. Chris looked like a man about to be stuffed into a cannibal's pot.

Half an hour later, Carmen descended the stairs. "Mercy's asking to go to the washroom."

Rob shot to his feet.

"Before you go up there," Carmen's voice carried a vaguely amused flavor, "I've been ordered to warn you men that if you try to take her to the clinic, she'll avenge herself."

Chris snorted. "Mercy wouldn't swat a fly. Her threat's all bluster."

Rob scowled over his shoulder. "Don't vex my wife, Chris." He went up the stairs and came back down with Mercy in his arms. She was bundled in a heavy flannel nightgown. Instead of wearing her hair up in its usual style, Mercy now had a single, fat braid swinging back and forth with each step Rob took.

From the way Mercy clung to Rob, buried her face against his chest, and moaned, she was embarrassed for them to see her in such a state. Duncan figured the least he could do was be casual about it. As they went past him toward the washroom, Duncan proclaimed, "The lass is whiter than her bedgown, Rob. Talk sense into her."

Ismelda shoved a soapy dish into the rinse water. "Shhh."

"Here you are," Rob said as he turned sideways to carry his wife through the doorway to their modern washroom. Duncan silently gave his brother credit for sounding so calm and remembering to turn so he didn't knock Mercy's head or feet against the door frame.

"Out!" Mercy's voice took on a shrill edge. "Out this minute, Robert."

Rob stepped out of the washroom, shut the door, and finally had the good sense to look concerned.

Chris kicked the chair Duncan leaned against. "Don't just stand there. 'Tis cold out. Rob'll be wanting to wrap Mercy in a blanket whilst he totes her to the clinic."

"I hhhheee–aaarred thaaaaat!" Mercy shouted.

"Now, Mercy," Rob wheedled.

Silence hung in the air. Rob shifted his weight from one foot to the other a few times, wiped his hands down his thighs, and cleared his throat. "Mercy?"

"Leeeeve meee aaa–looonne!"

Duncan decided it was a good thing Rob told them Mercy might be getting a wee bit testy. She seemed to be embracing the role with zeal.

A mere breath later, Mercy's voice changed to a bewildered, "Rob?"

"Aye, my sweet?"

She sounded so uncertain, so lost. "I don't know what to do."

A tiny wail rent the air. Rob yanked the washroom door straight off the hinges. Duncan collapsed into the chair. Having a baby was far more taxing than he'd expected.

Chapter 3

How's little Elspeth today?" Carmen called across the street to Duncan. He sat in the open doorway of his cobbler's workshop, stitching something.

"Fat and sassy." He grinned at her. "That garden of yours surely takes a lot of attention."

Carmen caressed a narcissus. "I hope these and the fern-leaf lavender bloom for the wedding."

Duncan nodded. "Those pinkish-red things behind you are a sight."

"The azaleas? I love them, but they're not easy to put in a wedding arrangement. Same with my crocus. Ismelda didn't want to wait until March when the whole countryside will be abloom."

"That tree Mercy calls a redbud is blossoming. Could you use a few branches?"

His offer pleased her. "Thank you. I'll keep that in mind."

He nodded and went back to work. All day long, every day, he'd sit out on the porch attached to his workshop. An eye-popping array of spindles, fans, turnings, and trim should have made the outside of his shop look tacky or garish; instead, it seemed whimsical. Folks would walk down the street, drop in and chat with Duncan, then meander off.

"What are you doing?" Ismelda asked from the corner of their yard.

"Checking on the flowers." Carmen turned around. "I need to water some of them a little more."

"Otto's mother offered to come help me pin up the hem of my gown, but I told her you would." Ismelda clasped Carmen's hand as she went up the four steps to their veranda. "I wanted to talk with you about something."

"Sure."

"You won't move into the Kunstlers' with me?"

"No, I won't." Carmen shot her sister a stern look. "You and Otto need to be husband and wife. I'd be underfoot and in the way."

"His mother is there."

"I know." Carmen stopped. "You and she get along well, and I know in my heart that it'll be a happy arrangement. But Mrs. Kunstler and I wouldn't be happy under the same roof. Besides, I love our home here."

"But I was wondering about something else."

Carmen waited for her sister to speak. Try as she might, she couldn't quite get past the hurt of everyone else finding mates and having babies. Her own sister didn't even hold out hope that some man might come along and develop affectionate feelings for Carmen. The reality that she was trying to make arrangements for Carmen's spinster years stung.

"Mr. Stein and Peter—they're faring decently, but with Mercy in town now, I think he'd be delighted to have a housekeeper. Why don't you talk with him about it? We'd be neighbors!"

Carmen merely shook her head.

"You already take a dish over there once or twice a week."

"If that is a reason for me to become someone's housekeeper, half of our neighbors would already employ me."

"But maybe it's time for you to get something in return for all the good deeds you do."

"I don't want anything, Ismelda. I'm content. I have a home and friends. Papa left us enough money that I needn't worry about finances." Carmen shook her head. "I'd be lying if I told you I would think about it. Go put on your gown. I'll wash my hands so I don't smudge it."

—⁂—

The heavy white satin felt smooth and cool in Carmen's hands as she pinned the hem. She forced a laugh. "I was just picturing Otto standing at the altar waiting for you."

"What's so funny about that?"

"I imagined him in one of the Gregors' kilts."

Merry laughter bubbled out of Ismelda. "Never. After church on Sunday, Otto told me if I have any plans to make him wear odd costumes, I'd better forget them."

"They're not odd costumes. The Gregors are proud of their heritage. I thought they looked. . .unified at church on Sunday." The pastor had called Mercy and Rob to the altar on Sunday to present Elspeth to the congregation and say a blessing over her. Duncan and Chris stood on either side of them. All of the Gregor men wore kilts, and the length of tartan Rob had draped over Mercy's shoulder for their wedding now served as the infant's blanket. "And I also think it was very touching how Duncan mentioned they'd named Elspeth after their own mother."

"It was." Ismelda sighed romantically. "I told Otto I'm wearing Mama's bridal mantilla as my something old. In a year or two, maybe I could drape it over our baby, too. Don't you think that would be a lovely tradition?"

"Mmm." Though tears filled her eyes, Carmen smiled up at her sister. *She's so sure I'll never be a bride.*

Ismelda pressed her hand to her bosom. "Oh, do I look so beautiful that you're in tears?"

"*Muy hermosa.* Very beautiful."

"You're such a wonderful sister to make me feel lovely in my gown."

"Never once forget how beautiful I think you are—inside as well as out."

"Are you done pinning me up?"

Grateful to break eye contact, Carmen reached for the pincushion. She pulled out another pin. "Just one more. Here."

"Now that we've finished my gown, we need to decide on yours. I don't care if the gringos here think red is for a loose woman. You look beautiful in red, and—"

"Be practical, Ismelda. I'd never be able to wear it again. If I put work into making a dress, I ought to get some use out of it."

Her sister made wavelike motions. "What about layers and layers of yellow and orange?"

"Since when did we wear layered skirts? Mama always dressed us in designs featured in *Godey's.*"

Ismelda shrugged. "You were talking about heritage. I thought it might be fun to have some of our heritage in my wedding."

"You could carry our Spanish Bible."

Eyes alight, Ismelda proclaimed, "You can! I'll hold a sheaf of flowers from our garden, just as I always dreamed, and you can carry Papa's Bible. In fact"—Ismelda clapped her hands—"you could read a verse from it."

"That doesn't seem right. Otto doesn't know any Spanish. A groom ought to understand the whole ceremony."

Ismelda wrinkled her nose. "I guess you're right. I know she doesn't mean to be rude, but his mother often speaks German to him in front of me. I'm so determined to understand them I'm having Otto teach me new words all of the time!"

"Chris Gregor rattles off German like he's one of them, and he's getting good at Spanish, too."

"I'm glad." Ismelda blushed. "He can translate for the doctor now. Duncan—he hasn't learned much Spanish or German, but everyone understands him, and he understands whatever someone else is trying to say."

Carmen started to unbutton her sister's gown. "That stream of people wandering past his shop and visiting with him—it's that way every day, all day long."

"Really? I hadn't noticed." Ismelda let out a trill of laughter. "I love Otto so much that I don't seem to notice anything else at all."

Carmen gave no reply. Duncan Gregor was a nice man. A good man—godly and gentle and kind. People couldn't help responding to his warm and humble personality. *He'll never be lonely, but I will.* That thought hit her hard. *What does he do that I don't?*

"You look so sad!"

Summoning a smile she was far from feeling, Carmen knew she didn't dare confess her fears. She wanted her sister to bask in the joy of her marriage, not to fret over things that couldn't be helped. She softened the truth. "I was thinking how empty the house will be. I'm going to miss you."

"So you're reconsidering my suggestion about becoming the Steins' housekeeper?"

"No." Carmen didn't have a hard time looking appalled at the notion. "I'm going to have to find ways to keep busy once you're not here to pester me."

"You can come visit me whenever you want." Ismelda carefully stepped free from her gown. "We still haven't decided about what you'll wear for the wedding."

"Leonard mentioned he's gotten a shipment of bombazine in at the mercantile."

"Bombazine is for widows and chaperones. You said you want to be practical—well, then we'll have your gown be a bright color in a lightweight silk or a challis. That way you'll be able to look festive all through the spring and summer."

"Come spring and summer, I'm going to want lightweight cotton so I can stay cool while helping you with the extra chores that come from being a farmer's wife."

"Then we'll have to be sure to get material for two dresses for you." Ismelda grinned. "In addition to the fabric for the dress you'll wear for the wedding."

Accustomed to her little sister's stunts, Carmen laughed and nodded. "Yes, *querida.* One for me and one for you." *And maybe a few more yards of cotton, besides. I could make Mercy's little Elspeth a couple of gowns, and with old Mrs. Lintz becoming bedridden, I'm sure she'd appreciate a crisp nightdress and soft pillowslips. And Mr. Rundstadt—it must be so hard for him to find shirts to fit his twisted frame. I'm going to devote myself to the people who need love and might not get it otherwise.*

Relieved to have come up with a solution to battling the impending sense of loneliness, Carmen went to fetch her reticule.

—⁂—

"Rob took Mercy and the baby home." Duncan offered Carmen his arm.

"It was nice of them to come to the wedding." She slid her hand into the crook of his elbow and walked toward the buggy with him. When she glanced up, her deep brown eyes carried a wealth of emotion. "I know Mercy loves Rob with all her heart, but it was especially nice of her to treat Ismelda so kindly. Some people were still talking about how just a year ago Otto was going to marry Mercy."

"It's time everyone let go of the past and embrace the future. It's plain to see Rob and Mercy love each other. As for Ismelda and Otto—he was a broken man, and her love did wonders for him. Both men are blessed."

As Carmen allowed him to lift her into the buggy, Duncan noted her new dress. He waited a moment while she gathered up the extra material from her fancy gown. "Your frock's comely. It puts me of a mind of the heather from back home."

"Thank you."

The buggy swayed as he swung up beside her. For all the fabric in their skirts, it was easy to forget how tiny most of the women were. Carmen was of average height but fine-boned. He saw how she tried to drag her left foot out of the way.

"You must be exhausted."

She bristled. "What makes you say that?"

He flicked the reins. "I'm thinkin' on how you've babied the garden so there were flowers aplenty and that you've stitched yourself a pretty frock. You cooked and cooked and cooked. And ooch, those Mexican wedding cookies—you baked hundreds of them. I'm not exaggerating, either, because I ate a good half dozen all on my own. Then you saw to any number of trifling details to make the wedding all your sister e'er dreamed of. Just reciting the list of what you've done leaves me weary."

The tension drained from her shoulders. "I'm afraid now that the wedding is over, I'll be bored to distraction."

"You?" Duncan chuckled. "I dinna think the word *leisure* is in your vocabulary. Rob tells me you've been cheering up old Mrs. Lintz, and I ken you've helped o'er at the Rayburns."

"Mrs. Rayburn's splint should come off next week."

"Aye, but a woman with a broken arm and a passel of children is a sorry sight."

"They're dear children—well behaved and affectionate."

"I've not been 'round them enough to agree or disagree." Duncan grinned. "You're a fine woman, and I'm sure they love you on your own merit. That bein' said, e'en the naughtiest of bairns would toe the mark just to have a taste of your *bunuelos* and *empan*-things."

"*Empanadas.*" She smiled. "I'll be sure you have some the next time I make a batch."

"I confess, I would hae never thought the Germans and the Mexicans to hold much in common, but the cinnamon-sugar desserts and the polka sort of music are startlingly similar. In the end, 'tis fun to see how much alike we all are."

She nodded. "I suppose it all boils down to a simple truth—we really all are the same. Young or old, blond or black-haired, we want to belong, to love, and to be loved."

Chapter 4

Duncan, did you think I wouldn't notice?"

Duncan ignored Christopher's bellow and assisted Mr. Rundsdorf up the single step leading to his workshop's porch. "I've been waiting for you."

"I can come back later if this is a bad time."

"Your timing couldn't be better." Duncan grinned. "Chris swears he canna stand all the frills that came wi' the house kit. Just to keep him on his toes, I've been tacking up a piece in or on the house every now and again."

Mr. Rundsdorf's gaze roamed the workshop. "Your brother's far ahead of you in the race."

"He likes to think so."

Chris stalked over. "Take it away by noon, Duncan, or I won't be responsible for what happens next."

"You gave me all the gingerbread. 'Tis mine to do with as I please."

"Bad enough we have enough scales to cover ten dragons on the outside of my house. Worse yet, you tacked a bunch of those stupid curlicue things together and hung them in the washroom."

"I made a shelf for Mercy," Duncan explained to Mr. Rundsdorf, who nodded in appreciation.

"But my bed?" Chris practically thundered the words.

"What did he do to your bed?" Mr. Rundsdorf asked.

Chris suddenly went ruddy.

"Dinna leave the man wondering." Duncan nudged his brother. "Tell him."

"He, uh. . .tacked something onto a post," Chris muttered darkly.

"What was it?" Mr. Rundsdorf leaned forward.

Chris gave Duncan a murderous look. Duncan shrugged. "Dinna give me that scowl. You're the one who decided to bellow. The least you could do is answer the gentleman's question."

"I don't feel like it." Chris rested his fists on his hips.

"Then I will." Duncan turned to the old man.

"He stuck a birdhouse on my bedpost!" Chris sounded livid. "Seeing it first thing in the morning was enough to ruin my whole day."

Duncan happened to glance across the street. Carmen stood in her garden. She held her hand clapped over her mouth, and he knew she'd heard every last word booming out of Chris. "I tell you what, Chris. I'll let you take down the birdhouse on two conditions: Carmen has to approve of it and you hang it over at her house."

"Done." Chris stalked off.

Duncan made a sweeping gesture. "Come on inside, Mr. Rundsdorf. I've got the brace all ready for you." A moment later, he threaded a strap through the device he'd created after conferring with Rob on the design. "The sheepskin ought to keep it from rubbin' you. If you feel a wider pad would help, dinna hesitate to tell me."

Mr. Rundsdorf wiggled his twisted torso within its new confines. He let out an appreciative sigh. "I can tell already this is going to work."

No brace in the world would ever begin to correct the man's deformity. Duncan didn't pretend otherwise. "Rob said the support might bring you some comfort."

"Unh-huh." Rundsdorf buckled the last strap into place. "Stamina, too—not that I expect this contraption to turn me into a schoolboy. But if I can stay up for two or three hours at a time, it'll be twice what I can do now."

Duncan picked up the misshapen shirt and held it for Mr. Rundsdorf to slide into.

"I'm twisted as mesquite."

"I'd never seen mesquite until I came to America. 'Tis a rare beautiful shrub."

A rueful bark of a laugh left the man.

Duncan went on to defend it. "Mesquite's got character. I've admired many a piece of furniture or bowl made from the wood. If that's not enough, the wood burns slow, and the flavor its smoke lends to Texas barbecue—" Duncan waggled his brows.

"I never thought of it that way."

"God made mesquite, just as He made pines and oak. He took pleasure in His creation and said it was good. If He took pleasure in that, how much more must He love a son who strives to live to serve Him?"

Rundsdorf stopped buttoning his shirt and gawked at him. A slow smile spread across his pain-etched face.

"I'm planning on having to fiddle wi' the brace so we can get a perfect fit. Dinna be shy about telling me what feels odd or where it puts too much pressure."

"It's perfect as it is."

"Aye, and I've heard the selfsame thing from plenty of folks when first they tied on a pair of shoes. 'Tisna just the fit when a body is at rest that matters. Pressure and rubbing are bound to happen—and that's when you discover the difference between bliss and a blister."

Fastening the last of his buttons, Mr. Rundsdorf cleared his throat. "You didn't say how much this cost."

The man needed to keep his pride, so Duncan gave him the answer he'd already made up. He swept his arm to encompass his workshop. "I used nothing but scraps and wee bits and pieces. They cost me next to nothing."

"But your time—"

"Has some value. I grant you that. But I wanted to help a brother in Christ, so here's what I've decided. More than a few men have said you've a talent with wood. In your spare time, using nothing but scraps, why don't you make something for my shop?"

"What do you need?"

Duncan let out a shout of a laugh. "That all depends on who you're listenin' to. Chris thinks I need ambition. Rob says I suffer from the affliction of clutter and wouldna recognize order if it bit me. My sister-in-law is the most dangerous of all. She's of the opinion that I need a wife." Duncan chuckled along with his customer. "Me? I'm content just as I am."

Rundsdorf looked pensive. "It must be nice to feel that kind of peace."

"The apostle Paul wrote of it—e'en whilst in jail. 'Tisna the circumstances a man finds himself in that matter. God is present with us and loves us. All we have to do is open our hearts to Him."

"Like Sunday's hymn, 'Just as I Am.'"

"Aye. And I canna help believing that since He takes us just as we are, then the grace He bestows ought to flow through us—not only to others but to ourselves. As for me, I've found when my heart's in tune with Him, He can fix my flaws." Duncan let out a diffident chuckle. "I've faults aplenty, so I keep the Almighty busy. But I'm content to serve God to the best of my ability."

"I'm thankful you do." Rundsdorf smoothed his hand over the front of his shirt. His fingers bumped up and down as they passed over portions of the brace. "Maybe that contentment is contagious."

—◊—

Later that afternoon, Duncan worked out on the porch. He looked up and bolted to his feet. In a matter of seconds, he'd crossed the street and yanked a bucket from Carmen's hand. "What are ye doin', woman?"

She turned three shades of red.

Duncan reconsidered his question. He'd allowed her no privacy. "I meant to ask, 'Why are you hauling water up these stairs and into your house?'"

"My pump broke."

"And you didna ask for help?"

"I'll ask Otto after church tomorrow. I'm sure he'll be willing to come look at it next week."

"Nonsense." Duncan stomped up the last steps and plowed into her house. "Did the pump just suddenly stop working, did it sprout a leak, or what happened?"

Carmen stayed in the doorway. "The handle's been getting stiff, and suddenly the works just stopped."

Duncan nodded and thumped the water onto her stove. He paused a second to appreciate her kitchen. Mercy kept their kitchen neat as a pin. The white cupboards and gingham curtains looked cheerful. In contrast, Carmen's kitchen was an explosion of color and scents. Chili peppers hung in exotic-looking spills from lengths of twine. Garlic did, too. The hutch held a cheerful display of red, yellow, green, and blue dishes that matched the same hues as the brightly striped cloth running down the center of the table. The place felt as vibrant as its owner.

"Thank you for carrying the water."

Duncan cast a glance at the red pump. "I'll take a look and see what's wrong with your pump."

"That's not necessary."

Duncan leveled a stare at her and slowly crooked a brow. "Why is it you can run all over the county, feeding and helping everyone else, but you shy away from accepting any help in return?"

"It's not that way."

"Oh? And how does this differ?"

"To begin with, it's not proper!"

Duncan made an exasperated sound. "I'm going to grab some of my tools. While I'm gone, gather up your sewing or some such thing. Whilst I'm here repairing the pump, you can sit out on the veranda." From the way she winced, Duncan gathered he'd spoken with more force than diplomacy. He softened his tone into a teasing lilt. "That way, you can admire your new birdhouse."

As he worked on the pump, Duncan's mood darkened. Carmen sat out on the veranda sewing a shirt for some little boy. The next-door neighbor called over and suggested that Carmen might think about taking supper to a certain family since the mother was ailing. Yet another woman appeared and dropped off her baby and a cranky toddler so she could go to the mercantile. She'd no more than retrieved her children before another woman dropped off three.

Duncan cleaned up his mess, washed his hands, and dumped his tools back into a box. It wouldn't be right to speak to Carmen about it in front of anyone. The next time he caught her alone, he was going to say something. Just because she had a big heart and a willing spirit didn't mean she ought to work herself into an early grave by doing favors for everyone in Texas. *I'm going to tell the lass she's a blessing to all who know her, but she canna let people take advantage of her.*

—⁂—

"I made empanadas." Carmen stood by Duncan's shop and extended a basket of the sweets to him.

He wiped his hands on a rag, then leaned over and took one. "One of these days, when Elspeth isna wakenin' Mercy every other hour, you'll hae to show Mercy how to make these." He took a bite and closed his eyes with a hum of appreciation.

"You don't need to wait until then to have more. Any time you'd like empanadas, just ask me." Carmen set the basket on a nearby table.

Duncan's eyes popped open. "I'd ne'er do such a thing!"

Stinging from his tone, Carmen stepped back. Her foot landed poorly, and she struggled to keep her balance. Duncan wrapped his hand about her upper arm, stabilizing her. The way he shook his head made her heart plummet. The one thing she couldn't bear was for people to pity her.

"What kind of man would I be, making demands of you? You're a friend and neighbor, not a servant."

"It's because we're friends and neighbors." She pulled away from his touch. "You fixed my pump and gave me a birdhouse. You fixed my roof last week, too. I'm returning a favor because you said you like empanadas."

Duncan held the other half of the treat up between them. "Dinna mistake me, Carmen. This is a fine mouthful, but on occasion when I come o'er and help out, 'tis without expectation of getting anything in return."

"I know." She wasn't willing to leave the topic. "Just as when I bring your family something, I'm not hoping to talk you into doing a chore for me."

"Fair enough." He finished the other bite. Like a small boy who didn't want to miss the last little taste, Duncan licked the cinnamon sugar from his lips. He was such a man of contrasts—so mature and wise at one moment, only to be delightfully childlike the next instant. Though huge and strong, he exhibited a gentleness that evoked a sense of trust. *He's such a fine man. Handsome, too. The next wedding will probably be his. Any woman would be delighted to have such a husband.*

"I've been meanin' to talk with you about something."

"Would you mind too much if we discussed it later? I need to be over at the Rayburns' in an hour or so."

" 'Twill only take a moment." He nodded toward a chair. Once she sat down, he folded his arms across his chest. "A man could get dizzy watching you going to and fro all day."

No man would ever watch me, so that's a ridiculous statement.

"You canna continue to allow others to take advantage of your kind heart. There's not another woman around who's constantly dashing off to lend a hand. You're going to be worn to a frazzle."

"I like helping others."

"And well they know it. Still, dinna feel that every single time someone mentions a need, you're the one meant to meet it."

Carmen couldn't fathom what he was talking about.

Duncan stepped closer. "They're taking advantage of you, getting you to mind their bairns, bringing them meals, doing all manner of chores. . . If you hae a hard time telling them no, then we'll work on that. But—"

"No one's making me do anything. I offer them my help, Duncan."

"Let me be sure I'm hearing you right." He tilted his head to the side, and his brows formed an ominous black V. "You got yourself into this fix, and you keep on volunteering?"

"Fix?" Carmen tried not to laugh. He looked so serious that it warmed her heart. "Duncan, I'm happy to be busy. There's nothing wrong with me helping our neighbors and church family."

"I'm going to disagree wi' you there." His voice held reservation. "Dinna be so wrapped up in actions that you fail to do as the Bible instructs—to be still and know that He is God."

"Of course I know He is God." Carmen rose. "And I know who my brothers and sisters are, because Christ is our Savior. It all fits together. By serving them, I serve Him."

The grooves along the sides of his mouth deepened. Shaking his head, Duncan said, "You've the cart before the horse. 'Tis by serving God that we serve others. When our hearts are in accord with Him, our cups run over and shower blessings on the lives of others. You canna rain showers of blessings forever on your own strength and merit. Your own cup will go dry."

His words left her feeling unsettled. Carmen resented that. *Instead of wallowing in self-pity because I'm crippled and alone, I'm filling my days by helping others. He just doesn't understand.*

"Think on it," he urged.

"Only if you hurry and eat another of those. I think you need to sweeten your disposition today." She forced a laugh and hobbled out of his shop and back to her empty house.

Chapter 5

"Things are wrong." Duncan did his best not to glower at Carmen.

"What's wrong?" She finished tying a ribbon around the bottom of a little lassie's plait. "Go ask Nestor to give you a cookie."

"Miss Carmen, are you telling me to get a cookie?" The lassie shot a jealous look up at Duncan. "Or are you telling him to?"

"I dinna have an appetite for cookies today." Duncan served Carmen a telling look.

The little lass tugged on Carmen's sleeve. "Do I getta have his cookie, then?"

"You and Nestor may share it, *chica*."

Duncan fought the urge to shoo all of the children back to their homes. His talk with Carmen had made a difference—but the wrong one. If anything, she'd taken on even more responsibilities. The woman looked tired. From clear across the road, he'd noticed how her steps dragged. As a result, he'd closed his shop and come over so she wouldn't have to mind the rowdy bunch of children who filled her yard all by herself.

Her flower garden wasn't the wonderland it used to be. Her walkway wasn't swept, either. Little things—none of them alone said much, but put together, they nearly shouted something was wrong. He'd stay here until every last child left, but then Duncan planned to nudge Carmen into seeing the truth.

"So you mentioned something is wrong?" She gave him an expectant look.

"Aye." She'd prodded him into the discussion before he'd anticipated, but Duncan decided he might as well get things out in the open. He fisted his hands and rested them on his hips. "Speakin' as your friend, I'm reminding you that Christ was happier with Mary for sitting at His feet than He was with Martha for dashing about."

"Miss Rodriguez!" The little girl ran back over with her lower lip poking out and quivering. "Nestor says he already gave away all the cookies."

"*Pobrecita.*" Rich with compassion, the word rolled off Carmen's tongue. She gave the child a hug and murmured, "Next time you come, I'll make sure you get two."

"I get two po-citras?"

Shaking her head, Carmen explained, "*Pobrecita* is a special word in Spanish that means I was feeling sorry for you and I care."

"Oh." The child's eyes brightened with greed. "But I still get two cookies the next time!" She ran off shouting, "Nestor!"

"It actually means 'poor little girl,' but it isn't in regards to money—it's just a sympathy word." Carmen absently brushed a smear of something from her skirt.

At times when he'd seen her with Ismelda, Duncan had overheard Carmen speak in Spanish. "Chris is the one who'd have figured that out. I dinna have a talent with words."

"I disagree. It's true, Chris learns languages so he can communicate." Her hands started together and separated outward. "Your gift is in choosing the right words to comfort." Her hands reversed the action, but she ended by pressing her hands to her bosom.

He'd never thought of it that way. It was a fine compliment, but Duncan refused to be distracted. "My words to you today won't bring you comfort. I'm aiming to urge you to take stock and make changes."

"I don't want to change."

Stubborn woman. He heaved a long, drawn-out sigh for her benefit. "Busy hands dinna mean a full heart."

She smoothed her skirts. " 'Faith without works is dead.' "

"Aye, and you'd best be glad you've held that faith when you work yourself to death."

Carmen's eyes flashed with ire.

He studied her beautiful golden brown skin. The dark circles beneath her big brown eyes alarmed him. Duncan gentled his voice to coax her into reason. "E'en the Lord God Himself took the seventh day to rest."

"And by keeping these little ones, I'm giving their parents a time of rest." Carmen lifted a crabby tyke who'd toddled over and now clung to her skirts.

One quick whiff let Duncan know Carmen was going to be doing those parents a bigger favor still.

She laughed. "You've turned an interesting shade. With Elspeth—"

"My niece has enough sense to wait until her mother or father is around to do that."

"Mercy said all of you Gregor men change diapers."

"We do." He nodded briskly.

"Then—"

"Elspeth behaves herself for Chris and me."

The speed with which he made that assertion sent Carmen into giggles. Her laughter floated out to him as she tended the baby inside.

Duncan sat on the steps. Kids were a joy. Why, the three scrambling to sit on his knees and hang around his neck were all full of sunshine and laughter. But their parents were wrong to take advantage of Carmen. Ever since her sister got married, everyone seemed to think the woman didn't have a thing to do.

"Piggyback!" Nestor pled.

"Sure, and why not?" Duncan was giving the second child a turn about the yard when Carmen came back out with the babe. She sat in a wicker chair and popped a bottle into the toddler's mouth.

By the time he'd given all the children two rides, their parents came to collect them. As they walked away, Carmen turned to him. "You'll make a good father someday."

"I'm looking forward to it. E'en promised Da I'd name my firstborn son after him, but that day's a long while off. Carmen, I was serious when I said 'tisna right, you doing so much."

"I'm enjoying myself."

"You're wearin' yourself to a frazzle. You dinna e'en hae time enough to tend to your flowers any longer. The garden's a sad shadow of itself."

"But the children have more room to play."

He yanked the diaper she'd slung over her shoulder as a drool cloth. "They can do that at their own homes."

Carmen yanked the cloth from him. "Yes, they can. But I like them to come to my house just the same. Our town is friendly. I enjoy spending time with—"

"The old and the sick and the lonely?"

"They are my friends and neighbors." Her eyes flashed.

"That doesn't mean you have to be responsible for other people's children, too. Not a day goes by that you aren't minding someone else's bairns."

The passion he'd seen in her eyes just seconds ago dimmed. The spirit in her voice did, too. "I'll never have children of my own. Why do you want to deny me the few hours I can enjoy someone else's?"

Before he could answer, she turned and fled up the steps. Her awkward steps made it difficult, and he could have easily caught up, but Duncan stayed behind. He tried to meet her gaze as she turned to shut her door, but she kept her head bowed. That was bad enough, but her shoulders—the way they lifted and fell wasn't due to exertion.

I made her cry.

Duncan lumbered up to her door and knocked. He didn't know what he was going to say, but he couldn't set a woman into tears and just walk away. When she didn't answer, he stood there and knocked again—harder and longer.

The door opened a mere crack—just enough for him to catch sight of a tear-streaked cheek.

Suddenly, he knew exactly what to say. He felt badly and wanted her to know he cared. "Pobrecita—"

"I'm not a child, and I don't want your pity." The door clicked shut.

"I'm a cobbler," he said at a pitch he knew would reach her. "I'm good at making shoes, but I'm e'en better at stickin' my feet in my mouth." She didn't respond. After another minute or two, Duncan went back to his shop.

Needing to wear off his frustration, he yanked out a case of metal stamps and a hammer, then started whacking the stamps with notable force to impress a design on a strip of leather. An intricately tooled design emerged.

It's not half as complicated as that woman. I vowed to Da that I'd hae a son, but I didna think through all that meant. I'm going to look long and hard to find a placid woman. Someone fiery like Carmen would be the death of me.

—w—

"She'd be here with you for about four months. Preferably five, if you don't mind her staying a month to recover."

Carmen set down her coffee. "Even six months is fine."

"If you have any reservations at all, it's okay." The doctor didn't so much as blink. "I've not mentioned this to a soul, so no one need e'er know if you feel 'tisna right for you."

"You didn't even mention it to Mercy?"

Dr. Gregor shook his head. "Nae. My wife honors the way a man of my profession must hold confidences. If you agree to boarding the young woman, you should know part of the usual arrangement is that she's to help about the house with normal chores. She's also to attend church."

Folding her hands in her lap, Carmen sought a polite way to ask how she was supposed to coax a soiled dove to worship. "Is she accustomed to attending church?"

"Not as of late. But when she asked for assistance, she specified she wanted her baby to go to a good Christian home. It's my hope that during her months here, she might turn her heart toward the Lord."

"That would be wonderful. How soon can I expect her?"

"Her current situation is undesirable. The sooner, the better."

Carmen nodded. "I just finished my spring cleaning. Ismelda's old bedroom is ready. I could take her today if necessary."

"She's a full day away by train."

"Tomorrow then." Carmen bit her lip. "Shall I say my cousin is coming?"

Doctor Gregor stood and leaned against the veranda railing. "Carmen, I didna seek you out because of your Mexican heritage. This lass—Jenny—I've been told she's Swedish. I asked you because when Mercy discovered she was with child, your support for her never wavered. You looked past the sad circumstances and poured out Christian love and charity. If Jenny is to turn her heart toward the Lord, I'm thinkin' you and the Gregors are goin' to hae to drench her in His love."

"I'll expect Jenny tomorrow."

—⁂—

"No!" Duncan thumped down his coffee mug, and everything on the supper table jumped from the impact. He glowered at Rob as he got to his feet. "Meet me in my workshop." Without waiting for a response, he stomped out of the house.

Rob sauntered into the shop a few minutes later. "You canna bellow like a wounded bull whene'er you take a mind to, Duncan. You woke Elspeth again."

"Dinna try to distract me. It willna work." Duncan glowered at his little brother.

Rob simply stood in the center of the shop and said nothing.

"It willna work, I'm tellin' you!"

"It must have. You've forgotten why you dragged me out here."

"Are ye daft? Maybe you're goin' deaf. I told you, it willna work. You canna expect Carmen to give shelter to that woman."

"I met with Carmen yesterday, and we settled all of the details. She made Jenny feel right at home today."

"Aye, Jenny felt fine, but what of Carmen? I'm askin'—what of her?"

"What of her?"

"We've been here for a year now. I've ne'er once seen a single gentleman pay a call upon that fine lass. She's married off her kid sister and put on a good face, but she's hurting deep inside. I didna see the truth till a few days ago. She's brokenhearted o'er the fact that she'll ne'er marry and hae bairns of her own—and what did you go do?" Duncan stabbed an awl through the center of a choice piece of leather. "You go and rub her face in it, that's what you've done."

"I gave her every opportunity to refuse. Instead, she expressed an enthusiasm that convinced me this was the right thing to do."

"And how was she to refuse? Carmen's heart is bigger than Texas. Once she learns of someone else's needs, she puts them ahead of herself." He shook his head. " 'Tis a rare day I disagree wi' you, but that day's come. I've been trying to make the woman stop playing a dangerous game."

"What game is that?"

Duncan fought the temptation to tell Rob to mind his own business. But if speaking confidentially to him would spare Carmen heartache in the end, it was worth it. "The lass is forever doing something for someone—baking treats, taking a casserole somewhere, minding another woman's children. . ."

"And she's happy as a lark."

"Nae, Rob. She isna. Just look into her eyes and see the sadness there. That wee little limp of hers has her convinced she's not worthy of love, so she's trying to fill up the aching hole by working to earn appreciation. God doesn't care about the deeds one does—He cares about the soul. I've been tryin' to get her to see that."

"Have you, now?"

"And you went and ruined it all with this scheme of yours. I canna support this."

"It's too late to change things now."

"No, 'tisna. Move that mother-to-be into one of the bedrooms in the clinic. She can join us Gregors for meals and e'en help out your wife." Duncan nodded. "Aye, that's the solution."

"It's a foolish plan. Once people figure out that Jenny's unwed and carrying a child, her reputation will be in tatters. Leaving her alone in the clinic is a sure invitation for disaster."

Duncan glowered at his brother. "So you've asked Carmen to protect Jenny? What man asks that of a woman?"

"There's a world of difference between sheltering and protecting."

Duncan let out a loud, derisive snort. "Only in your feeble mind."

"As I said, it's too late to change things now. We'll have to make the best of it."

"Wipe that smile off your face, Rob, before I do something rash."

Rob sauntered over, picked up a shoe, and pretended to be fascinated by it. "Just when," he asked slowly, "did you appoint yourself Carmen's guardian?"

Chapter 6

Someone has to look out for her. The woman doesna give a moment's consideration to her own needs."

"Hmm." Rob set the shoe down with exacting care. "And how is it you've paid attention to whether men have called on her?"

"Her house is directly across the street," Duncan snapped. "Take a look—her garden and porch are the view from where I work. I've not been skulking or spying on her."

Rob went over to the window and clasped his hands behind his back. He nodded sagely as he examined the view for himself. "Duncan?"

"Now what?"

"I like Carmen."

"You've an odd way of showing it, putting her in this painful predicament."

"Much as I like Carmen, Mercy loves her even more."

Duncan let out a low growl of frustration.

Rob turned around and grinned. "We'll be happy to have her as our sister-in-law."

Duncan gaped at his brother.

Rob held up a hand to forestall any response. "Dinna deny it. You've feelings for the lass. Your reaction tonight shows those feelings run deep."

"Friendship doesna mean I'm marching down the aisle."

"Good thing, that. We dinna have any more of our plaid. I'm thinkin' by the time 'tis ordered and arrived, you'll be wanting a length to drape o'er your bride's shoulder."

The image of Carmen dressed in a bridal gown with the Gregor tartan gathered over her shoulder hit Duncan so hard he dropped down onto his bench.

Rob grinned like a drunken jester. "You love her."

"I'm a rough man. Why would a fine lass like her hae anything to do wi' me?"

"Remember that song the sailor was singing when we were waiting for the train?"

"About America? What does that hae to do with this?"

"You're in America now. This is the land of the free and the home of the brave."
Rob snickered. "Only if you're brave, you'll no longer be free—you'll be married to a
fiery little woman."

Duncan shot his brother a dark look. "You're far too amused by this."

"Aye, that I am. But what you just did is telling."

"What did I do?"

"Actually, it's more what you didna do."

Duncan got up and started pacing. "You're driving me daft. Will you make up
your mind whether it's something I did or didna do?"

"What you didna do was deny what I said. You love her. If your heart weren't
involved, you'd have challenged me."

Duncan folded his arms across his chest. In that moment, everything fell into
place. His brother spoke the truth, and Duncan couldn't deny it. He didn't even want
to. "I've made up my mind. Aye, I have."

"About what?"

"I'm going to court the woman. She's not had a swain, and I'm going to ease her
into this slow and sweet. When we're old and gray, she'll look back and feel every last
tender hope she e'er held in her heart was fulfilled."

"Women are romantics. If you plan to fulfill every last tender hope, you'll be old
and gray and still not be married to her yet."

"You'd best watch what you say. I'm still sore at you for sticking that young girl
into Carmen's care."

"You ought to be thanking me. Now that Carmen's not alone, you can go over
there without raising any questions of propriety."

"The only thing I'll thank you to do is keep this conversation confidential." He
stared out the window. "There's every chance Carmen might not love me back."

—∞—

"'Tis a bonny day to go fishing," Duncan announced as he crossed the road with a
shovel in his big hands.

Only a few days had passed since Carmen had blurted out the shameful fact that
no man would have her and she had to resort to borrowing children. That alone left
her wanting to crawl off somewhere. But Duncan had listened to that appallingly
personal confession and rumbled "pobrecita" at her as if she needed his pity. Carmen
decided she didn't want to crawl off somewhere after all; she'd rather bake a special
batch of empanadas for him and dust them with cayenne and chili instead of cinnamon. She wouldn't, but just the thought brought a tiny measure of glee.

"Aye, I'm going fishing."

She pretended not to hear him and stooped down to pick a weed.

The hulking Scotsman kept coming.

Carmen fought the urge to tell him to stop wasting time and go fishing. *This is all his fault. I don't have a hard time minding my manners with anyone else. Duncan— he's polite and kind to everyone else. Why can't he just leave me alone and keep his opinions to himself? The man's an insensitive brute and needs to mind his own business instead of prying into mine. If he says anything—*

Boots stopped half a yard from her. Ordinary brown boots. Carmen hadn't figured out yet why Duncan's boots were so basic and plain. A cobbler could wear the finest and fanciest, yet he didn't. She looked up to tell him so.

"I'm going fishing," he said again as he reached down to assist her up.

Carmen accepted his help, then snatched her hand back and wondered why she'd let him assist her. Scrambling to find something to say, she blurted out, "Most men take a pole fishing, not a spade."

He chortled softly, and the fine lines crinkling from the corners of his eyes reminded her that he laughed often. " 'Tis the truth. I've some method to my madness, though. This time last year, you were planting flowers. Why dinna I turn the soil for you and swipe a few worms whilst I'm at it?"

Astonishment and relief flooded her. He was acting as if they'd never had that horribly awkward and embarrassing exchange. "That would be nice. Thank you." *And I'm going to bake you some empanadas with cinnamon, not cayenne and chili.* "Duncan, I have a friend staying with me for a while."

"Rob told me." His voice took on an undertone that she couldn't interpret.

Carmen called, "Jenny?"

Jenny stepped out of the house. "Ja?"

"Come meet our neighbor." She waited until Jenny reached her side. "Jenny Sigrids, may I present you to Duncan Gregor. Duncan, my friend, Jenny."

" 'Tis a pleasure to meet any friend of Carmen's. Nice to meet you, Mi—"

Realizing the fact that Jenny was unwed would cause for awkward moments, Carmen interrupted. "Oh dear, I should have mentioned that with three Gregor men across the street, it makes for a lot of confusion if we use formal address. Duncan, I hope you don't mind if Jenny follows my example and calls you by your Christian name."

"Not a-tall."

"And, Jenny, it's only fair that you reciprocate. There." Carmen smiled broadly.

"Duncan, since you're turning the soil, maybe Jenny and I can go to the mercantile and choose flower seeds today."

"You already have a beautiful garden," Jenny said.

"Actually, it's a pitiful mess right now. Isn't it, Duncan?"

"Shameful as 'tis to confess, I did tell you that just a few days back. Last year, the blossoms in your yard rivaled all of God's flower-strewn fields about us."

"Oh my." Jenny sighed. "I never had a garden. It will be so fun to grow something."

"You know," Duncan said, stretching, "if you'd like, we could go on a walk. I'll take a wheelbarrow, and we could transplant some of the wildflowers so you can enjoy them until your seeds sprout and blossom."

"What about the worms?" Jenny asked.

"I'm sure we'll happen across a few." Duncan's glance skimmed down their gowns. "You're both wearin' lovely frocks. Best you go change into ones that willna be spoiled by layers of dust."

"Though it sounds like a delightful notion, I'm afraid Jenny and I need to do something else today."

"Perhaps later in the week." Duncan didn't ask—he told. When had he become so bossy?

"Oh, that would be so much fun," Jenny said.

Carmen couldn't dash Jenny's enthusiasm. Though Jenny was tall and large-boned, she still seemed startlingly childlike in some circumstances. So far, she and Jenny had politely limited their conversations to impersonal things. Carmen wasn't sure how old her guest was. For now, she would indulge the girl. "We'll be able to go in a few days. The timing would be better. By buying seeds first, we can transplant the wildflowers to places in the garden where they'll have the best effect."

"Best effect?" Jenny wrinkled her nose. "I thought they were just supposed to look pretty."

"Me, too." Duncan grinned at Jenny.

He's impossibly handsome. He's charming her, just as he charms everyone else. He turned his steady blue gaze back onto Carmen. "Why dinna ye tell us just what kind of effect you are talkin' about?"

"What I meant was, we don't want to plant whistly blue behind paintbrush or bluebonnets. They're tall and would block out the flowers that are low to the ground."

He nodded. "That makes sense. Good thinking. Back home, Rob always kept an herbal garden so he'd have medicinals on hand. Each plant belonged in a specific location, but I dinna ken whether 'twas so he could tell them apart or because one might taint another if they grew too close."

"He didn't put in an herb garden here." Carmen frowned. "Why not?"

Duncan compressed his lips for a moment and then grimaced. "Chris dug straight through it when he put in the basement. He thought the herbs were weeds. Best you not mention it to either of them unless you're set to witness a shouting match."

"You Gregors don't fight," Carmen said.

"They don't?" Jenny sounded completely flummoxed. "Men always fight."

"Now I suppose that depends on the men." Duncan shrugged. "I've known many a man to lose his temper, but of all the men I've known, I admired my da the most. I canna recall a single time when he lost his self-control."

"He must have been quite a man," Jenny said softly.

"Humility, meekness, self-control—those are all traits a man of God strives for." Carmen looked at Duncan. "Your father must have been a godly man."

"The finest, and I thank you for sayin' so."

"Jenny, why don't we wash up and go to the mercantile?"

"All right." Jenny shoved her hands into the pocket of her apron. "I hope the fish are biting once you go fishing, Duncan."

"Now there's a grand thought."

Carmen didn't mention how she'd noticed Jenny's hands remained fisted deep in the apron pockets. Was she truly excited to go on the walk, or was she just afraid to have to be out and meet people here in town?

They went inside, and Carmen went to the washstand. "It never fails to amaze me how filthy my hands become after just a few minutes in the garden."

Jenny didn't respond.

As she dried her hands on a scarlet towel embroidered with big, sunny yellow flowers, Carmen turned to her. "I like to sew. Do you?"

"For my grandmother, I used to sew all of the time. She was a dressmaker."

Carmen smiled. "Wonderful. My friend Mercy—she's the doctor's wife—she recently had a baby. I remember her making special dresses during the time she was—" Carmen caught herself just before she said, "in the family way." Jenny wasn't going to keep the baby, so mentioning family would be cruel. Instead, Carmen simply said, "—increasing. I'm sure you're going to need some roomier clothes, too. Maybe we could drop in on Mercy and ask her for advice before we buy fabric."

"My other dress is bigger." Jenny paused a second then blurted out, "I don't have much money. I had to run away from the saloon. Bart thought I was going to the doctor to get rid of the baby, so all I have is what he gave me to pay the doctor."

"Jenny!"

Jenny hung her head. "I'm sorry. A nice lady like you shouldn't rub elbows with—"

Carmen stopped her by wrapping Jenny in her arms. "I'm so proud of you. You're a brave girl. You did the right thing."

Jenny drew away and looked nonplussed.

"It must have been hard for you to get help and keep everything a secret."

Jenny bit her lip and nodded.

"But here you are. And we have those three big, strong Gregor men across the street to protect you if that awful Bart finds out where you are."

"Why would they want to protect me?" Just as quickly as she asked it, Jenny answered the question. "Because of the baby."

"No. If you'd run away from a bad situation and weren't with child, they'd still defend you. They're noble men." Carmen squeezed Jenny's hand. "Mercy and I both enjoy sewing and doing embroidery. Won't it be pleasant to sit together in a shady spot and stitch together?"

A stiff shrug tattled on Jenny's reservations.

"Tacky as it might be for me to discuss money, you ought to know that on occasion someone chooses to be a secret benefactor to a woman in your situation. I know that's true in your case. You'll have an account at the mercantile, so it shouldn't be a problem for you to purchase fabric and other necessities."

"Someone would do that for me? A stranger? They didn't know what kind of woman I am."

"What that person knows is that you are a woman who is willing to give her child the wonderful gift of a family who will cherish him or her in ways you know you cannot."

"Don't you think whoever that is would want me to spend the money to make blankets and clothes and diapers for the baby?"

"Absolutely not!" Carmen released Jenny's hand. "The couple who receives the baby will take care of those details. Why don't you freshen up while I jot down a few things?"

While Jenny took a turn at the washstand, Carmen sat at the ornately carved oak secretary her mother once treasured. She didn't have much time, so she dipped the pen in the inkwell and quickly wrote:

CONFIDENTIAL.

Dear Leonard,

*Set up an account for Jenny. Twenty-five dollars. No one—
especially Jenny—is to know I'm funding this. Thank you.*

She hastily signed only her initials and glanced over at Jenny.

"I'm in no hurry. If you'd like to tame your hair, feel free."

"Oh. Okay."

Carmen took another sheet of paper and hastily started writing down anything she might vaguely need from the mercantile.

"That list must be getting long," Jenny said as she patted one last strand of hair into place.

"I've been doing a lot of baking. One peek into my pantry and you'll think we're in danger of starving." Carmen blotted the list and folded it to hide the note.

Chapter 7

Duncan yawned and stretched. He'd gone to bed late and gotten up early so he'd have today's work done by breakfast. That freed him to take Carmen for a nice stroll. Women liked to walk and have a man pick flowers for them. Surely this would be a time she'd remember fondly. It would be a fine start of their courtship.

The thought of taking a picnic lunch along crossed his mind, but Duncan decided he'd use that as another outing. Aye, he'd plan a string of pleasant activities and idyllic afternoons, and he'd make a point to go over to her house more often to handle some minor repairs and do general upkeep.

Small gardening hand tools jostled merrily in the wheelbarrow as he wheeled it across the street. Duncan mentally traced the route they'd take again. He'd wandered the nearby fields to plot out a leisurely walk that wouldn't tax Carmen. Though she didn't complain, he knew her leg pained her—and she loathed having anyone notice that ridiculously paltry limp of hers. But because she'd be mortified to be unable to exert herself, Duncan circumvented the difficulty by planning everything in advance.

"Good morning!" Carmen stepped from her house. The morning sun glossed her raven-black hair and made Duncan wish he could yank out the pins and run his hands through her tresses to see how long they were.

"Yeah. Good morning." Jenny stepped out of the house, too.

"Aye, 'tis. And it just got better, what with a pair of pretty ladies to go on a walk wi' me."

They sauntered down the street. Pride squared Duncan's shoulders. With Carmen by his side, he felt ten feet tall. The moment they reached a fork in the road, he started to veer south.

"Have you ever seen such a sight?" Jenny stared in rapture at the field that went north.

"I don't know what it is about flowers." Carmen smiled. "I always think the one I'm looking at is the most beautiful ever."

Jenny shaded her eyes with one hand and pointed into the distance. "Could we get some of those little blue ones?"

"What a wonderful idea. I'm always charmed by wind-blown."

Duncan tilted his head to the side. "Aren't all wildflowers windblown?"

"Most are," Carmen allowed. "But that particular flower's name is wind-blown. Jenny, I'll show you more of them. It's amazing, but wind-blown comes in a huge array of colors. If you keep watch, you soon see them in everything from a pale blue to a bright pink."

To Duncan's consternation, the women headed north toward the wind-blown. He wanted to snatch Carmen back to his side. He told himself it was simply because he wanted her to take the easier route he'd planned. He promptly called himself a liar. He didn't want her away from his side—and that was the truth of the matter.

"You mentioned whistly blue the other day," he said to Carmen. "I've found several stretches of it, but I'd rather hae them be among the beauty we gather after we gain a collection of taller varieties."

Carmen smiled. "That's good planning."

"I was wondering"—Jenny scanned the field—"can we fill the wheelbarrow today and put the flowers in the garden tomorrow?"

" 'Tis up to you, Carmen."

Carmen shook her head. "It's too dry and warm today to do that. We'd run the risk of losing them. It would be a shame to pluck up a flower, only to make it so it won't survive."

Jenny made a wry face.

"You're unhappy with my decision?" Carmen gave Jenny a surprised look.

"The only thing I've ever seen dry out in a wheelbarrow is a man. At the saloon, they'd dump a drunk into the wheelbarrow and push it over by the ditch."

Carmen's eyes widened.

"Oh, they did that so when he woke up and puked, no one would have to clean up the mess."

"They treated a man like that?" Carmen's voice sounded both sad and outraged.

Jenny shrugged. "A real man can hold his liquor."

"A real man doesna need liquor a-tall," Duncan said. "But any man who's weak enough to drink to that kind of excess still deserves better than to be treated like refuse."

Jenny's mouth twisted wryly. "Neither of you have ever had to mop up after a drunken fool."

"I far prefer having flowers in your wheelbarrow, Duncan."

Duncan flashed Carmen a smile. She'd bent the conversation away from Jenny's unfortunate past and back to something pleasant. Admiration for her diplomacy filled him. He nodded. "Flowers and ladies on a beautiful day are definitely to my taste." He managed to steer them all back toward the route he'd chosen.

At one point, an almost two-foot-wide crack in the ground broke the path. Duncan knew it was there, and he'd intentionally led them toward the rift. It provided an excuse for him to cup Carmen's waist and lift her.

"You ladies wait a moment whilst I get the wheelbarrow over there. If the edges here take a mind to crumble, I'd rather it not be under your feet." Proud of that excuse, Duncan made short work of hefting the flower-filled wheelbarrow over to the other side. Straddling the divide, he reached for Jenny first. That way, Carmen wouldn't feel as if he was making allowances for the insignificant problem she strove so hard to deny.

"You're so strong!" Jenny cooed at him as he swung the big-boned lass over the divide.

"Compared to the things he hauled when they built their house, you weigh nothing at all." Carmen smiled as she vouched so casually for his strength.

Her praise meant a lot to him, but the fact that she'd been watching him gave Duncan a glimmer of hope. Maybe the attraction was mutual after all. "I'm ready for you now, Carmen." *And not just to lift you across this.* He slowly cupped her waist and made sure he had a secure hold.

Unlike Jenny, who'd rested her hands on his shoulders, Carmen carefully rested her hands on his upper arms. The shyness in her beautiful brown eyes beguiled him. She was normally confident and saucy, so he'd not seen this side of her. *Give me time, lass. I'll show you just how lovely you are and that you can entrust yourself to me entirely.*

"Is something wrong?" Embarrassment colored her whisper.

"Not a bit." Duncan grinned. "I was appreciating your perfume. It's a tad spicy—like you."

"I like it," Jenny said.

"Aye, as do I." Duncan lifted Carmen. He would be content to stay there the whole day, holding her and inhaling her scent. Instead, he set her down by Jenny and waited a second to be sure she was steady before releasing his hold.

By the time Duncan returned to his workshop that afternoon, he couldn't stop grinning like a fool. Aye, he'd set his heart on that black-haired, brown-eyed woman, and courting her was going to be pure delight.

"Holes?" Carmen glanced at her windows in consternation. "I didn't notice any."

"Aye, a close look at the screens will tell you I'm right." Duncan clomped across her veranda and pointed at a few spots. "They're wee small holes yet, but that's when we need to catch the problem. If they get any larger, you'll be plagued with flies in the house."

"Thank you for pointing that out. I think I have a scrap of screening material somewhere."

"A scrap willna do."

Carmen gave him a patient look. "I can sew little patches if the holes are tiny."

"That brings to mind the verse about not putting new wine in old wineskins."

Carmen noticed Jenny's perplexed expression and made a mental note to explain the biblical verse to her later. "Wineskins are different. A more accurate analogy would be resoling a pair of boots." Pleased that she'd countered his assertion with something Duncan would relate to so well, Carmen gave him a smile.

Duncan's brows rose. "I'd not recommend resoling boots that dinna have enough life left in them to make it worthwhile."

"How old are your screens?" Jenny poked her finger at the screen door. It went straight through and left a jagged little tear. "Oh, I'm sorry!"

"There you have it." Duncan nodded. "They're all wanting replacement."

Otto was busy on the farm. Carmen knew he couldn't afford the time to accomplish the job. "I'll decide which ones are the worst and ask Otto to do one a week."

"Ooch, lass. And why would you be doing that when I'm willin' to get the job done now?"

"You're a busy man, Duncan."

"Not too busy to help out a neighbor. I'll do your screen door first, here on your porch, so you'll still be able to catch a breeze for the rest of the day. Elsewise, your house will be miserable as the inside of an oven."

"You've already done so much, Duncan. You turned the soil for our garden and helped us get the flowers."

"Dinna forget that I helped myself to some worms to bait my hook and caught several fish. Aye, and I had the joy of your fine company for a stroll the day we gathered flowers."

"You shared the fish." Jenny pointed out.

"Aye, but then you ladies shared your flower seeds with Mercy. She wept for joy when she discovered you'd started a garden for her."

"Elspeth keeps her so busy, we knew Mercy wouldn't have an opportunity to plant flowers." Carmen turned to Jenny. "Isn't that so, Jenny?"

Jenny nodded. "Carmen and I had fun planning where to put each flower."

"And you turned the soil so the ground would be ready, Duncan. You were every bit as much involved in the project."

"I just finished making that saddle for Mr. Stuky. This is a good time for me to take on doing your screens. I dinna like to start a new pair of shoes or a saddle when I'll have to skip working the next day."

"Oh." Jenny's voice went flat. "Tomorrow is Sunday."

"So there you have it." Duncan folded his arms across his chest as if he'd won an important debate.

"What do I have?" Jenny glowered at him.

"You hae the reason why you ladies ought to accompany me to the mercantile. We'll get the screening so I can fix Carmen's windows by sunset."

"It's been three days since we went to the mercantile, Jenny," Carmen remarked. "Those things you ordered are probably in by now."

Jenny wilted into a wicker chair. "Could you pick them up for me? I'm hot and tired."

"Sure we could." Duncan spoke before Carmen could insist Jenny come along.

On their walk to the mercantile, Carmen tried to think of a way to broach the delicate topic. Several different phrases occurred to her, but she dismissed them.

"You're quiet as can be."

She sighed. "It's Jenny."

Duncan stopped. "If things are strained, I'll hae Rob find a different place for her."

"No, no. She's not been here a full week yet. Settling in will take time."

"You're dillydallying around. Why dinna ye just say what needs to be said?"

Heat tingled in her cheeks. "It's not that easy."

Duncan tilted her face to his and spoke in a low, soothing tone. "We're friends, Carmen Rodriguez. We're trying to help a lass who's got a dark past and a difficult future. You're a cultured woman. I ken there are matters not normally discussed between a lady and a man, but this isna a normal situation. Troubling yourself over finding the proper words is silly. I'll not think less of you for doing what's necessary to help Jenny. Deep down, she's a sweet lass, and I'm wanting to help her, too. Speak to me from your heart."

His earnest words helped. Carmen blurted out, "Jenny doesn't want to go to church. She didn't even want to go to the mercantile the other day. Once people understand what she is, she's sure they'll shun her."

"Mmmm." Duncan stretched out the sound. "I see."

"Remember how long it took for everyone to face Mercy once her tragedy happened?"

"Aye. 'Twas a harsh time for her. Once we stood firm on her side, folks came around. We'll do the same for Jenny."

"There's a difference between their cases. Mercy was innocent."

"True." Duncan let out a long sigh. "Times like today, when I mentioned the wineskins, she's baffled. From what I gather, she's not a believer. We canna expect her to hae walked the straight and narrow path when she wasna shod with the preparation of the gospel of peace nor protected with the shield of faith."

"Ephesians six," Carmen murmured. He did that—slipped biblical references into his conversation. Often, it was so seamless anyone who wasn't steeped in the Scriptures would miss it.

"Exactly. 'Tis wrong to judge others. No one makes it to the Lord by good deeds or based on the opinions of others. 'Tis grace through the blood of Christ Jesus that redeems us. I'm thinkin' 'twill be our example of grace and love that will woo Jenny to the Lord. If others judge her, they'll be accountable to Him."

"So there will be the Gregors and me."

"To start with." Duncan began to walk again. "But just as surely as God can do a work in Jenny's heart, He can supply compassion to others so they can show it to her."

"As long as we're talking, Duncan, I may as well confess another worry to you."

"You can always share your worries with me."

She gave him an appreciative look. Duncan wasn't a glib man. He spoke directly and from the heart. That invitation wasn't just a platitude. He'd meant what he said. "Remember when Otto's mother dragged that awful man into my house so he could beg Mercy for her baby? It didn't occur to me until yesterday that once Mrs. Kunstler comes to church tomorrow and finds out about Jenny staying with me, she'll bring that man back again."

"We've discussed that at home. Mercy received a letter from Chester Heim that same week. He apologized and sought forgiveness. He and his wife are so verra eager to hae a bairn to call their own. In thinkin' back, Mercy said he'd implored her to gie them the babe, but 'twas actually Mrs. Kunstler who'd spoken the harshest words."

"Since Ismelda married Otto, Mrs. Kunstler is family, and she is my elder. Part of me says I owe her respect, no matter what. On the other hand, I feel if she dares to say anything, I'll lose my temper. So what do I do?"

"Just as you came to fetch Rob last time, you can always run to us for help. Neither Rob nor Mercy thinks Chester Heim will trouble Jenny. Though 'tis true Mrs. Kunstler is kin to you since Ismelda wed her son, I'm not mincing words. I think it best if ever she comes to pay a call that you instruct Jenny to come help Mercy."

"Thank you. I'll do that."

They'd arrived at the mercantile. Before he opened the door, Duncan gazed at her intently. "Dinna forget, Carmen, I intend to be your partner."

Partner. Such an odd word. It suggested both a union of minds and a distance of hearts. All at once, Carmen felt supported and yet very, very alone.

Chapter 8

O och, Carmen, you're looking grand today."

A blush filled her cheeks. "Thank you. Wait till you see Jenny. She's wearing her new dress."

Duncan nodded and winked. Carmen made for a good partner in this project. By mentioning Jenny's gown, he'd have something to praise her over so she wouldn't fret as much while they walked to church. The church bell began to toll. "Best we get started."

Once Jenny stepped onto the veranda, he mused, "I'm not a man who knows much about posies, other than to say they're charming wee things. But your gown— 'tis the same shade as those bachelor buttons in the garden."

"Leave it to a man to know the name of a flower named bachelor." Carmen laughed as she shut the door.

Duncan escorted the women down the street. Jenny held tightly to his arm, giving away the fragile state of her nerves. "Elspeth kept Rob and Mercy up half the night. They're going to sit in the back pew. I hope you dinna mind sitting with me today."

"We'd be happy to. Wouldn't we, Jenny?"

"Yes."

Duncan ignored how she sounded as if she'd rather have Rob pull all her teeth than attend worship. "Mercy directed me to invite you both to lunch."

"You just said she was up half the night." Carmen frowned. "Maybe some other Sunday."

Duncan intentionally waited until the church bell rang so Jenny wouldn't get mobbed by everyone and feel overwhelmed. Even then, as they reached the church door, Carmen found it necessary to introduce Jenny to a few people.

As they sat in the sanctuary, Duncan stared at the cross behind the pulpit. *Lord, 'tis good to be in Your house again. Teach me what Ye would hae me know, and if it be Your will, begin to prepare Carmen's heart so she'll become my bride. Most of all, Lord, open*

Jenny's soul to Your salvation. Blind her to any unkindness and grant others a special love for her so she can see the difference Ye make. Amen.

The sermon was about the woman at the well. The pastor kept echoing Christ's admonition, "Go and sin no more." He applied the concept to the sins, great and small, that are so common to man. Duncan considered the sermon outstanding.

It wasn't until he escorted Carmen and Jenny back to the Rodriquez house that Jenny finally spoke. "I don't want to go back. Ever. I know it's part of the arrangement, but can't we change it?"

"What was so bad?" Carmen sat beside her.

"He told that story just because I was there. Why didn't he just point his finger at me and tell them all I'm a—"

"Sinner, just like the rest of us?" Duncan cut in strategically. "I venture to say everyone is probably sitting at home thinkin' the parson's been spying on them. Impatience. Gluttony. Greed. Gossip."

Some of the tension in Jenny's shoulders eased. "He did say those things, too."

"The Bible says we've all sinned and fallen short of God's glory." Duncan met Jenny's troubled gaze and confessed, "I can only speak for myself, but I cringe and squirm inside when those dark things are brought to light, because I know I have room to improve."

"Me, too." Carmen took Jenny's hand in hers. "I'm guilty of vanity."

Duncan didn't breathe a word, but he thought Carmen had plenty to be proud of. No other woman on earth was half as pretty. Her eyes were aglow with intelligence, and her skin matched the shade of sun-warmed honey. The lively chatter and laughter bubbling from her lips lifted a man's spirits, and, despite her limp, the woman carried herself like a queen.

"You're not vain," Jenny objected.

"Oh, but I am. I'm crippled and I limp. If I used a cane, I'd be more stable, but I won't because I'm vain. Proud, too."

"What the parson said was the most important thing, Jenny." Duncan looked at her. "Jesus Christ didna stand there and condemn that woman. He forgave her and told her to start anew. What's done is done. He instructed her to change her ways and do better."

Jenny didn't look the least bit convinced. "I went to church. I don't want to think about any of that stuff until I have to go again next week."

"But you will go." Carmen's voice rang with authority.

"Aye. And I'd be honored to escort the both of you."

—◊—

"Duncan!" Mercy's alarmed voice wavered in the air.

Duncan bolted out of his shop and toward the house. "Aye?"

Mercy held Elspeth over her shoulder and shouted, "The sky's gone green!"

He halted. "So it is. An ugly—"

"Hurry and fetch Carmen and Jenny. This is tornado weather!"

He needed no further urging. Duncan raced across the street. Without bothering to knock, he burst right in. "Come along now."

Carmen held Jenny's wrist and was dragging her into the hall. Jenny cried out, "I thought tornadoes didn't strike here!"

"I've seen a few," Carmen said. "The safest place—"

"Isna here. You're coming home with me. We've a large basement. I'll keep you safe."

Carmen turned loose of Jenny, and Duncan felt a spurt of relief. She was being practical and cooperative. At least she was until she turned into a room.

"Woman!" he bellowed.

Carmen ignored him, so he chased after her. A man had no business being in a woman's bedchamber, but Duncan figured survival rated above etiquette. He'd never seen a tornado, but from what he'd heard, no one tangled with one and came out the victor. Knowing Carmen was in danger sent him blustering into her room. She eluded him by ducking under his arm and called, "Jenny! Go with Duncan. I'll be right behind you!"

"This is absurd. We're leavin' this verra minute."

"Give me a second." The daft woman swept back the magnificent star-patterned quilt covering her bed and crawled onto the mattress. "Grab that quilt—just in case."

Duncan didn't know precisely what she meant, but that didn't matter, anyway. He grabbed for her. "Woman!"

She half stood on her bed and grabbed a beautiful mahogany and gold crucifix from the wall. "This was Mama's."

When Carmen gasped as he cinched his arm about her waist and yanked her down, he declared, "I'm takin' no chances."

"Stop blustering and help me gather the quilt for protection."

The woman was daft as a drunken duck if she thought a quilt was a match for a wind that could knock over a barn. Realizing he'd waste more time arguing with her than in snatching it up, he kept hold of Carmen and grabbed the quilt.

Jenny waddled out of the other room. Duncan had no idea what she'd managed to stuff in the pillowcase she held.

Carmen smacked him on the chest. "Put me down. You can carry Jenny's bag."

"I willna!" He shouted at Jenny, "Drop that and come on!"

Jenny shook her head.

Duncan wanted to drop the quilt, grab the lass, and haul them both across the street. He couldn't though. A woman in Jenny's condition oughtn't be squashed about the middle. He dropped the quilt anyway and grabbed her wrist. "I'll come back for that junk."

In the blink of an eye, Jenny shoved her bag into Carmen's hands, jerked free from Duncan, and slapped him. She scooted back and wrapped her arms around her ribs. "Don't grab me. Don't ever grab me."

He hadn't let go of Carmen yet. She wiggled away and ran to Jenny's side. "It's okay. He's not mad at you."

"We're wasting dear time here." Duncan swept Carmen into his arms again. "Let's go!"

"You go ahead." Jenny's words were hard to hear over the wind.

"You run ahead of us, lass." Duncan jerked his chin toward the door. "I'll no' leave you behind."

He finally got them to his house, and Mercy called from the basement, "Come on down here!"

Duncan didn't want Carmen to have to limp down the steep stairs. "Jenny, scamper on down. There you go." He followed right behind her with Carmen held close to his chest.

"I'm so glad you're here." Mercy set Elspeth in a crate she'd lined with a blanket and then hugged the women.

Duncan headed back up the stairs. "Stay," Carmen called to him.

"I'll be back."

"Hail starts to fall right before a twister." Worry vibrated in her voice.

"I'm sorry." Jenny's voice sounded shaky.

Duncan turned around. "You've nothing to be sorry about. When I return, I'll give you my apology. You stay put." Duncan turned to his sister-in-law. "Mercy, what about Elspeth? What do you need for her?"

"I already have blankets and diapers here. Please stay."

He didn't reply. After carefully closing the door to the basement, Duncan ran to the clinic. "Rob!"

Nothing but the sound of wind met him. Satisfied that his brother wasn't there,

Duncan scanned the street. Not a soul stirred, so he went back to the women.

"What do you need down there?"

Carmen shouted, "You!"

His heart soared.

———ww———

"Ismelda!" Carmen embraced her sister. "I'm so relieved that you're okay."

"I'm fine. So is Mercy's grandfather. The twister was small. It left a zigzagging path about a mile from us."

"So no one got hurt?"

"We're all fine." Ismelda grabbed Carmen's hand and cast a quick look over at Jenny. Since Jenny didn't speak any Spanish, Ismelda said very quickly, "I think it's wonderful how you've taken this girl in. My mother-in-law is very upset, though. She feels you've tainted yourself by association. Otto and I talked it over. We want you and Jenny to be sure to sit by us in church tomorrow."

"Of course we will," Carmen replied in English. "After church, you and Otto ought to come here for Sunday supper. I'm teaching Jenny how to make tortillas. For a *gringa*, she does a good job."

Jenny let out a small laugh. "When I was small, my grandmother would give me the scraps from pie dough. When I pat the tortilla between my hands to flatten it, it feels just like when I played with that dough."

"We'll make lots of them and bake enchiladas. Why don't we have the Gregors over for supper, too?"

"There's not enough room at the table for that many of us." Jenny hitched a shoulder as if it didn't matter to her one bit as she said, "I'll just eat in my room."

"*No. Absolutamente. ¡Absurdo!*" Ismelda and Carmen said in unison.

Ismelda giggled. "Mama used to say that."

"And she'd say that here and now, too." Carmen shook her finger at Jenny. "There's always room at my table for you."

After Ismelda left, Carmen and Jenny sat together and made tortillas. Carmen hesitated, but her curiosity wouldn't let her remain silent. "You've mentioned your grandmother. Since she was a dressmaker, why didn't you go into that profession?"

"I didn't have a choice." Jenny slapped down a tortilla and began another. "I was thirteen when she died. No one would hire me—no one but Bart."

"You were just a baby!" Carmen stared at her in shock.

"It was a long time ago." She shrugged. "But I want better for my baby than what I had. My mother—she wasn't married. She died when I was a small girl, and all I had was Grandma. This baby—the doctor promised it will go to a husband and wife. There will be grandparents and cousins, too."

"Your baby is fortunate, Jenny. Not just because of the family it will go to. It's blessed because you've thought matters through and are giving it to a better home than you can provide."

"I can't keep it, you know. After I have the baby, I thought I'd take the train west. Now that I'm sixteen, maybe someone who doesn't know about my past will hire me. But I won't be able to work if I keep the baby with me, so I couldn't even keep a roof over our heads."

Aghast, Carmen echoed, "You're sixteen?"

"Unh-huh. I don't know if this is going to be enough tortillas. Those Gregor men eat a lot."

"Why don't I go over and make sure they can come for supper? You ought to lie down and rest awhile, anyway. Dr. Gregor said you should nap more."

Carmen stumbled into Mercy's parlor and finally gave vent to her outrage. "Mercy?"

"Yes?" Mercy remained in the rocking chair. The Gregor tartan draped over her shoulder, hiding Elspeth as she suckled.

"Jenny's only sixteen! I thought she was much older."

Duncan appeared beside Carmen. He pressed his handkerchief into her hand. "Hard living ages a body. 'Tis plain to see that's the case with Jenny."

She should have been surprised or even embarrassed, but Carmen didn't feel either emotion when she realized she was weeping. She let Duncan pull her close, and she soaked his shirt with her tears. "It's so dreadful. We have to help her. She can't go back to a life like that."

"Sure and enough, you're right. We'll come up with a plan, won't we, Mercy?"

"Of course we will."

"Now dry up." Duncan tilted her face to his and brushed away the last of her tears with astonishing tenderness.

How can a man be so big and strong, and yet so gentle?

He reached down and took her hand. "I'll walk you home. I have a little something to give to you and Jenny."

"Actually, I came over to invite you all for Sunday supper tomorrow—enchiladas."

Duncan's eyes lit up. "Those are the rolled up tortillas with stuff in them and sauce atop?"

Mercy laughed. "Carmen, he'll eat an entire pan of them all by himself. What can I bring?"

Carmen thought for a moment. "Do you mind giving me a little cheese?"

"Duncan," Mercy asked, "could you go fetch a wheel?"

He went down into the basement.

Drawing the baby out from beneath the tartan, Mercy chided softly, "Since when didn't I have enough cheese to share?"

"But it's such a chore to make it."

"Going to Grossvater's farm twice a week is a joy for me. The things I do while I'm there—they're no burden. I'd have no room here to make cheese. It's my excuse to go, because Grossvater worries that I should be here all of the time."

"Here we are." Duncan reappeared with a twelve-inch wheel of cheese. "I need to stop by my workshop for a moment."

After saying good-bye, Carmen accompanied Duncan to his workshop. He snatched something off his table. "Okay."

Jenny hadn't gone to take a nap, after all. She'd been making more tortillas and was just now washing her hands. "I couldn't seem to stop."

Duncan set the cheese on the table and stepped closer to her. "I made you something." After she dried her hands, he placed a green leather book in her hands.

Jenny ran her fingertips over the vine pattern he'd tooled into the center of the leather to form a heart. "This is so pretty."

"I thought that maybe you'd like to write letters to the bairn. That way, when he grows up, he'll hae some of your thoughts and hopes to let him know you loved him. I asked Rob, and he said 'twas okay."

Clutching it to her bosom, Jenny didn't say anything. She just nodded.

Duncan then turned to Carmen. "And this, 'tis for you, Carmen. Mercy tells me you keep a journal, but 'tis spring already. I thought you might like to hae plain pages so you could sketch or keep a record of your garden since it's always brought you such great joy."

He'd stained her book's cover the shade of a pomegranate. An odd interlocking circle design filled the center. She traced it with her finger.

"That's a Celtic endless knot called the Four Seasons. It represents not only time, but friendship."

Her fingertip kept going round and round. "It is endless. How clever. Thank you, Duncan."

That night, Carmen lay in bed and stared at the book. *Friendship.* Duncan extended friendship to everyone. The man could charm a rabbit into a stewpot. But the book he made for Jenny had a heart on it. Was he falling in love with her? He'd been coming over much of the time—and that started after Jenny's arrival.

Rob married Mercy and they're raising her baby. I can see Duncan marrying Jenny and loving her baby, too.

Tears filled her eyes and slid onto her pillow. *Lord, I don't understand. I try to live according to Your will. Your Word says man looks on the outward appearance and You look upon the heart. I'm so tired of my twisted leg scaring men off. Why can't You send me a man who sees me through Your eyes?*

Chapter 9

W ell, what do you think?" Duncan stepped back and grinned at Carmen. She looked at the windows. "It sort of reminds me of that design you made on my book."

"Aye, it does." Duncan stepped forward and dabbed paint on one last little wooden curlicue. Once he'd put up new screens, he'd used that as an excuse to sand and paint all of the windowsills—and now he'd tacked on some of the gingerbread left over from the Gregor house kit. "As long as I'm painting, I'll do the veranda, too."

"You don't have to, Duncan."

"I know I dinna, Carmen. I'm happy to, though. I brought o'er a few odds and ends. Let's decide what pieces of that wooden lace will look best where."

"Jenny!" Carmen beckoned. "Come here."

The lass knelt over by a row of flowers. Getting up had to be difficult, so Duncan strode over and assisted her. She always looked stunned when he extended common courtesies to her. *Puir wee lassie doesna count herself worth anything. If only she could see that the King of Kings longs to have her as His daughter!*

"I'll go get some sweet tea and bunuelos," Carmen murmured as soon as they approached.

"Better still, I'll go fetch them." Duncan grinned. "Whilst I do, why dinna ye both lay out a blanket, and we'll hae a picnic. 'Twill be easier to move about those bits of wood if we're already on the ground."

"Those are pointy; these are round." Jenny pushed away a few pieces. "Since Duncan put swirly ones for the windows, I think the roundish pieces would look best."

"Thank you," Carmen said as Duncan handed her a glass of sweet tea. "Jenny's leaning toward using these pieces."

Duncan took a gulp out of his own glass. "You dinna hae to limit yourself. You can hae e'ery last piece there. There's still more in a crate at the back of my shop."

Carmen smothered a laugh.

"What's so funny?" Jenny's brows knit.

"Suppose," Duncan said as he sat between the women, "you tell us what's amused you."

Carmen gave him a sly look. "Am I to assume you're keeping a supply on hand so you can nettle Chris?"

"Trials build character." Duncan smirked. "I'm doing my best to see that Chris's character is fully developed."

"Chris isn't fond of architectural embellishments," Carmen explained to Jenny.

"That doesn't make sense." Jenny craned her neck to look across the street. "He built the house and workshop, and they've got all sorts of fancy details."

"Much to Chris's dismay, the kit we ordered came with a plethora of frills." Duncan reached across the blanket and flipped a piece of gingerbread.

"Depending on his mood, Chris has called the place everything from an Easter bonnet to a wedding cake," Carmen said.

Jenny laughed.

"Dinna be forgettin' him sayin' the place has enough scales to cover a legion of dragons."

"Oh. The last time I heard, it was only two dragons."

"Chris was just a tad surly that day. When he's vexed, it's a legion." Duncan grinned. "He'll be none too happy tonight, once he sees what I've done."

"What?" Carmen and Jenny asked together.

"I took two of these and one of these and tacked them together just above his washstand."

"A gingerbread heart? Oh Duncan!" Carmen dissolved into giggles. "Chris is going to have a conniption."

"Oh, that's only half of it. I hung his razor strop from it—with the help of a wee porcelain knob that has roses on it."

"What will he do to you?"

The worry in Jenny's eyes and voice halted Duncan's mirth. "He's my brother. He'd not harm me. Oh, he'll bellow and bluster, but in the end he knows 'tis his own fault. He didna want a single piece of it on the house, so he made a pact with Rob that I'd end up with it all. Rob's a clever one, though. He forged the promise without Chris specifying what I could or couldna do with all those pretties."

"So he tried to trick you and it backfired." Jenny wrinkled her nose. "You mean to tell me the times I hear him roaring at someone, he's not punching or throwing things, too?"

"I told ye before, lass. We dinna fight. Rob's patched too many foolish men together to think violence solves anything. I enjoy horseplay, but when tempers flare, I know full well a soft answer turneth away wrath. Chris, he believes law and justice are the routes to peace among men. Connant Gilchrist keeps trying to convince him to become a deputy."

"I like this *corazon*." Carmen touched the example he'd made of the heart.

"Cor-a-zone?" Duncan looked into Carmen's bright eyes and willed her to see how he wanted to please her. "Does that mean heart?"

"Yes."

"I thought 'twould be pretty to hang this corazon to the side of your front door." She smiled at him. "I'd love that."

Ahhh, lass, but if only you'd love me, too.

—※—

"I've never understood the whole notion of getting a certificate that stands for money when the value of it isn't stable." Carmen cranked the agitator on the washing machine. "First, the stock market did that crash thing in May. Now the paper says many of those certificates are worthless and there's talk of a depression."

"I'd never trust someone else with my money." Jenny's brow puckered. "You can't trust anyone but yourself."

"I trust a few people." Carmen stopped cranking and lifted the lid. Judging the garments done, she drained the metal drumlike machine. "The only One who won't ever fail me is Jesus, though."

"Then why bother?" Jenny helped her pull out the soggy clothes and dropped them into a galvanized bucket with a splat. "If you don't depend on anyone, then you won't get hurt."

Carmen looked at Jenny. "There's pain in loneliness, too."

"How would you know?" Jenny shook her head. "You have a sister who adores you. You and Mercy do everything together—from cooking to canning to sewing. Duncan and his brothers are around all the time, and children drop by almost every day. Just talking about it makes me tired."

"I do manage to stay busy. Family and community are important to me. Very important." Carmen summoned a smile. "But you forgot to mention someone who matters a lot to me."

"Who?"

"You, Jenny. We've been doing practically everything together for months now." Carmen lifted one handle of the bucket.

Jenny automatically lifted the other. With Jenny's waddle, Carmen didn't have to push herself to hurry as they walked to the clothesline.

"After I have the baby, I'll be leaving. We both know it. I'm not going to let myself miss you. You shouldn't miss me, either."

"Of course I'll miss you. I've grown so very fond of you. Haven't you noticed?"

Jenny turned away and started to hang up clothes. The action didn't fool Carmen. Jenny guarded her emotions with a desperation that nearly broke Carmen's heart. Bravado was all she had. Nonetheless, Carmen wanted Jenny to know the truth. "From the first day you came, Jenny, I felt a special spark. Our time together has been wonderful for me. I hope you feel the same way. Even if you can't allow yourself to feel anything for me, I want you to know how I've come to love you."

"You're fond of everyone. I'm not like that. Some folks are just plain nice, but most only care about themselves. You were sheltered, so you've been spared learning just how ugly men can be. Women, too."

Carmen thought for a moment and admitted slowly, "I don't know how I would have turned out if I'd been reared differently or been through other circumstances."

"If you'd lived like I have," Jenny said in a jaded tone, "you wouldn't be so trusting and caring. You'd have to look out for yourself."

"I'm an independent woman, Jenny. I do look after myself." Carmen detected Jenny was seeking information in a roundabout fashion. "There's something I do know, deep down in my heart. Jesus will never fail me."

"I bet a lot of people who have those worthless stock certificates wonder why Jesus failed them." Jenny finished pinning up a petticoat.

"God isn't like a genie in a children's fable. He doesn't jump at our commands and give us all we wish for."

"Then what is He good for?"

"He forgives our sins and never forsakes us. No matter what we have to endure, He is faithful to carry us through. Joys or sorrows, God remains with us."

"I think it would be nicer if He was a genie who did give me whatever I wanted."

"What do you want?" Carmen waited for a response.

Silence crackled between them as they finished hanging out the laundry. Jenny finally said, "I want this to all be over."

Carmen didn't say anything.

Jenny, ostensibly watching water drip from a petticoat to make tiny little plops that turned the earth into a polka-dotted mud patch, finally said, "What I don't want is to feel the baby kick all the time. It just reminds me over and over that I don't even know who the father is and that I won't know who his new father will be. I don't want to go through the labor. I don't want to go back to living in a saloon just so I'll have food to eat."

The sadness in Jenny's voice and eyes made Carmen want to weep. "We have to have faith, Jenny. There will be good that comes from this, and Doc Gregor will make certain the man and wife who rear that baby will do a fine job of it. As for you—we'll make certain you never have to go back to that way of life. I promise you won't."

—⁓—

Duncan carefully placed Carmen's gift in a hatbox and smiled to himself. *She's going to be so surprised.* The ornate leather strap he'd created out of frustration went with the purse perfectly. The lid to the box didn't want to go on. Why, when he could create even the tiniest baby shoes, did his fingers suddenly fumble at this simple task?

So far, his plan seemed to be going well. Carmen appreciated his gifts and praised the work he'd been doing around her home. And she often brought treats she'd baked to his shop. A woman didn't cook for a man unless she held feelings for him.

"Duncan?" Mercy walked into the shop. "What a beautiful hatbox!"

"Aye. Think Carmen will like it?" He ran a rough hand over the elegantly striped pasteboard then rubbed his thumb along the red velvet ribbon running along the top's edge.

"Crimson is her favorite color."

"So I guessed. All the bright shades she wears—they make her match her beautiful garden."

Mercy smiled. "You certainly helped her have a spectacular garden this year."

"Jenny helped, too."

"Chris mentioned Grossvater wanted to spend a day with you, tending to his harnesses and such. Last year it kept him busy as he healed."

"I'll be happy to go out to the farm."

"That's so kind of you."

"Your grandda—he's surely taken Jenny under his wing. I'm sure 'tis his example that has many of the old men growing tender toward her."

"Grossvater has a big heart."

Duncan drew a deep breath. "Mercy, I aim to broach a topic wi' you. 'Tis less than polite."

"Did I do something wrong?"

"Nae. Carmen's limp. I'm thinking I could fashion shoes for her that would even out her gait."

355

" 'Gait' makes her sound like a horse."

Duncan filed away that little detail. Insignificant things like that mattered a lot to women. "When you pin up her hems, what's the difference in length from one side to the other?"

His sister-in-law's brows rose.

"I warned ye, 'twas a touchy subject. I need your help, Mercy. I canna proceed without knowing, and I'd not shame my Carmen by posing such a delicate matter to her."

"I'm a little surprised—but more at the thought of no one thinking to solve the matter this way than in the topic itself."

"I didna mean to shock you."

"You mean to help my friend. Of course I'm willing to assist you. The left side of her hems. . ." Mercy held her thumb and forefinger apart. "About an inch. Maybe a tiny bit more. But the measurement won't help you any. You need to trace her foot, and she'd never allow you to."

"I ken, 'tis true, so I cheated. She left footprints in the mud after watering the flowers she planted for you. I measured those and drew a pattern."

"You're very ingenious."

"Whilst you're here, I want to ask something. I ken you're busy as can be, but whene'er you bake, could you see fit to make wee little cookies for me?"

She nodded. "You'll have to tell me just how small."

"About the size of a quarter would be grand. I'd like to offer them to my customers."

Bless her, Mercy simply nodded.

Duncan reached for the mesquite bowl Mr. Rundsdorf had made for him. "I'll keep them in this."

"Ohhh! Duncan, that's breathtaking!"

"I think so, too. I'm supposing when folks see it, they'll be going to him, seeking something else he's made." He put down the bowl and stroked the hatbox. "I'll be back after a while. I'm taking this to Carmen."

"It would be nicer if you gave it to her when you're alone. Why don't you go over and bring Jenny back? I've been talking to her so she'll know what to anticipate."

Appalled, Duncan blurted out, "You're not going to hae her birth her bairn in the washroom!"

Despite her blush, Mercy assured him, "Of course not."

"Chris and I still think you kept your vow," he muttered.

"What vow?"

"If anyone breathed a word about you delivering your babe at the clinic, you'd avenge yourself." When she had the nerve to laugh, Duncan swallowed sickly. "Twitter all you want, Mercy Ellen Gregor, but you left a dreadful, bloody mess for us to clean up."

Mercy shook her finger at him. "You have no right to complain. After all, I did what you asked. I waited until Rob got home to have Elspeth."

"Good thing, that. With your next babe—"

Mercy's eyes grew huge. "How did you know?"

Delight speared through him. " 'Twas hope speaking. So you're carrying another wee bairn?"

"Rob and I are keeping it a secret for now."

"I'll not breathe a word." He patted her arm. " 'Tis kind of you not to celebrate your glad tidings when you know Jenny's going to give away her babe."

"Go ahead and send her on over to me."

Duncan didn't have to be told twice. He hastened across the street. No one answered the door, but the smell of lye soap reminded him it was Carmen's laundry day. Duncan went around behind the house and heard weeping. "Carmen?"

"Car–men's—not—heeeeere."

Duncan pushed between two sodden towels on the clothesline and stopped dead in his tracks when he discovered Jenny huddled on the bench by the flowers, sobbing. Cold dread washed over him.

Chapter 10

"You're not having the bairn—not now!"

Jenny shook her head.

"Good!" Relief added zeal to his voice. A moment later, Duncan frowned. "Are ye hurtin'? Do I need to fetch Rob?"

She shook her head.

Duncan stepped closer. "You're weeping. Why?"

"Carmen said Jesus would never fail her."

"Aye, and she's right. Our Lord Jesus Christ will ne'er forsake us."

"I don't have anyone like that. Everyone dies or they just use me and walk away."

"Puir wee lassie." He drew closer. "I canna imagine how sad and lonely it must be, you tryin' to face life on your verra own. You dinna hae to, though."

"No one will have me."

The sadness in her tone tore at him. "Jesus would welcome you with open arms."

"I'm not dying."

"Glad I am of that. He's more than eager to have you as His daughter."

Tears spattered her bodice as she shook her head. "Not me. I'm just a cheap wh—"

"You," Duncan cut in, "Jenny Sigrids, were bought by the blood of Christ. Never consider yourself cheap, because the price was paid in full—and 'twas the Son of God who paid the ransom for your eternal soul."

"Ransom? Like with a kidnapping?"

"Aye, only in this case, 'twas the devil who stole your soul. All you need to do is believe that God loves you so much, He sent His beloved Son to pay the price that would redeem your soul."

"You don't know what I've done."

Duncan shrugged. "What you've done in the past is of no importance. Remember how the preacher has mentioned stories in the Bible of women who lived in sin?"

"Like me," she murmured.

"Aye. Jesus forgave them. He gave them a new chance at life by telling them to go and sin no more."

"But other people knew what those women were. Everyone knows what I've been."

"Aye." Duncan nodded. "And Christ told them they could cast stones at the woman only if they'd ne'er sinned themselves. You see, sin separates each of us from God. 'Tisna our own goodness or the deeds we do that redeem us—'tis because Christ paid the cost. I'm heartily thankful He did, and I took Him at His word. I accepted salvation and let Him wash my soul free from the past. Carmen and Mercy and my brothers—they all did likewise."

He let that sink in for a moment and then quietly asked, "Would you like to ask Him for forgiveness and a fresh start?"

"What do I give Him back?"

"Your thankful and obedient heart."

Wrapping her arms around herself, she sighed. "It can't work that way. It's too simple."

"Carmen cares for you like a sister. Even when she didna know you, she opened her arms and heart and home to you. If she could do that, think how much more God can and will do."

"I don't know if I can get up if I kneel down."

Duncan glanced at her middle and silently agreed. "It won't matter. God is delighted to have you just as you are."

"Like that church song last Sunday?"

"Aye. 'Just as I Am.'"

"At church, folks have to get down on their knees."

She wasn't being quarrelsome. Duncan saw the sincerity in her eyes. She wanted to do this correctly. It mattered to her. "Since we'll be praying together, why don't you sit there, and I'll kneel."

—⁂—

Carmen heard the low hum of conversation and limped around the clothesline. The breath froze in her lungs. Jenny sat on the garden bench, and Duncan knelt at her side.

I knew it. I knew he had tender feelings for her. Rob married Mercy and—

"Carmen!" Joy brightened Jenny's voice.

Duncan rose. "Carmen, we have the most wonderful news."

"Do you?" Her voice sounded strained.

Jenny beckoned her over. "Duncan just asked me if—" her voice broke.

"Jenny's decided to ask Christ into her heart."

"Jenny!" Carmen hurried over. Every step made her repent for the jealousy she'd felt.

"You can help me pray, too. I want to do it right."

"Nothing would make me happier than to share this moment with you."

Duncan motioned to her. "Why don't you sit next to Jenny?"

Carmen sat down and embraced Jenny.

"I don't know what to do," Jenny confessed. "Am I supposed to fold my hands, or are we supposed to hold hands together?"

"Either way is fine," Duncan said. "What would you like?"

Jenny thought about it for a minute. "I think I'll fold my hands. I'm afraid if I hold your hands, I might crush them."

Duncan knelt again. He reached out and held onto the wrought iron arms of the bench, and the action gave a special sense of intimacy to the moment.

Jenny bowed her head and whispered, "What do I say?"

"Prayer is talking to God." Carmen exchanged a look with Duncan then asked, "Would you like to have one of us say a prayer, and you repeat the words?"

"That's a good idea. I'm afraid I'll forget something important."

"All right then." Duncan bowed his head. "Lord Jesus, I'm sorry for my sins."

"Lord Jesus," Jenny repeated, "I'm sorry for all my terrible sins. I've done a lot of bad things."

Duncan patiently waited. "You died on the cross so I could be forgiven."

Jenny echoed the sentence.

"So I'm asking You to forgive me and come live in my heart. Amen."

"God, I'm asking You to please forgive me. Since You're washing all the bad out of my heart, there's a lot of room in my heart for You to come live there now. Amen." Jenny looked up. "I feel so. . .right. Deep down inside, I feel. . .good."

Carmen squeezed her tightly. "I'm so happy for you."

"I'm happy for us all." The corners of Duncan's eyes crinkled. "You know, Jenny, now you're our sister in Christ."

Jenny smiled, but just as quickly, her smile faltered. "At least till I leave after I have the baby."

"Nae, lass. E'en if we're parted here on earth, we'll all be together in heaven."

"Absolutely! And after you go, we'll write to one another." Carmen emphasized her assertion with a passionate nod. "I'm going to insist on it. How will I ever come to visit you if I don't know where you are?"

Jenny's eyes grew huge. "You'd come visit me?"

"Yes. I'm inviting myself. I know it's rude, but you're my sister, so you'll ignore my bad manners."

As he stood, Duncan chuckled. "Carmen's a strong-willed woman, Jenny. Once she determines something, there's no dissuading her. She'll be sure to visit you. Why don't the two of you go see Mercy? Jenny can give her the grand news."

—⚬⚬⚬—

Mercy cried for joy.

Though Duncan hadn't accompanied them to the house, he entered a short time later. Carmen's breath caught as she recognized the item in his left hand. She'd looked at it a few times over at Leonard's mercantile. "Jenny, lass, this is for you." He handed her the beautiful cherrywood presentation box.

"For me?" Jenny opened the box. "A Bible! My very own Bible?"

"Aye. Read and reflect on the truths. 'Tis how we walk close to God."

He hadn't dashed out and snapped up the cheapest Bible in the store; he'd parted with money at a time when the nation's finances were strained. The gesture bespoke a deep affection. Until now, the biblical command not to be unequally yoked kept him from courting Jenny. Now that she'd accepted Christ, there wasn't anything that would preclude him from making her his wife. *He's not wasting any time at all. I suspected he was sweet on her. This proves it.*

Duncan turned and lowered a hatbox onto the table in front of Carmen. "And this is for you, Carmen."

"Ohhh." She looked at him. "Why?"

He stared back at her. "Because."

Tracing her finger over the velvet ribbon, she whispered, "It's gorgeous. Elegant."

"Open it up."

"There's something inside?"

He chuckled at her surprise. "Aye, there is."

Slowly, she opened the lid and looked inside. The sight before her left her speechless.

"What is it?" Mercy stood on tiptoe and peered inside.

"A purse made from an armadillo—just like Mercy's grandmother had." Pride rang in Duncan's tone.

"Hers is the only other one I've ever seen," Carmen said faintly. It was all she could concoct. The thing was hideous.

"You didna say exactly how your grandma's was fashioned, so I did the best I could."

Carmen gingerly lifted the leather strap. "Oh, look at this strap. Have you ever seen such intricate tooling?"

Duncan's chest puffed out. "I'm glad you like it."

Mercy reached over and tentatively touched the odd, half-curled hide. "Carmen, something this rare should be used for very special occasions."

Grateful for the way Mercy just gave her an excuse for not having to carry the monstrosity with her all the time, Carmen nodded.

"Grandma only used hers when she paid calls on sick friends. She kept healing herbs and powders in it."

"You go see sick folks all the time." Jenny reached over and fiddled with the creature's funny ear.

Carmen found the urge to shiver. "I've always loved traditions. Perhaps this is a way for me to keep the tradition."

"I've noticed how you treasure your traditions." Duncan folded his arms across his chest. "No matter where we go or what we become, 'tis always important to re-member and honor the past."

"Like when you wear your kilt," Carmen said. From the way he beamed, Car-men knew she'd managed to say the right thing and diverted his attention from the revolting purse. *But one of these days, he'll ask me where it is.*

—⚬—

"Where is she?" Duncan took the seat next to Carmen as some of the parishioners met at the parsonage to discuss church projects.

Carmen froze for a moment. He hadn't asked about the armadillo purse yet, but he was looking at her hem—possibly to see if she'd carried it with her here. She looked at him. "I beg your pardon?"

"Did Jenny come along with you?"

Of course he'd ask about her. Just look at the twinkle in his bachelor button–blue eyes. Well, he won't be a bachelor much longer. Carmen shoved aside her musings and an-swered. "No, she's spending the afternoon with Mercy."

Mrs. Kunstler sat on Carmen's other side. "Mercy—she is a good wife for the doctor. Ismelda told me Mercy helped the doctor when he saw her."

Carmen stared at Mrs. Kunstler and strove not to let her shock and hurt show. "Ismelda?"

"I told her to tell you. Well, now you know." Mrs. Kunstler twitched an embar-rassed smile. "She's trying to spare your feelings since you're older and—"

"You'll be a wonderful aunt," Duncan said. "Children flock to you. Ismelda probably wanted to get you alone to share her good news. She's got a kind heart and wouldn't want to flaunt her joy in front of Jenny, knowing the lass is going to give up her babe."

Carmen summoned a smile and nodded.

"Maybe so," Mrs. Kunstler shrugged. "But Jenny—she got herself into this fix."

Carmen set aside her own hurt and rushed to defend Jenny. "She's confessed her sins, and God's forgiven her."

"Aye, and we've all fallen short of the mark in some way or another." Duncan bobbed his head. "Forgiveness is ours for the asking—and I admire Jenny for knowing her babe would be better off with a stable married couple. She's suffering from the consequences of her past, and yet she's giving someone else a gift beyond words."

"I've told the doctor it's only right that my cousin's cousin should get the baby." Mrs. Kunstler rubbed her hands together. "Since Carmen is housing the girl and Ismelda is my daughter-in-law, we've kept this within the family."

"No." Carmen shook her head. *How could she condemn Jenny and then still claim the baby?*

Duncan patted her hand. "You're in the right of it, Carmen. The adoptions are secret. Only the doctor knows who gives or receives which babe."

"Well, he should give this one to Chester," Mrs. Kunstler grumbled. "Especially after he kept Mercy's baby for himself."

"My brother," Duncan said in a low, slow tone that dared anyone to challenge him, "cherishes Mercy. We all do, just as we adore Elspeth. You canna be suggesting he acted out of anything but love when he wed her."

"No one would ever say such a thing," the pastor said.

Carmen shot the pastor a startled look. She'd been so intent, she'd forgotten where they were.

"Let's begin," the pastor said as he motioned to a handful of people to come take seats. They all complied, and he opened the meeting with a prayer. After that, he smiled. "It's good to see so many of you here. God must be pleased to see so many of His children eager to serve Him with their talents. I've started a list of the needs within our congregation and community. Let's pour out God's love upon our church family and neighbors."

The first needs the parson brought up seemed so urgent, Carmen quickly volunteered.

When the parson said the church ought to be painted, Duncan signed up for that task.

Knowing she couldn't do that kind of work, Carmen thought ahead. In a few weeks, Jenny would have the baby. In less than two months, she would recover and leave. With loneliness looming, Carmen determined to stay busy. She even mentioned a few families who needed help.

At one point, Duncan scowled at her.

She frowned right back. He was a strong, healthy man. He didn't have a wife and children or a widowed mother to support. Surely he could commit to more than just helping paint the church.

Unless he wants the church to look fresh in time for him to marry Jenny. When Mrs. Kunstler spoke badly of her, he rushed to her defense. A man with a new wife and a baby wouldn't have much time for projects. Is that why he doesn't jump in to do more?

Chapter 11

As the meeting broke up, Mrs. Kunstler tugged on Carmen's sleeve. "When Ismelda tells you about her baby, you act surprised."

"Why would I lie?"

"It's not lying. You *were* surprised. She deserves to have the delight of seeing that."

"Then you should have held what you knew in confidence." Carmen shook out her skirts. "When I see Ismelda, she'll know how thrilled I am for her and Otto."

Duncan offered, "I'll walk you home, Carmen."

Thankful for the excuse to leave, Carmen nodded. "I'm ready to go." Carmen didn't say anything until they were out of earshot from anyone. "I keep reminding myself that she is a good mother-in-law to Ismelda. That's all that matters."

" 'Tisna all that matters, but I grant you, I'm glad for Ismelda's sake 'tis the case."

"Jenny's baby—"

"Dinna fret o'er the bairn. I can say with every confidence the arrangements will be good."

Carmen twitched a wry smile. *He might as well just announce that he's going to claim Jenny and the baby as his own.*

"I'm fit to be tied o'er something else, though." He stopped.

"What?" Carmen halted, too.

"Reading to old Mrs. Lintz. Organizing a meal for after the Warner funeral. Helping sew the quilt for the bazaar. Playing the piano every other week at church. Polishing all the wood inside the church. . ." He continued as if reciting a litany.

"There's nothing wrong with my helping out."

Duncan looked as if he'd sucked on a lemon.

Carmen started walking again. *He has no right to dictate how I spend my time.*

Duncan strode alongside her and bellowed out a prolonged sigh for her benefit.

"Maybe you're reacting this way because you're convinced that you're not doing enough." She shot him a look. "Painting the church is a good start, but there were other things you could have offered to do, too."

"I dinna run off and sign up for every last thing. What I'm to do is go where the Lord calls me. In the future, when He leads me toward other projects, I can put my hand to them then. But until He calls me, I'll wait."

His words nettled her. Her skirts swirled about her as she halted. "Are you saying I don't?"

"Come along." He grabbed her elbow and took a step.

Carmen jerked away. "I can walk just fine. Don't treat me like I'm a cripple."

His eyes narrowed. "I'd help any woman o'er these jagged roots. Ne'er once have I treated you like a cripple. Heed me well, Carmen Rodriguez, a special pair of shoes could even out your walk, but 'tisna the insignificant difference in your stroll that hinders ye. No, 'tisna a-tall. 'Tis your heart."

"There's nothing wrong with my heart."

"Ooch, lass, there is. Let's go to your veranda where we can discuss this privately."

"No one is eavesdropping here. Say what you have to say."

Duncan glanced up and down the street. His brow furrowed, but he gave her a curt nod. "You've a sickness in your heart of hearts, and 'tis twisting your spirit. I've spoken wi' you on other occasions, but ye've not listened. God doesna need you to do the work of a dozen and find an early grave just to enter the kingdom of heaven. Nae, He doesna, for Christ paid the price."

"I know that!"

"Do you?" He stared at her solemnly. "Then all these works you take on—what is the purpose?"

"To help others."

He wagged his head from side to side and let out a profound sigh. "You're a bonny lass, Carmen Rodriguez. Aye, you are—not only on the outside, but in your heart, as well."

She stared at him. No man had ever complimented her, yet this wasn't exactly a compliment.

"Anyone who needs you to do labor on their behalf ought to be thankful for all you do. Nevertheless, their caring for you ought ne'er be based on what chore you accomplished but on the fact that you're a fine woman."

Though tempted to respond, Carmen held her tongue.

Duncan seemed more than intent on speaking his piece. "You dinna hae to earn your way into the hearts of others by exhausting yourself. And if you dinna think that's what you're doing, then you need to wonder why 'tis so important for you to fill every last waking hour with rushing about. 'Tis in stillness that we calm our hearts and commune with the Almighty."

"You heard the sermon last Sunday, about the gifts God gives and expects us to exercise. The gift of helps—that's mine. I'm being a faithful follower to go forth and help others."

"I agree 'tis your gift."

"Then there's no problem."

He gave her a long, intent look. "Your gift is not to be a burden that strains your every waking moment. I'm concerned."

"Over nothing." When he'd looked at her, he'd ended at her hem—and it all came back to the same thing. He considered her feeble.

"Carmen, you've gotten so caught up in staying busy on the account of others that you've forgotten to listen for the Lord to direct your efforts."

"I don't need thunder to shake the heavens to direct me where the needs are. God gave me eyes to see them and ears to hear the pastor and others mention how someone requires help."

"Those people can be His messengers—but had you considered that others present are meant to assume some of those responsibilities?"

"The Lord loves a cheerful giver."

"Aye, He does. But I dinna recall e'er reading in His Word that He loves a frantic giver."

"Frantic!"

Duncan nodded. "Pray, Carmen. You're so caught up in deeds that you're losing sight of the One to whom you're devoted."

Carmen reared back. "Did it ever occur to you that some of us wouldn't have to do so much if others of you would step up and do your share?" She didn't wait for his reaction. Carmen lifted her skirt and hastened over the tangled roots as fast as her crooked leg would allow.

—⁂—

Duncan reached over and buffed the toe of a boot. He used buttery soft kidskin and created a pair that would yield ultimate comfort. Though he'd never once heard Carmen complain, Duncan knew her feet and legs had to bother her after she exerted herself. An elastic gusset would make it quicker for Carmen to pull on the boots, but Duncan opted to make the ankle-top boots lace up. They'd give more support.

At first glance, someone might think one boot was propped up on a small block, but it wasn't. Fashionable women's footwear featured heels that narrowed down to a three-quarter-inch circle. Both heels on this custom-made pair measured an inch in diameter, but he'd added a full inch in height to the sole and heel on the left and subtracted half an inch from the heel on the right. The net result was a pair of shoes that would compensate for the difference Carmen's twisted limb caused. Aye, she'd be able to walk more smoothly and even leave a footprint that wouldn't tattle on the compensations.

Kept busier still by the things she'd volunteered to do, Carmen didn't seem to be home much. Duncan wasn't fooled, though. He'd hurt her feelings. Since he couldn't catch her to give an apology, these boots and a note would speak for him.

Three crumpled, ink-blotted tries later, Duncan scuffed his own boots on the floor of his workshop. He'd not been this ill at ease with a pen in his hand since he'd been a schoolboy and had been forced to write a treatise on peregrine falcons.

He dipped into the inkwell again.

I did not mean to hurt your feelings. If you felt I was taunting you, I apologize. I'm a rough man, a mere cobbler. Though I spoke what was on my heart, my words were stark. I humbly ask your forgiveness.

He didn't scribe her name at the beginning nor his at the end. The boots themselves made it clear he was addressing her. Satisfied with this note, Duncan crossed the street, set the shoes by Carmen's door, and tucked the folded note between them.

—◊—

"You didn't come to church yesterday." Carmen took the egg basket from Ismelda. She'd intentionally waited until today because she hoped her sister would come to her. She hadn't.

Ismelda let out a nervous little laugh. "I wasn't feeling well. In fact, I'm not feeling good at all in the mornings anymore."

"You should have told me. Didn't you think I'd be delighted that you and Otto are going to be blessed with a baby?"

"Otto and I—we decided not to tell anybody because Mercy and Rob just shared their good news. Especially after what Mercy went through the last time, I thought it would be nice for her to have everyone get excited for her."

"That's sweet of you, but I'm not just anybody. I'm your sister!"

Ismelda wound her arm around Carmen's waist. "And you're going to be my baby's aunt. You don't know how happy that makes me. I promised Otto that I wouldn't tell a soul, though. You wouldn't want me to break a promise I made to my husband.

Since I missed church yesterday, I'm sure people must suspect the truth."

Carmen nodded. Telling Ismelda that her mother-in-law had said something would spoil her joy. "I knew this day would come. I've already bought some fabric, but I hid it away in my bureau."

"It would be too hard for Jenny." Ismelda smiled softly. "You know, when you first took her in, I wondered if it was such a smart thing. But the moment I met her, I knew God had a reason for sending Jenny here. Otto and I—we've been praying for her. Knowing she's accepted Jesus is so exciting. Now we're praying that maybe God will put a man in her life, just as He did for Mercy."

"Maybe so." *He probably has—it's Duncan Gregor.*

"Stay for the day. We could make tortillas. Otto's mother can't make them right. She keeps thinking they should be rolled out like pie dough."

"You'll have to teach my niece how to make tortillas."

Ismelda laughed and rested her head on Carmen's shoulder. "We'll come visit you all the time, and you can teach her that yourself. Yours are always perfect circles. Mine are as lopsided as those eggs you're carrying."

—⁂—

After spending the day with her sister, Carmen headed home. She'd rented a buggy from the livery and driven it back without any trouble. From the day she'd fallen off a horse and broken her leg, she'd never again ridden. Ismelda told Jorge at the livery about how horses made Carmen nervous. He always made sure she didn't have to be near the horses, so as soon as she reached the livery, he hopped into the buggy and drove her home.

"Look!" Jenny greeted her at the door and gestured toward the settee. "I must have been napping when Duncan dropped by."

Carmen stared at the floor and clapped a hand over her mouth to muffle her scream.

Chapter 12

I knew you'd be thrilled." Jenny pushed her toward the boots waiting on the settee. "Try them on. Aren't they beautiful? The leather is so soft and supple."

Pulling away, Carmen mumbled something that she knew didn't make sense and raced for her bedroom. She shut the door, threw herself across the bed, and slammed her fist into her pillow. Mortification and rage left her shaking. Duncan told her special shoes would correct her step—and now, he was proving his point.

Tap, tap, tap. Jenny slowly opened the door a mere crack. "Carmen? You don't have to be embarrassed. Ever since my grandma died, nobody loved me—but you have. Don't you think I love you enough to be glad that you can wear such clever shoes so it's easier for you to walk?"

"I—" She couldn't find words.

"It's just Duncan. He probably put the shoes there so neither of you would have to say anything about it. Most men blurt out whatever they want. Believe me, I know. Duncan's not like that. He cares. Come try them on."

"Maybe later." Once she mouthed those words, Carmen knew the truth. She'd never put them on.

—∞—

"I'm coming. I'm coming." Duncan trudged toward the door.

Chris stood at the head of the stairs, holster in hand. He'd been helping Connant keep law and order whenever necessary. Anyone banging on the door at this time of night either wanted the doctor or the law.

"What do you—" Duncan started at the sight of Carmen. She wore a sapphire blue robe, and her hair billowed out in a dark cloud past her waist.

So that's what her hair looks like down—wavy and shiny and longer than—

"Jenny," she said.

Duncan jolted and hollered, "Rob! Jenny's needing your help." He stepped out of the house only to realize he was barefoot. So, too, was Carmen. "I'll take you home and then carry Jenny back to the clinic."

She nodded and spun to take flight.

"Wait!"

Carmen shook her head. "I can't leave her alone!"

"Fine, then." Duncan swept her into his arms. When she stiffened, he rasped, "She willna protest me carryin' her if she sees me totin' you in the door."

When they reached her front door, Duncan dipped and ordered, "Turn the knob, lass."

Carmen complied. She barely allowed him to cross the threshold before she struggled free of his hold and hobbled to Jenny's side. "How are you?"

Jenny sat huddled in a tight ball and moaned.

Duncan fought the urge to moan, too. Instead, he cleared his throat. "Well, so this is the day. Or night. Well, I'm supposin' it'll be daytime when—" He shut up. Any medical issue turned him into a blithering idiot.

Carmen patted Jenny's arm. "Duncan came to carry you to the clinic. Dr. Gregor will meet us there."

"Okay."

Less than reassured by Jenny's tiny voice, Duncan slid one hand behind her back. "Wait now." Rob came in.

Duncan wondered how his brother managed this feat. In a matter of a few minutes, he could wake from a sound sleep, dress, comb his hair, grab his satchel, and calmly face whatever emergency God plopped in his lap.

"Jenny, let's just check you here in your bedroom. You'll be much more comfortable there." Rob motioned to Duncan.

Duncan carried her to the bedroom and darted back out as soon as humanly possible.

Carmen and Rob spent five minutes with Jenny, and then Rob came back out. He slapped Duncan on the shoulder. "It'll be a long while yet. Carmen will come get us when the pains are four minutes apart or so."

"She should be at the clinic!"

"Nae, Duncan. She's got hours of laboring ahead of her. Come on home. I'm going to have to ask you to fill in for me tomorrow."

"Fill in?"

"I'll tell you when we get home."

Duncan wouldn't budge. "Carmen? I'm going home only long enough to change into my jeans. I aim to stay on your veranda—"

The bedroom door opened, and she hissed, "You will not. Go home, Duncan Gregor. Go home this instant!"

He scowled at her. She didn't seem intimidated in the least. Come to think of it, the sassy woman had a habit of ignoring his scowls. He'd have to work on that flaw of hers. With Jenny laboring, this wasn't the right time though. He announced, "If you need help, you just shout. I'll be here in an instant."

Walking back across the rutted road, Duncan muttered, "You do surgery in the clinic. You stitch up wounds and set broken bones. Just what do you have against bringing a bairn into the world there when you've every modern medical convenience at your fingertips?"

"Bairns have a way of entering the world without a lot of fanfare. Mothers labor best where they're comfortable."

"You're daft, Rob."

Rob had the nerve to chuckle.

A minute later, Duncan repeated, "You're daft! Daft, I tell you. I am not gallivanting off to fetch a bairn and take him to the Heims. Not when Jenny's baby's about to arrive right here!"

"Do you need my help, Rob?" Mercy called out.

"Not for a long while yet, my love. Catch a wee bit more sleep if you can."

Rob turned back to Duncan. His face hardened. "You'll do no good here. You canna stand to be with anyone who's sick or bleeding."

"Chris will do it."

"Stubborn, hardheaded Scot," Rob growled.

"Aye, Chris is those things, but he'll help you." Duncan nodded. "If he's hesitant, tell him I'll not pester him with a single piece of gingerbread for a whole week."

—⁂—

"E'er again," Chris demanded at the breakfast table. "If I fetch this babe and take it to the Heims, Duncan canna e'er again bedevil me with those benighted wooden frills."

"A week is as good as you'll get from me," Duncan snarled. He'd not gone back to sleep, and his nerves were on edge.

"A year," Chris barked back.

"You're fetching a baby, not a wife. And you're giving it away this afternoon, anyway." Duncan gave him a sour look. "One month. 'Tis the best you'll get out of me, and there's not a reason in the world why you shouldn't have gone in the first place."

"What," Mercy said in a frosty tone as she thumped the coffeepot onto the table, "is wrong with having a wife?"

"Nothing." Duncan gave her an affronted look. " 'Tis the wooing and getting one that's so aggravating."

"Just when did you make any effort to—" Chris snickered. "Jenny or Carmen?"

"Carmen, you dolt!"

Chris hooted. "All this time she's been thinking you were sweeping her walk, and you were tryin' to sweep her off her feet!"

"You've no room to tease him, Chris. You're the eldest, and you've yet to court a lass." Rob spooned a bite of egg into Elspeth.

"I'm in no hurry." Chris cracked his knuckles.

"Yes, you are." Mercy laughed. "You have to be on the eight o'clock train for Austin."

Chris wolfed down his breakfast and accepted a slip of paper from Rob. As he rose from the table, he groused, "I've spent my life watching out for my baby brothers. How'd I get saddled with another bairn?"

"I thought you didn't mind watching Elspeth every now and then," Mercy said quietly.

"Of course I dinna! She's not a bairn. She's a beauty!" Chris bent down, planted a kiss atop Elspeth's downy head and strode out.

Mercy waited until he was long gone and then dissolved into giggles.

"What's so funny?" Rob asked.

She looked at both of them. "Mrs. Kunstler is going to find out that Chris took that little baby boy to her cousin. The woman has her flaws, but she sure tries hard to take care of those she loves. Your brother is going to be her hero."

Rob choked on his coffee.

"I dinna care how great a doctor you are, Rob. There's no cure for the agonies our brother will suffer once that woman takes a shine to him."

—⁂—

"By this evening, there's going to be a foot-deep rut in the road going from my house to yours."

Carmen smiled at Mercy's comment as she watched Rob cross the street and go back to the clinic.

"Duncan's been here twice as often as your husband." Jenny pressed both hands to her lower back and winced as she rubbed.

Carmen brushed aside Jenny's hands and massaged her. "He cares about you. We all do."

As if to prove that point, Duncan thumped on the door and barged in. "Traditions are important."

"What prompted that announcement?" Carmen gave him an exasperated look.

"Fetch your healer's bag. I'll hae Rob put the essentials in it. Then you can carry them o'er to the clinic." Once she gave him the monstrosity, he left.

"Well, that hideous thing did serve a purpose." Mercy smiled. "It kept him busy."

"He's going to have a conniption when he finds out you've decided to have the baby here, Jenny." Carmen rubbed her back again. "When he finally figures it out, we'll tell him how glad we are to have whatever he stuffs in that purse."

Carmen exchanged a look with Mercy. They'd made plans for this day months ago. Keeping Jenny distracted would help a little.

"Jenny, has Carmen ever told you how she kept the men occupied when I was having Elspeth?"

"Noooo." Jenny's answer got swallowed up in another moan.

Carmen began telling Jenny of Mercy's memorable labor.

Not five minutes later, Duncan tramped back in with Elspeth over one shoulder and the bag over the other. "She's growing a mite cranky."

Carmen grinned to herself. *What baby wouldn't when faced with the terrifying sight of that armadillo?*

As Mercy took her daughter, Duncan decided, "I'll wait on the veranda. Once you're done, I'll take the wee little lassie home."

"Go use my bedroom," Carmen murmured to Mercy. Since Jenny wouldn't keep her baby, Mercy thoughtfully left her own babe at home when she came to help with the birth. After Mercy nursed and calmed Elspeth, Duncan carried his niece home.

"I spent a good part of my labor in the rocking chair." Mercy nudged Jenny to sit down. "Try it."

"Mercy tried to cook while she was in labor." Carmen shuddered. "She tried to turn apple cider into gravy."

"And I added a cup of sugar to the mashed potatoes." Mercy laughed. "But Carmen's the one who put it all together with apples and flan as dessert. Happenstance, she called it. You've never tasted anything half as good."

"Good?" Carmen looked at her in disbelief.

Mercy headed for the kitchen. "I distinctly remember enjoying it. Maybe we could make some today."

"Only if you're planning to stuff that dead armadillo with it," Carmen muttered.

Gunshots drowned out Jenny's weak laughter.

Chapter 13

He's dead." Rob remained on his knees in the middle of the street as he turned to the next man.

"It's Connant," Duncan said in utter disbelief.

"Connant's dead," Rob rasped as he shoved at Duncan's shoulder. "Give me your bandana."

His brother's command made no sense, but Duncan complied. He stared at their lifeless friend. A trio of other men lay bleeding in the street.

Mercy demanded, "Rob, what do you need me to do?"

"I'm putting a tourniquet on Rundsdorf's leg. Stay with him while I check the others. Duncan." Rob jostled him. "Duncan! Get some men to help you carry him to the clinic."

Duncan ignored the order and lifted Mr. Rundsdorf by himself. Mercy scrambled alongside of him as he hastened to the clinic. Once he laid Mr. Rundsdorf on the examination table, he gawked as Mercy took a pair of shears to the hem of the man's britches. "I'll do that."

"No, you won't." Mercy barely spared him a strained glance. "You're already green. Get out of here before I have two of you to take care of."

Others spilled into the clinic. "Doc said Kondrad's to go upstairs," the preacher said.

"Duncan," Mercy said sharply, "you know where the gutta-percha sheets are. Throw one on each of the beds up there."

He dashed upstairs and threw the rubbery, waterproof sheets on the beds. Jorge grunted in pain as they laid him down. Duncan couldn't understand a single word of the rapid-fire Spanish pouring out of the man's wife. *Is there anyone who could help? Chris is gone delivering that baby. Carmen—Carmen! She couldn't possibly come translate. She has her hands full.*

Duncan stood out of the way as they carried the third man up the stairs and put him to bed. He herded everyone back down the stairs and loudly announced Rob's standard rule in times of trouble. "One family member can stay with each man. The rest of you, go on home."

Rob promptly shouted, "Eliza Wagner, Harriet Brun, and Gertrude Besselmen, you stay. Each of you keep watch on one of the wounded. You know what to look for. The rest of you, go. Pray."

The parson managed to get the rest to leave. Duncan strode over to Mr. Rundsdorf. "I'd take it as a favor if you wouldn't get in the habit of collecting bullets."

"He didn't collect it," Rob declared. "It went straight through. Mercy, get the ether."

Duncan's nose twitched. The smell of ether invariably left him woozy and often made him puke.

"Duncan, go see to Elspeth."

Glad for the reprieve, he left. In the midst of the excitement, he'd run to Carmen's to protect the women. Once he made sure they were fine, he and Mercy left Elspeth in Carmen's care so they could go help. It hadn't been that long ago, but he'd forgotten Elspeth was at Carmen's. Right on the heels of that realization, Duncan recalled Jenny being in labor. He decided he'd grab Elspeth and leave. It was a sound plan.

———ᴡ———

"Thank God, you're here!" Carmen yanked Duncan inside and leaned against the door. She didn't want to chance having him rush back out. The disturbance across the street following the gunshots told her the doctor and Mercy would both be busy for a long time.

"I just came to grab El—"

"You can't leave!" She kept her voice as quiet as she could, but it cracked with terror. "I don't know what to do!"

"Neither do I." Duncan gave her an appalled look. "You're a woman. You're supposed to be able to tend to such matters."

Jenny let out a long, guttural moan from the other room.

Duncan reached past Carmen for the doorknob. "I'll go get some help."

Carmen didn't budge. "Mercy and Rob are saving lives. They're not coming."

"I'll grab someone else!" He wiped the sweat from his brow on his sleeve.

"Who? Eliza Wagner?" From the way he swallowed hard, Carmen knew Doc had Eliza helping him. Frantically searching for any other possible prospect, Carmen asked, "What about Gertrude Besselmen or Harriet Brun?"

Even as he shook his head, he swiped across his brow again. "Think of someone else."

"All of those women are busy?" The words came out in a strangled gasp.

"Three got shot, and Connant's dead." As she gasped, Duncan tried for the doorknob again.

Carmen slapped his hand away. "You're not going anywhere, Duncan Gregor. So help me, if you try to walk out this door, your brother's going to have another patient."

Rushing over to the table, Duncan practically tripped over his own feet. He grabbed the armadillo bag. "Here. Whate'er you need, 'tis in here."

Carmen shoved the bag back at him. "Your brother packed it. You know more about medical things than I do."

He shoved the bag at her. "Go tell Jenny she'll have to wait."

"I'm not telling her that!" She forced the bag back into his keeping. After all, she'd never liked the stupid bag to begin with, and now it wasn't just ugly, it was frightening.

"I know! I'll prop up the foot of the bed. That way the bairn will be sliding toward her head. 'Twill buy us some time."

I can't come up with a better solution. "Do you think it'll work?"

"It has to." Putting an end to their demented game of hot potato, he shoved the armadillo bag into her keeping. "I'll get something to do the propping."

"Carmen!" Jenny sounded panicky.

"I'm coming!" Carmen gave Duncan a piercing look.

"We're coming," he said.

He'd given his word. Satisfied that he'd not leave, Carmen rushed to Jenny.

"Hurts," Jenny cried out as she writhed on the bed. "Hurts. Hurts-hurts-hurts-hurts-hurts-hurts-hurts-hurts."

"Pobrecita." Carmen grabbed a damp cloth and blotted Jenny's face. "It'll be over soon."

Duncan came in with an armload of thick books. He looked just as scared as Jenny. Just as quickly, his features altered into determination. "We're here. Aye, we are."

"Duncan!" Jenny reached for him.

Carmen blinked back tears as Duncan dropped the books. He strode to the bed and smoothed back Jenny's hair. He didn't say a word, but everything about him radiated loving strength.

Jenny grabbed his hand. "Can't do this!" Her face twisted, and for the very first time since the day she'd arrived, Jenny began to cry.

"Ooch, lass, 'tis hard. But Carmen and I—we'll pull you through."

Carmen nodded. Frantic as she felt inside, she knew Jenny needed them to be calm. For the past half hour, her prayer had narrowed down to a desperate, "*Dios, ayudame.* God, help me. Dios, ayudame. Dios, ayudame." He'd sent help in the form of a cobbler who didn't know anything more than she did—but God was faithful.

"Hurts." Jenny arched her back and began the heartrending chant again. "Hurts-hurts-hurts-hurts-hurts. . ."

Once the contraction ended, Duncan squatted at the foot of the bed and started to gather up the books. Carmen went to help, and he muttered, "Lord, give me stones for my slingshot." He glanced at Carmen. "I'd rather face Goliath than this."

"Propping up the foot of the bed won't work," Carmen whispered. "The pains—they're starting to come hard and fast, just as they did for Mercy toward the very end."

Duncan bolted to his feet.

Jenny let out a cry. This time she clutched Carmen's arm with bruising force.

Duncan pried her free and let Jenny crush his hand. When the pain was over, he murmured something nonsensical and pushed Carmen back to Jenny's side. He picked up the books, but instead of raising the bed with them, he set them aside.

He moved them so I wouldn't trip.

The last one he lifted made his brows rise and the corners of his mouth lift. As he flipped through the pages, he nodded with great satisfaction. "Instructions!"

Whether hours or minutes passed, Carmen couldn't say. Time seemed to stretch out for an eternity during a pain and then speed up in between. Then Jenny started to strain down.

Duncan pointed toward the bag. "You'll be needing that soon, Carmen." He cupped her face between his hands. "You can do this. Aye, you can. Not only do I have faith in God, but I believe in you, too."

Warmth poured through Carmen. "I'm so glad you're here." She was. Even if he knew nothing more than she did, Carmen knew for certain nothing disastrous would happen. God and Duncan wouldn't allow it.

"What—is—happening?" Jenny panted.

"Time's short," Duncan explained. "I've the instructions. I'll read them to Carmen, and she can tend to matters." He picked up the book and headed toward the door.

"Don't go!" Carmen wasn't sure whether she'd cried the words or if Jenny had.

"'Tisna proper, my being here."

Jenny made a funny sound. "More than a hundred men have—"

"Nae, Jenny. You're a new woman in Christ. Your past is forgiven and forgotten."

Carmen fought the urge to weep at the poignancy and mercy of his words. There wasn't time to indulge in those feelings now. She pointed to a chair. "Pull that up by her shoulders, Duncan. I'll need you to help with the baby."

Jenny started to strain down again. "Something's"—she gasped and strained—"wrong." She panted and strained again. "I'm all wet!"

Duncan yanked the chair up by the bed and turned so he'd be facing the headboard. He flipped open the book and rifled through the pages as Carmen whipped back the sheet.

"Here." Duncan cleared his throat. "The bag most often ruptures when birth is imminent."

Jenny let out a low groan as she strained again.

Mercy dumped the contents of the armadillo bag onto the bed. The scissors and strips of gauze looked daunting. "Tell me what to do."

Duncan pored over the book. "Hooves will appear first, with the muzzle between the forelegs."

Thunderstruck, Carmen still knew she couldn't yell at him. Besides, the baby was partway out. "What about the cord?"

Duncan turned the page. "If necessary, the mother will bi—" His voice died out.

Chapter 14

Carmen and Jenny exhibited grace under this ordeal, and he was blithering. Duncan cleared his throat. He couldn't let them down. He scanned farther down the page to give Carmen useful instructions. "We're to dry the newborn off immediately. Blankets or straw. Um, blankets." He slammed the book shut. "You have blankets, right?"

"Oh. Oh!" Jenny strained until she turned purple.

"Almost there. Almost." Awe colored Carmen's voice. A small gurgling noise was followed by a cry. "It's a girl, Jenny. A perfect little girl." A minute later, Carmen handed him a blanket-wrapped bundle. "Go dry her off and diaper her."

Duncan took his cue from Carmen and left the bedroom. "Ooch, you wee little lassie. Dinna cry." He gently jostled her and began to sing. "Jesus loves me, this I know. . ."

Duncan calmed the babe only to have Elspeth start squalling. Since Mercy allowed her food from the table, Duncan poked through Carmen's cupboard and located molasses cookies. He ate one and gave another to Elspeth to gum.

Boiling water filled the reservoir and three kettles on the stove. Carmen slipped out of the bedroom and took a kettle back with her.

Determined to help as best he could, Duncan decided he'd bathe the baby. On occasion, he'd helped with Elspeth's bath, so he pumped water into a dishpan and added enough boiling water to make it a comfortable temperature.

Mercy rushed through the door. "How—" She stopped cold.

"A lass, and a hefty one at that." Duncan pulled back the blanket so his sister-in-law could inspect the babe.

Mercy swept up Elspeth in one arm and trailed her finger across the new baby's forehead. "She's beautiful. How's Jenny?"

"Carmen's seeing to her. I thought to tub this wee one."

"No. Remember when Elspeth was newborn? Just sponge her."

"How're all the men doing?"

"They'll all pull through. I'll go help with Jenny."

Duncan methodically set out the water, soap, a towel, and a diaper on Carmen's table. He'd just started to wash the babe when Carmen joined him.

"Mercy's bathing Jenny and taking care of things. How's the baby?"

"See for yourself."

Carmen kept her gaze on the baby. Tears filled her big brown eyes. "Mercy didn't say anything, but I know something bad happened."

Duncan kept one hand on the newborn as he slid his other arm around Carmen. "The bank was robbed. Three men were injured, and Connant Gilchrist was killed."

The sound of pain curled in her throat.

Duncan nestled her closer as if to shelter her from that dreadful truth. Jenny's baby gurgled, and he decided to redirect Carmen's attention. "We ken Connant's with the Almighty this verra moment. The Lord took home His boy and gave us a wee little lass at the same time. I'm thinkin' we'd best tend to her."

Carmen was more of a hindrance than a help. She kept touching and smearing soap bubbles on spots he'd already rinsed. "She's perfect. Look at her. Isn't she beautiful?"

"Absolutely."

"Her grip is strong. How's her other hand?" Carmen chuckled. "It's fine, too. Oh Duncan, isn't she just perfect?"

"She's getting noisy."

"That means her lungs and heart are healthy. It's a good sign. Oh, look at her pretty little feet!"

Duncan listened as Carmen exclaimed over and over about the baby. Once he finished the bath, Carmen diapered the little one and swaddled her in a blanket. "It's a shame to cover her up. She's so..."

"Perfect?"

"Yes!" Carmen glowed.

"I'd have ye tell me, would this lassie be any less worthy of love if she weren't perfect?"

Carmen reared back and blinked. "How could you ask such a thing?"

"Because you keep assuring yourself that she's hale and bonny." Duncan led her over to the settee. He made sure she and the babe were comfortable then dared to sit on the settee, too. It was a bold move. A man didn't sit alongside a woman on her settee unless he had honorable and lifelong intentions.

"Don't be ridiculous, Duncan. Anyone would love this girl. Just anyone."

"You've my most hearty agreement. She's as sweet a miracle as I've e'er seen."

"Yes. A miracle. And sweet. Perfect." Carmen cooed softly to the baby in Spanish.

Lord, I've asked You for an opportunity to say something to Carmen. "Love doesna consider whether someone is perfect—either in body or in behavior. We're all flawed in our own ways. Love overlooks imperfections and doesna demand that someone strive to earn a place in the heart. At least, love that is worth having."

"God loves like that. Men don't."

He fought the desire to declare his love. He wanted an armful of flowers and carefully thought out words. "Some men do. Just as God is able to love us even though we're cracked vessels, we can love one another—ofttimes not in spite of those imperfections, but because of them. Think on that." *Please, think on it.*

———

Jenny's room lay empty. She'd left, but just to the Stein farm. Mercy's grandfather asked if she'd be willing to become his housekeeper. It was a happy arrangement.

Since Rob and Mercy needed to mind the wounded, Duncan was the one who went away carrying Jenny's babe and the dark green leather book she'd filled with her loving thoughts for the child. He'd left with tears in his eyes and returned the same way. Though he'd not reveal where he'd gone or who received the baby, Duncan repeatedly reassured Jenny and Carmen that the baby's mother and father were wonderful, loving Christian parents.

But the house was so very quiet. Carmen walked through it and felt so empty. The boots Duncan made for her peeped out from beneath her bed. She'd been so angry and humiliated about them, she'd shoved them out of sight. Pride kept her from saying anything to Duncan.

It's not in Duncan's character to taunt someone. He sat me down and said imperfections didn't halt love. Once he even called my limp insignificant.

She sank to the floor and drew out the boots. *I'd rather have my shoes look clumsy if it meant I wasn't so awkward.* She took off her boots. The new right boot fit wonderfully. The leather felt so soft and comfortable. But she stared at the left one. Duncan raised the sole like a platform and even angled it in such a way that it would conform to the twisted shape of her foot. The heel was stacked twice as high as the right one, too. It was ugly.

Until she put it on.

It fits perfectly. How could he have known how to do that?

For the first time in years, Carmen stood and didn't wince at the pain of putting weight on her left leg. She tried a few steps. Then another. . .and a few more. . .until the new boots carried her to Duncan's workshop.

A magnificent saddle rested over a frame. He stood behind it, buffing the leather until it gleamed. Every time she saw him working, Carmen noticed how his features bore the stamps of contentment and concentration. Today was no different. He happened to look up. "Hello, Carmen."

"You're busy." The last thing she wanted to do was leave, but it wasn't right for her to take him away from his labors.

"If e'er I'm too busy to spend time with a friend, then I'm too busy." He set down the cloth he'd been using and motioned toward a bench.

Would he notice how evenly she walked? Carmen slowly crossed the plank floor and sat down.

"Mercy baked cookies last night." Duncan carried over the beautiful mesquite bowl he treasured. Mr. Rundsdorf had made a similar one for her when she'd sewn shirts for him.

After Carmen accepted a cookie, she raised it to her mouth and lowered it without taking a bite. "My house feels so empty."

" 'Tis just you there now."

She stared down at the cookie and confessed, "I'm lonely, Duncan."

"So am I."

Her head jerked up. "You? How could you ever be lonely? You have a wonderful family, and everyone adores you."

He tapped the center of his chest. "In here, I'm lonely. Though 'tis true I've a fine family and many a friend, I'm in sore want of the woman I love."

Carmen set aside the cookie. "Jenny."

Duncan gawked at her. "Jenny? That wee lassie? She's a sweet friend, but I feel no more than brotherly love for her." Shaking his head, he drew closer. "There's but one woman in the world for me."

"You're strong and kind and good, Duncan. Handsome, too." As soon as she'd said that, Carmen felt mortified that she'd let slip that she considered him so masculine and handsome. For some odd reason, she kept babbling, though. "Any woman would be happy to have you. Your lonely days are numbered."

He cocked a brow. "Are they?"

"I'm sure they are." Carmen blinked back tears. He deserved a fine wife. She wanted that for him. Truly, she did. But once again, the lonely life stretching out ahead made her ache to the depths of her soul. "I'll be happy to help with the wedding."

"That's a fine offer, but you'll be too busy."

Carmen shook her head. "No, I won't. I'm not volunteering for everything anymore. You were right—I was trying to earn love and a place for myself in our community. Now I'm waiting on the Lord and asking Him to direct me instead of charging ahead and reminding Him the work of my hands was dedicated to Him."

Duncan's rough hand slid over hers. "You're not the only one who's done that. It nearly shook me out of my boots when I realized I was playing that same foolish game—only 'twasna with the Almighty. 'Twas with the woman I love. I tried to win her heart by making myself indispensable."

"She should have been flattered. I know I would have been."

Duncan's mouth tilted upward. "Nae, Carmen, you weren't."

"You're wrong, Duncan. Words can't begin to say how thankful I am for your friendship and all the time you've spent helping Jenny and me. Just think of that day when we took that walk and filled your wheelbarrow with wildflowers. And what about the picnics? I could go on for hours reciting things we've done and times we've agreed to pray about something. Don't you think for one minute that I don't appreciate you—and not just for the things you've done—"

The way he trailed a finger down her cheek silenced her.

"Carmen"—he stared into her eyes—" 'tis you I love."

His words hovered in the air. Carmen couldn't tear her gaze from him. Heat shot through her. "But I'm a cripple." As soon as she finished her mortifying confession, she rushed to add on, "But I'm wearing those beautiful boots you made for me. I barely limp at all in them. Did you notice?"

"Nae. And why should I? 'Tis an insignificant thing, and if all that matters to a man is how his woman walks or dresses or cooks, then he's a pathetic wretch. You're beautiful from the top of your raven black hair to the tip of your turned-in toes, Carmen Rodriguez. Most of all, you're beautiful on the inside."

Duncan rose and pulled her to her feet. "You've some thinking to do. I'll walk you home, and after you've thought on it and prayed o'er it, you can tell me whether you'll allow me to court you."

"You've given me a garden full of flowers. You've laughed at my jokes, complimented my cooking, and walked me to church. You made that pretty journal for me."

The side of his mouth pulled. "The design on it—"

"The interlocking rings that form the four seasons and friendship?"

"Aye. Well, tradition also says the design stands for a love that has no beginning or end."

"You've had feelings for me since then?"

"E'en before then."

And I was jealous because I thought he wanted Jenny. How could I have been jealous if I didn't love him and want him to love me in return? "What more is a man supposed to do to pay a woman court?"

Duncan brushed his thumb back and forth on her wrist. "He has to win her heart."

"You have, Duncan. I love you, too."

Then and there, he got down on one knee. Holding her hand as if she were a princess, he looked up at her. "I want to do this right."

"Oh Duncan!"

"Quiero compartir todavia de mi vida contigo, mi amorada."

Tears filled her eyes. *"I want to share all the days of my life with you, my beloved one."* He'd gone through the trouble of learning how to say something romantic to her in Spanish.

"¿Me se casará usted? ¿Será usted mi esposa?"

"Oh, yes! I'll marry you. I'd love to be your wife. *Te amo,* Duncan. I love you."

—⁂—

Mama's lace mantilla flowed gently around Carmen as she knelt at the altar beside Duncan. The golden band Duncan had just slipped on her finger gleamed in the candlelight. He kept her right hand in his while the pastor read the thirteenth chapter of First Corinthians from Duncan's father's Bible. The pastor then asked God's blessing on their marriage. After the prayer, Carmen joyfully accepted Duncan's assistance to rise. He wasn't helping her because of her leg; she knew his actions stemmed from affection. She smiled up at him.

"Duncan Gregor," the pastor said, "you may greet your bride."

Just as Rob had done with Mercy, Duncan freed a length of Gregor tartan from his waist and began to gently drape it over her shoulder. She remembered the Gregor tradition was for the groom to recite the romantic Burns poem. Duncan's tender smile told her he would mean every word of it.

"Como la feria usted es, mi chica bonita," he began.

Her lips parted in amazement. Spanish. He was reciting the love poem in Spanish!

"Tan profundamente son yo;
Y adoraré usted de todos modos, mi querida,
Hasta que todos los mares vayan secos."

After those precious words, Duncan drew her close and gave Carmen her very first kiss. It was worth the wait.

TO DO JUSTICE

by Cathy Marie Hake

Chapter 1

I'll be leaving in the morning." Chris Gregor waited until supper ended to make his announcement. No use spoiling a good meal with the inevitable conflict that would ensue.

Rob gave him a piercing look. "You gave me your word you wouldn't set foot in the Thurber mines again."

"And I won't."

Mercy patted Rob's arm. "Your brother wouldn't go back on his word. He's a Gregor. Will I need to pack a meal for you, Chris?"

"You rest." Carmen gazed pointedly at Mercy's pregnant tummy and started to rise. "I'll do it."

"No, but I thank you for the thought." Chris looked at his family. He'd always watched out for his younger brothers, but they were both married men now. Duncan had just moved in across the street after marrying Carmen, and Mercy was expecting her second child. No one needed him here.

But he had a job to do.

Duncan chuckled softly. "I'm thinking Chris is going to try to sneak away ere Mrs. Kunstler comes to pay a call again. He's fearing for his reputation."

Everyone laughed; Chris glowered.

"Come now, Chris." Rob plucked little Elspeth from her high chair. "No use in you being sour o'er a joke. We all think it endearing, how the woman keeps droppin' by with a treat to thank you. After all, you did deliver that strapping baby boy out to her cousin and his wife."

"Aye, and I rue the day."

Again his family laughed, but their laughter died out when he didn't join in. He gritted his teeth. "I should have been here that day." Until now, he'd never spoken the thought aloud.

The only things filling the air were Elspeth's babbling and the lingering aromas of pork chops and coffee. Chris stared at the center of the table and repeated himself.

"I should have been here."

"You couldn't have saved Connant." Rob handed Elspeth off to his wife. "They shot him straight through the heart."

"If I had been in town instead of playing stork, Connant would have acted differently. He had no one he could count on to back him up or cover him."

"Other men responded." Mercy's voice sounded soft and low.

Her tone might have been for Elspeth's comfort, but Chris suspected she'd used that voice to soothe him. It didn't work. Matters were far past words; the time had come for action. Instead of getting mired down in suppositions and conversation, he said what he needed to. "I'm becoming a Texas Ranger."

"No." Rob glared at him. "I barely managed to pry bullets out of the other men and keep them alive. I dinna need another patient—I need my brother!"

Jaw hard, Chris said, "My mind's made up."

"You're out of your mind!" Rob snapped.

Duncan shook his head. "Vengeance belongs to the Lord, Chris. Dinna take it into your own hands."

"Justice. That's what I'm seeking. An eye"—he pounded his fist on the tabletop—"for an eye." He repeated the action.

"We need a sheriff here," Carmen said quietly.

Shifting Elspeth to her shoulder, Mercy started to sway from one side to the other. "Having you here with us is a blessing, Christopher. I feel safe knowing you're close by."

"No one is safe—not with Whelan and his gang out there."

"So once Whelan is captured, you'll be done with this nonsense?"

"Nae, Rob. I willna. Not too long ago, Dalton and his gang terrorized Kansas. Evil men exist. 'Tis an unchanging fact. Get rid of Whelan and his followers, and the devil will make pacts wi' other men."

"My wife is right." Duncan slid his hand over Carmen's. "We do need a sheriff here. You've the heart of a warrior, Chris. But there's every bit as much valor in protecting our friends and neighbors as there is in chasing after the devil's brigade."

Chris stood. "I made my decision."

"We promised Da we'd all stay together." Rob stared at him. "You gave your word."

"Aye, and I'm not breaking it. I'll still be in Texas. Be assured, I'll come 'round often enough for you to grow heartily sick of me. I swore an oath today to serve as a Texas Ranger. As Mercy said, Gregors keep their word."

Duncan's features remained taut. "I'll not pretend to like your decision, but I'll honor it. You hae my support."

Carmen nestled into Duncan's side. "And our prayers."

Chris dipped his head in acknowledgment. He'd already thought this through and knew Duncan would respect his decision. Rob might well take a few years to get around to accepting it. Nevertheless, Chris looked to him.

Rob's heated glare could have sterilized his medical instruments.

Tension crackled between them, but Chris stood his ground. *Lord, I dinna want to leave at odds with my brother. Soothing words are his talent, not mine. Even so, I'd take it as a favor if You'd give me something to say.*

Rob shook his head. "If I wouldn't have to patch you up afterward, I'd be tempted to beat you to a bloody pulp."

"I'd be bloodied, all right." Chris paused a second. "But the blood would all be yours. You'd break your fingers and lose all the skin on your knuckles after the second blow."

"You arrogant—"

"Confident, not arrogant." Chris folded his arms across his chest.

"You're brothers." Mercy's voice held both censure for their scrapping and a plea for them to make peace.

Carmen laughed. "The Gregor men bellow and bluster, but they'd never come to blows. Duncan even told Jenny so. Isn't that right, Duncan?"

" 'Tis true. I did. Fretting's not good for the bairn, Mercy. Dinna let this upset you."

Chris faulted himself for having broached the topic in front of his sisters-in-law. Gentle women oughtn't be caught between warring men. Rob slid his arm around his wife's shoulders and drew her into the shelter of his side. *'Tis wondrous how he loves Mercy.* As soon as that thought flashed through his mind, Chris knew God had given him the way to make peace with his brother.

"Think back on the day Da passed on. Are you remembering how we read from his Bible on the *Anchoria's* deck?"

Duncan and Rob both nodded.

"Micah 6:8. 'He hath shewed thee, O man, what is good; and what doth the Lord require of thee, but to do justly, and to love mercy, and to walk humbly with thy God?' We made a pact that day to live that verse because God mandated it and because 'twould be a tribute to Da. Rob, 'tis undeniable that you love Mercy." Chris turned to Duncan. "And you—you and Carmen walk in step with the Lord and serve Him in the kind and gentle ways. Justice is left. Aye, 'tis, and I'm to fulfill that mandate. As a ranger, I'll do justice."

"You could do justice as the town's sheriff." Rob's molars might crack if he gritted his teeth any tighter.

"Mollifying you 'tisna what I'm called to do."

Resignation stamped Rob's features. "You're going, no matter what I say."

"Aye. You hae your calling. I hae mine. I'm doing what I must."

"Then God go wi' you."

The tension knotting Chris's neck melted away. "Aye, I'm counting on Him being with me. But I'm also relying on Him to stay here and keep His hand on the lot of you."

—⁂—

Color streaked the dawn sky as Kathryn "Wren" Regent left her shack and headed for Hepplewhite's Emporium. The clopping of horse hooves caused her to halt at the boardwalk and shove her glasses up a bit. An enormous, dust-covered man rode into town. He squinted at the buildings lining the street, then nickered softly to urge his mount onward.

Two men followed after the large man. He'd shackled their hands behind their backs, tied rope around their waists, and half dragged them toward the jailhouse.

A bounty hunter, Wren decided. Judging from what she'd overheard her brother say, bounty hunters weren't any more law abiding than the criminals they chased. It wasn't her business, though. She ducked her head and hastened to Hepplewhite's Emporium.

Every morning she drew a steadying breath before unlocking the door. Hepplewhite could have posed as an ogre in a child's book. Uglier on the inside than he was on the outside, he filled her days with misery and strife. *But what I have is better than anything I've ever had before.* She shoved the key into the lock and gave it a savage turn.

Wren hurriedly went to work preparing breakfast. She soon set a plate of biscuits and gravy and a slab of ham in front of Hepplewhite. She always ate as she cooked so she wouldn't have to join him for meals. While he slurped his coffee and belched over the plate, she set out the spittoons she'd polished the night before, dusted shelves, and cleaned the glass display cases. Washing the breakfast dishes stripped the ammonia smell from her hands, but that was part of the routine she'd created. Now she could handle yards of fabric without spoiling them.

Her shop took up the back corner of the emporium. Though Hepplewhite owned the bolts of cloth, spools of thread, lace, ribbon, and buttons, Kathryn owned the sewing machine. The Singer was her pride and joy. With it, she provided for herself.

The morning passed quickly. A bachelor brought in a shirt that needed a new button. Another brought socks that needed darning. Old Widow Marsby toddled in to get her new petticoats, which Wren discreetly slipped into an empty sugar sack.

Around those little tasks, she put the finishing touches on Ella Mae Tolliver's dress. Made of gold, water-stained taffeta, the gown was a nightmare to work on. The fabric wanted to fray, so Wren painstakingly candled the edge of each piece to fuse the threads. If that weren't enough, Mrs. Tolliver ordered that thin black braiding be stitched onto the skirts in an ornate pattern. That detailed embellishment took days of work, but *Godey's Lady's Book* could easily feature the resulting garment. Mrs. Tolliver would be in tomorrow, so Wren sewed jet buttons down the back of the garment.

The bell over the mercantile door clanged, and Mrs. Tolliver trundled in. Kathryn swiftly took one last stitch, knotted the thread, and snipped it. "Mrs. Tolliver." She stood. "I didn't expect to see you until tomorrow."

"You were wrong. I distinctly recall telling you at church Sunday that I'd come on Thursday."

"Today's Wednesday," Hepplewhite announced. He and Mrs. Tolliver were cousins, and they shared the exact same ugly disposition. Both were tall, blocky, and had mean-looking dark eyes and a permanent sneer. Once they started quibbling, Kathryn turned away and shook out the gown.

"Well, don't keep me waiting all day." Mrs. Tolliver snatched the dress from Kathryn's hands. "It's taken you long enough to get this done."

Defending herself wouldn't do any good. Kathryn knew the minute she so much as opened her mouth, Mr. Hepplewhite would suddenly remember Ella Mae was his kin. The last thing Kathryn wanted was to trigger his temper. Instead, she motioned toward the screen.

Mrs. Tolliver swept past her and declared, "It's taken you so long to finish this dress, the price should be discounted."

Wren didn't reply. The contract for the dress rested in the top drawer of the treadle machine's stand. The cost and date were clearly stipulated, and she refused to budge. She couldn't afford to. Mr. Hepplewhite made her pay for every spool of thread and inch of fabric out of her own pocket whenever she started a project. He also took 30 percent of the price she charged her patrons.

The emporium's bell jangled once again, but this time the bounty hunter filled the entire doorway. He scanned the store as he stepped inside. Kathryn's heart jumped as he started toward her.

"Hey, Wren!" Mr. Hepplewhite leaned on the pickle barrel. "Git movin' and make my dinner!"

After several muttered comments and a lot of bumping around, Mrs. Tolliver emerged from behind the screen, yanking at the cuff of her gown. "You can wait, you old goat. Wren has to alter this at once. It's abysmal. I'd be ashamed to be seen in it at all!"

"She ain't gonna stay on to do her stitchin' iff'n she don't make me grub quick like. 'Sides, Ella Mae, you can't much expect her to fit you into anything less than a tent. You ain't lost anything you put on 'tween babies."

The bounty hunter came to a stop about five feet away. For being such a big man, he walked with the lithe grace of a cougar. He took off his hat and waited patiently. Since she'd seen him earlier, he'd managed to dust off and wash up. Now his hair was wet, so she couldn't determine whether it was black or a deep sable. Silvery blue-gray eyes gave him an air of aloofness.

Mrs. Tolliver continued to splutter and cluck over her gown.

The stranger jutted his chin toward her. "Ma'am, I think that's a fine gown. I was in Chicago just a week ago, and none of the fancy society matrons wore anything that would put yours to shame."

Ella Mae stopped midtirade and gave him a withering glare. "Mind your own business."

"As a matter of fact, I came in to do business with the young lady. Her reputation—"

My reputation! Wren's mouth went dry.

"Wren!" Hepplewhite bellowed.

The stranger shot her a bolstering smile and continued on as if he hadn't been interrupted, "—is well known. I need to get a shirt."

In the background, the ringing sound of metal dropping on a hardwood floor failed to drown out a nasty stream of oaths. "Wren! You ain't even seen to the spittoons yet!"

"I did. The Clancy boys came by for eggs—remember?"

Hepplewhite snorted. "Gal, you gotta git me my food! My ribs are rattling!"

Mrs. Tolliver struggled with the waist on her dress. "You were intentionally mean-spirited when you made this. You tried your hardest to make me look fat!"

"Wren! I'm gonna starve!"

Wren took a deep breath. "Mrs. Tolliver, if you give me another day, I'll work on your gown. Sir," she paused and shot a wary look at the bounty hunter, "I have to cook. If you'll but wait, I'll gladly give you my portion."

His face darkened. "If you'll forgive me, ma'am, you look like a stiff wind could take you clear to the coast. I'd far rather see you eat whatever you're fixing. Go on and see to things. I can look around."

"Thank you, sir. Mrs. Tolliver, do you need help with your buttons?"

"I'm not a lackwit! I can take care of myself!"

Mr. Hepplewhite slouched over. "Gal, I done tole you, you gotta work to keep yer space. Yer long overdue for dinner, and I full well 'spect pie after supper tonight. And see to them spittoons again."

Wren's shoulders sank with weariness.

"What are you a-standin' there fer? Go cook!"

"Yes, Mr. Hepplewhite."

The storekeeper grabbed her arm and glowered. "I want somethin' good. None of them chicken an' dumplin's or chicken stew."

"Other than the ham for breakfast, you've allowed me only one chicken to feed us for the week, Mr. Hepplewhite."

"Don't get snippy with me!" He let go, reared back, and smacked her across the face.

Chapter 2

Chris didn't believe his eyes. He reacted out of sheer reflex and caught the poor girl as she flew toward him. After he set her to the side, he automatically spun back around. "That's more than enough!"

"Shuddup. Ain't none of your affair." The storekeeper sneered at the lass and took a menacing step toward her.

Chris stepped between them and growled, "Don't."

"This here is my place."

"Owning a place doesna give you license to harm anyone." Chris slowly closed his hands into fists. Hepplewhite might be big, but none of it was muscle. His eyes narrowed and the veins in his neck bulged—both telltale signs of a building temper.

"Get outta here," Hepplewhite sneered.

Chris didn't budge an inch, but when the storekeeper threw the first punch, Chris didn't hesitate to defend himself. A left to Hepplewhite's middle and a right uppercut to his jaw dropped the man like a ton of bricks.

"Miss Wren, are you all right?" Chris turned back in time to see her try to re-adjust her spectacles, only to find they were mangled from Mr. Hepplewhite's smack. Tears filled her eyes, making them look like the flowers Carmen called lobelias. If her tears weren't enough, a big red handprint, complete with rapidly growing welts, painted her cheek.

"Oh no!" she whimpered.

"You're white as a sun-bleached bone. Let's sit you down. I'll go get a wet rag to press to your face. Come on, sit here in this chair before you swoon." He gently cupped her elbow and led her to a battered cane chair. The poor woman's knees gave out on her, and he caught her in the nick of time. Easing her onto the seat, Chris couldn't help but note how thin she was.

The whole while, Ella Mae Tolliver screeched at an ear-splitting level. Chris gave her a nasty look and snapped, "Hush up and get out your smelling salts."

"I'm not about to aid that. . .that. . .*trollop*. I'm not going to help a murderer, either!"

"He's not dead. Dump water over him, and he'll come to."

The door burst open, and the sheriff entered with his pistol drawn. "What's going on in here?"

"That man," Ella Mae screamed as she pointed at Chris, "tried to kill my cousin!"

Having turned two prisoners over to the sheriff this morning, Chris reported, "He struck Miss Wren, continued to pose a threat, then took a swing at me. Self-defense."

"Now what did you do, Wren?" the sheriff asked in an exasperated tone as he holstered his weapon.

"She did nothing at all," Chris asserted.

The sheriff glanced at the tiny woman's face and grimaced. "He got you pretty good this time."

This time? Chris roared as his blood went from a heavy simmer clean into a rolling boil. The poor wisp of a woman didn't deserve even one smack—how could any man ever raise a hand to a woman? And from the sound of it, this wasn't anything new.

Miss Wren deserved her unusual name. Plainly dressed in a mud-brown day gown and wearing her ordinary brown hair scraped back in a schoolmarm bun, she seemed as dull and dreary as a common wren. Even the bright yellow tape measure she wore looped over her neck seemed to fade and droop.

Dark moons hovered beneath her eyes, and she bit her lower lip—most likely to keep from crying. Chris felt an odd need to shelter the little wren from the storm. He scowled at the sheriff. "This woman deserves protection."

Wren's lids lowered in shame, and she leaned away from the sheriff's touch. Once his hand dropped, she dipped her head. Chris watched how badly her hands shook as she tried to fix her mangled eyeglasses. Something deep inside him twisted. He paced across the worn plank floor, snatched a red bandana from a display stack, shoved a dipper to the side of a tin water bucket, and dunked the cloth inside. After wringing it out, he hunkered down by Wren and gently reached up to press its cool dampness to the fire in her cheek.

She threw up her arm in an instinctively defensive move and flinched.

Chris wrapped his hand around her stick-thin wrist and slowly lowered it back into her lap as he made a soft sound of reassurance. Folding the bandanna so another cool surface was available, he ordered in a tone milder than a spring breeze,

"Miss Wren, you'd best go on and hold this to your face. It has to be paining you a fair bit."

Once she took the cloth, Chris rose and glowered at the sheriff. "The man flat out assaulted her."

"Oh, he had cause!" The old battle-ax pointed at Wren. "She only got what she deserved—could've gotten more and had no cause to whine. My cousin took her in out of the goodness of his heart. He lets her work here and even feeds the girl. She got fresh-mouthed."

The sheriff scratched his shoulder. "It strains a man's imagination thinkin' Wren could muster even a few fresh words."

Hepplewhite started to rouse. He groaned and rolled onto his side before struggling to his feet. Rubbing his jaw, he cursed vividly. "He done went an' busted me in the chops. Go stick him in the jailhouse!"

"Can't. You struck Wren, and then you threw the first punch at him."

Mr. Hepplewhite turned on Wren. "I put up with more'n enough, gal. Git out. Now."

Wren's mouth twisted as she cried out.

"Git, I say!"

The sheriff sighed. "Wren, he owns the place. Go on and gather up everything that belongs to you."

"She ain't takin' a thang! I git a third of everything she sews, seein' as it's my place, but she ain't paid this week."

"You owe her for cooking and cleaning," Chris gritted. "Call it even."

"I don't owe her a cent."

"That wasn't the agreement you made with her," the sheriff growled. "We all thought you gave her a wage for her extra work."

"Thangs change."

"That does it," Chris said. "Miss Wren, do you have any kin?"

"Only a stepbrother. I haven't seen him in years."

"Fine." Chris gently flipped over the compress and set it back in place. "Let's send him a telegram."

Hopelessness tainted her voice. "I don't know where he is."

Poor woman. He looked to the sheriff. "Where else can she go?"

Ella Mae simpered, "No decent folk are going to take her in."

Mr. Hepplewhite held his jaw and snorted. "Told ya. Folks have dirty minds. All of 'em think you an' me—"

"Say one more word—" Chris snarled. He didn't need to finish his threat. Hepplewhite shut up, but the damage was done.

The blood drained from Wren's face, making her horrified expression all the more stark.

Chris glanced at the sheriff, his eyes asking an unvoiced question.

"Ain't much I can do. Hepplewhite's been drinkin' like a trout, an' he's been tellin' tales."

"Don't even think to ask me to take her in. I've got children. No scarlet woman is going to taint my home!"

The sheriff heaved a sigh. "Now, Ella Mae, you just heard your cousin. He's just been spreadin' lies—"

"She's opened herself to lurid speculation. I won't have men riding out to my place because they figure they'll have a turn with her." Mrs. Tolliver disappeared behind the screen and reappeared a few minutes later. She tossed the golden dress onto the floor. "I don't want this after all."

As the sharp-tongued woman sailed out the door, Wren bowed her head.

"Miss Wren," Chris said as he tilted her face up to his, "go on and get packed. I'm taking you out of here."

Flinching again from his touch, she wailed, "You lost me my job!"

"No, songbird. I freed you from slavery."

She eased away from him as she rose unsteadily.

Chris looked her over slowly, taking in her mussed hair, trembling lips, and shy, deep blue eyes. He saw how her shoulders squared with pride, just as he noted her breaths came far too fast and choppy to indicate she felt sure of herself or her situation. She held her clasped hands right at the base of her ribs, and her knuckles were white.

Chris clenched and unclenched his fists as he realized this defenseless woman had the tiniest waist he'd ever seen. Her drab dress hid her assets, and he began to wonder if she hadn't planned the effect.

"Old Pickersly's wagon." The sheriff shifted from one boot to the other. "It ought to last long enough to get you to a new place. Don't know what to suggest about an animal to pull it."

Chris tamped down a moan. The last thing he needed was to be saddled with a helpless female. Then again, he couldn't turn his back on her. *Mercy could probably use some help. I'm on my way home anyway.*

He locked eyes with the sheriff. "Miss Wren will come with me. I'll find her a good placement—safe and happy."

"Wren, this is Chris Gregor. He's—" Chris gave him a slight warning shake of the head, and the sheriff recovered. "Believe me, I know plenty of his friends, and they're all fine men. Real fine men. The very best. You'll be safe as can be with him. He'll make sure you land on your feet somewhere. I'd trust him with my life."

"But, Sheriff! I've never even met Mr. Gregor and—"

"Now, Wren, some situations you have to look at as being put into motion by the hand of the Almighty. You can't very well stay in these parts. Things just aren't workin' out. What with Mr. Hepplewhite spreading lurid tales, you'll not be safe here."

Wren flushed deeply but still managed to whisper, "I'm not a woman to follow a stranger out on the open trail."

"No one in their right mind would ever figure you and Gregor were. . .ah, misbehaving."

"But they thought Mr. Hepplewhite and I were!"

The sheriff frowned at her. "Consider the caliber of man you're dealing with, Wren."

"I'm not able to! I've never met him before."

"He's good friends with several of my buddies. That's the best recommendation you'll ever get."

Wren looked at Chris's face. She stared with great intensity, a fact that surprised him since she'd been so timid until now. Uncertainty painted her unremarkable features.

Chris no more than decided the woman was being rude when he realized her eyes looked cloudy. She couldn't focus well enough to scan him for a polite instant. "Miss Wren, I'll help you get spectacles straight off. It'll make you feel better, seeing where you're headed and what's going on."

"There you are, Wren." The sheriff absently helped himself to a fistful of gumdrops. "Mr. Gregor's got things well in hand. And now you've got that buckboard. It simplifies the move."

"She ain't goin' till she pays up!"

"That's more than fair." Chris nodded sagely. "And we'll make sure she gets what you owe her, too."

"Me? I don't owe her one red cent. She owes me rent!"

"Rent?" The sheriff reared back. "She cooks for you in return for her space here. I was here when you came to that agreement."

"I told you thangs change. She ain't all that good a cook."

The sheriff studied a red gumdrop. "Church socials and such—I've eaten what she made. Only woman around who can hold a candle to her is my wife. Wren, did you get paid for the weeks you minded the store when pleurisy laid up Mr. Hepplewhite? Or all the times he's busy and tells you to help customers?"

She shook her head.

He popped the gumdrop into his mouth and frowned at a black gumdrop. "What about all the dustin' and sweepin' and window washin' you do? You get paid for that?"

"No," she said in a shaky tone. She took a deep breath. "He's demanded one-third of my commissions, too."

Chris kept silent.

"Well, Wren, that seems fair enough to me. After all, he's got a stake in the project—it bein' his fabric and all." The sheriff flicked aside the black gumdrop and popped a half dozen other gumdrops into his mouth.

"I have to pay him for everything I use at the outset."

While the sheriff choked on the gumdrops, Chris took a menacing step toward Hepplewhite. "It's plain to see the woman owes you nothing. Sheriff, you're the law around here. What do you estimate this *gentleman* owes the lady?"

"Plenty. Cabin next to Wren's belonged to Pickersly. He kicked the bucket last week. Buckboard's a sorry sight, but it'll make one last trip. Go hitch it up, and I'll make sure Wren gets what she needs to start a new life. Wren, run along home and pack your belongings."

"She needs spectacles first." Chris scanned the mercantile.

"Ain't got none." Hepplewhite glowered.

Chris threaded her hand into the crook of his arm. "I'll escort you home. We'll get you glasses as soon as possible."

"Thank you," she murmured.

When he stopped at the door to the place she lived in, Chris felt a spurt of gratitude that she couldn't see his grimace. The place was no more than a shack. When she opened the door, he fought the urge to slam the door shut and set a match to the place. The only furniture was a single chair by the window. She slept on a pallet on the floor.

"I won't take long, Mr. Gregor."

There's an understatement. "I'll hitch the wagon and load things up." In the few minutes he used to hitch the wagon, Wren bundled her meager possessions into a blanket. Chris silently placed it in the buckboard and drove up to the front of the mercantile.

"You're robbin' me blind!" Hepplewhite whined at the sheriff as they entered.

The sheriff slammed down the lid of a trunk. He kicked Hepplewhite's leg out of his path and sneered, "Servants get room and board and wages for their work. Clerks earn a salary, and renters don't have to give back anything more than a percentage. To my way of thinking—legal-like, you know—you owe that gal a whole year's wages for two jobs. Thin as she's gotten, you ain't fed her much, neither. Count yourself lucky all I'm doing is taking it out in goods and not takin' it outta your sorry hide."

Chris helped him heft the trunk and load it into the buckboard. "What's in this?"

"Kitchen stuff—silverware, coffeepot, skillet, and such. Spices, towels. . . Oh, I put in some soap and a washboard, too."

It would take three days to get home. "She's going to need a warm blanket or two."

"Reckoned as much. We'll use them around the sewing machine to protect it."

The heavy machine would weigh them down. Chris shook his head. "Hepplewhite's cheated and mistreated her, but sewing machines are costly."

"I own the machine."

No wonder she doesn't have much else to her name. "Then we'll take it."

The sheriff motioned to a pair of young men. They came over, and he ordered them to load up the machine. He grinned at Chris. "The thing weighs a ton."

Chris watched as Wren tucked shears, a pincushion, and sundry other sewing notions into a small box. She'd need fabric or money to start up shop somewhere. He'd rather it be money. "Sheriff, how much do you estimate Hepplewhite still owes?"

"I kept tally of what I packed. Including the trunk, the total's just shy of twelve bucks."

"While I was in Chicago, I heard some of the lasses from a factory talking. Until May, they earned almost seven dollars a week. Since Black Friday and the market's drop, it's been cut to just under three." Chris yanked a strip of brown paper from the wrapping roll and started scribbling. "How long have you worked here, Miss Wren?"

"Since May of last year."

Chris worked out the arithmetic. "Twelve months at seven bucks, and three more at three comes to ninety-three dollars."

"I been feeding her and giving her space!"

"Which is why she cooked for you." Chris stared at Hepplewhite. In a matter of seconds, the man started squirming and blustering. "You took advantage by taking part of her commissions and exacting all sorts of labor. I willna allow her to take what she didna earn, but she's leaving here fairly compensated. Subtracting the twelve dollars' worth of goods already out in the wagon, you need to give the lass eighty-one dollars."

"I don't have that kind of money!"

In the end, Wren had fifty-three dollars in her reticule and a wagonload of fabric, lace, and every sewing folderol ever invented. She went to the back room and returned with her arms heavily laden.

Mr. Hepplewhite erupted from his chair and tried to grab the clothing she carried. "Oh no! You can't take those! I'm selling them!"

Chris tensed, ready to spring into action, but Wren surprised him. She held tight to the clothes. "You wouldn't allow me to take deposits at all, and none of these garments was paid for. They're rightfully mine. I'll need samples of my work when I begin anew elsewhere."

"Git outta here and don't come in for one more thing!"

"I'll be back in just a sneeze. I still have several garments back there."

Chris smoothly unburdened her and shoved them into the sheriff's arms. "I'll help you go get the other clothes, Miz Wren."

"Thank you, Mr. Gregor." She gave him a nervous smile and sidled closer.

Wren carefully selected a shirt before stepping back to allow the men to tie the clothing beneath one of her quilts in the buckboard.

Since she was out of earshot, Chris murmured, "The poor thing's scared of her own shadow!"

"She's got a nervous constitution. Sorta shy, too, but she's helped out here and there when one of the ladies had a young'un or someone took sick."

"Why didn't anyone help her out? It's plain to see he's mistreated her."

"Hepplewhite's richer than just 'bout anyone else in the county. Most everyone's had a bad time, what with the depression and drought. They all owe him big money on their accounts. Wren never complained. I tried to get her to talk a few times, but she'd just go real quiet."

"Was he just boasting, or do you think he's. . .hurt her?"

"Not a chance. Get a few beers in Hepplewhite and he lies about everything."

The lady tied on a sunbonnet and handed the sheriff a shirt she'd kept aside. "Thank you."

"Farewell, Wren."

Chris wrapped his hands about her waist and lifted her onto the seat. He climbed aboard and flicked the reins. As soon as they'd drawn away from the town, Wren broke their silence. "I'll be happy to purchase a horse if you give me some advice.

Soon as I do, you'll be free of your obligation."

"Where would you go?"

She shrugged. "Wherever I find a town. There's one a day or so south of here."

"Dogtail? You don't dare go there. It's worse than Sodom and Gomorrah. Don't you have any relatives at all?"

"I have no one upon whom I can depend." She inched a bit farther away. "Mr. Gregor, we've not even been properly introduced, but I must tell you I'm not a. . ." She blushed vividly. "That is to say, Mr. Hepplewhite made inferences, and I want you to know I won't. . . If you think I'll—"

He squinted at the horizon and added matter-of-factly, "We're traveling companions—nothing more—so you can stop fretting and fussing."

For all of her acute chagrin, she still manufactured a grateful flash of a smile, but she sat as far away from him as she could and wouldn't look him directly in the eye. Chris didn't mind the silence, but her tension grew palpable with each passing minute. "What you said was right, Miss Wren. We weren't properly introduced. I'm Chris Gregor. I had some business in Chicago and am on my way home. How about you?"

"Forgive my curiosity, but will there be a wife, children, a few dogs, and a crop waiting?"

He chuckled softly. "No ma'am. My work involves a fair bit of traveling. I built a house in town, and my brothers live across the street from one another. I thought to take you to Rob and his wife. He's a doctor."

"Oh, I couldn't possibly impose on them!"

"Mercy'd be tickled pink to have you there. She's got a wee little daughter and another on the way. Now suppose you tell me about yourself, starting with your full name."

"I'm truly not of any interest, Mr. Gregor. My name is Kathryn Regent. I'm a very drab spinster."

He thought it interesting she chose the adjective *drab*, since that was the very one he'd mentally assigned to her. Nevertheless, it would be terribly rude to confirm her assertion. Instead, he moved his boot half an inch as he wondered aloud, "How'd you ever get stuck getting called 'Wren'?"

"It's from my school days. I've always been plain as can be with unremarkable brown hair. I'm not very big, either. Given the last syllable of my given name and likeness, the name was inevitable."

He cocked his head to the side. "Wrens might be wee little birds, but they sing a grand song. Do you?"

Wrapping her arms about her ribs, she curled forward a bit and shrugged. Her bonnet shaded her face entirely, so he couldn't read her expression. In a dull tone, she whispered, "I haven't had call to sing in a long while."

He fought the wild urge to pull her close and soothe her. He simply reached over and hitched her shawl up a bit toward her nape. "Dinna worry anymore, little songbird. I'm taking you to a bonny new nest."

—⁂—

A short while later, Kathryn stretched a little and looked down at her brooch. The tin heart nestled a small timepiece in its center. She squinted and sighed. "Excuse me, Mr. Gregor, but I can't quite manage to tell the time. Do you have an estimate?"

He glanced down at the shadows. "Close to half past three."

"I don't mean to tell you your business, but shouldn't we be going due south?"

"Not a chance."

A frisson of fear danced up her spine. After steadying herself with a deep breath, Kathryn pulled her shawl more closely about herself.

"You getting cold, Miss Regent?"

"No."

"You're shivering."

She heaved a sigh. "Frankly, Mr. Gregor, I'm concerned. I'm not particularly good at remembering directions, but the nearest towns were almost due south of us as we set out."

"Aye, that they were."

Her hand fisted in her lap. "Without my glasses, I can't see well at all, but the shadows make me think we're traveling southeast."

"Aye."

His casual tone alarmed her even more. "What must you be thinking? We could have sought the relative safety of a town and spent the night under proper circumstances."

"I told you Dogtail was like Sodom and Gomorrah, all rolled into one." His tone made it clear he considered his outrageous plan to be perfectly reasonable. " 'Twas the first town, and I'd be a fool to take you there. You'll have to take my word that neither safety nor proper circumstances are to be found there."

Shawl edges fisted in her hands and pressed to her breastbone. She croaked, "Do you mean to tell me you planned for us to remain unchaperoned for the night?"

Chapter 3

Th「hat's about the size of it."

"Oh, dear Gussy!"

"There's nothing sweeter than bedrolling under the night sky, Miss Regent. It feels like angels are peeping at you from behind each and every star."

"Sweet Almighty, might You please arrange for one of them to be my guardian angel?" Wren hadn't realized she'd spoken her prayer aloud until she heard Mr. Gregor's chuckle. Scorching heat rushed from her bodice clear up to her sunbonnet.

"Dinna be mortified, lass," he said once his laughter died down. "I canna blame you for being a shade man-shy. Here's what we'll do: I'll keep to one side of the campfire, and you can have the other. Does that ease your mind a bit?"

"No." She turned toward him. "You know I have that money. Since we'd stop at my request, I'll gladly pay for two hotel rooms."

"We're nowhere near a hotel, and we'll be even farther from one by the time we stop tonight. You'll have to put up with things as they are."

Her heart thundered, and she could taste the salt of her own blood from having bitten the inside of her cheek.

"I appreciate a fine tune now and then, Miss Regent. Why don't you promise me you'll sing a bit as soon as I manage to bring down our supper?"

The way he switched subjects took her off guard. "Are you suggesting I sing for my supper, sir?"

His voice lilted with humor. "Could be."

"I'll sing whatever you request as soon as we reach the hotel."

He made an exasperated sound. "Nagging willna change what canna be changed."

"Had I known you intended not to have proper evening arrangements, I'd never have come with you."

"You can trust me."

Kathryn shook her head. "I have yet to meet a trustworthy man."

His head swiveled toward her. He dipped close so she could see his piercing gray-blue eyes. "You have now."

She gasped and held that breath for so long, her lungs started to burn. *Should I apologize? No, I'm not. I won't. Thanks to him, I lost my job. Now he's compromising my reputation. Why should I think he's—*

"I'm not perfect." His Scottish burr sounded far more pronounced. "Nae, I'm no'. But ne'er once hae I harmed a woman. And ere ye ask, I'll confess I've tangled wi' a few men—and then, only because they'd broken the law or hurt someone."

I knew it. He's a bounty hunter.

"I'm accountable to the Lord for all I do. Rest assured I'll not hae to stand afore the Almighty on Reckoning Day and say I e'er took advantage of a lass. You're perfectly safe wi' me." He nodded for emphasis. "Aye, you are. And I'll e'en give ye my Bowie knife to clutch during the night. 'Tis wicked sharp."

His offer didn't amount to enough to allay her fears, but she'd have a means to fend him off if necessary.

"I'd give it to you now, but I might hae need of it to see to supper."

Kathryn still didn't trust him. He could talk until the Second Coming, but they were just words.

Mr. Gregor heaved a prolonged sigh. She knew it was for her benefit. He leaned closer, and she fought the nearly overwhelming urge to slap him and scream. Just as quickly, he straightened back up. He'd removed his knife from his belt sheath and placed it in her lap. "Here. I've used it on occasion to shave and near cut my throat. I hold a healthy respect for that blade. Now will you calm down a mite?"

Curling her fingers around the bone shaft sent waves of relief through her. Nonetheless, Kathryn didn't want to discuss her fears. She thought it over and promised herself not to repeat the mistakes she'd made in town. By being meek, she'd given men an opportunity to push her into bad situations. With no alternative, she'd made the best of it. *No more. I'm not going to do that again. I've learned my lesson.*

Kathryn chose to redirect the conversation herself. "Mr. Gregor, I'd best tell you I'm not a woman to touch a snake. Should you kill one, you'll need to prepare and eat it on your own."

His brows went skyward. "You plan to cook our supper?"

"I presumed that to be the plan. If you hunt it, I think it only just that I prepare the meal."

"Do you even know how to cook over an open fire?"

"As long as it's not raining, I can give a fair accounting of myself."

Chris smacked his thigh. "Grand! A lass from the city who can do more than scorch coffee and burn meat over a fire."

Just how many women has he had cook for him under the stars? She worried afresh for her safety.

The buckboard jounced along the rutted road, and even at their slow pace, the horses kicked up a fair amount of dust and grit. Chris produced a canteen and offered it to her. She took a dainty sip before handing it back. "Thank you."

"Drink as much as you'd like, Miss Regent. I packed two kegs of water, and we've a jug of apple cider, too."

She took another drink, then reached for the reins so he could have his share.

"I've got it." He tilted his head and drank deeply. After capping the canteen, he set it aside. "You didna eat this noon."

"It doesn't matter." The way he stared at her made her want to writhe.

"You're starting to wilt in the sun, songbird. A short rest in the shade and a bite to eat'll perk you right up. When folks travel, they have to be careful, and they have to be up front about things. You're starting to feel poorly, and I was hoping you'd tell me yourself instead of me having to bring it up."

"I may not be at my best, but I'm scarcely ill."

"You're splitting hairs. I'll not scold you for this, but I'll get riled if you pull such a stunt again." He halted the wagon, leapt off, and reached up to help her down.

As his hands cupped around her middle, Kathryn tried to hide her surprise. For the past year, she'd not left town. The simple contact of a man spanning her waist hit her with stunning force. His fingers moved to give him a better grip then clamped more tightly. She lightly rested her hands on his shoulders to help balance herself. Mr. Gregor gently lifted, pivoted sideways, and lowered her. For a brief second, they were eye to eye. She saw kindness in his eyes, then a flash of anger. She found herself suffering the embarrassing position of being held several inches above the dirt.

"You're nothing more than skin and bones!"

"Sir, you forget yourself! You've no call to be so appallingly personal."

Instead of setting her down as she fully expected him to, Chris Gregor swung her up and took better hold of her by sliding an arm beneath her knees. "You're not walking until I get you fed. If I put you down, you'd fall flat on your face!"

"You're exaggera—"

"I told you I dinna split hairs. If you believe you've got room to talk me out of my observation, you'd best think again." He set her down in the shade of a shrubby-looking hackberry. "Best for you to have something straight off. We'll cook at supper time. For now, jerked beef and some apples might do, along with some bread. Stay put."

Kathryn watched him stalk off to the buckboard. He knew what he was doing, because he quickly located the desired food and brought it back. Everything about Chris Gregor struck her as self-assured and capable. He got a little too domineering with her, so she'd have to stand her ground. To his credit, he'd gotten her away from Mr. Hepplewhite, but would he settle her anyplace better? Only time would reveal an answer to her thorny questions.

After she ate enough to satisfy him, they were under way again. Mr. Gregor leaned toward her and asked in a conversational tone, "Just how well can you see without your spectacles?"

"I'm blind as a badger."

He chuckled. "That was alliterative but not informative in the least. Suppose you wax a bit less poetic and a heap more practical. What distance do you see well, and when do you lose your focus?"

She held out her arm three-quarters of the way. "I can see well this far. The horse is hazy, and I can only see a blur of brown and green beyond him."

"And you offered to take the reins?"

She heard the disbelief in his voice. "I supposed I couldn't do much damage for a few seconds."

"Until we rustle up some spectacles for you, dinna e'en think to be holding the reins or touching a rifle!"

Pressing a hand to her bosom, Kathryn gave him a shocked look. "Mr. Gregor, I would never even think to touch one! Papa was quite firm about ladies staying clear of men's weapons. Mama told me men didn't pick up crochet hooks or knitting needles, so women shouldn't pick up men's firearms."

He snorted.

"And just what is unreasonable about that?"

"Only those well prepared weather life's roughest storms. As soon as we get you settled in, you're going to learn to shoot a rifle. As a single woman, you have to be able to defend yourself."

"I hadn't given that much consideration." She sat quietly, and after a lengthy pause, she half whispered, "Mr. Gregor, I thought you said you were taking me someplace safe. Why would I need any protection?"

"Consider it an ounce of prevention, Miss Regent." His hand smoothed over her fists. "You were neither safe nor happy back there. This change is for the better."

She nodded mutely. *Lord, please let that be true.*

"You'll fall in love with my sisters-in-law. Carmen's forever busy with some project to help one of the locals—making a dress for some widower's daughter, going with the parson on his sick calls, and such. She's got quite a garden, too. She and Duncan live across the street. Duncan's a cobbler.

"Rob's a doctor. He's the youngest—smartest, too. Mercy's his wife. Wee Elspeth is a year old now, and Mercy'll be having another bairn in the next month or so. She's just as busy as Carmen—wi' the bairns and because she's taken to assisting Rob whene'er he needs help."

"They sound like wonderful helpmeets."

"Aye, you've the right of it, there." A second later, he shoved the reins into her hands and grabbed his rifle. Kathryn couldn't help but let out a sharp scream as he fired it. Afterward, she gave him an apologetic look.

"Dinna go lookin' so sheepish, lass. I surprised you is all. Looks like we got us some supper, though." He grinned at her a few minutes later as he carried a jackrabbit back to the wagon. "I hope you remember a fast tune or two."

She flashed back a self-conscious grin. "I know all fifteen verses of 'I Come, O Savior, to Thy Table.' Will that suffice?"

"All fifteen? By the time you finish singing, I'll have this old jack skinned, spitted, roasted, and eaten."

"I take it you don't care for that hymn."

"Maybe Mr. Perronet's 'All Hail the Power of Jesus' Name' or Wesley's 'Love Divine' if you're of the hymn-singing persuasion. They're a bit more upbeat."

"I believe I could manage that." *So he's a churchgoing man. He's told me about his family but nothing about himself.*

"You're pondering something. Mind sharing what it is?"

Figuring he'd opened the door wide for questions, Kathryn decided to take advantage. "You told me of your family but nothing about yourself."

"I'm a Scot. Was a miner back home. Since I've been here, I've done a wee bit of everything—farming, mining, construction." He shrugged.

He's being evasive. "What do you do now?"

"I work for the grand state of Texas, going around and solving problems."

"Oh." When he didn't say anything further, Wren fell silent. *He expects me to trust him when he's keeping a secret. It serves me right, though. I'm keeping a secret of my own.*

Chapter 4

Chris stopped just before sunset. "Wind'll kick up tonight, so we'll bedroll here."

They were so far away from everything, from everyone. Wren shuddered.

"Here, Miss Regent. Sit on this rock whilst I fetch your shawl. The shadow of the boulders might seem a wee bit sinister, but you'll soon note it serves as a windbreak and will bounce heat from the fire back at us. Aye, and better still, there's a wee little spring on the other side of the rocks."

"Then why don't we set up camp over there?"

He slid her shawl around her shoulders with enough solicitude to be mannerly but not so much as to hover or seem fawning. "Wind's blowing in the wrong direction. You'd be too cold."

"If it would make things easier, I could wear my other dress over this one."

"Nae, lass. 'Tisna worth fussing o'er. I'll go water Nero."

The thought of him being close frightened her, but the thought of him leaving her scared her witless. "Do you think coyotes might come around?"

"It's always a possibility. The campfire will keep all but the most brazen creatures at bay. My gun will scare those off." He rested his hands on his hips. "I'll give you the Bowie knife again for the night, but I'm needing it now so I can go dress the rabbit."

After supper Chris shoved another stick into the fire. "I dinna think I've ever tasted better rabbit, Miss Regent. You did a fine job cookin'."

"It didn't take more than a few quick turns over the fire."

"Must've been the way you basted the rabbit with your songs. You surely can sing. It was a pure pleasure sitting and listening to you."

"Thank you, Mr. Gregor."

"You look bone weary, lass. Sleep. I'll have one last cup of coffee and hit my bedroll, too."

Kathryn nodded and sidled over to her bedroll. While he'd been busy dressing the rabbit, she'd laid out their bedrolls—one on either side of the fire. Now she sat

411

down and tentatively lifted her arms, removed all of the hairpins, and let her hair uncoil. She dragged the brush through the heavy tresses, then swiftly wove them into a single, fat braid to keep her hair from tangling during the night. That done, she opened her quilt, laid down, and flipped half of it back over herself. She didn't know if she could ever fall asleep. *At least I have his Bowie knife.*

—⁓—

It took Kathryn a long while to coast off. Christ angled his stance so he could see her. Working in the mines taught him a man had to prepare for the unexpected. That being the case, he made a habit of carrying a knife up his left sleeve. Duncan had created a clever sheath that lay hidden there. Wren remained blissfully ignorant about it, so she'd finally fallen asleep. Even in her sleep, she clutched his knife. *Puir wee lass.*

He looked closer and scowled. Shivers wracked her frame. He got a second blanket from the buckboard and carefully sneaked over to her.

The softest, sweetest smile he'd ever seen tilted her lips when the extra weight descended. Chris fought the urge to hunker down and run the backs of his fingers down her cheek. He wanted to touch her hair, too. When she'd taken it down, he'd almost choked on his coffee. All twisted up in that stingy schoolmarm bun, it wasn't worth a second look; but hanging loose and free, it took a man's breath away. Abundant tresses flowed in luscious waves clear down to her hips, and the firelight brought out golden highlights. She had no notion how stunning her hair was. If she did, she'd have worn it in a softer, more inviting style—one that tempted a man to steal a quick touch but still prim enough that he'd have to concoct an excuse like a piece of fuzz or a speck of dust. She'd smile her thanks, and he'd melt.

Then Chris reconsidered. Maybe Wren knew how beautiful her hair was and hid it away, just as she dressed in a homely mud-brown dress to downplay her appeal. With a man like Hepplewhite bothering her, she might have hoped looking drab would discourage any attention.

In his line of work, he'd seen all sorts of people assume disguises. It took a lot to throw him off, but she'd succeeded. Beyond her ugly dress and hairstyle, beneath the dark circles under her eyes and timid ways, Kathryn Regent possessed a natural beauty. Without the thick spectacles, her eyes were an incredible color—one that drew a man closer and enticed him to examine their depths. Yes, the little wren was far more than her plumage promised.

As he did when on the trail, Chris dozed very lightly. Whenever he lifted his head to check on her, she was in the very same place. The poor thing was so exhausted, she didn't have the strength to toss and turn. He'd tell Mercy and Carmen to make sure to feed her well and make her take naps.

Moving quietly, Chris broke camp as the sun rose. Letting Miss Regent have an extra bit of sleep wouldn't hurt anything. Hazy beams peeped over the rock, filtered down, and kissed her awake. The wisps of her hair that broke free during the night coiled in a nimbus, and the golden light turned them into a buttery halo. Sleepy eyed, she looked up at him, then scrambled to her feet.

"Good morning, Miss Regent. We've a long day's travel ahead of us."

"Good morning." A fetching blush filled her cheeks as she bent, shook out her blankets, and folded them.

Her bashful nature gave her a certain maidenly appeal. *What am I thinking? I dinna care how sweet and innocent the lass is, I'm not about to be tied down.*

"I'll refill the canteens."

"I've already seen to that and watered Nero. Here. Eat up." He pushed a wedge of cheese and a chunk of bread into her hands.

"Thank you, but I'm not hungry."

"You'll eat, regardless." He glowered at her.

Wren gave him a disgruntled look. "You're going to hound me until I eat this, aren't you? Of course you are. Why did I bother to ask?"

"The better question is—why don't you take better care of yourself?"

"I can't very well talk and eat at the same time." She took a bite.

Chris threw back his head and chortled. "I never imagined beneath your prim and proper ways you had a feisty streak."

After swallowing, she started to lift the cheese to her mouth. "In Scotland, don't they quote the maxim of not judging a book by its cover?" Straight, white teeth sank into the cheese.

If a little witty repartee would make her eat, Chris was more than willing. He crooked a brow. Just in case she couldn't see him well enough, he teased, "Whoever made up that saying never saw those dime novels. The cover is just as absurd as the contents."

"Mmm." The corners of her mouth tilted upward. "You have to have read some of them to be able to speak with such authority."

"If this were a court of law, I'd have to plead guilty to the charge." He folded his arms across his chest. "And you, Miss Regent? Have you indulged in frittering away time reading them?"

"No." She ate another bite.

Something about her tone made him suspect she hadn't told the truth. "Now how did you manage to step outside the courtroom?"

"You were in that pretend courtroom. I wasn't."

"Feeling sassy, are you? Well, well." He smirked. "I've attended some trials. If people don't want to appear but they're forced to be witnesses, they're called hostile witnesses. I'm now dragging you into my courtroom, Miss Regent."

"That's not very gentlemanly of you."

"Do you swear to tell the truth, the whole—"

"I beg your pardon!" She didn't look in the least bit upset. Instead, her eyes sparkled and her smile grew. "I'm a lady. Ladies do not swear."

He refrained from mentioning that ladies didn't speak with their mouths full of breakfast. After all, the whole notion of him standing here, goading her, was so he'd be sure she ate—and she was. "Then promise you'll be honest."

"Sir, you wound me, implying I might be dishonest. If you wouldn't believe me in times past, how could you possibly give weight to my words now?"

"If you ever give up on being a seamstress, you might think about becoming an attorney."

"Never. I wouldn't want to have to deal with the unsavory types. But I will confess, I've read some of the dime novels. They span from insipid to inspired."

"We—" He went silent as the sound of hooves in the distance reached him.

"Yes?" She looked at him expectantly.

"Someone's coming." Chris strode over, grabbed her by the arm, and tucked her into a small cleft in the boulder. "Stay there and dinna make a sound." He turned away and grimaced. Even if Wren obeyed his edict, the riders might still spot the buckboard. Dogtail was by far the nearest town, and from the direction the riders were coming, Chris feared that was their destination. *Lord, let me be wrong. Let these be good people, or at least let them pass by on the other side of the boulders. I brought the lass out here, and I'm responsible for her.* Just in case, he reached for his weapon.

Three men stopped on the other side of the boulders. Chris silently thanked the Lord for the wind—it had caused him to camp on this side of the rocks, had obliterated any footprints he might have left, and had long since blown away any lingering scent of food or fire.

"Let's see what we got," one of the men said.

Three of them. I have the element of surprise. But I've got the woman. If something happens, she'll be at their mercy.

"Money's easy to divvy up. The rest—well, I reckon whatever each of us took, we ought to keep."

"Listen up, kid. You get what the boss decides. Get it?"

"Sure." After a short pause, the young voice added, "I've never had a timepiece."

"You fancy this one?" another voice asked.

"Unh-huh. Wow. Thanks."

A gunshot echoed off the rocks. Wren's scream mingled with it.

—◁◁—

Wren clapped a hand over her mouth, but she knew it was too late. She'd given away their presence. One of the men on the other side of the rocks just killed his partner in cold blood. From the voices, she thought there were three of them, but she couldn't be sure. She couldn't tell where Mr. Gregor was either.

She huddled behind the bush and prayed she'd go undetected. Just to back up her plan, she carefully slipped her fingers into the pocket of her dress and withdrew the tiny pocket derringer.

For a split second, she clutched it to her bosom. Wren couldn't help but wonder if she'd loaded it correctly. After all, she'd read the instructions countless times by the flickering light of her barely lit lantern. She'd gotten the tiny weapon from Mama after Papa died. Mama told her it was a ladies' gun, so he wouldn't have objected.

Now, though, she'd have to use it. How could she shoot another human being? How could she even manage to aim the weapon? Without her spectacles, she was virtually blind.

Curses filled the air. They came closer, too. Kathryn ducked down and pressed as far back into the cleft as she could. Gunshots fired from above her. Others came from several yards in front of her. At the same time a body tumbled from the rocks and landed mere feet from her, another man shot from around the side of the rocks. From the pause in gunfire, Wren assumed Chris was reloading his weapon. He'd stepped in to defend her. She could do no less. Her hands shook so badly, she couldn't hold the derringer. Wren threw herself down on her stomach and rested both elbows on the hard ground to steady her hand.

The man sidled around the rocks and stood close enough that she saw a star shape branded into the leather on the side of his boot. Kathryn looked upward, saw badly worn trousers, a dirty plaid shirt, and a face that was too far away to focus upon distinctly. The sound of his pistol cocking made her blood run cold, and she shuddered. The action discharged her weapon.

"Whelan!" Chris fired as he shouted.

The man shot back, but just as he did, he jerked to the side and began to fall. His loud, raw words made it clear he wasn't near death. He tumbled to the side and pulled the trigger, but the empty sound tattled he'd used all his ammunition.

"His gun's empty!" Wren cried out.

Chris shouted, "Wren, get back!"

"Wren?" Whelan scrambled away. Mere seconds later, a horse galloped off.

Chris charged toward her. He halted briefly to confirm the other man was dead, then reached Kathryn's side. He grabbed her by the arms. "Are you hurt?"

Tears slid down her cheeks.

He shook her gently. "Lass, are you all right?"

Eyes swimming with tears, she looked at him and lifted her right hand. She rotated it a bit, and he sucked in a sharp breath. Her hand started to shake, so he peeled the tiny vest-pocket derringer from her fingers and tucked it into his belt.

"So that's why he flinched and missed me."

"Dead."

"Nae, lass. You dinna kill him." He stayed close. "There's blood on the ground. I probably got him. I know you did, too. I canna say for certain 'twill keep him occupied. Whelan might double back on us. I'm getting you out of here."

Wren shook her head. Her voice quavered but still held conviction. "He won't come back."

"You canna be sure."

"His gun was empty." *Gregor's a bounty hunter.* Her shaking grew worse. "I shot him."

"Aye."

Her knees gave out on her. *I shot my brother.*

Chapter 5

Wren huddled under her shawl next to Chris on the seat of the buck-board. Two horses plodded along, tied to the back of the wagon where Wren couldn't see them. A dead body was draped over each saddle. Chris scanned the landscape. The road with virtually no good ambush points led to the nearest town: Dogtail.

Once again, Chris assessed the situation. If Miss Regent weren't so rattled, he'd gladly leave all her possessions behind. As for the thieves—dead was dead. Taking care of the living rated as the priority here. He longed to dump off one of the bodies, put her on the horse, and ride like the wind. He couldn't. The poor lass would fall right out of the saddle.

"Whelan." The name came out in a low, angry rasp. He'd been tracking the man ever since Connant was slain. If he didn't have Wren along, he'd have followed the outlaw and apprehended him. As it was, all he had were two bags of loot and a pair of dead bodies.

And a witness. Wren would be able to testify that the men had brought the loot. But could she identify Whelan? "Wren, you saw Whelan."

She shuddered. "I couldn't see his face."

"Tell me what you saw."

"The man fell." Her voice quavered. "He was dead."

"Aye." He frowned at her pallor, then patted her. "But we're alive. 'Twas either them or us. They started the shooting." His words should have given her comfort, but it would probably take some time for a delicate lady to get over the shock of see-ing a dead body fall within a few feet of her.

Whelan got away, but Wren would be a neutral witness who could at least con-nect him to the stolen goods. Pitiful as that charge was, if he'd killed anyone to gain those possessions, the connection would prove vital in court. "The one who got away—Whelan. What else did you see?"

"I didn't have my glasses."

"I'll help you get some spectacles right away. Aye, I will. You willna feel so lost and helpless then. In the meantime, I'll help you. I need your help, too. Was there anything else you did make out?"

"Just blue jeans. And boots."

His breath caught. "Was there anything special about his boots? Plain, or any designs?"

"Plain. Only one star," she said in a vague tone.

"A star? You're positive of that, Wren?" The star on Whelan's boot was a trademark piece of evidence. Lawmen knew about it, but they didn't let common folk know. It was the sort of thing, if blabbed about, would make Whelan shed his boots. "What did it look like? How big?"

Her hand shook as she lifted it. Holding her thumb and forefinger apart about two inches, she said thickly, "This big."

Whelan's boot. Clear as could be. "Tell me anything else you saw and heard."

"I shot him." She doubled over, as if in agony, and shook her head.

He took off his bandana, folded it, and poured water from the canteen on it. "You feeling sick?"

She moaned.

"You'll be feelin' better soon. Sure you will," he soothed as he brushed several darling little curls from her nape, then pressed the cool cloth to her soft flesh. "The day's turning hotter than the hinges of Hades. This'll help. Just keep your head down for a few minutes and breathe slow and deep. Slow and deep. There you go. Take your time. When you're ready, you can tell me more of what happened."

After taking a few shaky breaths, she said, "I don't want to talk about it. When we get to a town, I'll speak with the marshal."

"Whelan and his gang killed a dear friend of mine. I'm longing to get him."

She nodded slowly and tried to straighten up.

He continued to apply pressure to keep her head down. Judging from her extreme pallor, he was sure she'd faint dead away if he let her up too soon. "So you know it's Whelan."

"You called his name, Mr. Gregor." She turned her face toward him and opened her eyes. They'd darkened to pools of blue anguish. The bandana slithered away, and he glided his hand down to her shoulder and drew her upright. She started to tremble again, so he nudged her into resting her cheek on his chest.

"Worse, I called your name," he confessed grimly. "Wren is, unfortunately, a unique name. He's shrewd. Once he overhears someone mention you, he'll be able to track you down. I've put you in terrible danger."

"No one will talk about me. I'm utterly forgettable."

Chris snorted at that proclamation. Less than twenty-four hours after meeting her, he'd come to realize little Wren wasn't at all what she masqueraded as. Just scratching the surface showed her to be intelligent, well-spoken, and resourceful. A good cook and a fine seamstress. Pretty, too. Some man was going to get a prize when he wed her. *If I can capture Whelan before he finds her.*

"From now on you're Katie, not Wren. Not even Kathryn. Are you understanding me?"

She nodded slowly.

"Aye, and I'll be sure you learn how to fire a rifle." His brows knit with a sudden realization. "You lied to me!"

Looking indignant, she huffed back, "I did not!"

"You said you didn't handle firearms."

Blinking at him, she tilted her head. "Mr. Gregor, I told you I didn't touch *men's* weapons. We were discussing rifles, and I assure you, I haven't touched a rifle. I've not lifted any other pistol either. Mama specifically purchased the derringer as it was listed as a lady's firearm."

"I imagine a derringer, however small, can still kill a man. Why draw distinctions? If it shoots bullets, it's deadly."

Katie blanched. Her eyes went wide with shock, and her lips began to quiver. "Mr. Gregor, do you think my bullet might *kill* Whelan?"

"Only if we pray real hard."

Her face twisted with revulsion. "I couldn't ever think to pray for the death of any soul!"

"I figured as much. Tell me, though—just what were you aiming at when you fired the gun at Whelan?"

She blanched.

No one in her right mind aimed a gun, fired it, and hoped the bullet wouldn't do any damage. She was plumb crazy. *No, not plumb crazy,* the voice in the back of his mind corrected, *just very tenderhearted.* He steeled himself with a gusty breath and asked in a voice he considered to be remarkably conversational and restrained, "Miss Regent, gunshots can be—and often are—fatal. What possessed you to draw a weapon if you didn't plan to inflict damage?"

"Please, don't shout at me!"

"I'm not shouting!" He caught himself raising his voice enough to make the horse skittish. Embarrassed, he stated, "I'm merely being forceful. You cannot have the derringer back unless I'm absolutely certain you understand it has the capacity to take a life."

"Oh, I'd never take deadly aim! It would be sinful! I simply. . ." She tore her gaze from his angry glower and looked at her hands as she twisted them in her lap.

"What was your intention?"

She whispered faintly, "I didn't want him to hurt you. But don't think I was brave. I was shaking so badly, the gun went off before I even aimed."

"Courage isna the lack of fear. 'Tis acting in spite of the fear. You should be proud of yourself."

She shook her head. "I'm ashamed of myself. All we've done is talk about me, and I never once inquired as to whether you were injured."

She kept taking him off guard. She shifted like a prairie wind from one direction to the next without so much as a warning. For every irritating grain of sand the changes brought, there was also the sweet scent of wildflowers or a welcome gust of refreshing coolness. It made it impossible to be mad at her.

"I'm fine. I've got the Lord to thank—and you, too. I'll not forget 'twas you who shot him."

She rewarded his words of praise by scrambling down the side of the moving buckboard and getting violently ill.

—⁂—

She felt hideous. Mortified, too. Mr. Gregor actually held her head as she lost her meal. It served him right. After all, he'd forced her to eat breakfast. But she couldn't bring herself to be mad at a man who'd been gentle with her. Patient, too. Never once did he say a harsh word about the spineless way she handled all of the feelings roiling inside.

"Miss Regent? Katie? We canna afford to stop and let you rest. I dinna know how bad off Whelan is, but he's meaner than a stepped-on snake, and I want us as far from here as we can get. Are you understanding me?"

She nodded.

"There's a good lass." He lifted her into his arms, and she slumped against him like a rag doll. Katie tried to at least lift her head away from his shoulder, but he used his chin to nudge it back down. "Hold still. You've been through too much. 'Tis a wonder you've not swooned yet."

She missed his warmth and strength when he put her back up on the conveyance. He went to the rear of the wagon and plowed through some of the things. She was too weary to even keep her eyes open long enough to discover what he wanted.

"Take a few small sips, lass. Go slow." He held the speckled, granite-wear cup and tilted it to her lips, even though she'd tried to hold it herself. As badly as her hands shook, she couldn't very well question his judgment. The cider made her mouth taste far better. She granted him a wobbly smile of thanks.

"You're shivering." His soft tone made it clear he'd merely made an observation, not an accusation. "You've suffered more than your share of shocks these last few days. I want you to lie down, and I willna listen to a single argument. You have to rest, else you'll slow us down."

"I—I just need a minute."

He tucked a few errant tendrils of her hair behind her ear. "I made a place for you in the back."

Wrapped in a cocoon of both his kindness and her quilt, moments later, she closed her eyes.

—⁕—

The next thing Katie knew, she woke to a pat on her arm.

"Miss Regent, I know I told you we'd avoid Dogtail, but 'twas the closest place. We'll be coming to the edge of town in about ten minutes or so. I'm going to take us someplace decent folks don't talk about, let alone go to. Keep quiet and stay wrapped in the quilt. I'm going to pass you off as an ailing lass."

She sat up and gave him a groggy look. "But why did we come here?"

"I'll wire lawmen about Whelan, and we'll drop off the bodies." He extended his hand to help her climb onto the seat beside him.

"A temporary stop seems more than reasonable, Mr. Gregor."

"One other thing—there's someone here who will store your belongings."

The man had the gall to sound as if he considered his plan quite reasonable. She fisted her hands in her lap and gritted, "I'm not leaving my things behind. I need them to start up again in a new town."

"That sewing machine—"

"Was obscenely expensive," she interrupted. At the moment, her future survival rated far above the social convention of not interrupting someone else.

"It weighs a ton. I won't have a hunk of iron and oak slow us down."

"I need that 'hunk of iron and oak' to make a living."

He crooked a calloused finger, tucked it beneath her chin, and tilted her face to his. "You won't be around to make a living if we drag that contraption behind us. The only good it'll serve is as a headstone on your grave."

Whelan won't come after me, but I can't tell him that.

"Whelan holds no regard for life. You heard him—he shot his own partner in cold blood—and for nothing more than a greater share of the loot. Revenge on us for shooting him is a far greater motive." He dipped a little closer. "The sewing machine might be costly, but life is priceless. Dinna waste your breath. I've decided, and you'll not sway me."

"If Dogtail is such a pagan town, isn't it a poor choice for a destination?"

"I have a reliable contact. Fact is, I'm not concerned with your possessions a-tall. 'Tis your safety. No matter what happens, you're to obey my orders."

She caught herself right before making that promise. *Being agreeable about everything only got me into trouble last time. This time I'm going to take charge. There's no reason a rational woman would blindly obey a man she's just met.* "I'll be certain to listen." *But that doesn't mean I'll follow every last order spilling out of this man's mouth.*

"I'll have to ask you to take your hair down, Miss Regent. Put it into two plaits. You can pass for a schoolgirl if you do, especially with you being a wee snip of a woman."

It took little time to take down her already mussed bun. Katie finger combed the tresses, then hastily plaited lumpy-looking braids. She gave him a lopsided smile. "If they're too neat, no one will believe I'm a sleepy child."

His features tightened. Perhaps he wasn't satisfied with her appearance. "Do you suppose I ought to draw the quilt up over my shoulders?"

"Clear up to your neck. Even up higher in the back. Slump against my arm, too. It'll make you look shorter and more pitiful."

More pitiful? So that was what he thought of her. He viewed her as a pathetic spinster.

He shot her a whimsical smile that erased the sting of his thoughtless words. "Too bad you still manage to look so tidy. Kids always seem to get grubby. A streak of dirt or a runny nose would do the trick."

"Dirt?"

"Would you mind?"

"I'm sure it will wash off."

A few minutes later, he chuckled as he leaned back to view his handiwork. Half a teaspoon's worth of dirt and a drop from the canteen were his paints, and he'd mixed them with avid concentration before dabbing his finger against her cheek. With a quick, downward swipe, he smeared it. "There."

A habitually neat individual, Katie fought the urge to reach up and rub it off.

He looked too pleased with himself for her to do that. They got under way, and she murmured in a rather embarrassed tone, "Mr. Gregor, you'd best call me by my given name. Children aren't addressed formally."

He nodded curtly. "Lying goes against my grain. We're both believers, so I'll be telling the truth when I say you're my little sister. You leave matters to me."

Katie sat there and thought what a clever man Chris Gregor was. She cataloged his strengths and virtues. He was compassionate, respectful, and a champion of the mistreated. He was moral and good and resourceful. But that resourcefulness and his protective nature troubled her. Those qualities would compel him either to apprehend or to kill her brother.

"Aye, you leave matters to me." Mr. Gregor's voice resounded with confidence. "Your life is bound to change now."

In more ways than you know.

"I'll help you. In fact, our town is in sore need of a seamstress. Old Mr. Rundsdorf is gnarled as mesquite, so his clothes canna come out of a catalog. And he's just the start. You'll be making a whole new life as soon as I get you home. Set your mind on that."

" 'Finally, brethren, whatsoever things are true, whatsoever things are honest, whatsoever things are just, whatsoever things are pure, whatsoever things are lovely, whatsoever things are of good report; if there be any virtue, and if there be any praise, think on these things.' "

"Ahhh, yes," Chris stretched out those two simple words in such a way that she knew he relished them. "Philippians chapter four and verse eight."

Self-conscious, she confessed, "I can't ever seem to recall where verses are in the Bible. I've memorized countless verses, but I jumble up the books and chapters and verses."

"Da and Ma worked on that with me and my brothers. They knew 'twas important to drum things into our impressionable minds during those tender years."

"You were blessed to have good parents." *How would my brother have turned out if his father had been a good man instead?*

"Aye, I was blessed. But hear me well, *Katie*." He stressed what he called her and paused until she looked directly at him. "Regardless of how rough things might become, you're to think on the good that lies ahead. You'll have a safe and happy future. I'll see to it. Aye, I will."

"Thank you, Mr. Gregor."

"Chris," he corrected.

"Thank you, Chris." Burrowed in the blanket, she lapsed into silence. If it weren't for her worries over her stepbrother's gunshot wounds and the guilt that she'd inflicted one of them, life would be incredibly sweet. As it was, things couldn't become more complicated. Even so, Chris Gregor's good-hearted ways impressed her and made her feel safe and secure.

Chris told her Dogtail was Sodom and Gomorrah all rolled into one, and the short drive through town more than confirmed his estimation. She scooted closer to him on the buckboard bench. He even took the liberty of wrapping his arm around her shoulders. Under normal circumstances, she'd never allow a gentleman to behave so boldly, but this was as far from normal as she could imagine. Chris promised to make sure she was fine, and she knew he'd keep his word. . .until he pulled her buckboard to a stop before the last in a string of tawdry-looking buildings.

Katie squinted in an attempt to see where they were. Even without her glasses, the sign was clearly legible. Huge, garish red hearts had been painted before and after the lettering on the place's false front: Lucille's.

Chapter 6

*T*he man's a rascal! He probably chats with Lucifer on the banks of the River Styx each week. Earlier, he said it was as hot as the hinges of Hades. He ought to know.

Katie clutched the quilt around herself more closely and shrank into its folds. Dear merciful heavens, he'd driven up brazen as a bottle-stealing sot and sat there in broad daylight so everyone could see who he was and what kind of business he wished to transact. She closed her eyes and moaned.

"Well, well!" a deep, oily voice schmoozed from beside her. Someone touched the blanket right over her knee. Her eyes shot open. She stared in horror at the bristle-faced, rheumy-eyed man. "New kitten comin' to the cathouse? I'll have to visit and listen to you purr."

Chris drew his Bowie knife. "I'll thank you to leave my sister alone."

"Hey!" The man jerked back his hand.

Another man elbowed the first. "Stop gawkin' at the woman and take a look at who's on them horses!"

"Who cares? They're dead."

Chris leaned forward. "You know who they are?"

"Not one. T'other's Skip Freelon. Wanted dead or alive."

"Well, he's dead, and I don't regret it." Chris turned the knife so the blade glittered in the hot Texas sun. "I'll slice the neck or plug a hole in anyone who tries to hurt my sis."

"She ain't really your sis, is she?"

Chris pulled some of the quilt off of her head to give the folks in the general vicinity a quick peek at her dirty face and tiny shoulders before flipping it back up. "Aye, sister. She's been sick."

"Don't look none too sick to me. Mite pale, but that's all."

"Best you think to step back. She lost her breakfast this mornin'."

The man warily shuffled back.

The other stranger scowled. "How come you got black hair and your sis gots blond?"

"Different mothers. Same Father." Chris thrust his face close to hers. "He gave us both blue eyes. See?"

She tilted her head toward Chris's. At the moment, he seemed the lesser of the evils. He hadn't told a lie, but he sure did manage to twist the truth to suit his needs.

"She's weak, my wee sister. Couldna take another day on the trail. Seein' as I didna see a hotel here in your town, I thought to ask the only place with beds to rent us a room for the night."

She made a sound of distress. He couldn't possibly expect her to set foot in that place—let alone spend a night!

"You don't happen to know any church ladies who'd come watch my sister for me for a short while, do you?"

"Dogtail don't have a church, and shady ladies is all we got. That there kid's looking right puny."

"Betwixt her ailin' and me needing to drop off the vermin who tried to jump us, I was glad to spy your town. I need to get her set."

As soon as the men ambled away, Chris gave Wren a quick squeeze. "Sorry, little one. We have to make do. You're playing along just fine. I'll dash inside for a minute and then come back out after you. If you think to cough every so often, it'd be a good idea."

She dug her fingers into his arm and hissed, "You don't mean to have us go inside there! You're just doing this to confuse Whelan, right?"

He raised his voice, "No, Katie honey. Father would understand that I'm just trying to take good care of you. We'll stay just till you're feeling a wee bit better." He wrapped the reins around the brake lever and jumped down.

Appalled at his plan, she decided this might be her only opportunity to get away. She reached for the reins.

Chris reached for her. He was faster.

—⁂—

"Katie, lass, are you runnin' a fever again? Your cheeks are all red. Come here." He deftly kept the quilt wrapped about her as he hauled her into his arms. She couldn't possibly extricate herself from the bundle. "We'll go inside. You gotta lay down and have somethin' to drink."

"Please, I beg of you," she whispered thickly against his neck, "don't take me in there!"

He patted her and said in a normal tone, "Everything'll work out." When he'd joined the rangers, he'd been given contacts where he'd find help. Though he'd never been here—or any other house of ill repute—Chris knew another ranger had saved this woman back when she'd just opened her establishment. Out of gratitude, she had an open door policy for every Texas Ranger. They were welcome at any time, for any reason. Reportedly, she provided an excellent cover for them, and she'd been good about sending telegrams and passing notes when necessary. All any ranger had to do was ask for Rahab—the biblical prostitute who helped the Israelites.

"Stop your wiggling. Trust me."

"No. Not if you plan to take me into one of those places!"

"Dinna go jumping to conclusions." Chris tightened his hold of her. The sight of her trembling lips cut straight through him. "Appearances can be deceiving."

"You said we were coming here to drop off those men and store my goods."

"And we will."

"Turn loose of me, you scoundrel." She twisted and smacked at him.

"That's some wildcat you got yourself."

Chris clamped still tighter around Katie and turned toward the sound of the entertained voice. A buxom redhead in a garish red-and-black dress lounged against the brothel's door.

Irritated by the fact that he hadn't been able to give chase to Whelan, that he was stuck with a woman who suddenly summoned gumption she should have displayed years ago so he wouldn't have had to rescue her, and that his presence provided entertainment for the residents of Dogtail, Chris wanted to snarl a response. He tamped down the urge and said in the blandest tone he could, "I'm looking for Rahab."

The woman's eyes widened very slightly, and she straightened up. "You've found her." She tilted her head toward her door. "C'mon in."

"If you try to take me in there, you'll be sorry." Katie resorted to pinching him because she couldn't do much else.

He glanced down. "Behave yourself."

"You behave yourself!" She stopped pinching him. For an instant, Chris thought she'd finally realized he didn't have any scandalous plans, but she slapped her hand onto the center of his shirt, scrunched in her fingers, and yanked the hair on his chest. "Listen to me," she ground out.

"No, you listen to me." He pried free and tossed her over his shoulder. "We're doing things my way."

Chris walked into the red brocade parlor of Lucille's and scanned the place. No telling who might be here. Even with Katie over his shoulder, he kept one hand on his pistol. The madam's cloyingly sweet perfume made his nose twitch.

"Rahab" led him into a private parlor, shut the door, and motioned for him to dump Katie into a chair. He shook his head.

An amused look crossed the redhead's face.

Before she opened her mouth and revealed he was a ranger, Chris said, "Miss Rahab, Katie's not been feeling much like herself—"

"You try hanging upside down and feeling decent!" Katie pummeled his back. "And speaking of decent—"

Chris went on speaking as if she hadn't said a thing. "She needs to rest and have something to drink."

"Follow me upstairs. I have a room available."

Katie began to thrash more desperately. "No! Please, no! You can't sell me to her!"

Chris half dumped Katie onto a nearby settee and growled, "How dare you think I'd betray you!"

She struggled to break free of the quilt and stand up. "First, you cost me my job. Then, you compromised my reputation by dragging me out overnight. Then, you killed a man. After that, you brought me to a. . .a. . .house of ill repute." She stammered, but with every accusation, her voice rose. "Now you have the nerve to order me to trust you?"

He stepped closer and towered over her. "I've dealt with thickheaded, stubborn mine mules that would look docile compared to you."

To his utter astonishment, she inched closer, stood on tiptoe, and prodded him in the center of his chest. "Don't you forget that. I'm stubborn, and I'm getting my way. I'm going to make you miserable until you listen to me and get me out of here!"

"It's not going to work." He reached down and brushed her finger away from his chest. "You made me miserable a minute after we first met. It hasn't made me follow any of your ridiculous instructions yet."

She clutched his hand. "I confessed I was stubborn. I'm not going to give up."

"If you're so intent on getting out of here, why are you hanging on to me for dear life?"

"Because I'm my brother's keeper. I can't leave you in a den of iniquity. It's fallen to me to drag you out of here and put you back on the straight and narrow."

She tugged. He twisted his wrist at that same moment. He broke free from her, and she stumbled backward to fall in a heap on the settee.

"You are a perfectly dreadful man. I can hardly wait to get away from you." She turned toward the soiled dove. "Miss Rahab, you are worthy of far more than any of this. The Lord Almighty sent His Son to redeem us all. I'm marching out the door. You're welcome to join me." The crazy woman started smoothing her skirts as if she were preparing for a Sunday stroll. "I'll help you establish a respectable new life."

"Katie," he growled.

"Everyone deserves a second chance," she snapped back. "God's forgiven me, and I have faith He'll do the same for Miss Rahab. Don't you interfere, Christopher Gregor. I want her to have this opportunity. I'm breaking free of this place, and she can, too."

"You couldn't find the door. How do you propose to escape?"

She heaved a huge sigh. "Honestly, Chris. You promised you'd help me get spectacles right away. Instead, you've dragged me across Texas and stuck me in the middle of a gunfight. Miss Rahab, do you see me wearing any spectacles?"

"No."

Katie folded her arms across her chest. "There you have it, Christopher. You have to take me out of here this instant and fulfill your promise. Miss Rahab, you're still welcome to come along."

"You need glasses?" Rahab laughed. "Go no further. I have a box full of them."

"There *you* have it, Katie." Chris relished turning her phrase back at her. "You can get your spectacles while I tend to other matters."

"Is there a doctor in town?"

He frowned and looked at her more carefully. "Why?"

"If you try to leave me here, you're going to need his services. It'll be your fault. You're provoking me."

"If that was supposed to scare me, it failed. I still have your derringer."

"It's past time that you return it. I need to dig through the wagon so I can get what I need to reload it."

"They're called bullets." Chris didn't bother to hide the wry tone in his voice.

"I know they're bullets." She sounded exasperated. "What I need are the instructions on how to load them. Never you mind. Miss Rahab, could you possibly assist me with that task?"

"No, she won't. I'm not giving that firearm back to you."

"Rahab" laughed. "Miss Katie, he'd be a fool to arm you in your present state. On the other hand, Mr. Gregor, a woman has the right to own and carry a firearm. Once she settles down, you should give it back to her."

Katie huffed. "You should listen to her. She's the voice of reason. Miss Rahab,

I'm sure you can see how calm I am now. Why, I'm utterly serene. Just look at me." She stuck out her hand, palm up. "I'll take that weapon now, Mr. Gregor."

"It'll get in the way while you try on spectacles. Rahab, Miss Katie's possessions are slowing us down. Whelan's on the loose nearby, and we shot two holes in him. He'll seek revenge. Can you temporarily store the wagon's contents?"

She thought for a moment, then nodded. "Darlene left. We'll put the stuff in her room. Was that a sewing machine under the blankets?"

"Yes." Katie's voice shook.

"I thought so. I have one myself."

"You do?" Chris blurted out the words.

"What's wrong with that?" Katie bristled. "Many women enjoy sewing. Like any other person, Miss Rahab needs clothes." Just after delivering her staunch defense, Katie turned three shades of red and said in a tiny voice, "Isn't that true, miss?"

"She really can't see." "Rahab's" brow puckered. "I'll have her things unloaded while she sorts through the box of glasses and you dispose of those bodies."

"You can't leave me here!"

He thought he'd calmed her down, but the panicky edge to Katie's outraged words triggered his anger. "Much as I'm tempted, I won't."

"You tend to things," "Rahab" said. "I'll have Miss Katie sit in the kitchen and give her the box of glasses."

"Fine." Chris started toward the door. "Don't take long, Katie. I want us out of here as soon as possible."

"You're the one who hauled me in here to begin with."

"She needs a disguise." He looked at Katie, then at "Rahab," and back to Katie. "See what you can do. She's scrawny. Turn her into a boy."

"Whelan isn't going to have to track you down." Katie glowered at him.

"Because you're going to kill me yourself?"

"Of course I wouldn't. I'm a lady. But your charming ways must have earned you dozens of enemies by now."

He smothered a laugh. For as much of a bother as she'd been thus far, at least the woman was finding her backbone. That might make the difference between life and death. Instead, Chris locked eyes with "Rahab." "Do whatever you need to. We'll leave in half an hour."

Chapter 7

Katie sat at the kitchen table, blinked, and tried to read the label on the coffee tin. Though the lettering grew bigger, it also started to blur. "No," she muttered to herself. She pulled off the spectacles and winced as the right arm of the pair caught in a wisp of hair. "Ouch."

"Find a pair yet?" "Rahab" asked from the doorway.

"No." Katie sighed. "But at this rate, you won't have to put me in a disguise. I'll be bald."

The cook plunked a plate down on the table. "Things'll look a lot better once you eat."

"Thank you. I hope so." Katie's stomach lurched as she glanced at the plate. "Things couldn't look any worse."

"Spaghetti today, Lucille," the cook proclaimed proudly.

"Wonderful!"

Katie stared at the plate. It looked like a mess of bloody worms. But it did smell good. Unable to summon the courage to pick up her fork, she opted for another pair of glasses. *I'm an ungrateful coward. That's what I am. What kind of Christian witness am I being? These women need the Lord in their lives. Dogtail doesn't have a church. It's up to me to be a beacon of love and hope.*

"Well?" the cook said.

"I want to say a prayer and ask God to bless the hands that prepared the food."

"It's a waste of time. Dogtail is a godforsaken town," the cook declared. "But it's awful nice of you to wanna ask Him to think of me."

"He doesn't just think of you. He wants you to be His daughter."

The cook shuffled away. "One father was more than enough."

Katie shoved on the spectacles. Everything wavered before her, but through the ripples, she saw "Rahab" shake her head and press a finger to her lips, then tilt her head toward the cook. Without another word, she left.

Katie took off the glasses, bowed her head, and prayed. When she lifted her

431

head, she resolutely picked up the fork. By the time she lifted the fork to her mouth, nothing remained on it. *Proof that God is protecting me.*

The cook laughed. "Wind the fork 'round and 'round in the noodles."

By following the instructions, Katie managed to take a bite. "Ohhh, this is delicious!"

"Katie, do any of the garments in your wagon fit you?"

Katie nodded in "Rahab's" direction. "My clothes are in a pink flowered sack."

"Those are all the same brown as what you're wearing. We're going to disguise you by hiding you in plain sight. What about the gorgeous blue riding outfit?"

"I don't know." Katie smiled. "I'll try it. Anything's better than his plan to make me wear britches."

She'd copied the ensemble from a sketch Belinda's grandmama brought from Paris years ago when she'd been a bride. As far as fashions went, it didn't follow the current trends, but the resulting ensemble couldn't be any lovelier. Belinda failed to show up for the past two fittings, and before then, she'd sniped about how her Parisian wedding gown was of far better quality than anything Katie could possibly sew.

The broadcloth skirt was split, and ecru colored ruffles spilled from the hem in a blatant show of femininity. A paletot style jacket featured long, bell-shaped sleeves, and Katie had stitched a soft, ecru batiste blouse to wear beneath it.

While eating and trying on another pair of glasses, Katie started to think of the garments she'd brought. *I'm starting anew. I could wear something pretty instead of drab now.* The thought cheered her immensely. Swallowing a bite, she slipped on the last pair of spectacles.

"I can see!" She grabbed the coffee can and read the words painted on it, then hopped out of the chair and skipped over toward the shelves. "Borden's milk. Tabasco sauce. Quaker oats. Campbell's beefsteak tomato in a can. Wheatena. Oh! Dr Pepper! I can read far better now than I could with my own glasses."

"Excellent." "Rahab" entered with the beautiful blue outfit. "Now let's see to your transformation."

—⁓—

Chris paced back and forth along the hallway. His boots made a measured sound that wasn't dissimilar to the steady beat of a metronome. He pulled out Da's gold pocket watch and gritted his teeth. He'd given them half an hour. It had been fifty-eight minutes now. Snapping the case closed, he barreled toward the kitchen.

His plan had been to ride hard and get to the next railroad town. If they could hop the train, get off, backtrack, and zigzag, he could tuck her in with his family and be back out after Whelan.

But so far, nothing had gone according to his plans. As a result, he'd put together saddlebags for them. Small bags of jerked beef, dried fruit, and nuts would do. He didn't waste space with beans, rice, or coffee—those would require a cook fire. That would give Whelan a beacon. Still, Chris carefully wax-dipped the heads of several matches and stored some in each pack, along with a knife wrapped in a towel and a bit of soap. Most important, he supplied them each with two canteens of water. The second outlaw's horse was sound, so Chris loaded an extra blanket and water on him. That way, if one of the horses went lame, they'd not have to slow down.

"We're leaving. Now." He plowed through the kitchen door and stopped short. "What happened to your hair?"

—⁓—

Katie reached up and tugged one of the spiraling tendrils at her temple. "You wanted me to look different."

"You could have stuffed it up under a hat. You didn't have to go changing the color!"

"It's very attractive." "Rahab's" voice took on an edge. "It puts me in mind of cinnamon. You said you wanted to disguise her, and henna was an excellent solution. The reddish tinge is becoming, don't you think?"

He grabbed a hat from the table and shoved it toward Katie. "You look different. That's what's important. Lucille, thanks for all of your help. Katie, let's mount up."

"But I was going to see the marshal."

"I already dropped in on him." Chris took her elbow and hauled her to her feet.

"Thank you so much, Miss. . .Lucille." Katie turned to the cook. "And thank you for that wonderful spaghetti, too. Once I get settled, I'll be sure to send you my address so you can mail me your recipe."

"Lucille, I appreciate all you've done. One of the men I brought in had a bounty on his head. The sheriff will see that you receive it."

He took Katie over to the mare hitched beside his gelding. Katie turned back toward the cathouse. "We have an extra mount, Lucille. Why don't you come along?"

"I'll stay and guard your sewing machine."

"I'd rather have you with us than own a sewing machine."

His anger at her dawdling evaporated. She prized her sewing machine, depended on it for her living, yet she'd not given a moment's thought about sacrificing it.

"You darling girl." The madam smiled. "Off with you now."

Katie squeezed his arm and said softly, "Maybe she's afraid you don't want her along. Invite her."

"Dinna hound the woman, lass. She can walk away from there anytime she pleases. Just be grateful she was there to help us out today."

Katie cleared her throat. "Mr. Gregor—"

"No more." He scowled so she'd understand he wouldn't put up with any further delays. "We've lost precious travel time already."

"Fine." She glowered back at him. "But I ought to warn you, I've never ridden a horse."

"You'd best learn fast." He locked his hands around Katie's waist and hefted her into the saddle. "Stay close and stay quiet."

Chris wanted to make up time. He'd never planned to waste so much of it trying to stuff Katie into a disguise. Why Lucille chose this one was beyond him. With her hair up in a loose, soft swirl and dressed in that get-up, Katie looked like a princess. The way the waist on the riding outfit nipped in showed off her tiny middle. Even the spectacles looked nice. Instead of the stingy little round lenses she'd worn when he first spied her, this pair looked like jewelry and let him appreciate the fine sight of her blue, blue eyes. *Well, Whelan won't recognize her now.*

She seemed fairly stable in the saddle, but Chris forced himself to keep to a reasonable speed. She needed to get her bearings. When she sighed, he steeled himself for the inevitable complaints.

"She's beautiful. It's a pity we don't know her name."

"I dinna care what she's called, so long as she's swift and sure."

"She is quite swift."

Chris shook his head. "We've barely set a pace. I want you to feel steady in the saddle, so we've started out slow. I'll be speeding us up. It'll be gradual, so you can adjust to each change. You'll have to be able to ride at a full-on, dead run if Whelan comes close."

"I thought we were managing a remarkable pace."

He decided to give her a few pointers. "I'm not going to mince words or be delicate. If you don't want to get sore, I have to be blunt."

She hesitated a moment, then nodded.

"Always keep your thighs and upper calves right up against the mare. It'll help keep you balanced and tell her what you want her to do." Chris thought he'd heard her gasp when he mentioned the intimate parts of her "limbs," but he ignored her reaction. Instead, he went on, "Keep your knees and ankles bent so they absorb some of the jarring motion so you dinna slap against the cantle."

An icy voice inquired from behind her fancy hat's veil, "Is there anything else?"

"Aye. Dinna tiptoe. Heels down, toes up. When I get us to a fast trot, you'll see me actually stand slightly in the stirrups and rest my hand on the saddle horn. Bend at the hips and keep your elbows in."

He rode alongside her for a while, but her rigid posture and frosty silence let him know he'd offended her sensibilities. They went from a walk to a slow trot. Unwilling to put up with her snit, Chris pulled ahead. He knew the territory well. At one point, he stopped and ordered, "Have a swig from your canteen."

She nodded, loosened her veil, and obeyed. Up close, Chris could see through the veil fairly well. She seemed to be holding up satisfactorily. After she screwed the lid back on the canteen, he pulled a small, smooth stone from his pocket. "Suck on this for the remainder of the day. It keeps your mouth moist so you don't get so thirsty."

"Thank you."

"Miss Regent, this is a rough land. We're in a tough situation. I'm not trying to offend you by being straightforward in my speech. You canna get huffy because I'm a plainspoken man. If it means I have to remark on specific portions of your person to teach you how to do things, I'm not going to mince my words."

"I wouldn't expect otherwise, Mr. Gregor."

He took off his hat and wiped the sweat from his brow. "Then why are you so mad?"

She daintily arranged ruffles on the cuff of her blouse. In a tiny voice, she admitted, "I'm not angry, sir. I'm embarrassed."

He laughed in relief, then demanded, "Stop being goosey."

—༝—

Katie stopped outside the rail station, dampened her handkerchief, and blotted Christopher's forehead. He jumped, but she held him still. "Shhh," she murmured. "The sun's been too much for you."

"What gave you that cockeyed notion?"

She sighed. He'd just indulged in an embarrassing shouting match when he bought the tickets, claiming that the price was far too high when they'd be getting off only two stops away. "You bought tickets on the train."

"I know I did."

Her worries mounted. He'd already given vent to his ire, and she didn't want to set him off again. What would he do when she pointed out his error? She moistened her lips, then gave him a pitying look. "The tickets you bought are on the train going back the way we came."

A slow smile creased his tanned face. "I know." He took hold of her arm and led her down the boardwalk.

Her eyes widened. "You did it on purpose."

Minutes later, dressed in widow's weeds and a heavily veiled hat Chris had just bought her, Katie bought tickets for the train. He'd sent her to do it while he turned in their third horse to the local sheriff.

A short time later on the train, Katie fought the urge to sleep. The rocking motion and her exhaustion tempted her to close her eyes. She hid a yawn behind her hand.

"Sleep, lass."

She gave him a guilty look.

"You've earned a good, long rest. Go on."

The next thing she knew, something was missing. Motion. Sound. She opened her eyes and let out a gasp. In the dead of night, she'd used Mr. Gregor's upper arm as a pillow. Mortified, she sat ramrod straight and wouldn't look at him.

"This is our stop." He rose.

She disembarked and waited as he claimed their horses from the livestock car. The very thought of sitting in the saddle made her want to wail like a pinched baby.

In the early dawn light, Chris beckoned her. She pretended not to see him. "Katie, come, lass."

"You didn't have to bellow at me," she muttered as she gathered her skirts and joined him.

The man had the nerve to laugh.

"You're demented, Chris Gregor. And you're out of your mind if you think you're going to talk me into riding all day again."

"We willna ride all day."

She shot him a sideways glance. "I'm not going to ride even half of the day."

He cupped her elbow. "You've got a sassy streak, woman."

"It's your fault. Until you barged into my life, I was sedate and ladylike. Where are you taking me now?"

"You'll see."

One of the horses exhaled loudly, his loose lips causing a scoffing sound. Katie looked over her shoulder. "I couldn't agree more emphatically." A few minutes later, she heaved a loud sigh. "Had I known you planned a procession down the center of the street, I might have woven flower garlands for the horses so people would think we were a small parade. As it is, anyone spying us will be certain we've taken leave of our senses."

He tossed the horses' reins around a hitching post and dragged her around the building.

"What a darling little cottage!"

He let out a rude snort. "It's Duncan's cobbler shop." He tugged her to make her turn to the side.

Katie stopped so suddenly, he nearly pulled her over. She'd spent her life in rough cabins, squalid rooms, and shacks—but it never stopped her from dreaming that one day, she'd live in a big white house with airy-looking lacework and a veranda. The home of her dreams stood before her.

He slipped his arm around her waist. "You're almost there. Just a few more steps now."

Anticipation gave her a little spurt of energy. *I get to see this place.* As they walked up the steps to a wondrous-looking home, the sound of a baby's cries met them.

She balked. *I was an idiot to think this was his home and he was done dragging me all the way across Texas. A bachelor wouldn't live in such a grand place. Well, maybe I'll get to rest or freshen up.* The baby let out an ear-piercing cry. *I won't rest. That's for sure.*

"Whose house is this?"

"Mine." Pride rang in his voice. "I built it."

"It's magnificent."

"'Tis who's on the inside that counts, not what's on the outside." Anticipation colored his words as he opened the door.

A woman in the rocking chair beamed. "You're home!"

"Aye, that I am." Pleasure saturated those simple words. He slipped past Katie, kissed the fussy baby on the head, and then brushed a kiss on the woman's cheek. "Ooch, now, what's amiss with our wee little lassie?"

He told me he wasn't married.

"She's cutting another tooth." The woman patted her baby and smiled at Katie. "Hello, I'm Mercy."

Mercy is his sister-in-law. Recalling that fact made relief wash over Katie. *He could have told me they all lived together.*

"This is Katie Regent. I thought you could use a little help, and Katie is needing a safe place to stay awhile."

"You're more than welcome to stay as long as you'd like. Now that Duncan's married and moved across the street, his room is empty."

"Thank you."

A man came down the stairs. "Who are you talking—Chris!" He strode over and smacked his brother on the back with a force that would have felled an ordinary man.

"Rob!" Chris gave him a powerful embrace.

Clearly, they were brothers. Both had black hair and were tall and broad shouldered. Chris's profile was craggier, his voice deeper. He rested a hand lightly on Katie's shoulder. "Katie's come to stay awhile. Rob, I'm needing to speak with you a moment."

The men stepped outside. Katie cleared her throat. "Your daughter is beautiful."

"Thank you. Ordinarily, she's better tempered than this. She's calming down. As soon as she's asleep again, I'll get you settled in. You look exhausted."

"I'd be a liar if I pretended I wasn't."

Mercy laughed. "Between Rob and Chris having to come and go as they do and me with the baby, we all agreed long ago that sleep is a precious commodity. No one will think anything of you sleeping the whole day away."

The door opened and the men entered. "Oh Chris." Mercy's smile melted. "I know that look. Don't tell me you have to leave right away."

"I'll be going after breakfast."

Katie let out a dismayed gasp.

"It's the wisest course of action." Chris nodded curtly. "Whelan's at a disadvantage. I've got to get him."

"I don't care how much of a bounty he has on his head." Katie fought the tingling sensation behind her eyes. She refused to shed tears. "A cornered animal is the most dangerous. Let someone else assume the duty of getting him."

"It's a matter of honor and duty."

"You'll not sway him," another man said from the front door. Katie about jumped out of her skin at the unexpected intrusion until she saw the man's size and coloring. Clearly, he was the other brother. Face grim, Duncan said to her, "Texas Rangers always get their man."

It took a second for what he said to filter through the haze of exhaustion. The meaning hit her like someone had just doused her with a bucket of icy water. Katie shook so badly, she could scarcely even breathe. Slowly, she turned toward Chris. "Don't tell me you're a Texas Ranger!"

Chapter 8

Fury made Katie's voice shake. Aye and 'twas fury, all right. Baffled by her reaction, Chris attributed it to her exhaustion. " 'Tis true."

"Where's your badge?"

He let out an exasperated sound. "Rangers dinna wear badges."

"I've seen a ranger's badge!"

"I'm sure Katie isn't questioning your honor, Chris." Mercy stood and slipped Elspeth into Katie's arms. That show of trust let him know he'd better choose his words carefully. "Katie, it wasn't until Chris joined that I learned most rangers don't wear badges. They carry special warrants of authority."

Katie clasped the baby to herself and moved from side to side. Chris wondered if she was rocking the babe or trying to soothe herself. The dark circles beneath her eyes told the truth. She was reeling from exhaustion.

Katie looked down and rubbed her cheek against Elspeth's soft, blond baby curls. Her shoulders slumped, and she passed the baby back to Mercy. "It was nice of you to offer to let me stay, but I can't."

"What?" Chris roared.

Katie straightened her shoulders. "You've harped at me about how Whelan is bound to track me down. I've come to my good senses and realized staying here endangers everyone else—especially the baby."

"The only place you're going," Chris said through clenched teeth, "is to bed."

She stood toe-to-toe with him and tilted her head back to glare at him. "You're sinfully bossy, and I don't have to put up with it. I can come and go as I please."

"Nae, you canna." He waited a second as the air crackled with tension. "You're an important witness. If you dinna pledge to remain here of your own free will, I'll put you in protective custody."

"I believe I'll start breakfast," Mercy murmured.

"I'll help." Katie turned away from him, grasping at the opportunity to get away from him.

Chris grabbed her arm and spun her back around. "You'll not do a thing until you give me your word."

"You've got my money and my derringer."

"Nice try, Miss Regent. You didna distract me, though."

She shoved back an errant curl. "You have the winning ways of a rabid skunk, Chris Gregor. And nerve! You have the nerve to demand a promise when all this time you've been lying to me."

"I never once lied." He glowered at her. "My personal information was none of your business. Now are you going to be reasonable, or am I going to haul you off to the jailhouse and lock you up?"

"Personal information. None of my business," she muttered. "Fine. If that's how you want it, that's how you'll get it. I'll stay here."

"Until I give you permission to leave," he added.

A cry of outrage curled in her throat. Chris silently admired her cunning. He'd have done the same thing—plotted a way to keep his word and still get his way. Each time he looked about the house and spied a piece of the gingerbread embellishment, it reminded him of how a prompt agreement could come back to haunt someone. Instead of rashly agreeing to anything, he now took time to consider every angle someone might use to get the better part of a pact.

"Fine. I'll stay until you get so sick of me, you'll push me out the door. There. Are you happy now?" Before he could respond, she turned to Mercy. "I'm usually not like this. Even a saint would be liable to lose his composure around your brother-in-law. Well, I can't blame him for all of it. I did let him goad me into this. It's my fault, too. I apologize for bringing strife into your beautiful home. Truly, I do."

Mercy reached over and took her hand. "The Gregor men take getting used to. They're hardheaded, but when you get past that, you'll recognize that their motives are pure. Chris loves the Lord and is seeking justice. He's doing his duty."

"Besides," he tacked on, "you willna have to put up with me much. My responsibilities keep me busy."

Katie sighed wearily. "If that was supposed to make me feel better, you failed."

———

Chris ignored the kink in his back and watered his horse before setting out his bedroll. Frustration filled him. Almost two months earlier, he'd dumped Katie into his family's care and resumed his search for Whelan. Every other week or so, he'd drop by home. Each time he did reassured him that Katie was happy there.

Only something didn't feel quite right. He couldn't put his finger on it. Well, tomorrow he'd drift by on his way to Dallas. Maybe spend two days this time. With that thought, he bedded down for the night.

I'm making a fool of myself. It's probably just that I haven't managed to get Katie's belongings shipped to her. I'll do that soon. Real soon. And 'twill be good to see the lass again. She's won the hearts of my family, and Mercy canna sing her praises enough. And singing—aye, the little songbird is humming or singing a fair portion of the time. She's found contentment e'en without her possessions, but 'tis her worries that hold her back from being completely happy. That truth is undeniable.

Katie Regent is a bonny lass, and as soon as I've got Whelan behind bars, she can stop fretting. Certainly, there must be men calling on her. Instead of dreading Whelan, she can turn her mind toward marriage. A man couldna court and wed a sweeter lass.

—⁂—

Hot, dusty, and hungry, Chris strode up the steps at home the next day. To his keen disappointment, no one was there. Then he heard Katie's voice coming from the garden. Chris headed that direction.

The sight that met him ought to have been captured in a painting. He stood for a moment and stared. The henna Lucille had tinted Katie's hair with had finally rinsed away, so her hair was back to being the exact same soft shade as a newborn fawn. She'd lost her frail look and glowed with health. Aye, bringing her here had been a grand plan.

Katie held Elspeth's tiny hand and steadied her as she took a few halting steps along a stone pathway. "Aren't you a big girl! So big!"

"Bee-ah! Bee-ah!" Elspeth declared.

Chris chuckled as he headed toward them. "Is my niece asking for beer?"

Katie laughed. "She's saying she's a big girl. And you are, aren't you, precious?" She swept Elspeth into her arms. The sight of Katie cuddling a baby seemed so natural, so right. Every time he came home, Chris marveled at how easily she fit in. He cleared his throat. "Where is everybody?"

"Duncan's in his workshop. Carmen went to Otto's to help her sister serve the field hands. Mercy is assisting Rob over in his clinic. He's removing tonsils today."

"I see. I've arranged to have your things delivered. They ought to be here any day now."

"You did?" Her eyes sparkled. "Thank you!" Just as quickly, her smile melted away. "Does the livery here store goods?"

"I suppose they might. Why?"

She hitched her right shoulder. "After Mercy's had her baby and is recovered, it would be wise for me to move."

" 'Tis nonsense you just spoke. Utterly foolish. Just because Whelan hasna discovered your whereabouts isna license for you to venture far."

"He must be far busier trying to evade you than searching for me."

"I always said the man was a fool." *What got into me? Why did I say that?* Chris shifted from one foot to the other.

"I planned to go to the mercantile today. The reservoir on the stove is full. If you'd like, you can empty it into the tub and have a good, long soak."

"I confess I'm taking a shine to that notion."

She pretended to nibble on the fingers of Elspeth's bitty little hands. "Mmm. Mmmm. Mmmm!"

Elspeth giggled with glee.

The way Katie sometimes peeped over the tops of her spectacles made a man feel as if she were flirting. In fact, she used those glasses better than most Southern belles used a fan. Best of all, coyness had nothing to do with it. Her natural charm and the effect of her blue, blue eyes in their shy appraisals made his heart beat faster. So was the habit she had of slightly pursing her lips as she considered her words before speaking. Made a man want to pull her close and share a kiss before the opportunity was lost.

Whoa. What am I thinking?

"I'm serious, Chris. Mercy is due any day now, and I'll help her as she recovers. But after that, it's time for me to move on."

"You gave me your word that you'd stay until I released you."

"So, release me."

He shook his head. "You'd be helpless."

"You once told me you'd see to it that I learned how to fire a gun. Teach me, and then I won't be helpless."

"That would only lend you a false sense of security. It would take considerable time and practice before you'd achieve any accuracy." He could see his words didn't satisfy her. Chris decided to use the truth to scare her into behaving.

"The loot we recovered that day from Whelan and the men? It's been identified. Part of it is from another bank robbery. The watch belonged to the bank president. He was killed. The rest came from a ranch they hit."

The color drained from her face.

He gently eased Elspeth from her arms and used his other hand to tilt Katie's face to his. "Dinna think you'll be safe from him, lass. His soul is black as pitch, and he'll stop at nothing to get what he wants. You must stay here."

Tears welled up in her eyes. Her attempt to blink them back failed.

"I'm sorry to scare you, but running off will get you killed."

She pulled away from him and brushed away her tears. More trailed down her pale cheeks. "You have to let me go, Chris. You have to. For your family's sake. What if he finds me here?"

"If Whelan wanted revenge on my family, he'd have done so long ago. 'Tis no secret where we live."

"You don't understand." She'd taken to wringing her hands. The distress in her voice tore at him.

Cupping Elspeth to his chest, he used his mildest tone. "Are you not happy here?"

"I've never been so happy. But that doesn't matter."

"Of course it matters. I want you to be happy and safe."

"But I'm miserable!"

She wasn't making any sense. Chris stared at her. Maybe Duncan or Rob could explain this to him. As married men, maybe they would be able to clarify what feminine irrationality applied to the situation.

"I can't take it anymore. I have to go!"

"You're not going anywhere," he half roared.

Elspeth chimed in. "No, no, no, no, no, no, no."

"But Whelan—"

"Leave Whelan to me, Katie."

Anguish clearly twisted her features. "But. . .he's my brother."

Chapter 9

Your brother."

She couldn't see his face clearly through her tears, but his voice was calm. Katie bit her lip, started to nod, and then blurted out, "Stepbrother."

"Stepbrother." His voice grew deeper as he echoed her words.

Katie reached over and patted Elspeth's back. "I have to go now. You take good care of her."

His left hand shot up and manacled her wrist. "You're not going anywhere." He hauled her in his wake over toward the workshop, bellowing, "Duncan!"

Duncan shot out of his workshop. "Aye?"

"Take Elspeth." Chris gently transferred her and pressed a kiss on her cheek as she babbled a stream of sounds. His tenderness made Katie cry all the harder.

"What's amiss?" Duncan held the baby protectively.

"Miss Regent."

"Katie?" Duncan gave her a baffled look.

"You'll never guess what she's been hiding." Chris didn't even pause. "Whelan's her brother."

"Brother?" Duncan's brows shot upward.

"Stepbrother," she corrected tearfully.

"What other lies have you told us?" Chris demanded.

"I never once lied." Anger shot through her. "The night you brought me here and I discovered what you are, I begged you to let me go. You'd hidden the truth, and when I confronted you, you proclaimed you'd never once lied to me and that your personal information was none of my business."

"It wasn't."

"You can't have it both ways, Christopher Gregor. You can't fault me when you did the selfsame thing!"

" 'Tis not the same thing a-tall! My business is to bring that criminal to justice."

He marched her down the street, kicked open the jail door, and shoved her into a cell. The keys jangled loudly as he locked her in.

"What are you doing? You can't lock me up. I've done nothing wrong."

"Accessory after the fact," he said curtly. "You have knowledge concerning a criminal and did nothing to bring him to justice. Any blood he's shed since the day of our shootout—that blood is on your hands, Miss Regent."

"That's outrageous!" She clenched her fingers around the bars and rattled the gate. It made a horrible clatter but didn't yield. "How could I possibly know what he was doing when you were with me?"

"Criminals have hideaways. Where's your brother's?"

"I told you I didn't know where my brother was. I told you the day we met!"

"I scarcely believe you'd announce to all and sundry that your brother's face was on a WANTED poster and you knew his whereabouts."

"I haven't seen him in five years. Not until that day."

"That makes for a touching story, but I don't buy it. Not for one second. He's been all around Texas, wreaking havoc. You think I'm so thickheaded I would think his stumbling into you in the wide open spaces of Texas was just a coincidence?"

Slowly, she uncurled her fingers and let loose of the bars. Sinking onto the narrow wooden plank bed, she held her shaking hands tightly together. "Believe whatever you want to. I haven't done anything wrong."

Chris sat down at the desk and pulled a sheet of paper from the drawer. The only sound in the jail was the scratch of his pen's nib on the paper.

I've been such a fool. I knew this day would come and he'd be furious. I knew it. So why did I always look forward to him coming home? And why am I so hurt that he's acting just as I knew he would?

Minutes passed. Finally, she said, "The clock's not wound."

He kept his back to her and gave a maddening shrug.

"Just how long are you planning on leaving me in here?"

"As long as it takes." He swiveled the oak chair around. The smile on his face chilled her to the core. "The game has changed, Wren. I'm no longer chasing the rat. I'm setting a trap with irresistible bait: you."

It didn't escape her notice that he'd reverted to calling her "Wren" or "Miss Regent." The way he'd pronounce "Katie" accentuated his Scottish burr, and it always made her feel as if a tiny measure of affection or protection came with the name change. But that was gone now.

"Aye, Wren. He'll come to get you."

"You're wasting your time. He left me behind when Mama died. If he wouldn't take care of me when I was only fifteen, what makes you think he'll suddenly turn into a dutiful brother? Not everyone is blessed to have fine brothers like you do."

"Your story is touching, but it's hogwash, and we both know it. A lass out on her own at such a tender age wouldna be able to afford a fancy sewing machine. I dinna ken why I didna wonder about that earlier. But that alone condemns you."

"I scrimped and saved and sacrificed for that machine!"

He gave her a mocking smile and applauded. "I believe you missed your calling in life, Wren. You should have become an actress. 'Tis rare to find such talent."

Stinging from his insult, she backed away and sat on the board. "You don't want justice; you want revenge. You're mistaken, though. You loved your friend. My step-brother doesn't value me."

"We'll see about that."

—m—

"I'd like an envelope, please."

Chris held his hand out by the bars. "Pass me the letter."

"The United States mail is private!"

"Your letter isn't in the mail yet, and it's standard practice to review all communications entering and leaving a jailhouse." He stared at her.

"Oh, all right." She huffed, yet she carefully turned her hand sideways so the pages wouldn't become wrinkled.

An intelligent woman, Kathryn Regent might well have a code of some kind. Chris moved to a sunny spot and looked down at the paper. *Dear Lucille. . .*

Chris snorted. He'd not underestimate her. The woman was as wily as could be. He shoved the letter onto his desk. "You don't really expect me to send that."

"I do. Even the Romans permitted Paul to send letters from jail."

Duncan came in, and Chris spoke to his brother, "Stay here for a few minutes while I send off a few telegrams and do another errand."

"Have you taken leave of your senses?" Duncan gawked at him. "Open that cell and free that lass this verra minute!"

"I don't tell you how to make shoes and saddles. Don't tell me how to do my job." He kept possession of the keys and stalked out of the jail.

By the time he'd sent the necessary telegrams and arranged for an article to run on the front page of the *Gazette*, Chris dared to hope he'd finally bring down Whelan. He'd need to deputize several men in town and was making a mental list of likely prospects when he walked back into the jailhouse.

"What," he roared, "is going on here?"

Mercy was pushing a quilt through the bars of Wren's cell. Carmen finished making up the bunk in the adjacent cell. A canning jar with flowers sat on his desk. Rob tromped in with a fresh bucket of water and a dipper, and Elspeth slept contentedly in a wicker basket in the middle of the activity.

"You put the lass in our care," Duncan asserted. "Aye, you did. So we're caring for her."

"I remembered you saying something about protective custody when you brought Katie home to us." Mercy straightened out and rubbed her lower back. "So Carmen and I decided she needed help making this dreary place more comfortable. We'll each take turns staying with her. It's not proper for her to be alone with you."

"She's locked inside the cell."

"And a sad state of affairs that is." Robert gave Chris a baleful glare. "I'll not hold with blaming an innocent for the wrongs someone else has done."

"Does it occur to any of you that Whelan has managed to avoid capture even with two bullet holes in him? That she might be tipping him off?"

"And how would I be doing that?"

"Any number of ways. Telegrams—"

"Carmen and I would know if she's sent any." Mercy shook her head. "She hasn't."

"Letters. She wrote one today."

"To Lucille?" Carmen smiled. "I hope you told her cook how much we love that recipe for the spaghetti."

"See? She's been sending letters." Chris spied something and stomped across the floor. He opened the small, glass-fronted door on the clock and stopped the pendulum. After closing it, he opened the face and reset the hands. "No one touches that. No one."

"It's just a clock." Mercy gave him a baffled look.

"Connant's clock." Chris stared at them. "The hands mark the time of his passing, and there they'll stay until Whelan's brought to justice."

"Time waits for no man," Rob said.

"Time might not, but I do. God's put the means in my hands to capture Connant's murderer. I'll sit and wait. The rest of you, out of here. I'll not have you in danger."

"Oh, we're safer if we're all together." Carmen smiled. "Don't you think so, Mercy?"

"Absolutely. Why, if you are at your house and I'm at mine, then Duncan's in his shop and Rob is in the clinic, Whelan might sneak up on any or all of us. There's strength in numbers."

"You have a point." Chris paused a moment. He knew he had their attention. "Carmen, you and Mercy can go stay at her grandda's or with your sister. Rob, you can go along. Duncan, I'm deputizing you."

"But—"

"This isna a voting matter. I'm the law, and you'll obey my edict. Rob, Duncan—your first duty is to your wives and the bairns. You ken 'tis a dangerous trap I've set."

"If it's dangerous, you can't put Katie in the middle," Mercy protested.

"I am in the middle of it." Katie's admission surprised him. "Whelan is wicked. From the beginning, I've feared for your safety. Please, please go. I can't bear the thought of you being in danger because of me."

"Let's all have a word of prayer before you go," Duncan said quietly.

They started to join hands, and Rob slid his hands between the bars. "You, too, Katie."

"It's kind of you, Rob, but I don't belong."

Carmen opened her mouth to protest, but Duncan shook his head.

Chris joined them, but it felt wrong. He felt like an outsider in his own family, and they'd wanted to include his enemy's sister.

Chapter 10

Having slept on hard pallets most of her life, Wren decided sleep would be a refuge. She curled up with her back to Christopher and huddled beneath the summer-weight quilt Carmen brought her. All evening long, men came and left. They'd spoken in low murmurs and cast odd looks at her.

Lord, I don't know what to do. Everything is so mixed up. Only You can untie all of these tangled threads. Please, Father, keep each of my new friends safe. Don't allow harm to come to any of them. Set Your angels about them for protection.

My attitude was wrong. Deep in my heart, I knew I should have told Chris the truth a long time ago. He was kinder to me than anyone has ever been, but fear and pride led me to keep my secret. Through it all, I haven't had faith that You would work things out. I confess that shameful fact and beg Your forgiveness. Be my refuge and strength, Father, I pray. Amen.

"Katie, lass," Duncan called softly. "Dinna weep."

She hadn't realized she'd been crying. She took a few choppy breaths. "I'm sorry. I'm okay."

"Aye, you're fine. Chris, I'm rememberin' that prayer Ma taught us. 'Now I lay me—' "

Chris's deep voice joined in, " '—down to sleep. I pray the Lord my soul to keep.' "

" 'If I should die before I wake, I pray the Lord my soul to take.' " Wren said softly, "When I was a little girl, a friend at school taught me that."

"Ma didna like that last part," Chris said.

"Nae, she didna. I'm trying to remember. Something about say and day."

Chris cleared his throat. " 'In everything I do or say, I'll serve my God both night and day.' "

"That's so very dear." Wren snuggled into the pillow. "You were blessed to have such wonderful parents."

"Aye, we were." The brothers spoke the same words at the same time.

The unity they displayed stunned her. *What would it be like to have grown up in a home where the parents were godly and love flowed so freely? What would it have been like to have a brother who loved me?*

—⁂—

The next morning, the rail station manager showed up with Katie's belongings. Chris was off somewhere doing something secretive. Leonard from the mercantile had been deputized and left in charge. Uncertain of what to do, he allowed Wren to have her sewing machine in her cell so she wouldn't be bored.

Old Mr. Rundsdorf came in to pay a call on her. He sat outside her cell and sanded one of his mesquite wood bowls to a smooth finish. "When you get out of there, you can open up a shop and keep treats in the bowl, just as Duncan does."

"Thank you." She smiled at the dear old man. His show of support touched her.

"When you open that shop, I'll be your first customer, too. This shirt you made me—I've never had one fit this well."

After Mr. Rundsdorf left, Leonard allowed her scissors and a bolt of fabric, so she used the benchlike bunk as a cutting table. Desperate to have something to occupy her mind, she determined to make several baby gowns for Mercy.

"Miss Regent, I have some lunch here for you."

She looked up. "Oh. Thank you."

Leonard's ears were bright red. "I'll have to ask you to go sit on the bunk whilst I open the cell door."

"Of course." As he brought in the sandwich and apple, she let out a small laugh. "Somehow, I had the notion that the only meals served in jail consisted of bread and water."

"We'll make sure you don't go hungry."

Late in the afternoon, Leonard stretched. "You sure have been stitching up a storm. That foot treadle makes for quick seams. Puts the hand-turned wheel models to shame."

"The stitches are strong and even, too."

"Never paid much mind to how much work goes into itty-bitty baby gowns. Mercy Gregor's going to be tickled pink to get those."

"She's been a dear friend." Wren finished one last row of pintucking. "I'd like to hide them until the baby comes. Is there someplace you could put them?"

"I reckon one of the desk drawers will do. Since we don't have a sheriff, nothing's in them."

She handed him the gowns, and Leonard chuckled. "Lookie there. You fancified these everyday ones by stitching colored lines on 'em. The buttons match. You gonna sew like this once you open that shop Mr. Rundsdorf was talking about?"

"I'll have to see how God works things out."

"Plenty of folks 'round here are bendin' God's ear, telling Him what they think He ought to do."

"I've done my share of that, too." Wren started cleaning up. "It was foolish of me. I should have done a lot more listening and a lot less talking."

"Funny," Christopher said from the doorway. "I've been thinking you didn't do nearly enough talking."

"Mr. Gregor! Mr. Gregor!" Nestor scrambled through the door.

"Nestor, what's amiss?"

"José got my shooter and won't give it back."

"Hmmm." Chris turned around and squatted to be at eye level with the boy. Wren watched how he acted as if the boy's concern was the most important thing in the world. " 'Tis a pity. A sorrowful pity. Could you be telling me just how José took possession of such a fine treasure?"

"We were shooting marbles. It landed on the line. I say that means I keep it. José says he does."

"Now that surely does give me pause to think. I'm sure there's a rule about it, but it's been a good, long while since I played marbles."

Nestor nodded. "Yeah. You're really old."

To his credit, Chris didn't laugh or scold. He nodded his head. "Aye. And years of experience have taught me that 'tis important to play by the rules. Mr. Rundsdorf does considerable reading. I'm betting he has a book that has the rules for all sorts of games."

"You think so?"

"Aye, I do. You and José are good friends. 'Twould be a crying shame to ruin everything o'er a marble—e'en if it is a prized shooter. Why dinna the pair of you agree to follow the rule, then seek out what the rule book has to say?"

"That's fair."

"Off with you." Chris rose and sauntered into the jailhouse.

"To my recollection," Leonard mused, "anything on the line is out."

"I dinna rightly recall, but they can look up the answer together instead of squabbling. A fight is rarely worth the cost. Best the boys learn it early on."

He'll be a spectacular father some day. She sighed. *If we'd had the same upbringing, maybe Whelan would have turned out better. Well, it's too late now.*

By the third morning of waiting for Whelan to take the bait, Chris sat down at Connant's old desk. The rhythmic clatter of Wren's sewing machine barely even registered any longer. She'd been keeping busy, and that suited him fine. Otherwise, she sang or hummed hymns a good portion of the time. Granted, she had the voice of a songbird, but her selections were intentional—and she hadn't sung other than when specifically asked when they'd been on the road. Now she sang and hummed constantly. Just about the time she'd finished yet another hymn and he felt certain she was using those sacred tunes just to bolster her proclamations of being a Christian, she fretted that the sleeves on the shirt she was making were a tad long. Then she shifted like the Texas wind and launched into a rendition of a silly ditty he'd overheard children sing, "Do Your Ears Hang Low?"

When night fell and she couldn't see well enough to sew any longer, the woman would strike up a conversation with whoever happened to be on guard. He'd had to grit his molars at some of the things that came out of her mouth.

At first he thought she was weaving tales to get sympathy. Fanciful tales. Like the one where she'd walk the length of a hitching post while singing to earn a free supper from a diner. With a nickname like Wren, that tale took little imagination to concoct.

When Stu Key's sleeve popped a button, she stitched it right back in place while Stu kept on his shirt. She offered, saying she had the needle and thread handy. Besides, she'd done that same task a few times when her stepfather couldn't be bothered to leave the poker table.

Her stepfather might have been a gambler and her brother was a murdering robber, but she was undoubtedly the smoothest manipulator he'd ever seen in action. He'd almost get sucked into believing her tales but at the last moment would remind himself that she'd been able to live a lie for weeks on end without any trouble.

Mrs. Kunstler bustled into the jailhouse. Chris shot to his feet. *"Guten Tag, Frau Kunstler."* After greeting her in German, he continued to tell her very politely that because of the safety risk, he wasn't permitting women in the jail.

"Unser Katie—Sie ist eine Freulein."

"Yes, I ken Miss Regent is a lass. But she's also a prisoner." He fought the urge to sniff the air. The aromas coming from the covered basket Mrs. Kunstler held made his mouth water. No matter—she'd been baking him treats ever since he transported a baby to her cousin's cousin. Cinnamon. This time, whatever it was, it had cinnamon.

"Katie," Mrs. Kunstler called. "I baked cinnamon rolls for you."

What?

"How kind of you! Thank you." Wren left her sewing machine and approached the bars. "How is Ismelda?"

"Fat." Mrs. Kunstler laughed. "My grandson should come any day now. The quilt you made for the cradle—she loves it so much, we are piecing one to match for their own bed."

"Have you seen Mercy? I'm worried she'll work too much and tire herself out."

Mrs. Kunstler looked ready to settle in for a nice, long visit. Chris cleared his throat. "*Frau Kunstler, mussen Sie gehen.*"

She waggled her finger at him and answered in English. "Don't you tell me I must go. It is bad how you have her in here like a lonely chick in a big coop. My Otto—he is a good man, ja?"

Chris nodded.

"But did you know I had another son? No, you didn't. I do not speak of him. He shamed us all by coming to town and drinking the beer and whiskey. One day, with a broken bottle, he fought another man. They killed one another. No one talks of this. It was bad, shameful. But does anyone blame Otto? No, because he was not responsible.

"The pastor—when Otto was blaming himself for not being there to stop his brother—the pastor, he came and talked to him. He said in the Bible, you did not see the brother go seek the prodigal son. The bad son—he had to decide by himself to come back. The good boy—it was his job to stay home and be good. It is better that I have one good son than that I lost two bad ones."

Frau Kunstler mopped her face with a crumpled hankie. "What our Katie's brother has done—it is sinful. But it is not her fault." The woman thumped on her ample bosom. "In here, it hurts to know you cannot stop someone you love from doing wrong. Is that not enough? Why do you punish her?"

"Mrs. Kunstler, here." Wren extended a hankie she'd tatted around the night before. "I'm so sorry about your other son. I'm glad you have Otto. He's a fine man, and he's a good husband to Ismelda."

"Ja." Mrs. Kunstler accepted the hankie and straightened her shoulders. "I should be cheering you up, but I came and cried."

"You shared your heart with me. Even though it was a sad memory, you trusted me with it. That means everything to me."

"Ach!" Mrs. Kunstler kissed her own hand, slid it through the bars, and patted Wren's cheek. "It is a shame I did not have one more son. I would have him marry you so you could be my daughter."

As Mrs. Kunstler left, she called over her shoulder, "If soon you are not free, I will bake you a cake with a file in it!"

Chris picked up the basket and headed toward the cell. "Here."

"Please help yourself."

"I'm not hungry."

—⁓—

"Watching that won't make it do anything."

Wren's head jerked up at the sound of Rob's voice, and she almost dropped her cinnamon roll. "The basket is full. Help yourself."

"I don't know that I want one out of the basket. That one seems mighty interesting to you."

She nodded. "It's special."

"It's a roll—just like the others," Chris muttered.

"Yes, it is," she agreed.

Chris swiveled around and glowered at her. "Make up your mind. Either it's special, or it's like all the others."

"They're all special. Mrs. Kunstler made them"—Wren's voice cracked—"for me."

Rob regarded her solemnly. "Aye, Katie. She went to the trouble just for you, and 'tis because she cares for you."

Tears welled up as she nodded.

"Chris, this has gone on long enough. Look at the lass. She's miserable, locked away in there."

"I'm not miserable." Wren sniffled. "St. Paul was content in prison, and I understand why now. He took the time to ponder the things that matter most."

"Then why—" Chris started out gruffly.

"—are you crying?" Rob finished.

Wren took an unsteady breath. "Be–cause Duncan pr–prays with me. And—and Mr. Rundsdorf wa–wants to be my first customer. And"—she took a big gulp of air—"Mrs. Kunstler. . .another son. . .marry!" To her embarrassment, she dissolved into a sobbing wreck.

Chris clipped out, "Frau Kunstler came by and said she wished she had another son so he could marry Wren."

"Ahhhh." Rob stretched out the sound. "Now wasn't that a grand thing for you to hear? Folks here love you. Aye, they do. You're just now figuring that out, are you?"

She nodded as her tears dissolved into hiccups.

"Oh, for cryin' in a bucket. You'd think no people ever said they loved her."

Wren's gaze dropped to the cinnamon roll she still held, and she whispered, "They haven't."

—⁓—

Chris had to get out of there. Wren had everyone wrapped around her little finger. Her pity-me tales already set his teeth on edge, but this one—it defied any scrap of truth. "Stay here," he ordered Rob. "I'm getting some air."

Sitting around waiting for something to happen was driving Chris daft. After Da lost his arm, Chris knew he had to provide for the family. He hated going down to the mine—the walls always closed in on him—but he'd forced himself to. Rob pestered him about the few occasions when he'd gone to Thurber to give some advice on the mining conditions, but he could have saved his breath. Braver men than he would have to pry bounty from the depths of the earth.

Just sitting in the jailhouse left him restless. Cooped up, playing nursemaid to that woman. *Everyone's mollycoddling her. Have they forgotten Connant? Or the three other men her brother wounded?*

I canna fault them. I was taken in by her at first. I e'en brought her here. The most I can do is keep them away.

He scanned the street. A strange horse was hitched outside the mercantile. Actually two. He started striding that direction.

"Ja, Leonard. I'll tell her you said so." Mr. Stein came through the door. He unhitched one of those two horses and swung up into the saddle. He rode toward Chris and halted. "Chris Gregor!"

"That's a fine looking horse you have."

"I bought him last week. Perhaps it is foolish for an old man to buy a new horse, but I've told myself that when my grandson is a little older, he will need a solid workhorse."

"Peter will be a lucky man when you hand over the reins." From the corner of his eye, Chris saw a flash. He pulled his pistol as he slapped the horse. "Heeyaww!" The horse bolted, carrying Mr. Stein to safety.

Two men sauntered down the boardwalk. In the scorching summer weather, they both wore coats. At midday.

Mercy's grandda halted his horse at the far end of the street. "José! Nestor!" he called. "Come here. I have something to tell you!"

The boys dashed past Chris to relative safety.

One more man rode by.

Four. Four of them. Whelan's not here yet. Chris scanned the street as he took ground-eating strides cutting across the road diagonally toward the jail.

Jakob Wahl stepped out onto his veranda and shouted, "Everyone! God gave us a little girl!" Jakob and his brother lived in that home. They were both bachelors. They'd come up with that warning call, saying it was the truth. God had sent Katie to them.

The momentary distraction allowed Chris and two other men to close the net. They waylaid one of the men wearing a coat. Chris had yet to spot Whelan, but he knew one man was in the jail, and another just stepped into the doorway, as well. Chris kept his gaze trained on the remaining one in the coat.

Suddenly from somewhere behind him, Chris heard a shotgun blast. Gunfire started, but Chris spent only one bullet. The man pulled a rifle from his coat. Chris yelled, "Drop it!"

The man fired at him, but Chris dove behind a water trough. Whether it was his shot or someone else's he didn't know, but that man fell. Chris didn't pause. He saw the muzzle of a pistol from the jail's doorway and fired a mere breath later. The man dropped his weapon while cursing profusely.

Chris rolled to his feet and sprinted to the jail. That man was trying to shove the door shut. Chris kicked it open. It caught his assailant in the chest and knocked him across the room. His head hit the wall with a loud thud, and he collapsed into a heap. Chris didn't want Whelan sneaking in behind him, so he slammed the door shut and shoved the bolt into place.

The last man backed up to Wren's cell.

He had his gun to Rob's neck.

Chapter 11

D rop your gun, or I'll kill him!"

"He's the one! He's the ranger!" Wren, still in her cell, stood directly behind the gunman. From his angle, Chris couldn't really see her, but he knew exactly where she was. She kept yanking on the man, goading him.

His brother's life depended on the smallest twitch of a trigger finger. Chris had already resigned himself to the fact that she'd betrayed his trust—but it took all of his discipline not to roar at her. "Turn loose of him, Wren. He's got a gun on Rob."

"No one's gotten hurt in here yet." Rob's voice sounded slow and steady—it carried the same tone as when he handled medical emergencies. "If Whelan wants his sister back, I'm not going to argue."

"He's the one!" Wren's voice grew more urgent. "He's got the keys."

Sweat rolled down the man's temples. He rasped, "Drop your gun!"

"Easy now." Chris tilted his head toward the desk. "I'll set it on there. It's got a hair trigger, and I don't want it to go off." He slowly edged toward the desk. If he got the right angle. . . *Lord, please safeguard my brother. Help me. Give me guidance and perfect my aim.*

"Where's my brother?" Wren continued to pester the man. "Is he outside?"

"Shut your trap!" the man roared. "Whelan ain't payin' me half enough to put up with your mouth."

"He's here, isn't he?" Wren persisted. "Tell me he's here."

The man let out a dirty bark of a laugh. "That's far enough, mister. Set down your gun and put the keys on the desk, too."

Chris gave his pistol a longing look as he set it down on the edge of the desk closest to himself. He took the keys and started to put them in the center of the desk.

"Don't let his brother go get the keys." Wren stood on tiptoe and peered over his shoulder. "He could snatch the gun, too."

"You think I don't know that? I'm not stupid!" He waved his gun at Chris. "Just you step back until you hit the wall. Then toss the keys to me."

Chris intentionally threw the keys so they'd land short.

"Now keep your hands up where I can see them."

Chris raised his hands, threaded them together, and held them behind his head.

"Careful-like," the gunman rasped to Rob, "you stoop over and fetch me that ring of keys."

Rob waited a moment after he'd been turned loose, then inched forward. As his brother moved, Chris pulled the knife out of his sleeve. The moment Rob squatted down, Chris threw the knife.

The gunman reacted as soon as Chris's hand came into view, firing twice. The knife pierced the man's chest. Having not been struck, Chris assumed the worst: Rob had been shot. Chris let out a roar as he charged the assailant.

The man thrashed but didn't move far.

"Hurry," Wren pled. "I can't hold—"

Chris could see how she'd seized the gunman's sleeve in two places and fought to restrain him. Taking the gun proved quite easy. Chris grabbed for it, and when he met resistance, he dug the knife deeper into the gunman's shoulder. Curses and blood flowed as Chris took possession of the gun.

"Rob!" Wren finally stepped into view.

Chris couldn't turn and look yet, but the devastated look on Wren's face made him want to howl.

"I'm fine. Just knocked my hard head on the corner of that desk."

The air rushed from Chris's lungs. "Rob, get the handcuffs. Top drawer." He motioned with the gun. "You. Down flat on the floor. Face down."

A twist and a few curses later, the man spat, "I can't."

"Dinna tell me what you canna do. Down. Now."

"He can't." Wren grinned. "I tied him to the bars."

"You what?"

"His suspenders. He thought I was just yanking on his shirt, but that was a distraction. I slid material through and knotted—oh, just come look."

Why had she—? Chris couldn't distract himself with any questions just now. He shoved the confusing fact aside and kept the gun trained on the men until Rob had them both handcuffed. He also satisfied himself that the one who'd crashed into the wall was waking and suffered no real damage. Winding a temporary bandage over the knife wound, Rob declared, "When things settle down, I'll have to suture this."

Gunshots still resounded outside. Swiftly shoving bullets into the empty chambers in his own weapon as well as the gunman's, Chris ordered, "I'm going out there to finish this. Rob, get over here and bolt the door once I'm out. Dinna open it unless Duncan or I tell you to. Whilst I'm gone, lock them into the second cell."

"Be careful," Wren called to him just before he opened the door. Desperation and sincerity colored her voice.

He no more than looked out the door than something struck the boardwalk and rolled past. Chris scanned the area. The gunfire grew sparser, but something hit again. A marble. Chris cranked his head to the side. Mercy's grandda motioned to him, then disappeared between two buildings.

Chris reached him seconds later. "What is it?"

"The bank. There are men in the bank."

The bank was located on the opposite side of the street, on the other side of the churchyard. Chris knew at once Whelan used the jailbreak as a distraction so he could hit the bank again.

"How many?"

"Just two. I found their horses. Those bad men—they might come out, but they will not go far."

"Fast thinking."

"Rundsdorf, he said there are two men still on the street."

Chris nodded. He'd listened to the gunfire and had a good notion where each of those men were. "Do you know who's in the bank?"

"Mr. Meisterson was in the diner. I think Horst was alone in the bank."

Chris nodded curtly. Chris looped behind several buildings and sneaked toward the bank. Suddenly, the bank's door flew open. One man exited. He spied Chris and fired. Chris was faster.

"Surrender, Whelan!"

"I've got a hostage!" Whelan shouted back.

Bang! Thud.

Horst yelled from inside the bank, "He's wrong. The hostage has him! I got his gun and knocked him out."

Chris took a single step toward the bank. His leg didn't want to move. He glanced down and noticed red blossoming from just above his left knee.

—⁂—

"Kathryn Regent, I'm placing you under house arrest."

"House arrest!" Wren stared at Chris in utter disbelief. She'd stayed in the clinic with Duncan, waiting and praying as Rob removed the bullet from Chris's leg. The last thing she expected was for him to hobble out under his own steam. Well, the second to last. "Rob, check his head. He must have gotten another injury. It's the only reason he'd say anything so—"

"Dinna be kickin' up a fuss," Duncan warned, "else he'll put you back in the jailhouse."

"You're a material witness to several crimes." Chris stared at her.

"And I'm enduring another here and now. You're stealing my freedom and peace of mind, Chris Gregor."

"You'll survive," he responded in a dry tone. He folded his arms across his chest. "I wonder how 'tis you say I'm taking your peace of mind. You've got it twisted backward, woman. 'Tis you who's givin' me a piece of your mind every time I turn around."

"That's just another reason why I shouldn't be trapped under house arrest."

Carmen and Mercy rushed in. "Chris—is he—"

"Right as rain. No need to make a fuss."

"He's putting up a fine show, but he needs rest." Rob motioned to Duncan. "We'll take him o'er to the house. I dinna want him walking for a few days."

Chris glowered. "I'll walk."

"Mercy, you and I had better have daughters." Carmen gestured toward the men. "The Gregor men are all stubborn as mules."

"Aye. And dinna forget it." Chris took one hobbling step and halted. His eyes narrowed. "Duncan, you didna tell us!"

"Tell you what?" Duncan yanked Chris's right arm about his shoulder and supported him.

Chris shook his head. "Rob and I got all the brains, Carmen. Duncan, your wife just told us all she's carryin' a bairn."

Duncan turned so fast, he almost knocked Chris over. Instead of helping his brother to the house, Duncan insisted on carrying his wife there.

Wren lagged back. This might be a good opportunity to break free.

Chris must have read her mind. He ordered, "Mercy, I've put Wren on house arrest. Dinna let her out of your sight."

It seemed impossibly rude to fight with Mercy since she was carrying Elspeth and was due to birth her baby any day now. Wren made an exasperated sound. She swiped Elspeth and declared, "I'm only staying because I choose to. I promised to help Mercy until her baby comes."

Once they reached the house, she looked about herself. The house was sizable, but it had never seemed smaller to her. Chris Gregor nearly sucked the air out of a room, so commanding was his presence and so large his build.

Chris eased into a chair. "You'll stay as long as I say, Wren."

Wren gave him a dirty look. He'd locked her up and made it clear he thought she was in league with criminals, and now he displayed the unmitigated gall to think he could order her around? "One Gregor man isn't just stubborn, he's demented," she said to little Elspeth.

Elspeth's little hand came up and patted Wren repeatedly at the base of her throat. "Ya, ya, ya, ya, ya."

"Mercy, your daughter is very bright. She agrees with me."

"No matter when Mercy has the babe, you still are a material witness. You'll have to appear in court for the trials of all those men."

"I'll be an old woman before that's done," she moaned.

"No." Chris accepted a glass of water from Mercy. "We've already sent off for the judge. Those men will all get a speedy trial, just as the Sixth Amendment allows."

Her eyes widened. "You remember the amendments to the American constitution?"

"Aye, and why wouldn't I? 'Tis my new home, this fine nation. And I respect the laws of the land. 'Tis my responsibility and duty to see to it laws are upheld. So stay you will." He scowled. "Did you think I wouldn't notice, Mercy? There's laudanum in this."

"Doctor's orders," Rob clipped. "Drink it."

Chris set aside the glass and got to his feet. "The devil will be ice skating the day I need laudanum for a wee scratch."

Rob helped him up the stairs. A second later, Chris bellowed, "Did you think I wouldn't notice, Duncan?"

Duncan chuckled. "He's going to be fine." After a few seconds, he roared with laughter. "Katie, I have something I want to share with you. Seein' as how you'll be stuck here awhile."

"What is it?"

"Gingerbread."

Chapter 12

Chris gritted his teeth and sat in the desk chair at the jail. He refused to lie about all day. One day of convalescence at home drove him to distraction.

Whelan snickered. "Another day and that leg'll fester."

Chris ignored him.

"Yep. You'll get the gangrene and die."

"Don't you ever shuddup, Whelan?" One of the other men groaned.

"You ain't gonna fare any better." Whelan smirked. "Another day or so, and that hole he carved in you's gonna plant you six feet under."

"If it wasn't for your sister—"

Whelan cursed. "I told you all she was, was a distraction."

Chris kept his back to them and opened a drawer to get paper. He'd copy down what they said and use it in court. Only one sheet remained in that drawer, so he took it and opened the next. Instead of paper, tiny, frilly, white baby gowns rested there. Irritated, Chris shoved them to the side and grabbed for paper below them. The only paper he located was the letter he was to send to Lucille from Wren.

The whole while, Whelan argued with the men in the other cell. "I told you you'd get a share as long as you took care of the diversion. Didn't matter whether you sprung her free or not..."

Whelan's heated words took Chris off guard. *"He left me behind when Mama died. If he wouldn't take care of me when I was only fifteen, what makes you think he'll suddenly turn into a dutiful brother?... My stepbrother does not value me."* Wren's words flooded back.

He'd judged and condemned her, yet she'd sat there in his cell sewing clothes for Mercy's baby. And the letter. He scanned it.

Wren asked Lucille to thank the cook for the recipe for spaghetti. Little Elspeth especially loved it and made a comical mess of herself. Lucille was right in her last letter—the henna finally did completely rinse away. The flower, herb, and vegetable gardens at both Gregor residences were flourishing, but only because of conscientious watering. The church had just installed a lovely stained glass window, and Wren would love to have her come visit to see it. Three pages of woman talk. Newsy, breezy chatter. Woven amongst all those tidbits were gentle references to God or the Bible or something about a dear old soul in the congregation who'd done some small kindness. In the most unlikeliest turn of events, Wren had forged a friendship with, and was showing God's love to, a soiled dove.

She was right, Lord. I wasn't seeking justice. I sought revenge. It blinded me to the truth. I have to make this right.

—⟳—

"Wren, I'm needing to talk to you."

"Later." She continued to knead dough. Little bursts of flour swirled over her hands. "Carmen's not feeling her best. She and Mercy are both napping upstairs. After I'm done here, I need someone to take me to the mercantile so I can get her some Trenton crackers. Rob says they'll help."

"Trenton crackers?"

"The soda in them settles a sour stomach." She formed a smooth ball of dough, dropped it back into the yellow-striped earthenware bowl, and covered it. "Can you walk me there, or is your wound too sore?"

"You can go after we talk."

Washing her hands, she mentioned, "Rob's at the Kunstler's. Ismelda's in labor."

"Don't tell Mercy!"

Wren started to dry her hands. "She already knows. She wanted to go help, but Rob insisted she stay here with Carmen. Mrs. Kunstler has helped him with other births. We all prayed for Ismelda before he left."

Chris groaned and flopped into the nearest chair. "This is bad."

"Your leg?"

"No. Mercy knowing about Ismelda. The night she had Elspeth, Stu Key's wife had a baby. Mercy might think it's catching. Until Rob got back home, he oughtn't have told her."

Wren realized he was serious. She laughed.

"It was terrifying. I'm not going through a labor again—at least, not without him present."

"You didn't endure it, Mercy did."

Chris shook his head. "She'd like to have killed us. Baked cookies by the dozen, then put sugar in the mashed potatoes. Shouted her throat raw, too. And did she have the good sense to birth the bairn in that fine clinic? No, I tell you." He propped his elbows on the table and buried his head in his hands.

"Don't jump to conclusions."

Slowly he lifted his head. "Your advice is too late."

"Yes, well—"

"Not about the laboring. About me jumping to conclusions. That's why I'm needing to talk to you, Wren."

Wren. She heaved a sigh. She'd come to loathe that nickname. He'd not used it until he slapped her in jail.

"Sit down."

She shook her head. "The crackers—remember?"

"This is more important."

"At the moment, my friend is more important—"

"Than you? Nae, lass. 'Tisna so. You're hurtin' on the inside, and it's well past time for that to cease."

"I'm hale as a draft horse."

Chris shook his head. "I'm talking about your heart. You were right. Whelan didna care whether you were set free. He used your presence in the jail just to cause a diversion."

Wren shrugged. She'd not expected anything different.

"Mrs. Kunstler was right, too. As soon as I knew Whelan was your brother, I jumped to conclusions and judged you according to his sins. All this time, you've worked your fingers to the bone to scrape by. Then you came here and tended to my family."

"You have a wonderful family." *You cannot begin to imagine how blessed you are.*

"Lass, I'm asking your forgiveness. I wronged you."

Wren stared at him. "You don't have to do this, Chris. Awful as it will be, I'll still swear to tell the truth in court. What you say to me won't change what I must do that day."

He jolted. "I'm not talking about that. Nae, I'm not. I'm trying to tell you I might have a hard head, but the truth matters to me. Aye, it does. I canna have you thinking I'm proud of what I did. I canna let you go on believing I think ill of you."

"Okay. Thank you. Can we go get the crackers now?"

"Are you listening to me, Wren?"

"All of Texas must be listening. You don't have to shout. And once and for all, will you decide what you're going to call me?" As soon as she said that, Wren clamped her mouth shut.

"The ruse is o'er. There's no need for you to have to go by Katie any longer." His brows furrowed. "Dinna you like sharing your name with a songbird?"

She shrugged.

"Dinna feign 'tis of no consequence. You wouldn't have said anything otherwise. What's wrong with Wren?"

"Wrens are small and drab and common. Everyone who called me that shooed me off like a nuisance. Katie—" her voice caught. "Never mind."

"Oh, I'm minding. I'm minding a lot. Everyone here calls you Katie. Aye, and they cherish you. You even said so yourself."

She started shaking. "The crackers—"

"Will be there an hour from now."

An hour? She didn't want to talk to him for even one more minute. She felt vulnerable, raw.

"Katie—"

"Don't call me that." The words flew from her mouth before she even thought them through.

" 'Tis a pretty name for a lovely lass. But I'll respect your wish. Aye, I will. By your leave, I'll be calling you Kathryn until I've earned the right to call you Katie."

"You've better things to do with your time. Once Mercy's had the baby and the trial is over, I'll leave."

"You'll stay right where you are. I promised I'd see to it that you were settled in a happy location."

"I have been happy here—but it's time for me to move."

"Why? Because of me?"

She bit her lip and thought through her answer. "It's not just you. Other places, once someone learned Whelan was my stepbrother, the people figured I was cut from the same cloth." She shrugged self-consciously. "I'm accustomed to pulling up stakes."

"You willna do that this time. Nae, you willna." He nodded his head. "I was in the wrong of it, judging you by his measure. You canna forfeit your happiness because you judge everyone else here by my reaction. Think on it: I had to chase folks away. Aye, I did."

Wren shook her head.

"Lass, folks here learned a lesson several times o'er in the past two years. I dinna want to offend, but I'll speak the truth, because 'tis wondrous in the end. Elspeth is the child of a vile attack."

Wren's jaw dropped open. "But Rob—"

"Loves Elspeth wi' all his heart. Folks here didna know how to deal with Mercy's predicament, so they ignored her. It nigh unto broke her heart. Carmen—bless her—was a stalwart friend, and Rob discovered his feelings ran deep for Mercy. He wed her and named Elspeth after our own Ma."

Tears filled her eyes. "Oh, you're right. That is wondrous."

"Aye, 'tis. And so is how folks learned to look past the situation and care for Mercy. But the story doesna end there. You've met Jenny."

"Isn't she a dear? And she sews so beautifully!"

"Aye, that's how we all think of her—now. Has she ever mentioned her past?"

"But that's in the past! She found Christ."

"Aye, and we all celebrated her salvation and wanted her to find happiness. Folks here gave her a second chance. And then there's Carmen."

"Carmen?"

"She's a fine woman—inside and out. Men hereabouts looked at her limp and decided she wouldna be a good wife. 'Twas foolishness. Aye, and now Duncan and she are besotted wi' one another and anticipating a wee little blessing."

Joy lilted in his deep voice. Christopher made for a complete bundle of paradoxes. He'd spoken of indelicate matters very delicately. He could be gruff and abrupt, yet he'd been careful to get down to a little boy's level and treat his concern over a marble as if it were vitally important. He sat here, telling her about how other women found happiness regardless of the past issues in their lives, yet he'd jailed her. Trying to clear her thoughts, Wren shook her head.

"Attend to me, Kathryn." His calloused hand slid over hers. "Dinna dismiss what I've said. Everyone else for miles around—they learned what God intended. Instead of allowing human nature to take o'er and making snap judgments, they're striving to see others through God's eyes. Me? I'm as thickheaded and stubborn-hearted as a cantankerous old mule. Rob—he's the smart brother. Duncan? He's the one whose heart is attuned to the nudging of the Holy Spirit. Me? I'm the one who didna learn from my brothers' examples or pay heed to the message all our friends and neighbors learned from God."

She steeled herself with a deep breath and slid her hand away. The loss of warmth and shelter struck her hard. Nonetheless, she folded her hands in her lap. "Openhearted as they are, the people around here would be easy game for a wolf in sheep's clothing. God sets a hedge about His people for protection. You're prickly."

A prolonged sigh rumbled out of him. "I've thorns aplenty."

"Maybe it's for God's purpose. The Lord might have created that quality in your soul because He needed you to be a warrior and not a lamb."

"There's a bonny thought, but I canna agree fully. His sheep shouldna become ensnarled in the hedge He sets about them for their own good. I yanked you away from the flock and wounded you. Aye, I did. 'Tis a sorrowful thing I've done, and I'll do my best to make it up to you, little Wr—Kathryn."

The remorse in his eyes and voice tore at her. Carmen needed the crackers, but Chris needed her forgiveness far more. "There's nothing to make up, Christopher. Nothing. I admit, when you first imprisoned me, I was outraged. But I came to realize how my attitude revolved around my feelings, and I hadn't stopped for even a moment to seek God's will. I asked Him to reveal to me what He would have me know." Her voice started to tremble, and she blinked back tears.

"Ooch, lass," Chris moaned.

"Remember me crying when Mrs. Kunstler brought the cinnamon rolls? She labored and made a special trip and bared the ache of her heart just to comfort me. And Mr. Rundsdorf? Carmen and I have made him several shirts—but he wants to be my first customer. Regardless of how it pains him to sit up for a long time, he came and visited me each day. I wouldn't have ever learned God's lesson for me if you hadn't locked me up."

"What lesson was that?"

"That I'm not just a burden—a mouth to be fed or a pallet to be tripped over. Most people will see me as Wren, but there are a handful to whom I'm Katie." Suddenly feeling raw and vulnerable, she shot to her feet. "I really must go get those Trenton crackers for Carmen."

He rose. "I'll go along."

And that says it all. He'll never trust me. I have to leave as soon as Mercy doesn't need me. This is his home. By staying here, I'm pushing him away from his own family.

Chapter 13

I—" Wren stared down at her clenched hands. Their town didn't have a courtroom, and it didn't seem right to use a church as a site for a trial. The only other large building was the saloon. The Gregor men spent time this morning draping blankets over pictures that decent folk shouldn't see. Even so, Kathryn didn't want to look around. She swallowed and testified, "I didn't see his face."

The attorney scowled. "Your honor, I'd like permission to treat Miss Regent as a hostile witness. She's the accused's sister."

"Miss Regent is *not* hostile, and she's his *step*sister," Chris proclaimed. "The accused abandoned her when she was only fifteen, and she'd not seen him again until the day in question."

While the judge admonished Chris that he'd accept no further outbursts, Kathryn marveled that Chris defended her. Having already testified, he was permitted to sit on the front bench and stay as an observer. He sat straight as could be and stared at her. He even flashed an encouraging smile and nodded.

The attorney peppered her with multiple questions. She bore witness to what she'd originally heard and how she'd seen the star on Whelan's boot. As she started walking away from the witness chair, Whelan sneered at her. "Don't bother comin' by the jailhouse anymore to churchify me."

Chris rose and interposed himself between her and her stepbrother.

Whelan kept talking. "I only pretended I was interested so you'd show family loyalty today."

Chris squeezed her arm. "I'll take you home."

"You need to stay here."

The gavel came down again. "It's noon. We'll recess for lunch and start back up at one o'clock sharp."

"Chris," Mr. Stuky said, "I'll take the prisoner to the jailhouse."

"No, I will." Jorge from the livery came over. "Chris, you take that pretty little filly on home. She's had a hard day."

"Katie is not a horse." Mr. Rundsdorf shouldered his way between the men. "But she needs to go rest. Chris, I'll watch the prisoner."

Otto Kunstler curled his hand around Whelan's upper arm and pulled him to his feet. "Gregor, you take care of who's important. I'll mind this one."

No less than four more men volunteered. Chris gave the jailhouse keys to Otto. "Much obliged, men."

Chris threaded her hand through the crook of his arm. "Come, Kathryn." As he escorted her down the street, Chris grinned. "You've many a champion here. Did you see how all those men fought to have the honor of keeping Whelan locked away from you?"

"Even dear Mr. Rundsdorf." She managed a fleeting smile. "Never in a million years would I have imagined he could look so fierce."

"The old gent was quite a sight," Chris agreed. He stopped and trailed his rough fingertips down her cheek.

She fought the nearly overwhelming need to lean into his touch. Confusion made her mind whirl. The day he'd rescued her from Hepplewhite's Emporium, he'd told her she could trust him. Somehow, he'd overcome her defenses and actually earned her respect—only to obliterate it all when he towed her off to jail and believed the worst of her. *But he confessed he was wrong and championed me. Do I trust him again? Dare I risk that?*

"You're a rare woman, Kathryn Regent. Aye, that you are." Chris gave her a steady look. "A man would gladly put on the armor of God and battle a legion of demons just to protect you."

—⁂—

Her pupils dilated wildly. Chris could see he'd taken her by surprise. "I canna help thinking your brother's biggest regret must be having left you behind. He went off seeking riches and never saw the treasure he already had."

Tears filled her remarkable eyes. "I'm no treasure, and I'll not delude myself. His greatest regret is having been captured and knowing the evidence against him is irrefutable. Robbery and murder—he's done several of both. When the jury finds him guilty, he'll be sentenced—"

"Aye," Chris cut in, trying to spare her from having to speak the truth. In the days ahead, she'd come to accept the inevitable, but in the meantime, he decided to distract her. "He'll be sentenced. But for now, I'll get you home. Duncan and Rob both hold the opinion that their wives are overdoing. If you'd talk sense into them, I'm sure my brothers would be grateful."

"I'll do my best."

"Good. Good." He started walking again.

"Chris, you're trying to be kind by diverting me from thinking about what lies ahead. It won't work. Something truly dreadful lies ahead."

"Aye." He looked down at her. "Many a town would have held a kangaroo court and lynched him. We've bent over backward to give him a fair trial. Justice will prevail. With several murders and robberies against him, he'll receive the harshest sentence." He paused a moment. "You'd best prepare yourself for the worst."

She bit her lip and nodded.

His brow furrowed. "Do you hold feelings for him?"

Slowly, she nodded.

Surprise and a flash of jealousy shot through him.

"He's done wicked things, evil deeds—yet he'll always be my brother. I prayed that he'd be like the one thief on the cross and repent."

"So you've been praying for him."

"Yes." She shrugged—a tiny, tense movement. "You can be proud of Duncan and Rob. They're fine men, and they return your love in full measure." Pain flickered across her features. "Whelan's awful, but he's still my brother."

"Kathryn Regent, 'twas an understatement when I said you're a rare woman."

"Crackers," she rasped. "Carmen needs more of them."

"Did the ones we got that other time help settle her stomach?"

Kathryn nodded. "She's run out."

Though Carmen had his sympathy, Kathryn deserved his support. She'd been through so much already. If accomplishing this task gave her even a moment's respite, he'd gladly accompany her on a whole string of errands. "Then let's get them."

Once they reached the mercantile, he opened the door for her and walked beside her to the cracker barrel. Leonard hastened over. "Katie, Chris, I'm surprised to see you here—after this morning." He caught the look Chris gave him. "Thought you'd be eating lunch like the rest of us. What can I do to help you today?"

Gently wiggling the scoop so she wouldn't break the crackers, Wren said, "We just dropped in to buy a few crackers."

Chris gave the meager supply she gathered a dubious look. "That's only a quarter scoop."

She added just a few more of the tiny oyster-shaped crackers. "How's that?"

Chris curled his fingers around hers. "You dinna ration your comfort or your friendship, Kathryn. God doesna hoard His love, either. He gives abundantly above all we can e'er ask or think." Chris guided her hand, dipped the scoop, and lifted out a heaping mountain of crackers. Several fluttered down into the barrel again. "Are you watching, lass?"

She stared at the scoop. "That's so many, you're dropping some!"

"Leonard, go fetch us something to carry these in." Chris waited until the storekeeper was out of earshot. "Kathryn, canna ye see, lass? You're looking at the wee little crackers that fall. Leonard sees the ones in the scoop. God? Well, I'm thinkin' God sees not only those and the ones filling the whole barrel, but also all the ones that will e'er be made. You've lived on the fallen scraps far too long. Dinna tally your worth by who your stepbrother is. Your heavenly Father counts you as priceless."

Leonard arrived with a pasteboard box. "This ought to do."

Kathryn bit her lip and nodded. She didn't say another word the whole way home.

—⁓—

"To be hanged by the neck until dead." The sentence rang in Chris's head. The trial had progressed swiftly, and the evidence made for a compelling case—so compelling, the jury took only fifteen minutes to deliberate.

Whelan snorted. "Didn't expect nothin' different."

Chris rose. "Your honor, folks here love Miss Regent, and we don't want to see her suffer any more than she already has. If it's all the same to you, I'd request Whelan's sentence be commuted to life in prison."

"I'd druther be hanged!" Whelan shouted.

The judge pounded the gavel. "Order. Order. Whelan, you'll get what you want. Hanging's what the law dictates, and that's what you deserve."

The sheriff from the town whose banker had been murdered announced, "Plenty of folks in my town already picked out a hangin' tree. We'd be happy to oblige the court."

Chris left and went back to the empty jailhouse. He felt no satisfaction in having apprehended his friend's killer. He'd seen the job through to the end—as a Texas Ranger, he'd gotten his man. In doing so, he'd probably spared several more people from theft and murder. Slowly, he wound the clock, reset the hands according to his prized pocket watch, and started the pendulum with a faint tap.

Time is a gift. Don't waste it.

At that moment, he knew what he had to do.

—⁓—

"Kathryn, I'm needing to talk to you." Duncan stood by the front door and half shouted the words.

"I'm a little busy just now."

"This willna wait."

She swung around and gave Duncan an incredulous look. "Do you think Mercy's baby will wait?"

Chris stood beside Duncan. Both seemed to have lost their deep tans and gone an odd shade of green. Chris rasped, "We only want a minute."

"Go on. Hurry up." Carmen gave Katie a push.

Mercy sat on the steps and glared at her brothers-in-law. "Don't you dare try to convince my friend to drag me over to that clinic."

"They willna as long as you don't make any cookies or mashed potatoes today," Rob said as he rubbed her back.

Kathryn scurried out to the veranda. Duncan yanked the door shut, and Chris tilted her face upward. "Tell Duncan you dinna mind me having as much gingerbread as I want."

"You're hungry?"

Duncan patted her shoulder. "The wooden frills, lass."

Flummoxed, Kathryn shook her head. "I don't know why you're asking me."

"Dinna you recall me sayin' I'd share it all wi' you, lass?" Duncan nodded. "I gave my word, and I'll not go back on it."

"Chris is your brother. You Gregors all bought the gingerbread. I couldn't care less what happens to it—all I care about right now are Mercy and the baby!"

"I told you so." Chris slapped Duncan on the back and strode off.

Mercy moaned from inside the house.

A stricken look swept over Duncan's face. "Chris! You'll be needin' my help!"

Kathryn headed back into the house. Soon she was busy bathing Rob and Mercy's newborn baby. As dawn broke, footsteps sounded on the veranda. The door barely opened, and Chris stuck his head into the house. "How's she doing?"

"Fine," Kathryn whispered as she sat in the rocking chair coaxing Elspeth back to sleep.

"I didna mean Elspeth."

"Mercy's doing beautifully." Kathryn smiled wearily. "You'll have to go on upstairs. The news is Rob's to tell."

Relief flooded Christopher's face, and he swiftly entered the house. "So she's had the wee bairn?"

Yawning, Kathryn nodded.

"Go on to bed, lass. I'll tuck wee Elspeth in." He stole Elspeth from her and headed up the stairs. A moment later, delighted male chuckles echoed down the stairs.

The sound rolled over her, and Kathryn's eyes sank shut. *I should have known better. Chris wouldn't care that it's another girl. The Gregors all love one another. Lillith is such a fortunate little girl to be born into such a family.*

Chapter 14

Carmen laughed as she hung diapers out to dry. "I'm trying to figure out how many diapers to make for my baby. I never paid much mind to that, and suddenly it's important."

"A dozen a day," Mercy said as she nursed Lillith in a shady spot. "But I wish I'd made more than three dozen when I expected Elspeth."

"I'll get more cloth and hem up more on my machine. It'll take no time at all."

"Would you?" Mercy beamed. "I can't thank you enough, Katie. Chris? Katie's going to the mercantile. Didn't you say you had to get something?"

"Sure," he called back. He followed Katie out the door.

As they walked along the boardwalk, he suddenly stopped.

Kathryn halted, too. She didn't want to embarrass him, but concern caused her to ask, "Is it your wound? Do you need to sit down?"

Chris stared over her shoulder. "Rob did his best on my leg, and I've recovered well, but he claims I canna ride days on end as I once did."

"After riding a horse just that one day, I cannot imagine how anyone is able to ride for a prolonged period."

"The governor willna allow a ranger to remain in active service if he's impaired. Though I canna serve as a ranger, the town's asked me to become the sheriff."

She studied him closely, but it was hard to determine what he was thinking. "I can't tell whether you are resigned or upset."

"That all depends on you, Katie."

She blinked. He'd called her Katie—not Kathryn or Miss Regent. He turned her to face the opposite side of the street. Her breath caught.

The small storefront beside the mercantile had been freshly whitewashed. Pale green and forest green gingerbread adorned the eaves and windows. A sign out front read, "KATIE's."

Tears filled her eyes.

"None of that now." He escorted her across the street and threw open the door.

"Take a peek."

Her sewing machine rested in one corner. A deep green velvet settee lined part of a wall, and walnut-stained gingerbread hung from the ceiling to form clever arches. Lighter green curtains hung from them to form a dressing room. Shelves with little gingerbread flourishes in the corners completed the wall, and her measuring tape draped around the neck of a brand-new dress form.

Tears slipped down her cheeks. "But I'm s–supposed to l–leave."

"Why would you be doing that when this is where you belong? Everyone here loves you." Chris took her hand in his. He squeezed it. "Aye, they do—but not the way I do. I love you, Katie. Truly, I do."

"You do?"

"Ooch, Katie, I did you a grave injustice the day I let vengeance rule my head and heart. Nothing shames me more than knowing I hurt you."

"I told you that was forgiven," she said softly.

"You forgave, but I couldna forget. But Da told me time is a gift and isna to be wasted. I'm tired of wasting time on regrets. I'd rather spend my days knowing the joy of being your husband." He lifted her hand and kissed it. "I love ye, lass. With all my heart, I do. I'm askin' you, Kathryn Regent, if you'll do me the honor of being my wife."

"When I saw this"—she gestured—"I could scarcely believe my eyes. This is a gift far beyond my dreams—a place of my own, a place to stay. But it's nothing at all compared to what you've offered." Kathryn paused so she'd not spoil the moment by weeping. "You've offered me your heart, Christopher. No one has ever loved me. Not until now. I love the Lord with all my soul—but you. . .I love you with all my heart. Nothing would make me happier than to be your bride."

—⚉—

The Gregor men wore their kilts proudly and stood at the altar. Lillith took a mind to squall like a heathen the whole time the pastor prayed a blessing for her. Once that was over, the pianist started to play the "Wedding March." Mr. Rundsdorf proudly escorted Katie down the aisle. He refused to sit down until he got to kiss the bride.

Chris proudly wore his father's golden watch draped across the waist of his plaid. He pulled Katie close and spoke his vows in a booming voice. She said hers in one that quivered with emotion. Mercy and Carmen both wore lengths of the Gregor tartan over their shoulders, but they never told her why. She'd asked, but the two of them refused to answer her.

Once the vows were said, Chris pulled a length of the lovely plaid from a leather thong at his waist and draped it over her. "We've a tradition, Katie-mine. I've wed ye and given ye my name, and 'tis the Gregor plaid I'm placing o'er your shoulder to remind you always of a love that will warm and protect you and a family that claims you. There's another tradition, too. A man says this poem only once in his life. Hear me now, for 'tis from the depths of my heart these words come:

"As fair art thou, my bonnie lass,
So deep in luve am I,
And I will luve thee still, my dear,
Till a' the seas gang dry.

"Till a' the seas gang dry, my dear,
And the rocks melt wi' the sun!
And I will luve thee still, my dear
While the sands o' life shall run."

Epilogue

Five years later

Ian, don't you dare pick that. It's a carrot, not a weed." Mercy swept up her son and tickled him. "Remember? Mama said you aren't to pick anything until she says so."

Carmen pried a small sprig of green from little Micah's grubby hand. "I'm afraid my son set a bad example."

"At this rate, we're going to have to have Great-grandpa Stein and Jenny let us put a garden up over at the farm." Katie brushed back a wisp of hair. "If we had to survive on what we grow here, we'd all starve."

"There's no risk of us starving." Rahab smiled. Since leaving the bordello after Wren's continued urgings through her letters, Lucille had changed her life drastically, including a permanent name change, which, according to her, reflected the change God made in her heart. "God provides. But as much fun as it is to visit the farm, I'd love to have an excuse to go there more often."

Mercy waggled her brows. "I think you're looking for an excuse to be near Grossvater's new field hand. You have to admit, Barry is strong and handsome."

Rahab shrugged. "In a manner of speaking, that's true enough. But I'm not interested in marrying. Helping Katie run the dress shop is enough to keep me happy. Going out to the farm," she paused as a smile crept across her face, "well, I think Jenny and Barry fancy one another, and I enjoy watching them. Last Sunday I told him he ought to ask Mr. Stein's permission to court Jenny."

"How wonderful!" Katie gave Rahab a hug.

Duncan wandered over with his daughter. "Carmen, Anne's up from her nap." He laughed at Ian. "How did you get so grubby?"

"Weeds!"

Rob and Chris rode over. Each held one of Katie's twin boys. "Songbird," Chris said, "we've a problem. They climbed out of the crib."

Katie laughed and went over to take one of the boys. "That actually solves a problem, dear."

"Oh?"

She nodded. "We'll be needing the crib again in about seven months."

Leather creaked a bit as he dismounted. She'd never before paid attention to that masculine sound of a large body easing from a saddle and hitting the ground. Wren felt him close the space betwixt them with a few leggy strides and heard the grit scrape softly under the soles of his boots. His hands rested on her shoulders as he brushed her lips with a kiss of abiding love.

Kimberley Comeaux gets her inspiration from all sorts of places: travel, history, dreams, and once overhearing (okay. . .eavesdropping on) a conversation between a couple arguing in the grocery store line. She not only is the author of thirteen inspirational romance books, but also writes and produces church musicals. She is married to her best friend, Brian, and has one son, Tyler, and a brand-new daughter-in-law, Kellie! Kimberley resides with her family near New Orleans.

Cathy Marie Hake is a southern California native. She met her two loves at church: Jesus and her husband, Christopher. An RN, she loved working in oncology as well as teaching Lamaze. Health issues forced her to retire, but God opened new possibilities with writing. Since their children have moved out and are married, Cathy and Chris dote on dogs they rescue from a local shelter. A sentimental pack rat, Cathy enjoys scrapbooking and collecting antiques. "I'm easily distracted during prayer, so I devote certain tasks and chores to specific requests or persons so I can keep faithful in my prayer life." Since her first book in 2000, she's been on multiple best-seller and readers' favorite lists.